PRAISE FOR JE

Rising (Vincent and Eve Book 1)

"I felt fevered by the storyline, so besotted by Vincent and his mysterious life, so deeply connected to Eve and her dire circumstances. I felt like someone had PLUGGED ME INTO THIS STORY and turned me on, like a fire was lit inside me and the more I read, the hotter the flames grew until they were a raging inferno. It was crazy. Chaotic. And man, was I obsessed by the time I was done. I was invigorated and ready to scream it to the world."- **Angie, Angie's Dreamy Reads**

"Jessica Ruben's storytelling is hypnotic, her writing is nuanced, and her characterization is superb. It's difficult to comprehend that *Rising* is her debut. She's delivered an emotionally charged story with a well-conceived and intriguing plot, compelling characters and an intense, angsty romance, and it will keep you breathless in anticipation to find out what happens next."- **Mary Dube, USA Today HEA**

"I am practically giddy with excitement. My mind is awash with theories, potential plot lines and excitement with what is to come. I cannot wait to see where this author takes this story."- **The Romance Cover**

"If you love your impeccably written suspenseful romances that grab your attention and keep you invested throughout, then I cannot recommend Rising enough."- **Steamy Reads**

"A gritty, emotional, hard to read at times tale of how hard life can be on the "wrong side" of the tracks, while the over-privileged seek something simpler, the pureness of it. Corruption, fear, and the all consuming want of MORE. Which I now suffer from because I WANT MORE. Like now." -**Two Unruly Girls**

"A scandalous must-read!"- **Ellie, Love N Books**

"Jessica Ruben's debut novel will leave you breathless and addicted. From the first page, I was hooked on this fast-paced, sexy and unpredictable journey with a heroine I wanted to root for and a hero I was DYING to figure out. A must-read!"- **Author Ginger Scott**

Reckoning (Vincent and Eve Book 2)

The whole book brought it's angsty A-game! I can't even form thoughts! My head is a mess. THE FEELS! Dead over them! Ugh ugh ugh!!! LOVE THIS SO HARD.- *Angie, Angie and Jessica's Dreamy Reads*

Poignant, passionate, and powerful, Reckoning is ABSOLUTE PERFECTION and one of the BEST SERIES I've met! Reckoning OWNS every ounce of me. I was a GONER--so WONDERFULLY WRECKED by Reckoning. Hook. Line. Sinker. THIS LOVE STORY SLAYS ALL THE WAY!-*Karen, Bookalicious Babes Blog*

Historically book twos in a series fall a little flat for me, the middle part of the story that deals with the why, how and what doesn't always have the holding power to keep my attention, but Reckoning...it had me screaming for more. Depression setting in when I got to the end. Swiping, my kindle needing more. Please...MORE! I am SO SO ready for book three. MOOOORE!!- *Dawn, Two Unruly Girls*

Redemption (Vincent and Eve Book 3)
I devoured it just like the others and fell even more in love with Vincent and Eve. It was more than I could have imagined. MUST READ series! -**MJ Fields, USA Today Best Selling Author**

The Vincent and Eve series is everything. Passionate and steamy, emotional and gripping, utterly unputdownable. It's romance perfection that you have to read. - **Angie, Angie and Jessica's Dreamy Reads**

This is such a bang-up book with the intensity of The Godfather! This mafia series starring Vincent and Eve is among the BEST OF THE BEST in its genre. - **Karen, Bookalicious Babes Blog**

And with a bang, the series is over. I am so so sad to see it end. This final book by Jessica Ruben was utterly stunning and brilliant on so many levels that it just blows your mind. - **Suzanne, Goodreads reviewer**

6 I DON'T WANT THIS RIDE TO BE OVER stars! - **Jacquie, Unbound Book Reviews**

RISING completely shook me, RECKONING wrecked me and REDEMPTION broke me down and built me back up again. - **Chele, Goodreads Reviewer**

VINCENT AND EVE

THE COMPLETE SERIES

JESSICA RUBEN

JessicaRubenBooks, LLC

229 E. 85th Street

P.O. Box 1596

New York, New York 10028

Paperback ISBN:

E-Book ISBN: 978-1-7321178-8-4

Paperback ISBN: 978-1-7321178-9-1

Printed in the United States of America

Contact me by visiting my website, JessicaRubenAuthor.com

Cover Art Design by Okay Creations

Editing by Billi Joy Carson at Editing Addict

Editing by Ellie at LoveNBooks

Publicity by Autumn at Wordsmith Publicity

This is work of fiction. Names, characters, places, and incidents are the product of the author's wild imagination or are used fictitiously.

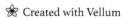 Created with Vellum

RISING (VINCENT AND EVE BOOK 1)

1

OAK DESKS, scuffed from years of abuse and handy knife work, stand single file in the back of the dingy public library. Curled up in a dark wooden chair, with elbows resting on the etched wood, I read the newest novel recommended by my teacher, Ms. Levine. I lift my head for a moment when my gaze lands on the nearly opaque second-story window, grimy from New York City pollution.

My eyes widen. "Oh shit," I say out loud, my voice ringing through the empty room. Eyes registering the darkness outside, my stomach liquefies with dread. I check my cell to confirm the time—it's ten fifteen.

Grabbing my ratty backpack off the floor, I slide the book inside and zip it closed as quickly as my shaking hands allow. Throwing it over my shoulder, I rush out the front door and make it to the dimly lit bus stop, just as the M-6 pulls in. I walk up the steps and swipe my metro card at the kiosk by the driver.

Noticing an empty seat by the window in the second row, I walk over, squeezing my small five-foot-one frame past the woman sitting in the aisle seat. She sighs as if annoyed, leaning back in an attempt to maintain distance. Wearing green scrubs, she has exhaustion written all over her drawn face. I take my seat and lick my dry lips, turning my gaze to the window.

As the bus approaches my stop on the Lower East Side, I raise the hood of my black sweatshirt. Anonymity is key in my neighborhood —particularly as a lone female walking at night. I live in the Blue Houses, a New York City housing project recently dubbed by the *Post* as "the hellhole houses." The nickname came as no surprise, as the complex is dilapidated and crime-ridden. It's common knowledge that cops always enter the building with their guns drawn, assuming that all tenants are packing weapons. To make matters worse, two gangs, the Snakes and the Cartel, are in a turf war for rights to push crack, the preferred pastime for many Blue House residents. The gutters run blood daily. Although I'm born and raised here, my time spent with my head inside the books has left me with street smarts that are at best decent, and at worst delinquent. My older sister Janelle reminds me of this constantly, and in this moment, I'm proving her right.

I'm so close to the building now, only about nine hundred feet away from the front yard. My eyes scan the eerily empty streets that, during daylight hours, are full of commotion. I force myself to stay calm by focusing on this morning when my sister's friends chatted about who's banging who, while old-school Tupac blasted on someone's iPhone speakers. I pull the hoodie closer to my head as my mind revists to the scene.

* * *

"Jem got pregnant—"

"Ohhhhh shit! No way! No fuckin' way! That poor mama of hers—"

"—I heard that Mark is gonna kick Sean's ass. He owes him money, but who's gonna pay that debt? Everyone knows he spends all his money on his—"

I shift my focus from the gossip mill to the girls jumping rope in front of me, crisscrossing and jumping with ease.

"Yo Eve, you listenin'?" I turn my head to Vania, one perfectly plucked eyebrow raised in frustration.

I plaster a smile on my face. "Sorry, what?"

She rolls her dark brown eyes. "Girl, you've got to get your head outta la-la land!" I flush with embarrassment; this isn't the first time I've been accused of spacing out. "I asked you if you saw Jason. He told Jennifer that he thinks you're: Hot. As. Fuck."

I shrug my shoulders. "Nah. I'm not really interested." She looks at me like I've got a screw loose in my head, and I immediately wish I said something other than the truth. Jason is tall with jet-black hair, blue eyes, and totally tatted from his head to his ankles. Most girls would give almost anything to be with a man like that. And while my eyes recognize his relative attractiveness, he doesn't affect me the way he does everyone else.

"I love your shade of lipstick!" My voice is full of forced enthusiasm, but I'm hoping to divert the conversation.

"It's called Honey Love. It's MAC." She purses her lips together, showing off the creamy nude shade.

I nod my head, relieved that the conversation of Jason is now behind us. "That's cool. I gotta tell Janelle to try it on me sometime."

Warmth fills her face. "Yeah, baby girl. And with your tan skin, pouty lips, and huge brown eyes...shiiiit. You'll have guys lining up." I blush, uncomfortable with the praise.

I turn to my sister, who is all long blond hair and legs for miles. While I share her small nose and bow-shaped lips, our physical similarities are minimal. Janelle is five-foot-seven and statuesque, whereas I'm short and curvy.

Vania clears her throat, rummaging through her purse. "Here. Let me put some on you." She takes out a lipstick and lipliner from her huge black tote bag that looks more like a suitcase than a purse, and gets to work on my lips. When she's finished, she leans back, seemingly pleased.

"Yo, Janelle. Take a look at baby sister over here." Janelle turns her head, smiling as she takes me in.

"You're smokin'. Je-sus!" She winks at me before turning back to Vania. "What color is that? Honey Love?"

"Of course, you know, you bitch!" They laugh together, Vania turning her attention back to Janelle. "I read that Mario uses this new color mix on Kim Kardashian—"

I slide up closer to them, trying to listen to their conversation, but everything they say goes in one ear and out the other. I'm the listener. The dreamer. The girl with her head in a book at all times. But even I know that in order to survive here, I've got to belong. Loners get picked on and picked off. But Janelle? She's the social butterfly. The girl everyone loves. And if not for her, I'd probably be floating in the Hudson by now. I move my body closer to the group, doing my best to fit in.

* * *

I STUMBLE on a hard piece of trash on the sidewalk, bringing my focus back to the present. The unnaturally silent air has alarm bells ringing in my head. I wonder if the gangs are roaming hard tonight. I look to the park adjacent to the Blue Houses, trying to find the regular late-night junkies. It's the most secure place for people to do drugs, as the cops never make regular patrols; apparently, they're too busy answering 911 calls. I take a sharp breath; the entire park is seemingly abandoned.

I tighten my hold on the straps of my backpack and quicken my pace, focusing on making it to the front door of my building. My heart rate increases as my imagination spirals. Maybe someone was shot earlier, and now everyone is home scared? Did someone die? Someone must have died. Is there blood on the sidewalk? There's blood. I know it. Fear takes hold, choking me. For all the laughter and friendly neighborhood vibes during the day, the reality is the Blue Houses are a deadly place to live.

When I hear the telltale *hiss* of the Snakes, the blood in my veins turns cold. I run as fast as I can, but the *hissing* only increases in volume. Risking a glance over my shoulder, I see a group close behind me. Janelle's voice enters my mind, *"If you run, you'll look scared. And looking scared makes you more vulnerable."* Even though my heart is pounding like a steel drum into my rib cage, I force myself to slow down. My legs beg to sprint forward, but showing fear isn't an option.

I make it a few more feet when they circle me, blocking any path of escape. My mouth opens, poised to scream, but my throat locks shut. It's so dark, but the shadows of the streetlamps bring their red and black colors into focus. My body quakes from my fingertips down into my toes. Dropping my head, I stare at the ground as the lieutenant of the Snakes moves in front of me. Focusing on his black steel-toe boots, a cold sweat breaks out on my forehead.

It's Carlos. As a kid, he used to torture and kill mice in the stairwell and leave them as threats for people by their front doors. He's been in and out of prison more times than I can count. In my mind's eye, I can see the blue teardrops tatted under his left eye down to the corner of his thin lips, each oval bead signifying a kill.

"Take that hood off. I wanna get a good look at you." His voice is low and menacing. I move to lift my head, pausing at his muscular bare chest. I shudder, making eye contact with his black-and-red snake tattoo. It peeks over his right shoulder, tongue hissing between two pointy white fangs like a beast from hell.

When Carlos sees I'm not doing as he demanded, he throws off my hood, roughly grabbing my chin and forcing my head straight. I can smell his rancid breath as he fists my hair in his hand. Staring at my face, he nods with what looks like appreciation.

"We found something good tonight, boys," he chuckles as if he's found a new toy he can't wait to play with. Bile rises up my throat as his smile widens.

My eyes dart from side to side as my breathing turns erratic. I'm fresh meat, and these animals are in it for the kill. Screaming won't make a difference. How many times have I heard yelling outside my bedroom window, but never thought to help the victim? Countless. Maybe it's karma. Maybe I deserve this for all the times I dropped my head and tried not to get involved. If I only listened to Janelle and made sure not to be alone on the streets at night—

Carlos steps back, pulling a cigarette from behind his ear and placing it between his lips. Taking a black lighter from his front pocket, he flicks it on and off, letting the fire burn at his will. Bringing the flame to the end of his cigarette, he takes a hard pull, turning the tip into a shining ember. With an exhale, smoke wafts around his face and blends into the night. He stands silently, assessing every detail of my trembling body.

"Looks like we're gonna have some fun," he laughs as his boys cackle in delight. My jaw slackens as my mind searches for an escape. If I can't physically get out of this, maybe I can force my mind to move elsewhere.

He grabs my upper arm. I can feel the bruising take shape as he turns me around forcefully, dragging me like a rag doll toward the Blue Houses. The others trail behind us, reminding me with every step that I have nowhere to go. Nowhere to hide. Nowhere to run.

Pushing through the front door of the building, we stop in front of what I always thought was a storage room. Carlos stuffs his hand in his pocket, removing a key. Shoving it inside the keyhole, he throws the door open, using his free hand to push me into the room. I trip over my own feet, the cement greeting me as I fall to my hands and knees. He flips a switch and the light casts a shadow below me. I lift my head and see a tiny barred window above a small bed. I look to my right, only to see a kitchenette with a round table surrounded by plastic chairs. Carlos bends down, grabbing me by the neck and pulling me up to face him. I want to scream, but my throat is closed. I see the exhilaration in his eyes and briefly wonder if death isn't the better option.

He loosens his hold on my neck, and I take deep, but shaky, inhales. The moment I catch my breath, he slaps me hard across the face. My body gets the message—he's the one in control. I open and close my mouth, shutting my eyes and willing my brain to tune out and turn off.

He grabs my chin. "I've been seeing you around. And get this?

You're just the one we need for tonight. You see, we've got lots of energy we need to burn off after where we've been." He licks his lips and I can see the dull yellow of his teeth. "I know you like to hide in those baggy clothes with those books in your hands, but I think it's about time you show us what you've got goin' on underneath all that shit." He laughs, pulling out a fresh cigarette and lighting it up. "Take your clothes off for us, and do it niiiice and slow. I think we're all in the mood for a little live show tonight."

A chair is pulled out and I lift my head to the sound. I make eye contact with one of the guys and his head snaps back in recognition. "Oh shit, Carlos, that's Janelle's little sister." It's Jason. His hair is styled in an undercut, buzzed on the sides and long on top. I'm shaking so badly it takes me a second to realize he's staring right at me, waiting for a reply.

"Y-Yeah," I stammer. "I'm J-J-Janelle's sister."

He shrugs casually at the guys. "Let's get rid of her. She's harmless. You know Janelle; she's the one who does all the old ladies' hair for free, and—"

Carlos throws a hand up in the air, silencing him. "Rid of her? Like, shoot her in the head?" He cocks his head to the side in question and the blood drains from my face. "Nah. I don't think I want to kill her just yet. Fuck her virgin brains out, yeah. Let all you guys take a turn when I'm done, hell yeah. Afterwards, you can kill her if you still want." He smiles and grabs my hand, lifting it above my head. I shut my eyes as he twirls me in a slow circle, showing me off to his crew. I hear wolf whistles and try to turn my thoughts into white noise.

A scratchy voice from the side of the room starts up. "Don't rough her up too much at first. I want her to have some fight left when I get my turn."

Tears drip from my eyes, burning as they fall down the sides of my face. "I'll d-d-do anything. Just let me go. Please..." I beg, dropping down to my knees and lifting my hands in prayer. "I'll do anything you want, but I don't want to die."

"Anything, huh? Get up," he commands. I stand on wobbly feet as

Carlos grins maliciously. "Ah, you take directions. That's good. Very good." He lifts his steel toe boot, kicking me in the stomach. I double over.

Carlos bends low, grabbing my hair to lift my head and bringing his lips to my ear, his voice a dark growl. "Let me give you a piece of advice. Shut the FUCK up and take what we're all about to give you. You may even enjoy it after the first few times." He puts his nose to my neck, smelling me deeply as he presses a sharp object against my side. My eyes widen; I feel the cold sharp edge of a blade drifting from my ribs up to my chest.

"Listen to what I tell you. Don't want to mess up that gorgeous face. But..." My breathing stops. "I will, IF you don't do as I say. You want to live? Shut up and take it." He moves his knife back to his pocket. "Strip."

He chuckles.

I oblige.

I remove every layer of clothing and stand crumpled. My shoulders are curled down and my arms cover my bare breasts. He thrusts my arms away.

His dirty fingertips grope my intimate parts as if he owns them. The body I thought belonged to me is now on loan. Finally, my mind separates from my body and floats away. But Carlos, unwilling to let me go in body or mind, pulls the cigarette out of his mouth and presses it against my shoulder.

I let out a scream from the burn.

He laughs.

Carlos turns to his boys, rubbing his hands together in eagerness. "I'm gonna make sure she's good enough for you all, first." They all chuckle at the joke, while one of them stares at me with rapt attention and a look of utter excitement.

"Poker—"

A cabinet opens and shuts.

The smell of old and wet laundry.

I close my eyes.

"Open your eyes and look at me!" Yelling, he grabs my neck to face him, forcing me to watch his ministrations.

My eyes connect with his, nothing but evil lurks in his depths.

I'm thrust forward, face down on the bed. I hear pants unzipping and falling to the floor. I hold my breath. If I hold it long enough, will I die?

"Yo, snake charmers! Cartel is In. The. Houssssse!" Voices and laughter radiate straight through the barred window and into the room. Carlos pauses, turning toward the glass and screaming, "We're coming MOTHERFUCKERS!"

My body shakes uncontrollably. I can hear him pull his pants back up, heaving. "The FUCK? If the Cartel is looking for a fight tonight, we'll give em' one!"

I dare to crack my eyes open, watching as they nod to each other. The rivalry between the Snakes and the Cartel is vicious. While the Cartel has fewer members, they make up for less manpower with intense and frequent bloodshed.

I'm in a state of shock, watching them pull weapons from their pants. Am I going to die? I shut my eyes again, moaning.

"Yo!" Carlos slaps my ass so hard I bite my lip, tasting copper. "Don't think you're off the hook, bitch. I got a glimpse, and now I want in. I'm coming back for you." He raises his gun and thrusts it into my mouth. I choke as he pushes it deeper down. Tearing it out, he nods—his version of a guarantee.

Seconds later, I feel warm hands on my naked back. "Open your eyes and get up." The voice is soft but urgent. Jason is on his knees by the bed, my clothes in his hands. "Put your clothes on, and get out of here!" he whispers loudly.

Somehow, I stand. I'm a machine, clothing myself like I've done millions of times before. He has the decency to turn his head as I put one foot and then the other into my underwear. As I slide my T-shirt and sweatshirt over my head, I realize I am no longer the priority to these criminals. If there is a time to run, it's now.

I take my bag and run out of the room with a speed I didn't know I was capable of. Opening the heavy stairwell door and running up the steps, I take two at a time as sweat pours down my temples. Are they after me? Are they coming? I want to turn my head back to see if they're behind me, but my fear won't let me turn around.

I hear cursing and some screams, but all the sounds are muffled by the whooshing sound in my ears. The stairs seem to vibrate with the sound of gunshots. Have I been shot? Adrenalin mixed with confusion pumps through my veins as I jet up the darkened stairwell; the lights are all out on the third floor, and it feels like I'm running through a black hole. My heart pounds into my throat.

In a blink, I'm back inside my empty apartment, staring in a trance at my gray threadbare living-room couch. I look at my feet and realize I'm barefoot. Oh shit, I'm going to need to buy a new pair of sneakers. I wonder if there's any in my size at the thrift store.

Turning toward my bedroom door, my mind registers the crack down the center. I briefly remember one of my mom's old boyfriends throwing a vase against it, splitting the wood. I walk into my room like a zombie and complete my nightly routine of brushing my teeth, washing my face with soap and scalding hot water, and changing into a clean pair of pajamas. In the recesses of my mind, I know what just happened to me is horrifying, but I keep telling myself if I just act normal, maybe it'll all just go away.

Before getting into my bed, I kneel on the floor, fisting my worn-out navy comforter in my hands. Prayers tumble out of my mouth to God, begging him to get me out of here before Carlos finds me. All at once, I feel punched in the gut. I run to the toilet, dropping my head into the bowl and emptying all the contents of my stomach.

Are they going to come for me tonight? Should I hide? I shut the bathroom door and curl up in the fetal position by the toilet, too afraid to go back into my bedroom where there's a window.

What feels like seconds later, I hear the front door open and close. As footfalls get closer to the bathroom door, my chest constricts, my mouth gaping open and poised to scream.

"Eve, are you in the bathroom? Get out, I need to wash up!" Janelle throws the door open and looks down at me on the floor, momentarily confused.

She gives me a once over. "You look like shit, girl." Her voice is quiet and laced with concern. "What are you doing in the bathroom? Are you sick?" I hear her, but can't manage a reply. She squats down, placing the back of her hand on my forehead.

"Holy shit, Eve, you're burning up! And your face is pale as hell. You think it's food poisoning or something? Let me get you some meds." She helps me up off the floor and walks me to my bed, letting me lean on her as we walk. A few minutes later, she drops two pills into my hand. I put them on my tongue when she hands me a glass of water. I swallow the medicine and a few minutes later, I'm plunged into sleep.

2

I WAKE up to the sound of the shower running and pipes groaning. I shut my eyes again, savoring the few minutes of relative quiet before Janelle comes back into our room. When I hear the water turn off, dread pools in my stomach. I can barely get enough air into my lungs to complete a solid breath. Every part of me wants to pretend like last night didn't happen, but I need to tell her if I want to stay alive. Oblivious to my anxiety levels, she shuffles into the room and hops into my small single bed, a fluffy pink towel draped around her tall and thin frame. She presses a hand against my head, checking my temperature.

"You're getting me soaked," I complain, my voice a morning rasp.

"I'm glad you're up! And I guess your fever is gone. It must have been food poisoning, right?" She hops off the bed and opens our shared closet, pulling out a white tank top and skinny jeans, getting ready for work. She's a hair stylist at the salon at Bergdorf Goodman. It's a job any girl in her industry would kill for. Most of the salon's clients are celebrities or rich uptown girls with trust funds; they book months in advance for a cut or highlights, ranging upwards of three-hundred dollars. After sliding on her jeans and a lacy white bra, she looks down at her phone, smiling at whatever she's seeing. Her face lights up.

"Oh my God, Eve." She turns to me with a smile and then brings her gaze back to the phone. "Guess who's coming into the salon today? Gwyneth!" She jumps up and down. "Louis just texted me." She looks down at herself, eyebrows low. "Shit! I need to change into something better than this." Reopening our closet, she rummages through clothes.

"Janelle…" I start. She swivels her head, turning to me.

"What is it?" she asks nonchalantly, pressing a navy blouse against her chest and staring at herself in our long mirror.

"Something really bad happened. We need to talk." I drop my head nervously. When I look back up, I see anxiety clear in her eyes.

Placing her phone beside her, she sits next to me. "What's going on?"

I have to swallow a few times, but eventually, find the strength to tell her about the Snakes. She sits in silence until I'm completely done with every horrifying detail. It's agony to recount the story, but I need to tell her the truth. I need her help.

"Oh, Eve." Her face crumbles and tears well in her eyes. She draws me into her chest as we both start to cry.

"The Snakes." She sobs. "Those guys are psychotic!"

"I know I messed up big time, Janelle." Embarrassment mixed with agony blazes through me. I'm old enough to know better. I was literally saved by a stroke of luck. I could have been raped and beaten. Left for dead.

"Janelle," I sob. "It's all my fault. If I had just listened to you and didn't lose track of time, none of this would have happened." I curl into her side, bawling uncontrollably.

She pulls back, staring at me hard. "Eve, stop this. This is not your fault. Do you hear me? It's NOT your fault. Walking home late at night does not mean that anyone has the right to take you or to touch you against your will." Her words echo in my head. "I never want to hear you talk like this. We live in a dangerous place and God knows you do everything you can to stay under the radar. But you have to live, right?" She pulls me closer to her body, holding me together when it feels as though I'm being torn apart. "I'll figure out how to get you out of this. He won't come back for you, all right? We'll figure it out together."

A memory rushes to the forefront of my head. "I forgot to tell you, but Jason was there." I stare off into space, remembering how he thrust my clothes at me and practically begged me to run.

"Jason Mendes?" A half smile forms on her lips and my face immediately falls.

"Don't even think about it, Janelle!" I hiccup, knowing what she's insinuating.

She has the decency to drop her head for a moment. "Come on, Eve. Chill out. He isn't one of them, just a hang-around. His mom is on the sixth floor and sick with cancer. I do her hair sometimes and met him when I was over there. He deals some drugs for the Snakes on occasion, but nothing really too serious. I think he's a mechanic or something, actually. Anyway, maybe if you were closer to him," she says, raising her eyebrows at the word *closer*. "They'd leave you alone. Wasn't Vania saying the other day that he's into you?"

"No," I tell her, my voice shaking. "Why don't you go out with him? If he was with you, he'd probably protect me too, right?"

"Everyone knows I'm with Leo these days. Otherwise, I'd hit him up in a heartbeat." She winks at me in an attempt to lighten the mood.

She and Leo have a crazy relationship. One minute he's the best guy ever, the next she'd be screaming at the top of her lungs and cursing the day he was born. I haven't met him yet, but I'm not too eager considering all the drama he causes. Just the thought of him has me rolling my eyes.

She looks at me and huffs. "Stop being so judgmental, Eve. I see the look on your face and it isn't pretty."

"It's not unwarranted judgment. The guy takes you on an emotional roller coaster on a weekly basis! You deserve better than him." I get out of bed, agitated and feeling weirdly hollow.

"Unwarranted judgment?" she repeats, standing up tall. "Okay,

Miss Big-Shot attorney." Her condescending voice is like a kick to the chest. "Anyway, he cares about me." She lifts her head up.

"A man who cares about you won't put you through that," I sass, surprised at my tone.

She places a hand on her hip and shifts her weight to one leg. "Did your books teach you that? Because one stupid make-out session with Juan doesn't qualify you as a relationship guru. And clearly, you don't exactly have the best intuition, huh?"

My heart sinks.

"I—" My face crumbles and her face falls in regret as she steps forward, throwing her arms around me. I lean into her, my tears running like a faucet.

She sighs, holding me by the shoulders. "Look. I'm sorry, okay? I shouldn't have said that. Especially after what you've just been through. I know jumping into a man's bed for protection is the last thing you'd ever do. But girl, we've got to figure something out!" Her voice is desperate as she pulls me back into her chest, rubbing my back. I keep crying, and she continues to shush me gently.

When I finally catch my breath, she sits us both down at the table. "I don't want you worrying about Carlos. I have so much goodwill in this building, did you forget? I'll cash in a favor. Someone will talk to him and tell him you're completely off limits, okay?" I manage to nod my head. "You know these morons have short attention spans. One second, it's all about you and the next, they're on to someone or something else." I look up at her and see hope shining through her glassy eyes.

As a favor to some of the older ladies in the building, Janelle sometimes spends her time cutting and coloring their hair for free. Especially when the elevator is dead, it becomes too hard for older people to take the steps and leave the building. Even if they are strong enough to walk all the way downstairs, most of them are afraid of taking the stairwell all alone, and rightly so. With the lights always going out, bad shit will often go down in there.

People are always looking to repay Janelle for her kindness. Usually, it's in the form of home cooking. But maybe Janelle is right.

Maybe she really can have someone talk to Carlos, and he'll leave me alone.

"Now go take a shower," she instructs. "You have work at Angelo's today, right? It's good for you to get out of here and clear your head. We'll take the subway uptown together and you'll call me before you come home so I can meet you."

"O-kay," I manage to stutter.

She bites her lip, and I can tell there is more she wants to say. "Don't get mad with what I'm about to tell you, because I know you won't like it." She lets out a loud exhale. "I think you need to consider talking to Angelo about what happened."

"No!" I reply vehemently. "I'm not talking about this with him. If he got the Borignone family involved, I'd be bringing a shit storm on myself." I angrily wipe the tears off my face with my fingers, feeling some scratches on my face. My stomach churns.

Janelle clears her throat, snapping me back into the moment. "Yeah, but what if my connections can't control Carlos? We've got to think of a backup plan."

"If I let the Borignones help me, I'll be indebted to them. I can't get involved. Once I start owing people, I may as well be dead. You know Antonio—no favor is free."

She sighs. "Okay. Let's see what I can do first." She hugs me again as I walk out of the room with my head down.

Entering the bathroom, I tell myself Janelle will be able to fix this for me. My tears are now laced with relief, because she's here and has my back. She'll talk to someone. She'll make sure the Snakes don't bother me again. I'm not alone in this. I take my clothes off carefully, making sure not to look at myself in the mirror. Just the thought of being naked sickens me. This body I've been given is up for grabs, belonging to anyone stronger than me who wants it. I turn on the water extra hot, practically scalding myself as I step under the spray. I want to clean Carlos' fingerprints from my body.

I know when Janelle mentioned the Borignone family, she did it because they are probably the only ones who could actually kill Carlos and get away with it. The Borignones are the most notorious

As WE GOT OLDER, we learned that when Mom was happy, the supermarket needed to be our first stop. She'd walk with us up and down the aisles, laughing and playing supermarket sweep. We'd buy up every dry good we could fit into our cart. Fresh food wasn't smart since it ultimately went bad, but we'd take lots of canned fruits and vegetables.

Over time, Mom's highs got higher and her lows lower and longer. Weeks would sometimes pass and we wouldn't see her at all. Our food would run low. Janelle dropped out of school at sixteen to get a job. She pays most of our rent now, too, and makes sure we have food at all times. Eggs and milk. Pasta. I try to help out in the ways I can by cleaning and cooking meals. But Janelle refuses to let me leave school and get a full-time job, no matter what. I know she only stays in this shithole so I'm not alone.

Janelle insists that she didn't need school to be a famous hair stylist, but I know how much she sacrificed for me. One day, I'm going to make sure I make enough money for the two of us to get out of here. I'm not letting anything or anyone stop me. I just have to survive long enough to make it out.

3

JANELLE and I walk underground and get on the six train, heading uptown. Quickly finding two empty seats next to each other, we drop down before anyone else can grab them. Janelle lets out a loud breath as we cross our legs, sitting in silence. I'm relieved Janelle isn't trying to talk, because I don't think I have it in me to speak right now. Just as the subway pulls into Fifty-Seventh Street, she stands up, holding the railing above us with one hand and telling me in a whisper and watery eyes that everything will be okay. She gets off, and I pull my bag closer to my chest, continuing my commute uptown to work.

I get to Angelo's Pawn, pulling out my key to open the old gray door. I glance up for a moment, noticing one of the electric-green lights on the signage is no longer on, turning the name of the shop into ANGELO'S PAN. As I push the door open, I make a mental note to remind Angelo to fix it. Getting inside, I immediately notice the frame of a man's silhouette behind the counter. My voice falls to my feet, my throat constricting. Carlos. He found me! Emptiness closes in with a threat of forcing me to pass out as my heart jumps from my chest.

Angelo turns around, and my knees threaten to buckle with relief. Shock lines his face while I feel myself begin to hyperventilate. My electric-red Mohawk, and he's literally snarling at his opponent. My heart beats erratically as I look from side to side, realizing these guys don't even have gloves on! My mind is finally putting together the pieces of what I'm about to witness. Something that feels a lot like dread pools in my stomach. I'm about to watch an illegal cage fight.

"The rules are simple," the announcer tells the fighters. "Don't kick each other in the balls. No biting or eye gouging. And for the fans..." He lifts his hands up, staring at us all. "Don't step into the circle, or risk becoming part of the maaaaadness!"

People begin to go berserk. I feel some spit fly onto me from someone standing near me and my body shudders. The fighters stand tall, glaring at each other. They're practically foaming at the mouth. The only thought repeating through my head is: *HOLY SHIT!*

I turn my head left and right, my stomach cramping; I'm in the front row. There is no way I can move as the crowd is totally closed in behind me. I see people across the circle with their hands up, fists pumping in the air. They're waiting for blood, and from the looks of these two fighters, the blood will definitely be flowing.

I turn to Janelle, grabbing her shoulders. "We're too close to the front!" I yell, staring up into her eyes. I'm willing her to snap out of her drug-induced trance. Unfortunately for me, her eyes have already dilated. She leans down and puts her sweaty forehead on mine, her smile so big I think it might split her face.

She throws an arm around my neck. "Don't worry baby girl, this will be amazing! God, I love you so much!" She squeezes me close to her. Letting me go, she takes a huge gulp of water from a plastic bottle and continues shouting along with the crowd. I try to stand on my tip-toes to get a better look at my surroundings. Is there an empty space I can run through?

Unfortunately, the entire circle is shut tight with bodies. When I realize there's no way out, I close my eyes and count down from twenty. Before I open them, I inhale deeply through my nose, trying to find a modicum of calm. *I'm going to be okay.* When I open my eyes, I feel like the wind has been knocked out of me. Right across from me is the most attractive man I've ever laid eyes on.

He's a head above the rest, black hair that's longer at the top and shorter at the sides; it's a little wild, but incredibly sexy. I have never seen anyone who looks quite like him. The entire fight scene ahead of me seems to come to a standstill as I study him, the breath catching in my throat. I hear screaming all around me, but it may as well be on mute.

I watch as he pushes his hair back and casually throws an arm around a redhead. She's tall and thin, with wide blue eyes and thick auburn hair, mirroring a model in a Neutrogena skin commercial. Laughing at something he says, it's clear she fits the mold of an all-American beauty.

Turning back to him, I take in every single move he makes. Holy shit, he's gorgeous. I hear Janelle cheering wildly next to me, but the shrill sound barely registers.

He has something I can't put my finger on. Maybe it's the slight slant in his eyes or his razor-cut cheekbones and chiseled square jaw. It's just a trace of something unique, and it doesn't make him look kind. In fact, his face and entire demeanor is absolutely feral.

He whispers something into the girl's ear. I wonder what he's telling her. She bites her lower lip as she listens to him, and in that moment, I wish it were me in her spot. For the first time in my life, I'm practically vibrating with awareness over a man. Just then, he decides to raise his head. He glances around, seemingly looking for someone. His eyes immediately pause at mine, catching my stare. I've been caught! My heart stutters; I'm a deer in headlights as embarrassment runs through me.

Strangely, he isn't staring at me like a weirdo. Instead, his eyes seem to see straight into my soul; it's unnerving, but in some unexpected way, feels *right*. I open my eyes a little wider, feeling my lips part. He squints as a smile spreads across his full lips, settling into his eyes. I can't help the flush rising through my body.

We continue to watch each other, and it feels as if energy is passing between us. He pushes his hair back again, and I see the wide expanse of his chest. I try not to swoon from the visual. I see boys all the time, but none of them make me feel like *this*. Who am I kidding?

She purses her lips seductively, not willing to give up too quickly. "You gonna give me your real name one of these nights, Bull?"

He chuckles. "Just two cups of water, please." He gives her a panty-dropping grin that has her squirming. She moves to get the waters when I realize that I actually know his name. Vincent. My heart flutters that he's given something to me that he hasn't given to the sexy bartender.

After bringing the water, Vincent hands one to me first and picks up the second for himself. I watch his Adam's apple bob as he swallows his entire glass without a breath. I try to drink mine the same way, but end up choking. He starts to laugh at me and I roll my eyes. "I'm trying here!" I tell him, embarrassed.

"Damn, you're sweet." His eyes sparkle and my heart thumps.

Picking up his beer from the bar, he leads me over to where his friends are standing. The music blares as throngs of people walk down the steps.

"The place is packed." I feel my anxiety rise as strangers move against me. My heart pounds; I still can't handle being touched. Immediately noticing my discomfort, he backs us toward a wall and stands in front of me, not letting anyone other than him get in my space. I should be scared, but for whatever reason, his presence makes me feel secure.

"Yeah, it's definitely full tonight." He turns his head, looking around the room. "The deejay is a friend of mine and he's pretty good. Brings in a decent crowd." He takes another swallow of his beer as I nod my head, trying to act cool. Meanwhile, I'm anything but.

"So, you like what you saw tonight?" His voice is inquisitive as he licks the corner of his lips again. I'm trying not to stare at his mouth, but I can't help myself. When I glance back into his eyes, he smiles at me knowingly. I flush, self-conscious that he keeps catching me.

Unsure what he wants to hear, I go with honesty. "No, underground fights aren't really my thing." I shift my weight from one foot to the other. I finally have the strength to look straight into his eyes and when I do, another connection passes between us like a zing.

"You aren't a regular."

All I can do is nod my head at his statement.

He looks around the room and takes my hand again, walking us to a lounge area that's roped off. The bouncer greets Vincent with a fist bump and lets us inside. "Sit. It'll be more comfortable for you here." I gingerly move to the edge of the couch, waiting for him to come next to me.

He sits, spreading his knees and leaning back against the cushions. "You know, these fights have picked up a lot of steam in the city." He casually drapes an arm around the back of the couch. "When I first started fighting at places like these, it was a small crowd and just for fun. But it's really turned into something." I watch as his eyes move from my eyes to my lips, then back up again.

"Well, aside from the obvious injury or death, the whole thing seems horribly stupid. What if one of these fighters has AIDS? I doubt anyone is getting tested and meanwhile blood is flying all over the place." Clearly, the alcohol has removed the filter from my brain and loosened my tongue. *Holy shit.* The look on his face is one of utter shock.

"Not that I'm saying you have AIDS—" I stutter, trying to backtrack.

His eyes open wider and he starts laughing, clapping his hands a few times as if I said the funniest thing he's ever heard. "Well, you have a point. But all fighters know what we're getting into when we sign up." He tilts his head to the side, daring me to keep going. Unfortunately, the side of my brain that no longer has a filter wants to rise up to his dare.

"Yeah, so do people when they're trying to score drugs. The state should know that this goes on and just admit it so they can regulate it. By turning a blind eye, they're letting people put their lives in danger." Apparently, my voice has been found, because I can't seem to shut the hell up!

He keeps chuckling. "And you think it's the job of New York to make sure I don't put my life in danger?" He smiles broadly.

"Of course I do. The health and safety of its citizens should be the number one priority of any government." I look him in the eye nervously, realizing that my rant may have just screwed this whole thing up. Turns out my braniac alter ego is on full display tonight. One drink and it's unstoppable.

"Priority of the government, huh?" He lowers his head, getting close to my ear and whispers. "Well, the truth is I never go into a ring in this setting unless I know I'll pummel the guy. I've got a lot going on and can't risk getting hurt. I train like a monster too, so losing is really not possible. Most of these guys are untrained; beating them is a given."

His warm breath at my ear travels straight down into my core; I press my legs together. A guy drops down next to him and he moves his head away to chat.

Am I imagining all of this? I have an internal freak-out the size of a tornado going on in my brain. Thankfully, I have the mental capacity to text Janelle. I pull out my phone. I'm not sure if this is a one-way thing or if he's feeling it too. My lack of experience is rearing its ugly head.

ME: OH MY GODDDDDDDD I'm with the HOTTEST GUY EVERRRR
JANELLE: Yay!!! Be safe but don't forget a thing, I want to hear all about this tomorrow
ME: He's so friggin' hot I can't see straight. I really can't. I need help!
JANELLE: Relax. You're gorgeous. BE HAPPY!!
.... Text me if you need me.
.... And taxi home, no late night bus!
Nice out tonight—Blue Houses will be packed with people, so no worries!
ME: k.
JANELLE: I'm going to hang out at Leo's place for a while...;-)

I close my phone and drop it down in my bag. Part of me is scared as hell to be out all alone, but thoughts of the man next to me are keeping me afloat. A few guys have walked into our section and Vincent stands up to greet them. They're intimidating, all with slicked-back hair and suits. I stand up as Vincent grabs one of them in a friendly hug. "Eve, this is my boy, Tom." Vincent smiles.

As Tom starts talking about the fight, Vincent walks away. My brain screams, "What? No! Come back!" Tom takes a sip of his drink, not breaking eye contact with me. He seems nice enough, but I can feel his interest, and it's making me uncomfortable. I move my eyes away from him, trying to see where Vincent went. I hear Tom's voice, but none of what he actually says registers.

I turn back to him. "Huh? Sorry, my mind was on something else."

"The fights. Did you like em'?" He looks at me expectantly. He's tall, with sandy brown hair and light eyes. He's wearing a suit like the other guys. Actually, Vincent is the only casual one here.

"Did you all come from work or something?" I'm gesturing to his clothes and he starts to laugh. I immediately feel self-conscious, as if what I said was stupid.

"I guess you can call it that." He winks, taking a sip of his drink. I can easily imagine him driving to some college on the West Coast with his top down and girlfriend in the passenger seat of a Mercedes Benz.

He clears his throat.

"Yeah. The fights were cool. I've never seen anything like that before." I immediately realize how naïve I must have come across with my reply. I need a conversation redo.

He chuckles. "You're gorgeous. Have you ever thought of modeling?" He's getting closer, placing his hands around my waist. I shuffle backward as my breaths become labored; I can't deal with his proximity.

He squints at me, seeing my unease and immediately letting go of me. Before things can get weirder, my brain pushes into gear. "Modeling?" I awkwardly laugh. "I think being five-foot-one is probably a barrier to entry, no?" I'm trying to pretend that I didn't just freak out from his touch and luckily, he goes along with it.

"Touché." He snickers, dropping my mini freak-out without worry. I turn to find Vincent again. "Ah, I see." His voice is knowing.

"The Bull, huh?" He raises his eyebrows at me in question, and I shrug my shoulders.

"Do you also fight?"

"Nah." He takes a sip of his drink. "My boy is tough as fuck though; he got his nickname for a reason. A lot of pent-up aggression. It works for him to get in the ring." It's clear Tom is a nice guy, but *nice* isn't on my radar right now.

I zero in on Vincent while he talks to two burly men, each standing on either side of him. They take turns talking while he stands tall, listening and nodding his head. He seems to be scanning the area, looking for something or maybe, someone. Luckily, Tom seems to take the hint as he walks away from me.

Finally, Vincent and I lock eyes again. I give him a small smile, asking—no, begging—him to come back to me. He reads me easily, walking over.

"Wanna get outta here?" His gruff voice does something to my insides. I've gone mute again and can only nod my head *yes*. I catch the gleam in his eye as he takes my hand, leading us back up the steps and into the night.

6

I TRAIL behind him with anticipation, our hands locked together. It feels so incredible to hold his hand. I wonder how it's possible that I've gone eighteen years without it.

We get outside and I wait patiently on the corner as he walks to the street to hail a taxi. One pulls up and Vincent opens the door, waiting for me to step in first. For a moment, my mind catches up with me and I hesitate.

He seems to notice my nerves. "I can take you home, or we can go somewhere to eat if you're down," he says to me gently. He's assuring me. And for some reason that I can't fully comprehend, I trust him.

I shrug my shoulders casually, believing the feeling in my gut that I'll be okay. "Sure, I can always eat." I slide into the back seat of the cab and scoot over to the far window. When the door shuts, I feel like I've got skates on my feet and I'm being propelled forward. There is no stopping what's happening to me. I'm in a taxi with a complete and utterly gorgeous stranger. I must be insane.

My buzz is simmering down, but I wish it wouldn't. I feel his gaze on me and my breathing shallows. Instead of turning toward him, I sit silently, looking out the window and watching groups of people walking around enjoying the night. My brain is still shocked that I'm sitting next to him; making eye contact would be impossible right now. Luckily, he doesn't seem to mind the quiet. From my side eye, he seems totally at ease, his long legs spread wide across the seat.

Finally, the taxi pulls up to a corner; I notice we're still in the Meatpacking District. We get out of the car in front of a restaurant, Albero Di Limoni. Next door to the restaurant, there's a club called Lemon Bar. I see a bouncer standing by the club entrance, looking imposing. There's a line of people that spans the block, trying to get in. Vincent opens the door to the restaurant for us and I move inside.

I look around, gasping at the beauty. Dark, wood paneling covers the walls; in the center of the restaurant is a row of lemon trees. Fresh lemons, ready to be picked, dangle off thin branches. The smell of the restaurant is citrus-perfect. Fresh lemon, roasted garlic, and other spices permeate the air. Vincent takes my hand, leading me to a table in the back. I can't believe I've just walked into this; it's like a dream.

"Wow, this is incredible," I say in awe as I look around the restaurant, taking in the scene. I lower myself into a plush, red-velvet chair still looking around. I notice him smiling at the fact that I'm so amazed. I want to be embarrassed at my excitement, but for some reason, he seems pleased by my reaction. The red chairs look spectacular against the backdrop of yellow lemons. I can barely believe where I am!

The waiter comes over, at first happy to see Vincent. But before he can get a word out, Vincent stares him down, his face glacial. It's almost like he's trying to communicate something to him, but I can't understand what. On one hand, I'm happy as hell not to be on the receiving end of that look. On the other hand, I'm confused as to what's going on here. The waiter clears his throat, asking what we'd like to eat—a perfect professional.

"We're going to have a bottle of Pellegrino and she'll have a glass of Sancerre. She'll also have a filet steak, medium rare. Also, the Cornish hen. Side of roasted potatoes and green beans. Let's do mashed potatoes too. You know what, also bring her a salad to start. I'll have the wild salmon, simply grilled with no butter, no oil, no salt, and steamed broccoli on the side, also no butter, no oil, no salt." The waiter rushes off.

"Wow, that's a lot of food." I lift my eyebrows at him, feeling overwhelmed. I'm not used to eating out and if I do, it's usually at McDonald's. I clasp my hands together nervously under the table; I can't imagine how much this dinner must cost.

"Yeah, I guess so. I wasn't sure what you'd like. Anyway, the food's great. You'll enjoy it. I know the owner... personally." He leans forward with his elbows on the table.

I'm not sure what to say, so I go with something simple. "No butter, huh?" I smile. I'm doing my best to look into his eyes without melting into a puddle.

He laughs at my question, not bothering to answer. He looks pretty rough and I see some scratches on his jaw.

I turn toward the waiter as he places a salad and cold glass of wine in front of me. Vincent looks down at my food expectantly, waiting for me to start eating. I take the fork and dig in. The lettuce is so crispy and perfectly chilled, and the dressing tastes like mustard and vinegar. It's simply incredible. When I sip the wine, I hum. My taste buds are in a very happy place right now. "So, I take it you workout a lot?" I ask, trying to go for another easy conversation topic.

He seems bored with my question, licking his lips and glancing around the room. "Yeah, I've been doing MMA for a while now." I stay quiet, waiting for him to continue. But a few minutes of silence, I realize that he isn't going to answer me.

"Do you plan on going pro or something?"

"Nah. I just do it for fun, actually. It started with me just messing around and sort of grew from there."

Our conversation seems to halt after that. Luckily, the wine seemed to numb any filters I usually have. Before I can think twice, I open my big mouth and ask, "So, what do you think about all the problems going on in the Middle East?" His eyes widen, and he starts to laugh. I'm relieved my attempt to shake him out of his seriousness worked. He probably thinks I'm a dork now but well, whatever.

Without hesitating, he leans closer to me. "I gotta say that

Netanyahu doesn't mess around. He's all about keeping Israel safe and I gotta respect that. Yeah, he pushes boundaries. And the UN hates Israel's guts, that's for sure..." His voice trails off, but my heart starts to pound.

I lean forward, putting my elbows on the table. "Have you read his autobiography? Netanyahu's, I mean. I went through a phase where I was trying to understand the Middle Eastern conflict better. It was actually really good."

"Believe it or not, it's sitting on my desk. I usually buy ten or fifteen books at a time and tell myself that I've got to finish them within the year. I just finished *The Autobiography of Malcolm X*."

I swallow hard. "I read that," I tell him quietly. My heart is filling up; that's one of the most influential books of my life. Thoughts of my childhood reading partner, Javi, enter my mind, and all of a sudden, I feel a combination of hot and terrified.

His throat moves as he drinks from his cup of water. "Yeah? What did you think?" He places the glass down, entirely focused and waiting for my reply. I'm not used to this type of conversation, and it's both nerve-wracking and exciting. He's looking at me as if he's actually interested to hear what I have to say. Even though I'm scared to sound stupid, a large part of me yearns to rise up. I push away any anxiety and reply.

"Most people stick to what they know because they don't know that any better option exists. They have no one in their lives who shows them a path that's different from the one they see everyone around them taking. Or, they make certain choices in their youth that result in shutting down any possibilities for the future. By the time they get older and understand the mistake, it's too late to back out. They're incarcerated or dead. Or maybe they're involved in some gang that won't let them out."

He chimes in. "But sometimes, things happen to us that propels us toward a different destiny. And I think that when Malcolm X goes to jail and makes a conscious choice to refrain from eating pork, that one small act was the catalyst in changing the entire course of his life. So, change is possible, right? If, of course, you can survive long enough to get to that point." He's staring at me seriously, and this time the feeling goes way beyond the physical. I'm gazing into his dark eyes, and somehow, his presence makes me want to rise up in all senses of the word.

I swallow again. His expression turns thoughtful, as if he's really waiting to hear my reply. I want to show him what I think; I feel as if I don't have to hide with this man. I push my worry in the back of my mind again, and allow myself to speak freely. The alcohol is definitely helping the situation, shutting up my nerves and loosening my tongue.

"I hear your idealism. And I know it seems possible to believe we can all change, especially when reading about a man like Malcolm X. But for most people, experiencing a world outside of their poverty is near to impossible. I mean, it's easy for a rich guy to believe that a kid from the ghetto can turn his life around if he just stopped with the violence, or picked up a book, or got into religion. But, you can't protect yourself from violence with a book. The streets are danger-ous, Vincent. And most people do the best they can to protect them-selves. And when protection is on your mind, and feeding your family—or when other basic necessities are at risk—there is no time for introspection or higher knowledge. That makes changing really, really difficult, although not impossible."

"Well, jail is certainly a place where you have nothing else to do but think and reach higher knowledge, huh?" He exaggerates his shrug, and I start to laugh.

A flicker of amusement passes through his face at my reaction, but his stare somehow intensifies. I feel my face growing red.

He continues. "Well, let's get real for a second. If you're willing to die to get out of your circumstances, that may be the answer. I mean, you can easily say, fuck it. Forget protection and basic necessities. Forget being smart on the street. My goal is getting out, even if I may die trying."

I'm in a state of utter shock right now and I'm sure my face shows it, because he's smiling like he just won a game. I'm not sure if he real-izes that he just pegged me, but he did. He hit my nail on the head.

I take another huge swallow of my wine. "Well, what do you make of the fact that once Malcolm X finally found peace, he was assassinated?"

He leans forward, even closer. "I think that America likes to claim that in this country, there's mobility within the classes. But in reality, even if you transcend your upbringing, there's someone who will push you back down again. Maybe in reality, change is actually impossible."

"No!" I exclaim, dropping my fork onto my plate. His eyes widen in surprise at my outburst, but I can't believe that what he's saying is true. "Change has to be possible..." I turn my head down, trying to process my thoughts.

"Eve," he starts. "It's not just people in poverty who suffer from this... I mean, shit, there's always someone controlling all of us. None of us are really free, are we? In every single realm from impoverished up to Arab Sheiks, we're all victims of how we were raised. Did you read *The Short and Tragic Life of Robert Peace*?" I nod my head.

"He may not have been assassinated, but he was brought back down and into the rabbit hole of his upbringing, regardless of the Ivy League college he attended and all the schooling in the world combined with incredible natural brilliance. Because change is—"

"No," I stop him. "Change is not impossible. It has to be possible! And yeah, I see what you're saying. But Rob didn't have to sell drugs. He chose it in the end, and that was his downfall. His bad choice. His refusal to let go of where he came from."

"So, you're saying that if you want to change, you need to cut ties with your past?"

"Yes." I nod vigorously. "I do. I think that sometimes you need to burn bridges. I think that in order to transcend a life of poverty, you've got to do just that—leave the hood behind."

"But what if your past isn't necessarily bad blood? Like, maybe you're poor and live in the ghetto, but you've got a huge amazing family. You still want out, though. Do you have to leave all those people behind? It's not always one-dimensional."

I immediately think of some friends from the Blue Houses, with huge but loving families. "Well, yeah. I think you can bring them into your new life, but I don't think going back to your old life is smart. You'd be surprised at how impoverished cultures aren't interested or supportive of people breaking out of the mold; it's almost as if they feel like if you leave the community, you're denying their value. Like, if you leave, it's because you don't think they're good enough or worth staying for. It's offensive to them. Maybe your own family is supportive and proud. But the community as a whole, not so much."

He stops and we get quiet, looking at each other. My chest constricts from the intensity of our conversation, and he looks at me with all the interest a set of eyes can convey. Deep down, I feel angry and upset. He doesn't know that I'm that person. I'm that girl with nothing and a shitty upbringing. I'm the one who is willing to die trying.

"Eve, look at me." I bring my gaze back up to his. "I wasn't trying to say that it's impossible to change. I mean..." he swallows. "I'm not poor by any stretch," he admits. "But, I've been raised in a certain way. I've also made choices that were in line with expectations placed on me. I've also picked a path that maybe, under other circumstances, I wouldn't have chosen. But now I'm here. In that life. And there's no way out."

I'm surprised by his admission, but assume that he's talking about being forced into grad school or something. A man like him doesn't have real problems. I mean, look at the place he brought me! Everything about him screams confidence and money.

"But Vincent, you don't have to live that way if you don't want to. You can wake up one morning and leave. You aren't behind bars or dead. You aren't in some gang where the only way out is in a body bag."

He pulls his head back, looking as if I've slapped him. Maybe I said something that touched too close to home. I want to say more, but before I can continue, dish after dish comes out of the kitchen and onto our beautiful table. I can't help myself as I dig into the delicious food. He watches me quietly as I eat my dinner. We're silent, and I'm glad for that. The silence with him is comfortable and somehow, full of warmth. We went from challenging each other to enjoying each other.

I've never eaten a filet steak in my life, and the meat melts in my mouth like butter. I moan from the taste, and he gives me a heated look.

"What?" I ask him, smiling with my mouth full, taking another sip of the cold wine. I look at my glass and realize that somehow, despite how much I've drunk, my glass is still full.

He leans closer to me. "Watching you eat is... let's just say that I don't usually see girls enjoying food like you do. I like it." His voice is a whisper, and I feel it straight down into my core.

I put my fork down and lick my lips, feeling the urge to engage him once again. "Yeah, you're probably used to girls picking at their salads, huh? No butter, no salt, no pepper, no taste?" I reply, starting to laugh. I'd be lying if I said I wasn't enjoying the hell out of the moment. Apparently with Vincent, I can go from serious conversation to banter in a matter of minutes.

"Oh baby, you have no idea. Between my usual clean food diet and these super skinny girls I'm normally with, we're like a restaurant's worst nightmare." Realizing he's making fun of himself, I can't help the giggle that erupts from my mouth. He chuckles with wonder when he sees my face.

"So, are you saying I'm not super skinny?" I raise my eyebrows, daring him to call me fat.

He drinks me in with his eyes, staring at me from my face down to my chest and back up again. "You're perfect; that's what you are." I open my mouth and then snap it shut.

"You know, when I saw you enter the ring, I was afraid for a few seconds. That meathead was practically foaming at the mouth." I cut up another piece of steak.

He snorts. "Yeah and that name Jack *the Ripper*?" Putting his fork into his food, he takes another large bite.

"Yeah," I nod enthusiastically. "That name is too ridiculous to take seriously." I roll my eyes, putting the meat in my mouth and moaning again. He looks at me incredulously as if I'm groaning for his sake. I ignore him and keep eating; nothing is going to stop me from enjoying this incredible meal. Just a few hours ago, I was sitting in my shitty apartment, eating Dominos with my sister. And now here I am, eating a however-many-course meal with the most gorgeous and intelligent man I've ever laid eyes on!

My mouth is full, but I continue, "I mean, I can think of a hundred better names than that stupid one." I swallow, clearing my throat. "If I were a fighter, I'd call myself *the Raven*." I can't help the smile that forms on my face.

He chuckles. "Is that your alter ego?" He's joking around with me and I...well, I freakin' love it!

"Oh yeah, that's me...poverty-stricken-book-nerd by day, pecking on people's windows by night and scaring the crap out of them," I deadpan.

He laughs out loud and the sound fills up a spot inside my chest. The table next to us turns around, but I barely register them. All I can see is the man sitting in front of me.

"Or you can go really wild and call yourself Poe's Raven." He's waiting for me to catch his drift and I'm squealing for joy inside. I want to scream, *I'm nerdy too! I know the poem!*

I can't help myself but recite it. I'm just really dorky like that and apparently, drunk enough to show it. "Once upon a midnight dreary, while I pondered, weak and weary..."

He stops me, a look of shock passing over his chiseled features. "Over many a quaint and curious volume of forgotten lore—"

My eyes widen and he guffaws. We're quoting poetry right now and my heart is so full I want to jump up and down and scream. Who the hell is this man? No, really. Who? An MMA fighter from an underground fighting ring? A poet? A few seconds pass. Or maybe it's minutes. But we're quiet, staring into each other's eyes. We're not even waiting for someone to talk. We're just staring. Glowing. Something is passing between us that I can't rationally explain.

Before I can stop myself, my subconscious blurts out, "Do you see me?" I immediately drop my head, shocked I just said that out loud. I'm not even sure what I meant! I turn red again, embarrassment blazing. I risk a glance at Vincent only to see him grinning, apparently pleased by my word vomit.

He moves forward in his chair, leaning closer to me. "Yes, Eve. I see you. And for the record, I like what I see. A lot." His eyes actually twinkle with his words. It dawns on me that this may be the first time I've ever been truly looked at. I never knew how much I ached for this feeling, until now.

"How did you get the name *the Bull*, anyway?" I'm smiling so wide that my cheeks are starting to ache.

"Well, you want the true story or the story I tell people?"

"Hmm." I press my lips together and stare at the ceiling, as if deep in thought. "Give me the truth." I stare into his eyes. "Always the truth." I drop my elbows on the table, not wanting to miss a word.

"How about I tell you both. And you tell me which one is real and which is the lie?" I nod my head, excited to play along.

"All right," he clears his throat. "Once upon a time, Zeus sees Europa. The second his eyes are on her, he knows he wants her. But he also knows she would never come to him out of her own free will. So, one day he disguises himself as a beautiful white bull. After a few minutes of petting the bull, she decides to sit on him, expecting him to be as gentle as he is beautiful. But as she sits on the bull's back, he runs away, stealing her and bringing her to Crete." He takes another bite of his food. "So basically, Zeus saw what he wanted, and he found a way to take her." After swallowing, he lifts a glass of water to his lips.

"Um, doesn't the story go that he steals and *rapes* her?" I ask, my eyebrows furrowing together.

He's silent until bursting into laughter, clapping his hands like my response was the funniest thing he's ever heard. "You little genius, huh? When can I watch you on Jeopardy?" His smile is blinding me. He's playing with me, but he isn't being condescending. I've never had more fun in my entire life.

I roll my eyes. "I do know a ton of useless shit. I gotta call them and get on that show." He's shaking his head incredulously, and I can't stop myself from smiling. Gah!

"Well," he clears his throat. "Some people say it ended in a rape. But I don't believe that. He just took what he wanted and didn't let anyone stop him."

I smirk. "All right. So, you're the bull who looks all perfect, but really, you're a selfish god? Totally possible for you to believe that about yourself, cocky bastard you obviously are. And what's the second story?" He's staring at me as if I'm something special. My heart warms. No, it's not warming. It's actually on fire right now. I feel like a side of myself, which I've never dared to show, has been brought out of me. I wish it would never end.

"Well, believe it or not, I wasn't always this big." I make a face, ready to call bullshit. I can't imagine him ever being small.

"Just listen. I was in second grade, and I was getting picked on at recess. This kid, Jack Ford, kept pushing me around with some of his friends. At first, I tried to ignore them. But somehow a shadow came over me and I went berserk. I fought the kids and took them all down, breaking one of their noses in the process. Not that I knew any fighting skills, but I was an angry little shit. Apparently, everyone who watched me said I looked like an angry bull. The name stuck."

I sit back in my chair, looking at him intently. "I don't know which story is real. Both seem kind of plausible." I'm about to take another bite of the steak, but stop before it reaches my lips. "Stop staring at me, Vincent! I'm sorry for the moaning and groaning, but it's just too good! You have to try some." I hand him my fork. He takes it from my hand, placing the meat in his mouth. He lets out a grumble as he chews, the sound coming from deep in his throat. All kinds of signals are sent straight from my ears down through my body.

His eyes move above my head and he squints, looking surprised at whatever he sees. I turn around, wondering what it is he saw. A group of men have come into the restaurant, all in dark suits. Most of the people eating turn around to stare at them; their presence is noticeable.

"We should go," he tells me abruptly, standing and waiting for me to grab my purse off the back of my chair. Without even asking for the check, he lifts my hand into his and we jet through the restaurant, still completely filled with people. I'm confused, but too nervous and uncomfortable to ask what the hell is going on. I guess he did say he knows the owner—I assume he'll pay later.

While Vincent hails another taxi, I look behind me to see the line for Lemon Bar has doubled. I know how weird it is that I'm born and raised in New York City, but never went to a nightclub. Maybe I'll go soon with Janelle. I turn my head, ready to abandon thoughts of dancing when Vincent moves next to me.

He looks back and forth between the door of the club and the restaurant. "You want to go inside?" His smile is infectious and before I know it, I'm nodding my head *yes*. It seems whatever had him running isn't following us out. Looking at some people handing their ID's to the bouncer, it dawns on me this club is probably for twenty-one and over.

"I don't have an ID. You need that to get in, right?" I'm not even sure how old Vincent is, but he definitely looks older than I am.

"You don't need an ID when you're with me." His smile is so warm. "Come on, let's go
have some fun."
Before we move, I ask, "How old are you, Vincent?"

He grins, as if my question amuses him. "I'm a junior in college." My heart skips at the word *college*.

The bouncer notices Vincent and immediately stops, opening up the velvet rope for us to pass through. I hear some people grumble with annoyance, but Vincent struts forward like he owns the place. We get inside the club and walk straight to the bar. The room is completely packed, but he easily slides himself between two people to get a spot.

He turns to me. "You want water or another drink?" I'm already feeling more than buzzed from the wine at dinner. "Um, just water, please." He nods his head, seemingly happy at my response. The bartender trips over herself to get to Vincent, and I grimace.

After I take a few sips, he drops my glass on the bar and takes my hand, bringing me to the center of the dance floor. I start to move, but I'm relieved to see that he's kept a slight distance. The music is amazing and I can feel the bass in the center of my chest. Throngs of people surround us, and it's easy to just get lost in the mix. Before I know it, I'm completely letting go and dancing with my whole body. His hands move around my waist, but he still isn't bringing me flush against his chest like I wish he would. A few times I try to move closer to him, but he's in total control. I want to be upset that he doesn't want to feel me against him, but I'm too happy to let myself pout.

I touch my shoulder, feeling the dampness on my skin. Looking up into his face, I notice he's hot as well. I've never had fun like this in my life!

He puts his hand in his back pocket, pulling out his phone and looking at it closely. "I've got to make a quick call. Wait for me, okay?" he's yelling over the music, and I hear him clearly. He leads me back to the center of the bar. "Don't move!" He winks, giving my hand a squeeze before walking off. At first, I see his dark head over everyone else, but then he's gone. I'm standing and minding my own business when a man I don't know slides up next to me.

"Hey, sweetheart. Can I buy you a drink?" I barely notice anything other than he's tall with blond hair when I reply.

"No, thank you." I keep my back straight and turn my head away from him, not wanting to give him any ideas.

"Come on, baby. Let me buy you something." He tries to get closer and I immediately feel my body tighten with anxiety. I want to move backward, but the bar is so full of people, the only way I can escape him is to leave the bar entirely—and if I exit this area, what if I don't find Vincent again? It occurs to me Vincent may have left me here. What if his plan was to ditch me and he doesn't come back at all? I mean, sure we've been having a great time. But he doesn't owe me anything. Janelle has told me about countless guys who she thought were crazy about her, but ultimately left her high and dry. I'm sweating again, except this time, it isn't from chemistry or the heat of the room. I check my watch, realizing it's getting close to two and I'm all alone. I didn't even consider how I'm going to get back into my apartment. I need to call Janelle, but my hands are shaking too badly.

After taking a good look at me, the man's flirtation turns into concern. "Hey, sweetie, are you all right? I wasn't tryin' to upset you. Look, let me get you some water. Calm down, okay? I had a girlfriend once who had bad anxiety." He turns to flag down the bartender. He orders me a cup of tap and I swallow it down.

"Feeling better?" I blink a few times, wanting to reply. I'm afraid if I open my mouth, I'll burst into tears. I never should have come here with a complete stranger. I never should have drunk any alcohol. I'm clearly inept at judging situations. I'm obviously incompetent, just like my mom always says.

"Take a few deep breaths," he instructs calmly. I'm holding onto the edge of the bar, my knuckles turning white. "Do you have a friend here? Maybe we should get some fresh air." I nod, but still can't manage speech. I turn around to leave when Vincent steps in front of me.

I must look like I'm having some sort of panic attack, because his wide smile turns down the second he sees the state I'm in. "You okay, baby? What the fuck happened here?" My bar neighbor turns to him to say something but freezes when he sees the look on Vincent's face.

"Did this guy mess with you?" Vincent's aggression should be making everything worse. Instead, I feel the anxiety drain from the soles of my feet. I grab his shirt, turning him toward me before he gets in this guy's face.

"No, Vincent, I—" My body trembles as relief courses through me. Vincent is back. Half of me wants to jump into his arms and thank him for not disappearing. But the other half wants to smack him across the face for walking away in the first place.

He leans into me, putting a hand on my arm to calm me down. "Let me take you home, okay? I shouldn't have left you alone—"

"I'm not a regular in places like these..." I'm moving my head from side to side, trying not to sound desperate. But the truth is I'm scared as hell. This is too much too soon.

He nods his head and grips my hand tightly, letting me know without words that it's okay. We walk out of the club together and back onto the street corner. Even though it's late, the block is full of people. He continues to hold my hand as he lifts his free arm to hail a taxi; one immediately pulls up to the corner.

Vincent opens the door for me and I climb inside first, moving to the far window. He follows me into the back seat, sitting flush against me. I feel his thigh pressing against mine; I'm not sure what I should do. Should I move my leg? Stay where I am? Does he notice what he's doing, or am I just overthinking it? Maybe this is how he normally sits, with his huge, muscular thigh touching the person next to him? I look up at him and he turns his face to mine. It dawns on me this man is used to getting everything he wants, whenever he wants it. I'm nervous, but holy shit do I want to please him. The realization is instantly sobering. I can't look away from his dark, gorgeous eyes.

The driver bangs his steering wheel, his voice instantly breaking our moment. "Where you headed?" he asks in a heavy Middle Eastern accent.

We both turn toward him. "I'm on Avenue D and Fifth," I reply. My voice doesn't falter, but I'm nervous, hoping Vincent doesn't recognize the address.

Sure enough, though, his eyes widen in disbelief. "You're in the Blue Houses?" The tone of his voice is unmistakable; he's surprised and seems to pity me.

"Yeah." I look back at him, shrugging my shoulders. I want to tell him sure, *it's a pretty horrible place to live, but it's home for now.* As I turn away from him to stare out the window, he takes my hand and gently rubs his callused thumb back and forth over my knuckles. It's both soothing and arousing at once. I swallow hard, trying to steady my heart rate. I cross my legs and let out a sigh, keeping my eyes focused on the city streets.

A few minutes later, the cab stops short in front of my building. I let myself out of the back seat and look up, wondering what it looks like to an outsider. Three tall gray buildings are clustered together and fenced-in balconies frame the facade. The result is a prison-like structure. Pockets of people stand around smoking. On a night like this one, with clear skies, people don't like to sit in their small apartments. I see a couple of guys on the stoop, observing everyone coming and going from the entrance. Luckily, they aren't wearing any colors; I know they may be thugs, but they aren't gang affiliated.

Vincent swipes his credit card to pay the taxi driver and steps out, insisting on walking me to the building's front door. I want to protest to prove that I'm independent, but my innate sense of self-preservation tells me not to let him go. Even though there are people around, it's late and dark—and being alone, even if I'm armed, isn't the brightest idea. He slightly raises his chin, looking straight-up lethal. The intelligent man from the restaurant is gone, and in his place is the Bull from the ring.

Taking my hand, Vincent walks us inside the building with purpose, as if he's the one who lives here. He makes it clear that he's taking me all the way up to my apartment's front door; he's a man on a mission, and I'm not planning on stopping him.

He opens the door for me and we walk into the dingy gray lobby. The elevator has a sign on the door that says: OUT OF ORDER. I shut my eyes, cursing my luck. Looks like we'll have to walk up the steps—just another sign pointing to my background, unworthy of a man like him. I lead him to the stairwell. Like a bad horror film, the lights flicker when the door slams shut. The light settles on a dim glow. He stops at the base of the steps, squeezing my hand and cursing. "This is dangerous. Tell me the lights normally work."

"Uh, maybe I should tell you two stories. One real and one made up. You tell me which is which." I internally slap myself five for giving back what he gave me just a few hours earlier.

He chuckles. "Okay." We begin the trek up the steps. Luckily, he can't see my face right now, because my body short-circuits every time his chest or hand brushes my back. It feels like I'm being stalked up the stairs; he's just so close, but at the same time, not nearly close enough.

I try to sound upbeat. "There's a fantastic super who fixes everything anytime tenants call. I'm sure all the bulbs will be replaced by morning." He lets out a noncommittal grunt.

"Ready for the second story?" Our pace seems to be slowing down as his hand lightly grazes my lower back. He continues to touch me, and I get the feeling it isn't by accident.

"Go on." His voice is rough, and I blink a few times to steady myself.

"I'm lucky the light is even flickering. Sometimes it gets so dark, I may as well be walking through a black tube."

I stop when we get to the fourth floor, turning around at the top step to tell him this is it. Before I can continue our little game to ask him which story is the truth, he puts his hands on my waist, waiting for me to look up at him.

I may be standing on a step above him, but he still towers over me. I watch as he licks his full lips, and my core begins to pulse from the visual. I'm not sure what the hell is happening to me, but my mind can't focus on anything other than Vincent. The darkness is impairing my vision, resulting in a heightening of all of my other senses. I put my hands around his neck and feel the warm sinewy muscle under my fingers. With both his hands, he pushes my hair behind my ears and angles my head up to face him. He's asking me with his touch if I want this. I let out a loud sigh and lean toward him as every cell in my body screams *YES*.

When he presses his lips to mine, I freeze. But he doesn't let it deter him. Instead, he continues kissing me with a surprising gentleness, moving his mouth against mine and finally sliding his tongue alongside the seam of my mouth, begging entrance.

I open my mouth, letting him inside. His taste combined with the softness of his tongue has my legs weakening. He wraps a strong arm around my waist and holds me up, steadying me. Within seconds, his soft kisses become demanding. I'm trying to keep up with his pace, but it feels so good, all I can do is take it. He lifts me up and I instinctually wrap my legs around his waist. As if I weigh nothing at all, he walks us up to the landing and pushes me against the concrete wall. My phone drops to the ground, but I barely hear it or notice. He starts to rub against me rhythmically, pressing his hardness against my jeans in slow and deep strokes. I let out a moan as he hits a spot that's starting an electrical current in my veins. Sweat beads on the back of my neck and between my breasts. My body is on overload; heat traveling from where he's pushing against me out into all of my limbs. I'm shaking as my hands clutch his strong shoulders. He moves his lips from my mouth to my neck and I lean my head back against the wall, offering myself to him. God, it feels so good. Too good. Moments later, his lips suck a trail up to my ear. I'm burning up.

His lips move to my ear. "Fucking gorgeous, baby. Watching you dance, I had to talk myself down from taking you right there in the middle of the club." Replying is not possible; the only sounds coming from my lips are moans.

My body is climbing higher and higher toward something. I feel him unbuttoning my jeans and I'm letting him. I'd do anything to soothe this ache. And right when I think I'm about to incinerate, his hand reaches down and presses into a spot that literally short circuits my brain. My head slams against the wall behind me and I'm completely lost, a scream tearing from my throat. I have zero control as my body melts on and on. He holds onto me, wrapping his body around me tightly as I come down from the high.

"What the hell was that?" I pant. I can barely see him as the lights flicker on and off, but the questioning look he gives me is clear.

"Was that your first orgasm, Eve?" All I can do is nod my head. He sighs, dropping his head into the crook of my neck. "God, baby. I can't lie to you. I like that. I like that a lot. You're so innocent and stunning. Fuck." My eyes close again when I feel his lips back on mine, his tongue slowly dragging in and out of my mouth.

I let out a hum and give myself over to him; I'm so pliable right now; he could do anything he wanted, and I would say *yes*. When he pulls back, I open my eyes and touch my hands to my face, noticing how hot it is to the touch. He slowly lowers my feet to the ground and all I want to do is beg him to keep me up here, close to his body. I button my jeans as he bends down, picking up my phone and handing it to me.

We walk together to my apartment door. I turn toward him and look up into his intense eyes, wanting to thank him. But when I hear a couple fighting, I'm immediately brought back to my reality. I drop my head, irrationally wishing he either didn't hear or didn't notice. I'm one-hundred percent sure this isn't the type of place Vincent is used to.

Noticing my discomfort, he slowly lifts my head back up. "Hey, Eve. Look at me." My eyes meet his again. "Give me your phone and let me give you my number." He waits patiently for me to pull out my phone.

I reach into my purse and hand it to him, breathing deeply. All of a sudden, things have gotten quiet between us.

He opens my contacts and types his information. I'm pressing my lips together, waiting for him to ask me for my number in return. But when he hands me back my phone, I can't manage any words. Leaning against the doorway, he looks down at me and pushes some errant hair out of my face. "You're different from other girls I know." Licking his lips, he bends down, pressing a chaste kiss on my forehead. "I'll see you around, okay? Promise you'll call me if you ever need anything." He turns around to leave, and I'm stuck speechless and quaking.

I float into my apartment, my brain short-circuited and high, but sublimely happy. I go into the bathroom to wash up, wishing I could savor this feeling for eternity. Before removing my makeup, I look in the mirror. Staring at myself, I try to see what he could possibly see in me.

My eyes shine brown and my hair looks glossy and full. My lips are puffy and pink from all the kissing. I touch my lips and sigh. When I'm all clean, I get into bed, replaying my night over and over. If I sleep, will it all just disappear? I try to keep myself awake to prolong the feeling and the memories, but with enough time, my body gives into exhaustion and I fall asleep.

7

SATURDAY MORNING COMES TOO QUICKLY. By the time I wake up, Janelle has already left for work. I wash up as fast as I can, not wanting to be late for my meeting with Ms. Levine at her apartment. I take the Six Train Uptown to Eighty-Sixth Street and walk out of the station, immediately coming face to face with Ms. Levine's tall glass building—a gorgeous brand-new condominium called the Lucinda.

I have a definite bounce in my step today. I'm not sure I'll ever see Vincent again, but just the potential is enough to lift up my spirits. I can barely believe a man like him exists in this world. I also can't believe all of the incredible things he made me feel. *He's here in this city,* my heart whispers. Maybe my luck is finally changing? I feel the hope move around in my chest.as I smile wide.

I stop at the desk in Ms. Levine's fancy lobby, letting the concierge know who I'm here to see. I turn my head to the front door as a bellboy pushes a large cart filled with suitcases. "The car should be out front," the woman tells him with a stony face.

Ms. Levine used to make some serious bank as a high-powered attorney in the city but left her white-glove life to help the city's neediest kids change their lives. Unfortunately for her, aid is almost impossible to give in a school system that's utterly broken and with kids who refuse to change. But I guess, there's me. And there's no denying the fact that she's changing the hell out of my life.

I remember when she walked into my ninth-grade English class. We all knew she was a brand-new teacher, and most of the students were ready to give her their version of a warm welcome. She walked into the classroom in a designer-looking suit and high heels that screamed, "I'm ready to take on the world!" Before she could put her briefcase on the chair by her desk, someone launched a calculator at her head. Laughter ensued, but it was just the beginning.

By her fourth day, kids were throwing textbooks from the fifth-story classroom window. It's safe to say her idealism took a hit pretty early on in her teaching career.

Even though the classroom drama persisted, she still assigned *The Great Gatsby* as the first required reading, followed by an essay on the book's portrayal of the upper versus lower classes of society. Because I happen to love that book and read it with my old friend Javi in eighth grade, I wrote the paper. I handed it to her quietly after class, writing: PLEASE DON'T TELL ANYONE I WROTE THIS at the top. The last thing I needed was to draw negative attention to myself.

Javi Dante was a friend of mine. He was *smart*. We'd pass books between ourselves—hiding the books as if we had cash inside our backpacks—reading for pleasure and for the possibility of a better life one day. Our hunger to get the hell out of the Blue Houses was insatiable. We would stick Post-Its inside the pages of borrowed classics, scribbling notes to each other. We read everything we could get our hands on. Malcolm X. Paulo Coehelo. Zora Neal Hurston.

The morning of his death, I passed him *The Invisible Man*—a book that shook me to the core but was ultimately left undiscussed. The cops found the book in his bag, wondering who wrote on all the green Post-Its. No one ever found out it was me. Janelle knew everything, though. She told me to shut up and stay low for a while. People can smell the stench of potential, and somehow, it never ended well for most of them.

The community went crazy for a few weeks, wondering who killed this innocent boy.

"Another youth wasted!"

"He had the highest grades for math. He could have been a doctor!"

"His mom applied him to one of the best prep schools in the country; they already accepted him for high school!"

"He could have been something. Done something for this comm-u-nity!"

"We need better schools. Someone, tell the mayor!"

It all fell on deaf ears. Debts are owed, and sometimes lives are used as payment. Here, our bodies are nothing but currency. I later found out his brother cheated the Snakes out of some drug money. To show their power, his brother had to pay in blood. Javi was the blood.

A few days after I handed in the paper, Ms. Levine pulled me aside and insisted my intelligence was being neglected; she wasn't going to stand for it any longer. According to her, I was never able to translate my intellect into academic potential. She intended on being the one to change that.

Since then, Ms. Levine has been on a mission to get me out of the ghetto and into an Ivy League college—insisting with her help, I could change the path of my life.

In the past three years, our relationship has grown from teacher and student to mentor and mentee. She's had my sister Janelle and me over to her beautiful apartment for countless dinners and gives us all sorts of advice, which goes way beyond the academic. When Janelle had a pregnancy scare last year, Ms. Levine's apartment was where she took her First Response test, which was thankfully negative. And when my mom came home on a drug-induced rampage and cut up all of my clothes with meat scissors, Ms. Levine is the one who brought me to Target on 117th street and replaced all of my old thrift-shop clothes.

Finally, the concierge nods at me, letting me know without a word that I can head up. Stepping into the wood-paneled elevator, it brings me directly to the fifteenth floor.

I walk down the carpeted hallway when her door swings open. "Hi, Eve! Application time!" she says in a sing-song voice. She hugs me tightly, genuinely happy to have me here. Ms. Levine is tall and thin with long caramel-colored hair. Normally, she wears it in a tight bun; right now, it's down around her face, making her look much younger.

"Eve, I already printed out ten copies of your transcript. I made copies of your best essay to attach to each application as a writing sample, and I wrote you a recommendation letter, which I really think is going to be the kicker!" Her voice rings with excitement as she brings me over to her dining table, grabbing stacks of papers off the console.

The apartment is modern and sleek with floor-to-ceiling glass windows on the entire west side. I look out at the city streets, wondering for the millionth time what it would be like to have an apartment this perfect and safe. One day, maybe.

I turn around, walking toward the wall where a large rectangular Peter Lik photograph hangs: a huge tree stands tall, the sun shining like a star through lustrous orange and red leaves. Living in a concrete jungle, I love seeing nature, even if it's only in a photograph. I'm shaken out of my fog when she hands me a plate of hot eggs, bacon, and toast.

"Take this and eat, you'll need your energy up for us to work." She stares at me expectantly with a huge smile on her face, but I'm confused by her demeanor. She's always kind, yet all of this feels a bit contrived. I take a seat at the dining table while she sits across from me. She's staring straight at me, seemingly waiting for something. The moment I see the pity and sadness pass through her eyes, I realize she knows about what happened with Carlos. I try to find the words to ask her about her day. I want to change the subject, but tears run without my consent down my face. She moves to the chair next to me as I crumble into her arms, looking for solace. She hugs me close to her, supporting me.

"Janelle explained everything already; she called me last week. Just...calm down, we're going to get you out of this."

I look up, worry sinking into my gut. "Are you going to tell someone about what happened to me? If you do, there's no way I'll live to see the day..." My breaths become shallow as my panic rises.

She drops a warm hand on my shoulder. "Eve, please calm down. I won't tell, okay? I know how things work here. I could get into serious trouble for not telling the authorities, but I'll take that risk for you."

My crying intensifies as relief sets into my chest. "This is the plan," she starts. "We're going to get you into college and out of here. A summer program, first. We're applying to these ten schools." She gestures to the paperwork already organized and laid out in the center of the table. "I'm using school funds for your application fees, so we can apply anywhere you want. And I've already cleared it with the principal; so don't worry about the money. You've got to hang on for six more months, and then you're free." I nod my head, swallowing. "You think you can lay low and out of harm's way until we get you out?"

My mind starts to race. "But what if I don't get the scholarship and grant money? I can't have Janelle support me anymore—"

"You took your SATs, and you did unbelievably well. I know you'll qualify for a full scholarship. And we both know it's highly likely Columbia will accept you. You know I've got pull at that school. There are so many grants and scholarships available you qualify for. I mean, if not for you, who the heck would that money be for?"

I chuckle, shrugging my shoulders. She has a point. "The thing is, I can't just keep letting Janelle handle paying for me. I'm letting you know now if I can't find a school that'll hook me up financially, I'm not going."

She puts her hands on mine. "You'll get it, Eve. You'll get it and you'll get the hell out of here." She takes a deep breath. "Have you spoken to your mom about college?" I raise my eyebrows at her in surprise and annoyance.

"Okay." She lifts her hand up as if to say she won't harp on the subject. "Let's just forget your mom for now. You know what? Forget everything. Let's just start by applying. When you get in, we'll figure out how to make it happen. You're a brilliant girl, and it's time to put that brain of yours in a place that's right for you."

I look down at my feet; my boots are Janelle's hand-me-downs. They've got a few holes in the heel, but since I lost my sneakers, I've had to make do. I know Janelle would easily give me the cash to buy a new pair, but the guilt I feel from taking money from her at this point is enormous. My job at Angelo's is okay, but two days a week isn't enough to give me much spending cash. I need to get those grants and the full scholarship. And maybe Ms. Levine is right; if not for me, who would it be for?

We spend the rest of the afternoon filling out applications, making sure to include everything the schools requested. Grant applications take even more time, as do the applications for scholarships. Ms. Levine wasn't kidding; there are so many places willing to give money to a kid like me. I just need to stay organized. Ms. Levine has a large spreadsheet detailing what we need and what we've taken care of, so we don't lose track. Without her, I'd be completely lost.

"Ms. Levine, do you think I'll fit into these places? I mean, no one I know has ever gone to college, and..." I feel insecurity pounding in my chest. "I mean, I know I'm different from the people I grew up around. But, that doesn't mean I'm gonna fit in with people like *them*," I say, pointing to the picture on the brochure folder for Columbia University. College kids in Polo shirts are throwing Frisbees to one another on a beautiful green campus lawn. "I've never touched a Frisbee in my life.... And like, what about Janelle? I'm nervous to leave her—"

She cuts me off. "Listen, Eve. Don't feel guilty about leaving. Imagine the life you will bring to yourself and Janelle once you graduate college. Doors will open. Law school, like you've always dreamed! I've lived that life, and I know you can make it there. And, Janelle wants this so badly for you..."

I take a breath and gather my thoughts. Images of my mom barge into my head, unwelcome. "You know my mom would go insane if she thought I was continuing my education. If she had her way, I would have dropped out of high school at sixteen and gotten a full-time job already." I bite my lower lip.

Ms. Levine clicks her tongue, and I look back at her. "Look, Eve. I want to speak to your mom. Maybe I can get through to her? Your mom has issues; we both know that. I really believe she only acts this way to you because she can't understand your potential. She's just trying to teach you how to survive. In your mom's opinion...now, this is just a guess, but I think in your mom's opinion, the books you read don't prepare you for actual life. But if she understood how much more is possible for you..."

I stare at Ms. Levine with hope, wanting so badly to believe her. Even though nothing in my entire life has ever pointed to the fact that my mom would support me, she's still my mother. Unfortunately, there's a part of me that wishes for her approval.

Instead of replying, I pick my pen back up. When we're finally done filling out the paperwork, she makes us some hot cappuccinos from her fancy Nespresso coffeemaker. "One day, I need to buy myself one of these," I tell her as I lift the mug up to my lips.

"Ready to write your last personal essay?" She turns her laptop around to face me. "You have to write about your biggest character flaw."

"Well, with so many to choose from..." We both chuckle.

"I'm going to run out and take care of some errands. Get comfortable. Write the essay. I'll review it when I get back in a few hours." She grabs her purse, letting herself out.

I go through a few drafts, feeling relief to get lost in the writing. I'm so involved in the work that somehow, hours pass without me getting up or needing to use the bathroom. By early evening when she returns, I have cramps in my legs, but also something I'm pleased with. She reads what I wrote and tears well in her eyes. "This is superb, Eve. Best one yet!"

Before the sun sets, I tell her goodbye and get on the downtown

Six Train. This time though, Janelle is waiting at the stop when I get off. We walk together to the Blue Houses and I fill her in on the details of my day. She jumps up and down, thrilled about the possibility of my going to Columbia. "This way, you won't be far!"

8

THE FOLLOWING SUNDAY, I get to work early and open the shop. Even though it's tiny and rundown, I take pride in keeping the place immaculate. I turn on the lights and straighten the items around the store before removing the gun out of my bag and placing it close to my hand under the counter.

The gun has turned into a security blanket for me. I don't ever want to feel like my life is up for grabs; I need control over my safety. The reality is where I'm from, I need muscle to combat terror, and I intend on using whatever is available to keep my life intact.

I'm sipping my second coffee of the day while dusting the shelves when Angelo starts frantically banging on the front door to get my attention; he doesn't always remember to keep his keys on him. After pressing the buzzer to unlock the door, he walks straight up to me and puts his hands on my arms.

Alarm moves through me as I notice the sweat pouring down his face. "Listen, Eve. Something's come up." The lines in his forehead crease. "Antonio Borignone may be coming in here today with some other guys."

"Antonio? I thought you told me when I took this job I'd never have to see him." My distress has my heart thrashing. Of course, I know the mafia owns this shop, but I didn't think I'd actually have to deal with them. Coming face to face with one of the biggest mobsters in Manhattan is a nightmare I hoped never to see. I haven't seen Antonio in person, but his reputation is vicious. Guns, women, gambling, murder...the list goes on.

Seeing the agony on my face, Angelo continues, "Look. Antonio isn't all bad..." His tone is softer as his voice trails off. "He gives to charity—"

"Angelo," I snap. "Don't give me that. I don't want to be an accessory in his crazy mobster shit, and if he's coming in, it can't be good!"

He has the decency to look apologetic, opening his hands to me like a peace offering. "Look. He gave me the heads-up he has a lot of business to take care of and this shop is the place it's going to happen. Just continue doing what you normally do while you're here, and don't look at anyone too closely."

I would walk out right now, but I need the money badly. On top of it all, I love Angelo too much to ditch him. The only thing to do now is to get as much information as possible about what's about to go down. "Well, is he going to try and talk to me?" I manage to squeak out the words, trying not to let the fear take over my body.

He shrugs his shoulders in a questioning motion. "Look, I'm not part of the family. I'm just an associate. I have no clue what he's planning to say or not say to you. All I know is he's going to be coming in here with some of the crew, and they'll be using the basement. Typically, they don't all walk in together. They stagger themselves. Your job is to not look too closely at him or anyone else who comes in, okay? I don't want anyone to see your gorgeous face and get any ideas." I look at him incredulously, shocked he'd think such a thing.

"For fuck's sake, just do me a favor and keep your head down, okay? No eye contact. No speaking. Just look down." His no-nonsense attitude straightens me out and brings me back to earth.

I know Angelo cares about me and just wants to keep me safe. It's not as if he asked for this. "Okay, Angelo. I'll stay quiet and keep my head down."

"That's a good girl, doll," he replies, his tone softening. "Now, can I buy you a bagel or something?"

"Yes. Feel free to buy me breakfast for the next week." I say, trying to calm myself down. As he steps out of the shop, I take a novel out of my backpack. I'm getting to the good part when I hear the buzzer. Absentmindedly, I press the button to open the door, assuming Angelo is back with the food.

I lift my head happily, but freeze when I see an incredibly handsome man in a fitted navy suit walking inside. I gulp, praying this isn't Antonio. Whoever he is though, he's got a dominating presence and walks like a man of importance. He has black hair, sprinkled with some white at the temples. I take him to be a bit over six feet, with wide shoulders that taper into a narrow waist. When he steps up in front of me, I'm met with eyes so blue it's shocking. There's something about him that feels so familiar, but I can't put my finger on it.

He smiles casually, but his jaw is tight and the cold look in his eyes is at odds with his nonchalant smile.

"Can I help you?" I ask nervously, tucking my book away beneath the counter and putting my hand on the gun. The way he's looking at me has me shifting from one foot to the other. His handsomeness is quickly eclipsed by the fear he's putting out.

He slowly licks his lips. "I think you can. Where's Angelo?" He brings out a pack of cigarettes from his pocket and casually pulls one out. My heart starts to thump and eyes widen; this must be Antonio. I can feel it. There is no smoking in here. But there's no way in hell I'm about to tell this guy that.

He puts his cigarette into his full, pouty mouth. "You know who I am, sweetheart?" He's raising his eyebrows at me and again I'm struck with the feeling I've seen him before. He's staring at me while he lights up and inhales, and I can do nothing other than gulp while my internal alarm shrieks.

He blows the smoke out of his mouth and leans against the counter while I stare at him dumbly, unable to reply.

"You must be Irina's daughter, right?" He takes another inhale and smiles.

I try to manage words, but I end up stammering. "Uh, yeah." I attempt to keep my face straight as my panic builds.

"I see the resemblance, although you're a lot more beautiful than she is." His mouth widens in a half smile. "Look at you." He moves close to me, pushing an errant hair away from my face with his free hand, studying me. I can smell his cologne and can instantly tell it's expensive. I hold my breath, afraid to breathe anything of his into my body. I blink my eyes a few times and turn my gaze to the left, trying not to make any eye contact. Even though it doesn't feel sexual, his touch brings on a terrified buzz that's rising from my chest down into my toes.

He raises his eyebrows. "You're afraid of me. Good. Your mom tells me you're smart. She doesn't like it much." I drop my head and he bangs his hand down on the counter. "Look at me when I speak to you!" I jump at the sound of his voice, facing forward.

He chuckles. "That's better, sweetheart." His voice is lower now and somehow even more terrifying. "You want to go to college?" When I hear the word *college*, my mind focuses on my future. I straighten my back and grip my gun with all my strength, ready to do whatever I may need to do. Feeling the cool metal against my hand centers me. I have control. I can handle this.

"Yes. I'm going to go to college," I say with as much strength as I can muster.

"Hm, I see." He smirks. "You're strong and intelligent. Still blooming, though. Just gotta grow up some. It's basically impossible for a girl like you to get out of this life. You know that though."

I nod my head.

"If one of these shitty street gangs in your neighborhood got their hands on a pretty piece like you, it wouldn't go so well. Angelo tells me that you're a good girl. Still innocent. Always got your head in the books and helping Alex with his work."

I swallow, wondering if he's mentioning the street gangs because he knows something about Carlos. Every part of my body is freaking out right now. This is the man who has my mom and half of New York City wrapped around his pinky finger. He can order my death and burn my body without anyone noticing. Hell, even if they noticed, the cops would probably help dig my grave. Antonio's got everyone in his back pocket, and I'm nothing but a blip on his radar.

From the corner of my eye, I watch Angelo running back across the street. In some strange reaction, laughter bubbles up into my chest. I want to control it, but it breaks free, straight out of my lips. Antonio looks at me like I'm a lunatic as I'm cracking up, but there is no stopping it. The combination of Angelo running toward the shop while the most dangerous man in Manhattan stares me down has my wires crossed. I'm still laughing uncontrollably as I hold my finger on top of the buzzer, waiting for Angelo to open the door.

Angelo jumps inside, holding a plastic bag full of food. "Antonio, how are ya?" he asks gregariously, dropping the plastic bag on the counter and wiping the sweat from his face with the back of his hand. I blink as the laughter finally dies down and realize that my face is full of tears. Christ, Antonio must think I'm certifiable.

They shake their hands like old friends as I hiccup, trying to compose myself. I wipe my face dry with a tissue from the counter as Angelo slicks his hair back in a nervous gesture. "Go into the back, Antonio, everything should be comfortable for ya. Just text me if I can bring anything down." Antonio nods, not unkindly, and lets himself into the basement without a second glance backward.

When the door closes, Angelo makes eye contact with me, letting out a deep breath. "Good job, sweetheart. You've met the big boss. Just calm down now, all right? He won't hurt you. I wouldn't have left if I knew he was about to come. Now as the others come in, keep your head down. I'll do all the talking." I turn around and grab some paper towels that I use to wipe down the counter, handing some to Angelo. He nods in thanks and uses it to wipe the sweat off his temples.

I walk into the bathroom in the back, splashing some cold water on my face. Staring in the mirror and gipping the counter, I tell myself to relax. Okay, so I've met Antonio Borignone. It doesn't mean anything.

I step back to the front and one at a time, in intervals of twenty minutes, seven other men come into the shop. Each man is wearing a suit, but none of them are as good-looking and charismatic as Antonio.

Angelo comes over to the desk. "Listen. Why don't you head out early? Someone else is still on his way, but I don't want you to be here when he comes." He hands me a wad of cash with a wink. "A little extra for putting up with today, doll." I take it from him with a smile and grab my stuff to leave the shop, thankful to be away from the Borignones.

I stop at a small bodega and order a hot coffee while I read my book. I'm not in a rush to go home and it's not close to dark yet. At the very least, I want to turn my mind away from Antonio and jumping into the book world always helps me to relax.

A few hours later, I meander toward the bus stop. I'm about to sit on the bench when I see Vincent striding down the street. I stare at him dumbfounded, not sure what he's doing here. I'm frozen, with my mouth agape.

"Eve? Is that you?" He walks up to me, shock written all over his gorgeous face. His eyes widen as he takes me in, full lips quirking up in a surprised smile. He's wearing a fitted gray suit and looks sexier than any man has a right to look. My heart pounds.

"Yeah, um, I work nearby," I stutter out, pointing around the corner.

"Where?" he asks, brows furrowed in question.

I would bet money he's never heard of it. Vincent is the epitome of uber-wealthy and finely educated. Trying to sound casual, I clear my throat. "Angelo's Pawn." I keep my head up after I tell him, not wanting him to see me as pathetic to work in a dive like that. I know that Angelo is amazing and the work is decent, but to a man like Vincent, it may seem like I work in a complete shithole.

Surprisingly, his eyes instantly widen when he hears the name, as if he knows the place and can't believe I work there. Before I can come to terms with the look on his face, he reins himself in. I'm left wondering if I just imagined the whole thing.

He pushes his hair back with his hands. "You heading home? I can drop you off."

The bus pulls up. My eyes flit between Vincent and the driver. Oh, who am I kidding? I've been dreaming of this moment for days and there's no way I'd let this moment pass me by.

"Okay," I tell him, biting back a smile. We walk a few blocks together in silence when I finally get the nerve to ask him what he's doing around here.

He pauses, thinking for a moment. "I train at a gym nearby." I want to ask which gym, but don't want to seem nosy.

We get to his car, a sleek black Range Rover. He opens the door for me and I jump in. It's impossible not to notice the beautiful leather seats and high-tech gadgets on the console. I let my fingers touch the buttery leather, trying not to freak out.

"Do you feel like eating?" he asks, buckling his belt.

I immediately remember how incredible the food was at the restaurant. Of course, my stomach chooses that moment to grumble.

"I take that as a yes?" He glances at my stomach as he puts the car in drive.

"Sure," I reply nervously, casually lifting one shoulder in a shrug. We pull up to a French restaurant with a black awning. From the outside, it looks incredibly fancy. My eyes scan my clothes and I realize that I'm seriously underdressed for a place like that. I'm in loose-fitting, low-rise jeans and a white T-shirt. I quickly pop down the visor and thankfully, see a mirror. Unfortunately though, the girl who gazes back at me is frizzy-haired and tired looking. A five-star dinner can't happen tonight.

"Uh, Vincent, I'm not so sure I can do something so extravagant." I gesture to my clothes.

My breath stops as his eyes take me in. "You're damn near perfect, Eve. But if you want, we can grab some pizza instead. I know a great place nearby."

I sigh in relief, trying not to blush at his compliment. "Yeah, let's do that." We park the car a few blocks over on the street and walk to Gino's Pizza on the corner. The bell chimes as we enter the restaurant. It's small and cozy, with red and white checkered floors and black tables. He tells me to take a seat in the back while he orders. I walk toward a table, choosing one near the window.

I sit and stare at Vincent as he checks his phone. Whatever he sees isn't making him happy; his forehead is creased, giving him a look of agitation. His turn is up to order and he lets go of whatever was bothering him, making small talk with the guys at the counter. They're so friendly as if they've known each other awhile.

He turns to me, catching me staring and mouths, "Hi." He stares at me openly, without any reservation; it lights me up inside. A few minutes later, Vincent walks over to the table, holding a large covered pizza box in his hands.

"That's all for us?" My eyes widen. There's no way we could eat all of that food!

He places it on the table and drops into the seat right next to me.

"I'm a growing boy, Eve," he jokes.

"Well, I'm starving, so thank you," I tell him appreciatively. I'm waiting for him to open it, but before he can, a booming voice sounds from the back.

"Yo, Vincent, you didn't tell me you were coming by!" A huge middle-aged man comes barreling out of the kitchen, wearing a white apron and smiling ear to ear. His accent is all Brooklyn.

Vincent stands to greet him. "Pauli, I miss you, man." They embrace each other warmly as if they're genuinely happy to see each other. Vincent is much taller, but Pauli looks heavier and undoubtedly solid looking.

Pauli looks at me, a pleased look on his smiling face. "And what's your name, darlin'? Always got the most gorgeous girl with ya, huh Vince?" I smile outwardly, but immediately feel slightly let down. How many girls does he bring here? Clearly, I'm not the first. I'm surprised by my reaction. I want to be special to him; I want to be unlike the other girls before me. Because to me, Vincent is all I can see.

Vincent moves next to me, placing a hand on my shoulder. "Pauli, this is Eve. Eve, Pauli is an old friend of my family." I smile up at him, standing as I put my hand out to shake his. Before I know it, he swings around to my side of the table and hugs me to his chest. My eyes widen in surprise at his friendliness.

Pauli chuckles. "Damn, Vince. Sweet as hell, this one." His touch is kind, but still, I feel shy from the attention. I watch as Vincent's throat moves in a hard swallow. My reaction to his disapproval is to take my seat. Vincent lets out a half smile, and I feel relief. Something about him is just so dominant; I can't help myself but try to please him.

Pauli turns his attention back to Vincent. "So, how's life going?" He moves back around and drops himself into the chair across from mine.

Vincent takes his seat next to me, placing a possessive hand on my thigh. "You know how it is. Never a dull moment." The men chuckle together when we hear a group speaking Russian loudly. Vincent looks at them, his face deadly. I suck in a breath, unsure what just brought on this change.

"Aw, shit," Pauli says, bunching up a dishtowel in his fists.

"These guys been giving you trouble, Pauli?" Vincent asks. "I thought the Russians knew to stay out of your way." I sit still as he visibly hardens, his eyes impossibly darker.

I blink for a moment, looking between Vincent and Pauli, who seem to be engaging in a silent conversation. Vincent stands up from the table and stalks over to the group. They all seem to be talking for a second or two until the Russians run out of the pizzeria, practically tripping over their own feet in what looks like terror.

I eye Pauli nervously. When he sees the look on my face, he begins to laugh. "Oh shit, Vince," he calls out. "Got yourself an innocent girl, huh? Much better than that redhead." I'm taken aback by his comment, still not understanding what the hell is going on.

Vincent moves back to us, smirking. "All right, Pauli. Get the hell outta here; make some pizzas or something." They hug again before Pauli leaves.

"Come back anytime, sweetheart," he winks at me. "For you, pizza is always on the house." He leaves us and I'm left with questions.

"Vincent, w-what happened with those guys?"

"The Russians? They're always causing trouble around here. Just got them to move along."

"Yeah but—"

"Let's eat before this gets cold." I want to press him, insist that he can't just silence me. But with one look out the window, all thoughts of the Russians flee my head. It's almost dark, and I'm still not home.

"Shit," I say out loud, anxiety hitting me square in the chest. Noticing my nerves, he grabs my hand.

His face is full of concern. "What's wrong?"

I press my lips together. "I don't really like getting home when it's dark out." I feel a pounding headache starting up in the back of my skull. What if the Snakes are around? I'll have to find somewhere safe to wait until Janelle can come to me.

"I'm going to drive you home and walk you straight to your apartment door." His eyes are full of reassurance and understanding. "Nothing to be nervous about when you're with me, yeah?" He is confidence and strength. Rubbing his thumb across my knuckles, I'm immediately put at ease. I trust that when I'm with Vincent, no one will ever hurt me.

As he strokes my hand rhythmically, I let myself get lost in his dark eyes. They're gleaming, reminding me of the ocean at night— endless. He lets go of my hand and I feel immediately colder. He moves to open the pizza box, and I'm awakened from my trance.

He smiles. "Still hot." We eat together while he tells me about the best pizza spots he's ever been to.

"Last summer, I went to Capri for a few weeks. The food was incredible and the pizza was something else." He takes a huge bite.

I move in closer to him, wanting to hear more. "Who did you go with?"

"Remember Tom from the fight?"

"Mmhmm."

"Yeah. I went with him and...a few other friends." His eyes look down for a moment. "We took a flight to Naples and then a boat to Capri. It can get too touristy, but the beaches are insane and the food is probably some of the best in the world." He tucks a stray piece of my hair behind my ear, and I move closer to him.

I lick my lips, the motion bringing his gaze down to my mouth. "I've never even left New York," I tell him honestly. "I can't imagine what it must be like to travel so... freely."

"Never?" He seems surprised. "Not even to like, Jersey?"

I start to laugh and then click my tongue. "Not. Even. Jersey." I punctuate each word in a way that has him laughing. My tendency is to feel ashamed, but he isn't looking at me like I'm pathetic for never having traveled. Instead, he's looking at me in what feels like wonder. "You know, there are people in this world who don't just pick up and go whenever they feel like it." I raise my eyebrows at him.

"Yeah, yeah. But you're the type who'd love it. Maybe one day we —" He starts but immediately stops himself. Picking up a napkin to wipe his mouth, my chest warms with the words he didn't say.

"Yeah. One day, maybe." I sigh. "Anyway, as of now, I go lots of places. In books, of course." I wink.

"Cheapest way to travel, eh?" His eyes sparkle.

Our conversation picks up again and before I know it, I've eaten three slices and it's after eight o'clock. He stands to throw away the empty box and takes my hand to leave.

Arriving at the Blue Houses, I'm relieved to see that the elevator works. He brings me upstairs and walks me to my door, as promised.

"Thank you for dinner and for bringing me back," I tell him quietly.

"My pleasure, Eve." I wait a moment, wishing he'll kiss me. Instead, he looks at me with a satisfied smile on his face. He can tell what I'm waiting for, but for whatever reason, he's decided not to give it to me. I sure as hell won't ask for it if that's what he's waiting for.

I clear my throat. "All right. Well, bye, Vincent," I say in an exaggerated voice, waiting for him to go before I let myself inside my apartment.

"If you say bye, you gotta go inside before I leave," he tells me, as if everyone in the world knows this.

"No." I place my hands on my hips. "You walk away first. After you leave, I'll go inside." What the hell? I'm not backing down. It's not even that it matters who walks away first, but I'm tired of him always deciding everything.

His face turns to stone and I immediately take a step back. "Eve. Walk through your door." He points behind me. "I'm not leaving until I hear it click shut and until I know you are safely behind it." He crosses his arms in front of his chest, stance wide. His face is serious, but I'm not going to budge. Sure, he's huge and sexy and strong. But screw that! I'm not a docile idiot he can order around!

"No one is going to snatch me away from the door, Vincent. You go first!" My voice is laced with attitude and he raises his eyebrows at me in surprise, lips quirking up. "I refuse to do what you say. You think you can just push me into doing what you want like you probably do to everyone else? Wanna throw me out like you did those guys at the pizza shop?" I cock my head to the side. I don't usually give this kind of lip, but it feels freaking good.

He takes a step closer, crowding me. I step back, my hands pressing against the door. I'm technically trapped, yet surprisingly, unafraid. "When I tell you to do something—" his voice is gruff as he moves even closer "—you should listen to me, Eve." The way he says my name, like a warm caress, sends a flutter straight through me. Common sense is telling me that I should be afraid, but I want him so badly, I'm aching. Is it possible to be nervous and this turned on at the same time? Apparently, my body says *yes*.

Before I know it, he lifts me up in his arms, pulling me hard against him as my legs wrap around his waist. His lips move to mine as my hands grab his thick hair. We both moan as our lips lock. He pushes me against the door, his kiss demanding and controlling. I'm completely helpless, but God, it feels amazing. I want him to come inside my apartment, but there's no privacy. For all I know, my mom is home. I'm feeling frenzied as he puts his mouth on the side of my neck and sucks in deep. It feels so good that my mouth drops open and I gasp. I can't control the sounds coming out of my mouth as I feel his hot wet tongue on my skin. I pull his shirt up from his suit pants and with my shaking hands, manage to open a few buttons. I need to feel him. Oh. My. God. His chest is hot and taut over hard muscle. I move my hands upward and feel him tremor; I've never felt so powerful in my life. All thoughts disappear as he continues to kiss me like his life depends on it. He sucks on my tongue and my entire body bucks forward, asking for more.

I'm in a daze by the time he puts me down. I look him up and down, trying to commit to memory his sexy, rumpled appearance. "Forget the Bull. You're Batman." I put my fingers to my numb lips, giggling.

"Why Batman?" His eyes shine.

"Because you're like, underground fighter one second and all suited up the next. The duality, you know?" I cock my head to the side.

He shakes his head from side to side. "Baby, you have no idea how right you are. My entire life is duality. One foot in one world, one foot in another." I'm not sure what he's talking about, but the way he's staring at me has me wanting to jump back on top of him.

"How's it going?" I bite the side of my lip, trying not to smile.

He sighs. "It fuckin' sucks. But hopefully soon, I'll be able to simplify."

"Simplify?" I repeat, my voice full of question.

"Yeah. Simplify."

He leans against the doorway, legs crossed. He's clearly waiting for me to let myself in. With a sigh, I turn my body around and finally turn the key in the lock. Before I can step inside, he gently pushes me into my apartment and shuts the door on my face. I can hear him laugh and I mentally curse him. He always wins, damn it! I stand on my tiptoes to look through the peephole, watching as he leaves, a smile on his face.

When I go to the bathroom to shower up, I notice he's left a huge bruise low on my neck. What the hell? He marked me! I start smiling like a fool. Maybe I won, after all.

9

It's three fifteen on Monday, and my mom just walked into Ms. Levine's classroom. Surprisingly enough, I haven't heard any yelling yet. I tried telling her earlier this week that meeting with Mom is pointless, but she insisted that maybe a different tactic would work. Hearing their voices increase in volume, I know I made a big mistake letting them meet.

Sitting on the floor of the empty hallway, I keep myself busy by reading the graffiti on some of the lockers. Apparently, Joaquin has a small dick and Chanel likes to suck it. Another locker is tagged with Snakes' symbol: a red circle with a capital *S* inside. My stomach does a slow churn as I stare. I try to turn my thoughts to Vincent, but there's no room for beauty in my mind right now.

When I hear Ms. Levine yell, I close my eyes and raise the hood of my black sweatshirt over my head. It's a men's hoodie and completely hides my shape, but I feel more comfortable having armor between my body and the world.

"Your daughter should go to college. Look at these scores! Her SATs are unbelievable. Don't you want her to go places other than *here*?"

"Ms. Levine," my mom screams, her voiced laced with aggression.

I can only imagine her standing tall right now, getting all up in Ms. Levine's face. "How many fuckin' times do I have to tell you people? When she's done with high school in a few months, she's going to get a job like everyone else we know! Stop putting nonsense in her head! Do you think living is free? That I can just continue to support her while she studies?" I hear my mother's sarcastic laughter. "You don't know shit about our reality. If she's going to survive, she needs to thicken her skin. Not be deluded into thinking that there's a way out. There is no way out for her; this is her real life. You want to do her a favor? Toughen her up. Teach her some goddamn street smarts in that class of yours; don't I know she's got none of those!"

I hear Ms. Levine speaking, but can't make out her words.

"No!" my mom yells again. "You aren't listening!"

I expect the conversation to be over, but Ms. Levine continues. "That's the point! She doesn't have to live this life! Give her a chance to make something of herself one day!" Her voice pleads.

Not one ever to let someone else get the last word, my mom goes on. "My kid is staying where I am and where her sister is. Fuck this school. You think those rich people will accept a girl like her? I know people who tried to leave. Yeah, she's white. But she's poor and those rich assholes can smell poverty in seconds."

I hear the skid of a chair against the floor and not a moment later, my mom comes barreling out of the room. She stares down at me sitting on the floor, her face tight. I try to stand up, but she bends down and grips my hand like a vise, roughly pulling me off the floor. Her manicured nails pierce my skin as she tears us out of the building, high heels *clicking* at an amazing speed. We move through the metal detectors while the security guards are too busy checking out my mom's impressive cleavage to notice or care that she's on a rampage.

The bus pulls up to the stop at the same time we do, and we get on quickly, taking two seats in the back. Dread pools in my veins when I see the manic look in her eyes. This turned out worse than I imagined. I try to calm down and make myself invisible by putting the hood back on my head, but having my mom so physically close to me when I feel her mania on the rise makes it impossible to focus on anything other than fear.

We get off the bus and go inside our building. My mom walks straight to the elevator and presses the *up* button with a sharp red nail, but the light won't come on.

"Fuck!" she exclaims. "Of course, the shit box is dead again. Someone gotta get shot before anyone fixes anything 'round here."

I see the "storage" room next to the elevator and blink a few times, feeling lightheaded. I need to get out of here and into our apartment. She pulls her cell phone from her bag and turns on the flashlight as I open the heavy fireproof door for the two of us. We start up the steps. Her phone is raised above her head, casting a small spotlight in an otherwise dark stairwell. The lights in here have been dead for some time; it's like a black hole right now.

When we get to the fourth-floor landing, I open the stairwell door and start down the hallway for our apartment, hoping maybe she's mellowed out some since the conference. But before the thought can exit my brain, I feel her take hold of my shoulders from behind and turn me around to face her. She slaps me hard across the face, the smack echoing through my ears. My head swings to the side from the force, my long and dark ponytail whips around my face.

"Eve. How many times have I told you to stop showing off in school? Stop dreaming! You think you're better than me? Than all of us?" Even though I know there isn't any blood, it feels like the bones in my face have been shattered. My eyes fill with tears as I stare at her forehead. If I look into her eyes, she'll think I'm talking back, but if I don't look at her face, she may think I'm disrespectfully avoiding her stare.

"You need to learn how to toughen up. Do you hear me? This life is what you've been given. Reading books and going to college won't get you anywhere but dead!" She's yelling now, shaking me hard with both her hands. In her own sick way, she's just trying to get me to see something that I already know: I'm not suited to live this life. I know I'm different from my neighbors and it doesn't serve me well. I keep my head down and hide, hoping to just get through my days without getting hurt. My mom keeps trying to wake me up—thinking that if she pushes hard enough, I'll learn how to navigate the streets and save myself.

"You think I don't know about what happened with you and the Snakes? I heard about it from some girls at the club. You're lucky your sister is so well-liked in this building and she saved your ass. But one day, your luck will run out. You've got to *grow up*! You see this place? This is where you live. This is who you are. You'll never be more than this. If you read every book in the world, you'll still be you. A nobody." Her words sear my insides. "If you want to do something good for yourself, go be Carlos's girlfriend for a while. He'll eventually get over you and you can move on with your life. The more you resist, the worse it'll be when he finally catches you."

With those parting words, she turns from me and walks to our apartment door, opening it forcefully and slamming it shut behind her. I close my eyes, leaning against the corridor and sinking down until I'm crouched on the dirty floor in a daze. I put my hood back on my head and lean into it, letting the black cotton cover my eyes. Her words are sobering; the truth in them rattles around my head. I want to think about Vincent, but it's useless. A man like him has no business with a girl like me. It isn't until I hear someone nagging about the electric bill that I'm shaken out of my thoughts.

Picking myself up off the floor, I walk into my apartment and straight into my room. Closing the door behind me, I strip out of my clothes and put on a pair of old and worn sweats before crawling into my bed. I'm relieved to see it's only five o'clock. I love getting into bed early and reading the night away. I take the new book Ms. Levine recommended off my bedside table, and escape my life by entering someone else's.

When I finally doze off to sleep, I dream of Vincent. He's lying on a white sandy beach with a group of friends while I'm drifting in the ocean on a small red raft. I see him and call out, but no matter how loudly I yell, he doesn't see or hear me.

I wake with a start when I hear the front door open and close. Checking my bedside clock, I see it's two in the morning. My sister comes toward me in the dark. I can see her tiptoeing, trying not to make noise. "Hi Janelle," I croak, rubbing my eyes and wincing, feeling my face sting.

She turns on a small lamp in the corner of the room and lets out a gasp. "Holy shit, what happened to your face?" She flips on the rest of the lights, inspecting my cheek with her warm hands.

"Mom. She came to school today to talk to Ms. Levine and went berserk afterward."

Janelle goes to the kitchen and comes back with a pack of frozen peas, placing it gently on my face. She sits on my bed as I sit up. "Girl, you're gonna bruise from this. Je-sus she hit you good. That Ms. Levine. Always lookin' on the bright side..." She lets out a sigh, looking into my eyes sadly.

"Let me do your makeup tomorrow, okay? Keep this ice on your face as long as you can stand it." She turns away from me and walks into the bathroom. I press the cold bag to my face, shuddering from the sting. When I can't take it anymore, I close my eyes and curl back under the covers, letting my body relax into sleep. It's fitful.

I wake up the next morning in exhaustion, and my face is sore and bruised. Janelle tries to put some concealer and powder on me to take the discoloration away. When I look in the mirror, I see that it actually looks a lot better with the makeup. With no time to wash my hair, I put a black baseball hat on my head and jump onto the bus to get to school. I get off and walk directly to the English Department. When I see Ms. Levine sitting in her office, I walk inside and slam the door behind me.

I put my fists on her desk and lean my body forward, getting in her face like I've seen countless students do to intimidate teachers. I've never acted like this before, but my hurt has taken over.

"Don't say anything to my mom anymore. I'm never leaving this place, and I want you to pull my applications out!" The tears start to run down my face as she looks at me with sympathy. Fury takes hold, and I have an urge to smack the compassion off her face.

My hands shake. "My mom is doing this for my best interest, and in the best interest of my family. I have to stay here. I'm graduating in six months, and then I'm getting a job!" I yell.

She stands from her desk and closes the blinds, making sure none of the other teachers or students witness my outburst. She stands next to me in front of her desk, trying to take my hand. I ball them into fists, hating the feeling of her kindness.

She steps back, eyes gentle. "I know you, Eve. And I'm not pulling those applications. Do you hear me? I know you're scared. But one way or another I'm getting you out of this life. You deserve better," she pleads. "I see your face right now. You can't cover bruises like that with makeup and a hat. I made a bad judgment call bringing in your mother. I should have listened to you. Regardless, you're too smart for this," she states firmly. "I'm not giving up on you."

"I'm nothing. Stop trying to turn me into something. It's only making my life worse, can't you see that? All these promises, it's all bullshit. I don't know anyone who ever went to these fancy schools, except YOU. I wouldn't even know the first thing about doing well at a school like that...and...this—" I glance around the shoddy room "—is who I am." My voice breaks off at the end.

She shakes her head woefully, stepping closer to me again. "We'll hear back from colleges shortly. I'm still crossing my fingers that you can start somewhere in June. Just hang in there a little while longer, Eve." She finally takes my hand, and I let her. "I'm not leaving you alone, all right? Don't be afraid." Her eyes show concern, and I know she's doing this because she cares, but I'm too hurt to accept it. When the first bell rings, I walk out of the room, no longer having the energy to speak.

I go to my first period math class and zone out, telling myself I need to calm down and let the applications stay in motion. Ms. Levine is right. I can't just give up after all I've put into this. I look out the window and watch as a delivery truck parks illegally to bring crates into one of the bodegas. While he's away, three kids jump into the back of the truck and run out with their hands full of loot. Only a few minutes after that, the cops come and give the truck a ticket for double-parking. I'm living in Gangland.

10

THE NEXT MORNING, Janelle wakes me up by vaulting into my bed. The box spring and mattress is so old that I immediately bounce up.

"Today is gonna be a great day!" She hugs my exhausted body to her chest, lifting me like a ragdoll. "It's the freakin' weekend, baby, I'm about to have me some fun..." she sings, quoting "Ignition" by R. Kelly.

I rub my face, my voice coming out in a rasp. "Ugh, get off me, or at least wait until I've had my coffee." I get up, dragging my body to the bathroom. How Janelle has this energy in the morning, I'll never understand.

After washing up, I walk into our tiny kitchen to put the coffee on. I take out a pan and put it on the stove. I take out eggs and some milk, and immediately scramble them together. I don't cook anything fancy, but Janelle always tells me I've got a gift in the kitchen.

I put some toast in the oven and when it's all ready, call for my mom and Janelle. My mom lazily walks to our table with a short pink silk robe wrapped around her tall frame. She sits casually and waits for me to serve her.

I put the full plate in front of her, and she tenses. "Where's the butter and jam?" Her tone raises my guard. I quickly open the refrigerator, taking out what she needs and placing it on the table. Moving to the sink, I immediately begin to wash the pan I've already used, making sure to give her a show as to how diligently I clean. My mom will never lift a finger to maintain the apartment, but expects it to be spotless nonetheless; she has an obsession with cleanliness—and as far back as I can remember, always has. The sight of a mess really sets her off, so I do my absolute best to keep things organized at all times. While it's annoying to be constantly scrubbing, the stress of keeping things perfectly tidy is nothing compared to her wrath if things aren't up to her standard. I continue to scrub the dishes as my mind wanders back.

* * *

IT'S MIDNIGHT. I'm officially thirteen years old. Mom barges through the door, unable to stand up straight. Janelle had just paused the show we were watching to wish me a happy birthday. We're in an embrace when she speaks.

"What the hell is this shit?" Her voice is low and gritty as she stares at us in the darkness.

"Mom?" Janelle asks, sitting up from the couch as my mom pulls off her patent-leather, sky-high platforms, dropping them to the floor. They clatter like dead weight onto the ground. We haven't seen her in over two weeks.

"What are you girls doing awake?" I feel goosebumps rise on my arms, and I pull the blanket tighter around me.

Janelle clears her throat. "Mom, we were just having fun...it's—"

"Having fun? I work hard for you girls!" She comes to the side of the couch, grabbing my arm and forcing me to stand.

"You like to stay up late? You're a little loser, you know that?" She cackles like she's never heard anything funnier. "I think you'll make a great housekeeper one day, Eve. Tonight, you better clean this shit-hole until it's sparkling." She flips the lights on, temporarily blinding us. "I'm waiting." A dark smile settles on her face.

My mother watches me wash every inch of the apartment until the sun rises.

* * *

I FINALLY BLINK the memory away, realizing I've been scrubbing for way longer than necessary. I hear her voice over the running water. "So, how are you?" I shut off the faucet and turn toward my mother as she takes a long sip from her coffee mug, looking more tired and worn out than usual. It's a rarity that she asks how I am, and her question catches me off guard.

"I'm good, Mom," I say hesitantly, drying off the pan with a dish towel. I take a seat at the table across from her, wondering if she'll be decent this morning.

She hums. "You look good." She stares at me from the tip of my toes all the way up to my face. "You're beautiful?" It comes out more like a question than a statement.

I shrug, not replying. I'm not sure what she wants to hear and would rather stay silent than say something that may incite her. Somehow, she always manages to take my kindness as arrogance.

"You're still working at Angelo's, right?"

"Yeah, I am. It's still cool."

"Don't embarrass me while you're there," she snaps. My mom is forever trying to stay in the good graces of the family, and she'd probably kill me if I ever did anything to jeopardize her relationship. The Borignones are so powerful; I'd never—in my right mind—do anything that could even be potentially construed as messing with them.

She glances around the kitchen, her eyes skittish. "You need to clean this place better, Eve. I can see dust in all the corners. Can't you see it?" Her voice accuses.

I gather myself before replying. "I'll make sure to go over it again today." I try to speak with as much decency as I can muster; any trace of an attitude is a surefire way to get her angry.

"I'm taking a nap. When I wake up, I don't want to see this disgusting mess."

"Yes," I reply calmly.

Janelle walks in, smiling happily. My mom's gaze turns to my sister. When she's in these moods, anyone in her path is going to get run over. "Why do you look so happy, Janelle?" Her eyes move from Janelle to me, completely distrustful. Anxiety fills me. She's rising.

Janelle's voice is scratchy as she starts. "It's nice out and I have a full day of clients. Cha-ching!" My mom huffs as I bite my cheek, trying not to laugh.

For whatever reason, my mom never hurts Janelle in the way she does me. I'll never understand it. Not that I'd ever wish Janelle to feel how I'm feeling, but I just wish I knew why I'm always the one singled out.

My mom's face turns to ice, her eyes shrinking into slits. She's obsessively touching her bleached-blond hair, pushing the strands back from her face over and over again. Janelle and I watch as her mood morphs. She stands abruptly, leaving her dirty dish on the table for me to clear and wash. I take a breath of relief when she finally slams her bedroom door, retreating into her cave. Janelle brings her coffee back to our room, leaving me alone in the kitchen.

Sitting by myself, I feel totally relieved. Grabbing my cell off the counter, I scroll through the *Post* headlines while enjoying my eggs and hot coffee. When I'm done, I wash all of the dishes by hand and put them away neatly in the cabinets where they belong. I step into my room, dropping my body on my unmade bed and wishing I could see Vincent again. I only have a few hours before I need to get to work, and I don't want to waste any more time on anything other than him. I curl under my covers, shutting my eyes and trying to replay both of our times together for what feels like the trillionth time, when Janelle drops onto my bed, making me bounce up and shaking me out of my reverie. "So, you never told me about what happened with the hot guy you met from the fight." Her smile is all-knowing, and I flush inside.

I open my mouth, ready to spill every detail, but quickly shut it. I don't want to tell her anything about Vincent. The whole experience was so new and incredible, I'm afraid if I tell her that it will become less mine somehow. Like once I discuss it, it'll be out in the universe —and I just want to keep it close to my heart. Who knows if I'll ever have something like that again. I got lucky twice, and something tells me a third time isn't in the cards.

Yes, I felt his want for me, but it was also more than that. He looked at me as if I'm someone worth knowing. He didn't see me like an uppity bookworm. And he didn't look at me like a poverty-stricken girl to pity, either. For some reason, he just seemed to actually like me. The real me. The me I almost never let anyone see. And God, I liked him. Almost too much.

"Nothing..." I say hesitantly, my eyes darting down for a moment while heat rises into my cheeks. She notices my blush and rolls her eyes.

"Wait," she asks me nervously. "You didn't have sex, right?"

My eyes widen with surprise and I laugh. "No! Absolutely not. We just made out and like, some other stuff..."

"Some other stuff?" She immediately sits up, wanting to know every detail.

"Yeah, like, I don't know. We made out. He touched me...uh, a little." I take a nervous breath. "I kind of had my first...you know..."

Her eyebrows rise up as she turns to me, smiling with surprise and shock. "Je-sus, Eve. Orgasm? If you can't say *orgasm*, God won't ever let you have one again. You know this rule, right? If you want it, you need to be mature enough to say it!" She's laughing hard, practically doubling over.

I'm so embarrassed I cover my face with the pillow. When I finally move it away to look back up at her, her eyes are sparkling with excitement.

"Eve. I'm seriously dying right now. God knows you're old enough. I need details! Did the guy have a huge dick? How was his tongue?" She raises her eyebrows up and down and I quickly bring the pillow over my head for a second time. "Well?" she asks expectantly, moving it away from my face.

"Janelle...it was..." All I can do is let out a heavy sigh, focusing my gaze on the ceiling. She lays back down next to me. "I know. When it's like that...it's everything."

Words just can't describe it. Instead of pressing me for more information, she throws her leg over mine and pulls me close to her. Janelle understands I'm not ready to talk, and she gives me the space I need. God, I love her.

"I'm so happy for you right now, Eve. I feel like my heart is about to burst. Whenever you're ready to talk, I'm here."

I let out a *hum* in response. I finally shut my eyes again, and he's all I see.

11

THE FOLLOWING weeks pass in a blur of school during the week and Angelo's on the weekends. I haven't heard from Vincent at all, but I'm too nervous to reach out to him. If he wanted to talk to me, he would have taken my number, right? Regardless, our times together are still on repeat through my head.

I grab my bag to leave Angelo's and type in the numbers for the alarm. I step outside and zip up my light jacket. It's going to be a cold winter for sure.

Shutting the door behind me, I pause when I see who's waiting out front. Vincent is casually leaning against his car, looking down at his phone. I stand there for a moment in wonder. Is he here for... me?

He glances up, dark eyes drinking me in as if I'm the first good thing he's seen in quite some time. I tentatively walk up to him, but he doesn't let my shyness dictate the moment. Instead, he takes my hand and pulls me flush against him, swallowing me up in a warm bear hug. I let out a sigh as I melt into his warmth. He smells so good. Part of me wants to ask him where he's been. But the bigger part of me is so deliriously happy, I can do nothing other than gush at the fact that he's here.

He finally lets me go and wordlessly opens the car door, inviting me inside. I hop in and buckle up as Vincent shuts the door behind me. The car is so warm compared to the cold temperatures outside right now. He takes his seat, immediately grabbing my hand and smiling as if we were just together yesterday.

"How are you?" he asks, his voice full of gentleness.

"I'm great!" I tell him overenthusiastically. He chuckles at my excitement. "So, where are we going?" The happiness pulses through my veins; I can't contain it!

"I thought maybe we'd go to Wolman Rink in Central Park. Have you ever been skating?"

My smile stretches from ear to ear. "Oh, I've always wanted to do that!" I stop myself before I tell him that I used to dream of being a figure skater, even though I've technically never been on ice. I've skated lots of times in my mind though, so it's sort of like the real thing, right? I mean, how hard can it actually be?

He winks. "I guess I'll have to show you how." I'm staring out the window, daydreaming about how he'll hold me close to his body as we skate, hand in hand. It will be so romantic.

We pull into a parking garage near Central Park on Sixth Avenue. Vincent tells me to wait as he steps out of the car, throwing his keys to the valet before coming around and opening my door.

"Do you know him?" I ask, turning my head for a moment to get a look at the attendant. Maybe that's the normal way people treat car attendants, how should I know? From what I see about Vincent, he lives in a world that's totally foreign to me.

"Nah. But I know the owner of the garage, so most of the guys who work there know me." He's so nonchalant, walking forward like he's the master of his universe.

We walk through Central Park from the Fifty-Seventh Street entrance. Walking down a small hill toward the rink, the first thing I notice is how packed it is with people of all ages. I'm looking around in awe of the entire place with the city skyline as the background, while Vincent pays the admission fee and skate rental. We walk together into the pavilion when what feels like a million kids run past us. I grab Vincent, trying not to get mowed down. He laughs as I cling to him for dear life.

They finally leave the vicinity and I shake my head. "Kids these days, huh?" He laughs harder, and I join him.

People sip hot chocolates and coffees while munching on churros and soft pretzels. Vincent asks me for my sneakers and I pull them off, handing them to him. He gives the rental guy my shoes, who quickly goes to the back and returns with skates in my size.

"What about yours?" I ask curiously as we walk away.

"I've got my own pair of hockey skates with me." I finally notice that he's got a black sports bag with him, and I roll my eyes.

"Next thing you're going to tell me is that you were about to go pro with the NHL or something."

"Hah! You think I'm that amazing, do you?"

"Nope. But you definitely think you are," I quip, smiling.

"I'm not too bad, am I?" He gives me a sly grin and I try not to melt in a puddle on the floor.

"So, when did you learn to skate?" I ask, trying to get as much information out of him as possible.

"I used to take lessons when I was a kid. I showed a lot of promise, but I preferred football." His eyes gleam.

"Really? That's so cool." My heart flutters. "So, how did the fighting start?"

"Well, martial arts has always been important to my father. It started out simply enough, we'd go together and learn. A bonding thing, I guess. But over time I got really good and started sparring with my coaches. They encouraged me to fight." he shrugs.

"Your parents know about it?" I ask suspiciously. I simply can't imagine any normal or decent parent encouraging their kid to brawl in the underground.

"My dad hates it," he replies coolly, finishing with his skates.

I finish tying mine, but I'm unsure if I pulled my laces tight enough. Without a word, he drops down on one knee in front of me, tightening them. I smile, an idea taking shape in my head. "No, I will not marry you, Vincent," I'm loud, garnering the attention of some people around us. He starts to snicker, shaking his head at me.

"Please, Eve," he replies loudly. "You're the most intelligent, kind, and beautiful woman on earth. Say *yes*! Don't keep denying me!" I do my best not to die of embarrassment as more people turn toward us. I know I started it, but I didn't think he'd continue. "How many times do I have to ask? Marry me! Be my wife! Be the mother of my children," he pleads.

I huff, looking left and right and pressing my lips together in a firm line. "Fine. You've worn me down. I'll do it."

Some people cheer as he stands up, wrapping me into his arms. We rub our noses together in a cheesy but oh-so-sweet gesture, while my insides melt. I have to ask myself, who am I right now? Vincent brings out a side to me that I never knew existed.

When he finally pulls back, there's an undeniable electrical current between us, and I can feel it down into my toes.

"All right, wife." He winks. "Let's finish putting these on." He moves back down to my feet and finishes lacing up my skates, pulling the strings tightly. We stand up together, ready to get on the ice. Before we can leave, he pulls out a white hat, scarf, and gloves from his bag. He slides the hat on me and I blink hard in utter confusion as soft warmth blankets my head.

"I know I didn't tell you we were coming here, and I didn't want you to be cold."

"You, b-brought this? For me?" My mouth literally drops open when I realize what he's done.

"Yeah," he replies easily, draping the scarf around my neck and tying it closed. Lifting each of my hands, he slides the gloves on one at a time. "There," he says, looking into my eyes. "Just right."

I'm totally struck dumb. Whatever he got me must be made from the softest material I've ever felt in my life. I turn over the tag from one glove and see it says 100% CASHMERE. Holy crap! I want to thank him, but I can barely muster the words.

"Uh, Vincent, I hope you kept the receipt—"

He lets out a chuckle. "Eve, it's for you. Keep them."

"No way. I can't keep something like this..." I shake my head vehemently.

He looks at me with confusion on his face, as if he can't imagine a girl saying *no* to a gift. "Look. I brought you here. I passed by Bloomingdales today and wanted to make sure you wouldn't freeze. It's my treat, okay? They're yours."

I wait a few moments, not sure what the protocol is for this. I can't even imagine what this gift must have cost. "Okay," I finally tell him, swallowing hard.

"Good. Now stay warm and try not to fall on your ass. Let me just put this in the back with your shoes." He gestures to his bag and I watch him walk away. I already feel much warmer, and I vow to take the best possible care of my new accessories.

He comes back to me and we start to walk toward the rink. I find myself losing balance and luckily, he grabs my waist, letting me lean into him. It's harder to stay steady on these skates than I originally thought.

When we finally get onto the ice, it's nothing like I imagined it would be. For starters, I don't feel graceful; I feel completely and utterly idiotic and clumsy. I try to move, but every time I slide my skates forward, I feel myself falling backward. Vincent takes hold of me as I cling to the wall for dear life.

"Okay, Tara Lipinski," he tells me jokingly. "Just stop a moment." I want to glare at him, but as I turn my head, my skates skid forward and backward again. I let out a huff as I grab the wall, realizing this is real life, not the fantasy. Little girls are gliding past me—twirling like swans—while I'm trying not to collapse to my death onto the cold and hard ice. Vincent keeps trying to stabilize me, but I can't stop myself from moving.

"Stop moving, Eve!" he stresses. I can tell from the tone of his voice that he's doing his best not to laugh his ass off at me.

"I'm trying, Vincent. But it's ice for God's sake!" I'm irritated by this turn of events. I was supposed to be naturally amazing at this and instead, I'm a failure.

"Watch your mouth," he whispers. "There are kids around."

I huff and try to stop my legs from falling out underneath me. I look up when I see someone ahead of me wipe out, landing on his ass. "Oh shit, Vincent! Did you see that guy?" Vincent throws his huge arms around me, securing my body to his.

"Just focus on your breathing," he tells me soothingly. I let myself follow his order, and before I know it, I feel myself calm. "There we go, Eve."

Somehow, the breathing really does work. "Okay, I think I can stand now."

Vincent gently lets go of me and I stand up tall, without hanging onto the wall. I hold myself like a statue while he moves behind me, carting me around the ice with complete grace. For a man so huge and strong, it's amazing how he's able to be so agile. After the fifth turn around the rink, I feel comfortable enough to lift my arms out to my sides. "I'm flying!" I yell, giggling, turning my head to glance at him. Have I ever been this happy in my life? I don't think so.

After we've gone around the rink what seems like dozens of times, he pulls us back over to the side, turning my body to face him. I grab his waist, so I don't collapse, and look up into his eyes. "Oh my God, Vincent! That was the best!"

"Well, I'll give you an *A* for enthusiasm, that's for sure." The look on his face is all play.

I purse my lips. "Oh, come on! Once I got the hang of it—"

"The hang of it?" He squints his eyes and holds back a smile. "You mean, the hang of staying still while I carted your tiny ass around?"

"Yes! Exactly!" He pulls me into his hard stomach and I breathe him in, feeling his body move with a laugh. It just feels so undeniably right.

He pulls me back a bit, still holding me securely. "I brought us some food. Let's go back inside." He kisses the top of my head. Helping me off the ice, he pauses for a moment as I turn my face up to his again. His skin is warm from the exertion; eyes so dark and glassy they're almost black. I'm not sure where his parents are from, but I'd bet his ancestry is something unique. I try to study each of his features, wondering what combination of ethnicity may have given him these incredible looks.

"You like to stare, huh? I hope you like what you see." His smile stops my heart.

"I'm just wondering where your parents or grandparents are from."

"My father is originally from Italy and my mother was Native American," he easily replies.

Did he say, *was*? I would bring it up, but I don't want to spoil the happiness we've got going on right now. "Oh my God," I say out loud, smiling. "I can actually totally see that. The wideness of your cheekbones and the slight slant in your eyes. It's like nothing else."

He chuckles. "And what about you?"

"My mom is Russian. She tells me my father was from Brazil."

"Mmm," he says, nodding his head in understanding.

"What do you mean, 'mmm?'" I ask.

"Just that you're sexy as hell, that's what." I flush from his blunt compliment, immediately dropping my head. He's so forward and confident, it's disarming.

"Okay, my gold medalist. Let's go inside." He drapes his arm over my shoulders and I do my best not to lean on him as we walk. He abruptly stops, seemingly annoyed. "I've had enough of this wobbly walking. I'm afraid you're gonna fall."

"Well, what exactly do you want me to—" I'm cut off when he lifts me in the air and throws me over his massive shoulder. I want to protest, but I can't stop laughing; all the blood rushes down into my head. We get inside and he places me down at a table in the back corner with a gentleness that's completely at odds with his tough demeanor. I look around for a moment; our table is completely hidden behind a beam. Did he bring us here on purpose?

He unties my skates, pulling them off my feet. I feel instant relief as I wiggle my toes around in freedom. "Feels so good to take these off!" I exclaim.

Vincent pulls off his own skates. "It does, huh?" I nod my head in reply. I look down and notice how massive his feet are. I swallow hard, wondering if that old saying is true. Big feet, big...

"Let me take your skates up." He picks them up off the floor, walking back to the rental desk. A few minutes later, he brings my shoes back along with his gym bag.

Unzipping his bag, he pulls out bottles of water, four huge sandwiches, and two colorful-looking salads along with napkins and plates. I'm looking at all the food with wide eyes. He gets up again and walks over to the snack counter, bringing us back two large cups filled with ice.

I sit on the edge of the table and watch while he finishes setting everything up. I'm not used to being taken care of like this. He opens up the sandwiches, each overstuffed with meat and vegetables and cut in half. I can't wipe the grin off my face when I see all that he's done.

"You're a perfectionist, huh?" He places the food on the table in perfect symmetry and with a neatness I'm shocked he possesses. "I can't believe you did all this."

"The food here sucks, and I thought you'd like something else." He smiles casually, as if bringing food this amazing is not a big deal. To me though, it's everything. And it's not just the food. It's the thought. It's everything. It's him.

He looks down at me as something dark and filled with promise moves through his eyes. I swallow hard, the smile from moments ago wiped off my face. He's looking at me so intensely that I feel my breath quickening.

He picks up a sandwich and hands it to me, breaking our heat. "You'll like this," he says gruffly. I close my eyes and take a bite.

"Mm, it's delicious." And I'm not bluffing. It may be the best sandwich I've ever had. I open my eyes to see him watching me intently, his gaze moving from my eyes down to my lips and back up again.

"It's from Eataly."

"Oh, I've always wanted to go there—" I want to continue, but stop myself. Not that he doesn't already know, but girls like me don't get to eat at fancy restaurants with even fancier chefs. I can't stand the thought of him seeing me as lacking or even worse, pitying me. Thoughts about my poverty disappear though, as he continues to gaze at my mouth as I chew. I swallow my food as heat finds its way into my lower belly. He picks up his own sandwich and takes a gigantic bite.

For some time, we do nothing but eat and stare at each other. We're quiet, but the silence is completely loaded. It's weird how these things don't take prior experience to understand; something inside me, on a basic and carnal level, knows what's happening. Our eyes, full of energy, say everything.

My eyes: "God, you're gorgeous. Sexy. Brilliant. I love this."

Vincent's eyes: "I'm so happy you're here with me."

Some of his hair is messy on his forehead and I put my sandwich down, leaning forward to brush it off to the side. His look softens and I wonder for a moment if he had a mom who took care of him—if she used to pack him lunch and make him breakfast and dinner, if she tucked him in bed at night, reading stories. Did Vincent have his parents' bed to run to in the middle of the night if he ever had a bad dream? Even though he seems to have it all, something is telling me that his life may not be all roses. I want to ask him, but feel shy.

I take my last bites of the sandwich when I start to consider getting some sauce on my cheek just so we can have one of those movie moments where he wipes it off and kisses me. But as I squeeze the remainder of the sandwich in attempt to get the sauce on my face, I screw it up and somehow end up getting mayo on my pants.

"Shit!" I gasp, clicking my tongue and grabbing a napkin.

He starts to laugh and I quickly try to explain. "I didn't realize that the sandwich would squirt from just a small squeeze! I mean, shouldn't it take more than that?" His eyes seemingly widen with disbelief at my comment, and he starts cracking up. I'm not sure what's so funny about what I said, but something in the way he's laughing tells me he's laughing at me, not with me. His laughter is intensifying as I get redder and there is nothing else to do but hide my face with my hands.

When I realize he isn't planning to stop his laughter, I lift my hands off my face and hit him on the shoulder.

"Oh, shut it. Stop!" I feel so juvenile. My face is probably the color of a beet right now. "Stop laughing at me, Vincent!"

"I can't help it. You're so damn sweet..." He drags me onto his lap and I put my head into the crook of his neck. I feel his body shake with the remnants of his laughter and I take a sharp breath. All of a sudden, I realize I may have just found the greatest spot of all time. I nuzzle into his neck, inhaling his scent. I hope he doesn't think I'm creepy right now, but the truth is that I couldn't stop myself even if I wanted to. I want to crawl inside this man and never leave. For all his hugeness, we manage to fit so well. He finally stops laughing and brings his arms around me, pulling me flush against his chest and holding me firmly. I guess he likes this too. I receive confirmation when I feel him hardening under me. I pause. Slowly, I pull my head back.

Some young kids start nagging their mom about wanting churros, but it all becomes background noise as our lips connect. It's slow at first. Gentle lips and warm tongues. But the moment his hands go beneath my ass, he presses me down into his erection and all common sense flees my brain.

"Fuck." His voice is a growl and my eyes shut, the feelings overwhelming me.

Blood pools down low as he rubs me rhythmically against him. I move over a little to the left and let out a moan into his neck; he's hitting that spot. "Vincent..." I say into his skin. I can't even be bothered to realize where I am or what I'm doing. All I can do is grip onto his huge shoulders as he presses me down harder and harder. I feel myself start to sweat and I welcome it; the heat is devouring me from the inside out.

I lift my head for a moment and look into his eyes when he stops. When I realize he isn't going to continue, I exclaim, "What? No!"

He chuckles as he gently moves his hands from my back to my shoulders and takes a breath, turning me around so I'm sitting back on the bench beside him. "Later, okay? Here isn't the place for you."

His eyes are filled with promise, but somehow, I'm left with this hollow and desperate feeling.

My body finally starts to wind down and I plunge my plastic fork into the salad, internally stressing about what is going on. And anyway, why did it take him so long to reach me? When we're together, I feel like we've got something more than just attraction. It's deep; I can feel it. But he disappears. And then he's back. I'm having emotional whiplash and frankly, I'm angry. I should have been pissed at him when he picked me up, but I was too overwhelmed by the emotions he brings out in me. He's too gorgeous. Too big. Too smart. Too everything!

I decide I may as well just get out with it and ask him. I turn my head to the side to get his attention, my anger fueling my tongue. "Vincent?" My voice comes out angrier than I intended. He looks into my eyes and smirks, as if he knows already what I'm going to say.

"Yeah, babe?"

I turn my body around so that instead of being side by side, I'm facing him. "What are we?"

"Hm. I think I'm a man, and you're a woman..." He starts to joke.

"Come on. I'm serious. What's happening here?" I gesture my hands between the two of us.

He takes a few moments before answering. "We're friends." His eyes are saying we're more, but his words obviously differ.

I startle for a moment and want to disagree with him. "But—"

He turns to face me. "I live a very complicated life, Eve." His eyes bore into mine as if he really wants me to hear what he's saying.

"Are you... with other girls?" I ask, my stomach sinking with dread.

He sighs but keeps his head up. "Let's start like this for now, okay? Let's just be friends." It seems to pain him to use the word, but it sure as hell feels like I've been knifed.

I try to silently communicate with my eyes how much I want him to be mine, but my chest pounds with feelings of inadequacy. I don't have the guts to tell him so.

Tears start to well in my eyes as I remember the mention of a redhead, but I swallow down my pain and try to keep my emotions in check. Why doesn't he want me? He watches as confusion and hurt cross my face. He looks as if he's about to say more, but he stops. Vincent has the self-control of a saint; if he chooses not to speak, nothing will leave his lips.

The truth is, I know why he doesn't want a girl like me. I'm a nobody. I'm a poor girl from the ghetto. What would a man like him want with someone like me? The answer is that he wouldn't.

He touches my shoulder. "No." He shakes his head. "I see what you're thinking, and I don't like it. There's a lot you don't know about me. Let's just finish eating, okay? We're cool. We're here right now. Let's be in the moment." He turns back around to face the table, essentially dismissing me.

"So tell me. Tell me what I don't know," I ask him desperately.

I wait, but he doesn't say a word. Finally, I turn myself back and finish my salad quietly. I'm not good enough, but this shouldn't be a surprise. My mom's words come back and hit me in the chest. I'm nothing. I look down at my shoes and feel the tears welling up again. He knows how poor I am, and probably sees me as nothing more than a toy to pass the time with. I try not to cry as I eat my salad. My mind is moving so quickly, I barely know what it tastes like.

When he finally brings me back to my front door, my shame is raging. I want to cry and scream at the top of my lungs. I wish he didn't drop me off here; it's nothing but a reminder to him of who I am and where I come from. But at the same time, I can't just waltz back home at this time of night. It's not safe, and it's undeniable that with him, I'm secure.

He leans against my shitty white doorframe. I want to ask him if I'll see him again, but I know that any words that come out of my mouth right now will sound desperate. He checks his phone and his face turns to agitation. I open my apartment door and let myself inside. Before closing it, I turn back around, thanking him again.

He puts his hand on my hips, bringing me closer to his body. I look down at the floor and back up to his face.

"Eve," he says, shaking his head. "Thank YOU for coming with

ME. You're too sweet for a man like me. Too good. I've got more going
on than you can imagine...but trust me, what I've got going on is not
about you. You're perfect." I want to believe him. Hell, I'm begging
inside for him to elaborate. But he doesn't. On one hand, he sounds
so genuine...and the scarf and gloves and hat...and the food! The
connection we have seems undeniable. But then again, it feels as if
he's breaking up with me. I've never been broken up with, but if it
feels like my heart is being ripped out, I guess this qualifies.

I shrug my shoulder sadly, and for a brief moment, I think I see
regret pass through his eyes. "I guess I'll see you soon, Vincent." I
stare up into his face one more time and see so much pain pass
through. He sighs, looking up at the ceiling and back down at me.

Moments pass and he's still silent. Somehow, I get the nerve to
turn away from him, shutting the door behind me. I hear his heavy
steps as he leaves, and I do my best not to cry.

12

A MONTH PASSES, and Vincent feels like a distant memory. I never discussed him with Janelle, and so in the daytime, it's almost like what happened between us didn't even occur. But every single night, he's the only thing I can see, smell, and taste.

Missing him began as an acute ache, and slowly filtered into the rest of my body. Ever since he disappeared, I feel like I'm always missing something. I leave home and feel it in my chest—it's not a sweater; it's not my phone or my wallet; it's HIM. He managed to fill a part of me I didn't even know was empty. And now that he's gone, I feel the hole gaping inside my chest.

This morning, Janelle and I are sitting together for breakfast before we head off to work. She sits across from me while I sip my coffee and read the newspaper. She looks nervous, so I drop my paper and ask her point blank. "What's up, Janelle? You look like you're going to freak out."

"Carlos is out," she says in a rush. I look at her face, feeling my stomach sink. She's playing with the hem of her shirt and glances at me nervously. Finally, her gray-blue eyes bore into mine, and I know that she's gearing up to tell me some serious shit.

With trembling hands, I put down my coffee mug. "Tell me."

"Yeah. Well, I heard he made bail—" She stops, clearing her throat. "I also heard that he's, um, angrier than usual." She stands, bringing the rest of the carafe of coffee to the table and pouring more into my cup.

I lick my dry lips. "What do you mean?"

She moves to the edge of her seat, pushing sugar my way. "Well, I was on the stoop yesterday. It was my day off. I was hanging out with everyone and listening to Mr. Samson talk about a new jazz club that recently opened up in Harlem. We were all getting high with some-one's hash, shooting the shit—"

"And?" I raise my eyebrows, waiting for her to get to the point.

"Juan came over, and sat with me." She slightly shifts her head to the side and presses her lips together. "Well, he told me that Carlos is out now. And, he's been talking shit all over town that he and you have some unfinished business. Juan wanted to tell me because he's scared for you. I know he's an annoying little shit, but after he heard..." her voice trails off.

I blink once, twice, three times.

"There's more," she says on an exhale. "Apparently, he hooked up with some girl last night. Beat the shit out of her. Ms. Santini from Three-A was on her way to work and stopped to drop off her trash by the dumpsters. Apparently, she heard a moaning sound. When she saw the girl, her clothes were torn. She was beaten up and started bawling about Carlos..."

My head gets dizzy, but I force myself to hear every detail. "An ambulance took her away, but she was in pretty bad shape."

I want to ask more questions, but the terror has a clamp on my throat.

"I think you need to stay close to me for a while, okay? The Snakes are getting more aggressive. They want the Blue Houses as their own territory, and it looks like they're trying to instill some bigger fear on the streets." She drops her gaze. I know she's afraid. Every girl in the Blue Houses probably heard the story by now.

"Yeah. Okay. I'll make sure Angelo knows I need to leave before it gets dark out."

"Good idea. We need to sync our schedules so you aren't walking alone at night. I'm gonna talk to some other people and try to get their schedules down so that everyone has a buddy or something at night. I'm sure when everyone hears about this, we won't be the only ones who are scared." I nod my head and stand up mechanically, rinsing my mug and walking to my room to digest the new information. After grabbing my stuff, I check my purse to make sure that my gun is still inside. I lock myself in the bathroom and load and unload the gun a few times, reacquainting myself with the weapon. If Carlos comes, I'll be ready for him.

Getting to work, I let Angelo know the details of what's new with Carlos. He's angry and continues to tell me that I shouldn't be so stubborn and I need to let the Borignones get involved. But I refuse. I still don't want any debts to my name. I've made it this far, and I believe I can wait it out a little longer.

Work passes in a blur. I'm convincing a girl to sell her diamond ring while Angelo sells the two violins and a Cartier watch to an elderly couple who want to buy something for their grandchildren.

When the day is done, Angelo insists on calling a car to take me home. I sigh deeply, knowing that the driver will be one of Angelo's associates. But considering the fact that Carlos is out of jail, I'm not going to complain. I nod my head and take his ride in the name of safety.

I get in the huge black Escalade and see a massive man sitting in the driver's seat. Swallowing hard, I remind myself that he's not an enemy, but on my side. He drives me right up to my building and I gingerly walk out, my shaking hand inside my purse, gripping my gun. I'm scared as hell, but it makes me feel a modicum of control. The driver enters the building with me and steps into the elevator as well.

We reach the fourth floor when I tell him he can go. "I can get into my apartment fine now." He nods his head wordlessly and recalls the elevator to bring him back downstairs.

I get up to my door without incident and let out the breath I was holding while I pry my fingers off my gun. "I'm okay," I say out loud, turning my head and letting my gaze run up and down my hallway. It's empty. I pull out my key and step forward onto my threadbare Welcome mat when I feel like I've kicked something. I look down, confused at what's on the floor. It must be Janelle's sweater that she dropped on her way out. I bend down to pick it up and freeze.

A cat. A dead cat. Its neck is broken with eyes that are bugging out. Blood is smeared all over its gray-and-black fur. Images of dead rats being left by Carlos in people's doorways pile into my head. The moment the stench of blood hits my nose, I turn my head and vomit in the hallway. Carlos. He's back. And he hasn't forgotten about me.

13

WHEN MY STOMACH IS EMPTY, I step over the dead cat and enter my apartment, locking myself in the bathroom. My mind races. "What do I do? What the fuck do I do? I need to call Janelle." With my body shaking, and sweat pouring down my face, I pick up my phone and manage to dial her number. It rings and rings, my heart pounding. *Pick up, Janelle!*

When I get her voicemail, I hang up and dial again. On the fourth try, I realize she isn't going to answer. "Help! I need her. I need help!" My heart is pounding harder now, and I feel like I'll be sick again. I focus my gaze on the bathroom wall, paint cracking along the edge.

I drop onto the floor, dropping my head into my hands. "Carlos. He's back and he's going to kill me. My mom said I should just give into him. Maybe I should end my misery and just call him. At least I won't have to wait for him to find me. No, I can't do that. Could I?"

I force myself up and into my bedroom, opening my side table, and pulling open the drawer. I find the stack of folded papers for prospective colleges underneath Janelle's beauty samples from Sephora. I sit on my bed and ruffle through them. Princeton. Yale. Columbia. I try to take in a few deep breaths, but my nausea intensifies. "I can't give into Carlos. I need to stand strong. Just a few more months. But how?"

Visions of the dead cat flashback in front of my eyes. I run back to the toilet to dry heave. When my body understands there's nothing left inside me to puke, I sit up and lean against the cold tile wall. "I've got a dead animal and a pile of vomit by my front door. I need to clean it up, but I can't. I just can't do it."

Like a flash through my head: "Angelo. I need to call Angelo. He'll know what to do. Does removing the dead body of a cat count as a favor to the Borignones? Maybe it does. But I have no other option right now."

He answers on the third ring. "Hey, doll. Everything okay?" His voice is laced with concern.

"No, Angelo. Something's happened. It's Carlos—"

"Take a breath. I can't hear you and everything sounds muffled."

I inhale and exhale deeply a few times, opening my mouth to speak again. "Carlos. He's b-back. He left a dead cat on my doorstep!" I pant. "It's there." My voice is frantic, chest shaking. "I threw up—" Gasp. "I puked ev-ev-everywhere." I exhale, trying to compose myself so I can speak while fluids fall from every crevice of my face. "I can't go back out. There's b-blood. A cat. He left me a dead cat—"

"Okay," he says calmly while I grip the phone like a lifeline. "I'm out in Jersey right now on business, and won't be back until work in the morning. But don't worry—I'm going to send Stix back to you, all right? He'll be there. Same guy who brought you home. Remember, he's very tall and built. Long black hair and green eyes. He'll knock three times on your door. Do not open the door unless you hear that knock, got it? Three times."

"Y-yeah, Angelo. I got it. I r-r-remember him."

"He'll clean it all up for you. Do you have a friend you can call and stay with tonight? You can't be alone there. Janelle workin' late?"

"Uh-huh. I think she said she was staying at her boyfriend's after work... I—"

"And that good-for-nothing piece of shit mom of yours. Fuckin'

Irina." He practically spits out her name. "Probably on some bender."
He lets out a breath over the phone.

"You gotta call a friend, okay? No stayin' alone tonight. Get outta
that shit hole. If you can't think of anyone, I'll arrange for you to go
somewhere. We'll talk about all of this shit when we see each other
tomorrow. I'm not letting you get hurt, do you understand me? If I
need to send a friend a' mine over to stand guard at your door, I'll do
it. Maybe you gotta live with me or with that teacher of yours for
a while—"

I listen to him intently, my stomach feeling raw. I grip the phone
harder, my knuckles turning white. "I'll think of someone to call for
tonight."

"I'm gonna call Stix now. He'll be there soon. Call me and we'll
make sure you got somewhere to go." He hangs up the phone and my
head spins.

Who the hell can I call? Other than Janelle's friends, I have none
of my own. I'm afraid if I tell anyone from the Blue Houses, it'll get
around what happened to me. And gossip always makes things
worse. I bet that's what Carlos wants. He wants to scare the shit out of
me and everyone else. He wants to hear that I freaked-the-fuck-out. I
know that piece of shit; he gets off on terrorizing people. Even if I
could call a friend from the building, I wouldn't put them in that kind
of danger. And, if people knew Carlos was after me, they wouldn't
want to come anywhere near me! Even Janelle could be in danger
right now. What if he uses her to get to me?

My mind keeps moving through all kinds of scenarios when I
hear three consecutive knocks at my door. I jump up and nervously
walk to my door.

"Who is it?" I say with a shaking voice.

What if Carlos knocked three times? Three times is a perfectly
normal number of knocks. I stand on my tippy-toes and stare through
the peephole in the front door. It's the driver, Stix. I was so concerned
with getting home earlier I didn't take in all of his features. In this
moment, I realize how stupid that was. Through the peephole, I give

him a once-over, making sure he isn't some random thug pretending to be Stix.

He speaks. "Eve? It's me, Stix. Angelo sent me," he says through the door in a deep voice. "Why don't you just wait inside and let me take care a' this. I'll remove the, uh, animal, and clean the floor for you. Got all my cleaning supplies with me; it was already in the back of my car. Just relax, a'ight? Angelo told me you're like a daughter to him, you don't gotta be scared of me. I'll be quick."

I let out a small squeak in reply before turning around, leaning my back against the door, and sliding to the floor so I'm sitting against it. I press my head back against the door, listening to him work. The sound of him cleaning is soothing.

I hear him grumbling about something and he barks out, "You there?" I knock against the door, letting him know that I'm near.

"The cat is gone now and I'm cleaning the mat with something that's pretty damn strong. Got any Lysol?"

"Uh huh," I reply.

Seconds seem to pass. Minutes maybe. "I'm waitin'."

I finally stand up and walk to my cleaning closet, grabbing the spray. Holding the can reminds me I have a gun. I run into my room and pull it out of my purse. I instantly feel better. I want to open the door, but my stomach suddenly drops. I can't open the door. Terror starts to build again. I feel wetness pouring out of my eyes. I can't do this.

"I can't open the door," I say, my voice quivering.

"Okay. No worries. I got a daughter myself, okay? I said it, but I'll tell you again. I'm cleanin' shit up. No worries." I hear a scrubbing sound again and try to focus on it.

"You still there?" he asks again.

"Yeah," I reply against the door.

"Call a friend. This shit is all clean now."

And with those parting words, he leaves. I look through the peephole to make sure no one is near and let out a breath and text Angelo.

ME: Stix came and left. It's done

If I can just find someone to be with me for a few hours, maybe Janelle will finally answer the phone and I can be with her tonight. Maybe I can even crash with her on Leo's couch. I try calling her another few times, but still, no answer. My heart pounds. What if she's gone?

I pick up the phone with my heart in my chest, calling her salon. They tell me that she's in the middle of doing someone's highlights and she won't be done until close to ten-thirty. Relief hits me so hard that I try not to bawl.

Janelle may be safe for now, but I still need to get the hell out of here in the meantime. I scroll through my contacts until I find Vincent's name and open up a message. I need to do this quickly before I think too hard about it and chicken out. The cursor blinks and I have no idea what I should type. There's no way in hell I'm going to tell him what happened to me. If he knew, he'd just think of me as some pathetic loser living in a crack den. I want him to see me as more than that. At the same time, I can't stay here alone right now. My lock is bullshit and can probably be cracked open within seconds. Vincent is strong and can protect me...and just the thought of him, of being with him, makes me feel secure. But, I haven't spoken to him in over a month! What if he doesn't want to hear from me? I look up again at the stack of college stuff spread out on my bed, and it gives me the strength I need. I'm doing this. Deep in my gut, I know that being with him right now is the right move. I need to at least try.

My fingers move at lightning speed as I type Vincent a text; I need to move quickly before I change my mind.

ME: Hey. What's up? It's Eve

What if he doesn't reply? Shit. Maybe I made a mistake?

VINCENT: Eve. Hey.

Oh my God! He replied. My hands shake as I type out the next message

ME: Want to hang out tonight?
VINCENT: Yeah, was just about to workout. Wanna join?
ME: Sure
VINCENT: I'll be there in 30
ME: OK

I lock myself in the bathroom and sit against the white tile wall, clutching my gun with one hand and my cell phone with the other. Thirty minutes, that's all I need to wait. Vincent will come, and I'll be okay. I know that I'll be safe with him. I have to be.

I shut my eyes, trying to focus my attention on the man I'm about to see. Vincent's huge callused hands. Vincent's strong body. Vincent's deep and dark eyes. Vincent's brilliant mind.

I finally stand myself up and head to the sink, washing my face methodically. I need to calm myself down if I'm going to see him. Stepping out of the bathroom, I move to my bedroom and change out of my jeans and into some loose sweats; I barely notice what I'm putting on other than the fact that it's comfortable.

I glance at the clock. It's been twenty-five minutes since we texted. Is he almost here? I risk a peek out my bedroom window when I see some thugs from the Snakes hanging out on the steps by the front door, their red and black bandanas clear under the lamplights by the stoop.

"Shit!" I exclaim. The last thing I need is for Vincent to have a run-in with Carlos' crew on his way to me.

Another dose of dread runs through my veins as I watch Vincent's black Range Rover park in front of the building. He walks out of his car, his steps sure and gait long. I can only imagine the don't-fuck-with-me face he's probably sporting. I briefly wonder again who this man is, completely unafraid? Vincent steps up to enter the building when the Snakes stand to greet him. I swallow back the bile rising in my throat. Should I run downstairs and warn him? Yell out the window?

I want to open my mouth to scream, "No," but all that will come out is a low and painful rasp.

Vincent takes the hat off his head. The Cartel stands up. A moment later, I watch as they run off the stoop. "What?"

He walks up the two small steps, looking left and right, entering the building confidently. I walk to the kitchen, grab a cup and turn on the faucet. I fill it to the top and drink it all down. I'm under so much stress right now that I can barely think straight. I probably saw wrong. I must have. Maybe they got a phone call and ran off, having nothing to do with Vincent.

I hear a knock at my door. What if it it's Carlos? My feet are frozen to the floor. I hear another pounding noise, like brick against wood. I force myself to step to the door, my body quaking as I stand on my tiptoes to look through the peephole. A whoosh of relief covers me when I see that it is, in fact, Vincent.

"Just a second," I manage to stutter out.

I look inside my bag, making sure my gun is still where I left it last. Breathing deeply, I remind myself to act upbeat. Nothing happened. Everything is just fine.

I swing the door open and step out before he can get a look inside my apartment. But as my feet touch the Welcome mat, I jump off as if I've been burned while my stomach sinks with echoes of memory.

He watches my skittish behavior with concern. "Eve?" His brows are furrowed as he bends down, getting a closer look at my face, seemingly trying to see what's got me acting so strangely. My eyes must look red-rimmed and inflamed considering how much crying I recently did.

"Hey Vincent!" My voice is so phony I barely believe it myself. "Ready for the gym? Wild night you've got planned. Hope you don't mind me crashing." I'm talking too quickly and let out an awkward laugh.

He holds my hand possessively, eyes roaming up and down the decrepit hallway.

"You've been crying." It's a statement, not a question.

I blink, but he doesn't say more.

As we get off the elevator, I start second guessing all of my choices. Maybe I shouldn't have left my apartment? What if Carlos is downstairs? Before Vincent notices my stress, he opens the front door. I let out a whimper of relief; the stoop is completely empty.

He opens his car door and helps me step inside before slamming it shut. Jogging around to the driver's seat, he gets inside, buckles up, and starts the engine.

I'm still reeling as his thumb begins to graze across my knuckles.

His touch is so soothing. Ninety-nine percent of myself wants to curl into a ball in his arms and just tell him everything. But that tiny little one percent has some pride. I simply refuse to look any more pathetic to him than I already do.

I stare at his strong profile, wondering how many women he's been with. He's probably slept with more girls than I can count on both of my hands a few times over. And here I am, a naïve virgin from the hood.

He stops the car at a red light and turns to me. "Eve? I can see the stress in your face." I immediately clam up with his observation. The light turns green and I watch as his eyes dart between me and the road, waiting for me to reply.

"It's nothing. Just a stupid fight with my sister," I lie, my eyes glancing out my window.

"You're lying," he tells me simply.

He parks in a small outdoor parking lot and steps out of the car, and I let myself out before he can walk around to open my door. We cross the quiet street to a large warehouse. Vincent rings up to Floor Two, the buzzer sounds and the lock opens. He holds the door for me as I walk inside. The staircase is narrow, with just enough room for us to walk in single file. Vincent starts up first, and I quietly trail behind him.

We get up to Joe's Gym—which is a lot larger than it seems from outside—a standard boxing ring is in the center of the room, surrounded by clusters of red and blue mats, jump ropes, boxing gloves, and other gym equipment. Vincent walks us to the far corner and tells me to hang out while he uses the locker room. I don't need to change, but I pull off my sweatshirt and use it to cover my purse, leaving it all in the corner. I drop myself on a large blue mat and look down at my outfit.

"Oh shit," I say out loud, grimacing. I'm in a pair of ratty old gray sweatpants and a T-shirt Leo gave to Janelle last year. It's long and baggy, hanging down to my knees. At least it's black.

Vincent steps out of the locker room and jogs over to a muscular guy in the middle of the ring. They talk and keep looking over at me while I self-consciously bring my knees to my chest. Is he going to tell me to go home? I can't go home yet. I turn around and dig into my purse, checking to see if Janelle called me. She still hasn't. I just need Vincent to stay with me until Janelle is off from work.

"Ten-thirty," I repeat to myself.

He jogs back to me. "All right. I'm not gonna fight tonight. Instead, I'm gonna teach you some shit."

"Um, me?" I squeak, looking up at him nervously.

He chuckles, throwing a heavy arm around my small shoulders. "Yeah, you. I'll teach you some kicks and punches. How to get out of some holds. Maybe even a little grappling."

I step back to protest, but he immediately crosses his arms in front of his chest in a stance that's telling me he isn't taking *no* for an answer. I sigh.

"Whenever shit gets tough in life, it's good to exert some physical energy. I'm not going to push you into talking, but we both know that something went down tonight. You'd be surprised, but working out has a way of clearing shit up mentally." I want to argue, but he shuffles me forward to the center of the mat before I can get a word in.

He turns me to face him. "Don't ever lie to me, Eve. I'll always know it. Understand?" I swallow the saliva in my mouth. I'm staring at the Bull right now, who clearly does what he wants when he wants.

I've still got at least two more hours to waste before Janelle can call me. If I want to stay with him right now, I have no choice but to go along with his plan.

I shake out my shoulders, trying to focus. "All right. Let's do this," I tell him. He smiles, trying not to laugh at my attempt to warm up.

"Let's start on the bag." We walk to a large red punching bag hanging from the ceiling. He demonstrates basic kicks and punches. I do my best to mimic his stance and the way he turns his arms with each punch and kick. Shifting my body this way and that, he's seemingly obsessed with proper form. When I've got the hang of the basics, Vincent shouts out my first combination.

Again and again, I front kick, jab left, and jab right. "There we go,

Eve. Very good." He nods. "Let's do that another seven times." He counts off, pacing around me as sweat beads on my forehead.

"Stop," he commands, his voice deep. In some strange way, it feels good to just trust him and take orders. I'm not in any state of mind to make choices right now, even small ones. He may be dominating, but he isn't cruel.

Vincent steps back to the bag, holding it steady with both hands. "I want to see round-house left, round-house right, jab, jab, punch, and elbow." He demonstrates and I stare with heavy breaths and rapt attention. The strength and power of his body is obvious in every move he makes; he's so thick and muscular, but at the same time, has so much speed and agility. It's clear why he's such a monster in the ring. I copy his moves again and again, hitting the bag with all of my might, while he circles me, yelling, "Harder, Eve. Three More! Punch harder!" All I can hear are his shouts, and it's keeping my mind focused on nothing other than the task at hand.

He tells me to stop, and I drop my hands to my knees. My entire body is no longer simply damp, but wet with perspiration. Ignoring my exhaustion, he shows me how to swing my arms laterally from wide angles, so that a punch to the temple can be easily followed with an elbow straight to the chin. I stand tall and lift the bottom of my shirt, pressing it against my sweaty forehead. Vincent's eyes roam my body and stop at my face. My breath catches as his pupils dilate. I can't help but stare back, my breathing still labored. His T-shirt is tight against his chest while dark jersey shorts hang low on his narrow hips. He still has his hat on, and it showcases his straight Roman nose and chiseled jaw. He looks intimidating and sexy as hell.

He steps forward, pressing his lips together in a thin line. "I want to show you how to get out of a hold." His voice comes out hoarse. "Let's assume that someone is coming at you from behind and holds your arms against the side of your body." He moves behind me, acting out his words. I feel him harden. I clench my fists, glad that he can't seem my face as I swallow hard.

"You're going to want to drop your weight down as if you're doing a squat. Especially if he's much bigger than you. There's more to the move, but let's begin with that." He slowly releases me.

Vincent steps behind me again and again, restraining me. I do as he asks and drop down in a squat. "Keep your feet wider than hip width," he commands. My thighs burn, but I refuse to give up.

I'm about to squat down again, but this time, he doesn't allow me to drop. Instead, he holds me firmly in place. While I'm not in any pain, it's clear he isn't about to let me move without his consent. The rational side of my mind lets me know that he's probably about to show me the rest of the move. But another part of my mind begins to panic.

I struggle against him, but his huge, masculine body is unshakeable. I can feel his dick against my back, and my entire body starts to buzz, terror filling every crevice of my body.

I hear my name being called, but it's nothing but a distant sound on a stranger's lips. I feel someone turning me around, but I can't look up. I hear a voice, but it's muffled as the whooshing sound in my ears increases in volume.

I see Vincent gripping my shoulders and staring into my face. But my vision feels fuzzy as the panic pulls me under. Am I drowning?

I think I hear my name, but it's far away. Little by little, it gets louder and louder until finally, it's clear.

"Eve," Vincent calls. "It's me. Breathe, baby." His voice full of worry and anguish as his hands move up and down my back. "Calm down. It's just me. I'm here." He gently places me in a chair and drops to his knees in front of me. Somehow the tension in my body settles, turning into numbness.

"Vincent?" I croak. He wipes the tears off my face with his thumbs. "It's over now, okay?" He holds me tightly and I can feel exhaustion settling into my bones.

"Over? No," I say, staring up at the clock. Janelle isn't done with work yet. I can't go home. "It's not done. I'm not ready to give up. I want more, Vincent—"

"Baby, we've been going at it for over an hour. This isn't giving up—"

"I want to do more! I can handle it," I beg. He shakes his head, not understanding what's happening. "Don't take me home, Vincent. Please. I'm not ready to go home," I sob, pleading with him.

He seems to understand that going home is not an option. "Let's go back to my apartment. You aren't going back there," he tells me firmly. My breath hitches and I nod my head in utter relief.

"I should call my s-sister," I stutter.

"No problem. Call her. Tell her you're out tonight."

Before I can put on my sweatshirt, Vincent grabs his and slides it over my head, pulling my damp ponytail out of the hood.

"I have my shirt," I gasp. The tears won't stop running down my face.

"I know. But mine is warmer." Without thinking, I lift the bottom of his sweatshirt and put it to my nose, inhaling deeply. It smells just like him, and the scent soothes me.

I take my phone out of my bag and with shaking hands, text Janelle.

ME: I'm staying out tonight. Stay at Leo's. DO NOT GO HOME.
JANELLE: What's going on?? It's Carlos, right? Who are you with?? I'm waiting for client's color to set. I need another forty min before I can call...
ME: Ms. Levine. Don't worry.

I type out the lie and immediately bite my lip. I can't get into the details of Vincent right now, especially not over text. I'll explain it all to her later. She'll understand.

JANELLE: OK.

I put my phone away as Vincent lifts me up off the mat and into his arms. "Vincent, I can w-walk," I tell him, my voice still staccato from crying.

"No. I want to take care of you right now. Let me." I lean my forehead into his neck and relax into his arms.

I shut my eyes while he drives and slowly doze off. "Eve, we're here," he whispers, putting his hands on the side of my face. I open my eyes with a start and look around. We're in a parking lot on the corner of Houston and Wooster Street. Vincent opens the door for me and we walk together into a beautiful white building. The doorman nods to us as Vincent shuffles me to the elevator. At the penthouse floor, we step off. He pulls out his keys, unlocking three different locks. After typing in a complicated-looking code to an alarm panel, he opens the door. The minute my eyes take in what's around me, I gasp. The entire kitchen, living room, and dining room is an open floor plan. The kitchen gleams in marble and chrome, a beautiful white marble island separating it from the dining area. A long wooden table surrounded by black chairs serves as the dining room. Farthest away is a living area, complete with a beautiful L-shaped black leather couch, coffee table, and big screen TV.

He clears his throat and I snap my jaw shut. "Let me show you to the bathroom. You wash up and I'll order us some Chinese. Cool?" I nod my head in silence as he takes my hand. Opening a door at the end of the living area, we walk through a short corridor. "Here's my bedroom," he points. The room is cozy in whites, grays, and blacks. A large bed sits in the center of the room with two wooden side tables flanking it. A wooden desk is in the corner, piled high with books and a silver laptop. The space is clean, orderly, and masculine. It's exactly what I'd imagine Vincent's room to look like.

"I've got some clean clothes in the drawer by the bedside table. Take whatever you need. The bathroom is right there." He points to another door and I nod my head. "Let me just get you some fresh towels." He steps into the hallway and returns a moment later with a large fluffy white towel and a smaller one. He hands them to me and then steps out.

"Holy shit," I say in a whisper as the door closes. Walking to the window, Vincent has the perfect view of West Houston Street. I can see the Angelika Theatre straight ahead. Stepping into his bathroom, my eyes widen; it's completely white marble. Turning on the shower and taking off my clothes, I step into the spray. I sigh in relief at the heavy water pressure. I grab his shampoo, washing my hair and focusing on the clean scent. I use a simple bar of Dove soap, and I shut my eyes, imagining Vincent using this same bar to clean his own body. I swallow, set down the soap, and lean against the shower wall. I wish I could stay in this apartment forever.

Shutting off the shower and stepping out, I wrap myself up with the towel. Moving back into his bedroom, I pull out a plain white T-shirt and a pair of sweatpants from his drawer. I have to roll them up on my hips seven or eight times to keep from falling off me. I brush out my hair with a comb that I find underneath his sink and tie it back in a braid using my hair tie. I'm going to eat with him, ask to see a movie, and feign sleep on his couch. I realize I'm being a liar right now, but my life is at stake here.

I finally garner the strength to leave the room. My bare feet pitter-patter against the wooden floor as I enter his living area. Vincent leans against the marble kitchen island, staring at his cell phone. He lifts his head, noticing my entrance. The moment our eyes lock, I swear to God, my heart stops. He looks me over from my toes up to my face, his eyes darkening. I immediately feel nervous. Should I not have used his clothes?

"Food is on its way up." His voice is deep and low.

I take a seat at the dining table, curling my feet beneath my butt. The doorbell rings and Vincent moves to get it, handing cash to the delivery guy and telling him to keep the change. Moving back to the table, he sets everything up. I dig in, eating like I haven't had a decent meal in days. It dawns on me that I skipped lunch at work, assuming I'd eat a big dinner at home. But obviously, those plans didn't work out.

"Where have you been?" I ask quietly, chewing a piece of steamed broccoli covered in garlic sauce.

"Busy." I wait for him to elaborate, but he doesn't. "You ready to tell me what that was about before?"

I drop my head as my heart beats heavily. "No...I...I can't." I shake my head.

"Eve," he places his fork in front of him, turning to me with warm eyes. "You can and you will. Do you trust me?" His hands move to my thighs, but it isn't sexual. It's comforting.

I slowly nod my head as he moves closer to me, taking my hand in his. "Talk to me. Let me help you." My guard lowers from his gentle words.

I open my mouth, and like an open faucet, the words burst out in a rush. I give him the backstory on the Snakes. Surprisingly, he barely shows alarm. I tell him how the Cartel somehow managed to come at the right time, saving me from a potential gang rape. When I get to the dead cat, I'm shaking so badly that he has no choice but to hold me tight to keep me from crumbling.

"Holy shit, Eve." He gently caresses my back. "Okay. I'm here now. You don't have to worry." His voice sounds strong and confident. He continues to secure me to his body as I cry harder, unsure how many more tears I have left to shed. My body feels exhausted and rung-out.

"You deserve more than this. So much more. I've done enough selfish shit in my twenty-one years on this earth. And for all the messed-up things I've done, I'm going to do right by you. I'm going to take care of this. Do you hear me?" I shudder in his arms, wanting so badly to believe him. "Let me get you a glass of water." He moves to stand, but I grab onto him, refusing to let go. He sets his body back down.

"Vincent, who a-are you?" I ask, searching his face for answers.

"I don't want to give you details. Let's just say, you don't have space in your life right now for a man like me." He slowly exhales. "But you already know who I am in here, don't you?" He presses my hand to his heart.

I raise my eyebrows, vaguely remember our conversation by my front door. "Does it have to do with duality, Batman?" I let out a shaky smile.

He rubs the side of my face with his palm. "Yeah, baby. Exactly that." He pushes his hair back, resigned. "What we have between us right now may not be total openness, but I won't ever lie to you, either. If I can't answer something, I'd rather stay quiet than give you a bullshit story. You deserve better than that."

"But, how will you take care of this for me? These men—Vincent, you don't understand—they're dangerous!" My voice comes out as a plea.

He smoothes the lines on my forehead with his thumbs while he lets out an ironic laugh. "My life is seriously fucked up, Eve. Let's just say, my father runs a major business. My family and I, we're very well-connected people. You can trust I'll get this taken care of." He locks his eyes with mine and I tilt my head to the side, still not completely comprehending; I wish that he would give it to me straight.

"Are you going into business with him after college?"

"I already work for him. Have since I turned eighteen. And until I met you, I never let myself imagine another path was possible. I've got some ideas going through my head now, which I'm trying to make work. But until then, all we can be is friends. That's what I've got to offer." I blink a few times, trying to hold back my tears. "But even if you don't want my friendship, understand that Carlos is finished."

I slowly nod my head, my breathing settling down. I want to argue with him! I can handle whatever it is he's hiding. I want more than just friendship. Hell, I want it all. But a nagging part of my brain tells me that he's right; I can't add more to my plate right now. "I'm just so tired, Vincent," my voice is low.

He stands, taking my hand in his and walking us into his bedroom. I climb into his huge bed as he turns out lights and flips on a small lamp, casting shadows around us.

"I want to be able to see you," he says softly, sitting beside me. I sit up on my knees, staring at his features.

He opens the drawer in his nightstand and takes out a bottle of lotion. Squeezing some into his palm, he starts to methodically massage my hands with the cream. I let out a hum, feeling soothed by his touch.

"The hands hold a lot of tension." His voice is gruff. "This should relax you." I open my eyes. The heated look on his face sends a zing straight through my core.

"Vincent?" I say his name reverently, wanting to repeat it over and over again. His name on my lips feels undeniably right. "Do you...like me?" My voice is so quiet, I can barely hear myself.

He sets his hands down, moving them to my sides. "Eve." He lets out a troubled sigh. "I like you more than I've ever liked anything. I've never given a shit about any woman before you. There have been so many girls—" he winces, realizing his mistake as my heart plunges down. "But they've all been faceless and nameless. Since I met you, there has been no one else. You're all I can see."

"But, why do you keep disappearing on me? Why can't we—"

"Listen closely, okay? My life, as it currently stands, is not meant for you. One day, maybe. But not yet. You have your own journey right now. You've got to get your ass out of the Blue Houses. Get into college, right? Nothing else matters other than that."

I move back as if I've been slapped. "Not...meant for me?" I repeat, my voice stuttering. Does he mean I'm not good enough for him?

He takes my hands back in his. "It's not what you think. But right now, this friendship we've got is all there can be. I won't get you wrapped up in my life. Promise me that you will focus on nothing other than your studies." He touches the side of my face and I screw my eyes shut, unable to stop myself from leaning into his warm palm.

He clears his throat. "Repeat after me." I gaze up at him, unable to look away. "Vincent thinks I'm gorgeous."

I stay quiet. "Come on, Eve, I want to hear it."

"Vincent thinks I'm gorgeous," I hesitantly repeat.

He smirks, continuing. "Vincent thinks I'm brilliant." I can feel my face turn pink. "I'm waiting, Eve. Tick-tock..."

"Vincent thinks I'm brilliant." I shut my eyes again and smile wide, too shy to look at the man giving me this praise.

"Vincent thinks that I'm going to leave the life I'm living behind me, and be whoever I want to be. He won't let his shit fall on me." His voice is full of promise.

I open my eyes and stare at him openly, wishing that everything he says will be true someday. "I want to be a lawyer," I tell him reluctantly, unsure of what his response will be.

"Oh yeah? I can see that." He quirks his lips to the side.

I can feel a glimmer of hope turning in my chest. "Really?"

He moves his head without doubt. "Yes. I can help you with that too when the time comes. Go to sleep now. You're safe here with me." I settle down with my head on his pillow as he lightly strokes my hair.

"Vincent?" I ask quietly.

"Yeah, baby." His hands move to massage up and down my back.

"What do we have between us? We have something special, right?" I turn around to face him. We may not be able to be together, but I know in my heart that we have something more than just friendship. This can't be one-sided; I know deep down he feels it, too.

He pauses, seemingly thinking of the right response. "Yeah, we've got something. But what we have has nothing to do with anyone else on earth. What we have between us, is just for us."

He moves me on top of him and lets his hands rub from my toes all the way up into my hair. Even though he's obviously holding a hell of a lot back from me, something inside me is pushing me to just enjoy this moment and trust him. His touch feels so good. So right.

"Can I kiss you?" I suck in a breath, wanting him so badly but also, so afraid.

His hand slides over my hip, slowly dragging the sweatpants from my legs. "I love how delicate you are. Soft. You're a siren on a quiet street. You're all I hear." His words tune and bind me to him.

I feel his warm mouth against the side of my lips and a tiny moan escapes. I want him to be on top of me but he grips my thighs, not letting me move. "You're in control tonight, understand?"

He sits up with me straddling him and I immediately turn my head to the side, too nervous to look into his eyes. "Don't turn away from me," he orders. I slowly turn back, nervous that it'll be the hard version of Vincent in front of me. Instead, there's nothing but warmth shining from his face. "It's me here, just me. I'll never hurt you."

I feel his lips on my neck and gasp as he trails his warm mouth up, pausing beneath my ear. Moving to my lips, he kisses me chastely, over and over again.

I want more, my body hums. I grind my hips down onto his pelvis. I can tell he's keeping himself steady, letting me set the pace. His warm tongue dips into my mouth and my body melts deeper into his lap. His parts press against mine, and I yearn to feel more of his weight on me. I tug on his arm and move off his lap, laying down on the mattress. With my eyes, I'm urging him to follow. He's hesitant, as if he really needs to make sure that I'm okay and feeling stable. He checks me over and I give him a small nod of approval. My throat is dry, but I have never felt safer in my entire life.

His hands move into my hair, pulling out the tie. My damp strands fall around us as he pushes himself into me, wrapping his arms around my back and pressing me harder against his solidness. We're kissing mindlessly when his knee snakes up between my legs. It's as if an alarm goes off in my mind and I immediately want to tear off his clothes. *Oh, God.*

I tug on the bottom of his shirt desperately. He sits up, pulling it up and over his head.

"Ohhh," my voice says of its own accord; nothing we've ever done comes close to *this*. His body looks as if it's been chiseled from granite. He sits me up, taking off my shirt. I melt as his eyes take their fill, clearly liking what he sees.

He lowers his head, letting his tongue lave at my nipple. I liquefy, grabbing his hair with my hands and moaning as he nips and tugs at my breast. Moving to the next side, he kisses and sucks until I'm writhing against him in pleasure.

He moves himself, pulling up one of my thighs and wrapping it against his waist. Pressing himself into me as if we're having sex, I can't stop moaning. His pants are still on and so is my underwear, but I swear on my life I never knew that something could feel this good.

"Everything about you, Eve," he rasps. "I want to strip you naked." He presses again, deeper. "I want to lick you until you're screaming my name."

My body is shaking so hard right now that I think I may pass out. "Vincent, Vincent, Vincent," is all I can manage. "I'm so—" my voice is hoarse as he grips my thigh harder, lifting it up over his shoulder.

"Look at me." His voice is hard and demanding. I open my eyes, locking my gaze to his. He leans his head down, breathing in my breaths. Open mouths. Tongues. I'm sweaty and wet all over. He slides his hands up, brushing his callused fingers over my nipples again and again. I'm squeezing my core in pulses, my body finding a rhythm. All at once, my legs straighten out and my toes curl as I come apart beneath him.

He stops, holding me tight as he whispers in my ear. "You're perfect. Do you know how wonderful you are?" I wrap my arms around his back, my throat raspy from how loud I must have been. "You're shaking." He turns me so that I'm back on top of him, holding me tight while our breathing settles.

"D-do you need—" I feel how hard he is, and realize that he probably needs something in return.

"You don't need to do this tonight, Eve," he whispers in my ear. "This isn't about me."

"I want to." I push forward, eager to feel him.

"Are you sure?" he continues, lowering his mouth to my nipple, taking a slow and lazy lick. "My tongue sucking on your nipples while you touch me? Or maybe, you want to feel my stubble rubbing between your thighs while I take my time?" My body short-circuits from his words as I stroke him over his pants.

"I want to drink you in. Just the thought of licking you..." I gasp as he sucks hard at my nipples. "You feel how hard I am?" We're both dripping with sweat as I finally put my hand into his underwear, feeling his hardness jump directly into my palm. I felt how big he was through his clothes, but this is entirely different. He's huge, hot, and velvet soft.

I'm tentative, unsure what I should do. He moves his hand over mine, covering my fingers with his, showing me how he likes it.

I continue at the pace he sets when he finally lets go of my hand and brings me closer to him. He slides his tongue around my nipple again, bringing it back into his mouth. I let myself grip his dick harder and we both moan until we're panting again from pleasure. "Don't let go, baby. I'm so close."

He screws his eyes shut and comes with a guttural shout. I feel him coat my hand and my eyes widen. I don't dare to move as his body tremors. I'm in awe; watching Vincent come is amazing.

"Holy fuck, Eve..." His wide chest glistens with sweat, and I lick my lips.

"I should wash—"

He nods, sprawling himself out on the bed while I stand up and walk to the bathroom. Looking at myself in his mirror, I take in a breath at what I see. My face is flushed pink, hair wild. My lips are puffy and my nipples are all red. I'm in a state of utter amazement right now; intimacy with Vincent is bliss.

Vincent steps into the bathroom, moving directly behind me. We're both staring at each other in the mirror, smiling and satisfied. The top of my head hits the center of his chest, and for the first time in forever, I decide that I love feeling so small. Even with all our physical differences, or maybe because of them, we look perfect together.

I turn on the warm water and place my hands in the sink when he slides his hands on top of mine. Taking the soap, he cleans each of my fingers one by one. I lean back into his chest, savoring the feeling of his touch while he cleans me off.

We move back into the bed together and I giggle as he jumps on top of me, putting his nose into my neck and scenting me. He holds my hands together above my head while he puts his face between my breasts, nuzzling me. I'm wheezing with laughter as Vincent's playful side comes out.

"You're embarrassing me, Vincent! Stop! I probably stink!"

He finally moves himself back up, face turning serious. "No, baby." He rubs his nose against my neck. "You literally smell like heaven on earth. Don't you know?" I wrap my legs around his waist, locking him against me.

Part of me wishes we were naked. But another part knows the beauty of this moment is amplified because of the innocence. We both know that he could have taken everything from me, but he didn't.

I burrow my head in his chest, so thankful for him.

"I'm gonna shower now. Give me a few." He kisses me on the

temple and stands up. I turn to my side, getting an eyeful of his perfect butt.

After he shuts the door, I check the bedside clock; it's just after midnight. I wait patiently for him to finish. Climbing back into the bed, I burrow into his hard and clean chest and finally, doze off to sleep.

15

THE NEXT MORNING when I wake up, I find myself alone in Vincent's huge bed. Finding a spare toothbrush in the cabinet in his guest bathroom, I wash myself up as best I can without my usual toiletries. My eyes are still red-rimmed and puffy from all my crying, but deep in my soul, I know that somehow, Vincent will take care of Carlos for me.

Vincent, Vincent, Vincent. I want to say his name a million times, but every time I even think of his name, I flush. The man has somehow taken over everything. I was with him all night and now I feel as if I'm going through a withdrawal. My body aches for more of him. Where is he?

Walking into his beautiful kitchen, I see a note on the dining table. He went out for a run and will be back at nine. Looking up at the clock hanging on his wall, I see that it's already eight forty-five in the morning. I open his fancy refrigerator—surprised to see it's completely stocked. Taking out eggs, milk, and bacon, I hope that when he gets back he's hungry. Opening one of the refrigerator doors, I find it full of fresh vegetables.

The front door opens and shuts, and I turn toward it, nerves fluttering in my stomach. Vincent's hair is damp with sweat and his white T-shirt sticks to his muscular chest. Dark stubble is already growing on his face, even though he was freshly shaven last night. He's so insanely hot that my heart skips at the sight of him. But when we make eye contact, I realize that something's missing. It's Vincent, but his eyes look...uncaring. I feel whiplash from the coolness of his stare. Did he change his mind?

"Morning," he says curtly, and my heart sinks.

He struts into his bedroom without another word, and I hear the shower turn on. I hurry up and scramble fresh eggs with some milk, turning the heat on another pan to fry up the thick-cut bacon. Quickly looking at a recipe from the Food Network on my phone, I put together a small tomato and cucumber salad. God, to have this much food in your fridge at any given time!

Ten minutes later, he's back out in the kitchen freshly showered, and I'm pulling out the whole-wheat toast from the toaster oven. He comes up behind me and I shut my eyes tightly for a moment, savoring his fresh scent.

"You cook?" His voice is full of surprise as he watches me plate the food.

"Yeah. I cook a lot actually..." I want to say more, but the vibe he's giving off is completely closed. Did I say something to anger him? "I hope you don't mind—"

"I don't," he abruptly replies. "And thank you." He nods as I hand him his plate. He stands, waiting by the table until I wash off my hands and come next to him. He doesn't sit until after I do.

We eat together in silence, but the quiet has turned to painful. In the light of day, it's like he's completely shut down from me. I want to yell, ask what the hell happened? I spend my entire breakfast playing our night over, wondering what I said to make this all go so wrong.

"The food is amazing." I turn to him, my heart fluttering from his compliment. I never would have imagined that feeding him would feel this satisfying, but it does.

"You're welcome," I tell him quietly, searching his eyes for a sign he still cares.

Soon afterward, he drives me back to my apartment. The car ride is completely quiet, I can hear horns beeping and fire trucks screaming in the distance. I remember that it's Sunday, and I need to open Angelo's in two hours. On one hand, I'm dreading work, but on the other, I could use something to keep me occupied while my mind runs circles.

He brings me up to my door, and I feel my heart rate pick up. There are a million things I want to ask him.

"Let me come in, check out the place before you go inside."

"No!" I exclaim, putting my hands up. He looks at me skeptically, but the truth is that the last thing I want is for him to see my shit-box apartment. Especially after I just saw his place—I can't imagine what he'd think if he saw mine.

"I'm sure my mom or sister is home. You don't need to go in."

He looks like he wants to argue with me, but thankfully, he doesn't. "I'm going to wait here. You go inside, and when you think everything is okay, come out to tell me. And if something is wrong, yell and I'll run right in." I nod my head, swallowing back my tears. I need to get inside before I lose it in front of him.

His eyes are full of anguish as he steps closer to me, letting his fingers run across my face. "Everything I told you last night—it's still on. No more fear, okay? Trust me. Carlos will never bother you again."

I nod my head, feeling true relief. At the same time though, it seems like he's saying goodbye in a final sense.

"We're still f-friends, right?"

He sighs. "I'll always be your friend, Eve."

The man is holding so much back, and I wish he wouldn't. Before the tears fall, I turn around and open my door, moving inside before he can get a look. Scanning the room, I notice that nothing is out of the ordinary. I step back to the front door, checking through the peephole. He's still there.

I want to tell him all is well, but my tears start falling. I refuse to let him see me cry again. Instead, I pull out my phone and shoot him a quick text. I hear his phone ping and look again through the peephole, watching as he reads it. He curses loudly, slamming his hand down on my door in what looks like anger and frustration. He turns around and stalks away from the door. When I can no longer see him, I feel the emptiness creep back into my chest, as if he took a piece of me with him. I want to throw the door open, chase him down and beg him to take me with him. But instead, my fear cripples me, and I spend the next twenty minutes crying over him in the shower.

Once I calm myself down, I go to work where I talk to Angelo. Again, I refuse any help from the Borignones. I tell him that I slept at a friend's last night who has pretty deep connections. I've got a guarantee that Carlos won't bother me anymore. He looks at me incredulously, but I stand firm. I've still got hope that Vincent will fix this.

When work is over, Angelo insists that he wants to bring me home so he can check out my apartment before I go inside. He's thinking about installing some cameras at my front door for extra surveillance, and I agree it might be a good idea.

Getting back to the Blue Houses, he struts inside the building, glaring at anyone who dares to look at him. We enter my apartment and he searches every possible crevice. When he finally decides that all is safe, he heads out, hugging me to his chest. "You sleep with your phone next to you, okay? And the gun under your pillow. I wish you'd stay with me tonight—"

"I know. But Janelle will be home. And I'll be okay," I tell him nervously.

"You don't always gotta be so tough, Eve. I'm here." He looks at me with pain in his eyes.

"I know you are. Look...I'm going to call you before I sleep, okay? And when I wake up."

"You better." He brings me back for a tight embrace and I realize that in all the ways that matter, Angelo is my father. "Bye, sweetheart." He walks out, shutting the door behind him. I'm closing the front door lock and move to the refrigerator to take out something to eat when I see a note innocuously taped to the door. I pause, confused at first. But when I see the sloppy handwriting, dread pools low in my stomach.

Eve,

I know you've been talking to the cops bout me, and I'm gonna pay U back for that shit. You think I don't see how you think you're better than everyone round here? People like you run to the cops. You're a snitch. A bitch. But before I end you, I'm going to fuck the hell outta you. It's time to pay up.

You see, the truth is that I've been watching you for years. With your baggy clothes and bag full of books. You think that no one noticed you hiding behind your sister? With a face like a fucking angel and a body made for fucking... hiding ain't possible. And now that I've seen what you got underneath all those clothes...you bet I'm gonna tap that. I'm gonna tap it nice and hard until you're begging for fucking mercy.

That cat is just the start, bitch.

I sit at my kitchen table in a trance. He was in here. With the locks being so shitty, I don't know why I should be surprised. Carlos is a sick thug who loves the terror; he loves the game. I have to think of something. I've got to get myself out of this. Vincent said he'd fix it, but maybe Angelo is right. Maybe I need to get the Borignones involved. Obviously, calling the police is completely out of the question. I swallow hard, mind pinging back and forth. He isn't going to stop until someone puts an end to him. That much is clear. How long will it even take for Vincent to fix this? And that's IF he can fix it. I don't think Vincent understands who Carlos is and who he's dealing with. The Borignones are looking more and more like my only option.

Before I make any rash decisions, I should make a list. I've got too much shit piling up in my head and it's adding to my stress. I take out a pen and piece of paper from the cabinet drawer.

1. TEXT MS. LEVINE TO ASK ABOUT APPLICATION STATUS
2. TEXT JANELLE TO TOUCH BASE AND MAKE SURE SHE'LL BE HOME TONIGHT
3. CRAWL INTO MY BED AND SHUT MY BRAIN OFF

4. WAKE UP AND MAKE ANOTHER LIST DETAILING PROS AND CONS TO LETTING ANGELO TAKE CARE OF CARLOS

I drop my pen and walk into the kitchen, gripping the papers like a lifeline. It's all too much! I need the universe to give me some time —a break to sort out my issues. I can't handle the way my cards are unfolding. While undressing, I take a deep breath, telling myself I can complete things one at a time.

I pull out my phone to text Ms. Levine.

ME: Hey. Any word yet on schools?
MS. L: Soon, Eve. I think in the next week or so, you'll have your answer. Hang in okay?
ME: Yeah. Is there a way you can call admissions? Maybe they can rush their answer or something?
MS. L: I'll call. Don't worry.

I exhale and cross out number one on my list. It's weird, but it feels good to cross off an item. Now it's time to reach Janelle. We texted a few times last night, and I told her we really need to catch up on lots of shit going on. I haven't been able to tell her about the cat or Vincent and now the letter... I need to talk to her.

ME: Hey Janelle. A lot of shit going on—we need to talk
JANELLE: Is everything all right??? I'm actually at Leo's now. We're going out tonight. I'll be home super late, don't wait up. But I promise I'll be there in the morning.
ME: Ok. Tomorrow morning breakfast before I go to school?
JANELLE: Yup! Love ya. Lock the door! And Juan is home tonight. Call him if you don't want to be alone.
ME: OK. Thanks. BTW, where has Mom been? Haven't seen her in weeks
JANELLE: Lucky 4 U. I saw her yesterday. You guys are on opposite schedules—count your blessings...she seems to be worse lately

I put my phone down, and cross off number two on the list. Now it's time to shut my mind down and go to sleep. I take out my gun and place it under my pillow. As I'm dozing, I think I can still smell Vincent on me. I put my arm up to my nose and inhale as deeply as possible, but the scent disappeared. My body is under so much stress that within mere moments, I'm completely asleep.

Somewhere in the recesses of my sleeping mind, I hear the front door open and shut. My bedroom light flicks on and Janelle jumps into my bed. "Eve! Wake up!" Her hands are on me and she shakes me awake.

I sit up in a shock and my heart skips a beat. When I see it's Janelle, I blink a few times, my eyes adjusting to the light.

"You don't know—I have to tell you—holy shit! Eve!"

"What? What happened?" My voice is raspy and sounds strangled. Janelle's eyes are wide and she's...smiling? I rub my eyes.

"You don't understand, Eve! It was epic!"

"Huh? What the hell is going on?" I look at the time and see that it's two am.

"I was in the Meatpacking district tonight. There were fights on, but it was a really small thing. Not like the gigantic crowd I took you to." I shrug my shoulders and rub my eyes again, still trying to get my body to understand that it's awake now.

"All of a sudden, the announcer tells us that the Bull is fighting. He wasn't on the roster."

When I hear his name, my heart stutters in my chest.

"He got in the center of the circle, looking angry as hell. And PS, angry Bull is like the hottest man on the planet! It should be illegal to look that good." She fans her face and I resist the urge to roll my eyes. "But forget that." She waves her hand around as if to push the thought away. She still doesn't know that Vincent is the Bull. And that Vincent is...Vincent. But now isn't the time to mention it. I need to hear the entire story.

"Okay—so...?" I'm waiting for her to continue.

"So, he gets into the ring. Angry. Somehow, Carlos, YOUR Carlos, gets thrown inside." My eyes feel like they're bugging out of my skull.

She pushes her hair back with her hands. "So, Carlos gets pushed into the ring, looking around like a deer in motherfucking headlights!"

"Oh. My. God." My stomach turns and I feel like I may throw up.

Janelle's smile is practically splitting her face apart. She gets back out of bed, jumping up and down like she just won the lotto. "The Bull tears off his shirt in the middle of the circle, Eve! Not normal-like, but like a man enraged! The entire place was going berserk!"

Janelle paces the room, her excitement so huge that sitting isn't possible. "Carlos's fear disappears, and he looks like he's going to tear the Bull's head off! Clearly, there is some shit between them..."

"Wait. C-Carlos?" I can barely say his name.

"Yes, Eve. Are you lis-ten-ing? Carlos! Sergeant of Arms for the Snakes. The same fucker who tried to rape you, Eve. The same Carlos! Are you awake?

I swallow hard, my voice sounding panicked. "And?"

"And the Bull went apeshit. I've never seen him fight like this. Normally he does what he has to do and has some fun. He always wins, obviously, but gives everyone a little show first. This time? It was total annihilation. At first, everyone was yelling, excited even. After three minutes, it was silence. It looked like he broke every bone in Carlos's body!"

"Wait. What? My voice is monotone; my mind in so much shock it can barely process what she's telling me.

"YES! No one was stopping him! The announcer stood there in silence, letting the Bull do whatever the hell he wanted. At one point, Carlos was a heap of blood on the floor. His nose was totally shat-tered. I saw his arms were both bent in a crazy direction. The Bull literally, like, publically humiliated him and broke that motherfucker, limb by mother-fucking limb!"

Laughter starts to bubble up inside my chest. I'm in a state of complete shock and apparently, this is my body's reaction. Janelle joins me, and somehow, we're laughing our asses off! Tears are pouring down her face from glee.

"Carlos had to be carried out by two bouncers and probably

dropped off at the hospital! It was the scariest thing I had ever seen. In. My. Life. He may be dead! And when the Bull was finished? Oh. My. God, Eve! When the Bull was finished, he spit on Carlos's body, picked up his shirt, and walked out of the circle like it was just another goddamn day!"

"But, what..." I'm shaking my head, still in disbelief.

"You obviously have a guardian angel, Eve. I mean, he's gone! Carlos is done! God, I can't wait to tell everyone!" She kisses me on the forehead and skips into the bathroom, leaving me alone in our bedroom.

I shut my eyes, not sure how to deal with this new development when my throat starts to burn. I let the tears flow. I'm free.

16

I'VE GONE BACK and forth a million times in my head over it, but I think that it's probably best this way. If he wanted to reach out to me, he would have. He has my number.

On a daily basis, my mind goes through something like this:

"He killed, or almost killed, someone in my honor. What am I supposed to do, call him and thank him?"

"Holy shit—Vincent is a killer! I can't be friends with a killer!"

"I'm being crazy. Vincent is amazing. Vincent is perfect for me."

"No—a man like Vincent isn't perfect for me. He's dangerous, and I have plans for myself. Big plans, including college and grad school and a big job!"

"But if not for Vincent, I might have been killed by now. Or raped. Or who knows. The man saved my life. And more than anything...I miss him."

"I've never had anyone in my life understand me bone-deep like that. I know I'm young, but something tells me that he is IT. He is the one. I'm trying to ignore the nagging feeling that Vincent is love, but it won't stop knocking on my heart."

I drop my head in my hands, sick of my thoughts. I need to focus right now on finishing off my year well and praying on getting into college. My phone chimes, shaking me out of my obsessing. I check the text and see it's Ms. Levine asking me to call her. When I get her on the phone, she tells me to come over—she has good news for me!

Right before I can head out, my mom struts into the apartment, teetering and swaying on high heels.

"Well, if it isn't my second daughter," she slurs. Her makeup is smeared and the blond highlights in her hair have grown out, leaving a limp brown line at her roots. For a woman who is obsessed with appearances, I'm shocked she looks so unkempt. She steps closer to me, her voice lowering as if she wants to tell me a secret. "I haven't seen you in quite some time, huh? You're not avoiding me, right?"

"No. I guess our schedules have just been—"

"Don't talk back to me!" She screams. I instantly drop my head, knowing that when she's at this point in her mental state, nothing but silence will do.

Her breaths shortens, and she starts huffing. "One of the girls at the club told me that she heard from Angelo that you applied to college!" She starts to laugh as if it's a big joke. "I told her that there is no goddamned way you did. You wouldn't go against my wishes, would you, Eve?" She steps closer to me as I move backward to avoid her. "My own daughter. My own flesh and blood wouldn't do that to me, right? Not when you know that we need you to work full time. Not when you know that we need the money!" Her voice is shrill and I can feel my heart pick up its pace. "...Not when you know that you should have dropped out of school years ago!" she says with a scream.

Before I think about what I should say, the words come tumbling out of my mouth. "Mom, you're wrong. It's only a few more years of time. And imagine the job I could get! So much more money!"

"WHAT?" Her shriek can probably be heard around the entire floor. "I'll kill you! I brought you into the world and I have every right to take you out of it! I owe people money and I need you to bring some in for me!"

I blink hard, understanding finally dawning on me. At the end of the day, my mom is a selfish and jealous woman who has absolutely zero care about me; all she knows is what she wants. After everything that's happened in my eighteen years of life, I simply can't let her hold me down anymore. I just can't keep hoping that one day she'll change. It's enough already! Somehow, the truth after all these years becomes obvious. If I want to move on out of the Blue Houses, I've got to move on from her. I need to stop hoping and wishing that she'll eventually become a real mother to me and just focus on my own path. She's not on my side and she never will be.

She raises her hand to hit me and I duck, running out the apartment door. She turns around, yelling, "EVE! YOU GET FUCKING BACK HERE!" Her voice is a high-pitched screech. Instead of stopping, I open up the stairwell and go flying down the steps.

Before I get to the first floor, I see George in a corner with his usual bottle of whiskey. "Hey, Eve. In a rush?" I stop myself, breathing heavy, but manage to put my hand in my purse to pull out a dollar bill.

"I hear you're going to college," he says as he takes the dollar, the unmistakable shine of pride in his eyes.

"Yeah, I hope so. I'm waiting to hear back." I shrug, still catching my breath and looking up the steps, trying to hear if my mother is following me down.

"Don't give up, okay? Irina... don't listen to her. You're going to go places. I know it. Knew it since you were a little kid." I nod my head, surprised by his comment.

His voice is scratchy. "Hurry. If she comes down here, I'll tell her I didn't see you," he says with a wink.

I can't help the smile that forms on my face. "Thanks, George. I'll see you soon, okay?" I leave the Blue Houses and jog to the subway.

I jump on the train uptown, heart thudding. Twenty minutes later, I get into Ms. Levine's building and race to the elevators, ignoring the door attendant calling out to me. When I get to her floor, I rush to her door and knock hard. She opens up and engulfs me in her arms.

"Columbia accepted you! You're in!" We both jump together, embracing. I do a happy dance, my arms up in the air.

"Come in!" She pushes some forms toward me as I step into her foyer. "Full scholarship! Grants to cover living expenses and books! Get these signed by your mom..." She hands me pages of documents and winks, walking to the bathroom. I take my shoes off, leaving them by the door. Sitting at her dining table, I pull a pen out of my bag and quickly sign where necessary, forging my mom's signature without blinking an eye. At this point, nothing would stop me from accepting admission.

A few minutes later, she walks back into the room. "You wouldn't believe this, Ms. Levine, but while you were in the bathroom, my mom came over. Signed all these documents. Then ran out!"

She shakes her head and chuckles at me, but takes the forms nonetheless.

A sense of relief comes over me as I realize I'm finally taking my life into my own hands. Before I can enjoy the feeling, a deep sense of anxiety settles into my chest. The truth is, I'm worried. What if I don't fit in? What if I get there and can't handle the workload? I peer at my loose, holey jeans and large shirt from Goodwill. I'm obviously going to have to put a mask on in order to blend into this school. Or maybe, I'll have to take off my mask? I've been covering up for so long, I'm not even really sure who the "real me" is anymore.

"Ms. Levine, I want you to know how thankful I am for everything you've done for me." I tuck my feet under my butt, and she seems to immediately sense my discomfort.

"Of course! But what's wrong?" She squints, tilting her head to the side and sitting beside me.

I lick my lips, clasping my hands together. I know I should confide in her. She is, after all, the only person I know who has ever even been to college. "What if I don't belong there?" I ask. She gives me a half smile as if she was waiting for me to bring this up. "I know that I live in the city with all different kinds of people. But these kids have never been inside a classroom that makes them nervous for their lives. I know that most of them will come from the best prep schools. They can barely fathom the concept of their lives being up for grabs."

"Yes," she says, clicking her tongue. "They are quite different from what you're used to. But you have this opportunity, and I want you to take advantage of it. I don't want you to shrink back. When you're there, shed the fear and insecurity, and put on confidence. As I always say, turn the fear you harbor into resilience and make it all count. You deserve this opportunity, Eve. More than anyone else, you deserve this."

Self-doubt continues to plague me, despite her confidence in me.

She grabs my hand, forcing me to face her. "You'll have to stop wearing hats and your hood over your head. You can start to wear clothes that are more fitting for a girl. You're stunning, Eve. And it's not easy for you to hide. Think of it this way. When you get to Columbia, you don't have to try to hide yourself. You can be the gorgeous and intelligent girl you actually are! I want you to finally be free. Sure, some of those kids will be assholes. But that's part of life, right?"

I think about Vincent for a moment and his upper-crust life. Tears threaten, but I hold them back and focus on what's in front of me. Columbia. Maybe one day, after I graduate, I'll be able to, with confidence, look a man like Vincent in the eye and feel deserving of his time.

I still haven't told Janelle anything about Vincent. Maybe I should tell Ms. Levine. Not everything, but just some parts. I feel lost after what happened with him, and I'm still unsure why things turned out the way they did.

"Actually, there's something I wanted to talk to you about. There's kind of been a guy. But he's sort of ghosted out on me. And I'm not really sure what to do about it..."

"Okay," she says anxiously. "Go on."

I give her the general details of what happened, nothing sexual or detailed about Carlos, either, and ask her what she thinks.

She stares at me apprehensively. "Something sounds a little fishy about this whole thing, Eve. You've looked him up, right?"

I click my tongue for a second. "Uh, no, I haven't." I turn my head to the side, attempting to avoid her intelligent gaze.

"Eve," she snaps. "You gotta get on a computer and check him out. Is he on Facebook? How can you just go off with him? You met him at some underground fight, got into his car, let him take you out to eat, and you don't even know his last name?" Her voice is skeptical as if she can't believe my naiveté.

I swallow. "Yeah, okay, I'll look him up." The moment the words leave my mouth, I realize that I don't want to know more about him. I'm afraid to uncover something that I won't like. I just want to stay in this little bubble I've created for myself. There's definitely something different about Vincent. But then again, I'm used to seeing aggressive men. Plus, he's obviously rich. That's all it is, right? Okay sure, so he almost killed someone on my behalf. But he's a fighter. He did it to help me. He isn't connected to anyone or anything. Well, at least I think he isn't. His family is in business.

She takes my hands in hers. "You must be careful, Eve. Don't bury your head in the sand. I'm glad he's been decent to you so far, but even the fact that he just comes and goes of his own accord—randomly working out near your pawnshop—nothing is near that pawnshop! Drives this fancy car? Something smells wrong here. He's got *gang* written all over him." Her voice is apprehensive.

I take my hands out from hers feeling agitated by her questions. "There's no way he's gang affiliated. He's too rich and powerful for that."

"Eve, we both know that not all gangs are roaming the streets. Maybe he's a dealer?" I think for a moment, but Vincent is too sophisticated for that.

"Well, I know him now. Maybe not his blood type or his last name, but I've spent a lot of time with him and he's been nothing but respectful. He isn't like the other gang guys I know. Or even dealers." I shake my head vehemently. "Not at all."

I imagine the gangbangers I know from the Snakes and the Cartel. At heart, those guys are chaos. Disorganized. Street smart. Book stupid. Vincent is nothing like them. Nothing at all.

When Ms. Levine sees my mind operating, she lets out a breath and gets up, pulling out an old laptop of hers. "Eve, promise me that you'll go home and look him up. I want you to keep this computer for school anyway, okay? Now that you have this, you don't have any excuse not to know."

I hug her tight. "Thank you for everything."

"You make me so proud, Eve. Truly. Now, get your stuff together! Summer classes start in June, right after graduation!"

After lots of hugs, I get on the subway and head downtown. Walking through my front door, I go straight into my bathroom and look in the mirror. Pushing thoughts of Vincent out of my head for the millionth time, I tell myself that my life is about to change for the better. I can't wipe the smile off my face when I realize I'm starting Columbia. Ahhh!

I turn my head for a moment, staring at the computer Ms. Levine gave me. I decide that I don't want to look him up. I'm not ready to learn anything more than I already know. And really, who knows if I'll ever even see him again. He hasn't reached out to me, and I'm too chicken to text him again. So, it doesn't matter who he is or isn't, right?

I swallow back my sadness, realizing I'm hung up on a guy who hasn't been in touch with me for weeks. A guy whose last name I don't even know. A guy who is technically a killer. I hope he doesn't go to jail for this. Oh my God. How could I not even have considered the legal implications of what Vincent did? If it gets back to the cops that he killed Carlos, he could go to jail. Or even worse, maybe the Snakes are going to try to retaliate against him! I blink hard a few times and try to breathe. Should I warn him? I told him all about Carlos and the Snakes and he didn't seem surprised at all. He's also not stupid. He must have considered the ramifications of what he did, right?

Luckily, Janelle comes home and my mind is instantly occupied with good thoughts. We celebrate my admission by ordering Domino's thin-crust pizza and cheesy bread and dancing to Drake.

Eventually, she lowers the music and we drop onto the couch. I turn to her. "What the hell are we going to tell Mom about school?"

"Ugh, who cares?" Janelle says nonchalantly, throwing her bare feet up onto the coffee table with a smile on her face. "She's hardly home, anyway. We'll tell her you've got a new boyfriend and you're staying with him. Since you've got grants and scholarships covering everything, there shouldn't be a money trail." Janelle does an evil-sounding laugh and I join in, as if we're conspiring to take over the world. And maybe in some ways, we are. Moments later, we erupt into genuine laughter, feeling high over the fact that college is now no longer a pipe dream, but an actuality.

17

THE SCHOOL YEAR goes on uneventfully, finally ending in a blur of standardized testing and Advanced Placement exams. I am the valedictorian, and I make a simple speech at the graduation ceremony about perseverance and never giving up in life, no matter the odds. While I'm embarrassed to speak in public, I'm surprised the amount of pride I feel standing up there. It may only be the old gymnasium in my high school, but getting to this point means something to me. When I'm finished, the audience and other students clap politely while Janelle screams like crazy. With a red face, I walk away from the podium and take my seat. It's hot as hell in here; the air conditioning must be broken. I press the long blue gown to my chest, trying to soak up the sweat.

I turn to the students next to me when it finally dawns on me that hardly anyone I started with during my freshman year is sitting with me now. Out of two hundred and fifty students from my freshman class, it looks like only about one hundred kids are graduating. I guess the rest all dropped out or got their GED certificates. I know that technically, I saw it all unfold. I mean, I lived it. I watched as boys who were my friends as children grew up and joined gangs. I don't believe they were looking for bloodshed, at least, not at first. They just wanted to belong. Understandably, they looked for protection on the street and some respect from their peers. Isn't that all it is? Can I fault them for that?

I look out into the audience, seeing some Blue House families gathered together with pride. Janelle's face stands out among them all; she's staring at me, glowing with joy. It hurts me that she never got to graduate, but at the same time, I know I'm doing this for both of us. The reality is—without her support, I never could have made it to this point. I drop my head for a moment and say a little prayer to God, thanking Him for giving me my sister. As usual, Vincent's face comes into my head. I drop a line of thanks for him too. Because without him, I'd probably be dead by now. He may have only popped into my life for a short period of time, but damn did he manage to come at just the time I needed him most.

When the graduation is over, Ms. Levine takes Janelle and me out for a surprise celebration lunch. We drive down into the Flatiron district and I see the restaurant. My throat tightens. We're at Eataly, where Vincent picked up sandwiches for us all those months ago while we skated in Central Park. I walk inside, trying to keep cool as fancy-looking people walk with baskets full of fresh fettuccini and gelato. I see a line of people waiting for fresh cannoli. The entire place is like a vibrant marketplace straight out of my dreams.

I thought I was doing okay without hearing from him, that I could just take his help with Carlos and all the emotions he brought out of me and box them up in a quiet part of my brain. But the moment I see those special sandwiches on display, I have to swallow back my tears.

Ms. Levine seems to notice my distress. "Don't you like it here? The restaurant is just around the corner over there." She points to a perfect spot that is roped off: Riso e Risoto. "I thought you would..." Her voice trails off as her face scrunches up as if I've upset her.

Janelle looks at me, confused. This is one of the coolest restaurants right now, and I know that I'm so lucky to be here. They're probably sensing my unease and imagine me to be ungrateful. Meanwhile, nothing could be further from the truth.

I shake my head, needing to say something to let them know how thankful I am. "No. I absolutely love it. I-I can't thank you enough for bringing me here. I guess I'm just nervous for college to begin." I shrug.

She clicks her tongue, draping an arm around me in a motherly gesture. We walk into the restaurant where a beautiful and young hostess immediately seats us.

"Don't worry, Eve." We take our seats. "You should be excited! Everyone is nervous at first, but just wait until it all begins!"

While we all scan our menus, the waiter takes our drink orders. We chat about move-in dates and signing up for classes. I already got my room assignment, and apparently, I'm living with a girl from Texas.

Janelle looks at me, a huge smile on her face. "Eve, there's something I wanna tell you."

"What's up?" I take a sip of my soda, my mouth around the straw while I look up at her.

"Well, you know I only stayed at the Blue Houses because you were still there. Now that you're moving out, I decided I'm going to rent a place with some girls from the salon. It's a small place in midtown, but—"

"Janelle!" I jump out of my chair and run to hers. She stands up and we embrace. Our lives are really changing. We're truly moving on! Ms. Levine turns to us both, grinning.

The waiter comes back and I order a risotto with honeynut squash, sage, and black truffle butter. Janelle and Ms. Levine agree that it sounds great, and decide to order the same.

Ms. Levine turns to me. "Don't forget, Eve. With your full scholarship and grant money, your only job is to maintain a 3.2 GPA and to enjoy life for a change. If you want extra cash, there are work-study programs like the library help desk."

I smile broadly in excitement.

We finish our delicious food—and holy shit is it amazing—and then hug and kiss Ms. Levine goodbye. Janelle and I take the bus together back to the Blue Houses. Now that Carlos is dead, the Cartel seems to have risen in power and the fighting seems to be slowing down.

We walk into our quiet apartment that we'll both be moving out of soon enough. Janelle pulls out a bottle of vodka from the freezer and some seltzer water from the fridge. After cutting up a few lemons, she makes us drinks. Handing me a glass, I take it happily. We're alone at home, and I have nothing to worry about with Janelle by my side.

She raises her cup in a toast. "You're gonna go to college. There are gonna be frat parties and stuff. You've got to know what it's like to be wasted in a comfortable environment."

I laugh at her comment. "And anyway," she continues, "I want to say that I'm proud of you. I'm so happy right now. To our futures!"

"To getting out of this hell hole!" I add.

"To moving on and up!"

We clink our glasses together and moments later, ask for another. By our third, I'm swaying as I walk to the bathroom.

After I'm done peeing, I realize that I miss Vincent so much my chest aches. In fact, it hurts even more now than ever. I thought drinking was supposed to make me forget?

I'm washing my hands and staring at myself in the mirror, becoming angry. Why am I being such a baby about him? Why can't I go ahead and text him? I mean, I'm all about women's lib! He doesn't have to reach out first. I take out my phone and find his name in my contacts. *There he is!*

ME: Hey Vincent. Hi!!! Where are you???

I blink a few times when I see the dots show up, letting me know he's about to reply. "Oh my God, he's going to reply!" I jump up and down, squealing.

VINCENT: Are you okay? Do you need me?
ME: Yupppp all's well. Just home with my sister....
VINCENT: Ah, that's good. What are you girls up to?

ME: Just drinkin' too much :-)
VINCENT: I see. So, this is a drunken text, huh?
ME: Yupppp. Why haven't you called me?
VINCENT: Been busy.
ME: Of course MR. FANCIEST PANTS ON EARTH

I laugh out loud to myself, thinking I'm the funniest person ever. Why did I never realize before how funny I am?

VINCENT: Hah. Not that fancy...

I roll my eyes.

ME: Not fancy my ass!!!
VINCENT: =-)

I huff. What is that supposed to mean? Stupid emoji. Behind my eyes, all I can see is his stupidly perfect smile, and I suddenly feel the urge to wipe it off his face! I've been waiting for him. Pining, for fuck's sake! And he's what, smiling with an emoji! The NERVE!

ME: You're an asshole!!!

"There!" I huff out loud.

VINCENT: ???
ME: You heard me. You think you can just waltz into my life and then waltz out? Who the hell do you think you are?

My heart pounds. I can't even believe him right now. And he isn't even replying! I deserve a reply. I'm a human being, too!

ME: Ah, now you don't reply? I'm not good enough for your perfect world? Well guess what! I'm going to college! Starting summerrrrr!

And I'm gonna be someone! And one day you'll see me and I'll be like, I'm busy motha-fucka!!!!

ME: I hate you!

I turn my phone off and the tears start to fall. I'm crying. Did I do something wrong? Is the room spinning?

"Yo, Eve." Janelle walks into the bathroom. "What's wrong?" I screw my eyes closed but can hear the concern in her voice.

"Nothing. Juuuust ..." I try to speak, but nothing is coming out right.

"All right, you little drunkard. I think you've had enough. She opens the bathroom cabinet, pulling out a bottle of Advil and filling a cup with water from the sink. She hands the pills to me with the water and somehow, I swallow it down.

Lifting me off the ground, she practically drags me to my bed. "Now go pass out and I'll see you in the morning. Leo is calling, I'm gonna go spend the night." She tucks me under my covers.

All I can think about is Vincent. And how much I hate his face. I hate his brain. I hate his huge gorgeous warm body that makes me feel insane things. I hate how he always carries me around and it feels like home. His intelligence. I hate how he looks at me like I matter. Like, I mean something to him. I love him. I love him so much.

I cry harder into my pillow until I finally pass out.

I wake up the next morning with a pounding head. It feels like someone is hammering into my skull. I turn around and see Janelle's bed is still empty. The clock says it's six in the morning. What the hell? Why am I up so damn early? I slowly stand, my hand pressing against the wall for balance as I go to use the bathroom. I drop my head in my hands while sitting on the toilet seat, trying to soothe the ache when I spot my cell phone on the floor. I pick it up and turn it back on.

Oh shit. Oh shit, shit, motherfucking shit! What did I do? I read my texts to Vincent and I want to die of shame. I have to fix this!

ME: Hey. Sorry about the texts... was drunk, not sure what came over me.

I close the phone, realizing that there is no way in hell he's gonna reply at this hour. But when my phone buzzes, I turn around and grab it.

VINCENT: It's ok. We're cool, Eve. And congrats on school. You deserve it.

I want to reply. Hell, I want to talk to him. I want to see him. I turn on the shower and get under the spray. First, shower. Second, coffee. Then I'll figure out how to reply.

But after I'm done with all that, I stare at my phone and feel the nerves fluttering in my stomach. His last comment wasn't exactly asking for a reply, right? Maybe he doesn't want to hear from me. I mean, if I were him, I wouldn't want to hear from me after last night. I re-read my texts to him, feeling more embarrassed each time.

I remember the new book I took out of the library is in my backpack. If I read it, maybe it'll relax me. Then, I can decide what to do.

I'm shaken out of my book-induced trance when Janelle walks in with a huge box in her arms. "Hey girl, this came for you." She has her phone on her ear as she drops the box on my bed before walking out of the room.

I glance at the clock and see that it's already three o'clock in the afternoon! Going into the kitchen, I take a knife from a drawer and bring it back into my bedroom. I jump onto my bed and lean over the box in excitement, slicing the taped seam with relish.

I open it quickly as if it were Christmas. A beautiful travel coffee mug in pink, a cozy sweatshirt that says: COLLEGE, a pair of warm Ugg slippers with fur inside that I guess I can wear around the dorms! I slide them on and they fit perfectly. There are six packages of beautiful fountain pens, and four spiral notebooks, with dividers. Sticky pads! Whoever did this, obviously went to town at Staples and holy shit, I'm not complaining! I pull out a scientific calculator. Wow! I open up an envelope and see a gift card to Barnes and Noble for $500.00. What! I guess I can use this when I need to buy books! I keep rummaging through, and see a box of Kind bars! I guess they will be useful when I'm running between classes. My heart is pounding with excitement. College is coming! I need to call Ms. Levine. She's the best!

When I finally empty the box, I grab my phone and with shaking fingers, dial her number.

"Hey Eve!" Her voice is happiness.

"Oh my God! I can't believe what you sent me. SO amazing, I'm freaking out!" My words come out in a rush.

"Uh, Eve. I'm sorry, but I didn't send you anything."

"Wait, what?" My heart beats erratically as my eyes zero in on all the goodies on my bed.

"What did you get?" she asks probingly.

I breathe silently over the line. No. It couldn't be.. "Oh, um, okay... Ms. Levine. I'll, um, call you back." I hang up the phone quickly and go through the box again.

I put my head in my hands and realize that I can't ignore this. It's too much. Too...thoughtful. Damn him!

ME: Hey
VINCENT: Hey you. I assume you got the package?
ME: How can I thank you? It's too much
VINCENT: No. It's not enough.
ME: It really means more than you know. Truly. I wish I could do something back
VINCENT: When you finish college and get into law school, that'll be my thank you. Don't give up. Focus. And don't party too hard.
ME: Thanks, Daddy... I'll be moving on June 23. Should I write it on

one of my new Post-Its and leave it on the kitchen table as a reminder?

VINCENT: Daddy, huh? :-)

I roll my eyes, but smile so hard my face hurts.

ME: Thanks, friend

VINCENT: My pleasure, baby. Kick ass and good luck.

I lay on my bed with all my stuff around me. Janelle and I are both planning to pack our things together in the next week. She'll help me move, and I'll help her as well. Being so close to home has its perks.

"Vincent," I say loudly. I want him so badly, but I also know that he is staying away from me for a reason. Maybe it's for the best. And I've got an entire life to live, right? I know that until I reach my goals, I'll never feel confident or comfortable around him. I'll always be afraid that he just sees me as some nobody. I need to fix myself before I can be confident enough to be with a man like him. Maybe it's best that he backed off. And like he said, I've got to focus now, anyway. I've got to get my head in the game! It's time to accomplish my goals.

I stand up and decide to start packing my things. One more week! College, here I come.

18

Two Months Later

I'VE KEPT MY WORD. My life is about more than first love...if you could even call it that. I have goals and right now, my education comes first.

Columbia is awesome. It's everything I could have ever hoped for and then some. I did the six-week summer session to get a jump-start on classes. A few girls in my dorm arrived early too, and we've all instantly clicked. a

Ms. Levine and Janelle ended up surprising me with a shopping trip to some decent consignment stores, so I finally dress like an eighteen-year-old woman, not a fourteen-year-old boy hiding in baggy clothes. After enduring almost two decades of hell in the Blue Houses, I finally feel like I could fit in. This is my place; this is where I'm trying to belong.

The summer heat is still stifling, but most of the students are finally on campus. I came with my friends from my dorm; we're walking through the extracurricular activities fair, moving from booth to booth and jotting our names down for random activities. Debate Club. Model Congress. Finally, I found myself at the PanHellenic Counsel table, filled with information about the sororities on campus. The girl sitting down, her name-tag says: CLAIRE, seems pretty cool. Her hair is braided in a 1960s flower-child way, and she's wearing a long and flowy blue dress.

I sign my name down for sorority rush while Claire asks me some questions. We chat for a few minutes about prospective majors, and it turns out we're both pre-law.

"Actually, I'm supposed to meet up at eleven-thirty with some girls from my sorority for lunch. Why don't you join us?" I'm unsure what to make of this. Sororities aren't really my thing. But before I could think too much about it, I blurt out, "Yes, I'd love that actually."

"How about we meet at the Coffee Cup at eleven-fifteen and we'll walk together to the dining hall? By the way, we're in Phi Alpha." She winks like she just let me in on a secret.

"Okay, cool. I'll see you there." I give her a soft smile and say goodbye.

I find the girls to tell them I'm leaving for class. The rest of the morning moves quickly. Tons of work gets assigned, and I'm anxious to get started.

I meet Claire outside of the Coffee Cup as planned. We walk side by side through campus, discussing our schedules for the spring semester. Luckily, she talks a lot. She tells me all about her sorority, and I'm trying to keep up with all the parties and fun they apparently have together.

We walk into the dining hall that has turned into chaos. Over the summer, it was pretty quiet with no one other than jocks and kids taking summer classes. But now, with most of the students back on campus, it's frenzied.

The two of us wait in the lunch line and talk about bands we like. Turns out we have really similar taste in music. Our energy is connecting, and I'm actually feeling really good. Maybe joining a sorority would be a good thing for me.

"Do you play any sports?" She's looking straight ahead, getting annoyed that the line seems to have frozen to a standstill.

"Nah, I'm more of the bookworm type." I may want to hide where I come from, but my lies end there.

She looks me up and down. "Ugh, I hate girls like you who just wake up with a body to kill." She rolls her eyes at me playfully. "I play volleyball. Tryouts are coming up, and I really want to make the varsity team this year."

"With your height, I don't doubt it. You're probably awesome." I didn't realize when she was sitting down, but Claire looks like she's even taller than Janelle.

She points to some sandwiches underneath a little heater-looking thing. "Oh, the chicken sandwiches here are the best!" I watch as she takes one and I go ahead and pick one up as well, grabbing a bottle of water to go with it. The sandwich is warm and I can't wait to dig in. We leave the line after paying and carry our lunch trays to the seating area while she looks around, trying to find her friends.

"There they are!" she exclaims, walking to the left. I follow her and take a seat beside her. All of her friends at the table are smiling and dressed similarly in blue jeans and collared shirts. I'm in Pleasantville!

"Hey guys, this is Eve. I met her during the extracurricular fair!"

They all look me up and down and say polite hellos. Claire goes around the table introducing them to me. A few of them are sophomores like her, and two of them are juniors. I give a small wave to everyone, feeling really nervous by their inquisitive gazes. I sit down and unwrap my chicken sandwich, realizing at that moment how hungry I am.

Ms. Levine made sure the school gave me a food credit. I can eat anything in the dining hall at any time—it's like my personal pantry. Pretty nice of the school to take care of me like this, but Ms. Levine always says that you can't get what you don't ask for. Now here I am, eating like a queen in the best school in the country, all for free. Life is good!

I'm taking a bite out of my food when I feel a presence. I'm obviously not the only one, because the noise level seems to have quieted down and as I look up; I notice that everyone has their heads turned toward the front doors. I follow the collective gaze, wondering what they're looking at.

That's when I see him.

He's just so much taller and bigger than everyone else. He's a man among boys. My jaw actually drops when I take him in. He has a few girls giggling behind him, and guys on either side. What. The. Fuck.

"Wow," Claire says in a breathy voice, momentarily shaking me out of my thoughts.

Allison sees the look of shock on my face and takes it upon herself to fill me in. "Oh, that's Vincent Borignone. He's a god around here. I would say you'll get used to him with time, but no one ever does. He's just that insanely sexy. Brilliant! And he's also one of the most connected people you'll ever meet. Some people say that he's the son of the infamous Antonio Borignone. Like, you know, the crime family. But that's probably just a rumor—"

I lift a hand, stopping her. "Wait, w-what?" The name Vincent Borignone echoes in my ear. Rumor. It's a rumor. I never knew his last name. Suddenly, it all clicks—all the puzzle pieces falling into place. It's him. He never told me his last name because he's a mafia prince! And he goes here. To Columbia. To MY school. Where my future is supposed to be happening. My mind is working on overtime right now. I blink, staring out into space while my heart beats into my throat.

Claire turns to me, shaking me out of my fog. "Well, goddamn! It's only been a few months, but he's even better looking now. The man just gets hotter with age." They all start laughing.

"Eve, are you okay?" Claire asks, putting her hand on my back.

I slowly turn toward her, plastering a fake smile on my face. "Is he in a fraternity?" I squeak, trying to move the conversation forward.

"No way! But he doesn't need to be in one; he just goes where he wants, and I swear, it's like the entire student body rolls out the red carpet for him. He can get into any party at any time."

I bring my bottle of water to my lips when Allison points to his table. "By the way, that's Daniela." My body freezes at the mention of a girl in connection with Vincent; the water I was just swallowing moves down the wrong pipe—I'm choking. Claire taps my back as I cough like crazy. "Oh my God, are you okay?" I clear my throat, trying to regain my composure.

One of Claire's friends, I think her name is Jen, starts talking. "Daniela is such a bitch. She's gorgeous, and no one knows it better than her. Of course, she's in O Chi A...that's the slutty sorority, FYI."

We all turn as a unit to stare at their table when Jen starts up again. "She's always up Vincent's ass. But I'd bet he messes around on her all the time. Last year, Jillian Samson said she gave him a blow job—" She keeps talking, but my mind has gone static.

He has a girlfriend? Holy shit. And she's gorgeous. Actually, I remember her from the fight the first night Vincent and I met. The redhead. She moves from her own seat onto his lap, wrapping a pale, skinny arm around his back with a smile on her face. Her hands move to his hair; he looks relaxed but disinterested. She puts her lips near his ear for a moment and then looks around the room, making sure that we all see she's with him. I want to scream and cry right now. Instead, I take a slow sip of my water, keeping my face as neutral as I can while I continue to watch. No wonder he didn't want more with me. He already has someone, and she looks like she just walked out of *Vogue* magazine.

Vincent Borignone. My life just got a hell of a lot more complicated.

RECKONING (VINCENT AND EVE BOOK 2)

1

EVE

MY ANXIETY PEAKS as I listen to the sorority girls gossip about Vincent and his stunner of a girlfriend, Daniela. Vincent's past words ricochet around my mind... *"One foot in one world, one foot in another."* The doors of realization are now flung open, and there's no stopping the onslaught of truth. This man is Vincent Borignone, a member the largest crime family on the East Coast. He is also a student at one of the best colleges in the country. *"My entire life is duality,"* he said. My head throbs. I try to calm down by focusing on my immediate surroundings—starting with my table in the dining hall.

Claire, who I just met at the activity fair, sits on my right. With golden brown hair in a messy high bun, a light dusting of freckles on her nose, and a blue floral dress falling around her shoulders, she looks effortlessly beautiful. Her sorority sister—who I've nicknamed *Preppy-in-Pink* because I can't remember her name—sits on my left. The collar of her rose-colored Polo shirt is popped and a string of white pearls sit around her slender white neck; she blends in seamlessly with the blue-blood crowd of this Ivy League University.

The conversation gets loud again, and I can't help but listen in.

My heart pounds into my stomach as the girls take a poll about whether or not sex with Vincent would be hot or scary as hell. They're likening him to a sexy vampire; a man everyone lusts after, but who may or may not take a vein. My mind is in overdrive as they all crack up with laughter. I need to get the hell out of here and look him up.

Ms. Levine's warnings ring in my ears. I should have done my research, but instead chose to stay in the dark. The truth is banging on my brain, echoing through every organ in my body. I jump out of my seat, interrupting their conversation with my unexpected movement. Claire and her friends stare at me in confusion.

"Sorry guys, I, um...uh...forgot something in my room," I blurt the excuse, trying not to stutter. I swivel my head to Claire. "Sorry, but I need to go." I turn to the rest of the group, my ponytail swinging. "It was nice to meet you all." I smile, but I'd bet it looks more like a grimace.

I drop down to the floor to grab my black backpack. Standing up too quickly, I smack the top of my head on the corner of the table. My eyes screw shut as I wonder what hurts more, the embarrassment or my skull.

Finally getting the nerve to reopen my eyes, I see the girls staring at me, trying not to laugh.

"Are you okay?" Claire's biting the side of her cheek. I resist the urge to rub the top of my head.

"I'm totally fine." My voice sounds higher pitched than usual.

She lets out a little chuckle. "Listen, we're all going out tomorrow night, maybe you wanna come with?"

I shuffle from one foot to the other, itching to go. "Um, sure. Text me?" I don't take another glance at the girls as I pivot, running to the front door like my ass is on fire.

At this point, I couldn't care less what they think. I just found out the man I thought I loved is Vincent Borignone, son of the biggest mafia Don on the East Coast. There's got to be some mistake. I get to the steps by the dining hall's entrance. Just as I'm about to leave, I pause.

Maybe I saw wrong.

Maybe that Vincent they're talking about isn't my Vincent.

I turn my head to get one last look. Even sitting down, I can see how much bigger he is than the boys around him. My eyes cover his ink-black hair styled in an undercut, his chiseled jaw beneath his high, widespread cheekbones, and his slight slant in the eyes, making him appear broody. The girls weren't wrong; he looks dangerous as all hell. I let out an involuntary groan as I spin back around, high-tailing it out the door.

I'm jogging to my dorm room as my mind runs in circles. Sliding my backpack from my left to my right shoulder, I plunge my hand inside the small zipper pocket, searching for my phone. I pull out the first hard thing I feel, and it's a tube of Janelle's coconut lip balm. *Shit!* I stuff my hand back inside again and pull out my cell. I'm about to open my browser when I realize I need to calm down and do my research in the privacy of my room. I don't want to open this can in public, which will most likely be full of something worse than worms.

I know that what I'm about to see will probably annihilate me, but there can be no more hiding my head in the sand. Vincent's here and it's time I face the truth. I drop my phone back in my bag, trying to walk the rest of the way calmly. A few extra minutes won't mean anything.

I make it to my dorm room and fall into the chair at my desk. Flipping my laptop open and clicking on Firefox, I type in: Vincent Borignone. There are hundreds of photos of him with his girlfriend. *Holy shit.* My belly drops like a sack of cement.

I move my mouse through the images.

The first photo I see is Daniela in a tight white nurse's jacket, tits pushed up and pouring out. Her thin arms wrap themselves around Vincent's strong neck. She makes a kiss face to the camera, show-casing high cheekbones and full, blood-red lips. Vincent looks a bit rumpled like he hasn't shaved in a few days. Dressed in green doctor's scrubs, he's the sexy doctor to her overly styled nurse.

I continue scrolling through photographs, clicking on another

one that catches my eye. The caption reads: WINTER WONDER-
LAND GALA. Daniela is in a long, pink sequin gown that pools by
her feet. Vincent wears a gorgeous navy tux. It's dawning on me that
they are socialites.

The next photograph is of the two of them at an event for poor
inner-city children. The irony that I'm that poor inner-city child isn't
lost on me. I continue to surf the internet, weirdly feeling like I'm
researching a complete stranger.

After looking at hundreds of photographs, I enter the world of
YouTube and click on a video of Vincent wrestling at Tri-Prep Academy. He's wearing a black singlet with a yellow lion on the front. I
swallow hard, staring at every perfectly defined muscle in his body
as he takes down his opponent. Raising my eyebrows, I take a look
at his gigantic...package. My body immediately flushes. Why the
hell did I never know how hot it is to watch guys wrestle? The
crowd is going berserk when he wins. He looks up for a moment,
and I can immediately tell that he was younger here. But still
gorgeous.

My stalking knows no bounds as I read and watch anything and
everything I can get my hands on. Columbia seems to have a gossip
column of its own, *High and Low*, and Vincent and Daniela are on it
weekly, spotted around campus like celebrities.

The first story I find is titled: "Vincent and Daniela, They're Just
Like Us!" I assume it's a satire of *US Weekly* gossip magazine. Photo
one shows them drinking coffee at a local cafe. The second shows
him holding her hand, entering the mathematics center. The third
has them at a back table of the library, books scattered around the
desk while they study. The fourth has them in side-by-side
photographs at the gym. On the left, he's bench-pressing a barbell.
On the right, she's jogging on the treadmill. Her workout outfit is a
white sports bra and matching white leggings with shiny stars.

Finally, I find a photo of Vincent with an older man at a charity.
My throat tightens. He's with Antonio Borignone. They look so much
alike; I can barely believe it. His father's eyes are electric blue, just as I
remember from that day at the pawnshop. In fact, their physical simi-

larity is so strong that it's almost ridiculous I didn't notice right away. Vincent is taller and more muscular, but he's his father's son.

I drop my head, forcing myself to see the truth. Vincent is the son of Antonio Borignone, the most notorious gangster on the East Coast. And his girlfriend looks like she's got the beauty of Grace Kelly and the brains of Einstein. I kick out my garbage can from beneath my desk, feeling like I'm going to puke. No. I'm stronger than that.

I move my hand back to my computer, staring at the most recent photo of them on *High and Low*. They're in the science lab conducting an experiment. Even with huge goggles and in front of a Bunsen burner, they look like perfection.

Finally, I pull out my cell phone and open up my Instagram account. Searching for his name, it's not difficult to find. His profile isn't private. I click on the first photo and see him drinking a beer on a yacht in Capri—tan chest and low-slung blue swim shorts. The next photo shows him training at a boxing gym in Bali with his shirt off. My body feels numb as I scan picture after picture, but when I glance at my fingers, I notice they're shaking. Moving back to the first picture, I see the last time he posted was a little over a year ago.

I check how many followers Vincent has. Two hundred thousand! And he's been silent for a year? Like a tempest, I feel a rush of anger and depression move through me. Clearly, I've been played. How could I have been so stupid to think that he would ever want me? And...how could I be even more stupid not to realize who he is?

I don't take a breath before I click on Daniela's name, tagged on one of Vincent's photos. I know that what I'm about to see will hurt me, but I'm on a masochistic binge right now, knifing myself with truth. For some reason, I feel as if I need to see all of this. I want to make sure that my brain, heart, and body all understand that whatever I thought I had with Vincent is good and done.

Finally clicking on her name, I see she has one point four million followers. I look at hundreds of photos, dissecting each and every detail. Her entire feed is about New York City glamour and travel. Even the mundane shit she does is perfect. In one photo, she's eating a hot dog in Central Park with her tiny little white dog on a leash. In another, she's strutting across a New York City street in sky-high heels and a cropped fur jacket.

In another picture, she's wearing a long, silver gown and hanging on the arm of the sexiest man alive—Vincent—for an event, Feed the Children. I read the comments.

BeachnSand472: Who makes your gown? LOVE!
PebblesnRox: You guys are perfect!
SheRaines: please grab his ass for me!
DocAllie: OMG! #GoalsAF
Jay_Har4572: DYINGGGGG. Love love love!
Candybaby999: OBSESSEDDDDDD need that dress, AND that man.
Fashon4more: He's hot AF!
Janananana: #couplegoals

Another photo. Daniela dives off a yacht, her pink bikini sparkling under the sunlight. Her caption: ST. BARTHS WITH BAE. Vincent's watching her with a smile on his face as if he can't believe how beautiful she is. Did he ever look at me like that?

I move to another photo and see them at the Robin Hood Gala, raising money to combat New York City homelessness.

Caption:

Enjoying a special night with the love of my life. #MileyCyrus #Coldplay #stophomelessness #lovemycity #bestmanever #heartofgold #goodcause #charity #giving #robinhood

I do a quick Google search and see that tables for this event start at over ten thousand dollars.

I move back to Instagram, staring at another photo of Daniela at the Robin Hood Gala. She's posing with a girl who looks just like her, but with blonde hair instead of auburn. The girl's name is tagged and I click, finding myself on Daniela's sister's page.

The first photo I check is in the middle of her feed. A group of friends smile around a huge white Christmas tree, decorated in what looks like hundreds of gold and silver ornaments. The caption: CHRISTMAS IN VERMONT! Enlarging the photo with my thumb and forefinger, I spot Vincent smiling in the background in a black sweater and jeans. Considering how tall he is, the tree must be over seven feet! My heart constricts; I've never seen a tree this perfect in my life.

I remember all the years Janelle and I would celebrate Christmas a week late, so we could take someone's old tree from the dumpster. I'd string Fruit Loops on a colorful lanyard, while Janelle would put a knot at either end so the cereal wouldn't slide off. And then I'd sit on her shoulders and scatter our stringed cereal around the tree. My eyes prickle with tears, remembering how beautiful and special I thought it was. Meanwhile, I was nothing but a poor gutter rat living in the ghetto with a big sister who tried to make it right. I swallow the thought as I read Daniela's sister's hashtags:

#après ski #sorrynotsorry #cheers #kissesunderthemistletoe #dontbejealous #lifeisgood

After finding myself on Daniela's sister's boyfriend's page, I know I've gotten out of hand. I shut my phone off because I don't trust myself not to go back for more. I sprawl out on my bed, shaking my feet until my shoes pop off. My eyes burn from staring at my phone for so long.

I should study. Read. I need to compartmentalize this and keep my focus on school. In fact, I should be happy all of this unfolded because it makes it clear that whatever we had is ancient history. Part of me wants to die, but another part of me wants to show his ass up. I never want to feel like this again. And I refuse to ever be that girl I used to be; I was naïve and stupid.

I spend the rest of my night with my eyes glued to my books, hoping if I just study hard enough, I can push the Vincent shit to the back of my head. I went through hell and back to be where I am, and I won't let a man stop me from succeeding.

With the help of the school's guidance counselor, I've already planned out my path to becoming an attorney like I've always dreamed. The possibility of a safe and secure future, complete with money in the bank, is so close I can practically taste it. As far as I'm concerned, nothing else matters. Vincent Borignone can go to hell.

2

VINCENT

THE FALL SEMESTER began last week, and I've got a shitload of work to get done in addition to work for the family. Unfortunately, I'm stuck sitting here at Maison Kayser, a fancy French coffee shop on the Upper East Side. Daniela snootily orders four different desserts and a skim-milk cappuccino from the waiter, requesting the shape of a heart in the foam.

This restaurant actually pays Daniela to eat here—just so she'll take a picture of her enjoying the food and post it on the internet. Apparently, millions of girls all over the world look up to Daniela and want to eat where she eats. Last week, she posted a photograph of her lip gloss, and within an hour, the color was sold out almost everywhere.

"Y-yes, miss." The waiter stumbles over his words before scurrying away. She smiles like an evil cat; Daniela loves to make people fidget.

"You know, Vincent." She presses her overly plumped lips together, shifting forward to get closer to me. "The whole-milk cappuccino looks a lot more beautiful than the skim one. I feel like the color is whiter. I wonder if there's anything to that theory?" She looks at me expectantly, tilting her head to the side. She's put some shimmer or some shit on her cheeks, and it makes her face sparkle.

I stare at her but refuse to answer such a dumb question.

"Waiter," she calls out, not taking her green eyes off mine. She lifts her hand in the air, shifting her fingers around like an impatient child.

He walks back over to us. Before he can take out his pad and a pen, she barks her updated order. "I want a skim and whole-milk cappuccino." Her demanding attitude grates on my nerves. "And I'm in a hurry. Have them rush it."

I finally break my hatred-fueled eye contact to look at the waiter, stopping him before he can walk away. "Thank you." He nods at me appreciatively before leaving.

She snickers at the angry look on my face. "Oh, come on, Vincent. It's his job."

I shake my head slowly. "The way you treat people, Daniela."

"Oh, come on. You're the richest man in this place. Don't be so sour."

"Sour? What does money have to do with anything. You have no respect for anyone. All you care about is your social media bullshit."

"Don't talk down to me," she spits. "Social media is the new age."

"No one gives a fuck!"

"They don't? Tell that to my million followers or the designers who beg me to wear their clothes and accessories." She pulls out a green cashmere sweater from a shopping bag hanging off her seat. "Tell that to this gorgeous sweater you've been gifted by Armani. People would die to get this for free."

"I'm not wearing your shit." I crack my knuckles one at a time. "You ask me all the time, and the answer is always the same—*no*. You need me to come out, smile for a damn photograph, fine. But wearing the clothes you choose? Fuck no." I clench my jaw and she immediately pulls back.

She drops her lips into a frown. I can sense she's going to try a new tactic. Daniela is nothing if not a great actress.

"Vincent, you don't have to wear any of it, okay?" Her voice is five times higher than it was a moment ago, her eyes spelling out disappointment. But I know the only real thing behind her gaze is calculation.

I let out a cutting laugh. "I'm not your bitch, Daniela. I never will be. I don't wear what you tell me to wear. I do what I want, when I want. Feel me? I may be stuck in this fucking lie of a relationship to keep your father happy, but remember that you and I are nothing in real life. Don't delude yourself into thinking otherwise."

She tries to put her hand on mine, but I tear it away before she can touch me.

"I know, baby. Calm down. You're too wound up. It's because classes have started, right? I know how serious you get about school." She looks around, making sure no one is watching us argue, the idea that anyone might see us gets her nervous. "Tell me what I can do to relax you, huh?" She licks the corner of her lip seductively.

I practically snarl. "You've got to be kidding me." I throw my napkin on the table and push my chair back, wanting to get the hell away from her.

"Come on," she purrs with a gleam in her eye. "I know we haven't fucked in ages, but it doesn't mean you can't change your mind—"

I grip the side of the table, my knuckles turning white. "I will *never* touch you again, understand?" I take a deep breath, doing my best not to flip the table and walk out. Luckily, the waiter brings the two cappuccinos and a tray full of gourmet desserts, none of which she plans to eat. I've actually watched her take bites of food only to spit it out after the photograph has been taken.

The waiter glances at my hardened face and drops the dishes in front of us before speed-stepping to the back of the room.

"But why, Vincent? We were so good together!"

"No. We weren't."

"We used to fuck like crazy! You loved it. I know you did. I just don't understand—"

"My life isn't for you to understand," I growl in frustration. She can't take a hint.

She sits up with her lips pursed, knowing no matter how much I hate her guts, I'm not going anywhere. "Anyway, sit back. I don't want your shadow in the pictures. Oh, actually, do you think you'll eat a dessert for me? I think everyone would love to see you opening wide for something white and creamy." She raises her brows, smirking. Does she think she's funny?

I breathe hard, trying not to tear the hair from her skull. "You're a sick bitch. You know that?"

"If I remember clearly, it didn't bother you too much before. In fact, I think you liked it."

Daniela Costa is into some kinky shit—and that's saying a lot coming from a man like me, who has done it all, and then some. When we started out, I was nothing but a cocky kid, willing to lay it on her for two reasons: one, she was hot; two, the family wanted someone to keep a close eye on the business we had with her father —owner of the largest bank in Central America. Costa houses and cleans our dirty money. Daniela and I went to school together, and it was damn obvious she wanted my dick. It was no surprise my father tapped me on the back to handle it.

We all hate Alexander Costa, and everyone knows he's a loose cannon, but there really isn't another option to working with him. Not yet, at least. As our operations continue to grow and give off cash, the small-time pawnshops and strip clubs aren't enough to launder all of our money. Costa, on the other hand, has the capacity to clean tens of millions a year. The situation seemed easy; I fucked Daniela, kept an eye on business, and all was well.

And then I met Eve. She's genuine and smart and somehow, perfect for me. She just got me. The real me.

I knew I couldn't touch Daniela anymore. It's not that I was ever faithful to her and she easily accepted it. Once I met someone real, the thought of another woman wasn't appealing anymore. Simple as that.

I spoke to the family, letting them know business dealings between Costa and the family were functioning well, and we had no reason to keep such a close eye on him anymore. The man was making a huge percentage off our business; none of us thought he'd be dumb enough to jeopardize that kind of cash flow. But when I made it clear to Daniela that she and I were done, she went insane. I don't think anyone in her life has ever told her "no" before.

It took only an hour for Costa to call my father and go berserk, threatening the family. Keeping his princess Daniela happy was necessary, or he'd stop laundering and holding our cash. Apparently, she was in the midst of growing her social media empire, and my face was essential to her growing fame. A family vote was called, and everyone insisted I make it right with her. I was told to do whatever it takes to keep her happy. That is, until I build a new business to take over Costa's use of ours.

I've spent this past year working to build out my own hotel and casino complex on the Tribal Lands in Nevada. As the son of a Masuki Tribe member, I have some inalienable rights, which I plan to capitalize on. And if the numbers turn how I expect them to? Our dirty cash can easily be laundered within the hundreds of millions we'll be making per year in clean money.

Once I get the family out of Costa's grip, I'll be free of him and his leech daughter. And then, maybe, I can find Eve again.

The terms between Daniela and me right now are simple: I have to look and act as though I'm still with her. She doesn't care whether or not we fuck anymore, so long as I play the part. But if I refuse to smile for the damn camera? She'll get Daddy involved, and the family would be left with a boatload of cash that the FBI would love to get their hands on. I'm stuck being her public boyfriend until Gaming gets off the ground.

Daniela shifts a bony shoulder and shuffles in her seat, bringing my attention back to her. "I think the red raspberries look best against the white cup, don't you?" She moves the cappuccino slightly askew and snaps maybe twenty pictures of each dessert with the frothy drink. Standing up to get other angles, her jeans hug her flat ass. How do millions of girls look up to this shit?

Daniela stops taking pictures, putting her fancy iPhone down on the table and bringing the cappuccino up to her glossy lips. "Okay.

Talk to me. What's going on, Vincent? You're brooding and more pissed-off than usual." She rolls her eyes, putting down her cup.

I clench my teeth. "Just take the fucking photo already." We both know why I'm here today, and it isn't to chitchat.

"Okay, if you insist." She smiles. "Turn to the side and lean back on the chair with your foot crossed at the front."

The flash goes off and I grind my teeth together.

3

EVE

THE NEXT MORNING, I decide I will do everything in my power to forget Vincent goes to school here. I do my best to focus on starting my day, one small step at a time. After washing up and getting dressed, I take a quick trip to the dining hall for a gigantic coffee and a bagel. Bringing the food back to my desk and sitting quietly to eat, I do my best not to get any crumbs on the floor. Finally, I crack open my economics textbook.

My room is a simple square, located on the third floor of one of the old gothic buildings making up the freshman quad. The desk next to mine is empty; I was supposed to have a roommate, but she decided last minute to defer admission for a year. After living in the Blue Houses—where I could hear my neighbor's conversations and smell everyone's cooking twenty-four seven—this room has become my own little sanctuary.

Staring at the supply-and-demand curve, I again reread the same passage. I need this shit to make sense! I drop my head on my desk and groan. It's only ten in the morning, and I already feel tired.

And then, like a three-dimensional puzzle with a gaping hole in the center, my brain finds the missing piece and places it right where it belongs. "Oh, thank God!" I exclaim out loud. "I understand! I get it!"

I jump up from my chair, dancing to music that isn't on, shaking my ass left to right. My phone *buzzes* mid-dance, and I smile wide when I see it's Claire. After my weird stunt yesterday, I was worried she'd write me off.

Claire: Meet me at my dorm @ 10. Brearley Houses. Come earlier if you want to pre-game!
Me: I'm planning on studying today, not sure if I'll be feeling up to going out later. Can I text you?
Claire: Come on, girl! We'll have fun! Come out!

I look back at the economics book. I deserve to go out, right? I promised Janelle last week that I'd do my best to get out more at night. Now that I'm living in relative safety, I don't have to be a hermit. And, while it's hard to change my old ways, it's something I'm consciously trying to modify about myself.

"You know what?" I exclaim loudly into my empty room. "I'm going out."

Me: Okay. I'll be there. See you later!

The day goes by with my head in the books, my only break to run down to the campus deli to pick up a turkey sandwich and another large coffee.

By evening, my brain feels completely fried. I lift my hands to my hair and try to pull the rubber band from my ponytail. When it gets caught in a knot, I whimper, trying to pull it free. I finally remove it, but not without ripping out a bunch of hairs in the process. Ouch.

Looking at my old worn-out clothing, I take stock of my situation. I seriously need to revive myself if I'm going to be seen in public tonight. I quickly undress, slide on my blue robe and Old Navy flip-flops, and grab my lime-green shower caddy. Peeking out of my door to make sure the hallway is clear, I sprint to the girl's bathroom, praying with each step that I won't bump into someone. I know it's only girls on this floor, but I'm self-conscious about being seen in nothing other than a terry-cloth bathrobe.

After shaving and scrubbing as best as I can, I grab the fancy shampoo Janelle brought me from her swanky salon and massage my scalp with my fingertips. I inhale, smelling the creamy coconut scent. After rinsing, I take out the conditioner and let it sit in my hair for three-minutes, exactly as the instructions suggest. I'm standing and waiting for the time to pass when I hear a few girls walking into the bathroom, giggling.

"...saw them at the business center!"

"I seriously can't even—"

"You can't?" another voice interrupts. "Well, I can! Doesn't Vincent look like he'd be a total savage in bed? God, I bet he fucks like—"

Laughter.

I hear a swishing sound in my ears. I want to turn away, pretend that I didn't just hear his name in the context of sex with someone, but I can't un-hear the words.

Their high-pitched voices taper off until I hear the door *clang* shut.

My face contorts into an ugly cry. No sound is coming out of my mouth, but the silent moans wrack my chest. Tears run furiously down my face, mingling with the shower water. My heart moves low into my stomach, my mother's voice barging into the forefront of my mind. She's railing. I can hear her words echoing against my skull. *"You're nothing! A zero!"*

I lean my hands against my knees under the spray, trying not to heave as my stomach twists. I slightly turn my head and come face to face with my beautiful shampoo bottle. Even with Janelle's salon discount, it was still crazy expensive. But, she wanted me to go to school with "good hair." According to her, it would help me do better in my classes. Somehow, I manage a small chuckle along with my tears. Then Angelo forces himself into my mind, too. Angelo, who thinks I'm destined for great things. They're the scaffolding to the strong and independent woman I want to become. I need to lean on their opinions of me, and not let some asshole tear me down.

I put my hands back to my sides and stand taller. I rinse my hair, and with as much strength as I can muster, open the shower curtain and put my robe back on. Gathering my wits, I leave the bathroom with my head held high.

After getting into my room, I slide on an old band T-shirt that one of Janelle's ex-boyfriends gave her. I conveniently took it along with a few other items before moving out because, well, sisters! I take out my blow-dryer and a round brush, placing it on my desk while I separate my hair into sections, drying my hair piece by piece, just as Janelle taught me.

I look in my mirror, relieved that I managed to turn thick dark hair into something relatively smooth. I drop the brush at my desk, exclaiming, "Fuck love!" Better yet, fuck Vincent Borignone! I'm going to work as hard as I can while I'm here, and I'm not allowing a man to take advantage of me again. I'm a freshman with my head in the books, and it seems that he's the most notorious bad boy on campus. Why would our paths ever cross? They shouldn't. And thank God for that. I couldn't bear for him to see me. Would he laugh? I'm sure he would. I was so stupid.

I pull out a pair of tight black jeans and a simple white tank from the top from my closet. Sliding on a stack of gold bangles I bought from H&M, I finish myself off with some clear lip gloss and a little mascara. I feel casual, but a hell of a lot better than I did an hour ago.

I'm no longer that pathetic girl who hides behind her sister and her books. I'm new. I'm improved. And Vincent Borignone can kiss. My. Ass. At the end of the day, all that shit is behind me. It's done. And I'm... over it!

Like a horrible thunderstorm, memories of the two of us flash through my head. But this time, I inject my newfound knowledge into every past moment. We met at the fight, but he was with Daniela— who probably gave him a blowjob in the bathroom. He brought me to the skating rink, but he likely went home that same night to Daniela, who was waiting for him, wearing nothing but sexy black lingerie and high fuck-me heels. He took me to pizza but shot those Russians in the head while Pauli distracted me with conversation!

The Borignone mafia is nothing if not arrogant and powerful. Just last month, I read a newspaper article about an explosion killing an FBI agent and his wife in their car. Apparently, this agent was garnering evidence to bring forward a case against the Borignone mafia. And Vincent is part of this? I shake my head side to side, disgusted that I ever touched him. I vaguely wonder what part he plays. Is he simply a soldier at the lowest rung? No way. He's too intelligent for that. Maybe he's one of the Capo who reports to the boss? Even that feels like it isn't enough. As the son of Antonio, I have no doubt that he plays a crucial role in their sick schemes.

I grab the small black bag Janelle bought for me as a graduation gift, filling it with some essentials: lip gloss, cell phone, my ID, and some cash. I leave my room, taking the steps to the lobby. Pushing open the building's large wooden front door, I inhale the scent of flowers. The campus is simply beautiful and perfectly maintained— an oasis in the city.

I take my time walking to Claire's. Even though it's evening, the entire school is lit up with huge streetlamps. I pause to read a silver engraved plaque located on the back of a wooden bench: IN LOVING MEMORY OF DAN BROWNING, WHO ALWAYS LIKED TO SIT. I chuckle, rolling my eyes to high heaven. These rich people have so much money, and they spend it on this shit? I shake my head at the absurdity of it all and finish my short walk to Claire's dorm.

"Hey," the guy at the front desk stares at his phone intently. "Who are you here for?" His hair is long in the front and covers most of his eyes.

"I'm waiting for Claire, um, I'm not sure her last name. But she's a sophomore."

He finally lifts his head and pauses, his mouth hanging slightly open and cheeks turning pink. I look down at my clothes, self-consciously wondering if there's something wrong with me.

"Do you want to w-wait here, or go up?" His eyes flicker between my eyes, lips, and boobs.

"Uh, I'll just wait here," I mumble, pulling my tank higher to cover me better. I take a seat in one of the lobby's plastic chairs, typing out a message to Claire that I'm waiting downstairs.

I try to relax. I'm still unsure about the best way to cope with this new world. It's hard enough to sit in class with these entitled rich kids, but it's even harder to have to go out socially and try to act like I'm the same as they are. In my heart, I'm still the poor girl from the ghetto. I know technically, I've left my old life behind—I'm a student here, just like everyone else. But still, the past remains with me. The result is a sense of not really belonging anywhere. Maybe if I just pretend to be like them for long enough, my new persona will become me. Eve Petrov, Columbia-educated woman. Eve Petrov, attorney-at-law. I like the sound of that.

I look back up again at the guy sitting at the front desk. He doesn't look much older than I am. I once read that every passerby has a life as vivid and complex as my own. I wonder if that could possibly be true. He looks like any other preppy white kid, but then again, he's working here tonight instead of chugging beers at a frat house.

Claire walks out of the elevator. She looks beautiful in a fitted jean jacket and a long black cotton dress with a high slit in the thigh. Her outfit is casual but still manages to show off her toned body. When we look at each other, I feel a combination of relief and happiness. I know we've only just met, but it feels like we could be good friends.

"Hey, girl! I'm glad you decided to come out." Her voice is upbeat. I stand from the chair, and we head out into the night.

"Where are all of your friends?" I rub my hands up and down my arms. Since I left my dorm, it seems that the weather has dropped fifteen degrees.

"They may meet us there later," Claire replies. "It's just the two of us for now. Oh, by the way, the party is close, so we can walk. Totally beats having to get in a cab, right? Maybe we should go downtown to a bar in the West Village later if the party here sucks. Did you bring an ID by any chance?" Her voice is hopeful.

I nod my head, relieved that my age won't cause a problem. "Yeah. My sister called the DMV over the summer and told them she lost her driver's license, so they sent her a new one and I got to keep her old."

"Oh my God, that's so lucky! Mine is just one of the older girls in Phi Alpha, and she looks nothing like me!" We laugh.

Even though we didn't drive, Janelle thought it was important for us to have driver's licenses. Somehow, she got Vania's brother to lend us his old Volvo once a week so we could practice.

Claire and I finally get off campus. Everywhere I turn, college students are ignoring traffic signals, or running drunkenly from one corner to the next. A group of girls, all in short skirts, walk ahead of us.

Finally, we enter a small but obviously expensive-looking building. The uniformed doorman nods to us as we walk into the elevator. Claire pushes the button for the penthouse level and we smile at each other excitedly. The door opens directly into a huge loft. Claire immediately steps out, but it takes me a second to realize this is the party.

Hard-core rap music blares on the speakers. I step inside, doing my best to give off a casual vibe as if this social scene doesn't scare me. But the truth is everything around me serves as a reminder that I'm out of place. Floor-to-ceiling glass windows and an open floor plan give the apartment an airy feel. The walls are filled with beautiful black-and-white photography, framed in silver and gold. This place screams money.

I turn my head to see a green ping-pong table along the wall by the kitchen. Some people are playing a drinking game on it, throwing balls into cups on the opposite side of the table. There's a beautiful brown leather sectional couch in the center of the room. A coffee table is littered with ashtrays, red cups, and empty water bottles. Random pockets of students grind their bodies together to the music.

Before saying hello to anyone, Claire walks us into a large chrome and silver kitchen. Bottles of alcohol are spread out chaotically across a white marble island. She checks them out and finally picks up a magnum of vodka that's already half empty. She pours some into two large plastic cups, adding some Diet Pepsi to each. After handing one to me, and taking the other for herself, we walk to the side of the living room. Clinking our drinks together, we take our first sips. The swallow burns, but I do my best not to flinch.

"To new friends," she says.

"New friends." My heart actually warms in my chest.

Claire checks her phone while I look around the party. I put my lips back onto the cup's rim when I lock eyes across the room with a familiar guy. He's big and built, but also really preppy looking. It only takes a moment for me to realize that we're both staring at each other questioningly, trying to place the other. Wait. Is this who I think it is? Oh. My. God. Does he remember meeting me? Vincent introduced me to him the night of the underground fight in the Meatpacking District. Did Vincent ever tell him about us? Does he know anything? Is he also Borignone mafia?

He starts to move through the crowd, seemingly toward me.

My heart thumps.

Some girl stops him to say hello and he barely gives her a second glance. He's on his way.

He reaches his destination—me. Standing tall and naturally imposing, I'd peg him at over six feet tall, and in this moment, I'm wishing I wore a pair of higher heels. I feel like a kid in front of this man.

"Holy shit," he says, not unkindly. "You're Eve." His lips quirk up into a smile, but I can tell there are nerves behind his relaxed demeanor.

"Do you know Claire?" I point to her, deflecting. His eyes smile as he takes her in.

"Of course, I do."

Claire rolls her eyes as if she's been there and done that. "Yeah," she says. "I know Tom." She cocks her head to the side and crosses her arms over her chest, full of attitude. He doesn't look daunted.

"Oh, come on, Claire," he laughs. "We had some fun together, didn't we?"

"Huh," she says skeptically. "I vaguely remember sitting in the dining hall with the rest of my pledge class when we all got a text on our phone at the same time." Claire's face is reddening, but Tom looks like he's trying not to laugh.

"And you wouldn't believe it, Eve, but, it was the same exact message. From the same guy. And do you know what this text said to each and every one of us?"

I let my gaze bounce between the two of them.

"It said"—she lifts her hands to make air quotes—"Netflix and chill?"

Tom breaks out into laughter. "Come on—I was throwing out an option and figured someone would respond! How was I supposed to know you were all together?"

"We were all pledging Phi Alpha! We were together for the entire semester, you moron."

"All right, so I got busted. Doesn't mean you and I didn't have fun while it lasted though, right?"

I want to ask if Vincent is here, but I don't have the nerve. Tom glances toward the couch. I turn my eyes and—there he is, facing away from me while Daniela straddles his lap. The back of his head rests against the cushion while she grinds up against him to the music.

I turn away, trying not to stare. Tom looks at me with pity in his eyes and all at once, I feel like crying. He must know everything. I wish I could care less about this right now. Against all odds, I made it to one of the best schools in the country. I have everything paid for and taken care of. My sister is safe. I'm safe. I have a nice clean bedroom to sleep in every night. I'm on a path to success. I can't let this bother me.

Still, seeing them in front of my face feels like I'm receiving punishment for a crime I never committed. I need to get out of here before Vincent sees me. The last thing on earth I want right now is to bump into him while he's with his girlfriend.

Tom seems to notice my distress. He shrugs his shoulders as if to say that what I'm witnessing is just the normal course of things.

"You girls want another drink? Eve, you look like you could use one."

"We just got," Claire replies, lifting her full cup. "But I could use a bottle of water."

Tom nods. "No problem. Let me grab one for you." He turns, walking toward the kitchen.

Claire's eyes follow Tom as he saunters off. "Ugh, he is such a man-whore. Then again, we did have a lot of fun together."

"Yeah," I reply, taking another huge gulp of my drink. If she's still talking, I wouldn't know. I need an exit strategy, stat.

Claire turns her head toward Vincent and Daniela. "He's best friends with Vincent. That guy, over there." She points to his back. "I know Vincent's gorgeous, but he's so intense. I don't know what it is about him, but he always looks so aggressive...so, dominant. I obviously get the appeal, but sometimes he just like, scares the shit out of me."

"Tom looks pretty intense, too," I add.

"Yeah, but not in the same way. Tom is sort of free-spirited; he messes around and makes a lot of jokes. He's definitely got that aggressive side too, but not like Vincent. Vincent is like, brilliant. And huge. And rough." She laughs, taking another sip of her drink. "They say he got a full scholarship, even though he's a gazillionaire!"

"Oh." I shrug and take a deep breath, my gaze falling back on the asshole who cared for me—during my lowest moments—like no one else. I need to hold myself together, at least until I find somewhere private to cry.

A girl I've never met before walks over to Claire. "Do you see the bag Daniela has?" She's huffing, annoyance written all over her pale face. "How the hell did she even find it? I looked everywhere for that bag and it was sold out! Barneys, Bergdorf, Net-a-Porter, everywhere!"

I've recently come to understand that in this rich people's world —where everyone has the money, the looks, and the intellect— connections and access are what reign supreme. Because when everyone can afford the newest "it" bag, it's no longer exciting or special to have it. The goal becomes about having a bag that others can't get their hands on.

"Who cares? I think it's ugly anyway," Claire looks at me and winks. "By the way Alexa, this is Eve. Eve, this is Alexa. She's a junior in Phi Alpha."

Alexa turns to me, giving a genuine smile. "Nice to meet you. Are you planning to rush?"

"Oh, I don't know. Maybe?" I lift a shoulder in question.

"You totally should. We have a lot of fun and it's great to have a smaller community within the college scene. Especially since the city is so huge, you know? It's good to have that close-knit family feeling."

She turns her body again to face Claire. "A few of us are heading over to another party in the building next door. Come with?"

"We just got here. I think we'll stay for a bit." The girls air-kiss goodbye and Alexa waves to me as she walks away.

Claire plunges a hand into her huge purse, searching for something. "I almost forgot!" She pulls out two small bags of pretzels and hands one to me. "I brought these for us so we won't get too drunk tonight. Carbs to soak up the alcohol!"

I take the pretzels from her hand, feeling like crying even harder now. The fact that she thought of me enough to bring this little snack is beyond thoughtful. I've never really had anyone in my life other than Janelle who I could call a friend. And in this moment, Claire is seriously coming close to that mark.

Tom walks back over with a bottle of Poland Spring and within seconds, they're shamelessly flirting. I drop the pretzels into my bag and hold my drink in a death grip as my eyes move back to Vincent and Daniela. I just can't stop myself; watching him with her is like staring at an awful car crash. It's sickening to see, but impossible to turn from.

Apparently, I'm not the only one with a staring problem because Daniela's stripper dance is beginning to garner interest. Katy Perry and Rihanna's "Black Horse" booms on the speakers as a few preppy-looking guys move closer together, hooting and hollering as she grinds on Vincent. It's obvious she's loving all of the attention she's getting; her seductive dancing only increases with their cheers. Her narrow hips slowly circle as her long auburn hair sways down her back. The look in her eyes is seduction.

She spins around in an expert-looking move. While the front of her top was relatively modest, the back is entirely open and strung together with nothing other than a few delicate gold chains. The shirt showcases her milky-white skin. I wish I could see Vincent's face, but he's still sitting looking away from me.

Daniela finally moves off him when the music changes. I know it's not rational, but I feel instantly relieved. Some of the guys who were watching start to boo, begging her to keep dancing. She demurely shrugs as if she didn't even realize anyone was watching her. "Oh, please," I say under my breath.

Meanwhile, Vincent leans forward on the couch, seemingly ignoring everyone and focusing on a muted UFC match on the big-screen TV in front of him. I step closer to Tom and Claire. Strangely, it feels like Tom keeps darting his eyes toward me. He's not giving off any sexual interest, but he is for sure watching me.

I glance back to see Daniela walking toward her friends. Pulling out a phone from her bag, she leans into the group with her arm extended forward, posing for selfies.

I subconsciously lift my tank top higher, making sure I'm not showing too much skin. I let out a groan of irritation. I'm sick and tired of the same old issues that I've always had—the same boring flaws and anxieties that have been gnawing at me for years. Every girl here is dressed sexy and I can, too. I'm in college, a place for reinvention within relative safety. I have nothing to fear anymore. I pull my tank down just a bit so that the top of my breasts show. *There!*

All of a sudden, Daniela and her friends turn to me together. *Oh, shit.* They totally caught me staring. I do a quick about-face and try to act like I'm part of the conversation between Claire and Tom.

I feel a soft hand on my back and I immediately flinched, turning around.

"Didn't mean to scare you," Daniela says with a saccharine smile.

"Having fun?" Her perfectly plucked auburn eyebrows are raised in question.

I want to look happy, but my face won't move. Luckily, Claire turns to us then, her presence immediately breaking the potential for awkwardness. Tom casually drapes an arm around Daniela's thin shoulder and pulls her in for a hug. Of course, they're friends. This is his best friend's girlfriend.

"How was your summer, Claire?" she asks as she relaxes comfortably into Tom's side. She sounds just as a rich girl would: confident and perfectly measured. Claire, who I could swear was slouching just a moment ago, is now standing ramrod straight with her stomach pulled in and shoulders back.

"It was great. I was working in Malawi actually." She glances down for a moment before resuming eye contact.

"I always knew you were one of those do-gooder types. You're pre-med, right?"

"Yeah," Claire says proudly. "Did you declare your major?"

"Yeah. I'm business." Her voice is upbeat. "I plan to work with my father's bank after graduation; so this works for me."

I hate that she has a brain. If she were stupid, I'd feel a whole lot better about this entire conversation right now. I stand silently, hoping that everyone just forgets I exist.

Unfortunately, I have no such luck. Daniela turns her face toward mine, placing a hand on her chest. "I'm Daniela by the way." Pointing to a group of girls who are now standing behind her, she introduces them next. "This is Allie, Jenna, and Julie." She turns to another girl standing slightly behind them. "Oh, and that's Quinn."

"Hi!" they all reply in unison. I eye each one of them, their hair all long and highlighted in the same honey-blonde shade. The girls stand around Daniela as if they're her secretaries, ready to do her bidding at a moment's notice.

Daniela's smile is back on me. "You should take a look at Omega Chi during rush next semester." She looks me up and down, assessing me. "You're so pretty. I feel like you would really fit in with us." I blink a few times nervously, feeling confused. I know she's speaking English, but it's as if there's an undercurrent to her words that I can't catch onto.

"So, what's your name?" she asks expectantly.

I clear my throat, hoping that I can get a word out. "Eve." I rub my sweaty palms on my thighs, wishing she'd leave me alone.

She nods her head slightly as if my name is suitable to her. "Well, we're all about to head out. This party totally sucks. But I'm so glad we met. See you soon, Eve." She struts off in her black stiletto heels, her posse walking behind her.

The moment they're gone, I lean back against the wall, looking for support. Claire is about to say something when I interrupt her. "Do you know where the bathroom is?"

"It's in the back, second door to the left," Tom replies with a piercing gaze. Does he think I'm going to steal something? Jeez.

Before I walk away, Claire gives me a face like *holy shit I can't believe Daniela was here just now,* but then looks back at Tom to continue chatting. I walk away from them, moving as quickly as I can. For a moment, I wonder if I should turn around and leave the party. But Daniela may be in the lobby, waiting for a ride or something. I don't want to bump into her.

Luckily, I find the bathroom quickly and walk right inside, locking the door behind me. It's small, white, and thankfully still clean. I put my hands on either side of the sink and bow my head, my breathing labored. How long should I stay in here?

I finally lift my face and look at my reflection. My hair, which I painstakingly straightened a few hours ago, now has a wave to it and my face is flushed, lips puffy. I look down at my wrist and find a skinny black hair tie. Pulling my hair back in a tight bun, I immediately feel better. Turning on the faucet, I put my wrists under the ice-cold water, trying to cool my body down. I feel completely depleted from seeing Vincent and meeting Daniela. All I want to do is run back to my dorm room and cry myself to sleep.

What I need to do is leave this party. I let out a whimper and stare at myself hard, willing the tears not to leave my eyes. Everything with Vincent was blown up in my childish mind. He has his own life, and I was nothing more than his little sideshow. What a joke I must have been. A pathetic joke. I'm going to walk back into the party and tell Claire that I have a terrible headache. Hopefully, I'll be able to find her quickly and without incident.

I hear a knock on the bathroom door. "Just a s-second." I try to stop my voice from stammering. I take a few deep breaths when I hear another hard bang.

"Just a minute!" I yell again, my voice stronger. I stare at myself, trying to muster the strength to go back outside.

"Whoever is fuckin' in there, better get out." It's a man on the other side, his voice deep and angry. I turn around, swinging the door open with annoyance. What a jerk!

A huge body looms in front of me. We lock eyes, both rooted to our respective spots. The plot of my life just doesn't make sense anymore.

"Eve?" The tone of his voice registers that he's completely stunned. He puts his hands on either side of the doorframe, seemingly to steady himself.

"Uh…" My entire brain goes on mute as I drop my head and stare at dark denim hugging muscular thighs, my eyes track upward to a tight black T-shirt that stretches across a wide chest, and finally, my eyes lock with a dark and penetrating gaze that belongs to only one man.

"Eve?" he repeats. While I didn't think it would be possible, his stare deepens. All I can process is how vulnerable I feel in this moment. When Vincent looks at me, it's as if he can see within me. It's exposure I both yearn for and despise.

In a blink, he steps inside and locks the door behind him. He bends down and lifts me onto the counter, dropping his head in my neck and breathing me in. My legs immediately spread apart to make room for him to get closer. He wraps his huge hands on either side of my head, keeping me in place while he lowers his head to look straight at me again as if to confirm that I'm real.

"You're here? But, how—" his voice breaks off. I listen to his shallow breaths mixed with mine.

Seeing him face to face like this brings it all back in a rush. He's so *intense*. I swallow hard. How much time passes with us locked in the bathroom like this, I have no idea. I'm lost to him. All of my pain and anger seems to have gone up in smoke. I want to stay lost in his eyes and simply savor this moment and the way he's looking at me.

He keeps his hands on the sides of my face, thumbs gently rubbing my temples. It's soothing and arousing. I'd clamp my legs together to stop the ache if I could, but his huge body is still between them, not allowing me any movement. I'm melting for this man. And it isn't the fact that he's insanely sexy. It's more. It's *him*.

He wraps his arms around me again, pulling me into his chest for another firm squeeze. "Did you know I was here?"

I take a deep breath, confused by his implication. Is he saying that I followed him here? To school?

"What? I didn't know at first...but I, I saw you..." The truth comes rushing back into the front of my mind. Vincent has a girlfriend. Vincent is Borignone mafia. I physically shrink back from him.

His eyes change as if he notices the change in my demeanor and isn't happy about it. "When did you see me?" Lines form on his forehead. Clearly, Vincent isn't a man who is used to surprises.

I shrug, trying my best not to sound as broken as I feel. "I saw you with your g-girlfriend in the dining hall." I wish I were one of those girls who could look him in the eye and dare him to lie to my face. Instead, my voice comes out sounding insecure and small. I drop my eyes to the floor. Even though he's the liar, I'm the one who is embarrassed. He saw me as a girl who wasn't worthy to be his. He made me feel as though we had something special, but clearly, I was mistaken.

He presses his thumb under my chin to lift up my head. "There's a lot to that, Eve. But, I'm just..." he sighs, tracing my full lips with his finger, stunning me quiet with his gentleness. "I just can't believe this. I need to explain everything to you, and I promise I will. But, can we just chill tonight?" He lets out a deep breath as I sit, staring at him in confusion. He wants to hang out tonight? What. The. Hell? I stare at him like he's insane.

"I know you must be hurt by what you've heard." He has the

decency to look down for a moment, but when he lifts them back to meet mine, his dark eyes are full of hope. "Can we just pretend that we're all good, and trust that I'll explain it all later? Nothing is as it seems. Trust me."

My rational mind is saying no. Actually, it's screaming "FUCK NO" at the top of its lungs. But my heart is beating with the word "Yes." He's here and I can't believe how much I missed him. I almost forgot how good it felt to be looked at in this way. How could this Vincent I'm staring at be the man in the photos? It just can't be! The man I'm staring at is warm, loving, and gentle. He saved me from the hands of a madman. He doesn't gallivant around town with a socialite and then kill people after hours with the mob! I can't reconcile his sides.

He seems to sense my hesitancy because before I can make a final decision, he steps forward, hugging me into his chest, essentially making the choice for me. He lifts me back into his arms and gently sets me back on my feet. "I may not deserve this chance. But fuck if I'm not gonna take it." His voice is rough, and damn my traitorous body, but it melts a little more for him.

"Wait right at the door. Give me a second, yeah?" I step outside and the door closes. A minute later, I hear the flush of a toilet and the water turn on, as though he's washing his hands. Finally, he exits. The look of relief on his face that I didn't leave is evident.

Taking my hand, his steps are certain and strong as we walk. The crowd of people literally parts as he moves. I'm trailing behind, nervously holding onto his hand, but keeping my head down. We get into the kitchen when he picks me up with something that feels like tenderness, totally at odds with his hard demeanor. He places me on top of the marble counter.

I move my lips to his ear, whispering, "Why do you keep manhandling me?"

"Don't take that away from me," he whispers back, bending his head so we can continue to speak at eye level. "You know I love it. You're so tiny and it feels so good to keep you safe." He moves his gaze from my lips up to my eyes and back down again.

"But, Vincent, I don't need—"

"I know you don't need. But I want."

His dark eyes shine, telling me he sees me. And the truth is, he's the only one who ever has. He licks his full lips. "God, Eve, you look —" he stops. Raking his hands through his hair, seemingly to gather himself. "Are you happy here? Are you living in the dorms? You have everything you need, right?"

Instead of replying, I want to ask him some questions of my own. Like, where the hell has he been? And how could he see me when he had a fucking girlfriend? And how did he hide the fact that he's *Vincent Borignone*? I internally groan, feeling frustrated. Apparently, I talk a big game. But when push comes to shove, I have no backbone. Why the hell am I sitting here in front of him? If I were Janelle, I would have raged and caused a huge scene. I would make sure that he paid the price for lying to me! Better yet, she would have thrown one of these huge bottles of Vodka at his head. But, I'm not Janelle. And when I'm near Vincent, I lose all rational thought.

"Breathe," he says, giving me a crooked grin. "I promise we'll talk about everything, okay? You didn't change your mind now about hanging out, have you?" His voice is full of question and I manage to nod my head, albeit reluctantly.

"Yes. I mean, no, I...I haven't changed my mind." I feel my face turning beet red.

He steps between my legs again, moving his mouth to my ear. "Don't change." He grabs a bottle of water from the counter and drinks it down in a swallow. Dropping the empty bottle in the sink, he leans forward on his hands, caging me in. The party may be full, but we may as well be alone. His face is so close to mine that I can feel the energy coursing between us. Right now, it's no one and nothing other than us. My heart falters as he speaks to me with his eyes. Everything in this moment becomes so simple. I stare at his face, trying to memorize every feature. I can't believe how much I missed him.

Tom throws his arm around Vincent and I gasp from the intrusion. "Wake up, brother. You're at a public party, remember?" Tom laughs, but it seems there's a hard undercurrent to his words. He's looking at Vincent with a face that says *get the fuck away from her.* I turn to Vincent, who is scowling at him.

After their strange standoff, Vincent moves his face back to mine. "This asshole is always pushing me to come out to these fucking parties. Now that I'm here, he's unhappy." He shuffles to the side, shifting an enormous shoulder. For a moment, I remember what he looks like without a shirt on and I feel a throb in my lower belly. Vincent has a body that I'd swear was airbrushed if not for the fact that he's a living, breathing human and not on a billboard in Times Square. He's just so...big. Everywhere. I touch my hand to my face and feel it heating up again.

"Yeah," Tom replies. "You're supposed to come out to chill with your *girlfriend*, right?" He exaggerates the word girlfriend.

My breath gets clogged in my throat; I feel like reality just came over and bitch-slapped me. It's obvious Tom isn't happy that Vincent is talking to me right now. My hands grip the edge of the counter, wanting to jump off and escape when Vincent grabs my thigh with his hand, essentially keeping me frozen to the spot.

"You're a funny guy, Tom. Eve here is my friend. You better treat her with some goddamn respect, brother." He spits out his last word like a curse.

Tom stares at me hard. "Hello, Eve. Welcome to Columbia University." With those words, he steps back to Claire. I blink nervously.

"So, how are your classes going?" Vincent licks the corner of his lips as he leans his side against the counter, ignoring what just happened with Tom. I'm still staring at him dumbly, the stress making my throat immobile. "Ignore him, yeah? I'll deal with him later." I shiver at his words. They're laced with promise, and not the good kind.

I press my lips together. "My classes are actually p-pretty good. I like them."

I may be crazy about the old Vincent, but I'm not equipped to handle this new one. As if he knows I'm wavering, he places his hands above my knees, bringing me back into his orbit. I suck my stomach in and take a sharp breath; his proximity is intoxicating.

"There are a few kinds of kids at school. You're obviously the first kind." His words are teasing, but the way his hands are gripping my thighs are anything but.

"Oh?" My voice squeaks. My entire body is burning up from the heat of his hands and how good it feels to be touched—no—gripped by him.

He raises his eyebrows, fastening his hold. "You think I don't know you, Eve?" His heavy hands move slightly higher and my eyes widen. "I know you. I remember every single detail. I know you love the stress and the classes and the assignments. Pop quizzes make you giddy. You're like, 'Hell yeah! I did the reading; I'm gonna ace this test with my huge brain!'" He speaks in a high voice, making fun of me. Meanwhile, his hands keep roaming up inch by inch. I feel like I may pass out.

"Yeah, so what?" I bite the inside of my cheek but can't stop the laugh that's beginning to bubble in my chest. The asshole really does know me! I try to cover my face with my hands, but there's no stopping it. He picks up his hands from my thighs and brings me into his chest to laugh with me. My laughter only intensifies and I try to control myself, the result being a loud snort. He guffaws when he hears it and I want to die of embarrassment.

Moments later he stops, his face turning serious. It's as if yesterday I were in his apartment, sleeping next to him in his bed, feeling like I was finally home.

"Oh, Eve," he says on an exhale. "You're probably carrying your books around like a good little nerd. Tell me you wear a backpack! Wait..." he pauses, moving back from me for a moment. "Are you as good in math as you are in English?" As usual, for Vincent, I always want to rise to the occasion. I nod my head *yes* excitedly, but then die a little inside that I do, in fact, have a backpack. I'm going to go home and throw it into the garbage.

"Is Vincent laughing? Holy shit, but I never thought I'd see the day!" Tom shakes his head in surprise while Claire's mouth hangs open.

"I laugh," Vincent says, his face like stone. "I just never laugh with you because, well, you aren't funny." It's clear Vincent is still angry over Tom's words from a few minutes ago.

"I am funny as hell. Claire, tell him how funny I've been tonight."

"You're hilarious," she deadpans, rolling her eyes as if he is the most unfunny guy she's ever met. Her eyes then move to mine, and they're saying: what the hell is going on here?

Vincent chuckles silently and turns back to me. "Okay, Ms. Brainiac. What's forty-seven times fifteen?"

"Seven hundred five," I reply. He looks at me with surprise but continues.

"One hundred twenty-two times seven plus forty-six?"

I picture the numbers in my head. "Nine hundred. That's easy, give me more." We're both laughing again, and I feel like we're inside this warm and gooey bubble. Everything and everyone outside of us is blurry and dull and... silent.

Wait a second. I look around and realize that the silence is not just in my head. Every single person in the kitchen is staring at us. I hear a voice say, "Who the hell is that?"

Before things can get more awkward, I turn to Claire, relieved that she didn't leave our side. "Vincent, do you know Claire?" He smiles at her and her face immediately falters. He outstretches his hand in a greeting.

"Hey." With only one word, her face changes from white to red. Honestly, it's not her fault. Looking at Vincent straight-on is hard to do without crumbling. Tom rolls his eyes at her inability to speak and throws a possessive arm over her shoulder.

"Tell me something, Claire," Vincent starts. "Seven thousand one hundred fifty divided by thirteen."

"Five hundred fifty. Why?" Her eyes bounce between Vincent and Tom. Claire may be gorgeous, but she's obviously wicked smart.

"Damn, you two girls deserve each other."

Some of Vincent's hair gets into his eyes and I'm yearning to push it off his face. Instead, I look away. *I shouldn't be doing this.*

"Yo, let's play quarters!" Tom grabs a bunch of beers and cups off the counter.

Claire takes my hand and pulls me toward the couch with a face
full of question. She glances back and forth between Vincent and me
as if she's trying to understand what is going on. I shrug because I
don't have any answers.

We drop down onto the *L*-shaped leather couch and the boys sit
on the bottom of the *L* so that we can all see each other. Tom
explains the rules of the game to me; we each get a chance to bounce
a quarter off the table and try to get it into one of the cups full of
beer. If you get your quarter into a cup, you choose who in the group
has to drink it. The boys keep getting their quarters in and making
Claire and me drink. Before I know it, we're drunk in the best
possible way. I feel free and relaxed as I laugh at something stupid
Tom says. The alcohol has thankfully shut my inner voice up. All I
can see and feel in this moment is a blissful buzz and Vincent's
warm gaze.

Soon enough, the game is forgotten as Tom begins telling us
stories about my economics professor, Ms. Williams. Apparently, she
used to dance in a cage at Exit, a huge dance club in the city.

"Yo Vincent, remember the moment you noticed it was your
professor dancing up there? Jesus...her tits! I was ready to fuckin' sign
up for college after that show!"

"You don't go here?" I ask.

"Nope. Just come out to party with this asshole."

I look back at Vincent and my laughter abruptly stops when I
glance down at his pants and confirm that he's carrying a gun. Other
people wouldn't notice, but I'm not other people. I was raised in the
hood. How the hell did I not realize in the bathroom just now? Or any
of the times we were together last year? Vincent muddles my brain.

The conversation is continuing, but I'm not listening anymore.
Terror starts to move through my body. His last name isn't just a
name; this is Vincent Borignone. My heart thumps so hard I feel sick.
He's killed people. He's a thug. Borignone mafia.

He notices the change in me and sits up to move closer. I lean
back, not wanting him to come any closer. The look on his face tells
me that he knows what I'm thinking; I forgot how easily Vincent is

able to read me. My eyes flicker down to his pants, and he slightly nods, letting me know that yes, he's carrying right now.

Shrill laughter breaks me out of my mental fog and seems to be coming from above me. I look up only to see a tall blonde teetering in her heels. It's like slow motion as she falls into me, about to turn me into party roadkill. But before she can crash down, Vincent jumps up, catching her mid-fall. How can a man so big be so agile?

He sets her straight and when she looks at him, she freezes. "Oh, um, hi Vincent." He dismisses her by turning his back and taking a seat next to me.

"You okay?" he whispers centimeters from my ear. I blink for a second longer than necessary, remembering what his lips feel like. Soft and warm, but so demanding. I'm in the midst of emotional whiplash right now.

"Stop eye-fucking my girl," Claire says with a giggle. "I know she's insanely hot, but keep it in the pants, would you?" He jumps away from me as if he's been slapped. Meanwhile, Tom is looking at him angrily.

I turn around, noticing that mostly everyone in the party is gone. I need to get out of here. Before I can say goodbye, Claire stands up.

"Why don't we all go out? The night is still young! Eve has an ID too, right? We can go wherever."

"We?" My eyes open wide.

Vincent laughs at my comment as if it were a joke. "Let's head over to Goldbar. I heard DMX is coming for Shaun Roses' birthday."

I turn to Claire, moving my head side to side in the universal gesture for *no*. Not one to take no for an answer apparently, Claire grabs my hand and pulls me toward the elevator. "Don't back out, Eve. This is once in a lifetime."

"But—

"No buts. We're gonna end up having the best night ever! Tom and Vincent are probably the most well-connected men in the city, and if you don't go, I can't go. Please come. I'll owe you!" She puts her hands up in prayer and I huff, looking up at the ceiling. I can't say no to her right now. I'm trying to be social. I'm trying to change my life around. Backing out of this would mean ending a brand-new friend-ship that I'm not ready to lose. I guess I could go and then leave once we get there. I can use the headache excuse.

"Fine," I reply dejectedly.

She jumps up and down excitedly as the guys walk over to us. Vincent cracks his knuckles, a serious look on his face.

We step into the elevator. Vincent is next to me, but I focus on when I'll state my excuse. Should I wait until we're at the bar?

Exiting the building, we wait on the dim corner for a moment when a long black Escalade pulls up to where we're standing. The driver steps out of the car and opens the door for us. Claire goes inside first and Tom jumps in behind her. I walk inside next, my heart leaping from my chest as Vincent sits directly next to me. Claire and Tom are in the third row, behind us, giving us privacy I wish we didn't have. The driver slams the door shut behind us.

The inside of the car is dark. I try to breathe slowly and concen-trate on my own heartbeat. When we stop at the next light, I'll use my headache excuse and ask to be taken back to the dorms. That's all. Vincent may be a liar with a girlfriend, but he would never hold me against my will, right? I stuff my hand into my purse and grip my phone. I need something to hold onto; it's like a lifeline right now. I try not to notice that Vincent's huge legs are spread wide on the seat, brushing against mine. I can sense from my side eye that he's turning toward me.

I quickly turn my head and look up. "Vincent—"

"Shhh," he replies, moving closer to me so our legs are flush. "Tonight, let's have fun. I'll explain everything later. Trust me, Eve." He puts his hands up, tucking some loose strands of hair behind my ear with so much intimacy, my heart squeezes.

Right on the heels of that feeling, indignation runs through my blood. How dare he touch me after what I've learned?

"What are you doing? Back off!" I whisper-yell. Maybe it's the darkness, but my outrage and resentment are finally coming through. I didn't sacrifice everything only to get sucked back into this life.

He sighs, physically moving back from me. "Let's just be us tonight. I want you to give me that."

"No," I huff. "I changed my mind. I can't do this. Take me home." I cross my hands over my chest, trying to protect myself.

"Come on. Just one night." His voice is tight; it's obvious he isn't accustomed to pleading. "DMX is playing. How can you say no to that?" His white teeth shine and I immediately want to knock them out.

"Vincent Borignone." I state his full name like a curse. "You're a liar! And I want to go home," I hiss.

"Don't say that. I told you I'd explain." He's angry now, sitting taller than a moment ago.

"What could you possibly say?" My words come out with fury. We both look behind us and see that Claire and Tom are making out in the back, seemingly oblivious to what's going on right in front of them.

Vincent straightens. "Can you turn up the volume, please?" he asks the driver.

"Yes, sir." Britney Spears' "I'm a Slave For You" gets louder.

"Tonight, let everything go. I swear to God. I swear to Jesus. I'll explain everything to you later, okay? Don't go back on your word. You should trust me, after everything I've done for you."

"You're kidding, right? How dare you throw our past in my face?"

His entire demeanor sets in a hard line. This man isn't going to play fair and it's clear he isn't above using everything in his arsenal to get what he wants. He's right, though. He saved my life. I owe him.

"Fine." I angle my body toward the window. I may go out with him tonight, but that doesn't mean I have to enjoy it.

4

VINCENT

SHE PULLS the tie out of her hair and her hair falls in waves, draping around her small shoulders. I'm immediately assaulted by a sweet coconut scent blended with something uniquely Eve.

"Your hair...it got even longer. I love it like this." Even though I know that Tom and Claire aren't listening to us, I'll use their existence as an excuse to get closer. I watch her take a sharp breath as I bring my hand to her hair, gently pushing it aside to see her beautiful neck.

She stares out the window, the softness of her profile melting my insides. Her nose is small and slightly turned up, lips full, hair dark and natural...everything about her, on a physical level, works for me. I know I don't deserve it, but if she's willing to say yes, I'm not going to turn it away just because I had to bring up some hard shit to get her to agree. I'll explain everything to her later, but before I do, I need to remind her how good we are together.

I'm waiting for her to look back at me, but she doesn't. I'm not a patient man, and I have zero tolerance for being ignored.

"Eve." My voice comes out harshly, but it works. She finally moves her head, and everything is written clearly on her face; I have no choice but to pause. Does she know how obvious her love is? How pure? It takes my goddamn breath away and makes me curse who I am and where I come from. How can I see a woman like this, after all she's been through, and bring her back into my world of violence? Would she ever accept my life?

I always loved women. Being with Daniela had zero bearing on my extracurricular activities. I live in New York City, not some small town in Nebraska; there's no shortage of pussy here. But Eve was never the kind of girl who would just be a regular fuck. I knew it the moment I first laid eyes on her. I had only just met her and immediately brought her to one of my restaurants. I think there was a part of me that was always looking for her. And the moment our eyes met, everything clicked in place.

The vehicle stops and the driver jumps out, opening our door. We all exit the car and immediately walk to the front of the long line, my huge hand holding her tiny one as we step forward. She squeezes my palm nervously and I look down at her. "I've got you." She looks at me and slightly nods, seemingly reassured. She believes she's safe with me. Again, I ask myself, what the fuck am I doing?

"Vincent, what up man?"

I fist bump the enormous bouncer who I'd guess weighs over two-fifty. He moves to the side as he opens the red-velvet rope. I turn to Eve as we step into the club, noticing the wide-eyed look on her face as if she's never seen something so beautiful. Just like its name, the entire bar is gold. The walls are lined with golden skulls and even the drapes are gold. Giant crystal chandeliers hang from the ceiling, giving the place a warm glow.

We're ushered to a private table in the back with a perfect view of the dance floor. Eve and I sit together on one side, Claire and Tom on the other. Eve is watching raptly as half-naked bodies gyrate to the music in front of us; I take her hand, rubbing my thumb across her knuckles.

The table server saunters over to us in a tiny bikini top and shorts, her tits and ass pouring out of both. She bends down seductively, placing a large golden bucket on our table filled with bottles of vodka and glass jugs of cranberry and orange juice. She pauses before walking away, her eyes flaring with interest. Once upon a time, I'd take this woman up on her offer. We both know that with a nod, I could get this woman on her knees in the club's back room. The entire thing—like almost everything in life—is a transaction. She wants my dick, and I feel horny. One plus one equals two. Crazy how over the last twelve months, just the idea of a woman other than the beauty next to me is enough to turn my stomach.

"Can I get you something?" She slowly scrapes a long fingernail against the back of my neck. I grab her wrist, probably harder than necessary, turning my head so I'm staring at her hard.

"Don't touch me." Her eyes widen in fear. Finally, when I'm good and ready, I let her go. She scurries away.

I turn to Eve then, but her eyes are still trained on the dance floor. I'm glad she didn't catch that exchange with the waitress; most of these women are disrespectful as fuck. They don't deserve to breathe the same air as my girl. Dropping a hand on her leg and gently caressing her thigh, she turns to me, biting her lip, as if she's conflicted. She probably doesn't want to enjoy herself, but the music is amazing and the crowd is hot.

Still, this girl, she fills me up inside exactly how I need. Yeah, she's seen some bad shit. But somehow, she's maintained this... *innocence*. She may be better than a man like me deserves, but now that I've got her, there's no way I'm letting her go again. I want to do right by her, but I'm not a fuckin' saint.

She inches closer to me. "So, DMX, huh?" Her face is so expectant I have to hold myself back from not throwing my arms around her and mauling her right here at the table. I shift my body, adjusting my dick in my jeans. She has no idea how special she is. Other girls would be sitting on my lap, trying to do whatever they could to keep my interest. They'd be asking me what they could do for me. They'd beg to meet DMX. But Eve isn't other girls.

Instead of saying all of these things, I reply with one word: "Yes."

"Vincent..." she takes a deep breath, looking as if she's ready to go off on a rant. I stop her with a hand on her thigh.

"Shut that brain of yours off tonight. A promise is a promise, Eve." I move to the edge of the couch and pour three shot glasses of vodka. I hand one glass to her and pick the other two up for myself.

"Are you asking me not to think, Vincent? Because any time a man asks a woman not to think—"

"I'm not asking you. I'm telling you." I can't take my eyes off her. I go ahead and throw back one drink, waiting patiently for her to take hers. "I dare you, Eve," I say with a joking smile, trying to bring the moment down a notch. It isn't easy for me to be playful, but I want to be.

She purses her lips, doing her best not to laugh. "Listen. If I take this drink, it's not because you're daring me." She raises an eyebrow.

"No?" She wants to play? I'll play.

"No." Her lips slightly pucker at the end of the word, and I can't help but stare at them. "It's because I'm in college now, and I can drink if I want to. Understand?" Her attitude and this newfound strength only turns me on more.

"By all means, college girl. Be free to experiment." I pause. "But only with me, when I can make sure you're safe."

"I can take care of myself, Vincent. I've been through a lot, in case you've forgotten."

"I haven't forgotten anything. Not even a minor detail." I pause, looking her up and down until her face heats. "But getting drunk in a place where someone can easily spike your drink? That's not experimenting. That's just stupid."

She clears her throat. "So, right now, you're giving me this drink because?" She cocks that gorgeous head of hers to the side, waiting for my response.

"Because I want you to relax and let go a bit. Have some of that college fun you deserve. *Safely.*"

She lifts the glass to her pouty lips, swallowing the drink. Her face scrunches from the burn and I hand her a lemon. She takes a bite and breathes a sigh of relief.

"L-listen, Vincent." Her earlier bravado turns to hesitation. "I know you took care of some stuff for me in the past. But I'm not that girl anymore, okay? I'm not looking for someone to run my life. And I sure as hell am not trying to get wrapped up in your... family business. I spent close to nineteen years running away from that shit, and I'm not getting brought back into it—"

"—And I'm not looking to drag you into something you don't want. I helped you out, as a friend. You don't owe me anything, understand? I brought it up in the car because I wanted you to come out with me tonight. I felt like seeing you. Not because I wanted compensation."

She nods, letting out a relieved exhale. A better man may feel guilty for lying, but not me. Killing Carlos was never for the sake of friendship. Every punch and kick—until he was writhing in his own blood on the floor—every ounce of heat I gave that fucker with my fists, was payback. He thought he could torment my woman, nearly rape her, and get away with it? I made him pay like the dirty snake he was. I'm still the son of Antonio Borignone. And no one fucks with me and mine.

She lifts her face. "Can we have some fun now?"

Tom drops next to me, growling in my ear. "This bitch has you by the fucking balls, Borignone. Stop this shit!" He's seething.

I want to grab his throat, tell him if he ever speaks to me like that again, I'll put a bullet in his head. But Eve is next to me looking so happy, and there's no way I'd jeopardize that. I swallow down my anger, focusing on her instead.

Standing, I bring her with me to the center of the dance floor. She's got great rhythm, so obviously comfortable in her own skin when she's dancing. It's at odds with her regular shyness. I can tell she's holding back for now, and I can't wait until she lets go.

I maintain a slight distance, which is difficult for me; I always take what I want. But with Eve, I've always held back. The arrogant prick inside me knows that with her, everything needs to be different. I've gotta shut up and wait.

Song after song comes and goes, and we don't stop moving. It's

Eminem. We're still not close enough, but I can see her body relaxing. We're in our own orbit; I'm going to keep us here for as long as I can.

The song changes again and then again. It's "In Da Club" by 50 Cent. His gravel voice blares from the speakers and the entire dance floor cheers. We're sweating, and her cheeks are flushing pink. My eyes rove around her small and curvy body. She's wearing a simple cotton tank top with a white lacy bra underneath, but holy shit if it's not sexier than all of these girls who are walking around half nude. Her hair is down and free, the way I love it.

She finally takes a step closer, letting me know I don't have to keep a distance. I bring my arms around her and we immediately fall into step. How is it possible I can connect with someone in this way? My arms move to her small waist and she turns her body so her back is against my front. She's sweating, and it makes her scent more acute. My dick hardens. Eve may have been a book nerd for her entire life, but it's obvious she was made to dance. I stay with her, keeping control of our movements but at the same time giving her room to do her own thing.

She turns. "Vincent, I want another drink," she yells happily over the music.

I pull her back through the crowd to get to the table, immediately pouring three more shots. I hand her another drink, taking the other two for myself.

She's about to grab it from my hands when I pull it back. "You don't have to finish this, okay? Just a sip."

Smirking at me in defiance, she lifts it up and swallows the whole thing down. I shake my head as I give her a slice of lemon, watching her teeth sink into the bitterness. She lifts her shoulders, daring me to stop her. I can only laugh as I quickly shoot down my own drinks. I've been drinking alcohol for so many years now, it would take another five to get me drunk.

We're back on the dance floor when she starts giggling, leaning on me. She may think she doesn't need anyone, but why fight through life alone when you can have back up?

DMX gives the crowd his signature growl, and the entire room instantly starts screaming with excitement. I feel someone push against me. I open my eyes to look around, noticing the dance floor is completely full. I wrap my arms around Eve's shoulders protectively, making sure she's safe and comfortable. Somehow, we've landed ourselves in a mosh pit.

She's jumping up and down in excitement. I chuckle at her exuberance. Some guys bump into us and I turn my head quickly, glaring. They move to the side, but within a few minutes, the crowd grows aggressive. Eve won't feel comfortable in this.

She starts to lose her footing as people continue to push forward, trying to get closer to the stage. She looks at me with an anxiety-filled face and I immediately walk us off the packed floor.

The moment we get to the table, she starts in a rush. "I'm sorry. I couldn't. It was too much—"

I push an errant hair from her face and she quiets. "Don't ever apologize." I turn to Tom while Eve hangs on my side. He's staring at us, an angry look on his face. "Yo, Tom. We're out." He stands up to shake my hand goodbye; I squeeze his as hard as I can, letting him know without words that he and I have shit to discuss later. I know he's only thinking of the best for me, but if he ever disrespects my girl again, I'll make him pay.

Eve and I walk out of the club. The cool air feels good. I'm about to take out my phone to call the driver when Eve, seemingly out of the blue, says, "I'm lost." She lifts her hand to her lips, surprised that she said that out loud.

I turn to her. "No, baby. I found you, remember?" She stares up at me, all purity and trust. I need to get us out of here.

I pull out my phone from my jacket pocket and type to the driver to come get us. Her eyes are trained on my face; she's studying me. Never in my life have I given a fuck about my looks. I know women like what they see, but my face was never something I had to work for and therefore, it's not something I'm particularly proud of. But the way Eve is looking at me now—memorizing every feature of my face —makes me want to give God a high five.

"Your mom was Native American, right? You look it." She blushes. She's drunk, staring at me with wide eyes like I created the damn universe in four days. I do my best to resist the urge to lift her into my arms.

I put my phone away and pull my jacket off, draping it around her tiny shoulders. It hangs on her, falling to the middle of her calves.

"Tell me you have a coat." I pull the sides of my jacket around her so that the wind won't get through. It's not too cold, but she definitely isn't dressed warmly enough for a fall New York City night.

"Yeah, I do. I just bought a new coat from Barneys yesterday at the bargain price of five hundred dollars," she deadpans.

I chuckle. "Five hundred? Is that it?" She pulls my jacket closer to her body, smelling the collar and tightly shutting her eyes.

The black Escalade pulls up. As the driver moves to get out of the car, I shake my head, letting him know to stay put. Eve is mine tonight, and I want to be the one to hold the door for her. I open it and she climbs inside first. Taking a look at her perfect heart-shaped ass, I groan at all the things I wish I could do. I follow in behind her and shut the door as I sit inside. Without another word, the car heads downtown.

"Are we going to your SoHo apartment?" She clasps her hands together nervously. The last time I brought her to my place downtown, she opened up to me about Carlos. Hopefully tonight, I'll be able to have another honest conversation with her.

Moving my hands around her waist, I pull her to sit on my lap. She leans her head in the crook of my neck and shoulder as if it were the most natural thing in the world. When her eyes shut, I feel relief like I've never known. How can she fit so well in my arms? I ask myself for the hundredth time, what the fuck am I doing? Normally, I'm calculated. I don't do shit without thinking it all through. Consequences. Positive outcomes. Potential disasters. I'm a numbers and logic man. And this? This is something I never do: *emotion*.

We get to my building. The doorman holds the door and I strut through, Eve following right behind me. I still haven't said a word to her since we got into the car. Standing together in the elevator, she barely reaches the center of my chest. She's biting her lip, and fuck if I don't want to throw her against the wall right now.

We step off and walk to my door, where I type my security codes. Before pushing the door open, I pause to take a look at Eve and wonder if I'm not about to make an enormous mistake. She stares at me with absolute trust, and I know that I can't stop myself. I want this woman.

5

EVE

I WANT to act like he's the same Vincent I used to know, but he isn't. The Vincent I used to know wasn't this dangerous looking, was he? I look down at his pants again, noticing the outline of his gun. God, help me. How can I be so afraid, but so turned on at the same time?

We get inside and I try not to let my jaw drop at his perfect apartment. It's just as beautiful as I remember. We step into his open kitchen area, and he leaves his keys on the marble countertop. Grabbing two cold bottles of water from the fridge, he opens the cap before handing me one. I take a deep pull, letting the cold water wet my dry throat.

He said we'd discuss everything. Is that why he brought me here? To tell me about Daniela? I can't handle it. I don't think I'd survive if he told me he loves her. If he told me that I was a mistake. If he told me he never meant to hurt me, or some other bullshit. It's bad enough to hear about Daniela through the gossip mill and it's even worse to see them together. But to hear about their relationship from Vincent's perfect lips? It would break me. I'd rather just pretend we aren't at school together; move on and let what we had be a good memory. He can continue being the hot guy on campus, and I can keep my head in the books.

We stare at each other, time seemingly suspended. I'm desperate for him not to tell me more than I already know. How can I stop this conversation from happening? I notice his pupils starting to dilate and the quickening of his breath.

At once, we both step toward each other. I look up into his face when he lifts me in his arms. Before I change my mind, I press my lips against his. He pulls away, his eyes searching mine. I slightly nod my head. He starts by slowly kissing every piece of my lips as if I'm something to be savored.

When his tongue finally enters my mouth, I grab a fistful of his hair and moan. It must register with him how badly I want this because with that sound he finally starts to kiss me like his life depends on it. He consumes me with his mouth, moving to my neck as he nudges my legs wider to make room for his hips.

"You're shaking," he tells me between kisses. I feel out of my mind.

I'm hot. Cold. Soaked.

He moves his hands down my legs, pulling the shoes off my feet. They clatter like dead weights onto the wooden floor. I'm trembling like it's twenty below. He presses my body against the wall while he pulls his shirt over his head with one arm. My heart hammers. His body heat is off the charts. My hands move on their own accord up to his massive shoulders and down along his sides. I pull in a hard breath as I trace the gorgeous V-shape of his back.

"Get this off," he demands, tugging at my shirt.

I try to get myself out of my tank top, but it gets stuck on my arm. "There we go," he says as he untangles the fabric and lifts it up. I groan in relief, grabbing his hair with my hands and pulling him to my mouth again. I can't help myself.

He hums, and I feel the vibration straight into my core. His fingers graze over my nipples, up and down, until they're hardened peaks. My bra is on, but the cotton is so thin I can feel the roughness of the calluses against my sensitive skin. I want to tear my clothes off. I want direct contact. My lower belly clenches in anticipation.

He finally unhooks my bra, roughly pulling it off my shoulders and stopping with a hiss, taking me in with his hooded eyes. "My memory doesn't do you justice. Jesus Christ, Eve. You're fucking perfect. Perfect." His mouth lowers over my bare nipple and with his first hard suck, tremors instantly wrack my body. "Ahhhh!"

"Always so responsive to me." He moves his mouth to my other breast and I try to contain the pleasure. It's almost too much. I bite the side of my cheek, wanting to stay quiet.

"Moan for me, baby. I need to hear you. No one here but us." As if I have a choice! I'm gripping the back of his shoulders as the fire inside me rages.

He lifts his mouth, letting his thumbs graze against my neck. "Tell me, Eve, has anyone other than me touched you?" I can't manage a reply; it all feels too good.

He stops moving. "Answer me."

"N-no."

He moves his nose into my neck, scenting me as he pushes his hardness into my core. "You're mine, do you understand?"

"Vincent!" I cry, screwing my eyes shut.

6

VINCENT

With the moan of my name from her lips, I'm brought back to reality. I pull my mouth away. *You can't do this,* my mind echoes. I stare at her face, flushed from her high cheekbones down to her perfect cherry nipples. I want this so bad, but I need to control myself. It takes her a few seconds to realize that I've stopped. At first, her eyes open wide with so much joy...

And then she blinks.

The realization that something is wrong moves through her face. She must see remorse is written all over me because her smile falls.

"Eve," I pant, dropping my head into her neck, trying to slow myself down. She places her small hands behind my head, holding me close. She's comforting me when she should be slapping me across the face.

"W-what happened?" She looks at me openly, her eyes and body so full of tenderness that it makes my knees weak. I touch her face, smoothing out the stress lines on her forehead. I'm angry that she'll allow me to do this to her when she deserves so much more. I haven't even explained things yet!

"I'm not going to fuck you like this, here against the wall." My voice comes out harsher than I intended. I sigh, telling myself to calm down. "That's not who you are."

I set her down on the floor and she immediately bends down, picking up her crumpled clothes. Her dark hair is wild, draped around her shoulders and covering the tops of her breasts. She slides her shivering arms into her threadbare bra, hands moving to her back to shut the clasp. This is my fault.

I step behind her, gently hooking her bra together. Her body trembles, literally shakes like a leaf, while I put her shirt back on, adjusting her straps so they aren't tangled.

I need to talk to her. We need to be open and she needs to know what's going on. The time for withholding truth is over. If she and I have any hope for the future, we have to go about this the right way, with honesty.

"There are obviously things I didn't tell you. I need to start by saying that I shouldn't have given you those drinks. Tonight was entirely my fault. I was hoping for a little more time with you before I had to bring all of this shit up." I shut my mouth tightly, breathing through my nose.

Her head is down as if she's embarrassed by her behavior. Doesn't she realize that this isn't one-sided?

"Eve, don't put your head down." I take her hand, bringing her to my couch. I maneuver us so that the height difference isn't as pronounced. I want her to feel like an equal.

"You're Vincent Borignone," she says, biting the side of her quivering lip. "I need to get out of here." She makes a move to turn away, but I hold her in place. I move my thumb to her cheek, brushing the tears off with the pads of my thumbs. Her huge brown eyes have turned into a honey hazel blend. "How could I do that, Vincent? How could I, and how could you?" She starts to cry in earnest and I bring her closer to me.

"Don't cry, baby. I swear to you, I understand. What we have is difficult to control. What happened tonight was my fault, all right? Blame me."

"And you're...you've got a—"

"You heard things, right? About me? And Daniela, too. What do you think you know? Tell me everything, Eve, and we'll sort it out together. The time for secrets is behind us now." I'm waiting for her to break down and tell me everything she knows. And then I want to wrap her up in my arms and tell her the entire dirty truth.

She sniffles, trying to catch her breath. "You have a g-girlfriend. Your father is Antonio. You're B-Borignone mafia."

"The internet, and Daniela, in particular, have a way of molding reality. She is very talented at giving just enough honesty in her photography that the lies become camouflaged."

"Vincent—I don't want to know, okay? I've learned enough through the gossip mill and the internet."

"So, you used to hide behind your sister and your books, and you're trying to continue that? Eve, you can't live in darkness. If we're going to figure this shit out between us, you need to open your eyes—"

"Figure shit out between us? There is no *us*, Vincent."

This girl is mine. She can deny it all she wants, but I know what we have. "You think I'm letting you go again?"

"And what is that supposed to mean? You. Don't. Have. Me." She punctuates every word, but I hear the pain in her undertone.

"We're both here at school together. I'll never be okay with us pretending like the other doesn't exist."

"I don't want to hear it!" Her chest rises and falls with her heavy breathing. "I don't want to learn about how you treated me like I was y-your whore."

Her tears keep falling, but she doesn't stop. "I can't find out more about it because then, everything I believed we had would feel like a lie. I thought we had something; when really, I was nothing to you! You knew me, but I didn't know you. Did you see my mother and think, 'well, she's just like her?'"

"No—"

"You had a girlfriend the entire time! You turned me into a

cheater, Vincent! I can't find out more. If you care about me at all, you'll just leave it as a good memory, and move on." She is slashing herself with her words, but I'm the one who sharpened the knife. I need to find a way to dull the edge.

I move closer to her, opening my hands in front of my chest. "Eve. I swear to all that is holy that I never saw you that way. Look into my eyes and trust me. Let me just explain—"

My words come too late; her pain is obviously spiraling. "I can't believe how stupid I was! And you let me be the idiot. I can just imagine, rich and gorgeous Vincent Borignone. Standing in my shitty stairwell with the lights flickering..." She lets out a sardonic laugh. "I've seen countless men do this to my mother. But you would know that already, wouldn't you? She does work as a stripper in one of your—"

I lift my hand, stopping her. "No. You don't deserve to feel like I treated you like trash. I won't allow you to think poorly about what we had." The thought of never touching her again turns my chest hollow. But I calm myself, needing to continue. "I will not let you believe that your first experiences with a man, with me, were tainted. What we had wasn't a damn lie!"

She looks at me, fury surrounding her. "You won't *allow* me?"

I grit my teeth. "I will not." I wait, letting it sink in that there's no way I'm going to walk away from this. From us. "I see how you may think Daniela and I are together on social media. And yeah, we used to fuck." She winces, but I don't let it stop me from speaking the truth. "But things are complicated with us. If you'd just let me—"

I move forward, trying to touch her again. But the way she's staring at my eyes makes it clear that she wants nothing to do with me right now. Eve stands up off the couch, backing away. Even though every part of me is telling me to grab her and force her to listen, I don't want to hurt her any more than I already have. Maybe she needs a few days to process. She got a little drunk tonight, and I want her to be straight when she hears me out.

She turns her angelic face toward the ceiling, trying to look anywhere but at me. "I get it," she hiccups, still refusing my eyes. "You're the king and queen of New York and all that, right? How could you throw something like that away for someone like me?"

"No one is the king and queen of shit," I yell. "Like I said before, it's a lot more complicated than that. It's family business." I try to soften my voice at the end, but nothing is working. I'm not used to feeling so out of control; I hate it.

"Oh, that's great!" she replies sarcastically. "Family business. Let's add that to the list, huh? You're Vincent Borignone, a member of the hardest mafia on the East Coast! You think I don't know what *family business* means?"

"Maybe I'm an associate?"

"Don't give me that bullshit, Vincent. I see how strong and powerful and smart you are! You belong to the family, and they aren't dumb. They probably see you as their golden ticket! And as the son of Antonio—"

"Well, let's start with this," I tell her firmly. "You're right. I'm not just a member. The entire family operation? It's going to be mine one day. All the illegal shit we do? The drugs, the guns? I am my father's right hand." My chest heaves. "And you want to know something crazy? Ever since I met you, I knew I needed and wanted to make a serious change in my life!" I step closer to her, feeling the emotion run through me. "Because of you, I've been in the process of trying to change everything." I yell, my voice echoing around the room.

Instead of backing down, she rises up to me. "Why is it so important to you for me to know the truth? Why do you even care? Let's just stay away from each other. Let the past stay in the past where it belongs."

"Why?" I grumble, my teeth clenched. "Because I fucking lo— " I stop myself, exhaling. "You call to me on a hundred different levels. Because who you are has meaning in my life." I pause, gripping the ends of my hair. "When I thought I'd never see you anymore, the memory of you still mattered. What you stand for matters. Do you understand?" I point to my own chest. "The idea of you walking away from me. Ignoring me. Falsely believing that I took advantage of you last year. I won't have it. This apartment? It's mine and mine alone. No one other than my father, Tom, and my driver knows that it exists. You're the only other person I've ever brought here. You're the only woman who has ever put her head on that pillow. You aren't a side piece. Since the day I met you, you have been the *only* fucking piece!"

I look down at the ground for a moment, clenching my fists. "You've risked your life to get out of that shitty fucking universe you lived in. And I swore to myself then that I'd stay away from you because I didn't want to bring you back down the rabbit hole. But then tonight," I sigh, dropping my head in my hands for a moment. "You showed up. If you think I'm giving up on us now, you're wrong. I let go of you once, and I'm not making that same mistake again."

She opens and closes her mouth a few times, but she doesn't speak.

My phone pings with a text. I lift it from the side table. It's a 9-1-1 from Jimmy. "Fuck!" I roar. "I gotta take you home." I press my lips into a firm line. I've got no choice but to answer this. If a brother needs me, I'm there.

She moves to put on her shoes and I walk into my bedroom, pulling out one of my dark hoodies. It'll probably fall to her knees, but it'll keep her warmer than that thin tank she's got on. When I get into the living room, she's sitting on the couch with her knees up to her chin. I bend over to slide it over her head, pulling her hair through the hood while she threads her arms inside. I realize that she's in somewhat of a shock right now, and I immediately feel like shit. I want to protect her, not hurt her. What have I done?

We get downstairs and my car is waiting for us. She's silent. This time, I don't press my leg against hers. Our conversation will have to wait a few days until she processes what she's learned tonight. I need time with her, without any distractions.

The car pulls up in front of the freshman quad and I put my hand on the door, stopping her from leaving. There's a lot I want to say, but my head is too full. I watch as she shuts her eyes tightly, a lone tear sliding down her beautiful face.

I finally move my hand off the door. She steps out and walks to her dorm, not looking back. I slam my hand on the passenger seat. "Fuck!" I yell. "Take me to Jimmy's," I order the driver.

"Yes, Mr. Borignone."

7

EVE

I CRY MYSELF TO SLEEP, fisting my navy sheets. I feel like I'm melting from the heat, but I refuse to take his sweatshirt off. It smells like him —and even though part of me wants to shred the sweatshirt with my bare hands and burn it—just the thought of removing it from my body makes me cry even harder.

In my heart, I know Vincent has good intentions. He wants to make sure I understand what happened. He doesn't ever want me to believe falsehood. But what if he tells me he was fucking her the entire time he saw me? How am I supposed to know he isn't going to tell me something equally as horrible? I spent a year wishing he'd be open and honest, and now all I want to do is beg him to keep his mouth shut.

Finally, my body drifts into a restless sleep.

Sometime later, I hear a hard knock at my door. At first, I hear it in my dreams, but after a few bangs, I spring out of bed. Squinting at the clock, it's one o'clock in the afternoon. I stumble to my door and open it, rubbing the sleep from my eyes.

"Eve? I've been calling your phone all morning. Thank God you're here and not at Vincent's!"

Claire barges into my bedroom, shutting the door behind us. "Vincent." Her eyes practically bug out of her head. "Eve. You and Vincent!" She's practically bouncing on the soles of her feet, actively waiting for a reply.

"What are you staring at me like that for? I just woke up and I've been here all night, okay? Calm down."

"Well, if I didn't know better, I'd say that man wants you. Badly. He couldn't take his eyes off you all night! By the way, DMX was sick! But whatever. Wash up. Let's go out to eat and talk!" She looks me up and down, noticing the large black sweatshirt I'm wearing. I ignore her stare. For all she knows, it's my brother's.

She makes herself at home in the chair by my desk and pulls out a book from her enormous purse. I stare at her in confusion, but she isn't minding me. After a moment, she lifts her head. "Move it, Eve, and get your ass to the bathroom. I'm staaaarving."

I let myself out of the room, too emotionally exhausted to argue.

Under the shower spray, my mind plays back last night's events. Vincent. Vincent. Vincent. His lips. His hands. Dancing. Our fight. His half admission of love. What am I going to do? He wants to talk. He wants to tell me everything so there won't be any more secrets. Is he going to tell me about the family business with Daniela? And do I even want to know the truth? I've spent my life trying to stay away from that bullshit. How is this happening to me?

I walk back into the room physically refreshed, but still unsure what I'm supposed to tell Claire. I change on autopilot, lost in my own head.

She's so engrossed in her book that she barely registers I'm ready to go. I glance at the cover of the paperback she's reading and my eyes widen in surprise. It's a hot guy with a naked torso, covered in tattoos.

"What are you reading?" I ask, suppressing a chuckle.

She slams her book shut, turning red. "Um, nothing..."

"Tell me you're reading porn right now." I bite the side of my cheek, doing my best not to burst into laughter.

"It's not porn! It's really good actually!" I move closer to read the cover when she hides the book behind her back. "It's about this guy in a motorcycle club...and...this girl, well, she was a stripper at first, but then—" She stops talking and we burst into hysterics.

We leave the room to head over to the dining hall on campus. We both need coffee and greasy food badly. Taking a small booth in the back, my stomach growls louder than I thought possible. Claire tells me she'll get the food and I should grab the coffee in order to save time.

The cashier gives me a face when she takes my dining card for the two coffees as if she's annoyed to be helping some hungover rich kid whose daddy makes sure she has enough money in her account each month. I want to tell her that I'm not like that at all; I'm here on full scholarship and the school pays for my food—I'm not some rich asshole. Instead, I just thank her as graciously as I can manage, and walk back to our booth, holding both our mugs of coffee.

Claire sits down right after me, setting a green tray in front of us. Relief settles in my stomach as I unwrap a gigantic egg-and-cheese sandwich, immediately taking a huge bite. While I'm chewing, I pour a small packet of creamer into my coffee mug and watch the color turn from black to light brown. I put the cup to my lips and hum. "Ah, coffee."

"Okay, Eve. I'm ready. Tell me everything." Claire's eyes are shining with excitement as she scoots forward in her seat. Even though I'm a private person, I feel like I can trust her with at least a general outline of events. And the truth is, I'm relieved to have a friend to share this with. Everything has gotten so complicated, and I want support. I know that I need to come clean with Janelle, too.

I clear my throat. "Well, me and Vincent met one night in the Meatpacking District last year. And we ended up going out a few times."

Her eyes widen in shock with my admission. I could have told her I had dinner with the President and she probably wouldn't be as shocked. "Wait. Vincent Borignone took you out? Like, on dates?"

"Um, I guess so?" I stop and look around, making sure no one is eavesdropping. Luckily, everyone around us seems to be busy in their own conversations. "I asked him once what we were doing, but he just said we're *friends*." I shrug. "Look, we have this weird connection. He's gorgeous, but with him, it's more than that. I had no clue that he went to school here! And I definitely didn't know he had a girlfriend."

She breathes in deeply, sucking her bottom lip into her mouth. "Look, Eve. There's a lot I need to tell you because clearly, you don't have a clue. You've looked him up though, right?" She lifts the salt, shaking it over her eggs.

"Yeah." I nod. "I finally did, after lunch that day when I met the girls in Phi Alpha."

"Ah. That's why you ran out." She nods in understanding.

"Listen, we all talk about Vincent all the time because of how hot he is. And yes, there are rumors about his mafia connections. But Eve"—she lowers her voice and moves closer to me—"I don't think they're just rumors. They say he's the son of the biggest mobster in Manhattan! And there must be a grain of truth to that, right? I mean, otherwise, why would that rumor even start? And honestly, look at him! He's scary as fuck! And, Daniela, she's been with him since her freshman year. I guess that's three years now—and to my knowledge, they've never been on a break. I mean, have you seen her social media accounts? Millions of followers!" She's rushing to get the words out.

I feel the need to defend myself. "I didn't even know his last name until lunch! How would I have known he had a girlfriend?"

She lets out a breath but continues. "You know that she's a socialite, right? Her father owns a huge bank in Central America. They're billionaires. Her parents had a Debutant Ball for her at the University Club when she turned eighteen, and people said it was insane! They're not just a college golden couple. They're like, a global golden couple." Her green eyes turn to gray as my face drops. It's obvious that she isn't enjoying this.

"I'm telling you this because you need to know that they aren't"— she takes a breath, thinking of the right word—"*ordinary*. And it's obvious you and Vincent were into each other last night, but trust me, her claws are in him deep. And if Daniela ever found out about whatever went on last year between you guys, let's just say your life would be made into a living hell. She'd make sure you were black-balled from all of Greek life and probably every restaurant and club in New York City. Maybe even beyond that."

My throat tightens. I'm shaking from the anxiety of what I may have gotten myself into. Vincent knows I'm here and he isn't going to stop until he talks to me. He's nothing if not persistent.

"I'll take last night and our conversation to the grave, okay? Don't worry." Looking into her face, I see her honesty.

"But, I really didn't know—"

"I know. Let's change the subject now, yeah? Just promise me you'll stay away from him. Seriously, nothing good can come of it."

I nod my head in agreement, and we spend the rest of our break-fast discussing classes and how to get the best outlines. Apparently, Phi Alpha has an entire room dedicated to notes and exams from almost every professor at school.

When we're done eating, I hug Claire goodbye and get back to my room to crack open my books.

Around eleven o'clock that night, I get a call from Janelle. "Hey, love. How's it going?"

I let out a sigh and move to my bed, swallowing back the tears that are resurfacing in my throat. "I don't know. Something's come up and..." My heart starts to pound. "There's a lot I need to tell you."

"Okay. Now or in person?" Her voice is full of anxiety.

"In person."

"We'll do that. How have classes been this week? I hate hearing you sound miserable. Things were so good the last time we spoke."

I sniffle. "I actually made a new friend and she's pretty cool. Her name is Claire. But she's in this sorority and most of the girls seem like bitches. I'm not used to this..."

"Just take it easy," she says soothingly. "It's okay to have harder days. Nothing is ever simple. But this is what you've been waiting for. Just take it day by day and keep your eye on the prize. Your life isn't just a wish anymore. It's happening. Remember that, okay?" I feel the tears welling up heavily in my eyes, and I know if I open my mouth again, the dam will burst. The last thing I want is for her to worry, so I keep my mouth shut.

"Have you spoken to Ms. Levine? I bet she can help you with what you're feeling. She told me that you'd probably go through something like this at some point." I drop my head and breathe in and out, and the tears start to drop. I want to tell her about Vincent. No, I need to tell her. I can't keep it in anymore. But it can't be over the phone.

"Janelle, are you free tomorrow night for dinner?"

"Yes. And don't cry, Eve, okay? We'll be together and everything will be all right." I hear the kindness in her voice, and it makes my heart squeeze. She's always got my back.

"O-kay," I manage to stutter out.

"Cool. I'll be at your dorm at five. Let's also stop at Bed Bath, get some shit to make your room more like a home. That's bound to help, right? Go to sleep now. Everything will look better in the morning." She hangs up, and I curl into my bed and stare at the wall, images of Daniela and Vincent shifting in front of my eyes like a movie reel.

8

Vincent

TOM and I leave the meeting together. It's only ten at night, but I'm so tired it may as well be three in the morning.

"Let's hang out and order some food. I'm starving." He opens a pack of cigarettes, grumbling when he realizes the box is empty.

"No. I need to be alone," I tell him seriously. I keep wondering how Eve is doing. I want to run into her room and force her to talk, but I shouldn't. She has to calm down before I speak with her. And something tells me that after our discussion last night, a few days off from me is the right move.

"Vince," he says emphatically, a nervous look on his face. I cock an eyebrow. Tom only shortens my name when he's broaching a sore subject. "I still can't believe that Eve is actually here in school with us. What are the fuckin' chances? I mean, shit, I know you told me how smart she is. But there are so many other schools. I mean, fuck. Talk about a turn of events. We've gotta discuss this."

I let out a grunt. After the shit that went down between Carlos and I, I had no choice but to tell Tom about Eve and what happened between us. I needed him to do some damage control for me since I didn't kill Carlos on behalf of the family. Tom may be family, but he isn't Antonio's son, and he isn't in the inner circle—not yet, anyway. He can get away with more than I can. Ending the life of the sergeant of arms for a gang—even if it's only a pissant street gang, would be a declaration of war if it came from me.

It took a long time, but I was finally accepting Eve was good and truly gone from my life. In my head, she was off at some great school, living her dreams in safety and maybe even wearing the Uggs I bought her. And even though I felt like I gave up something bigger than the world as I knew it, I told myself that so long as she was doing well, it was enough for me. It had to be. I'd eventually get out from under Daniela's thumb, get off the East Coast, and maybe one day, have a chance with Eve again.

But all that came crashing down around me when I saw her at the party last night. I seriously just couldn't believe it. And God, she's so beautiful. I wish I kept her in my bed, head on my pillow, body wrapped up in my sheets. She should be with me, not in some cold dorm room. Instead, I sent her off like the asshole that I am after mauling the hell out of her. She must be mortified, thinking that I used her. With the life she grew up with, what else would she believe?

Tom clears his throat. "Let's stop at that deli. I need a fresh pack of smokes." He throws the empty pack in the trashcan on the corner as we step into the dimly lit bodega. The place is tiny and jam-packed with rows of junk food. There's a small counter in the corner selling lotto tickets and cigarettes.

"Can I help you?" The clerk looks between us nervously, probably grabbing his gun beneath the register. The truth is, he should be afraid. We're both huge—sucking the air out of this place and making it look more like a dollhouse than a store. We're also packing some serious heat tonight. I've got four guns and a knife on my body, all concealed. Although we do our best to tone it down when we're out in the real world, we're always Borignone mafia. We could set this entire place on fire and get away with it. We're dominant in this city, and everyone knows it.

Tom leans against the counter, giving his best smile to put the clerk at ease. "Marlboro Lights." Tom reaches into his back pocket and pulls out his leather wallet that we bought together in Buenos Aires last year. Dropping a hundred-dollar bill on the counter, the guy hands him his pack and opens the register to get him his change.

"Make that two," I interject. Tom turns to me, a smirk on his face. He pays for the packs and we head back outside.

He chuckles. "Behind that stone face you're sporting, you're really freaking the fuck out right now that she's here, huh?" Tom knows I only smoke when I'm stressed.

"Shut up, man." I open my pack while he laughs.

"Don't worry." He throws a meaty arm around my shoulder. "We'll eat and chain smoke on your balcony—and maybe we can even braid each other's hair—while we discuss the girl you killed for." He's laughing, but behind the smile, I can tell he's mad as fuck.

He moves his hands to the back of my head and I duck, shifting away from him. We walk to my building near school, talking shit until we finally get upstairs. My apartment here is a nice-sized one bedroom; it has a black leather couch, nice big screen TV, and a simple rug on the floor. It's totally different from both my room at my dad's townhouse and from my SoHo loft. In a weird way, it's appropriate though; all three sides of me are represented via different living arrangements.

Tom takes out his phone to order the pizza while I walk out onto my small balcony for a minute of privacy. I pull out another cigarette. Lighting up, I let myself take a deep inhale.

Most people in my world smoke. I try not to since I love to fight and don't want anything to slow my training down. But every so often, it feels damn good. It's completely quiet on my block, and that's by design. I can't stand the stress and hustle of the city. The truth is, I can't wait to get the hell out of here. I turn to the glass door to see Tom laying back on my couch and turning on the TV. Thank fuck. The last thing I need is for him to question me right now.

Tom and I have been Borignone family since before birth. My father grew up in Brooklyn, the American-born son of Italian immigrants. While his father didn't choose the life, two of his uncles rose to infamy in the early 1970s by taking bets on sports, eventually using their brand of muscle to manipulate games. Those uncles are the men who supported my father as he grew up. They bought him shoes when his were torn and gave him lunch money when his own father's pockets were empty. And so, after grade school, my father joined the family. And since his uncles' deaths, he's the Boss. Gambling, guns, and drugs are our main sources of income. Tom's father, Enzo, is my father's consigliere. The hope is that one day, Tom will be mine. Even though he's made, he isn't at the highest rung—yet. But I am. I've killed for the family, and I'd do a fuck of a lot worse if need be. I may be at a crossroads right now, but I'm a man of loyalty. Always will be.

What's funny is that once upon a time, being part of the family was all I ever wanted. I desired all the benefits that came with the notoriety. I knew, even then, that most men would sell their soul for a chance to live the life I was born into. They wish, if only for a moment, to walk into a cocaine den where naked women sort and weigh the goods—tits sprinkled with white powder. The vacations abroad on private planes. The non-stop cash pouring in. Hell, being above the law basically guarantees a life of debauchery. But that's just human nature, isn't it? Without being forced to tow a line, everyone would be running as wild as we are.

No other illegal enterprise is as powerful, organized, or as successful. We're the governing body of most black markets on the East Coast. Hell, Eve said it on the night we met. If the government turns a blind eye to illegal shit like fights, then control is lost and people get hurt. Well, she was wrong about something. Control isn't lost. It just falls into someone else's hands. And usually, it's ours.

I swallow hard, letting my mind wander back to the night that would change the path of my life forever.

* * *

WE THROW our blue caps in the air and cheer. Everyone slaps each other's backs, scattering to find family. My father comes to me, chuckling in both pride and amusement while one-hundred-twenty students gawk at us.

People know who we are, and they stare in nervous fascination. The Mafia Don and his intellectual son; I earned my honors status. We're both well over six-feet tall with chiseled, hard features. I'm already wider and thicker than he is. Where his eyes are electric blue, mine are coal black like my Native American mother.

I graduated in the top five percent of my class, and it wasn't done with anything other than aptitude coupled with hard work. My IQ took me far, but to get to the top level here at Tri-Prep Academy, nothing but keeping my head in the books would get me the grades I needed for an Ivy League. My father always knew my potential, and he was sure to capitalize on it. If we want to take our business to the next level one day, we need someone in the family with the academic credentials. An inside man to be the face of legitimacy.

Behind all the shit we do is love and loyalty; that's what we stand for, and it's something that regular society doesn't have. These boys around me would shorten their lives to be me. I don't give a fuck how many times they shrink back, talking shit about what we do. The truth is they wish they were me. If they had the brotherhood as I do—people who have their back no matter what—I'd bet my life they'd never leave it.

My father shakes his head, excitement in his eyes. "Tonight's the night, Vincent."

I nod, doing my best not to show how excited I truly am.

Tom moves next to me, his typically fun-loving face turning serious as he puts his hand out to my father, showing respect.

Tom never gave a shit about school and grades. He spent the last four years partying, fucking girls, and doing small-time shit for the family. Now that he's graduated, he plans to stay and work in the ports of New York and New Jersey with his father, who oversees our business there. The family dominates the waterfronts, and our stronghold could always use more loyal muscle. His father is a Capo—a made man of the highest rank, beneath my father, of course.

Most of the kids in school are getting into their limos to go to the Hamptons for post-grad parties, planning to get drunk and party. Meanwhile, my father and I step into the back of our Rolls Royce, heading to one of our warehouses in Long Island.

Sitting side by side in the back seat, my father takes a small black box from inside his suit jacket. "Open it." The warmth in my father's tone from earlier has disappeared.

I use my thumbs to pry the box open. It's a gold crucifix. I let my fingers touch the simple chain. Every member of the family wears this. Everyone's got ink, too. The Borignone insignia.

"You aren't getting inked," he says, reading my mind. I move my head in confusion. "When you're in college, you have to focus. I don't want people seeing you and automatically knowing you belong to us. You've gotta be smarter. Cleaner."

I look into his electric eyes. "Yes, sir." I keep my mouth in a firm line, my attention solely on him.

"And you don't wear this until tonight is complete."

I shut the box, sliding it into my pocket. I'm not sure what tonight will bring, but I'm ready for anything.

I may have a propensity for books, but I take my fighting and gun skills very seriously. People like to think that today's mob families are less dangerous and powerful as they once were. Well, that's an utter lie. We're just better at cloaking ourselves in legitimate work. Regardless, behind the surface of intellect and schooling, I still have my father's blood running through my veins.

During the ride, tiny pieces of doubt creep inside my head, but I shove them down, focusing on my future. It's time for me to man up and accept my destiny. Scenery passes by in a blur; before I know it, the city skyline is behind us. The traffic, as usual, is ridiculous on the Long Island Expressway.

"I swear to God, Vincent." He lowers the window before taking out a cigarette and lighting up. "They could add a tenth lane to this mother-fucking highway and there would still be bumper-to-bumper traffic at any hour of the day. Fucking bullshit."

"I heard the mayor is creating this traffic on purpose as punishment or some shit, for someone in the political arena for not supporting him."

My father laughs. "That's life. Tit for tat. Someone should leak that shit to the Post."

Other than that comment, he sits beside me without a sound.

Completely unmoving, other than taking slow and deep drags of his cigarette. A lesser man may be afraid by his silent demeanor, by the way he's trained his eyes to show no emotion. The government would argue Antonio Borignone is an enemy of the United States. They wouldn't be wrong.

About an hour later, we step out of the car and stand in front of a huge warehouse; the combination of heat and recently smoked cigarettes permeate the air. Sweat drips down my sides, dampening my starched Armani button-down shirt.

My father opens the heavy gray door and has me walk ahead of him; I'd be lying if I said exhilaration wasn't the primary thing I feel.

The warehouse is dim and damp. We strut through towers of gun-filled wooden crates while my father's shoes clap against the concrete floors, echoing through the space.

Standing at the top of a concrete staircase, my father taps my back. I look into his eyes and he nods, telling me in his own way that what I'm about to see and do will probably change my life forever. I stare at him unblinking, communicating that I'm ready.

I move ahead of him, my steps measured as I walk down the narrow staircase.

I smell it first: a twisted mixture of piss, puke, and blood. Two young-looking guys, at least from what I can tell beneath their broken faces, sit in plastic chairs. Their arms and legs are bound together with cable ties. They're crying like little bitches, noses broken, eyes blackened and shut. Pools of liquid saturate the floor under their chairs.

"Jesus Christ," I say out loud, lip curling in disgust. A tightening sensation moves deep within my bones.

I swallow hard and take a moment to look around. All the men in the family are here, jaws tense. My heart thumps. I crack my neck from left to right, relieving the tension before moving to my knuckles.

"Finish 'em." The order leaves my father's lips as easily as if he were telling me to take out the trash.

I've beaten up plenty of guys in the past, but killing—this is something new to me. I neatly pull off my suit jacket and hand it to my father, as if I have all the time in the world. I look around the room again. If the family wants these men dead, they must have done something deserving of this ending. Borignone mafia doesn't kill for nothing. But if you fuck with one of ours, payment will be due.

I nod at the ten Capos around me, giving my respect. And then I turn to the two men seated in front of me. Before I can question myself further, I pull out my gun and steady my hands, shooting each of them directly in the head. Their brain matter splatters around them, black and red, like some fucked-up Jackson Pollock painting.

My father places his hand on my shoulder, letting me know without words, that I completed the duty. I immediately turn the safety of my gun back on, sliding it into my holster. The men's faces register pride.

"These two gangbanged Sammy's daughter out in Central Islip a few weeks ago." I open and close my fists a few times. Sammy is an associate who we all love. He isn't here tonight, of course. But I know his daughter, Allison, well. She's a thirteen-year-old girl who I would guess is on the Autism spectrum. No one talks about it since weakness isn't ever discussed within the family. Here, we only strengthen our strengths. But she and I play math games together during Sunday night dinners. I've told my father already that when she's of age, we need to get her to help us manipulate some numbers; her ability is off the damn charts. And these motherfuckers hurt her? Took advantage of a disabled child?

I pull my gun out again, shooting each of these bastards again, and again, picturing sweet Allison in my head. I wish I could revive them just to kill them again. When I'm finished, I see the back of my father's suit as he walks over to the bodies, his shiny black Ferragamos clapping against the gray concrete. He leans over the dead men, spitting on them.

"Chop 'em up before you burn the bodies," he demands. One by one, each man in the family steps up to me, shaking my hand.

Single file, we walk toward another door in the back, entering a new room. It's small and completely wood-paneled, smelling distinctly of cedar. The table in the center is huge, taking up most of the space. My father pulls out a large knife with a jewel-encrusted handle and turns to me. "This part of your induction will represent sharing of blood. This is the Family," he says, gesturing to the men around us. "Nothing else comes before it. Leaving is only possible in a coffin."

He lifts my hand, slowly slicing the center of my palm with the knife. Surprisingly, it doesn't hurt at all; my adrenaline is so high right now; I can't feel a thing. My blood beads up to the surface of my skin. Taking a piece of white parchment paper from the table, he turns my hand over, letting it drip onto the sheet. The paper is then passed from man to man until reaching my father again.

He lights a match, setting the bloodied paper aflame. "Repeat after me," he says with a nod. "Honor. Allegiance. Family." With a steady voice, I repeat the oath, sealing my fate.

"There's still a little more, Vincent." He taps my back, motioning for me to follow him again. He brings me into another room, crates piled low to the ground. The men circle me.

"We all know how fuckin' smart you are. You all know that my son graduated Tri-Prep tonight? Columbia is coming this fall." They do a slow clap at first, which turns into whistles and hollers. "Sound mind, sound body. Now, show us what you can do in the ring."

I turn my head left and right. A few men wearing ski masks walk inside the circle. I can tell by the way they move their feet that they are trained fighters. Luckily for me, I'm a machine.

THE FAMILY DOCTOR stitches me up before sending me back to the townhouse. I walk up a few floors until I get to my bathroom. Dropping to my white tile floor, I vomit into the toilet bowl.

"What have I done?" I sit up against the cold marble wall, willing my body to stop shaking. I feel my teeth chattering in my mouth, but I can't will them to stop.

Dropping my head in my hands, I roughly grab my hair. The night's events need to be compartmentalized. I'm not a pussy. I can handle this. Somehow, I force myself up to stand in front of the mirror.

I grip the sink hard, my knuckles shaking with the pressure. "I'm a made man. This is my destiny." My voice is quiet. I look at myself harder, moving closer to the glass and repeating the words. I need my brain to believe! "I'm a made man. This is my mother-fucking DESTINY!" I scream, punching the glass with my fist, shattering the mirror to pieces.

* * *

A TAXI HONKS his horn and I'm brought back to the present. Shit, I need to calm the fuck down. I let an image of Eve float into my head and somehow, I exhale the tightness in my chest. It's not just how stunning she is. It's more. It's the way she moves. Thinks. Breathes. How she sees more than just the sum of my parts. When people look at me—with the family or during my fights—they see the muscles and the anger and a good-looking face. When people look at me in school, they see an image that Daniela projects. Somehow, my life has become increasingly fragmented. But with Eve? I'm whole. She's someone I can't afford to lose.

I lean against the railing when the balcony door opens. It's Tom. He moves next to me, lighting up his cigarette.

"Fuck, it's getting cold," he mumbles, rubbing his hands together like we're on the Titanic.

"Why don't you bring yourself a sweater from inside? Maybe make a hot chamomile tea while you're at it?"

He laughs. "Erez is coming in from Israel next week. How many men of his do you think we'll need? They'll have to be ready by spring."

"I expect things to be pretty tense when we get there. I already know the Tribal Council isn't down with us partnering up with them. We may need around fifty guys to convince them otherwise."

Tom exhales smoke. "Fuck, yeah. It's time to take what's ours." He spits off the balcony. "Don't let that bitch derail us now, true? You've gotta keep your head on the prize. You've got to be all about *your* girl right now. And I don't mean the tiny one with the big brown eyes. I mean the snake with red hair and claws."

"Yeah." I flick some ash off the balcony. The lie burning my throat. There's no way in hell I'm going to have Eve near me and not make her mine.

"So, you won't talk to her anymore?" He drops his cigarette on the concrete balcony floor, stepping on it with his shoe. "I know your vague answers. You say 'yeah yeah yeah,' but in the end, you always do whatever the fuck you wanna do." His voice is harder now.

"Think before you speak, brother," I reply firmly, daring him with my eyes to spew more bullshit at me. We stare at each other wordlessly, aggression fueling our stances.

"Fuck, Vince!" he seethes, stepping closer to me. "Swear to me you'll stay away from her! We've got plans. The family needs you to stay on the path. Shit between you and Eve almost ruined everything for us last year. Since that bitch, you can't even be with another girl! You know I've been telling you that it feels like a storm is brewing at the ports. On top of that, we can't be left with this much dirty cash. It's a bad recipe."

I grab his shirt, lifting him to my face. "Don't call her a bitch."

"Calm the fuck down," he yells. "I'm not the enemy!"

I try to blink the rage out of my vision. When I finally let go, he shakes out his shoulders, still fuming.

"She's turned you inside out. You don't want any pussy other than hers? Fine. Keep being a damn monk. You used to fuck a different girl every night!"

"Who I fuck is none of your goddamn business!"

"That's where you're wrong." He steps up. "That fake relationship you've got going on with Daniela directly affects all of us. We aren't done with her yet. And we both know that if you cut shit off with her too soon, we'll be up in a shit storm. You know how long they could put us away for?" His voice tempers at the end, but it does nothing to chill my anger.

My lips curl in fury. "Don't fuckin' lecture me. You think I don't know every detail of what you're talking about? I've got it under control. Whatever is going on with Eve has nothing to do with *this!*" I breathe heavily.

His eyes widen and he lets out a cackle. "Control? You find a girl with a face wars are fought over, and you think you can pull off *control*?"

"Yes. For her, I will do whatever it takes. Once I get this shit off the ground in Nevada—"

"You know what? You aren't thinking." He starts breathing hard, gripping the railing in rage. "Eve will cause a clusterfuck for the family. Let. Her. Go. You think you can keep a relationship alive with Daniela while having Eve? It's hard enough for you to be fake with Daniela right now, despite the fact that you haven't fucked her in ages. Your temper with her is borderline abusive. Three weeks ago at that charity event? The photos of the two of you don't look fucking convincing. Daniela will catch wind of another woman, brother. And when she does, there will be hell to pay for all of us."

"I'll talk to Eve. I'll explain everything, and she'll get it."

"That girl's got her finger hooked into your heart, and getting reacquainted with her again after working so hard on trying to move on, is going to fuck. You. Up." He looks at me with an incensed expression and I turn to him with an even angrier one.

"Don't talk to me like that, motherfucker. Not now, and not ever!" I take a heavy step toward him, and Tom immediately shuffles back. Instead of hitting him like I ache to do, I pull out another cigarette and light up.

"You don't give a fuck about anything but that girl. That much is clear."

I stare at his ashen face, taking another step closer until we're barely an inch apart. I use my height to my advantage, staring down at him.

"The family always comes first, but I'll never be fucking done with her. Understand? Never. I will walk through fire to keep her. And the next time you question me and my authority, I'll break your fucking face." My voice is quiet, but the rage simmers beneath my skin.

"Well, you'll have to walk through shit worse than fire in prison, 'cause that's where you'll be if you can't keep your dick in your pants and eye on the prize. Until we get our new business running, there are no other options."

The doorbell rings. Tom turns from me, stepping back into the apartment and sliding the balcony door shut behind him. I watch as he opens the front door and hands the delivery guy some cash from his back pocket. Dropping the pie on the coffee table, he opens the door and pops his head into the balcony again. "Hey fucker, come in and let's eat."

I walk back inside and we dig in, our conversation shelved for now. I'm biting into a hot slice, my mind running rampant when his phone pings. He lifts it off the coffee table to read the text. "Wanna fight tonight?" He looks me up and down, my posture rigid. "Looks like you could let out some steam." He raises his brows and leans back on the couch, crossing his feet on the coffee table and biting into his pizza.

I nod my head. "Fuck yeah."

THREE HOURS LATER, I'm in the basement of some underground warehouse, kicking the shit out of some faceless guy. And man, does it feel good.

9

EVE

MY ENTIRE DAY passes in a blur. I clean my dorm room and then get to studying. Before I know it, it's nearing five o'clock. I need to wash up and get dressed before Janelle comes. After showering and putting myself together as decently as I can, I hear a knock at my door. I swing it open and see my beautiful sister, blonder than usual.

"Nice hair!" My head pounds with nerves, but I want to keep it together until it's time to fess up.

"Thanks. I felt like lightening it up a few days ago." She fluffs her roots with her fingertips as she struts into the room, her black booties clapping on the wooden floors. "I can't wait to rearrange all the furniture."

Janelle is so creative; I'm sure she'll find a way to maximize my space. Our tiny room in the Blue Houses could have been horrible. But between her little touches and the way she set up our beds and my desk, she was able to transform the space into a small oasis. "Well, what do you think we should do with the place?"

"First of all, we need to push the beds together and make you a king. Then, we can ask your RA to get rid of this extra desk." She walks to the door, staring at the room from a different angle. "Should we do Target or Bed Bath for fresh bedding? Honestly, Eve, I'm sick of looking at those old sheets. They're old and full of shitty memories."

My eyes widen. "Janelle, I don't want to spend—"

She puts her hand up. "Je-sus, Eve. Stop with that shit! It's not that expensive, and knowing you, you probably haven't spent a dime of your grant money for anything other than books. That money is meant for you to actually live! I've been doing well in tips, too. You're buying yourself new sheets and maybe even a few pillows for the big bed we're about to set up for you. And then we'll reorganize the room and order in some takeout! Oh—maybe we should get you a small table too, with two chairs? There's room for that now."

"Here we go..." I say under my breath, nervous that Janelle is going to take this whole room rearrangement to an absurdly expensive degree.

"Now sit down. Let me put you together before we leave." I drop into the seat at my desk, knowing that with Janelle, there is no room for negotiation. Luckily, it only takes her a few minutes to apply eyeliner, mascara, and a little blush on my face. Moments later, we're knocking on my resident advisor's door to make a small request before heading to Bed Bath and Beyond.

"Oh, hey Eve." Her usual animated self is on display; I squint my eyes at her yellow polo shirt with the collar popped, and her matching hair ribbon. Alexandra is a brand of New England preppy that I never knew existed until college. My sister turns to me, furrowing her brow as if to say, is this bitch for real?

"Hey, Alexandra," I reply in my perkiest voice. "Now that I don't have a roommate, I was hoping you could have someone remove that second desk?" Janelle turns to me, her eyes widening at my tone, but I ignore her.

"Of course." She nods happily, ponytail swaying. "I'll call housing services tonight."

Janelle squeezes my hand three times and then turns to Alexandra. "Thanks for your help, sweetie." Her tone is so upbeat and unnatural that I have to bite my cheek not to laugh.

"No problem!" she exclaims, thankfully not understanding that Janelle is mocking her. She gently shuts the door and we turn down the hallway.

We're barely ten feet away when Janelle starts cracking up. "Seriously? Whatever Kool-Aid that bitch drinks, I need a sip a' that!" We continue our snickering as we walk out of the building.

Forty minutes later, we're arguing over king-sized sheet colors and plastic table sizes. Luckily, we manage to leave the store without tearing each other apart. Janelle is holding overflowing bags of jersey sheets in navy—while clutching pillows, a duvet puffy-thing to go inside a navy-and-white floral cover—along with a cute little area rug in silver that she tells me I absolutely need. Meanwhile, I'm hauling a small white plastic table, folded, and two white plastic folding chairs.

We get in a large taxi that fits all of our goods in its trunk and head back to my dorm. We both break into a sweat as we drop all of the new stuff by the door. They had delivery, but neither of us wanted to waste the twenty bucks.

After taking a breath and drinking some water from the sink, we get to the heavy work of pushing the single beds together in order to turn it into a king, pushing both to the left side of the room. Janelle answers the knock at the door and it's two big guys from student services here to remove the spare desk.

"Oh, hey guys," Janelle says with a sugary smile as she lowers her eyes, getting a nice long look at their denim-clad asses. I roll my eyes at her blatant ogling and can't help myself but laugh; I do a cursory glance and have to say, they look pretty good in those jeans. Not like Vincent, but—I quickly turn my head and breathe through the pain. Thoughts of him now are accompanied by agony.

She hops up onto the desk that's staying and crosses one long leg over the other. "So, are you guys students here?" She cocks her head to the side, her eyes twinkling with mischief. The guy with blue eyes stares back at her, clearly liking what he sees.

"Yeah," he shrugs. "We just do this shit for a little extra cash on the side." His accent is all Brooklyn.

Janelle turns to me, eyes wide. "You see, Eve? Everyone here isn't a spoiled rich kid!" I want to glare at her, but the guys laugh, and so I do too. After chatting for a few minutes about the uptight and spoiled kids at school, Janelle takes their phone numbers and they leave the room with the spare desk.

We clean up the dust from the corners of the room and Janelle finally unrolls the new area rug. My old sheets and comforter are now in a huge trash bag. Looking around my room, I'm in a state of utter surprise. "This looks amazing, Janelle!"

"Hell yeah, it does." She holds out her fist for me to pound and we knock them together saying "swish" at the end. It's a stupid hand-shake, but we both love it, so we do it anyway.

I clear my throat, knowing we're going to have to talk. I've got a shitload of stuff to unload on her tonight, and it won't be pretty.

"I'll order the Chinese. And then... we talk."

She's texting someone on her phone while she replies to me. "Make sure to get some spicy sesame noodles. The girls I live with barely eat a thing. Do you see how skinny I've gotten?" She tries to look appalled as she stares at her bony arm, but I know that she's actually thrilled.

"I can see your bones," I reply in all seriousness.

"Really?" She jumps up and down with glee.

"You're crazy; you know that?" I can't help but chuckle at her exuberance.

"Well, everyone can't just eat their faces off and be all perfect like you, you bitch." She winks. "Now, order that food before I eat you."

I roll my eyes as I place the order. I decided I'd better wait until she's full before I give her the Vincent saga.

The delivery guy comes and goes, and we sit at the small table to dig in.

"You see? I told you this was necessary!" She spears a piece of chicken with her fork and takes a bite.

"I've got shit to tell you, Janelle." I look down at the food I've yet to touch and finally lift my face to hers. My eyes must show anguish because she stops chewing.

"All right. Lay it on me," she says as she swallows her last bite.

"Some bitches giving you trouble? Because if they are, I have no problem kicking someone's ass."

I swallow hard, gathering the nerve. "No. But, Janelle, I'm going to tell you something kind of serious. And you have to swear not to be angry that I've...withheld all of it from you. But before I start, I want you to know that it's all over now. So really, there isn't a reason I'm telling you this except that I feel like you ought to know."

"Oh, shit. You're babbling. That's a bad sign. What is it?" Her no-nonsense stare propels me forward. Before I know it, I'm telling her every gritty detail I've kept close to my heart about Vincent. Once I start, I can't seem to stop myself. I thought that saying it all out loud would push everything farther from me. But it turns out, the opposite occurs. Talking about him and what we had only makes the entirety of my memories more vivid.

The dinner and club the night we met. Making out in the stair-well. Ice skating. I include the information about Angelo's pawnshop when I met Antonio. Hell, I say it all. I don't think I've ever talked so much in my life. When I'm done, Janelle sits completely frozen, staring at me with an expressionless face. For what it's worth, it felt amazing to unload. But watching the way her face is morphing into hurt and fury, I know I'm about to pay.

She blinks her eyes a few times. "So, you're telling me, that *the Bull* is actually Vincent Borignone? And he killed Carlos. For you. And now he's at Columbia. Here. But it turns out that he's had a girl-friend all along—and she's some billionaire's daughter and she's gorgeous and connected and all over social media? And last night you guys made out, but he stopped you. And he told you he loves you and that he wants to explain everything..."

I shuffle in my seat, gathering myself. "Um, I guess that's the general r-rundown..." I stutter.

"So, you're telling me," she repeats a little louder. "That you never touched a man in your life other than making out with Juan. And then you almost had sex with Vincent Borignone. And you never told me?"

"Well, I was never technically *with* him..." My voice sounds tiny to my own ears. "But, I didn't know who he was at the time..."

"Eve. Look into my eyes right now!" she exclaims. "Whatever is between you and him is O.V.E.R." She punctuates every letter, making sure I understand. "Am I being clear? That motherfucking killer isn't allowed anywhere near you."

"Janelle, I think you're—"

"Don't say I'm overreacting," she says angrily.

I turn my head to the door and then back to her. "Shhh! Someone might hear you!"

She takes a breath to calm herself down, but the anger is still slick on her tongue. "No fuckin' way. No, Eve. You don't realize what's happening. You're too naïve." She throws her arms up in the air. "This man is fucking dangerous." She stands up, pacing back and forth in the room. "I don't give a rat's ass if he's so smart that he wins that stupid No-Bell Prize or whatever the fuck it's called. He is bad news. He should not be ANY news. Vincent Borignone is Antonio's son." Her words come out staccato, she's panting, talking a mile a minute. "I never knew he was the Bull, but I've heard his name a million times. He's dangerous as all fuck. He'll probably be running the family one day."

She keeps moving, on a rampage. "He isn't an associate like our Angelo. He's a *made man*. You thought the Snakes were bad? The Cartel?" Her breathing turns rapid. "Holy fuck Eve, this man is a hundred times those guys." She sits back down, grabbing my hands in hers. "Swear to me right now that you will never. Ever. Speak to him again."

"Janelle..." My heart is pounding. I know that everything she is saying is the truth. But it hurts.

"Last week Vania, whose boyfriend works in the fish market by the docks, told her that everyone pays the Borignones. Anything moved through the waterfront is taxed by them. And what do you think happens if someone says *no*?"

I sit in silence as she continues.

"No talking. No looking. Whatever that shit was you had between the two of you is over. And, do you realize what he turned you into last year? How you could even think of defending him right now—is making my stomach turn."

Visions of my mother being a mistress to these rich guys flash through my mind. How many times was my mother the one they all made promises to? They swore they were ending their marriages. They promised her a new apartment. They swore everything under the sun. But inevitably, it all would blow up in her face.

"You want to be the side piece to Vincent Borignone?" she continues. "Because that's what he wants. It's what all powerful men like him want. He's got that fancy piece of ass he takes around town. She's the public one. She's the one with the life and the kids and the Mercedes Benz. You're the idiot on the side! It's all fun and games until he's got you on a fucking leash, living in his high-rise penthouse on Park Avenue until the day he gets sick of you. He'll handcuff you emotionally to him, and meanwhile, you'll never get to live your own life!"

I gasp as if I've been slapped. Janelle is hitting on every insecurity I've ever had. "It's n-not like that," I say, my voice breaking. A headache sets in the back of my skull; a pounding pain that's growing by the second.

She opens her eyes wider. "Yeah. It's exactly like that. He saw you as some charity case. Okay, maybe he's attracted to you. But he will never choose you over her, Eve. Ne-ver." She snaps, crosses her arms over her chest.

"You can't understand what we had—he swore there's more than it seems! And—Carlos—"

"Stop making excuses." Her eyes move wildly. "Let me be clear. Number one." She lifts a perfectly manicured finger in the air. "He's got a girlfriend. He had a girlfriend while he was hooking up with you and he cheated with you—on her. And I don't care that he didn't fuck you when he obviously could have. I mean shit, Eve! Did you listen to yourself recount the story?"

She lifts a second finger in the air. "And secondly, he's Vincent fucking Borignone. He's a killer. He fucking kills people for the mafia.

Are you lis-ten-ing to me? How do you even know that he killed Carlos for you? Maybe it was because the Snakes were rising in power and he had to take care of him?"

My stomach sinks. I know I have to hear it, and here it is.

"I'm serious, Eve. I refuse to allow this. I'm putting my foot down. If you can't stay away from him—or if he doesn't stay away from you —I'm calling Angelo. And I know for a fact he will go fucking insane on your ass. We all didn't bend backward for the past four years only to have you back in bed with the enemy!"

My face feels like it's burning as tears stream down my cheeks.

She lets out a sigh, her voice softening. "You can't let him do this to you." She gently pushes some hair off my face. "You can do better than him, Eve. I know it. A man like him will seriously fuck you up. The money and the power is an easy thing to get lost in. But at the end of the day, a man like him sees a girl like you or me, they see where we came from, and they try to take advantage. They make false promises. They lie—"

"He has a girlfriend. I know that. I stalked the hell out of them. I lived my life running from these gangs. The streets. I'm done with that and I'm done with him. It's over. Done," I say as she looks at me pointedly as if she isn't sure she believes me. "It's over and done, Janelle. I promise."

"Well, halle-fuckin'-lujah. It's not like you saw him all that much anyway, right?"

I drop my head. Our timeline may have been short in the way we normally think about time, as twenty-four hours a day. But the way time managed to move with us was...different. Heavier. Deeper. *More.*

10

EVE

IT'S MONDAY MORNING. I walk into my economics class, taking a seat in the center of the lecture hall. Jared, a starter for the school's football team, drops into the chair next to mine, giving me a grin that has most of the girls in class swooning. The girls on my floor put him on our hottest guys list and seeing him so close like this, it's obvious why. With his shaggy blond hair and sparkling blue eyes, he looks like the perfect farm boy who could probably tip a cow over with one of his bulging muscles.

After talking to Janelle last night, I realize I need to force myself to move on. I know Vincent said he wants us to discuss it, but there's no way in hell I'm doing that. God knows, my pain threshold has been reached.

"So, Eve, how's the year going for you?"

"It's cool," I say with a smile, opening up my red spiral notebook and pulling out a pen from my backpack. Almost everyone in class is sitting with a laptop open in front of them, but I find that it's harder to concentrate with a computer screen in front of me. Instead, I take handwritten notes in class and then type them on my laptop once I'm back in my room. It's probably overkill, but it's been working for me so far.

"Do you live in the quad?" His smile reaches his eyes. Jared's got swag, I'll give him that. He's really good-looking in that all-American way. I know I should feel excited, but I don't feel any zing. I take a deep breath, pushing these stupid thoughts away. What is a "zing" anyway? Zings are for naïve girls who don't know better.

I shrug my shoulders, feeling inexplicably shy. "Yeah, I do. Are you there, too?" I give him my best smile.

"Yeah." He's looking at me with blatant interest and I want to kick myself right now for not enjoying the moment. Guilt sits like a pit in the back of my throat. Why am I feeling this? I need someone to give me the Heimlich.

He shifts his thick, muscular arm so that it's flush against mine, and an irrational prickle of anxiety moves through me. I should feel thrilled, not frightened. Vincent must have changed my DNA or something. Now that my body knows a man like him exists, nothing else is a match. Everything else feels blatantly wrong. He set himself up as a benchmark for what a man should be; he was so damn impactful, he managed to change my vision for any other man. How am I going to get past that? Past him?

Luckily, the professor begins his lecture and I force myself to concentrate. Jared and I make eyes a few times while the professor talks and the truth is that it feels good to be wanted. And even if I still think about Vincent, I know my actions will *never* follow through with what's happening in my head. I won't allow it; I'm stronger than that. So, a new guy who is single and normal? Bring it on! I can add him to my list titled: Fake it 'til I make it.

Class is finally over. I slide my books into my backpack, laughing about something funny Jared says when I feel my skin prickle. I move my head up and immediately spot him. Vincent's striding toward me, confidently, as if he was expecting to see me here. A piece of his hair falls into his eye, but nothing can cover that piercing gaze. He's a hunter, and I'm the deer about to get speared.

Jared is completely oblivious to Vincent's approach as he gathers his books. I want to grab him and beg him to take me with him out of the classroom before Vincent reaches me. My heart thuds as Vincent steps right between us, ignoring Jared's existence as if he was nothing more than dust.

"Uh, bye Eve." Jared waves as he scurries away. Vincent leans against my desk, his eyes practically black.

"Who the fuck was that?" he asks angrily.

"You're joking, right?" I lift my backpack up on the table and open the zipper roughly. I drop my books inside, shutting it as if the zipper and I are mortal enemies.

"I know you're angry." His voice is gruff. I don't reply to him, because I can't. My voice literally won't work right now. I'm too hurt.

Vincent looks around the now-empty lecture hall. Grabbing my hand, he pulls me out of the room and into the hallway.

"What the hell, Vincent. Stop!" I whisper yell.

Of course, he doesn't even pause. He practically drags me behind his enormous body. With every step we take, my anger amplifies. He's handling me like I'm nothing more than a doll, and I'm tired of it. I'm a human being, not a tool to use whenever he feels like it. We finally stop in a quiet corridor.

"Fuck you!" I shout. The emotional pain ripping through my chest is so acute, I can feel my entire face turning red.

He tries to take my hand, but I ball it into a fist so he can't hold it. "Look," he huffs. "How about we go get a late lunch and talk about it. Let's figure it all out, okay? Are you hungry?" His voice is measured as if he expected this outburst from me. But I can't manage to calm myself down. The anger is too fresh. All of a sudden, another burst of indignation moves through my body. *I'm not taking his shit anymore.*

"I'm not a cheater. And I'm not a lunatic either to be dating the son of Antonio Borignone. I came here because it's one of the best schools in the country and I'm not ruining my life because of you. There is nothing we need to discuss." I take a heaving breath. "The. End."

He bends down to get closer to me and lowers his voice. "You're coming out with me, and we're talking."

"No, we are not." I turn my head, making sure no one is near us. The last thing I need is to be part of the Vincent gossip mill. "Actually, I have an idea. Go to lunch with your girlfriend of the past few years and be sure to snap a photo with your shirt off while you're at it. I'm sure your leeeeegions of fans would looooove to see The Vincent Borignone shirtless. And when you're done with her, go see your father and maybe shoot someone for not giving you a cut of their profits!"

He stares at me wide-eyed before bursting out laughing, which only makes me more furious. "Come on, Eve. How can I not laugh? You're funny."

"Funny?" If I were in a cartoon, smoke would be billowing out of my ears right now. I turn my body around, ready to walk away.

"Hey," he says, stepping forward so I'm pressed against the wall. "There's a lot about the situation you don't know. And yeah, she likes to post shit about us, but it never mattered much to me before. Let's go out. Let me just explain—"

"Before? Before what? Before or after you put me in your goddamn bed?" I shouldn't be speaking to him right now. I watch as resolve comes over his face. I'm about to yell again when he bends down and picks me up, throwing me over his enormous shoulder.

I want to scream, but I don't want to draw attention to us as we walk out of the corridor. My hair is dangling down, practically sweeping the floor. And for the first time in my life, I'm relieved that it's so thick and riotous because it's covering my face from any potential passerby. He's carrying me like a caveman and I'm absolutely powerless. If people are staring, I wouldn't know; my eyes are screwed shut. When I realize he isn't going to put me down without a fight, I try to pinch his side. Not only is he not ticklish, but he's a solid wall of muscle without an ounce of fat to grab. My voice is low as I threaten his life, but he completely ignores me. Blood rushes to my head and I stay quiet, hoping he'll flip me back over soon.

We get to the student parking lot, filled with fancy looking cars. Lowering his body and placing my feet on the ground, he holds my arms to make sure I don't fall over. When I'm stable, he puts his hands through my crazy hair, acting like he's doing me a favor by taming it.

"Your hair is wild, Eve." He's cackling, and I want to strangle him with my bare hands.

"Thanks a lot, jackass. Everyone can't have perfectly silky hair like you. I can't imagine how much you probably pay for conditioner. You probably get it cut at the salon Janelle's at, paying two-hundred-and-fifty bucks for a trim."

He guffaws, shaking his head in amazement. "I love this side of you," he smiles, checking me out from my toes up to my face. "Actually, from a certain angle with your face all flushed and your hair all crazy, it kind of looks like you've just been –"

"SHUT UP!" I yell, grabbing a clip from the bottom of my shirt. Before I can put it up, he stops me, his face turning serious. All of a sudden, things get quiet.

"Leave it. I want to see you just like this."

My breath catches as he strokes my cheek with his calloused thumb.

Letting me go, he casually walks to the driver's side of his gorgeous black Range Rover, my bag still draped over his shoulder. He gets in the car, immediately lowering the passenger-side window.

"Get in," his voice commands. I lick my lips and take a breath. I have two choices. I can either run and leave my backpack, or get in the car. Clearly, he won't take *no* for an answer. I think I have to run. I watch him unbuckle his seat belt and I freeze in my tracks. He steps out, walking back around the car.

"You think you can run away from me?" He's got a glint in his eye that's so sexy and arrogant; I'd slap the ego off his face if I could. I look behind us, trying to map out a route.

"Don't map out a route," he says, reading my mind perfectly with his ridiculously deep eyes.

"Stop reading my mind, Vincent! What the hell?" I stomp my foot on the ground like a petulant child. And because I want to do the opposite of what he thinks, I get into the front seat. I try to shut the door, but fail to pull hard enough. Again, I open and shut it with a loud slam. Finally, I put my hair up just to spite him. There!

Maybe it's good I'm going. I can finally tell him that this is the last time he's seeing me. Closure, right? Maybe once we talk, he'll leave me alone, and I can just get on with my life. Damn his perfect body and amazing face and brilliant mind.

We zip around campus until he pulls up to one of the older gothic-style libraries. We walk inside; the place is dim, covered in yellow light. The ceilings are so high and daunting. Even though it's completely silent, I can hear the walls talk: brilliant minds have studied at these desks. I want to touch all of the books, flip through their soft, yellowed pages—and imagine who must have studied here before me. I feel...lucky.

He walks us into the elevator and we exit on the fifth floor. We walk past the stacks and enter a study room.

I move to the corner of the room and watch dumbly as he shuts the door behind him. His phone rings, momentarily startling me. He immediately pulls it out from his jacket.

"Yes," he states seriously, clenching his fists. I watch as his normally dark gaze morphs to threatening. This Vincent is straight-up deadly. "I'm going to have to deal with this later. I've got an important meeting right now." He hangs up the phone and rolls out his shoulders, obviously trying to let go of whatever that call was about. Finally, he sits down. Staring at me, he's waiting for me to take a seat. I sit, keeping my back straight.

I need to start before he does. "Vincent, you've got a girlfriend, who I've been told will make my life a living hell if she sees us together. A girlfriend who has apparently been on your arm for years. And"—my temper rises—"how could you lie all that time about who you are and what you've been doing! I trusted you...I—"

"Eve," he states succinctly. "There's a lot I'm going to tell you. But if you want to rail at me first, be my guest." He leans back into his chair, crossing a huge leg over his opposite knee.

My jaw drops. Screw that! I'm not letting him set the rules. He doesn't get to tell me when I can be angry.

"You know what? No. I'm not yelling at you." I move my arms over my chest.

He reaches out, placing a hand in the center of the table. "You ready to hear it?"

"Why should I trust you? You swore you'd never lie to me." I'm surprised to see the torment on his face.

"I withheld. I told you as much as I could. Do you remember the stress you were under? How could I pile more shit on your plate?"

I shut my eyes, unable to look at him. That night I found a dead cat on my doorstep was terrifying. And Vincent saved me. But then, why? How? How could—

"Eve. Stop letting your mind go crazy. You know me. What we have is something entirely different. You know this," he begs.

"The world thinks you're the golden couple! What does that make me, Vincent?" He flinches at the desperation in my voice.

"No. Don't say that. You were never the girl on the side." He reaches out to me again, but I pull my hand away. "Eve—"

"Don't!" I turn my face away. "I'm here to tell you that we won't be seeing each other anymore. The whole thing is too fucked-up. I know who you are. And we both know what I had to do to get myself out of that hell I was living in. I'm not getting sucked back in! You made me believe you cared about me, and..." I take in a breath and swallow. "I was so afraid at that time when really, you were the one I should have been afraid of."

I look down at the floor, gathering myself.

He moves forward in his chair. "Eve, don't play that game with me. You may be innocent in a lot of ways, but you weren't exactly stopping me when I told you I'd take care of Carlos. You must have known that I had some reach."

"Don't you throw that in my face! I had no choice, and—" I let out a dark laugh. "I thought you were the better option than the Borignone family that Angelo was begging me to reach, how should I have known that you *were* the family?" My chest aches as the words leave my mouth.

"Yeah. And big bad Vincent took care of Carlos for you, didn't he?" He pushes himself back from the chair, looking up at the ceiling for a moment. "Let me go back to the beginning. You know now that I'm Borignone mafia. My father is Antonio, and I'm his only son. We do a lot of illegal shit and make a ton of cash doing it. A few years ago..." he continues, explaining the details of Daniela's father, Alexander Costa, and how his bank houses and launders the family money.

When he finally gets into the topic of Daniela, I can't help but drop my head. "Don't tune out, Eve. We were never exclusive. At the time, she was the one I was screwing around with in school. But right after I met you, I felt like I couldn't keep living the lie. Business is one thing. But I wanted real. I wanted more. I wanted—you." He throws his hands up in the air. "The faceless and the nameless girls. Daniela's constant manipulations. I put a stop to it."

I slide my hand to the center of the table; he recognizes the offering and gently places his hand on top of mine while he continues to tell the rest to me. All the grimy details of why he's stuck pretending to be her boyfriend in public make me feel ill. My heart actually aches for him, being forced to be near such a vile human. But he clearly has no other option right now.

"So, you're saying you haven't touched her in all this time?"

He nods his head sincerely, and I swallow hard, my mouth drying. I need a moment to process all of this new information. I meet his eyes and something passes between us; it's a magnetic energy that is impossible to stop.

"There's more. You know that I'm half Native American." I furrow my brows, confused why he's reminding me of this.

I hum my assent.

"There are tribal lands in Nevada that rightfully belong to me because of my birthright. Well, technically, they are lands that belong to the entire Masuki Tribe. But I'm part of them."

There are so many questions I need to ask, and I have to trust my inner voice more. I must learn to speak up. But before I can get a word out, he continues.

"I've got a plan to develop a hotel and casino complex. Seven men run the Masuki Tribal Council right now. I mean, shit, the place is a wasteland with nothing other than a few rundown gas stations and some trailers. I want to get out there and build out a resort to rival the current Vegas strip. All the bells and whistles and amenities, but minus the tacky glitz. Totally legitimate. And on the side, I will launder family money, too. And get us away from Costa's hold."

"Does your father know?" I ask, wide-eyed.

"Of course. I started thinking about it last year after I met you, and I've been doing the legwork ever since. It will be huge in scale, and I will be the one building and then running it. Most of the planning has been done on paper. I'm just waiting to graduate before I make the move and put the plan in motion."

I fixate on the smell of old books, trying to keep my emotions calm when a memory pops into my head. "The day I saw you around the corner when I was leaving work. And you took me out for pizza. You were at the meeting at Angelo's pawn, right?"

He nods his head in the affirmative. "I'm not ordinary, Eve. As Antonio's son, I'm not just a simple soldier who can come and go as I please. This has been my path since I was born." His eyes seem to swim with misery as he states this fact.

"And th-this is what you want?" My heart beats on overtime. I want him to say *no*. I want him to say he plans to leave the life behind —because I can't have him if he's Borignone mafia. I've worked too hard in my life to come back to this, no matter how much I love him. It helps that I've lived how I've lived. Violence and drugs aren't new to me. I just never thought I'd be here. This is exactly what I've been running from. I wanted to get away from this life, yet somehow, it has followed me. How can I turn back now?

He stands up from the chair and paces the room, stopping at the glass partition and leaning his hands on the sill, facing away from me. All I can see is the large expanse of his back, and I yearn to step behind him, put my hands around his waist, and press my nose into his shirt. Instead, I grip the arms of my chair.

He turns to me, his face settled in a grim line. "The choice has already been made for me, Eve. I'm made. This is my path. But understand that when I leave the East Coast, the heat will lessen. We aren't like these shitty street gangs. Being cloaked in legitimacy is necessary. And I'll be the face of that honest business."

My head lightens as he squeezes my hand on the table, leaning forward and looking at me pleadingly. "I'll be building something real, Eve. Taxpaying citizen. Yes, I have a gun. I'm armed. That's how it is for me. And, as of now, I have no choice but to continue being her "—he pauses for a breath—"fake boyfriend. Acting like we're together, in public. But Eve," he continues. "Our relationship is completely contrived. Do you hear me? She knows it, and I know it. She just insists on looking like a couple for her image. But once I leave, we can be free."

"Can't you just find her someone else? Maybe if she had another boyfriend, she'd leave you alone." I feel desperate and angry.

He huffs at my comment, seemingly annoyed. "You think I haven't tried that?" I've attempted everything, but apparently, she thinks that having me is important for her image."

I feel my anger rise up; the injustice of it all forces the words out of my mouth. "But if you act like her boyfriend...tell her you're her boyfriend...and everyone on earth believes you're her boyfriend... Then, I'm confused why you think you aren't? You are what you do and nothing else, Vincent. If I went to school to be a lawyer, practice law, hand out business cards that say 'Eve Petrov, Esquire,' can I now say I'm not really a lawyer?"

"I will start the new business and then I will cut her loose. That's it. And your metaphor isn't appropriate, because *boyfriend* and *girlfriend* implies sexual relations, which we don't have. It also implies fidelity, which we don't have either. As far as she and I are concerned, the relationship between us is in name only. She doesn't care who I fuck, so long as the girl doesn't infringe on the public image. That's all there is."

I drop my head. "What are you doing to me, Vincent? I'm not like these girls you know. I don't have brass emotions. I can't hear one thing, see another, and stay strong through it. And I can't navigate this complicated social stuff... I'm not made that way."

"Don't you know, from the minute I met you, it has only been you?" He moves his hands to gently cover mine, and I find it difficult to breathe. "I can't even smell anyone but you...touch a woman who isn't you..." He lifts his hand and caresses the side of my face while I shut my eyes tightly. "And no one, no one has ever turned me on like you..."

The door of the study room opens. I feel a gust of cold air as Vincent's hand moves off mine at lightning speed.

We turn our heads at the same moment and I look up, staring into the ice-cold face of Daniela—shining dark red hair down past her perky boobs, tight white V-neck shirt, cropped navy leather jacket, tight skinny jeans and heels—and a look on her face that says she wants to tear me apart.

"Hello." Her smile is tight as her eyes dart between Vincent and me, finally stopping on my face. Licking her pink lips, she presses them together angrily. "I had no idea you knew my boyfriend. Wait, what was your name again? Evelyn?" She tilts her head to the side, putting a hand on Vincent's back, possessively.

I blink a few times, not sure what to say. I introduced myself at the party, but I'm obviously forgettable.

Vincent sits up in his chair. "Daniela, this is Eve. She's a freshman. Eve, this is my girlfriend, Daniela." Vincent looks at me coldly. Just a moment ago he was an open telephone line, and Daniela just put a finger on the disconnect button.

She sidles closer to him; in front of me is the best-looking couple I've ever seen. They're perfect together. I cower in my seat, feeling awkward in my Target clothing—the one who doesn't belong.

Daniela turns to him, hand massaging his neck. "Vincent, what are you doing here, anyway? Don't you usually go to the gym Monday afternoons?" Her voice is accusing.

He leans into his chair confidently, turning his face away from mine completely. "Yeah, well, Eve has been hanging out with Tom. She's having a tough time in Ancient Philosophy, and he asked me to help her out."

"Wait, your Tom?" she says disbelievingly, moving her hair over her slender right shoulder.

"Yeah. Tom. They met at Cohen's party Saturday."

My heart starts to pound. *Tom? What?* "Eve and I decided to get to know each other some before we cracked our books open. You remember how hard Ancient Philosophy is, don't you? And the start of the semester is the worst." He leans back and puts his hands behind his head casually as if he's got nothing to hide. Meanwhile, she continues to stare at the two of us skeptically.

"Hey," Vincent says to Daniela with a honeyed smile, bringing her attention back to him. "Wanna sit down and study with us?" He glides his fingers over her knuckles in the same way he just did to mine. My heart feels like it's crumbling.

She lifts the strap of her beautiful, quilted, black Chanel bag on her shoulder as she steps closer to him. "That's okay." She looks at me again warily.

"Well," she continues. "I just came to grab a book for French. I need to get home and start this paper. Oh, I'm meeting with my father tonight."

I watch as he slides his fingers between hers. "Make sure you get those questions answered for me, okay baby?"

I want to tear her hair out and then run into a corner and cry.

"Of course, Vincent. We're still going to the movies tomorrow night?" She puts her hands in his hair, pushing his gorgeous dark strands back.

"Sure," he says with a smile.

Casually leaning forward, she presses her lips against his. I swallow back a gasp when he pulls out his hands to bring her closer. He's telling me with his body language that they're together. No—they're better than together. They're in love. The most influential couple on campus is sitting in front of me, and it's not just a simple photo on the internet. Their relationship doesn't look like a ruse, and I'm watching it in real time. Everything he just told me goes up in smoke. What's genuine and what's fake? I can't navigate this.

"Vincent!" She gently pushes away from him as if she's trying to calm him down. "Not here!" I've never felt jealousy to this degree in my life as if she just poured salt on a bloody wound.

She turns toward me again, her smile tight. "Why don't you and Tom come to the movies tomorrow. I mean, you are seeing each other, right? So why not all go together?" Her words sound calm, but there's a calculated edge. Is she testing me?

He chuckles casually. "Sure. I'll make sure Tom's free. But, are you free, Eve?" He cocks his head to the side. I have no way out of this right now; I can't think of an excuse fast enough. Although my mind protests, I shrug my shoulders in agreement.

"Good." She opens her bag and checks her phone. "See you later." She walks away from our table, and I feel totally shell-shocked.

I won't look at him; I just can't do it. Seeing her makes the entire thing clear as day. He has a full-on faux relationship with this girl, and she's gorgeous...and she's tall...and she's rich... and she's smart. I've got to get the hell out of here and away from him. I stand up and from the corner of my eye, can see that he's putting his jacket back on.

"Where's your coat? That scarf isn't going to be enough." His voice is concerned, but I'm too upset to give a shit.

I roll my eyes and finally dare to look up at him. "I didn't bring one, Dad." I open the door of the study room and with one step, he's beside me. I refuse to acknowledge his question, even though the truth is that I left my jacket at my mom's, and there's no way in hell I'm going back there again.

We walk outside into the fresh fall air. "I'll just walk back to the quad," I say, still refusing eye contact, taking wider steps so I can get away from him.

He grabs my arm, spinning me around so we're staring at each other. Pulling off his own jacket, he puts it over my shoulders. "I'm driving you back to your dorm." The man doesn't ask; he orders.

"I'm not getting into your car again." I say with as much strength as I can muster, pulling his jacket roughly off my shoulders, handing it back to him.

He steps closer to me, getting in my space. "Take my damn coat and get in the car. You're cold."

"I don't want your jacket!" I yell, shivering from the wind. My hurt is turning me into a crazy person.

"What you just saw wasn't what you thought. You aren't listening to me. I have to keep her off your ass. You're stronger than this, Eve." He moves closer, lowering his voice. "I've got to keep up the façade. If she thinks I have something going on with someone else—if she even smells that I've got feelings for anyone else—she'll go insane. She's just a lie, Eve. She needs everyone to believe we're a couple."

He stands unwavering, a block of stone. I walk to his car, slamming the door shut and throwing his jacket in the back like it's poisonous. I buckle my seatbelt and cross my arms in front of me, anger coming off me in waves. As we drive, my emotions simmer.

We arrive in the quad and he pulls into a parking spot. Leaning forward with one hand resting on the steering wheel, he turns toward me. Why is it that right now, all I want to do is straddle him and kiss him senseless? I want to imprint myself into him so that the entire universe knows he is mine. Not hers, but mine! My mind is fuming, but my body and heart are obsessed.

"Tom will text you about the movies." His mouth is in a tight line.

I let myself out of his car. Even with the tinted windows, I can feel his eyes on me.

11

VINCENT

I PULL OVER ONCE I'm off campus and dial Tom. After a few rings, he answers.

"Yo." I hear the smile on his face and girls laughing in the background. I raise my head to the roof of the car, annoyed.

"What the fuck are you doing? It's five o'clock on a Monday evening."

"Yeah, so? Everyone isn't as serious as you, motherfucker." The giggling gets louder. "Remember the days you used to actually enjoy pussy?"

I'd reply, but I don't have the energy to engage dumb-as-fuck. "Something's come up. We're going to the movies tomorrow night."

"Cool. Can we see that action flick?"

"Sure. But you've got a date with Eve."

The phone muffles for a second. "Hang on," he says, a question in his voice. I hear some girls complaining in the background and a door slamming shut. "Sorry, dude. Came into the bathroom to hear you better. These girls are seriously insane. Not that I don't enjoy the crazy, if you know what I mean. Anyway, what are you talking about? Why am I going on a date with Eve? I thought she's behind us."

"I was sorting out shit with her in the library. Fifth floor study rooms. Somehow Daniela found her way up there and caught us talking. I lied and told her I was doing you a favor, helping Eve study for Ancient Philosophy."

"Wait." He pauses. "Study. For ancient fucking philosophy? You've got to be kidding me," he scoffs.

"Yeah, study. Because the two of you are hooking up and she needed help. It's actually a pretty hard course." He's silent on the other end, but I can only imagine his red face.

"Fuck no," he spits. "Feed Eve to the wolves for all I fuckin' care. Tell Daniela you fucked her and she's out of your life. The end."

"You will come to this goddamn movie and you will act like you're into her!" I seethe, slamming my hand against the wheel. There's no way I'm letting Daniela hurt Eve...or spread a rumor that she's a whore...or blackball her from a sorority. I know the shit that bitch is capable of, and there's no fuckin' way I'm allowing it. The only way to save Eve from Daniela's wrath is to convince her that nothing has—or ever will—happen between Eve and me."

"Yeah, yeah. I get it. Don't get your panties in a goddamn twist. We'll all go out together. Make it look like she and I are hooking up. And then we're all moving on."

I stay silent, fuming.

"I've got two girls begging to suck my dick right now. I'm not going to sit here on the phone arguing with you. You're a smart man. Use your head. Money is flying into our shit right now faster than a wildfire out in California. We've got the Feds up our asses at the ports. Now isn't the time to ruin this connection with Daniela, brother. I've said it once. I'm saying it again. We're going to the movies and I will make sure Daniela believes that the two of you are nothing. And you wanna know why?" I can hear his hard breaths over the phone. "Because there IS no Vincent and Eve! And then you will delete that girl from your mind so all of us can live in goddamn peace." He hangs up.

I slam my hand against the steering wheel again, cursing.

12

EVE

VINCENT TEXTED me earlier with Tom's number, letting me know Tom will be picking me up for the movies at seven. It's six-thirty and I'm already dressed in a jean skirt and a simple black T-shirt. I was worried I'd be late, and so I overshot my timing. I'd pick up a book, but my nerves are too frayed. And every time I look in the mirror, I find something else about my face that I've recently decided I can't stand. After spending all of my life trying to cover up what I look like, it's weird to all of a sudden give a shit. I know all I have to do is get through this movie, make Daniela believe the truth—that is, there is nothing going on between Vincent and me—and then, move on.

The fact that I'm going against my sister's better judgment has me feeling incredibly guilty. Still, what choice do I have? If I can just get through tonight...

I pull up my phone and see Daniela's newest post on Instagram. She took a selfie of herself in a long mirror, showing off her outfit. Pointy blood-red pumps, light denim that's perfectly distressed with a hole at each knee, a plain white T-shirt tucked in at the front, a long camel sweater, and of course—a gorgeous red-quilted Chanel bag. Twenty-five thousand likes.

Out to the movies with bae tonight. Not sure I'll be able to watch the movie, though... #luckiestgirlalive #hotterthanhollywood #datenight

I stare, unable to take my eyes off the picture. I know he told me this entire thing is for show but it all looks so... perfect! He told me he can't turn from me, now he knows I'm here, but I don't have the type of personality to decipher between social media lies and truth. I can't understand the difference between what my eyes see and what my ears hear from Vincent. I Just *can't.*

My phone pings.

Tom: I'm in the front of the quad.
Me: K

I walk out of the building, breathing in and out. In front of me is a gorgeous white Range Rover, windows darkly tinted.

I open the door, sitting in the passenger seat and buckling up. He's silent next to me. I finally turn to stare at him. He's wearing a black shirt and jeans. Holy crap, he looks scarier than I've ever seen him. Gone is the smiling playboy.

"Let's talk a second."

I exhale loudly, mentally gearing up for what I know won't be a pleasant conversation.

"I know Vincent told you the truth about his relationship with Daniela and the family. And I know you guys had a *thing* going on last year." I stare at him, trying not to show any emotion.

"Tonight is about you and me pretending to be more than friendly. We'll do what we need to do to clean up Vincent's fuck-up yesterday." He stares at me expectantly, waiting for a reply.

"Yes, I know." My voice is full of attitude. I'm furious, and for whatever reason, not afraid to show it.

"Do you also know that I'm going to have to touch you so that she understands you are not a threat to her? I don't want you freaking out—"

"How do you know about that?" I ask accusingly. What has Vincent told him? Internally, I boil.

"I know a lot." The asshole actually smiles, perfect white teeth shining.

"Part of my job description is to have Vincent's back." I blink a few times, understanding that Tom isn't just a typical best friend. He's Borignone mafia—here to support the prince.

"For what it's worth," he continues. "He had no choice but to explain it to me. I mean, shit, after all that went down with Carlos, someone had to clean up that mess, right, Eve?" He says my name with disdain.

"Listen to me." I stare up at the roof of the car, gathering my strength. "I'm not sure what Vincent said or didn't say to you, but it doesn't matter anymore, does it?"

"That's right," he smirks, looking somewhat relieved. "So, I guess you really do understand that whatever you had with Vincent is *finished*. I was worried you had some hope in that pretty little head of yours. But you're too smart. And you'd never want to be the cause of Vincent going to prison, right?" I bristle from his condescending tone.

He pulls out a piece of gum, unwrapping it slowly and sliding it into his mouth.

I blink. "Prison?"

"Daniela's father launders our illegal cash. We can't bury that shit in the fields Pablo Escobar style, can we? Ending things with Daniela means ending business with her daddy. And ending things with her daddy, means the family having dirty cash. The cops will be on our asses in seconds." He chews his gum casually.

"And you've got plans for your own future, don't you? To be the cause of an important man like Vincent Borignone being put away in prison would make a lot of people very. Fucking. Angry." He blows a huge bubble with his gum before it explodes back into his mouth.

I swallow, understanding making my mouth dry up. This is a threat.

"Vincent is family, understand? Nothing comes before that. Not now, and not ever. Especially a piece of ass like yourself."

I clench my teeth. "I heard you, asshole." I stare at him, hard. I may be trying to run from my shitty upbringing, but I also refuse to be a scared little girl, threatened by the big bad mafia boy.

"Look, I'm not trying to hurt you," he says, shrugging a shoulder. "I'll make sure Daniela knows you aren't a threat. I know you've been through a lot—and that for whatever reason—you and Vincent seem to be connected in some really intense way. I'll play along tonight, and then we can all move on." He snaps his gum again and I pull the seat belt down, buckling it over my body. It closes with a *click*.

I raise my head high and with dignity. "Yeah, okay. I get it. No more Vincent or risk putting him in jail. Lie to Daniela. The end," my voice snaps.

"Quick learner." He smirks, facing the wheel. "I see why Vincent is so enthralled. Behind that shy demeanor, you're a damn shark."

We drive for ten minutes down the West Side Highway and finally exit into the city streets. Pulling his car into a private parking lot, the sign reads: $75 per hour. Holy shit! The movie is two plus hours long. I can't believe what he's about to drop in parking costs.

He throws his keys to one of the guys who works there. We finally get to the AMC Theater and through the doors. The place is huge, but I immediately spot him.

Vincent stands by the closest ticket booth to the door, with Daniela by his side. She's staring down at her phone in the same gorgeous outfit that I already saw...thanks to social media. Vincent and I lock eyes for a moment, and then I let my gaze take him in— from his dark jeans to his black hoodie. He's wearing a red and black baseball hat, showcasing his straight roman nose and chiseled jaw. He's scary and huge and sexy as all hell. My legs freeze up, but Tom grabs my hand, ushering me forward.

"Just breathe," he tells me as we walk farther inside. I take his advice and try to relax as I move toward him.

"Yo," Tom starts, pounding his fist with Vincent. Daniela puts up a manicured finger, the universal sign for give me a minute. "I just have to reply to this …" she says to no one in particular as she stares at her phone, furiously typing.

"Eve, I brought your jacket. You forgot it in the library the other day."

My eyes widen as he holds up a coat. What. The. Hell? I'm staring at a beautiful silvery gray puffer jacket, that until this moment, I've never seen before in my life.

"That's not mine," I say under my breath, staring at him in confusion.

"Yes. It's yours. You left it in the library, remember?" His eyes flit over to Daniela, who is still totally oblivious to us; her entire focus is on her phone.

I swallow hard, taking it from his hands. It's exactly what I'd buy if I could afford it. Tears prick my eyes, but I swallow them back.

I squeeze the jacket in my hands before trying it on. It's so soft and light. I zip it closed, tying the belt in a knot around my waist. It's a perfect fit. I touch the hood and my jaw drops to the floor when I feel it, realizing that it's lined in what feels like real fur. I look at Vincent, whose eyes have so much warmth in them that I die a little inside.

I turn to Tom, who looks like he's about to rail. He's squinting at Vincent with a what-the-fuck look on his face.

When Tom sees I'm watching, he looks me up and down, almost resigned. "Look at you. You look like a beautiful little Eskimo." He smiles not unkindly, throwing the hood over my head playfully so I'm practically drowning in warmth and softness.

I pull the hood back down and watch as he looks at Vincent. "Good thing you brought her jacket, man. It's supposed to be a freezing winter." The sarcasm drips off his voice.

"Yeah, it is." Vincent's standing tall with an almost dead-eyed stare when Daniela pops her head up, breaking the tension.

"Hey guys," she says happily, completely having missed the exchange.

"Daniela, you remember Eve?" Tom asks, throwing a heavy arm around my shoulders.

I stare up at her, probably looking as scared and nervous as I feel.

She is so tall, staring down at me with a wry grin as if she's trying not to laugh. Insecurity blazes through me.

"Yeah, of course." She raises a perfectly plucked eyebrow. "We met at a party and then the library. While Vincent was tutoring her. Right, baby?" She holds onto Vincent's arm possessively, pursing her lips that somehow look bigger today than the other night.

All of a sudden, her face morphs—as she looks me up and down—with something like shock. "Wait. Where did you get that jacket?"

"Uh, a friend bought it for me." I dart my eyes to the side nervously.

"How is that fucking possible?" she quickly replies. "I've been looking everywhere for that coat in that color, and it's impossible to find! Is it Moncler?" She's fuming. I'm ready to rip it off my back and hand it to her if she'll just calm down and leave me alone.

She puts her hands on the belt of my coat, and I guess it confirms her suspicions. "It doesn't make sense that you have it."

"You're hilarious, Daniela. It's just a fuckin' coat. Go to Bergdorf or whatever and pick one up if you like it so goddamn much."

"You're funny, Vincent," she says mockingly. "I can't just *pick it up* because that color is not available." She moves her hands to her hips, waiting for me to speak.

"Well," I say, my voice quivering. "A friend of mine works at Bergdorf, so I'm sure that's how she managed to get it." I shrug, trying to act as if one of the biggest socialites in New York City isn't about to rip my head off.

"What department?" Daniela counters.

"She's, um, at the hair salon," I say with my head high. The lie twists in my gut, but I do my best to act like the words out of my mouth are truth. And since Janelle does actually work at the salon, I'm sure I could back up my story if need be.

"Whatever." She pulls the phone back from her purse and furiously types, probably ripping her assistant a new one for not getting her this jacket before I did.

Vincent grunts something that sounds like, "The movie's starting soon," and gives the tickets to the bald guy at the ticket booth. He rips them in half, handing the stubs back to each of us as we pass. Vincent chooses seats in the back; no one is behind us.

"Anyone want popcorn?" Vincent asks. I'd love some, but there's no way in hell I'm opening my mouth to say yes. I need to get through the night in one piece.

"Get me a small. No butter. Not even a little bit. Totally plain, okay?"

I'm internally cursing Vincent. He couldn't just buy me a regular jacket from The Gap or something? He had to go and buy me something like this? God, it must have cost a fortune.

Vincent leaves the theater. I think about the crunchy, salty popcorn and sweet fake butter, and my stomach grumbles. Too bad I won't be having any tonight.

Tom takes my hand, lacing his fingers through mine. His hands aren't hard and calloused like Vincent's, but they are still warm. Daniela watches us with a smile on her face. One thing is for sure— Tom is in it to win it. I've got to get my head back in the game and make sure she believes that I'm here for Tom. I snuggle closer into his side.

"Aw! You guys are seriously cute together."

"Thanks," I reply, trying my best to act happy, even though I'm anything but. This movie couldn't start fast enough.

Daniela clicks her tongue. "So, Evelyn, where are you from?"

Tom laughs. "Come on, Daniela. What is this, the inquisition? And her name is Eve, not Evelyn." Tom squeezes my hand in what feels like solidarity.

"Get a life, Tom. I'm trying to make conversation." She smiles, and I feel my palms start to sweat. "If she's your girlfriend, I'm going to be spending lots of time with her, right?"

"She's from the city. Grew up downtown."

"Really? What part?" She seems happy, but a nagging voice in my head reminds me that this is a test.

"Near SoHo," he replies smugly, staring at me as if I'm heaven on earth.

She looks at us skeptically, and I do my best to stare back at Tom as if I couldn't be happier.

"What school did you go to?"

I put my hair behind my ears. "I went to a public school, actually."

"Public?" she says incredulously. "And you still got into school at Columbia? Holy shit, you must be freakin' smart then. Half of these kids got in because their families donate or went here themselves."

"Isn't she something?" Tom says, staring at me with stars in his eyes.

Daniela hums, looking me up and down. "You're so... small. Kind of like a little girl, actually." She's doing that thing again, where she's laughing at me with her eyes. She hasn't said anything so bad, but the energy she's giving off is vile.

"Little girl?" Tom stares at my boobs blatantly and my face heats. "Not in any of the ways it matters, she doesn't. She's definitely...fresh, though, if that's what you're implying." He licks his lips and I'm so embarrassed, I can't bear to look up.

Moments later, the previews begin and the theater darkens. Tom lets go of my palm and I feel relieved. I'm trying to settle into my seat when Vincent returns, handing Tom two drinks.

"Eve," Vincent whispers, handing me a huge popcorn and four different candy boxes. My eyes widen, and I want to jump up and down and scream in excitement. He turns to Daniela next, giving her a small bag.

Movies are expensive as hell, and add in all these treats? It's something I've never been able to afford. When Janelle and I were younger, we'd buy bootleg DVDs from the guys in Chinatown who would bring a camcorder to the movies, record the entire film, and then sell the recording for $1.99 to kids like us. The picture was always a little shaky because no one's hand can stay perfectly straight, and the screen would black out for a minute or two if anyone in the audience stood up to use the bathroom or something. But still, it was as close to a movie-going experience as I could expect.

My gaze moves to Vincent and Daniela, whose hand rubs up and down his leg possessively. His form is rigid. "Ugh, I can't see with this guy in front of me. Can we switch seats, Vincent?" Daniela asks.

They both stand and Danielle squeezes by Vincent, rubbing against his body like a cat before planting herself in his old seat. *Shit.* Vincent is now next to me. His muscular thigh brushes up against mine and I squeeze my legs together, sitting straighter in my chair. He reaches over to me, pulling out boxes of candy from my side. "You feel like chocolate tonight?" I turn to face him and swallow hard, nodding. He opens a box of Reese's Pieces and pours them into my popcorn. "Eat them together; it's the best. Used to eat this as a kid and loved it."

I stare at him dumbly.

"Go on," he says. I put my hands into the popcorn, pulling up a handful of popcorn mixed with the chocolate. The minute I put it all into my mouth, I let out an involuntary moan. "This is beyond good," I tell him with a mouthful. He chuckles and nods at me. "You sure you don't want some?"

He puts his hand in the popcorn, smiling. Bringing up a handful, he puts it into his mouth. "Delicious," he tells me, staring at my mouth. The tension between us is so loud nothing other than him registers.

He leans over me, lifting a drink from the holder next to my seat. "I brought you Cherry Coke and regular. Try them both to see which you want." I bend down, wrapping my lips around the straw. "Cherry," I tell him, my voice a whisper.

"Regular Coke for you," he tells Tom. His eyes don't leave mine.

"Damn. I love the cherry!" Tom complains.

"You want mine?" I immediately ask, turning my head.

"No," Vincent interjects, leaving no room for negotiation. I risk a glance at Daniela, who is thankfully completely focused on her cell phone.

Finally, the movie starts, and I try to relax. Staring at the screen, Vincent leans toward me, shifting his arm so we share an armrest. Then his leg rubs against my leg. I want to concentrate, but it's basically impossible with him this close. I can smell him, all woodsy, soapy, and clean. With each passing minute, he inches closer until his enormous hand is wrapped around my thigh. I clench my teeth, unsure what is going on right now. I shift forward to see Daniela; thankfully she's totally oblivious and still staring at her phone.

Vincent's fingers rove higher on my leg. I keep my head forward, staring at the screen, trying not to pant. My mind and body are engaging in a war right now.

A little higher...

I should make him stop!

His hands are so warm...

His fingers begin to move up and down in a steady rhythm, turning my body into a furnace. What is he doing to me?

I turn toward him, wanting to give him a what-the-fuck-are-you-doing look, but he's still facing the screen. I can see the outline of his dark lashes and the shadows across his sharp cheekbones and scruffy jaw. His face looks even more fierce in this dim light. I never thought it was possible for someone to be so captivating.

His hand roams even higher now, and I lean my head back against the seat, all rational thought disappearing. I'm assaulted by memories of what these fingers can do. Sweat beads on my lower back as his hand drifts upward, centimeter by agonizing centimeter, moving closer to my core. I forgot how possessive he is, but he's showing me right now—loud and clear—that he's the only one in control. Holy shit, but I want to straddle him and then punch him in the face!

I watch from my side-eye as he lifts my Cherry Coke, bringing the straw to his full lips. Tilting his head back slightly, I can see his Adam's apple move with each swallow. It's as if he is completely unaffected. Meanwhile, my panties are damn near soaked. I'm mindless, all rational thought exiting my brain.

Tom stands, walking past all of us to I guess use the bathroom.

Daniela stands up next. "I've gotta make a call."

We turn to each other at the same time; he puts his hands around my ass and lifts me straight into his lap. *Oh my God.* He's so hard. Insistent. Grinding me against him and kissing me like his life depends on it. His tongue drifts down my throat. Before I can even process being on *Vincent*, he moves me back to my chair. Not a moment later, Tom and Daniela both shuffle back to their seats. Can they hear my heavy breathing?

He doesn't touch me for the rest of the movie.

When the film is over, Tom throws an arm around my shoulders. I know I'm supposed to act like we're together, but after that kiss with Vincent, I feel confused and dazed, my heart still beating erratically. We walk out of the theater as a group, and I try not to stumble over my own feet.

Daniela seems relieved; as far as I'm concerned, mission accomplished. Now that I'm no longer an issue, I'm ignorable.

We all say goodbye and Tom drops me off at my dorm. Before I can get out, he locks the door, keeping me within the confines of his car. I turn around, wanting to ask what the hell he's doing when he starts. "Eve. Stay away from Vincent. Our life—and our lifestyle—isn't for a girl like you. Go meet some nice normal guy. You deserve that. That's what Angelo would want, too."

I exhale. For a moment, I forgot that my Angelo is an associate. He may be lowly in their ring, but he's still part of them.

I hear the *pop* of the door unlocking. As I walk to my room, Tom's advice is on repeat in my head. Still, I can't ignore what Vincent does to me—not just in body, but in mind, too. I need to stay away from him because when we're together, the tension is too much to manage. How could I have made out with him like that, and in a public place no less? He makes me completely mindless.

I wish I didn't know who he was behind the mafia man; I wish I had no clue how loving and caring and brilliant he is beneath the hard surface. I sigh, taking off my clothes and gently placing the jacket on my desk chair, and then sliding on an old band T-shirt I got ages ago from the thrift shop.

I know I should give the jacket back, but I don't want to.

Crawling into bed, sleep refuses to come. The thought of tonight being the last time my lips will ever touch Vincent's is killing me inside. I shut my eyes and somehow catch his scent; my heart slows down and I fall asleep, imagining him next to me.

13

EVE

SOMETIME LATER IN THE EVENING, I hear a knock. I wake up, startled. Checking my clock, it's after two in the morning. Must be some drunken frat guy. I put my head back on my pillow when the *bang* comes again. I finally stand to get the door, rubbing the sleep from my eyes as I drag myself across the room to open it.

It's Vincent. He steps inside and closes the door, twisting the lock behind him. "What are you doing here?" My voice croaks as my eyes adjust to the man in front of me. I didn't shut the shades when I got home tonight, and the city gives the room a dim glow. My eyes finally acclimate from being awoken and I notice blood trickling down his eyebrow. "Oh my God. You need a doctor!" I press my fingers to my lip in a gut reaction.

He chuckles. "It's nothing a little TLC can't fix." His voice is sure but tired.

I crouch under my bed and pull out a simple first-aid kit that Angelo got for me. Vincent sits at my desk while I grab a washcloth and wet it at the small sink by my door. He sits while I clean off his cuts and cover them with ointment. With him sitting and me standing, we're finally eye to eye.

"Your cheekbone is darkening," I tell him, gently grazing his face with my thumb. "What happened? Was it a fight, or—"

"Tonight, just a fight."

I shake my head, hating how he constantly puts himself in harm's way.

"It's fun for me, that's all. It's one thing in my life that really is that simple. I just do it 'cause I love it. Not for any end." He shrugs and then curses; the movement seems to have caused him pain.

"Did you hurt your ribs?" I help him pull off his shirt, noticing a dark bruise spreading across his side. I want to touch him, but I'm nervous. I gape at his body, my eyes glued to his chiseled muscles.

"Eve," he says my name reverently. I look up. The small towel drops from my grip and onto the floor. His fingers move to my face, slowly grazing my cheek and down to my neck. His touch is gentle but possessive. I shut my eyes, savoring the feeling. I let out a soft moan as he continues to stroke me. "I can't stay away from you. I need you. Don't you need me? I can't be near you and not have you."

14

VINCENT

STANDING UP FROM THE CHAIR, I move to sit on her makeshift king-sized bed. She comes next to me, biting the bottom of her lip. She's hesitant, but her face is flushed from my touch.

"My father was in prison." I'm not entirely sure why I'm divulging this information, but something inside of me needs this connection with her. I want to tell her everything. "I was seven at the time. Lived with Tom and his family for eight years while my dad did time."

She hums, letting me know she's listening, her body swaying toward mine as I speak. "My mom died while giving birth to me out on the rez. My dad barely knew her. He actually tried to get gaming off the ground, but the Tribal Council was against having anyone who didn't have Native blood work with them. Even with a Native wife, they didn't accept him. Once I was born, he brought me back to New York. Back to the family. This violence and this life is what I was raised on, Eve."

I shift, bringing her closer to me so that we're touching. I want to pull off her clothes, feel her naked skin on mine. But I have to get this off my chest—make sure she knows what she's getting with me. It goes against everything I know, but I can't just...take her. She deserves more than that.

"I'm technically perfect for this world. I've got enough self-awareness to understand that I'm built for it physically and mentally. But it's still not what I want. I want out. I want to be free. I can't leave the family in all ways; I understand that. But I'm physically leaving here soon. And when I go, I want you with me. I can't promise a life with a small yellow house and a white picket fence. But I can promise you... maybe a clean trailer out on the rez." She pushes an errant hair from my eyes, a small smile playing on her lips.

"Nothing surrounding us for miles." I raise my eyebrows, looking at her with thoughts of the future in my mind. "I'll buy us a motorcycle and we can spend our nights riding free. I'll work hard and build out the hotel and casino. You can be my lawyer. What do you say? Let's keep this secret, for now. I want the real, Eve. And you're it. I can't wait anymore."

"Vincent." She drops her head onto my chest, wetness moving from her eyes and dampening my skin. I pull her body to mine, wrapping my arms around her small shoulders.

"Say yes, baby." I'm practically groveling, the sound of my voice foreign to me. "Trust me. Trust in me. I have these last few months, and then I'm going out there. You can stay here and we'll do long distance if you want."

She sniffles. "What about the lies? And Tom told me about prison. And you're making it sound so perfect, easy, even. But it isn't, Vincent. And my sister. She—"

"It IS easy. And lockup is always a possibility for me. I'm not going to lie to you. That's the truth. But I'll make it as simple as it can be. We'll be careful. Your sister? She'll understand eventually. Just say yes to me, baby. Say ye—"

She grabs my head and presses her lips to mine, stunning me.

I pull her closer, so every part of me is touching every part of her. I slowly take off her T-shirt. She shudders, completely topless in my arms. Her body is my heaven; I want to worship it.

She moves forward, grabbing the covers to pull them over herself.

"Don't cover yourself from me. Not now. Not ever."

She drops her hands and lets me take my fill of her body with my eyes. God, this girl. Mine. Thank fuck it isn't dark in here; the city lights have me seeing every beautiful inch of her clear skin.

A thought crosses my head—that maybe someone can see through the window. I stand up hesitantly, shutting the blinds with a curse on my lips. It's a reminder that I won't be able to have her openly, and I hate it.

I move back into the bed, pulling her soft and pliant body on top of mine as her small hands frame my face. She leans in, lips to my ear. "Are we really going to do this?" Her voice is a prayer.

I flip her beneath me so she's lying on the bed and shift myself to the bottom, sliding off her underwear with my hands. "Yeah, baby. We are."

Moving back up, I press my hands against her core. She immediately pushes herself toward me. I know what she wants, but I need to drag it out as long as I can. I palm her, feeling wetness straight through her simple cotton underwear. She's soaked.

"Always so ready for me. Fuck. I'm going to give you everything I have tonight, and then some." She's panting now as I shift my hand rhythmically against her. Every single cell in my body is yelling to get closer. To brand her. I want to get so deep inside her I'll become part of her.

She stops for a moment, and my brain registers there's something she wants to say. "What's wrong?"

"Vincent, I—"

All at once, I decide I can't let her continue. I put my thumb over her lips to quiet her. I can tell from her expression she wants to say a million things. She's angry with me for withholding all of this from her last year. She's furious I have this bullshit girlfriend. She's mad I have duties to the family. I stare at her intently. "I know, Eve. I feel all your anger, too. Hang onto me through this, and we'll make it out together. All we need is time."

"How do you read me like this, Vincent?" she asks quietly, grabbing my hair.

"I read you because I listen to you. I listen to your body. I listen to your eyes." I lift her face and start kissing her, bringing the focus back to the moment. Eve is so tiny I can easily move my hands from the tips of her toes up to her entire body. I finally let myself just consume her with my mouth, drinking in her essence.

I take my time sucking on her neck, down her chest and onto her nipples. She doesn't realize what I'm doing, but something primal inside me is forcing me to mark her. She moans from the deep sensation of my mouth sucking on her skin. I know I'm intense, but I can be no one other than myself.

She grips my neck, pulling me down to her. I know she's ready for me. I put two of my fingers into her mouth and she opens wide for me. "Suck."

She does what she's told, twirling her soft tongue and coating my fingers. When I pull them from her lips, she looks at me with nervousness and love. I pause for a moment, swallowing hard and savoring the feeling.

"Eve, I love you. You know that, right?" I couldn't stop the words even if I wanted to.

"Tell me this is real, Vincent." Her voice is a plea.

"This is never-ending."

"Tell me you'll stay safe for me."

"I won't lie to you; I live a dangerous life. You see me here and in school, but I've got duality, remember?"

I slide one wet finger into her core, and she immediately gasps, gripping my shoulders. She's so fucking tight I groan, adding a second finger and curling them up, hitting that spot. I can barely believe that a girl this beautiful has never been touched before. She was made for me. Every second of this moment is mine and mine alone, and I plan on making sure I set a benchmark so damn high, no man on earth could ever compete.

When I look down, her entire body is coated in a light sheen of sweat. Fucking perfect. I finally move up over her. "You still want this? I need to hear it." My voice is a raspy whisper.

"Oh God, Vincent, p-please..." she begs. I slide a pillow underneath her butt, giving me a better angle to enter her.

Eve's skin. Eve's dark hair. Eve's lips, so pouty and beautiful. Eve's nipples, a perfect shade of rose. I see the red splotches all over her chest from my mouth and it spurs me on. Mine.

"Come inside me...don't wait anymore," she begs, hooking her legs around me in an effort to keep me in place. I laugh at her attempt to stop me from moving away. I'm so much bigger than her, there's no way she could physically restrain me. But the truth is with just one word from her, I'd bow at her feet. She's the queen, and I'm nothing but her servant. She doesn't want me to tease her anymore? Her wish is my command.

"I'm clean, but I want to get a condom on until we get you on the pill." I try to move off the bed, but she grips me tightly. "Just a sec, okay?" I kiss her forehead and move off. Pulling out a condom from my wallet, I slide it on. She watches with a wide-eyed stare, looking at my dick with anxiety.

I chuckle. "Don't worry. It'll fit."

"Are you sure? I don't know, Vincent. I don't think that's possible. I mean, I obviously didn't realize before how enormous it is. And I'm so much smaller than you. What if I break?"

I laugh out loud. "I swear it. You were made for me. Nothing will make you feel as good as this. Lay down."

She does as I ask, but I can tell from her body language that she's tightened up. I kiss her lips and neck until she's rolling her body beneath me.

She moves her lips to my ear. "Do it now, Vincent. I'm ready."

I don't listen. Instead, I slide my fingers around her clit, swirling them until she's writhing in pleasure. With a breath, I sink into her heat. It's been a while and I freeze, willing myself to hold back. "You okay?" My voice sounds strangled, even to my own ears.

"Vincent. It's too much—"

"It's okay. Just breathe through it and let your body relax." I smooth the hair away from her face. I know my dick is the first she's ever seen, but if Eve really knew how big I am compared to other guys, she probably would have run away at the sight of it. I don't want to hurt her any more than I have to, so I will myself to be as slow and gentle as possible. Sweat gathers on my forehead, dripping from my head onto her chest.

She grips my shoulders, staring deeply into my eyes as I finally push in all the way. The moment I feel the breakthrough, I have to stop. It feels too good.

I hear her suck in a breath. "It burns, Vincent."

"I know, baby. Keep breathing."

We're all tongues and groans. Never in my life did I kiss like this during sex. Holy shit, but every inch of me is begging for this connection with her. My body is tense from going slow, my movements driving us both to the brink of euphoria. I want to make this good for her. Make it last.

I watch as the electricity enters her bloodstream. "Ohhh," she says on an exhale as if bliss has hit her all at once. She's so close. I track every movement she makes. When her pussy starts to tighten, I think I may pass out. With every thrust, I'm marking her slow and deep. My ribs are aching, but nothing short of a gun to my head would make me stop. Finally, with a groan, I finish. She holds onto me with her legs still wrapped around my waist, and I can sense her unwillingness to let me go.

Pressing another kiss on her shoulder and then her lips, I stand again. After taking care of the condom, I walk to her small closet and pull out a fresh washcloth, wetting it with hot water from her tiny sink. Before getting back into bed, we lock eyes. She's waiting for me with her legs closed, looking at me expectantly. She's unsure what she's supposed to do, and I can't help but laugh.

"Open up for me, baby. I think things may have gotten a little messy." When she opens her thighs, what I see turns me from possessive to wholly insane. I clean her off gently, making sure not to miss a spot.

"You're in me now," she whispers. She has no idea how badly I want that to be true. I want every man who ever sees her to know that she's taken.

I pull her flush against me. "I want to own every single part of you." I grab her waist tightly.

"But you do, Vincent," she replies. "You have me."

The look I see in her eyes? It's more than love. So much is moving between us that I feel high. I shift, kissing her entire body. She's giggling as I find her ticklish spots, nuzzling between her breasts and behind her ear. We kiss and play around in bed and it's so innocent and yet, it's ecstasy. Something I never imagined possible.

Sometime around four in the morning, I stand to leave. She's watching as I dress myself, first with my pants and then sliding on my shirt. My ribs feel like they're on fire, but my heart is too damn happy to care.

"Vincent, don't leave me yet. Why do you need to go?" I hear her distress, but I need to leave before anyone sees me. The truth is, we should have done this at my place in SoHo.

I crouch down by her bedside. "This isn't goodbye, okay? I just don't want anyone to see me leaving here in the morning. I love you." Have words ever felt more natural rolling off my tongue?

She nods her head in understanding.

I lift my hand, scratching the back of my neck. "I'm a selfish fuck, Eve. I couldn't help myself last night. If you're bruised on your neck and chest, don't be afraid, okay? It's just from my mouth. You also might be sore down there. Just take it easy the next few days, yeah?" I know that Eve knows nothing other than me. She was so innocent before I came into her life...*Jesus, forgive me.*

She pushes the sheet down, staring at her skin. "You like marking me." She states it as a fact and she's absolutely right. I do love it. If I could, I'd go back over them now and make the bruises darker. Last longer. Everyone on earth should know she's taken.

I drop to my knees and put my forehead against hers, breathing in her breaths. She lightly pushes me back, forcing eye contact.

"I want to take the risk."

I press our lips together, pulling back for just enough time to get a few words out. "I love you." Kiss. "I fucking love you." Kiss. "So much." I don't let go, even when I taste the salt from her tears. I finally slow us down and push myself back up again.

"Vincent, you're everything to me." Her voice is laced with love, but also pain. "I'm a-afraid, though. I've worked so hard to get here, and—"

"I swear it. I'll never take your future from you." Taking the small gold crucifix off my neck, I push her hair to the side and close the clasp at her nape. Kissing the cross to the center of her throat, I blink into her large brown eyes. Her long lashes open and close, and then somehow, I get myself up and walk out her door.

15

EVE

I SPEND my entire day studying. Every time I move my body, I feel where Vincent had been. The reminder heats my blood and makes my heart ache at the same time. I hate the idea of sneaking around. But he's right about one thing; I'd rather have him this way than not at all. He's a risk I'm willing to take. I just have to hang on for the rest of the school year, and then he can publicly break it off with Daniela and we can just be normal. The fact that he's Borignone mafia worries the hell out of me, too. But when he leaves the East Coast, he won't be in the middle of the fire anymore. I believe him. I can handle it.

I hate that I'll be lying to Janelle. While we aren't technically cheating, if anyone else in the world saw us together, they'd assume we were. The idea has my stomach churning. Claire's warning that Daniela would make my life a living hell pounds in my skull, too.

I move my hand to my neck, pressing his necklace against my throat. He loves me. We'll be okay because we have to be. Life can't be so cruel to finally give him to me, and then take him away.

I have an exam in Ancient Philosophy in five days and I need a good grade to do well in the class. I turn back to chapter one, hoping if I read the passages over and over, it'll all become clear to me.

My phone pings.

Claire: Hey girl! Late dinner tonight?
Me:I'm so screwed for my Ancient Phil test. I don't know shit!
Claire:Ugh, it's the hardest class freshman yr. Buckle down!
Me:I'm going to have to pull a few all-nighters studying...
Claire:I wish I could help you but it would be the blind leading the blind. I got a C in that class by the skin of my teeth
Me:I'm not sure what the hell I'm going to do. I got a C- on the last paper and I need an A on this test if I'm going to pull a decent final grade. Plus, Prof Schlesinger is an a$$hole
Claire:Totally
Claire: OMG! We need to pull a Cher from *Clueless* and hook him up with some other prof. Maybe if he were getting laid, he wouldn't be such a fucking dickhead!
Me:LMAO!
Me:But all that shit aside, the test! I'm so screwed....

My night passes quietly. Vincent texted me that he was busy tonight with work, which I guess means family stuff. I hope he's okay.

The next morning I'm leaving my chemistry lab when I spot Vincent. We see each other, and I watch as his eyes light up. I want to run to him and say hello when Daniela struts out of a different room, walking directly into his arms and placing a slow kiss on his lips for everyone to see. Her back arches, long hair swishing to the side in perfectly curled tendrils. I struggle for breath while students watch the spectacle.

I shouldn't be dumbfounded, but I am. We're all stargazers in the show titled: *Vincent and Daniela*. Finally, as if the kiss was more like five minutes as opposed to a few seconds, she pulls back. Her hands move up his chest and then into his hair as her lips move. Acid burns

straight up from my stomach through my throat. I'm having a physical reaction to them together. I want to run away, but my feet feel as
though they're cemented to the floor.

They walk by me.

Vincent ignores my existence.

I drop my head, feeling utterly worthless. I check my cell for the
time and notice I'm going to be late for Calculus. I scurry on to my
next class, my backpack heavy on my shoulders. I can't think of him
now. I have class to attend.

I knew seeing him with her would be like this, but watching it in
real time is more painful than I ever imagined. Now that we've had
sex, it's as if everything I felt for him before is amplified. For a
moment, I imagine if this is how my mom felt when she was the girl
on the side for so many men. But then, I push the thought away.
Vincent and I aren't like that. We aren't. We really truly aren't.

I run out of the science center and enter the mathematics building. Thankfully, it's my last class of the day. I jog up to the third floor
and about to turn the corner when an arm snakes out, pulling me
into an empty classroom. I want to scream with fear as the door slams
shut behind me. But when I turn around, it's Vincent.

He lifts me up and presses me against the wall. Within minutes,
I'm moaning into his mouth, getting lost between his lips and the
heat of his body. Pulling back for a second, he stares into my eyes and
breathes heavy.

"Hi," he tells me, nuzzling into my neck. I'm in a fog of bliss, but I
know that I need to mention what I saw in the halls. If we're going to
do this, I can't be afraid to speak up.

"Vincent, I don't like what I saw." I push the words out of my
mouth before I can second-guess myself.

"What did you see?" His eyebrows are raised teasingly and I can
tell he's trying to play, turn the awkwardness from the hallway into
a joke.

"Stop. I'm serious." He doesn't respond, but his eyes turn
into slits.

"You know what you saw is what's expected. She needs that

public display of affection." His face reddens as if he's trying to stay calm.

"All you ever do is what's expected of you, huh?"

"You're kidding, right?" He lets out a breath, eyes narrowing at me. I swallow hard. "I don't fuck her, Eve. I walk around with her like we're together. That's all there is," he replies angrily.

"Put me down!" I say, struggling to be freed from his arms. He slowly lowers me to the floor and then runs his hands through his thick hair, pulling on the ends as he walks away from me to the other end of the classroom.

"You're unbelievable, Vincent. You're the one who kisses Daniela around the halls, and I'm the crazy one for being mad? How about I have lunch with Jared today?"

He pivots around and in a blink of an eye, he's back in front of me. I forgot how fast he is. The look on his face is terrifying, but I'm not afraid of him. "You touch another man and I will fucking end him. Are we clear? We have gone over this already. Daniela and I have to look like a goddamn couple! You can't get upset every time you see us together. It just won't work."

"I can't stand it. Just—stop touching her!" I stomp my foot on the ground as hysteria rises in my chest.

He lifts me, putting me on a desk and leans into me, his hands on either side of my thighs. "Look at me, Eve. I cannot—under any circumstances—end shit with her right now. I need to keep her happy. This is non-negotiable."

"I know." I hear the whine in my voice but can't help it. I know I'm not being fair but seeing them together guts me.

"Tell me what you want. Talk to me." He moves his hands around my waist, lifting me up and pulling my butt to the edge of the desk, closer to him.

I put my fingers on his lips. "I don't want her touching you here. Your mouth is mine." I move my fingers to his hair. "Or here." I run my fingers through his dark strands, it's wild and sexy as hell.

"I need a haircut," he tells me with smiling eyes.

"No. I love it long like this."

"Then I won't cut it." He presses me to his chest and I let out a long exhale.

I move out of his arms. "Actually, how does Daniela like it?"

"She likes it long too, I think," he grunts.

"In that case, I want you to shave it all off." He laughs out loud and I can't help but giggle. I put my nose into his chest, smelling him. "I love you so much, Vincent. You don't understand."

He lifts my head with his hands, forcing eye contact. "I swear I do." He pulls me against his lips again and I do my best to kiss him with every ounce of myself. "But you can't keep allowing your insecurities to affect you like this. Promise me you aren't going to get upset every time you see us together. I love you and only you."

My eyes inadvertently glance up at the classroom clock. "Oh shit, I'm missing Calculus!"

He shrugs. "Take the skip. You don't need that class anyway."

"Don't be a bad influence on me, Vincent! I need an *A*."

"I wouldn't have taken you out of a class that you were struggling in. You're going to get an *A*. And you're going to get into law school. And all of your dreams will come true."

We breathe each other in, our mouths so close, but not touching.

He lets out a playful growl. "Lips only belong to you. Hair only belongs to you. Dick only belongs to you..."

I slap him in the chest, laughing. I can't help the flush that comes into my cheeks. I love this man.

"Come downtown with me tonight at four. We'll study together."

"Really?"

"Of course."

"I'm doing shitty in Ancient Philosophy. I think you jinxed me that day in the library." I lift my brows.

"It's a good thing I wasn't lying when I said I got an *A* in that class."

"You're kidding me."

"Nope. You have Schlesinger?"

My eyes bug out. "Tell me there is something on this earth you suck at." I raise my head to the ceiling, looking for God. But when I bring my gaze back down to earth, all I'm met with are Vincent's laughing eyes.

"Not the way to speak to your new tutor, Eve."

"Oh hell, no! I'm not letting you tutor me." I pull my hair back with my hands, tying it back with a black tie from my wrist.

He stares at my lips and smirks. "Why not? I'm a good teacher. I have a paper due tomorrow, but I can get it done easily now that my outline is done." I give him a face as if nothing sounds worse. "Don't look too excited, Eve," he deadpans.

I sigh. "All right. Four o'clock?"

"Four o'clock. Don't be late."

"Oh? Or what?" I sass.

"Or you'll get punished." He winks before pulling me in for another kiss.

16

EVE

"WHEN IT COMES to Aristotle's Nicomachean Ethics, the most important thing to understand is his explanation of a good life for a human being. Aristotle's approach is a practical one. He sees the one big purpose of human existence is to reach the highest good, which must be both intrinsically valuable and self-sufficient. Remember those prongs."

Vincent is lecturing me right now about Ancient Philosophy. We're sitting together at his dining table, books spread out around us. My feet are bare, resting against his legs.

"Okay, but I don't understand how he understands those two concepts." I bite my bottom lip.

"If something is intrinsically valuable, then it's good in itself and never pursued for the sake of something else. For example, if you study to get an *A*, then studying isn't intrinsically valuable. If you study for the sake of studying in itself, then it is."

"Okay. So like, your underground fights are intrinsically valuable?"

"Exactly." His lips quirk up in a smile.

"Okay, and what about self-sufficient?"

"This means that by itself, it makes life worth living. The good life for Aristotle is a life in which we flourish. Make sure to use that word on the test, yeah? Schlesinger will love it. Anyway, all activity should be directed in such a way to give us that life."

I take a deep breath, feeling like everything is finally clicking. "Okay, Professor Borignone. So, what is the flourishing life?"

"Easy. For Aristotle, it's performing your specific activity, which is distinctive to human beings in general, in a state of excellence."

"Ah hah!" I exclaim happily.

"Let's move to the mean. For Aristotle, the mean is not about balance or moderation. Instead, it's about what is appropriate. Sometimes, it's appropriate to be angry. The mean for Aristotle is one which varies."

"This is where you use practical judgment to know what's right, using deliberation and calculation?"

"Yes!" His smile is blinding.

He takes another huge gulp of water as turns the page of the textbook.

"How do you drink this much and not have to pee every other second?"

He chuckles. "I'm just replenishing. You can't imagine the amount I sweat when I work out. I made the mistake a few years ago of not giving myself enough water and I passed out naked on the locker room floor."

I bite my cheek, shocked at the fact that something that crazy both happened to him, and that he'd tell me about it. Then the image of naked Vincent hits me like a train and I have to bite my cheek to stop myself from cheesing from the visual.

"That mind of yours, always in the gutter, Eve. Didn't your mama teach ya any manners?" His terrible southern drawl has me doubling over in laughter.

Finally, I stop, letting my eyes roam from his neck down to his perfectly cut chest and then back up to his dark eyes.

"Don't look at me like that. I'm trying to help you learn," he says, kissing the top of my head. "Plus, you need a break after yesterday."

I nod my head in agreement, but internally, I'm begging him not to give me a break. Because the truth is, I don't want to wait. Now that I've had him once, I want it again. And again. He pulls back and I let my fingers trace his face. He has two old scars through his right eyebrow. "Where did you get these?"

"Bad boys have scars, Eve." He winks.

"Well, apparently, bad boys aren't very bad these days. They like to be gentle and sweet."

"Gentle and sweet?" Lifting me in his arms, he runs full speed into his bedroom. "Let's see how gentle and sweet I can be, huh?" Throwing me onto his huge bed, he lifts up my shirt and blows into my stomach until I'm crumbling with laughter. The playful side of Vincent is so incredibly unexpected.

His face turns serious as he moves me to the edge of the bed, sinking down on his knees to take my pants off. Next, I raise my arms as he takes my T-shirt over my head.

For whatever reason, I'm feeling braver today than ever before. Maybe it's because I saw him in the hallway with Daniela, and I want to remind him of what he has. Or maybe it's because I'm tired of being the shy girl I used to be.

I stand, removing my bra and underwear. I'm completely nude in front of him. With hooded eyes, he swallows every inch of me with his gaze. Shaking his head as he lifts me up, he carries me into the bathroom. I have no idea why he brought me here, but any questioning thoughts in my head exit my brain as he places me on the marble countertop.

What starts as our mouths moving in a gentle caress quickly becomes frenzied. He's kissing me so deeply that my lips turn numb; I'm mindless from the pleasure. Letting go of my mouth, he lowers his head, licking and sucking on my nipples, moving from one side to the next.

"You like that, baby?" All I can do is whimper. My body is humming, core pulsing with need. Releasing one breast with a pop, I feel cold air take the place of where his hot mouth was. I open my eyes, wondering where he's gone. And why—of all places—he brought me to the bathroom when we were just in a perfectly warm and comfortable bed.

The flat of his tongue takes a long and deep sweep out of my center and my body jackknifes with surprise. Holding my legs open with both of his hands, he starts out slowly, taking his time. "You taste like fucking heaven, Eve. Better than I ever dreamed."

Any embarrassment I may have had disappeared with his words. It isn't long until my moans grow loud. I'm shaking and can't stop. Sweat beads between my breasts, the heat of his mouth consuming me. My body is undulating, completely out of control. Grabbing my hips with his enormous hands, he keeps me secured to the earth as he sucks and hums. Just as I'm climbing toward a high, I feel his calloused fingers trailing down my body, and pressing where his mouth is sucking. I'm seeing stars. All I can do is grab onto his shoulders as I ride out the most euphoric feeling of my life.

"I can't possibly handle anything more," I say to myself. But he brings his tongue back inside me, not stopping until he sucks every morsel of pleasure from me. With glazed-over eyes, I watch as he kisses back up my body. The warmth of his lips feels like heaven and I want to curl into a ball and sleep for eternity.

The thought that Vincent may end up running the biggest mafia in the country passes through my head. The photos I've seen with him and his Daniela enter my mind. And just like that, straight behind the most pleasurable experience of my life, I start to cry.

"Eve? You're crying?"

I nod my head, unable to control the torrent of feeling.

"I'm that good, yeah?" My tears stop and I stare at him for his asshole remark when a smile spreads across his handsome face. He's...joking!

"Oh, you!" I exclaim, laughter mingling with staccato breaths.

"Tell me. Talk to me."

"It's just, Daniela. And your family. And my sister would go insane if she knew, and I feel so guilty..."

"We're together now. I'm going to find a way out of this shit with Daniela. We just have to be patient. Can't you be patient for me?" He's talking, but I only cry harder, body wracked with tremors.

My mind registers Vincent is fully dressed. Meanwhile, I'm sitting here on a bathroom counter, completely nude with my huge boobs—that are way too big on my small frame—out in the open. I cover myself up with my arms. The strong girl from a few minutes ago is gone, and, in her place, sits a nervous nineteen-year-old.

He uses his hands to lift my chin. "I think you need to hear it straight. I'm a man with lots of needs, and I want it all from you. Do not cower in front of me. Ever. You're stronger than that. I know you've been through a lot, but you aren't weak." His voice is firm.

Every cell inside me wants to open up to him. I don't want to hide. I want to give him everything. I move my arms away from my body, baring myself to him.

"There we go." His voice comes out with a sigh.

I pull back, staring at each part of his face in isolation. His gorgeous chin and chiseled jaw. His sensual lips. His straight Roman nose and wide cheekbones, giving his face a perfect symmetry. My eyes move up to his dark eyes that see straight through me. In his gaze lives the most beautiful version of myself. It's where my strength lives. It's where I'm not a poor hood rat, but an intelligent woman who can achieve her dreams. The ideal version of myself lives within Vincent.

"You are everything right in my life. Understand?" His voice is deep and full of love.

Leaning his forehead against mine, he breathes heavily. Then he wraps me up in his arms, lifting me with one arm and turning on the shower with the other. When the water is warm enough, he places me into the spray.

From behind the glass, I watch as he takes off his clothes. I lean against the door to stabilize myself. His broad shoulders and muscular arms are incredibly sexy. His chest is sprinkled with some dark hair. My eyes move downward and I literally gasp, shocked again at how huge he is. There's no way in hell he's normal. The combination of seeing him naked after what he just did to me makes my legs weak.

When he finally joins me, my breath hitches. Our eyes lock as he lifts me up again in his arms, my hands finding the back of his hair. Steam billows around us as he presses me against the cold marble wall. I'm searching for answers within his kiss as we claim each other with wet mouths and water-slicked bodies. My soft body rocks against his hard, asking for more. More. More. "Please," I beg. "I want you."

He pulls away from my lips and looks at me, pushing my wet hair out of my face. "I know what you want. But I don't want to hurt you. It's too soon after yesterday."

"No. Now. I need this now. Want this now." His eyes darken, turning almost black.

"I'd kill for you. To make you a part of me, I'd do anything. I'm a selfish man, Eve. I'll never let you leave me."

With my legs wrapped around his waist, he enters me in one push.

I can feel him deeper than I ever thought possible—his dick pulsing and growing larger inside me. My throat aches from how loud I'm moaning. "Let me hear you. Let me hear how badly you want it." One of his hands is splayed on the tile behind me; the other grips my ass.

When I feel myself building up for another orgasm, he holds me tight against his chest. I unravel right into his arms. Not a moment later, it's his turn. He pulls out before he can finish inside of me.

Eventually, he lowers me to the ground, dragging my naked body down his. Turning me around, he squeezes some shampoo into his fingers and washes my hair. The act is so gentle and loving; I have to put my hands on the wall to keep from falling. After my hair is clean, he drops himself down onto one knee, turning my body toward him. When he lifts up my right foot, I lean my hands on his massive shoulders. He soaps me from the tips of my toes up my thigh toward my center. I gasp as his hands move upward, gently cleaning a place only he has ever been. When he's done with my lower half, he rubs his soapy calloused hands over my breasts and down the sides of my body. Then he turns me around and soaps my entire back, gently massaging me. When he's done washing me, he cleans himself. I can only stare in wonder as he lathers, raising his arms up one at a time to clear away the soapy suds.

Turning off the shower, he steps out before me to get fresh towels. He places one around his trim waist and then opens the shower door, wrapping me up in a second. I've never had someone take care of me like this. I'm trying not to cry again, although this time it would be out of sheer happiness. Holding my hand, and gently walking us back into his bed, I move to my side as he joins me.

We're face to face, lying together all cozy, wrapped up in his covers. He's smiling and my heart is soaring. "So, you think you'll ace this test? You need philosophy for law. Make sure to take Logic next semester with Professor Weiss." I brush my nose against his, breathing in his breaths, taking him in. I slide my legs between his, wanting our bodies to touch in every possible way.

I press my lips together. "You know I've watched like, every single *Law and Order* episode in history. I thought that one day I'd be prosecuting gang members." We start chuckling and before I know it, we're laughing so hard we're wheezing. When I let out my signature snort, his laughter intensifies.

We calm down and our eyes turn serious. "Vincent. How many weeks until you leave?" I stare at his chest, swallowing hard.

"Sixteen." I finally look back up at him again and he nods his head.

"What's it like out on the rez? I heard it's pretty crazy out there. Like, third-world in some parts, right?" I want to discuss this with him, but I also don't want to say something wrong. I'm hanging onto his every word, just hoping he tells me everything.

"You wouldn't believe this, but there isn't any water there. People literally drive their trucks an hour back and forth just to get fresh water to drink. I mean sure, there are watering points, which are just hoses in towns bordering the rez. But there's still no groundwork or infrastructure to bring water directly to people's homes. There are some windmills and wooden buildings which house wells, but they are totally contaminated. And people drink from that." His eyes are registering something like distress. I can tell he's passionate about this.

"So, yeah. I want to get back out there. A casino complex on the lands would change the face of tribal economics. And if I can get in there and make that difference, I'll do it even if I have to let the waters run red for a while. One of my main goals is to find a way to bring that infrastructure onto the rez. I'm sure Nevada would be willing to help out if I gave them a cut of profits. Tribes in other states have worked out deals like that."

"Sounds like some plan, Vincent." I stare at him in absolute awe.

"Don't look at me like that. I haven't done anything yet." His face is serious, and for a moment, I get a flash of Vincent ten years from now. He's already so powerful and magnetizing. This man is going to be someone important one day; I can just feel it.

"Yeah, but you will. It's obvious that you'll do this. People do incredible things all the time. Why shouldn't it be you?"

"You're looking at me right now like I'm a savior. But if you know half the shit I've done..." He lets out a breath. "I'm not a stranger to the life, Eve. The corruption out on the rez and what I'll be doing to get the Tribal Council to go into business with us will be extreme. I'm not going to lie to you and tell you there won't be violence at first."

"I know. But, sometimes wars have to be fought for the betterment of the people, right?"

His gaze turns reverent as he moves his hands around my entire face, tracing my eyebrows and down the straight slope of my nose with his thumbs. He runs his middle finger around my lips and I snake my tongue out, trying to lick his finger. He smiles but continues up my cheekbones and down my ears.

"Jesus, you're so beautiful." His hands are on my face, palms against my cheeks and then down, pressing the cross against my chest.

"Vincent, you're everything," I tell him, wanting to cry again. It's an emotional onslaught.

"Eve, you're perfect." My smile is so huge I feel my eyes crinkle in the corners. "I carry your heart. I carry it in my heart." His face must mirror mine because all I see in his eyes is love.

"Quoting e. e. cummings?"

"You know it." He laughs.

"Vincent, I was thinking—"

"Thinking?" he says the word with distaste and I slap his shoulder, holding back a laugh. He's obviously joking with me, and I love it.

"So, I was thinking...maybe I should transfer to a school in Nevada. I don't want to be far from you." I swallow hard, nervous to be mentioning this. But the truth is, the idea of being across the country from Vincent seems like torture. I'm sure I can still get a great education at another school.

"You're at one of the best colleges in the country right now. I'm not taking that away from you."

"No." I vehemently shake my head. "I don't want to be across the country from you. What if I go to California or find somewhere on the West Coast? I can find a great school out there. We'll still be separated, but at least I won't be all the way on the East Coast while you're out on the West." My voice is small but hopeful.

He takes a few breaths before nodding his assent.

Somewhere inside me, I realize if I thought I loved him before, this man is now imprinted within of me. All of my emotions buzz from the top of my skin down into my bones. I wonder if he can feel it.

He runs his hands along my arms until he reaches the curve in my sides. We're staring at each other in silence, the time passing. He pulls the covers over us again, kissing every inch of my body.

We're in so deep. I nuzzle into the palm of his warm hand.

"We're forever. I'll never stop loving you." His voice is a whisper.

He's on me again. I'm aching but saying no to Vincent feels like sacrilege. Instead of entering me this time, he kisses down my entire body and stops right where I wished he would. Oh, this man's mouth.

Time moves like a smooth current until we're soaked with sex and bliss. "Want to watch some TV?" He's smiling wide, playful, and sexy as hell.

I hand him the remote from the side table and he switches the television on. He props himself up on a few pillows against the headboard and I rest my head on his chest. Scanning some movie titles, we settle on an action-packed movie with a little romance.

I touch my hair with my hands and feel the frizz. He turns to me and laughs as I sit up, trying to tame my hair with a braid. Before I can finish, he pulls me back down and undoes my hair. He puts his hands through the strands. "Don't touch it."

We're staring at each other again, all lines of communication open. I want to climb inside him right now.

I wake in the middle of the night curled into his body. It takes me a moment to realize where I am. I put my nose to his side and breathe him in. I want to fall back asleep but can't stop twisting and turning —going back and forth in my head about whether or not this will actually work out. I want our love to win. I want it to be enough.

Sometime around four in the morning, my thoughts turn to fire as Janelle's words flash back to me. Has he killed people? *Of course he has*, a nagging voice in my head replies. Is he going to end up in prison? What if his dad never lets him leave? My heart pounds.

When he wakes, he turns over and takes a look at his watch. Moving toward me, he lets out a warm smile. I want to melt back into him, but I can't help the feeling of doom that's curling around my chest.

17

EVE
Three months later

I FINALLY FINISHED my last midterm exam—Spring break has officially begun. I'm not planning on leaving campus, though. This is my home now. Vincent and I have been amazing. Ever since we got together, we've spent almost every night downtown in SoHo at his apartment. He brings me with him twice a week to work out, too. It turns out I love mixed martial arts, and I'm pretty good at it. His trainer, Sergey, is awesome, and I've already gotten much stronger.

The only times we're separated are when we're in class, or if he has family business to attend. I know he sneaks moments in with Daniela for the camera, but I try to pretend those times don't exist. I've even gotten off social media. Watching them together, even if it's fake, is too much for me to handle.

Janelle is over tonight, celebrating the end of midterms. We're planning on hanging out in my dorm first, and maybe going out to a bar later. We haven't seen each other as much as we wish we did, but the truth is that between school and sneaking around with Vincent, my time is limited. I know eventually I need to fess up and tell her about what's going on. But I want to push that conversation as far into the future as I can. She just wouldn't understand, and I'm worried about losing her. Her threats still hang heavy in my heart.

Tonight, we're playing some Drake on her phone and drinking wine when I hear a knock.

I open the door to see Claire decked out in a tight black dress and black ankle booties. Her hand is wrapped around a magnum of wine.

"Eve," she squeals, hugging me with her free hand.

"Hey, babe!" I'm surprised but excited to see her.

"I've been texting you nonstop and you weren't answering, so I figured I'd just stop over."

She walks into my room, eyes widening at my sister. "Tell me you're Janelle." She drops the wine bottle on the table and then throws her arms around Janelle as if they've known each other forever.

They both laugh. "That's me. I've heard so much about you."

"Oh my God, I love your hair!" Claire starts.

"You've gotta come by my salon and let me highlight you." Janelle puts her hands through Claire's locks in that expert way, lifting up different pieces and analyzing her color.

"Yes! I want to go blonder. Maybe a few lighter pieces around my face, you know?"

"Absolutely. I can do it for you. Call the salon at Bergdorf."

"How amazing that you work there? When Eve told me, I freaked. Do you do all the celebs and stuff?"

"Yeah, I do a lot of them actually."

Claire turns to me as she takes her jacket off. "Get dressed, ladies. We're going to a club tonight."

"Wait, what?" I ask.

"You heard me." She pulls out a wine opener from her huge purse and proceeds to uncork the bottle. "We've all been studying like crazy, and finals are now over, so you have no excuse. We're going out to celebrate—everyone is going. See this outfit?" She stands tall, gesturing to herself. "I've got to be seen!" She pulls out the cork and reaches into her bag, taking out a plastic wine glass.

I laugh out loud. "Tell me there's a puppy in your bag, and I'll consider it."

"There's a horse in here, not a puppy!" We all laugh.

"We gotta get dressed if we're goin' out!" Janelle says excitedly. She moves to my closet, searching for clothes when she takes out a black halter-top that I conveniently took from her side of the closet before we moved out. "You little bitch!" she exclaims. "I was searching for this top everywhere!" She pulls off her T-shirt and slides it on.

I'm watching Janelle flit around getting herself glamorous, while Claire pours herself wine and kicks off her shoes. All of a sudden, they seem to realize that I'm not getting dressed.

In a blink, they huddle around me like I'm Cinderella, forcing on different outfits until they decide on a tight red dress, also conveniently taken by me from Janelle's side of the closet. I want to argue that I don't want to wear something so flashy, but another part of me wants to experiment, too.

Janelle immediately gets to work on my hair and makeup while Claire tops off my wine. When she's done, I stare in the mirror, stunned. I still look like me, but much older and a hell of a lot sexier. I'm bronzed, highlighted, and my lips are lined and filled to perfection.

Claire chokes on her wine. "You are a genius, Janelle. I mean, Eve is beautiful. But this takes her to a whole other level." Claire turns back to me. "You're definitely hooking up tonight!"

Claire's phone pings and she stares down to read the text. "It's Tom. He's also going to be at the club!"

"I guess we're clubbing tonight," Janelle says happily in a singsong voice, flipping her hair a few times. "Who's Tom?"

"He's a guy I used to hook up with. Oh shit." Claire nervously puts her fingers to her lips. "I wonder if Vincent is coming."

Janelle squints her eyes and my heart pounds.

"Vincent and Tom are sort of like a package deal," Claire explains. "They're both hot, but Vincent is like, off the damn charts. I'm sure Eve told you about him, right?" Her eyes flit between us as Janelle's gaze liquefies into fury.

"Wait. You mean, Vincent *Borignone?*" She purses her lips, waiting for the ball to drop. I hold my breath.

"Yup," Claire supplies easily. "The one and only."

"Oh, yes. Eve told me all. About. Him." She punctuates every word, seemingly trying to keep herself calm.

"I'm gonna use the bathroom before we go." I stand abruptly and run down the hall, with my phone in hand.

Running into the stall, I shoot out a text to Vincent.

Me: Hey. My plans changed. Claire came over and wants us to all go out. Heard you're coming?

Vincent: I'll be there. I know I can't touch, but I'll be watching

Me: I like that. Janelle is with us, too

Vincent: Cool

Me: She hates you, by the way

Vincent: One day she'll get over it. When we're together and all this shit is behind us

Me: I can't wait...

Vincent: Love you baby

Me: Love you too

We all walk together out of the dorms when Claire's phone rings. She answers and immediately begins chatting about tonight's plans. Janelle squeezes my hand and I turn to her.

"I'm going to nail that man's balls to the wall tonight for what he did to you last year!"

All of a sudden, Janelle pauses, eyes widen as she stares at my jacket. "Eve. Tell me where you got that coat."

"Janelle, stop it," I hiss, turning my eyes to Claire. Thankfully, she's too busy on her phone to notice our conversation.

"Oh my God. Tell me you did what you promised. Tell me you aren't seeing him."

"Now isn't the time to explain. There's so much happening—" I bite my cheek and look down.

"You had sex with him, didn't you? How long has this been going on?" Her eyes are murderous. "You swore to me you'd stay away."

I want to lie, but I can't. Instead, I keep my mouth shut. Claire hangs up the phone and tells us Tom is sending a car to pick us up at the dorm.

"How lucky are you two to have friends who are so well connected?" The sarcasm drips from her voice.

Claire moves her gaze between Janelle and me. "Why do I get the feeling something is going on? Is this about Vincent?"

Janelle puts a hand on her hip and stares at me pointedly.

"No, nothing is about him. We're just friends is all."

Claire's jaw drops. "Do you have a death wish or something, Eve? If Daniela ever finds out—"

"Exactly!" Janelle exclaims.

My face must be red; I can feel the heat traveling through my veins. "He has a lot going on, a-and..." My words are coming out in stutters; I'm not prepared for this.

They both stare at me unhappily. "It's your life. But don't say we didn't warn you." Claire shakes her head from side to side.

I look down when Janelle takes my hand. "Tonight, let's have fun. You deserve it after all your hard work. I just wish you'd use your brain and choose someone else. He's—"

"Let's just leave, okay?" I swallow hard, knowing how lucky I am that Janelle didn't fulfill her promise of never speaking to me again. She's not simply my sister or my best friend. In so many ways, she's truly my other half.

A large black Escalade shows up right in front of my dorm. The driver opens the door, and we all climb inside.

Stepping into the club, a beefy-looking guy walks us straight to a table on the right side of the dance floor.

I see Tom first; Claire must not have told him that she was with me, because he looks pretty mad I'm here. Trying to ignore him, I walk over to where Claire's friends are sitting. Everyone is in a great mood, celebrating the end of finals. I spot Vincent, sitting in a dark corner with his hat pulled down low. Even though it isn't easy to see him, I can feel his gaze on me. I force my feet not to run to him.

Looking around, I wonder if Daniela will show up tonight. I silently pray she is sick with the flu and stuck in bed, puking with a raging fever while her little white dog chomps on her favorite red-quilted Chanel bag. I chuckle at my evil musings. But deep down, I know she always is sure to be where Vincent's at in public.

Claire hands Janelle and me shot glasses full of Bacardi. I feel his eyes on me as I swallow it down. I see him from my side eye, nodding at me; wordlessly letting me know he's watching.

Claire and Janelle grab my hands and bring me to the dance floor. We grind up against each other as heat pulses inside my veins. I watch Vincent lean forward, elbows resting on his knees. I incinerate from his stare.

Claire bends down, putting her lips to my ear. "Holy shit, Eve. Vincent is staring right at you!" Her voice is nervous but excited.

My heart skips as Vincent stands up, seemingly walking toward me. My heart pounds so loudly, I'm sure the entire club can hear it. My eyes lock on his. I want him so bad in this moment, I could scream.

I hear a loud squeal before I see her. Turning toward the sound, I watch as Daniela glides in and grabs Vincent's shirt. Moving up to her tiptoes, she kisses him while their friends whistle at their display. Her tongue slides into his mouth and my heart drops into my stomach. I watch as Janelle surveys the scene. She's shaking her head angrily. I squeeze her hand, yelling into her ear, "Let's get another shot."

We walk to our table where I find a bottle of tequila sitting on ice. I pick it up and pour us four. I shoot two drinks, watching as Daniela whispers something to Vincent. I'm staring at them so hard I barely feel the burn of the liquor. She moves onto his lap as if it's her rightful spot, removing the hat from his head.

My eyes bug out as she screams, "You shaved your head?" Her shriek has the table craning their heads toward her. Vincent's hair is buzzed in a military style, and he looks like a total sexy bad ass.

He turns to me for a moment and winks. God, he looks gorgeous like this. With his chiseled face and sharp jaw, he's sin. I can't stop the smile spreading across my face.

When Daniela notices everyone watching her, she flips her shiny red hair to the side, composing herself. Smiling confidently, she possessively rubs a hand against his head, pulling him closer to her. Every cell in my body is screaming at her to stop. Didn't he swear that his body is mine? Mine! My rational mind knows this isn't real, but anger blurs all my senses. I want to yell like a maniac. I want to claw her eyes out!

Vincent is turning me into a monster.

All I can see in this moment is Daniela.

Daniela's perfect hair.

Daniela's gorgeous face.

Daniela's model-perfect outfit. Touching my tight red dress, I realize how cheap I must look compared to her. She is high-end-designer, and I'm the Chinatown copy. Insecurity blazes through me. I'm a wooden house and her perfection is like lighter fluid, her beauty and wealth the matches.

I turn to find Claire is next to me. I put my hand on her arm, desperately needing reassurance. "Do I look like shit? Is my hair frizzing?"

She stumbles back a bit but then rights herself, holding onto me for support and giggling drunkenly. "Eve, you might be the most gorgeous girl I've ever seen!" She hiccups while I look at her with hope. In one moment, Daniela managed to steamroll my self-esteem. "Everyone has been talking about you since you came to school. You're by far the prettiest girl in this club and I don't know what the hell is going on with Vincent, but he's obviously ob-sessed with you."

Her eyes move behind me for a moment. "Oh. Shit. Don't turn around, but Vincent's staring at you and like, isn't even blinking."

"Is Daniela still sitting on his lap?" I need Claire to be my eyes.

"The fucked-up thing is that yes, she is. She's on him, but his eyes are only on you. Oh no, she's—"

Hands grip my shoulders, spinning me around. It's Daniela, and her smile is so fake it sends an actual shiver down my spine. "Hi, sweetie!" she says, throwing her arms around me as if we're best friends. Taking my hand, she practically drags me to a corner of the club, away from prying eyes.

The corner is dark. She drops my hand as if it's diseased. "I see now that you have a little crush on MY Vincent. You like to look at what isn't yours, huh? Did you fuck Tom just to get closer to him?" My eyes widen with her accusation, tongue frozen in my mouth from fear.

"Wait a minute." Her smile turns lethal as her face darkens, as if she's realizing something for the very first time. "Vincent fucked you already, didn't he?" She rolls her eyes before shrugging. "That's Vincent. He's wild in bed; needs a lot to keep him satisfied. Do you get nice and dirty for him, how he likes? There are things he wouldn't dare do to me. I'm too classy for that."

She lets her eyes rove from my toes up to my face. "But you?" She chuckles, pressing a French-manicured nail up to her lips. "I can see how a girl like you would be up for anything. All desperate and cheap, giving it up so easily and willing to do anything he wants." My stomach drops, pain filling the space between my lungs.

"You see, no matter who he fucks, I'm the one he's going to show up with in public. I satisfy him in a way you never could. Meanwhile, you spread your legs for just a moment with him. Girls like you are a fucking dime a dozen," she sneers.

Flipping her hair to the side, she continues, "My rightful spot is next to him, and he wouldn't want it any other way. He and I go together perfectly. And your spot? Your spot is to be his *whore*. Because that's all you'll ever be to Vincent."

Stepping backward, she puts a smile back on her face before turning on a high heel. I try to focus on the world around, but it's spinning. Somehow, Janelle finds me, bringing me back onto the dance floor. I see Vincent and Daniela again. But this time, it's Daniela making eye contact with me as she kisses him, probably moaning into his mouth. He pushes her off, and I see his lips move. It looks like he's saying "enough," but I can't be sure.

Strobe lights flash, creating shadows on the walls around. I try to go with it, letting the music take me away.

The competitive part of me rears its head. I want him to wish it was me on his lap, not her! I want him to picture my lips on his, not hers! Even though the music is going fast and my head is spinning from the liquor, I consciously slow my pace. All I can process from my conversation with Daniela is that she thinks I'm no one. She thinks I'm just trash. Well, fuck her! That man is mine!

Licking my lips, I stare at Vincent. Moving my body seductively, I try to communicate with my movements how badly I want him. I shut my eyes and throw my head back, letting my hair drape down my back. I know how much he likes when my hair is wild like this. I want him to read my gestures...to understand that I need him now. I need him inside me. Everywhere, all at once. In the back of my mind, I realize that Daniela is willing to throw down, and fighting her is a really bad idea. But in my drunken haze, I couldn't care less about anything or anyone else. I want him to prove to me that I'm the only one.

As I dance, the entire scenario plays out in my head. I picture him coming up behind me, his hands pressing me against his hard body. I imagine him taking my hand, pulling me into the bathroom. Pressing me up against the stall, kissing me, and turning me mindless. He'd lift up my dress and give me what I've been both consciously and subconsciously asking for since the moment I met him.

I feel a man come up behind me. Instead of walking away from him, I press myself to his front, feeling him harden. I screw my eyes shut, imagining that it's Vincent. This guy is exactly what I need right now: a prop. I move against him, opening my eyes for a moment to see if Vincent is watching me. His jaw is ticking; I can practically see his teeth grinding together. Is he angry? I want him mad as hell. I want him to realize how it feels to see me with someone else. He used to have sex with that vile bitch, and it infuriates me. Everyone on earth believes they belong together, and it makes me sick. I'm angry at her for saying that shit to me, but I'm livid at him for putting me in this position. I hate being hidden. I hate being ignored. It's not fair!

He's got a drink in his hand and I watch as he brings it up to his full lips. He tips the drink into his mouth and I watch him swallow. I close my eyes again, slightly moaning, dancing against this random body.

When I finally re-open my eyes, Vincent is gone. I feel my stomach drop as I look around. Did he get so mad that he left with Daniela? What time is it? I need my phone. Where is my bag? Anxiety and alcohol are wreaking havoc on my insides. When the guy tries to pull me to him, I shake him off me, quickly running to the table.

Claire is sitting on Tom's lap, whispering in his ear. I interrupt them. "Claire, did you see Vincent?" I feel myself sway, my voice raspy and eyes dry. Even in my drunkenness, I can see that she's looking at me with pity. A scenario becomes clear in my foggy mind. It's everything I just imagined—except instead of me with Vincent in the bathroom—it's Daniela. Daniela is against the wall. Vincent's lips are on HER neck. She's moaning. Everyone knows they are in there. I'm stuck out here, the idiot. He's fucking her. She's better for him than me.

I'm completely messed up, engaging in this weird triangle I'm not equipped to handle.

Janelle moves behind me. "I think you should go home. You've had too much drink. Let me get us a cab."

I continue to look around the room. Where is he? I need Vincent. The tears well up in my eyes. Is he mad at me?

Tom stands, saying something to Janelle. Not a moment later, he's grabbing my arm. "Let's go, Eve. Your night is over."

"What the hell, Tom?" I'm furious as he hustles me forward, not giving me a chance to even say goodbye. I'm teetering on my heels as Tom drags me out of the club.

Right outside, a black Escalade stands with its engine running. Tom opens the car door, pushing me in and throwing my purse behind me, like used trash.

"Tom?" I'm confused, my brain muddled. He slams the door shut. Looking at the driver in front, it dawns on me this is the same car and driver that picked us up tonight.

The door reopens and Vincent jumps in the back. Fuming. I should be afraid of his intensity, but instead, I feel my own anger bubbling up—and my want.

"You're lucky I was there," he sneers. "You can't just grind against random guys at clubs. You know what you're asking for, right?" His voice is condescending and dripping with antagonism.

"Yeah?" I sass. "Well, I'm just trash, anyway. The girl who spreads her legs for nothing while you go out with the fancy girl in public?" The bitterness in my voice surprises me.

He gets closer, lowering his voice to a dark whisper. "You think I treat you like garbage, huh?" My eyes widen with anxiety. This isn't my Vincent. This is Vincent Borignone.

I press myself against the door, trying to get some distance when he reaches over me to buckle my seatbelt. "Don't touch me!" I shriek. In an instant, his huge hand is around my throat. I freeze. He's not squeezing or hurting me, but I know that he could if he wanted to, and that thought alone is enough to immobilize me.

His face is hard as stone. "You want to know what being treated like a whore feels like, Eve? Should I make you suck my dick right now and then throw you out of the car? Should I hand you my black AmEx and tell you to go shopping for a day before I share you with my friends?"

I can't breathe. I blink, salt water coating my face. I'm crying.

"I'm mad as FUCK right now!" He slams his hand against the seat in front of him. "You think you can walk around a club, touching a man who isn't me?" His voice echoes around the car.

He's scaring the shit out of me and turning me on like I didn't know was possible. My body is acting completely out of control and I have no wherewithal to rein myself in. He lets his hands roam down my chest and onto my legs, lifting my dress higher and caressing my upper thighs with his fingertips. My panties are instantly soaked. My body knows what his hands can do, and my legs immediately part for him.

"You wanted to make me jealous with that fucking guy? You got your wish, baby." His hands rove higher, calloused thumb skimming the edges my underwear. *Oh, God.* I tilt my pelvis up as I lean back into the seat.

The moment I shut my eyes, his body heat disappears. I sit up, noticing that he's no longer near me. It feels as if he's punishing me. Even though my mind is telling me not to, I move closer to him.

"Vincent, I'm sorry, okay? I hated seeing you guys together. Why did she even show up? She t-told me how you like to be dirty. Told me that I'm nothing." I'm shuddering, feeling cold and hot and nauseated. Is he going to leave me because I danced with someone else? I'd die if he leaves me. My tears fall harder down my face.

He turns back to me, his eyes frigid. "What else did she say to you?"

"She told me that I'm not the first, but she'll always be the only. She told me...she told me...you've been with a gazillion girls! But sh-she's the only one who matters. She's the wife; I'm cheap, and I'm the whore."

He pulls me onto his lap, shushing me while I ugly cry. Somehow, I fall asleep in his arms.

Before I know it, my door opens. I wake up seeing Vincent crouched down onto the pavement, angling my body toward him. Before I can ask him what he's doing, he pulls off my high heels. "Ahh!" I gasp as they drop off my feet.

"Oh, it hurts," I moan. He squeezes my arches with his thumbs and I cringe from the pleasure and pain. Lifting me up in his arms, I immediately wrap my legs around his waist and rest my head on his shoulder. He walks me up the flights of stairs to my dorm room as if I weigh nothing at all, putting his hands into my bag to pull out my keys.

Dropping my face into his neck, I take a deep inhale. "You smell so good, Vincent. I want to smell you forever. Tell me we're forever. Don't be mad at me about that guy. I was jealous, okay? I can be dirty too, if you want." Whoever said alcohol was a truth serum wasn't lying. He chuckles at my oversharing.

"We're here," he whispers, swinging open my door. He gently places me down on my bed.

"Lift your hands." I raise my arms and he pulls up my dress.

"Vincent, you really shaved your head." I put my hands on his head, rubbing the short scruff.

"Didn't I tell you I would?" His voice is low and deep as he gently pushes my hair back.

"But that was a while ago. I thought you forgot."

"I'll keep it shaved until we can be together openly. What do you think?"

I hiccup. "J-Janelle knows, now. And she's so mad...."

He licks his lips. "Because she loves you. Maybe you should tell her the truth. I don't want to isolate you from your sister."

He holds the back of my hair, staring at each feature of my face. "Why did you wear so much makeup tonight? I hated it." My stomach sinks at his displeasure.

"You did?" I raise my eyes to his nervously.

"Yes. Don't do it again." His voice is warm, but also sharp.

"But, everyone said it looked good. And that's how all the girls look here. I'm trying to fit in better—"

"How many times do I have to remind you? You aren't other girls. You'll never be other girls. When I look at you, I don't want to see them. They're fake, Eve. They've lost their innocence. You are nothing like them. Never will be."

"But, I want to be. I know the type you're used to..." I pause, my chest aching with the thought.

"No," he sighs, using his thumb to wipe my tears. "Don't you understand that you are my only type?"

I nod my head. "Okay, Vincent. No more makeup. Maybe just a little?"

He rolls his eyes and I shift to get under the covers. Pulling the comforter up and over me, he tucks it into my sides. I want to feel his lips on mine. His tongue in my mouth. Instead, he asks, "Do you have Advil?"

"Under the bed," I croak. I hear my plastic drawers opening and closing, and then the sink turning on. Finally, I feel his warm breath by my ear. "Sleep."

"Will you stay?"

"Not long. Can't bump into anyone in the morning." He moves behind me, pulling my body into his chest. I slide my legs between his so that we're entwined and let out a loud exhale. Vincent is my home.

"I wish you brought me to SoHo," I say quietly, nestling deeper into his chest.

"Me too. I was angry and wasn't thinking. Tomorrow night."

I hum my assent.

When I wake up, I turn to my bedside clock and see that it's five am. I sit up for a moment, my head pounding and muddled. I see the pills and a huge cup of water and immediately swallow them down. I'm not sure what was real and what was a dream last night. But when I put my nose into my pillow inhaling, I know Vincent was here.

18

EVE

VINCENT and I spend most of spring break in bed. I've cooked us every meal, and all we did was lounge around, make love, watch movies, and eat. We dance together too, because Vincent he knows how much I love it. He's tried a few times to discuss what happened at the club, but I told him I didn't want to talk about it. There's no use in rehashing Daniela's words when they do nothing but make me insecure.

Yesterday, I saw an episode on the *Food Network* of Giada making spaghetti Bolognese, and I wanted to make it for Vincent. I think he is going to be in heaven. At least, I hope so. I slice up a fresh baguette with garlic and olive oil, and pop it into the oven to get nice and crispy. The salad is already washed and sitting in the fridge.

I check the clock. Vincent will be home from his workout in about thirty minutes. While the sauce simmers, I decide now is a good time to wash up and get the smell of fried onions out of my hair.

I shower and then open up his side table to pull out a white T-shirt. It's snug on Vincent, but gigantic on me. I slide it on and grin; he loves when I wear his clothes, and I love it too. Just as I'm drying my hair with the towel, I hear the front door open and shut. "Hi honey, I'm home!" Vincent yells.

I laugh as he comes up behind me, but then cry out when I realize his shirt is soaked in sweat. "Ugh, Vincent! I just got clean, and now you're getting me all gross!" I'm trying to sound mad, but we both know I couldn't care less. I'll take him any way I can get him.

"Let me get you nice and dirty. I want you back in the shower with me."

"No. Dinner will be ready soon and I know you must be hungry."

"You know I love when you feed me. And the house smells fucking fantastic. But right now, I'm hungry for something else." He nips at my ear and my head rolls back.

An hour later, I'm drying my hair for the second time. I run into the kitchen to get everything ready for us while he makes some calls. Finally, he joins me by the stove, wearing jersey shorts and a T-shirt. His hair is still buzzed, making him look dangerous.

He moves to a seat and I bring everything to the table. "Goddamn, I'm a lucky man."

I smile and sit next to him. Vincent bows his head to say grace. I've never been religious before, but I know he grew up Catholic, and it's important to him. I press his cross against my chest, my own little version of a prayer.

We get to eating, and he groans that it's the best meal he's ever eaten.

"You really are an incredible cook. If law school doesn't work, there's always culinary school, huh?" I preen at his compliment. Looking down at his empty bowl gives me more satisfaction than I thought possible. If I could, I'd feed this man every single meal for the rest of my life. I know this is a negative for womankind and all, but cooking for him fulfills some emptiness inside my heart I didn't even realize existed. And watching him enjoy the food I made? Euphoria.

He pushes his chair closer to mine and I'm immediately assaulted by his amazing scent—fresh laundry and something purely Vincent.

He puts his hands in my hair, moving his fingers down to massage my neck. "Move in with me."

"I can't do that—"

"Why?" He wraps his hands around my face, smiling. He's genuine and delicious warmth. "Stay here. Bring your things over. You don't have to go back just because break is almost over."

He lets go of me and I crawl into his lap, nuzzling in his chest.

"I never want you anywhere else. In a few months, I'll be gone. I want to maximize our time together."

"But isn't it dangerous? Like, what if Daniela—"

"She won't know. She doesn't even know this apartment exists. And technically, you'll still have your room in the quad. I just don't wanna ask you to come over. I need to get home every night and have you here. In our home. I wanna wake up in the morning to you by my side. Drink my coffee with you."

"But the girls on my floor will start to wonder—"

"No, they won't. Didn't you tell me they're all in the middle of pledging sororities? Everyone makes all these friends first semester, but once they pledge, anyone who isn't in their sorority becomes a distant friend. That's the way it works here."

A smile spreads across my face and he laughs, his dark eyes twinkling. "I fucking love you. Want you in my bed every night of my life."

I curl myself around him. "It's gonna suck to be far from each other in a few months."

"Have you heard from any schools yet?" His voice is encouraging.

"Just waiting for interview dates. But you know, I can still apply to some places in Nevada—"

"No fuckin' way," he replies gruffly, dropping his fork. "We've discussed this already. I'm not letting you lower your standards, and California is close enough to where I'll be. You've worked all your life to get the best education; I'm not gonna be the reason you lose that."

His phone chimes, interrupting our conversation. He reads the message and curses. "Baby, I gotta go."

"No," I complain.

"Yes." He stands up with his plate in hand. "Dinner was amazing.

Beyond fucking good. Don't throw out any of it. I want leftovers tomorrow or later tonight."

"I'm glad you liked it." I fuss with my hair as he proceeds to move everything from the table into the kitchen. "So, where are you going?" I know he never tells me, but...

"We've been through this." His hard voice shakes me back to reality. "Don't ask. When it's family business, it isn't yours." His voice is firm, with no room for negotiation.

My stomach clenches. I hate when he acts this way. Doesn't he understand I'm afraid he'll get hurt? What if the cops show up? Who would even be able to tell me if something went wrong?

He cleans the table silently, and I know he's gearing up for whatever is to come tonight. When he's done, he moves to the bedroom. I follow him into his walk-in closet, which I now know houses his weapons arsenal. Opening his gun safe, he methodically takes out holsters and guns. He takes off his clothes after dropping everything onto the bed. He's so strong and powerful, but I yearn to take care of him.

He moves to strap himself when I step in front of him. "Let me," I tell him softly. He blinks as I take his ankle holsters and drop to my knees, wrapping them above his feet. "Is this good?" I tighten them, staring up at him and biting my bottom lip.

He nods, handing me two small handguns that I slide inside and then fasten. Walking to his drawers, he pulls out a fresh black T-shirt and a pair of black jeans: his standard outfit when he leaves for business. He puts on another holster over his shirt, and I stand on my tippy-toes to tighten it for him. The straps make his muscles stand out even more than they normally do. I take two other guns off the bed and drop one in the left pocket and the other in the right. When the guns are secure, he pulls my hair back with his hands, forcing me to look into his eyes. I can only imagine what my face must be saying, because my heart is pounding and my core is pulsing. I want him so badly; I'm practically shaking.

As if a cloud passes through him, his eyes turn impossibly cold. I feel his breath against my lips, so imposing that I pause. I wouldn't dare move when he's in this zone.

He presses his lips to my ear. "Check the desk in the bedroom. I left something for you." His voice is curt, but I manage to nod my head. Stepping away from me, he takes a dark zip-up sweatshirt from his cabinet before striding out of the apartment. My stomach tenses as the door slams; he's gone.

Seemingly out of nowhere, I feel a pang for my sister. Vincent mentioned I should come clean and tell her everything. Now that he's not home, it's probably a good time. I pick up the phone to call her, biting my bottom lip nervously.

She answers after the first ring. "It's been almost three fucking weeks since your finals. I know you have no classes right now. So where have you been? I keep calling you and all I get in reply are some stupid texts telling me you're *okay*?" She's fuming. "You owe me a goddamn explanation!"

I fill her in on all the details. We cry together through the honest talk, but after over an hour of back and forth, she understands I'm going to take the risk for Vincent—no matter what. He and I are in this together, for the long haul. We're in love, and there's really nothing anyone can do or say at this point that can change that. Once she realizes that arguing with me is virtually impossible, she promises to try and get over it. Still though, she's angry at the choices I've made. I hang up, feeling relieved that at least Janelle finally knows. The lying was like a deadweight on my ankle.

Next, I call Claire, checking in to see how her break is going. She tells me she's unpacking and we make a plan for lunch between classes tomorrow. Even though I adore her, I don't think it's possible to maintain a true friendship when I hold secrets as big as the one I'm keeping. One of the things that saddens me the most about my situation with Vincent is because it's under the radar; we can't just live like a regular couple. I wished for a typical college life with studying and some parties, too, but I guess it isn't in the cards for me.

After cleaning up the dishes and saving the leftovers, I shuffle back into the bedroom to find a beautiful set of fresh keys with charms on a keychain, a list of security codes, and a note from Vincent.

Eve,

Keys to our apartment.

Everything that's mine is yours. Forever.

19

VINCENT

I GET into the car and force myself to change faces. It's whiplash moving between loving the hell out of my girl and having to take care of business. Tom keeps telling me something feels off at the ports, and his text said as much. In the business we're in, trusting our gut is necessary.

Daniela has been asking some probing questions ever since the club. Thank fuck Eve got herself off social media; if she saw what I've been doing these days, she'd probably go insane. Since Eve and Daniela had words, I've had to go the extra mile to keep Daniela off our backs. That means more time with her out in public, where I've been doing my best to keep her happy; at this point, I deserve a goddamn Oscar. Just tonight, I let her come with me to the gym, where she snapped a sweaty picture of the two of us after working out. She keeps insisting that Eve and I have something going on between us, but I just continue to deny it. The damage she can inflict is endless. Not fucking her definitely makes her angrier. I know she wants to get back with me—but that's not something I'll ever budge on.

I get to the stretch between Newark Liberty International Airport and Port Newark. The newspapers have described this area as the most dangerous two miles in America. They wouldn't be wrong. I open the car door and see Tom waiting for me, a smile on his hard face. I crack my neck side to side.

"Hey, brother." We knock our fists together. "I've got the rat. Motherfucker has been compiling some data for the Feds."

"Let's see him. Is he ready for me?"

He nods in the affirmative. I crack my knuckles.

20

EVE

Spring break is now over. We only have eight weeks before the semester is finished, and then Vincent leaves for Nevada, and hopefully, I'll have transferred to a school out in California. Stanford is my top pick. I know some people would scoff at the idea of transferring schools for a man, but I don't see it that way. Vincent is my life, and if I can have both a great education and be closer to him, why shouldn't I try to do that?

I pour myself a hot cup of coffee from the dining hall, trying to stay calm—despite the fact I'm scared to death to bump into Daniela. The gossip mill says she went away with Chi Omega girls to Mexico. But now that she's back in the city, I'm not sure what to expect—especially after the club fiasco. Did she see Vincent run out of the club after me? Claire's warnings about her ability to ruin my life pound in my chest. Taking my coffee to go, I try to relax while walking to my first class of the day.

I take a seat in the center of the large lecture hall, pulling out my spiral notebook and a blue pen from my backpack. Strangely, a few students turn toward me before whispering to each other conspiratorially. I hope that it's my imagination, but I open up the mirror app on my phone anyway. Doing a quick scan of my teeth and face, I see nothing is out of the ordinary.

When class is over and I head out into the hallway, I bump into her. My gaze starts at her high-heeled black boots that tie up to mid-thigh, a short black skirt, and a beautiful cream-colored cashmere sweater; the color is bright against her perfectly tousled red hair. It hurts to admit it, but she looks like a million bucks.

My heart thuds as she looks down at me mockingly. "You poor thing." Daniela shrugs a bony and tanned shoulder. "You were totally wasted at the club before break. And the fact that it was photographed..."

"Photographed?"

"Well, you were dancing like a stripper. Do you even remember?" Her eyes move from my feet to my face disapprovingly. And then she lets out a little laugh as if I'm nothing but a joke.

"I—"

"Well, even if you don't, you should check *High and Low*. You're all over it. And let's just say, it isn't exactly flattering." She lifts a perfectly manicured hand up to her lips. "But then again, I guess you are who you are, right? I just hope the school doesn't find out about your behavior. I know they take scholarships away from kids like you who try to party with the rest of us."

Sweat breaks out on my forehead, but she continues, "It would be a shame if you got thrown out, wouldn't it? And after how hard you worked to get out of the ghetto you were raised in! What would your sister Janelle think if everything she sacrificed for you was all lost? Would you have to move back into the Blue Houses with your mom? She's a stripper too, right?"

My mouth drops open. How does she know? Cold terror moves straight down my spine and into my feet. Seemingly content with my obvious fear, Daniela struts off. I want to move, but I can't. I can barely breathe.

With a shaking hand, I manage to take out my phone and open the browser. I hear whispers in the hall, but I'm too focused on my task to pay attention. I quickly type in HIGH AND LOW in my Google search. I know this is what Daniela hoped for, but I need to know. I can't even think about anything other than finding out what is on the internet about me.

I click on the link, and there I am. Pages of photographs of me, dancing. My super-tight red dress leaves almost nothing to the imagination. A random guy stands flush behind me, his face slightly blurry. Every feature of mine is perfectly visible, though. As if the photos weren't enough, there's an article accompanying it.

Will Bitches Never Learn?

This freshman, Eve Petrov, was spotted before spring break at the hottest club in the city, Marquis. Word on the street is she tried to hook up with THE Vincent Borignone, who completely ignored her pathetic advances —obviously.

Bystanders at the club all laughed while she pounded shots, got completely wasted, and then slutted herself up to any guy who would give her attention. Ugh, gross!

When will this freshman girl learn more than just math? It's called self-respect. And by the way, no one told us here at High and Low that the drinking age was lowered to nineteen.

XOXO,
High and Low

I LIFT my head while mortification filters through my senses. I quickly type out a text to Claire. She responds right away, telling me to meet her by the no-smoking sign in front of Grant Hall —right now.

I run out of the building, not caring that people are watching. I burst through the front doors of the mathematics building, wanting to collapse in relief when I see Claire waiting by the tree.

She starts, "I read it. Everyone has. So, swallow your pride and let's figure out how to deal now, okay?" I nod my head. We're in crisis mode, but she's in control. It almost feels as if I'm an outsider looking in. My mind hasn't caught up to the fact that this is all happening to me.

"First thing you do, is a lot of really good stuff so when your name comes up in a Google search, the newer and more positive stuff about you comes up first. That means getting your name out wherever possible in conjunction with good things. Like, charities. Or, donating your time to a good cause. We don't ever want a future employer seeing this!"

The tears well up in my eyes. "Employer?" I gasp. This is my future. My life! What if one of the schools I plan on transferring to sees this?

She puts a hand on my shoulder. "It is what it is, Eve. Another thing you need to do is to speak to Vincent. Maybe he can find a way to erase it."

"B-but how?" I stutter.

"People have connections. I have no idea who is behind *High and Low*, but you never know. Girls would lick the dirty gym floor if Vincent asked them to do it. If he knows who wrote it, I bet they'd take it down if he asked. It's worth a try. At least your friendship can help you in this way, right?" She looks at me accusingly, but I drop down on the grass, bringing my knees to my chest.

She sighs, sitting down next to me. "Text him now, Eve." I look up to see urgency in her face. I can tell she knows I've been lying, but she has the decency not to mention it right now.

Pulling out my phone, I text Vincent, asking him to call me when he can. Three minutes later, my phone rings.

"Eve?" His voice is soft and warm, how it gets in the morning right when he wakes.

I start before I lose the nerve. "I'm on *High and Low*. Can you find a way to get it taken off?" My voice comes out in a rush. I'm not just mortified. I'm also ashamed.

"They wrote about you?" He sounds furious.

"That gossip site. They said..." I pause. I want to tell him everything, but I'm too upset to speak. I swallow the dryness in my mouth, willing myself to hold it all in until I get to the privacy of my dorm room.

"Give me a few hours. It'll be gone." He hangs up the phone. I'm sitting on the ground with Claire by my side. She takes my hand.

"Vincent to the rescue, huh?" Her smile is relieved, but also sad.

"Do you really think he'll get it removed?" My desperation is making my head pound, the tears finally starting to fall.

"Yes. I do." She's nodding, the hopefulness written all over her face. "But Eve, please stay away from him. If Daniela is out to get you, this is likely just the tip of the iceberg. Getting her angry is a really bad thing. She's so connected, Eve. I tried to warn you, and I hope it's not too late."

"I'm gonna go back to my room. I can't be out on campus right now."

I run-walk directly to the quad with my head down, swiping my key card to get into the building. After climbing the steps, I bump into my Resident Advisor. She's about to say something, but I quickly run past her; I can barely look up. Has she seen it? Has everyone?

I sit at the desk in my room, opening my computer and checking out *High and Low*. Tears of relief fall down my face when I see that the article and all the photos about me are gone.

21

VINCENT

Slamming my hand on my desk, I pace the length of my bedroom. I'm back in my apartment by school, here to grab a textbook for Number Theory. The fact that Eve was on *High and Low*—and her name was mentioned in connection with mine—is a huge goddamn problem. Thankfully, I know the girls who run it. The moment I told them to remove the photos and the article, they took it all down. But if Daniela saw the article, there will be hell to pay.

My doorbell rings, and I open the door to see her. The bitch has timing; I'll give her that. I take a deep breath as she waltzes into my apartment.

"Vincent." She drops her designer purse on the floor carelessly.

"Daniela."

Sitting on the edge of the couch, she crosses her legs—high-heeled boots and a skirt so short it's practically indecent.

"I saw you got that article taken down. So, contrary to everything you've told me, you obviously care about her."

"Care? She's no one to me," I scoff. "Now do me a favor and get out. I've got work to do."

"You think you can just get rid of me? You're funny, Vincent. Do you know how many men would give their right arm to get me in bed?" She puts her arms on her hips.

"Good for you, then." I laugh angrily. "Go fuck whoever you want." I walk into my kitchen, pulling out a bottle of water from the fridge.

She trails behind me. "Look at me," she says, grabbing my arm. "Me and you go together. Me and you are together. We. Are. Together."

I shake my head slowly, amazed that a girl this smart in the books can be so delusional. "We aren't anything, Daniela. Not now and not ever. You need to find another man and move on. I'm sick of this bullshit." I can feel the tendons straining in my neck. I know I need to calm down, but it's becoming damn near impossible.

"Another man? What other man? Look in the mirror, Vincent! Me and you make sense. Me and you are perfect. Our families—think about the connections! We'd rule the world. I totally accept your life. Hell, I more than accept it. I love it. We," she starts, gesturing between us, "make sense!" Her lashes flutter faster than normal; the girl is unhinged and clearly on something.

I put the bottle to my lips, swallowing the entire thing down.

"It's her! That fucking bitch charity case!" She's panting. "You think I'm blind? I saw how you looked at her at the club before break, Vincent. I know you bought her that fucking jacket! You help her with her studying. I already knew you were fucking her, but I figured she was a passing fling!"

"You need to be committed to a mental hospital, Daniela. She and I have nothing between us." The lie burns my throat.

She starts moving through my room, emptying drawers. "Does she have her shit in your room? Is she here every night in your bed, where I'm supposed to be?" She runs into my bedroom like a dog on a scent, throwing my drawers open and pulling out my clothes.

"Calm the fuck down!" I yell. My shirts and underwear are scattered around the room.

"Calm down?" she seethes, facing me with her fists balled up at the sides. "Don't tell me to fucking *calm* down! You swore to me you'd never bring another girl into our orbit. You could fuck anyone you wanted, so long as it didn't infringe on what we have. And when I get calls from my friends telling me that my man is staring at another girl and I better get my ass to the club to intercept it? People are going to think there is trouble between us! People are going to think we're breaking up! I saw how you looked at her. I watched you go after her in that club after she was dancing with that guy!" Tears start to fall down her face.

"Jesus FUCK Daniela. You don't own me! I'm done with you. Get out!"

She stands tall, a smirk growing on her lips. "First, I'm going to call my father to pull the plug on your business. Second? I'm going to get that whore of yours thrown out of school for indecent behavior. I read up on the expectations of scholarship kids. Underage drinking? That's *academic probation*. And third? I'm going to publicly humiliate her. I will make sure the entire world knows that she. Is. A. Home-wrecker!" Her breaths turn shallow and hard. "You think you can walk away from me? Humiliate me with some piece-of-shit loser?"

I step up to her. "Have you forgotten who I am?" My voice is terrifyingly low; I feel my jaw clench. My anger is catching hold of me. Part of my brain is telling me to calm the fuck down, but the other side is only getting hotter until my judgment is officially clouded over.

"A-are you threatening me?" Her voice turns shrill.

I pull out my gun from the waistband of my jeans. Pushing her against the wall, muzzle pressed underneath her neck. "Who the fuck do you think you are, Daniela? If you so much as even *attempt* to do what you just said, I will end your fucking life." She shudders, but I don't let up. "What? You think I'm going to be shitting in my pants over some dumb bitch like you? You think you can control me?"

I step back and she falls forward, tripping over her own feet and landing on the floor. Hysterical, she grabs her purse and runs out of my room, the front door slamming against the wall with a *bang*. I laugh as she runs.

* * *

I'VE BEEN STEWING for hours, pacing my room and going through every possible scenario that could go wrong when I get a call from Tom on my work phone.

"Yo."

"Serious trouble here at the port, man."

"What are you talking about?" My breath turns shallow. "Didn't we already deal with the rat?"

"Yeah, but someone is stalling our shipment out of Colombia. We were ready to accept today, but the flight turned around mid-fucking-air. My dad told me to call Antonio right away to let him know, but I wanted to let you know first. This isn't because of Daniela, right Vincent? Because I think one of the Feds infiltrated a labor union here, too. I can feel shit going down—"

"Got it. Thanks." I hang up the phone, cursing.

I pick my work phone back up, dialing my driver. I have to see my father. I check the time and know he must be home right now. I throw on a sweatshirt and take the stairs to my building's lobby; I've got a shit ton of energy right now I need to expend.

The car ride to the townhouse is quick. I grew up here, on Ninety-Third Street between Madison and Fifth Avenue. Unlocking the front doors, I strut through the hallways lined with money. Famous art hangs to my left and right, each piece valued between thirty-thou-sand to close to a million.

I stop in the living room and take a seat on a navy velvet couch, a red and blue Persian rug under my feet. My father will call me when he's ready; he knows I'm here. In fact, I'd bet he's watching me on the security camera right now. I breathe deeply, getting my head on straight.

"Vincent," my father's stern voice calls out on speakerphone. "Come down."

I exhale as I get to the staircase, walking down two flights of carpeted stairs into the basement level. Opening the second door to the left, I enter our meeting room. The walls are painted in black lacquer and a huge crystal chandelier hangs from the center, giving the room a dark glow. He sits in his black leather chair at the head of the table. In this moment, he's no one other than the leader and boss of the Borignone mafia, and I can tell from his body language he's angry as all fuck.

"I'm waiting for an explanation as to how all of this shit broke down. I already heard from some of our friends that Costa was behind stalling our shipment today. You're my right hand. Who the fuck is causing a crack in the empire I've built? Tell me you didn't piss off the daughter, Vincent." Sitting tall in one of his custom suits, he stares at me with fury in his eyes. He brings his cigarette to his lips, taking a heavy drag. The smoke wafts through his lips and nose, momentarily covering his face. I can tell he knows. He's waiting for the confirmation.

Without any preamble, I begin with the night Eve and I met. I fill him in on the important details, including what happened to her at the hands of Carlos and the fact that we're together right now, in secret. I end with Daniela's threats.

His breaths turn shallow as he drops his head, seemingly gathering himself. "Do you know what you've just done?" His voice is low, eyes turning to thin slashes in his face. "And for a piece of pussy? I expected more from you, Vincent. You aren't one of these dumb fucking kids who can't think without his dick!" He slams his fists against the table. "I raised you better than that! We had a vote. You weren't supposed to fuck shit up with her!"

"I'm a man. Not Daniela's bitch!" I spit out. "She doesn't control us, and she sure as fuck doesn't control me," I yell back.

"Ah, so now my son is twenty-two and knows it fuckin' all, huh? Our entire business is shaking right now because of this bitch! I don't need to remind you we've got three hundred kilos of cocaine on that plane. That's close to fifteen million dollars." His red face flashes.

"And on top of that, Lieutenant Wall called. The Feds are gathering evidence to file a suit against us under RICO. They're trying to bar us from any business involvement at the ports and in any union activity around the harbors. They're catching on about the unions being in our back pockets; according to all the shit Enzo has picked up, they're not going to grab us on drug trafficking, but instead, embezzlement of union funds."

I look up at his angry face. "For RICO, they'll need to show a pattern of racketeering activity. Do you think they've put surveillance inside the unions?" I pause, my mind running as it puts together different possibilities. If they've been listening in on union activity, we're completely fucked. We are so closely tied to labor that they're essentially another arm of our organization.

He grips the side of the table. "They don't need to prove criminal acts. All they need is to focus on behavioral patterns. Patterns, Vincent. That isn't difficult to show. And now that you've messed with Costa's daughter, we've got another fight on our hands." The cords in his neck strain. "If we don't get him to send our flights back here, we'll be taking a huge hit."

I swallow hard, my mouth completely dry. "The RICO case is just a continuing vendetta by the government to try to throw our name around. There have been decades of investigations, which have led nowhere. Maybe they're just trying to scare us—"

"The threat is real. And I'm going to bet that within the week they'll take in the labor officials. The FBI is knocking on our goddamn door. We've had a chokehold on shipping and all other waterfront activities for the last sixteen fuckin' years, and we're gonna to have to give them something."

"If they bar us from activity in the ports, they'd basically be putting an entire marketplace under court supervision. That's just not possible. All businesses will stall." Sweat beads on my forehead, dripping down the sides of my face.

"It's possible. And it's happening."

I drop my head into my hands. Everything I prayed wouldn't happen, just did.

"And Costa controls half of South America. Look what he was able to do within moments of you fighting with his daughter! Turning our planes around?" He curses, slamming his hand back down on the table. "He's obviously waiting for our phone call to clear up this goddamn mess!"

I exhale, trying to stay focused. "Call him. He'll want a bigger cut of the money we give him to launder and house. That should be enough to shut him up and free up our shipment." I grind my teeth, internally agonizing.

He stands before grabbing the phone; I can see a tremor in his hand. *Millions of dollars could be lost because of me.*

He tells Costa not to let the squabble of kids ruin up the goodwill they've got going on between them. I can hear Costa yelling through the phone. They go back and forth until finally agreeing that Costa will keep thirty-five percent of all monies sent to him for laundering. He'll also release the plane within the hour. My father hangs up the phone, pulling out his gun and aiming it straight to my head.

"You realize the loss we're taking? You fucked up big time, Vincent." He says my name like a curse; if I weren't his son, he would shoot me in the head. He brings the gun back down and lights up another cigarette.

* * *

AN HOUR LATER, twelve of us sit together around the table. Smoke billows around the room as my father updates the family. Everyone talks over each other, enraged that I went against their orders and pissed off Daniela. I'm not sure they realize that Costa is essentially turning into the largest shareholder of Borignone mafia. Now that he's taking this much of our profits, we all have to wonder who works for whom. Luckily, my father doesn't mention Eve in connection with all this drama. If anyone knew she was the reason all of this went down, it wouldn't bode well for her.

My father clears his throat. Voices simmer, but the anger level is still high. "It's fucking horrible what's happened, but it's done. We gotta send Vincent out to Nevada as soon as possible to start gaming and get us out of Costa's hold. We also gotta discuss this potential RICO charge that Enzo believes is coming on the quick."

Hell is pouring down. My shirt is soaked in sweat, but I continue to keep myself looking controlled. I can't let my emotions rule me.

Enzo shifts in his seat. He has the same sandy-blonde hair and big build as Tom, but probably fifty pounds heavier. "At least one of us has to go to lockup, Antonio. Someone needs to plead guilty to a lesser charge, or we risk seizure of all our assets under RICO. And I'm not talking about soldiers we can pay off to do time. The Feds are going to want someone from around this table."

My father turns to me pointedly, a cigarette dangling from the corner of his mouth. I can tell what he's thinking. Tom warned me. Hell, I knew the consequences when I got into it with Eve, but I took the risk anyway. My day of reckoning has come. I may not have been the one to tip off the Feds about our union involvement, but the fact that my fuck-up led to giving Costa this much of our money is all my doing.

"I'll do it." My voice comes out clear.

They all shift in their seats and stare at me, faces hard as stone. "I'll go," I repeat.

"No," my Enzo declares firmly. "The build-out in Nevada is the most important thing on our agenda. And you're the only one with the key because of your birthright. If you're in lockup, we'll be stuck with Costa for another goddamn decade."

"I'll still be able to work; I don't need to physically live out west to get it done. If I hire a lawyer to do business on my behalf, through a power of attorney, I can do it all from prison. I'm sure we can even arrange weekly meetings, too. Nothing about what I'm doing out west is illegal on its face; in fact, by design, it's one hundred percent kosher. We can all rest assured that within five to seven years, the complex will be operating and we can be free of that fuck."

Luciano's voice clears from the end of the table. "What if you get hurt? If somethin' happens to you in lockup, there will be no casino complex."

Everyone starts talking again, turning to each other in debate.

I clear my throat loudly. "Let's put it to the table. Let's vote." My voice is strangely calm.

"Why don't we send Tommy in there with him?" Luciano chimes in.

Enzo shrugs. "Not a bad thought. My son won't leave Vincent's side. Plus, we've got seven soldiers already in Canaan. We'll cut a deal to make sure the boys go there so they'll have protection."

"There's something else," Luciano says. "In Canaan, they've got tough regulations for e-mail and internet access. If we send Vincent, they've got to lax those rules for him. Otherwise, he won't be able to work."

"True," Enzo replies. "Let's make sure to bring that up with Goldsmith when he works out the plea deal. That's gotta be non-negotiable. In writing."

"And how about Daniela?"

Luciano shifts in his chair. "She'll find a way to spin it in her favor. Of that, I have no doubt. Anyway, shit with her is done, right? Antonio worked out that deal with Costa; his daughter's feelings don't matter to us no more." The men nod and grumble in agreement.

A part of my chest loosens. The days of Daniela owning me are done.

My father leans back in his chair and lets out a deep breath. "A'right. I'm gonna call Goldsmith. Let's get everything organized with him quickly. I'd say Vincent and Tom have about a week. Vincent, you think that's enough time to get your shit in order?"

Enzo chuckles. "It's gotta be enough. Right now, RICO is a hard threat. We gotta stop that train before it runs us over."

I crack my knuckles, one by one. The men all stand to leave, shaking my father's hand and then mine, as they exit the room. I'm taking the fall, which means I'll have paid my debt for this fuck-up.

Once the men are gone, my father sits up. "Prison." He shakes his head as if in shock and picks up another cigarette.

I pull his pack toward me, taking out a smoke for myself and light up. I take a deep inhale, thinking about the fact that I'll be behind bars for God knows how many years of my life. My exhale is long and slow. *What have I just signed up for?*

"We've all been there. And you're tough. Sergey will make sure to give you pointers before entering; he'll show you how to make weapons, too. Once you've established yourself, general pop will leave you alone. They will know who you are, and you'll have proven your worth. After that, it's just time. Time where you can get everything moving for Gaming. Whatever you need done from the outside, we'll make sure it goes through."

I nod my head, keeping my gaze strictly on him, and letting him know with my eyes that I'm both hearing and listening to his words.

He leans back in his seat. "I met her, you know. She was at Angelo's. I scared the shit outta her. Let me tell you, that girl looked at me like I was the fuckin' devil," he chuckles.

I look at him questioningly, wondering what he's getting at.

"Going to jail makes many alliances, but also many enemies. And a girl like her?" He raises his eyebrows. "I don't have to tell you that plenty of men would want to take her. Especially to retaliate."

Blood rushes into my head and my stomach churns. I clench and then unclench my fists. He has his own reasons for wanting her out of my life. Of that, I'm sure. Still though, he has a real point. I shuffle in my seat, not wanting him to see that my chest is caving in. If anyone knew I had a woman I was leaving behind...if she even came to prison for a visit...it could mean her death.

He puts his hand out to me, and I steel myself, shaking it firmly. Before I can let go of his grip, he squeezes my palm. "Get shit set for Gaming so you won't lose any time while you're locked up. The sooner we get it off the ground, the sooner we can cut Costa loose."

He's all business. I nod my head, swallowing hard. "I'll send you hard copies of my plans, and I'll scan and email myself everything. I already discussed with Erez about how many men we'll need to pressure the Tribal Council. As we discussed, it'll probably be bloody getting them to agree to this."

"You going away is a travesty for the entire family, Vincent. You'll come out stronger, though. No room in this life for love. Love is for pussies. Prison will teach you." He holds my hand for another beat and then releases me.

I move to leave, when he clears his throat. "One more thing.

Tomorrow morning, you gotta get inked. It's time to get the Borignone insignia."

"I'll call Shane, then."

He looks at me gravely. With a swift nod to the leader of the Borignone mafia, I walk out the door, my fate sealed.

22

VINCENT

I TAKE a car to the East River at Eighty-Seventh Street, sit back on a bench, and light up a smoke while staring at the lights of the RFK Bridge.

Eve accepted me and my life months ago. She won't be easily convinced to be done with me; even if I'm in jail, she'll want to stay close. And she'd wait the however many years if I asked her to wait. I know this because I'd wait a lifetime for her.

I have to break her heart—make sure she believes we're completely done. I need her to get off the East Coast, and then promptly forget I ever existed. If she has any hope, she'll hang onto me. If there's one thing my father is right about, it's this: if anyone hears there is a woman I love, they will come for her and use her against me. Not least, I wouldn't be able to sleep knowing she's waiting—for potentially ten goddamn years—for me to leave prison. What if I die in lockup? What if I come out a different man completely? She can't wait. I won't let her.

My father's reasons for that good advice are obviously purely self-ish. He sees her as the girl who shook our empire. I lift my head for a moment, realizing that the biggest threat of all may be him—Antonio Borignone. She has to leave and my father must know that it's completely over. It's shocking to imagine that my father would do that to me. But when he puts on that suit, he's only one man—the Boss. And the Boss makes sure every *I* is dotted and every *T* is crossed.

I exhale, wondering how I'm going to break us up. I imagine that the plan is for a fictional character, because every time I think of doing this to my girl, my stomach clenches.

Finally, I pick up the phone, calling Angelo. I'm going to need him to back up my story. I know how close they are, and he's the best man for the job as she trusts him entirely.

He listens intently to me before cursing me out. The only reason why I accept the way he's speaking is because I know it's out of love for my girl. He's furious I dragged her into this mess in the first place. He's shocked, but his fury only solidifies the truth; Eve deserves better than me and this life. When the conversation ends, I hang up the phone and drop my head into my palms.

All of a sudden, I'm assaulted by the memory of Eve's shitty stairwell back in the Blue Houses. I haven't thought of that shithole in quite some time. My breath grows ragged, imagining those darkened steps.

I MOVE BEHIND HER, one hand on my piece and the other at her lower back. I feel her tiny frame trembling at my touch. I want to turn her around and pull her into my arms, grab her and carry her up to her apartment. No, I want to grab her and carry her out of this fuckin' shithole. I just need to feel her lips on mine. Everything about her calls to me. She's whip-smart and intellectual and somehow, has no goddamn clue how gorgeous she is. My heart pounds with want. She's so tiny, and it brings out the caveman in me. Even two steps behind her, I tower over her.

I turn her around on the step and do my best to gauge her mood in the dark. Could I leave her in this building alone tonight? What I see in her face has my dick twitching; she wants me. Full lips parted, eyes slightly glazed. I go in for a soft kiss, not wanting to scare her. But the minute we touch, it's as if I've been electrocuted. Never in my life have I felt heat and energy like this.

* * *

MY MIND FLASHES to Eve in my kitchen, cooking for us a few nights ago.

"Vincent!" she squeals, running and jumping into my arms as though she hasn't seen me in a year. We were just together this morning. I laugh at her exuberance. "I'm making you the best dinner. Wash up and sit!"

I drop my backpack on the floor by the table and then move to the sink to wash my hands.

Turning, I watch as Eve pulls a foil-covered dish out of the oven using a set of black oven mitts that I never even knew I owned.

She's so beautiful. Fuck. I stand up and move behind her as she places the dish on the counter. Using my fingers, I pull off a piece of chicken straight out of the pan, like I know she hates.

"Vincent, no!" she scolds, trying to push me back.

"Eve, yes!" I mimic her voice, chuckling as I take another juicy bite.

"Don't eat like an animal. Let me put it all out for us; I just need a few more minutes to take the rice off the stove."

"I'm a growing boy. I can't wait, and you're moving too slow."

"You have zero patience, has anyone ever told you that?"

"Nope." I take another bite, trying not to laugh.

"You're a liar."

"Wait, Eve. Shush. Do you hear that sound?" I move my eyes left to right.

"Hear what?" She cocks her head to the side, listening intently.

"It's my stomach growling. It's angry, Eve."

"Oh, Vincent. Sit your ass down."

"My ass or your ass?" I grab her, lifting her onto the counter.

"Let go! I need to take the rice off, or it'll burn."

"You're giving me your bitch face. You know I love that face." I nuzzle
my nose into her neck, inhaling.

She pushes me back and I let her move me.

Lifting an arched eyebrow, she fumes in that sexy way of hers.

"Okay, okay, I'll sit." I bring her down from the counter and move to
my seat, watching her fuss over my meal, staring as she mixes the salad.
Watching as she scoops out the rice with a fork before tasting it, making
sure it's just right. Mine.

I BLINK, feeling wetness coat my cheeks.

23

VINCENT

I ARRIVE to SoHo and see Eve curled in the fetal position over my covers; she's fast asleep. "Eve. Are you awake?" I drop to my knees by the bed and put my nose by her throat, breathing in her scent. I don't want to touch her when my clothes smell like smoke and sweat.

She opens her eyes, groggy from sleep. "Vincent? You're home. I was so worried about you."

"Eve, do you remember the buried art?" I'm remembering a few months back when we were studying together. I had to write a paper on lost art during World War II. I explained to Eve how people buried their valuables in their backyards before they were taken by the Nazis. They were hoping that one day, if they made it home, they could find their valuables again. I wish there was a way to bury what we had underground instead of burning it to ash. I'm selfishly praying that somehow, she retains just a sliver of hope. Just enough that if I happen to make it out of prison alive, we may have a chance again.

"Mm hmm," she says as she snuggles down, immediately falling back asleep.

I remove my clothes and take a hot shower before putting on a fresh pair of boxers. Before getting into bed, I rifle through her purse to find our apartment keys. Holding the keychain up to the light, I pull off one of the charms, a silver boot. This charm, above all others, has a deeper meaning for me. I want her to know that I'd follow her anywhere. And, I want it to keep her safe when she leaves here. Pulling it off the key ring, I drop the charm into the small zipper pocket inside her purse. I need to know that whatever happens to these keys, the charm will stay with her.

I get in bed, pulling her under the covers with me. Checking the time, I see it's after one in the morning.

I want to wake her. Make love to her. Moving some hair away from her face, I can see her eyelids flutter; she's back in a deep sleep. I move my lips to her ear. I know she can't hear me, but I need to tell her anyway.

"Eve," I exhale, burrowing my nose behind her ear. "I want to take you to be my wife." Kiss. "I want to have you and hold you." Kiss. "From this day forward, for better, for worse." Kiss. "For richer, for poorer, in sickness and in health." Kiss. "Until death do us part." Kiss. "I'm so sorry for what I'm about to do. Forgive me, baby. I love you so fucking much." I fall asleep with my face buried in her coconut-scented hair, wishing things could be different, but knowing that come morning, I'll be shattering her life, and mine.

I wake up to pots and pans banging in the kitchen. I stand up and stretch for a moment before brushing my teeth. Washing up quickly, I can feel the clock ticking between my ears. I need to do this right away before I lose my nerve. This is about saving her and giving her the best possible life.

"Hi." I lean against the kitchen counter, arms folded across my chest. She's fluttering around, opening and closing cabinets and flipping eggs like this place is her home.

She beams at me. "You're awake!"

Is this the last time I'll see her smile? I blink. "We have to talk. You're skipping classes today."

Her large brown eyes squint in question. "What's wrong? Is everything okay?" She pours an oversized mug full of black coffee and fills a plate with eggs. She tries to hand them to me, but I don't take them from her.

Gone is the Vincent with stars in his eyes. In a matter of one night, I've managed to drown my old self. Resurrected is the man who does nothing other than represent the toughest mafia in the country.

"Do you know who I am?"

"Of course I know who you are. But, you aren't just one thing—"

I cut her off. "That's where you're wrong. I'm always Vincent Borignone."

"I- I don't understand." Her gaze moves from my feet up to my eyes, finally taking in my hard demeanor. She steps back, dropping the plate and cup on the countertop. They clang against the marble and I clench my fists, trying to stay straight.

"The Feds are coming after us. And I'm going to be taken in. Less than a week. I'm meeting with my lawyer tomorrow and we'll probably meet with the FBI the day after."

"Taken in? B-but—"

"I'm going to prison, Eve. Between seven to ten. Shit went down with Daniela and me after *High and Low*, and she ran to her father. He stalled a huge shipment. It all happened in tandem with a huge investigation into the ports by the FBI." I clench my fists. "One of us needs to plead guilty to a lesser charge before they bring forward a RICO case, and I'm the one who is going to take the fall."

"N-no. No, Vincent. You can't. It's not possible." I can see her pulse flutter in her neck.

"I'll be gone, and who knows what Daniela may do to you. You need to finish this year with your head down and leave for California like you originally planned."

"I don't care about her. I'll pull my applications and stay here with you. I only wanted to transfer because you were going to Nevada—"

I huff, stopping her from continuing. "We're finished, Eve. You wanna stay here and let Daniela ruin your life? Be my guest. She knows all about you, now. And it's only a matter of time before she goes public about us."

"No." She vehemently shakes her head. Her ponytail loosens, stray hairs falling in front of her face. I want to brush it out of her eyes, but I won't. I can't. "Forget her. I don't care about her, Vincent!"

I let out a hostile breath. "Do you know what I did a few weeks ago?" I step closer to her, my body language angry. "I personally took a knife to Rafa Vasquez's throat. Slit him from here...to here." I graze my middle finger across her beautiful narrow neck. "Then threw him off a boat myself. He's a captain in the Cartel. You remember the Cartel, don't you, baby?

"They've been skimming some cocaine off our shipments. Their entire gang has a vendetta against me, now. And that's just the beginning. We've spoken of who I am. What I do. But maybe you don't remember, huh?" I keep my hands loose around her throat, but still tight enough that she knows who's in control. "When Daniela tells the world about you, who do you think is gonna come knocking on your door? *The Cartel.* And where will I be? Behind bars."

"No, Vincent," she whispers. "You're my life. I- I can't live without you. Don't push me away. I know that side of you exists, but soon we'll be gone together. I can wait here. If I go, I'll never be able to visit—"

I laugh sardonically. "You think I'm a good man. You don't know who I am. What I do. You conveniently ignore it." My breath is low as I methodically rub my thumb back and forth across her neck, wanting to both strangle her and love her. I hate her for what she's done to me. She makes me weak. She makes me insane with love and lust. Instead of panicking, she shuts her eyes and raises her head, offering herself to me.

"Vincent," she whimpers. "I'm here. I'm right here."

I'm on her in seconds.

Tick-tock. Tick-tock. Time pounds at my ears.

It's messy. Teeth clanking. Desperate. Dropping on the wooden floor, I strip her completely naked, tearing her underwear off. I pull down my pants, sliding into her soft and willing body.

I spend the rest of the day inside her, but my anger won't stop pulsing through my veins. Nothing is lessening my need. I'm squeezing her too tightly. I'm holding her too roughly. I'm sucking on her perfect skin too hard. But I won't stop myself. I just can't. And she takes it all. Letting me do what I want. Giving me her essence. Offering herself up to me.

The reality of what will happen bangs against my chest—she must leave, forget me, not contact me again—but my body is refusing to listen. Not right now. Not fuckin' yet.

Tick-tock. Tick-tock.

"Moan for me how I like. I want to hear you." I drag her to the edge of the bed and drop down to the floor. I take a long, deep lick out of her center. I taste both of us on her, and it only spurs me on. I have to memorize this moment. Memorize *her*.

"Vincent," she pants. Her legs are shaking so hard I have to hold them down. I know how sensitive she is, but I need her to take everything I'm giving. *She tastes so good.* Her chest rattles in pleasure and pain; she grips the sheets, trying to keep herself from crying out again as she thrashes her head from side to side. It's too much. Her voice, hoarse, echoes around the room.

I finally let her go, moving back up and drawing her small body into mine. Her dark hair sticks to the sweat on my chest, but I lock her down so she can't move a muscle without my consent.

"Oh, Vincent," she cries. "I'm here, baby. I'm here. I won't leave you. Never."

I come inside her so many times, I'm convinced I've found my way into her bloodstream. She's my salvation. *How am I going to walk away from her?* I try to fuse our naked bodies together with my strength, moving my head so she can't see my face. Would she be able to see my pain? I know how much larger I am than her, but nothing is enough.

I turn her onto her back. She's so fragile. Perfect. I let my hands roam all over her body and stop at her flat stomach. I bend down to lick and kiss her smooth skin. I span my fingers around her waist, wishing she were pregnant right now with my child. I want love and intimacy and home-cooked meals. I want all of it with Eve, every day forever.

Instead, I'm leaving for prison. Giving up a decade of my life. The only way to survive in there is to give up my humanity. While I'm in lockup, I can be nothing other than cold-blooded. I need to let myself adapt to the change. Having a woman like her in the back of my mind would only weaken me.

While I'm kissing her, I let myself imagine her here in the city while I'm behind bars. I picture my enemies finding out about her and then, coming after her. Or my father, taking her away to punish me. My heart pounds, solidifying my decision.

I have only one fear in this world, and it isn't dying or being tortured. It's that my love will haunt her. Have I put a mark on her head? I was supposed to leave her alone. I should never have insisted on us being together. I was impulsive and reckless.

She lays on top of me. Breathing hard. Hands roaming up and down my biceps.

"Vincent?"

I move my head to see her. Something that looks like hope fills her large brown eyes. She brings her hands to my shoulders, so gentle.

"Don't make me go. I can't leave you. Don't you understand?"

"I gotta do what needs to be done. You have to leave for California, and not look back." I want her to scream at me and tell me that we're done. I need to hear her say she wants nothing to do with a murderer. I want her to slap me across the face, angry I had sex with her so savagely, and run out of this apartment. "Please," my heart begs.

She shakes her head. "No. I'm not leaving you. I can't! It's just not possible!" She moves over me, straddling my legs. "Once you're out of prison, we'll live out on the reservation together, right? I want to live far from everything and everyone. I've dealt with far worse shit my whole life. I can handle this."

Her words feel like a sucker punch to the gut. The plan has to stay in play. She isn't going to give me up. I remove her hands from my chest and stand; I need to get away from her.

"Vincent?" She sits up in the bed, but I move quickly.

I open my drawers, turning away from her in both mind and body. Pulling out a fresh pair of jeans and a long-sleeve gray Henley, I slide it on as if the love of my life isn't breaking down in front of my eyes. Hurting her right now feels like I'm cutting off my own arm, but I ignore it. Overriding every emotion in my heart is my need to keep her safe.

I pause for a moment to breathe. I want to press my lips against the cross around her neck and swear to her and Jesus that I'll be back for her. That she belongs to me. That I'll never love anyone else other than her. But I can't.

I hear her heavy breaths while fat tears drop down her face. "Don't, Vincent. Don't do this to me. I know you love me. You can't pull this cold routine anymore. You need me to stay close to you." She gets out of bed, walking on my heels as I step into the bathroom to brush my teeth. I stare at our reflection in the mirror; I double her in size. "Tell me you love me, Vincent," she begs, hands up in prayer.

I stay silent. Squeeze toothpaste on the bristles. Brush. Turn on the faucet. Put my hands into the water like a cup and draw it into my mouth. Swish. Spit. Clean the brush.

I turn around and see she's on her knees in front of me, crying. She clutches my calves, head bent to my legs. "I want to wait for you. However long it takes—"

"No, Eve. We're done. We had a good time while it lasted, but you have to move on. I'm done with you now." I bend down, grabbing her shoulders. Doing a quick survey of her body, I can clearly see all the bruises that I've placed on her with my mouth and hands. What have I done? I deserve jail after what I'm about to put her through. I let go of her and she collapses to the floor.

I walk out the door, leaving her broken, no traces of mercy behind me. I have to pray that maybe one day, she'll forgive me.

* * *

I'M on the couch at my apartment by school. Picking up my phone, I call Tom. At least I have no doubts of his loyalty. My brother will be by my side until the end.

"Come over tonight to my SoHo loft. Bring girls. There's something I need to do." I scratch the back of my head with my free hand.

"Yeah, no shit. We've got a limited time to fuck as much as we can. Or at least, I do. And by the way, fuck you, Vincent! Fuck you for dragging us into this shit and fuck that bitch for fucking it all up!"

I can imagine Tom's hands shaking on the other end of the line. He may be angry, but he's tough and will do just fine with me in prison. "One way or another, we'd have to do time for the family. Every man has done it. Now it's our turn."

"Well, I didn't want to go now! How about that, motherfucker!"

"Don't spend your last few days of freedom complaining like a pussy. I'm heading over now to Shane's to get inked. Then meeting with Goldsmith to discuss what we're going to plead. Tonight though, let's party." With the thought of this evening, my teeth clench together; I can feel the vibration in the back of my skull.

"I'll be there," he growls.

I hang up and the rest of my afternoon runs in a blur. By ten o'clock, I've got a solid plan with our attorney and feel pretty confident that he'll negotiate seven years. I shift my shoulder, feeling the residual sting from my new tattoo. Like the other men in the family, I placed it over my right shoulder and down the bicep giving me a half sleeve. *BM* is written in ancient script lettering, but I placed it within an intricate Tribal design. Shane is a seriously talented artist—I'll give him that. He also added Eve's name within the lines of the bands. It's unnoticeable to anyone other than me, but I wanted to feel her on my skin.

Eve's hair. Eve's lips. Eve's body. Eve's smile.

I lift my head up, praying for the strength I'll need to pull this off.

24

EVE

VINCENT IS GOING TO PRISON. My heart thumps.

There has to be another option.

Even if I move to California, there's still no way I would move on from him. How could I? I've given him everything of me—my entire being. There is no Eve without Vincent.

I stare down at my bruised body, hoping that whatever it was he needed from me, he got. Deep down, I know he wanted to scare me. He wanted me to see him as a hardened criminal. He wanted me to run away from him. Did he think he would scare me off with his strength, size, and aggression? Too bad.

I take my time to wash up and get dressed, gently soaping my sore body. I let myself cry for twenty more minutes before I force myself to toughen up. Vincent doesn't want me to be weak. He wants me to be strong. If he goes to prison, I want him to know that I can be a support for him. The first thing I need do is head over to the law library and make some sense of his predicament. Right now, I refuse to dwell. I'm going to invest all of my energy on the present moment, which is gathering knowledge about Vincent's situation. The more I know, the more control I'll have.

I leave the apartment, trying not to look at anything too hard as I make my way to the door. Every single square inch is full of memories; I don't want to start crying again. I stop at a corner deli and pick up a coffee and a toasted butter bagel before jumping onto the subway, heading back uptown to school. The train is full of people, but luckily, I squeeze into a spot where I can hold onto the pole. I flinch as my hand touches the cold metal, thinking about the article in *High and Low* that started everything.

Finally, I'm at my stop. I walk to campus with my head down, deep in thought. I've already missed a day of classes; one more won't kill me.

The law school library stands dauntingly at the top of a hill. I enter with soft steps, but I can still hear the echo of my shoes against the floor. Another woman may be overwhelmed by the gothic architecture and high stacks, but I'm not ordinary. If there is an answer to helping Vincent, I'm damn well going to find it.

I begin by scouring the internet for cases on the American mafia. I compile a list of keywords, including RICO. Once I've done enough of that cursory research, I find one of the librarians, explaining to her that I'm trying to get information on previous cases where the defendants were indicted under RICO. After a fifteen-minute crash course on how to search case law, I begin.

I review every court case I can find on the topic, reading and then re-reading in order to capture the details. So many of the results of these cases are simply changed based on what facts the federal government can prove. It's obvious now why Vincent is pleading to a lesser charge. If the Borignones were ever found guilty under RICO, they would be forced to forfeit everything the family has made under the assumption that all the money is somehow tainted from their illegal dealings. With just an indictment of RICO alone, the government can freeze all of their assets and property. Hours pass, and the reality only becomes clearer. Vincent has no choice but to plead guilty—to something other than racketeering. I feel sick.

Time continues to move at too fast of a pace. I'm sure I'd be better able to help Vincent if I weren't in the dark when it came to his business dealings.

Lifting up my head, I blink. I turn my gaze toward the window, surprised that it's already dark. I blink and rub my eyes that feel like sandpaper from hours of crying and reading. My phone rings—it's a number I don't recognize.

"Hello?"

"Hello, I'm looking for Eve Petrov." A professional sounding voice comes across the line, and I swallow away the rasp in my throat.

"Yes, this is she."

"Good afternoon. This is Anna from Mr. Farkas's office. I'm calling to see if you're available for an interview tomorrow morning at ten thirty. He can meet you at 347 Fifth Avenue, Suite 302, across from the Empire State Building."

"My interview?"

"Yes. Your interview with the Mr. Farkas of the admissions committee at Stanford." Her voice sounds annoyed, and my mouth runs dry. "Ms. Petrov, are you still on the line?"

"Y-yes," I stammer. "I'm here."

"I know it's last minute, but another candidate canceled while I was reviewing your file. I'm glad the timing works for you. Goodbye." She clicks off. My mind is spinning so quickly; I can barely form a coherent thought.

I inhale and exhale, attempting to get my bearings. I need to weigh the risks and benefits of staying here in New York City versus leaving. For one, if Vincent's enemies do find out about me, my life could be in jeopardy. On the other hand, I don't want us to break up. I can write letters from California—wherever. The thought of losing him—no! I can't even think of it. I breathe deeply. I need to go see Vincent and tell him about my interview and everything I've learned based on previous case law. Maybe once he knows I've agreed to leave the city, he won't force me away from him. Maybe I can help him to win this case. Or, appeal.

I shut the books in front of me and take care in putting them back where they belong. I pull my purse off the wooden desk and it hits the floor with a clang.

I get down to SoHo and square my shoulders, stepping off the subway. It's a cool night, but my excitement is keeping me warm. For a moment, I pause, wishing I had a better plan of what to say. Maybe I should stop by the corner deli, grab a coffee and a cookie, and plan my words. I'm debating my next move when a group of girls enter the building. They strut into the lobby, and for reasons I don't completely understand, I follow straight behind them.

They're in skirts so short, I can see the bottom of their asses. They're wearing sky-high heels and chunky rhinestone jewelry; add in fake tits and red lips, it's clear they're walking sex.

My heart pounds.

We enter the elevator together and I listen to them talk about a girl named Alessandra, and whether or not she brought the party favors. It doesn't take much to guess what they're referring to. I've never seen girls like this in this building; it's strange.

The elevator stops at the fifth floor, and we step out together. One of them flips her bleached blonde hair to the side and reaches into her bra to push her boobs up, instantly giving her the look of larger cleavage. I'm standing there, feeling like a ghost. They don't notice me, and I'm completely silent.

They strut to apartment 5B and I ask myself if I'm dreaming. I stare at the apartment number on the outside of the door. This is it. This is our home. I finally gain the courage to step inside.

The apartment is filled with smoke and loud music. Bodies are everywhere. Half-clad girls dance throughout the space, some dancing on top of our coffee table. Where is Vincent?

I see a man with a buzzed head. I move forward through the crowd quickly and touch his shoulder, my heart skittering in my chest. When he turns around, I suck in a hard breath. It's a complete stranger. The man looks big, dirty, and tough. Biting a cigar and staring me up and down, he chuckles. "Hey, baby."

I turn and walk forward, entering the kitchen that is now littered with bottles and cigarette butts. It looks like people are blowing lines near the stove—each taking turns bending down, holding one nostril as they inhale hard.

"Eve?" A hand grabs my elbow and I spin around. It's Tom. "What the fuck are you doing here?" His voice has no inflection, but I can see the anger pulsing at his neck. His bloodshot eyes tell me he's halfway to gone.

"W-where's Vincent?"

He laughs sardonically, his hand still wrapped around my wrist like a vise. "You shouldn't be here."

"Please, Tom. I know he's leaving. I just need to speak to him. For just a minute." I'm talking too fast, the desperation in my voice obvious. At this point, I'd beg on my hands and knees if I had to.

"Do you have any idea how much you have fucked up our lives?" His voice rises in volume. "I warned you months ago, and now because of you, not only is my best friend going to jail, but I have to accompany him there. You couldn't just keep your legs shut, huh? You had to tempt him with your 'I'm so innocent' act. Well, screw you! You deserve whatever happens next. Do me a favor and don't transfer. Stay right here where the wolves will chew you up." He drops his head, spitting at the ground in front of me.

What have I done?

He lets me go and I make my way into the corridor, my pulse rapidly beating. There's a couple by our bedroom door, practically screwing against the wall. Who are these people? Is this Vincent's other life? It feels like I'm walking through a nightmare.

I push open the bedroom door.

My eyes immediately lock with Vincent's.

He's sitting on our bed with his pants unbuttoned. Without a shirt, his tan wide chest is on display; from his right shoulder down to his bicep, I see an intricate tattoo. One hand is on a bottle of vodka, and the other makes its way up the shoulder of a blonde. He pushes her down to her knees. I hear her exclaim, "Finally!"

I stumble backward, the wall catching my fall.

Vincent chuckles. "Well, well. What do we have here? You came to say goodbye? See me off?" He looks down at the girl. "Did I say you can stop?" He grabs the back of her hair as she eagerly pulls his pants down to his ankles, leaving him in nothing other than his black briefs.

"Vincent?" My voice cracks along with my heart. "This c-c-can't be. No." I shake my head from side to side.

"Didn't I tell you we were finished? Get out of my apartment."

I feel bile rise up my throat. I must be losing my mind, because the next thing I know, I'm trembling and nodding at the same time. The room feels smaller as my breathing accelerates. "V-Vincent? P-please..." Tears blur my vision as I sink to the wooden floor. This can't be real. I hear laughter. This isn't him. This isn't me. Who am I? The girl turns to me, licking her lips. Her hands spread on his thighs.

I move my gaze, noticing that his eyes look dead. If I didn't know any better, I'd think it was Antonio Borignone sitting on the bed before me. I stand up, tearing his cross off my neck and pulling his keys out of my bag, throwing them across the room. For a moment, I notice the stricken look in his eyes, but I'm too distraught myself to care. I run through his apartment, and out the door.

I find a cab to take me back to campus. I'm hysterically crying, and it's ugly. Tears blur my vision. I throw some cash to the driver as I exit the car. I vaguely realize that people are stopping to stare at me, but I couldn't care less. Somehow, I take out my phone to call Janelle. I can do nothing but cry into the phone.

I get to my dorm room and immediately collapse to the floor; I can't make it the few feet to my bed.

Janelle shows up. I must not have locked it, because she walks right inside the door. Dropping down to her haunches, she immediately hands me two pills. I swallow them down without any water. Minutes pass, and I feel like I'm floating above myself. We move to my bed, where I tell her everything. She shushes me, combing back my hair with her hands.

"And tomorrow is my interview with Stanford. I was supposed to be there while Vincent was in Nevada. To be closer to him."

"Don't worry, Eve." Her voice is soothing and understanding. "It's for the best. You need to leave here. Vincent is right. It's not safe for you."

"I'm dying, Janelle."

"No, sweetie. You aren't dying. Your heart's just broken."

25

VINCENT

THE MOMENT EVE stumbles out of my apartment, I stand up and button my pants, throwing the girl off me. There's no way I'd touch her. The last woman I'm going to feel is Eve. Only Eve. I stalk out of the bedroom door, shirtless, and pound on the wall. "Everyone, get the fuck out!" I yell. People scatter like rodents.

I get back into my bedroom and take out a small envelope from my desk drawer. Picking up my necklace off the floor, I kiss the cross and drop it inside. I'll give it to Angelo for safekeeping while I'm away. This necklace doesn't belong to me anymore.

26

EVE

I WAKE up to people loudly whispering in my room. I see Janelle in a pair of my pajamas—and Angelo. His dark hair is slicked back. He's pacing my room.

They turn together when they see I'm no longer sleeping, and Angelo steps to me. "Oh, Eve. Oh, God." Tears fill his eyes. "I never shoulda let you come here. I didn't think he'd see you. I didn't know. I shoulda told ya that Vincent was here. Oh, Eve." He drops next to me, the tightening in my chest excruciating. "After all your hard work! We can't let you lose it. Come on. Let's get you washed up, and then we're leaving."

"L-leaving?" My voice croaks.

"Yes. Your interview with Stanford is in two hours. If everything goes well, and they accept you, you'll go out there."

"But, Vincent..." I say his name and the tears begin again. I know in my heart he was only trying to push me away. He just has to hear me out that I'll leave to the West Coast. I can forgive him for last night, right?

"Eve." Angelo clears his throat. "There's something you need to know. Now, you know I'd never lie to you, right?"

I nod my head and see Janelle staring at me. Her eyes are wide and sad.

"Eve, Vincent has been with tons of women this year. Your sister filled me in on what happened between you guys." He takes a deep breath. "He was lying to you, doll."

"No. That was all just for show. He only pretended to be with Daniela." I move my eyes to my sister, who stares at me with absolute pity on her face.

Angelo touches me compassionately with a warm hand on my shoulder. "No, doll. Not for show. Three weeks ago, he was at one of the clubs getting a blow job from one of the waitresses in the bathroom. Take a look at Daniela's social media accounts. He has been with her, too, quite a lot. They were never exclusive, but I know for a fact he's been with her. And recently, they've been together more than ever."

"That's impossible!" I say vehemently. "No. He just shows up to take pictures when she needs them. He just—"

"No, sweetheart." His face turns ashen. "I'm telling you the truth." I look down at

Angelo's trembling hand. "You trust me, don't you? Open your social media accounts. See for yourself. None of what you see are lies, doll."

I finally open up my social media, the same ones I've been avoiding for months. Typing in DANIELA COSTA into the search box—what comes up is enough to make me sick. It's all here, in color.

Vincent is a liar.

27

EVE

Surprisingly, the interview with Stanford goes amazingly well. Janelle gave me a Xanax while we headed over to Mr. Farkas's office; that shit works wonders. By the end of the interview, he actually shook my hand and with a wink, told me he's looking forward to seeing me in the fall, as a full-scholarship student.

The only thing left to do is finish off my semester as quietly as possible and find a way to reorganize my grants. Ms. Levine forwarded me an e-mail with all of the grant information on it. I should be able to contact everyone and let them know about the move.

Angelo brings me back to my dorm where he hands me off to Janelle. I hug him goodbye and then step into her arms, immediately crying again. We binge watch *Sex and the City* and fall asleep to Carrie screaming at Big to stop fucking up her life.

I wake up alone. Janelle must have left to work. For a moment, before my mind fully wakes, I breathe easily. But then, I take the phone off my side table, scrolling through today's headlines:

Mafia Boss, Intellectual scholar, and Scheming Mastermind Vincent Borignone Pleads Guilty.

Vincent is going to prison. Seven to ten years.

28

EVE

I MOVE my brain onto automatic. I have eight more weeks of school until finals, and then I'll head out to California. I put on a pair of comfortable sweats and grab my backpack. The second I enter the dining hall to get myself some coffee and a bagel, the entire room gets quiet. I glance around, knowing something is coming. Luckily, for me, I'm in too much emotional pain to even care. All I can think about is getting out of this city.

Daniela steps up to me, all long legs, skinny jeans, and loose sweater. She takes the coffee out of my hand and spills the hot liquid over my head. I gasp as the scalding wetness seeps straight through my hair, down to my clothes, and onto my pants.

"Oops," she enunciates every letter. The dining hall is so quiet, I can hear someone in the back clearing their throat.

"Does everyone see this girl?" she yells and every single person turns their head; it's a collective gaze. "This girl fucked Vincent behind my back. Ruined his life. Told the Feds lies to get him in jail, because he wouldn't be with her. Let's all make sure to give Eve Petrov a little extra attention, huh?"

I hear gasps.

My life is falling apart.

29

EVE
One month later

MY LAST FINAL came and went yesterday. I'm shocked to have completed my first full year of college. Angelo is on his way to take me to the airport, and I still have a few odds and ends to pack. Although I insisted I could get to California on my own, he surprised me with two tickets to San Francisco International Airport. From there, we'll rent a car and drive the thirty minutes to Stanford. He said he needed a vacation anyway, but I know that he just wants to make sure I'm settled and comfortable. Luckily, Stanford is allowing me to begin over the summer, which is quite a relief. At the rate I'm going, I'll be able to graduate from college in only two more years.

Saying goodbye to Janelle and Claire was difficult, but necessary. The past two months have been excruciating. Janelle has tried to come over as often as she can, but it's difficult with her schedule. Claire and I still chat, but it isn't easy for her when I've become the most hated girl on campus.

Daniela managed to spread every vile rumor possible about me. Not only am I called a whore to my face, but people are actually saying that I screw guys for tuition. People seemed to think it was funny to *accidentally* spill food or drinks all over my clothes or head. It didn't take long for me to realize that while I was no longer in the middle of the ghetto afraid for my life, the people here can be just as terrifying. The entire school now sees me as a slut. I'm the girl who put Vincent Borignone behind bars.

Vincent's warnings about his rivals finding out about me still knock around in my head. But I guess Daniela was good for something; the rumors she spread make it pretty clear that I'm not his ex-lover, but a bona fide enemy. I wouldn't be surprised if the Cartel sends me a goddamn fruit basket at this point.

I pull my stringy hair back with a tie, unconcerned with the fact that I haven't worn makeup in months and I haven't washed my hair since last Saturday. The only thing I care about now are grades and moving on with my life.

One thing is for sure: the world doesn't owe me shit. But, I'm prepared to work hard and succeed at my goals. I still intend on going to law school after I finish my undergraduate degree. None of my plans have to change.

I'm still working through the fact that Vincent and I are totally done. While I do think we had love, he always made it clear that there was another side to him. I guess I was too dumb and blind to notice. I wish I had someone to really talk to about it all. But the truth is, no one can relate to what happened to me. Talking about it is nothing but futile. I just want to bury my feelings, along with the memory of him. It's too painful to deal with.

That's not to say I haven't had compulsive conversations with him in my head. They go something like this:

"Vincent! Why? How could you do that to me?"

"I just wanted to know what it felt like to have someone at home."

Or, other times, he'd say:

"I just couldn't control my urges; I'm a sexual man, and I was never willing to say no to a woman."

And every so often, he'd say:

"No baby. I made Angelo lie. I had to save you from my enemies. I had to make sure you had no hope left so that everyone knew we were over."

Somehow, I vaguely remember him whispering something about art the night he came home before he broke things off. But for the life of me, I can't remember what he was talking about. But what good would it do, anyway? He wanted me gone, and he got his wish.

I look around my now-empty dorm room. I can't believe that only a few hours ago, this space was filled with books and clothes, and now, it's completely abandoned and empty. It's oddly wistful.

I can smell Angelo coming down the hall and let out a quiet laugh. Finally, he steps inside, placing a warm hand on my back. "Ready, sweetheart?"

Somehow, his scent makes me feel secure. I take a deep breath before handing him two pieces of luggage to bring down to the car.

* * *

LaGuardia Airport is mayhem, but Angelo and I make it to the gate with a few minutes before boarding. Before we get onto the plane, I stuff my hand in the small zipper pocket inside my purse, trying to find a piece of gum. I feel something hard. I pull it out and lift it closer to my face to inspect it. It's a silver boot charm.

"What is this?"

I hand it to Angelo, and he looks at it. "It looks like a boot."

"No shit," I laugh. "But why is this here?"

He chuckles. "How the hell am I supposed to know? You girls have tons of random junk in your bags." For a moment, I remember Claire's gigantic bag, and I smile.

But of course, my mind starts racing. The only charms I've ever had were from the keychain Vincent gave me. But, why is it here? Could it have fallen off the chain? Maybe Vincent had something to do with this—did he remove it off the keychain? Was he trying to tell me something? I swallow back tears as I get on the plane. My mind is probably playing tricks on me, looking for anything as a sign of hope.

I walk onto the flight, handing my ticket to the stewardess. She smiles kindly, gesturing to my seat.

I pause, turning around to Angelo behind me. "You didn't have to get us first class."

"Of course, I did. Your first time flying, gotta be the best." He winks at me, but I can see the sadness behind the smile. Even though I love him, I feel this inexplicable urge to push him away. Maybe leaving really was the right move. I need to start over. I can't face my past anymore.

California, here I come.

REDEMPTION (VINCENT AND EVE BOOK 3)

1

VINCENT

BEADS OF SWEAT trickle down my chest and onto my abs within mere moments of stepping onto the gray concrete. Squinting my eyes from the blaring sun, I crack my neck from side to side, letting out tension as my eyes take in the huge cement blocks around me.

Me and Tom, my best friend and brother in the Borignone mafia, are personally escorted off the prison grounds, our heavy strides silent against the dark pavement as we walk to our freedom. The warden and two highly armed officers flank our sides. A throat clears as a lone black Mercedes-Benz pulls up to the tall gates.

Tom turns to me, smirking like a beefed-up demon as his green eyes twinkle with triumph. Prison did nothing but make my boy tougher both inside and out. The guards step back. Tom swiftly opens the door, bending his thick neck low and entering the car.

I move to face the straight-backed warden, his bald head perspiring from the sun. He takes my hand in a firm shake.

"I won't forget what you did for me, sir. Thank you." I feel nothing short of honest gratitude. If not for the warden, I'd be leaving as nothing but an ex-con. Instead, I'm heading out of here as the board president of what will be one of the largest gaming companies in the USA.

"No doubt, son, you're one of the good ones. I hope to never see you again." He chuckles, his timber gravelly and strong as his hand continues to grip mine. I finally let go and step into the car, shutting the door firmly behind me. It closes with a satisfying *slam*.

I'm free, sort of.

It's been six years, three months, and two days; my sentence lessened due to good behavior. And now I've got six months on parole before I can leave New York behind me—for good.

The driver starts down the dirt road wordlessly, his orders likely already given by my father Antonio Borignone, the boss of the Borignone mafia. Tom and I face away from each other, staring out our respective tinted windows. Boxy white mobile homes come into view as my eyes slightly water from the smell of fresh leather seats. It's that new car scent everyone loves but always bothered me with its sharpness.

Green trees enter my vision next, and the unexpected burst of color has my eyes widening. Prison is all grays and blacks, all the time. Absentmindedly, I rub the center of my chest as an acute feeling of worry seeps inside, blocking the relief I felt only moments before. What if a cop pulls us over and says there was an error with my paperwork during discharge? There are rumors that a misplaced signature can get a person back inside on the quick. I shake out my shoulders, telling my consciousness to shut the fuck up. It's not like me to double and triple guess myself like this, but what can I expect after being locked up for over half a decade? Freedom is here, yet I have this sinking feeling someone is going to take it away from me.

Being locked up is hell, although I know I deserved the punishment. I made wrong choices, which led me to ruin my world along with both Eve's and Tom's. I was an impulsive and hotheaded kid, believing I could have my girl in secret while publicly dating a socialite for the family. But this compartmentalized life brought me nothing but divide. Unable to get a good grip on the world around me, my life fell apart.

I've had years now to go over my mistakes, and now that I'm free, it's time I redeem myself. Once, being the son of Antonio Borignone defined me. But now I understand I'm my own man. What I do is on me, and me alone.

The low growl of motorcycles ring in my ears. I've got to get myself a ride. Considering the fact that I've spent years caged like an animal behind steel and metal bars, the idea of being free on the road without the restriction of a roof and doors sounds incredible.

The car begins to shake as a swarm of bikes surround us; my body and mind switch to alert mode; I look left to right, forward and back. Four motorcycles are on either side of the vehicle, plus two in front and two behind. They're wearing leather vests but moving too quickly for me to identify the insignia on the back.

One of the bikers pulls dangerously close to our car. He turns his head as a dark grin spreads across his face—raising a hand in what looks like...solidarity. My pulse quickens. I finally get a good look at his leather. This is the outside arm of the Boss Brotherhood, also known as the BB.

They're a group of white supremacist bikers with nothing but stupidity, muscles, and drugs between them. The fact that they work with the family is the tip of the iceberg when it comes to what I see as the degradation of the Borignone mafia. It's a downward spiral I'm not interested in taking part in—not anymore. And if I get my way, I won't have to any longer.

"Holy fuck, man. This is insane. Enemies inside, friends outside?" Tom's voice has a hard and confused edge.

We both knew the family aligned with the BB but still, seeing it in real time is a new thing entirely.

"Christ," I mumble, fantasizing about opening the window and grabbing the fucker's throat.

I clench my fists but lean back. "Sit, brother. We're not packing and I'm not getting us back inside within twenty minutes of leaving. They aren't showing aggression and we have no reason to fight."

"Fuck!" Tom slams his fist into the empty seat in front of him. He presses his lips together in a thin line, his tell for when he's calming himself. "You're right," he replies after a few beats, his voice resigned.

Finally, the bikes take off, leaving us unharmed.

Tom leans forward and touches the back of the seat in front of me, getting the driver's attention. "Stop at a restaurant, man. We're starved."

I nod. "Good call." The thought of food has my stomach grumbling.

Thirty minutes later, we pull up to what looks like a 1950s-style diner. The structure is low and white with two rows of pink neon lights highlighting the roof. I strut inside, the door chiming with our entry. It's strange walking into a restaurant as if I were just a typical law-abiding citizen when just an hour ago I had cuffs around my wrists. Yet, here I am.

Tom follows me to the back corner booth where two over-sized white menus are already placed on the table along with silverware and a red and white checkered napkin. I've got a good spot, able to watch the entire diner as well as keep an eye on the parking lot. Can never be too careful.

I sit down and scan the food choices, letting my eyes ping-pong between appetizers, main courses, and desserts. In prison, we had no choice when it came to food. Hell, we barely had a choice when it came to anything. I'm staring at over fifty potential meal items and the list seems endless.

Frustrated, I drop the menu back on the table, noticing an over-weight trucker sitting alone in the booth in front of ours. His red face shows a tired contentment as he digs into a huge slice of apple pie with a dull silver spoon. My mouth waters.

"We did it, huh?" Tom's voice brings my attention back to him. "There were moments, I swear to God, Vincent, I thought time would never pass," he admits.

"We were lucky though."

"True." He nods his buzzed head in agreement.

Our prison stay wasn't as difficult as it is for most inmates. For one thing, the skillsets we were raised on easily translated into prison culture: mental toughness, physical strength, and ability to lead. We also had a pre-existing structure within the system to plug into, as seven of our boys were already doing time.

The waitress steps over to take our orders, a pink apron tied around her short white uniform. She's young with bleached-blonde hair; I cringe remembering the girl who Eve believes I was with in our bedroom that fateful night. Goddamn, but the memory of watching her heart break in front of my eyes still burns.

Mouth widening in excitement, the waitress stares at Tom as if she just hit the jackpot. His eyes rove her body hungrily, like an animal starved. Not that I blame him. It's been a long time.

I clear my throat and the waitress turns to me. I order a double cheeseburger, fries, and Coke with extra ice. Apple pie, the same one as the guy in front of me, for dessert.

Instead of writing down my order, the girl's gaping at me, frozen to the spot. I look at her notepad, then her eyes, silently telling her to get her ass into gear. She swallows, pupils dilating, before finally jotting down my order. She's attracted but also scared.

"I'll have the same," Tom tells her with a crooked smile, causing her to erupt in a nervous giggle.

"Uh, I'll go get you guys your order." She scuttles away with a bright red face, and I shake my head at Tom.

"Not even a minute, huh?"

"I'm just glad to see I've still got it," he laughs. "I know what I'm doing tonight, and it isn't jacking off like I've been doing for almost seven years. The first thing I wanna do, after this meal of course, is fuck my brains out." He grabs the edge of the table and pitches forward to get closer to me. "You think the waitress would take a five-minute break to suck me off in the bathroom? After the burger?"

"Five minutes? I'd put you at thirty seconds."

He happily shrugs his shoulders. "What about you? I'm sure she'd do us both. Although you might be too much for her."

"Yeah, you're right, my ten-inch dick would definitely scare her." I quirk my mouth in a half smile and Tom laughs out loud.

"Man," he says, shaking his head from side to side. "She took one look at you and almost pissed herself. You got a bad case of resting murder face. As scary as you looked before—you're worse now." He laughs. "Those Indian black eyes of yours. Shiiiiit."

"*Native American*, you fuck head." I casually shrug at the dig, but he isn't wrong. I'm bigger and harder than ever. We both are.

"Not my type, anyway," I reply, leaning back in the booth and crossing my arms over my chest. It's been a while since I've sat without guards watching my every move and the independence is shockingly unnerving.

"I won't say that bitch's name, because it makes me sick what she did to us. But tell me you aren't still thinking about her after all these years."

I immediately sit up, gripping the edge of the table. "I may be leaving the life, but if I ever hear you talk about her like that again, I'll kill you. I told you before we were locked up, and I'll remind you again now that we're out. She didn't do shit. I made choices." I point at my chest with my thumb. "I did those wrongs. What happened to me and you is all. On. Me."

He leans closer. "Man, this is why you're supposed to be the Boss." His voice is a conspiring whisper. "It's in your blood. Don't walk away from it, Vincent. You take responsibility for yourself. We both know if the tables were turned, I woulda said the girl had you whipped. But you—"

"I love you like a brother, but I'm not on board with the new direction the family's rolling in." I shake my head slowly from side to side. "Just can't do it anymore."

"Your dad is gonna freak the fuck out. I mean..." he exhales. "Maybe you wanna wear a Kevlar before you have your chat?" It's spoken in jest, but I can tell Tom is worried. While we've discussed my plans about leaving the family for good, my father doesn't know about my decision yet.

Tom's chosen to stay inside the fold, unable to see anything in his future outside of the family. If anything, prison solidified his loyalty. Still, we've lived our lives side by side since we were born. Leaving prison together was a given—the family made sure of it. While we'd never admit it to each other, parting ways is unsettling. Still, it's just the way life goes. I know the conversation with my father won't be easy, but truth? I'd rather die than keep this shit up and I've spent years now coming to terms with it.

The waitress walks back to the table with large white plates of food. The moment I see the juicy burger sitting between a toasted sesame seed bun, every thought previously in my head disappears; I take a huge bite and groan. Neither of us speaks until our plates are completely clean. Dessert is more of the same; not so much as shifting until every crumb is transferred into our mouths and rinsed down with gigantic ice-cold sodas.

* * *

THE CAR PULLS UP to Park Avenue and Seventy-Fifth Street.

"Wish it weren't this way, brother." Tom puts out his fist and I knock mine against his. He opens the door and steps out.

The driver continues uptown, taking me directly to my father's townhouse. My right leg bounces up and down as we swerve through city traffic.

"Sir, do you mind if I take First Avenue? My GPS is telling me there's an accident on Park."

"No problem," I reply, noticing the super high-tech screen planted on his dashboard. Goddamn, a lot changed while I was locked up.

The car turns east before taking a left on First. I squint my eyes in confusion, seeing designated bike lanes running up the street. The mayor must be insane to do this; I can only imagine the potential for accidents.

Turning west, we drive up Ninety-Second Street, pulling over between Madison and Park. I thank the driver politely as I open the door.

Stepping out of the car, I stand tall and inhale the city air. It isn't fresh or clean, but it's free.

My eyes examine the block as the clouds overhead cast a dull gray tinge on the row of brick and limestone townhouses. Three black SUVs sit idly, double-parked along the quiet tree-lined street.

Turning toward my father's townhouse, the home I grew up in, I count ten security cameras framing the mansion's entrance—five more than before I went into lockup. It still looks like an embassy opposed to a personal residence. I can just imagine him now, watching me like a hawk from the fifth-story window while he smokes cigarette after cigarette, stewing.

The car drives away and I feel a surge of heat rush over my body. With a rolling stomach, sweat breaks out on my forehead. I slick my short hair away from my face, feeling dampness at the roots. It must be stress. The combination of leaving lockup, entering this house, and the looming talk about leaving the family is giving me an emotional reaction. *Fuck*, I've got to get a grip.

I inhale through my mouth and exhale through my nose as I walk up the wide steps to the front door, imagining myself setting fire to this entire place and burning it to the ground. Still, I've got no choice but to deal with what's ahead. I move to ring the bell, but the door swings open before I make contact.

"Vincent." My father pulls me into the house before to the doorway, eyes scanning the street. Seemingly satisfied there's no one watching, he moves back inside and shuts the door; the crystal chandelier hanging above our heads sways from the force. Gripping my shoulders, he apprises me. His hands dig into my biceps as if to incapacitate. I can easily get out of his grip. Yet, I stand still, not wanting to aggravate him. In the last few years, he's become increasingly more paranoid. I need to do my best to keep him calm, especially today. With a man like my father, the less I say, the better.

Finally, he lets me go.

"Come with me," his voice is stern, "lots to go over."

I don't reply. I was never much of a talker, but my solitary demeanor only increased with time and circumstances. With heavy steps, I follow him up the red-carpeted staircase.

I crack my knuckles, noticing the place hasn't changed at all, still showy and ornate like an Italian palace. We enter the white-marble kitchen on the second floor and my eyes zero in on the surface of the dining table, filled with files. "All for me?"

His electric-blue eyes shine; the idea that my casino and hotel complex is close to completion and all the money that'll be rolling in excites him to no end. Still, seeing all my hard work in front of me like this is straight-up astounding. It was dirty business getting the Tribal Council on board to partner with me, but when one of the older board members died, there was a perfect spot open for the taking. The family managed to pressure them to grant me a seat within a year of my going to prison—with less bloodshed than we initially thought. Once that bridge was crossed, I let the Council know of my intention to start a gaming operation. Luckily, with a few well-placed and heavy bribes, my current predicament of being in prison while creating a gaming operation was dropped into the basket of *sovereign immunity* under the Tribal Nation.

I studied everything about building and development. Internet access could have been an issue, but my attorney had it worked out that the warden himself would monitor my emails. With nothing to hide, having him look through my electronic correspondence was the least of my worries. Every single detail of this business had to be perfectly constructed—and it is. I won't allow ignorance of any law getting between me and my goals.

Negotiating with the builders and architects was difficult considering the circumstances, but I managed. People came to the prison weekly, and meetings were held on bolted-down plastic tables in the far corner of the cafeteria. Deals were brokered, and slowly, I built a team of trustworthy and hardworking professionals. Concurrently, my lawyers worked on my behalf to obtain all construction and building permits, approvals, and bank loans.

The Tribal Council came to me on the first Monday of every other month, flying across the country so we could work in tandem. It started out as an angry and awkward partnership due to the fact that Borignone muscle was used to force me at their table. But it didn't take long for them to realize I wasn't there to screw them over. I took my birthright seriously and expected the Milestone to advance and better the Tribe's day-to-day lives; I made sure the Council understood that.

As the work took shape, the parts within me that were disjointed pulled together. The creativity. The business acumen. All my studies in school. Street smarts. Negotiation. My days of fragmentation were over and I'm proud as hell of what I've accomplished.

Taking our respective seats across from each other, I stare at the light shining off the corner facets of the crystal and glass dining table. My mind wanders into an idea for the front desk in the main hotel's lobby.

My father shuffles in his chair. "I set up a work area in your bedroom; monitors with large screens have been outfitted."

"Tomorrow morning I'll move to my own place." No way in hell I'd stay here willingly. A few weeks ago, I had my lawyer set up a rental for me in midtown; the lease begins tomorrow.

"What's wrong with this fuckin' house?" His voice is aggressive as he stares me down.

I squint my eyes, taking note of his overly exaggerated response. "I just want my space." My voice is calm, meant to take the situation down a notch.

He hands me a file with hostility. I force my hands to steady as I open it. It's the descriptions and numbers for the gaming floors, which I spent years meticulously planning out: 5,000 slot machines, 250 table games, as well as a race book.

I clear my throat, switching my gear to work-mode. "Economically, we should be able to employ roughly seven thousand locals. I've done the math— we'll have about $1.03 billion in revenue per year. Concerts and boxing events will also bring in further employment and money."

"Excellent," his voice is enthusiastic. "I think the more locals we employ, the better the goodwill with the state."

"A lot of people will move here specifically for the casino and hotel management positions. I've been toying with the idea of subsidized housing for the employees who live off the rez. We have

BB, though? They've got violent crime tatted all over them. In fact, the more obvious, the better off they think they are. Their style is extreme and caricature-like, so much so it's easy to dismiss them as absurd. But if I ignored them, I'd be making a mistake. Within these walls, the BB is a highly powerful group.

Crow lifts his hand in greeting. "Yo. Borignone. Let's go for a walk, eh?" He strokes his chin. I'd put him in his mid-thirties, although he could be younger. A hard life can age a man. A bold black swastika takes residence in the center of his pale throat next to the number 666. He sickens me.

I turn around, letting the guys know I'm going before giving Crow a small nod in agreement. We step away, walking toward the north side of the fence, facing C-Block.

"I think we could do some good shit together, Borignone," he starts, puffing out his chest.

I inwardly laugh. Over my dead body would I ever align with these pieces of shit.

He pivots to face me, standing ramrod straight. "How I see it is simple. Here on the inside, you and I are small in numbers, but strong. We can align. On the outside, you guys run guns up the West Coast. The BB would like to help you with that. Inside and out, we can benefit each other."

I keep my face passive and thoughtful as if I'm considering his proposal. Even though the answer is fuck-no, there's no use in creating enemies. "The family doesn't do work with outsiders. We've got our own routes and our own men. But I'll mention it to Antonio for you," I reply politically.

He squints his eyes, angered by my noncommittal response. "Well, I hear you can do more, eh? Or are you not as important as they're sayin'?" He moves to his tiptoes, obviously trying to get a rise out of me. I stand strong and silent, unmoving.

He gets within a few inches of my face. "You're the next king of the Borignone mafia. I may be living in prison, but I'm not under a fuckin' rock." His teeth are clenched as he speaks.

Silence, like heavy tar, sits between us before he lets out a slow and heavy chuckle. "Oh, I see. Daddy doesn't let you make any decisions, huh?" He points a skinny finger directly to my chest. "You're weak. Sent here to become a man, is that right?" He stares me up and down, laughing.

There are some truths in prison. The first one is the vulnerable get stomped. I've got to show this fucker and everyone who's watching I'm not to be messed with. I already know it's critical to fight as viciously as I can the first time I get into a confrontation. The best thing for me to do is act like I'm nothing but a sheep. Let him come at me and then, I'll show him what I can do.

He clenches his right fist. He must be holding a weapon. "You're a pansy, Borignone? Ready to take it up the ass, maybe? If that's what you like, I got boys I can arrange who'd love that GQ mug of yours. Maybe I'll even take a turn." He puts his hands down the front of his pants, grabbing his dick.

I take quick stock of his build; he's close to six feet and looks decently fit. I'm a few inches bigger, though. I purposely cower, trying to look scared. Meanwhile, I scan my surroundings to see if his crew is going to join him. I can feel a charge in the air. People seem to notice our tension and alerts have gone up among the prisoners. It's only a matter of time before the guards realize something's up. I don't have long to make this happen.

The animal inside me starts to pound as I keep my body steady, the beast within me ready to break free. I must maintain outward calm so he doesn't see my readiness.

I frown in mock fear. "Look, man," I start, darting my eyes around as if I'm scared. "I'm not gonna fight you. Let's just chill." I adjust my footing, waiting for him to jump.

He comes at me quickly, jamming a sharp object into my lower abdominals. It slices straight through my clothes and into my skin. He thinks he can hurt me? He has no idea who he's dealing with. I'm Vincent fucking Borignone! I see nothing but the blood I'm ready to spill.

Like a man possessed, I go after him, punching him so hard in the face I can hear a CRACK—shattering of bones. I grab his skinny throat with my opposite hand, squeezing until his lips turn blue. This time, I'm the one laughing as I smash the side of his head over and over again.

A swarm of guards surrounds us, but I easily pull back. My work is done. He coughs hard before moaning in agony, water and blood dripping from his nose and eyes. His face is obviously broken and dislocated, the *angle of his jaw harshly shifted from a few minutes ago. I'm smiling wide with adrenaline, staring at my blue shirt now stained black with blood.*

I spit on the ground, relieved to have solidified my place in this hellhole. I've made it clear I'm not afraid of anyone or anything. As the guards cuff me, I glare at every man ballsy enough to stare, telling them with my eyes: I will kill whoever stands in my way. There's only one alpha here—me.

The guards walk me to the infirmary and shackle me to the bed like the prisoner I am. After the doctor stitches my wound to stop the bleeding, I get sent underground to a blackened cell aptly named The Hole.

I sit in a concrete corner, shaking and sweating. Fever. How did my life land me here? My mind begins to struggle with the brutality of my hands. My father, blue eyes flashing as he locks me in the closet as punishment for disobedience. Faces of the men I've killed in the name of honor and allegiance. Piles of books in the school library. Professors lecturing to note-taking students. The man I always wanted to be, but couldn't reach...I'm so far away from him. Freedom, in the true sense of the word, will never belong to me—at least not so long as I represent the Borignone mafia. I'm staring at nothing but darkness, farther from redemption than I ever was.

On my knees, I pitch forward. Eve, oh God, she makes me whole. With her, I rise. I thought coming to prison was the right thing to do. The honorable thing. What a delusion I lived under. There's nothing here but death and degradation. I whisper prayers into the cell, begging for redemption as I roll in and out of consciousness.

✳ ✳ ✳

I HEAR the shower running and I'm snapped back to the present. Moving inside the spray and shutting the glass door behind me, I groan in pleasure from the heat and hard water pressure. Damn, but this feels like heaven. The water rains down, coating me.

Shutting my eyes, I find peace with the image of Eve. I haven't said her name out loud since entering the Pen. My only fear in lockup was that my weakness of loving her would implicate her.

I drop my head, envisioning her in the shower. *She's on her knees...my cock feels so heavy in her mouth. I bring her up to standing and stare at her gorgeous wet body. I slide my hand down to her center, curling my fingers up the way she likes until she's writhing in my arms. "I love you, Vincent. Don't stop. Don't stop..." she's begging me. Needing me.*

"Oh, Fuck!" I groan. "Eve," I yell, her name echoing against the shower walls as I come undone.

2

EVE

Six Months Later

"Hey, Lauren," I knock on the corner of her desk as I walk through the office, black Louboutins clicking against the marble floor. The law office of Crier, Schlesinger, and Hirsch is located in Century City, the business district in Los Angeles. I work for Jonathan Foyer in the real estate department, assisting him in transactional work. He's the biggest and most well-renowned real estate attorney on the West Coast. Landing this job straight out of law school two years ago was a dream come true. Not only is the experience of learning from him completely invaluable, but the caliber of work is high.

After pulling out my cell phone and dropping it on my desk, I place my quilted red Chanel bag in the bottom drawer and immediately log onto my computer to check the week's work calendar. I pause, confused at what looks like major changes to the schedule. This better be a mistake.

Lauren struts into my office in a skirt-suit, her blonde hair pulled back in a low ponytail. She places a hot cup of coffee and a protein bar on my desk. I look up at her pointedly, my face tight.

"I've got three closings this week and need conference room *A* for the large screen. I requested it, but now it's blocked?"

Before she can answer, my phone rings. It's an unknown number —again. Someone has been calling me over the last few months, not leaving any messages. Refusing to answer any call from an unknown, I tap IGNORE.

Staring at Lauren, I let her know with my eyes that my question still stands.

She dismisses my forceful tone, understanding I'm in work-mode. Clients want an attorney who's a shark, and the other lawyers here would eat me alive if I didn't have skin as thick. The moment I walk into this office and sit in this chair, I have to put on my emotional armor.

Leaning onto my desk, a mischievous smile spreads across her Botox-filled face. Even though Lauren is only thirty-two, she's had so many fillers done I'd categorize her as ageless. Still, it's undeniable that she's a classic beauty.

Lowering her head closer to mine, I'm accosted by her Creed Spring Flower perfume. "Jonathan is on lockdown," she says conspiratorially. "Apparently, there's a new development and he's dying to get his hands on it. He's using conference room *A* for the rest of the week, and he's got the DBC in there with him right now. The developer is coming in at three o'clock this Friday."

"How long have they been strategizing? Those douchebags are always trying to cut me out of the big deals," I exclaim.

We call the three other associates in the transactional real estate department the DBC, for Douchebag Boys Club. I'd feel bad for the name, but the truth is they deserve it and worse.

Crier employs over twenty-five attorneys. There are five partners, and each has three to six lawyers working under them as associates. Four associates work under Jonathan, including me. Instead of working together, the dynamic is one in which everyone is always trying to get one up on the other. As if the workload wasn't stressful enough on its own, I have three cutthroat men who would step on my head with their suede Ferragamo loafers if it would enable them to rise in the ranks. We all started at the same time, but they like to see themselves as higher up and more important than me. Lauren, our legal secretary, is the only one I can trust.

I strum my freshly manicured nails on my desk, a nervous habit I acquired in law school. I can't remember if I've heard of any new developments big enough to warrant this level of Jonathan's anxiety. It's probably located outside of California. All of the attorneys on our team have passed New York and California bar exams at a minimum to enable us to close deals around the country; this project could technically be anywhere.

"What if he doesn't choose me to help him?" I ask anxiously, biting my bottom lip. On average this past year, I've billed mostly sixty-hour weeks, essentially bringing in millions of dollars for the firm in hours alone. I know Jonathan is happy with my output, but my goal is to make partner within the next five years. If a huge client comes in, I *must* be the lead associate working on it.

Lauren snorts, waving a hand in front of her face. "Those assholes can't get rid of you. They don't have your capacity in brains or work ethic. Jonathan has to choose you to work on this deal if he knows what's good for business." She winks, and I want to get up and hug her. Instead, I take a big bite of my chocolate-brownie protein bar.

She walks to the door and pauses. "Oh, and don't forget, hair and makeup are coming here for you at eight Friday night for the Kids Learning Club gala," she smiles. "I have your gown and a pair of Louboutin heels hanging in your closet." She points to the small door on the right side of the room where I keep spare clothes.

"Okay, good." I can continue working while the glam squad does its thing.

For the last four years, I spend my Monday and Wednesday nights working at the Kids Learning Club, helping teens prepare for college entrance exams like the SAT. I remember how it felt to study all night long on my own when I knew that rich kids were all being tutored for the same test; it gave them a leg up and frankly, it wasn't fair. By doing this, I feel like I'm leveling the playing field. Not least, I want the kids to know that changing their circumstances is possible. I tell each of them about my difficult upbringing so they understand that if I could do it, they can too. Mobility is possible.

Every spring, the Club holds a large fundraiser. While I'd rather spend a free night sitting at my kitchen table eating kabobs from the Persian restaurant down the block and reading a new romance on my Kindle, I would do anything to support these kids. If that means wearing a gown and schmoozing, so be it.

"Is Marshall picking you up from work beforehand?" Lauren asks excitedly, practically bouncing up and down on her toes. I roll my eyes. Marshall is a doctor, clean-cut and preppy—the type of man most women would be happy to introduce to their family. In my opinion, the best part about him is he's busy and so am I. He expects little from me, and I appreciate that enormously. I'm all work, all the time. The last thing I want, or need, is a clingy boyfriend. I just can't handle the pressure of a relationship or the vulnerability that comes with it. Not least, I don't think I have the capacity for love in that way. At least, not anymore.

"No, he'll meet me there," I reply.

"Too bad, I was hoping to see him." She looks at me pointedly. "You do realize that whenever I mention Marshall, you cringe?" She opens her mouth to say more, but thankfully, my office phone rings.

"Hello?" My voice is sharp as if I was in the middle of an important meeting and whoever called just disrupted me.

Lauren exits the room as Jonathan's voice comes over the line.

"Conference room A. Now."

I stand up, straightening my navy suit. It's perfectly tailored to my frame and the right blend between stylish, classic, and covered. It may not be exciting, but it works.

Grabbing my long yellow legal pad and a blue ballpoint pen, I walk across the carpeted hallway and into the conference room. The DBC are clustered closely around the large rectangular table, designer ties loose even though it's still morning. Files surround them.

I hesitate. How long have they been working without me? The

door *clicks* shut and Jonathan looks up from his mountain of paperwork.

"Huge deal we're trying to land. Potential for years of billing; and that's without any lawsuits that will come up along the way. They want to open up their doors within the year, but they haven't actually closed tenants yet. We're looking at four hotels that need hospitality groups—huge closings. Huge." His smile is wide and unstoppable. The man is in his element right now.

"Read," he hands me a stack of files, with what looks like two-hundred-plus pages of documents. "Write up a summary of your findings—your most concise work. Fewer than thirty pages."

I can't escape the collective smirk of the DBC. They think they'll be talking and strategizing with Jonathan while I'm stuck reading in my office. But what they don't understand is I'm going to learn every single detail. And when Jonathan has a question, he'll always defer to me. I'll make myself invaluable to the project.

"No problem, Jonathan. When do you need this by?"

"Tonight," his voice is clipped. "Oh, and Eve? Bring coffees for all of us. Now."

I bristle as the DBC laugh under their breaths. I clench my fists in order to keep my calm. I won't jeopardize my career over being treated like a secretary from time to time. I'm tougher than that. And in the end, my persistence is what will bring me to the top. I just have to deal with this for a few more years and then I'll finally be treated with the respect I deserve. My past experience is actually helpful to me, because no matter how bad things get in this office, it's sunshine compared to the life I used to live.

I walk out of the room and drop the stack of files at my desk before walking to the small kitchen in the back of the office. I consider spitting into the carafe but decide against it. Returning to the conference room, I attempt invisibility. Brandon raises his eyebrows before his eyes dart to my ass; the asshole loves to watch me performing these menial tasks. I leave the coffee with a stack of fresh cups at the console and exit the room. I've got work to do.

I open up a Word document on my computer and stare at the

stack of files for a moment; another person may be daunted, but working hard is part of my DNA. I blow the air from my lungs, readying myself to learn the entire history of this deal.

I kick my shoes off my feet beneath the desk, getting comfortable. The first stack I pick up is a contract between the Masuki Tribal Council and the Milestone, LLC. My eyes freeze on the cover page as my stomach does a slow churn. My fingers tremble as I open the file and begin to skim. The purpose of this contract is to build a large-scale casino and hotel complex.

I do a quick scan of the other documents, noticing his name isn't here; everything has been signed via Power of Attorney. Is this Vincent? I blink, clenching my fists. It can't possibly be him. He's been in prison. But why would someone have an agent do business on their behalf, if not because they're not in a position to handle things themselves? Normally, one uses a Power of Attorney if he is unable to handle his own affairs as a result of illness or old age. I guess, technically, Vincent may have chosen this avenue due to his absence. The agent would have been able to do anything Vincent requested. Like, for example, build a huge hotel and casino. Sign documents. Pull out money from banks. Request loans. If Vincent trusted this person, a lawyer from what I can tell, that man could have been Vincent's hands and feet on the ground while Vincent masterminded everything from behind bars.

I drop my head into my hands and swallow hard. "This is work," I tell myself out loud. "I'm putting my conspiracy theory behind me and getting it done."

By evening, the summary is complete. I immediately email Jonathan and within seconds, he replies with a confirmation. I shake out my shoulders, knowing I've got another few hours of work to complete for other clients.

Checking my phone, it's already nine o'clock. I'll just bring the rest back home with me so I can at least be comfortable.

I get into my black Mini Cooper and throw my bag and files into the seat next to me. With the blinding Los Angeles traffic, my mind roves to the man I've kept locked out of my consciousness; no amount of mental toughness will save me now.

I should just call Angelo and find out if Vincent is behind this. But what if he says, "Yes, it's him." My mouth dries.

The reality is—whether or not Vincent is part of this deal—it's actually none of my concern. He's an ex-boyfriend, and whatever happened in the past is over. I refuse to ever let myself go back into that black hole.

When I first got out to California, my life was in shambles. I was emotionally broken, physically weak, and all alone. I questioned myself a million times. Did he lie in order to make sure I left the East Coast or was the joke on me? Angelo's insistence that Vincent was never faithful made the waters harder to muddle through, and I suffered in that space between. Questioning. Constantly wondering.

The silver boot charm I found in my bag the day I left New York continued to burn a hole in my psyche. Night after night was sleepless and filled with a profound sense of helplessness—did he give me this charm, or did it simply fall off the keychain? If he gave it to me, what was he trying to say? Am I leaving him to rot in prison when I should be helping him? Guilt was one of the primary things I felt, as if I abandoned the love of my life.

My mind plays the word "no" on repeat. He cheated and lied; that's what Angelo swore. But my heart refused, and still refuses, to fully believe it.

Traffic lights switch from red to green and I pull over to the side of the road, not trusting myself behind the wheel right now. I shift my car into park and lean my head on the steering wheel before letting my thoughts wander back to that night, a month after arriving in California. I was nothing but a nineteen-year-old kid—heartbroken.

* * *

THE BEACH IS SO DARK. *There are no stars in the sky, only the black expanse above. I focus on the curling ocean waves moving at a steady rhythm. Last week,*

Janelle told me our mother died of a drug overdose. She was dead for a long time in the apartment, but it took five days for someone to realize she was missing and go check on her. God, so much unfinished business between us. Should I have tried harder to help her? Did my leaving without a trace make her worse? For the second time in my life, I'm left to wonder if dying isn't the better option.

I dig my toes into the sand, the cold grains nestling between my toes. How am I going to live without Vincent? I gave him all of myself. And when he left to prison, he took the fabric of my insides with him. I'm nothing now but an empty casing. I can almost understand my mother's twisted solitude.

I strip naked as the salty wind rushes my limbs.

I don't know how to swim. Still, I want to go inside. If I drown? Relief hits me with the thought.

"Vincent," I cry, stepping into the cold, shallow water.

Trembling, I move deeper into the dark. "Vincent? Can you hear me?" I call out into the night, wondering if maybe he can feel me calling. I shiver.

With tears burning down my face, I continue my slow steps until the ocean pools around my thighs. Waves roll up to my breasts and back down again, leaving goosebumps in their wake. My nipples become painfully hard. It's so cold. Still, I welcome it. Should I go in farther? Yes. I continue to step forward.

In the distance, I hear the unmistakable song "Hot Line Bling"—my ringtone for Janelle. I want to ignore the call, but the song persists, taunting me. "What if she needs me?"

Turning around to face the beach, I wrap my body with my arms and wade back through to the shore. The sand sticks to my legs, coating my feet and calves. I bend down to pick up the phone from the top of my clothes pile. The ringing is done, but there's a new text. It's Janelle, telling me to open my email. My body continues to tremble, wet and wind-chilled, but I click the envelope on the bottom of my phone screen. Reluctantly, I read.

EVE,

I can't sleep. I know you've been suffering and it kills me that you're all alone out there. Since Mom died, you've gotten worse. Angelo keeps calling, too. I hoped that maybe when you left to California, you'd feel as though you were reborn or some shit. But I guess your demons have followed you.

Mom hated you because you were better than her. She was jealous. We always ignored her abuse, but that's on me. I thought talking about it would make it all worse. I knew how badly she hurt you and the truth is, I should have done more to protect you. I know she's still sitting on your conscience, but I want you to kick her ass out! She's dead now, and I want all of her taunting to die, too. I know you're probably thinking you wish you did something else. Well, Eve, there's nothing you could have done. She was damaged goods, and honestly, I'm glad she's dead.

And Vincent, that motherfucker. You've been out in California a month now and still mentioning his dumb ass and questioning the truth. It's time to let him go. Tell yourself this: Regardless of what happened or didn't happen, the results are the same. Vincent is locked up and you're free. If he really cheated on you and all that, then fuck him—go live to spite him. And if he lied just so you'd move out to Cali, then live life FOR him. You see? No matter what the reasoning, the bottom line is LIVE LIFE.

Now, I want you to read through this list of dares and swear to me you'll complete them. Maybe it'll give you the push you need to finally step out of your depression.

1. Monday: Spend twenty minutes today making friends with the girl who lives next door to you
2. Tuesday: Get a guy in one of your classes to join you for a day at the beach
3. Wednesday: Ask two girls on your floor for dinner
4. Thursday: Pick up your books and study in the library—not in one of the closed rooms, but on the main floor where everyone talks; no headphones
5. Friday: See a movie with the girl who lives across the hall
6. Saturday: Go to a frat house with a new friend and drink a beer

By the way—the weather sucks in New York. Love ya.

I SOB HYSTERICALLY as I put my clothes back on over my damp skin and head home in a daze. Another girl may be afraid of walking unaccompanied in darkness, but I've been through worse. And I'm not afraid of death.

The next morning, I wake determined to follow Janelle's orders. I'm not sure if I could ever fall out of love with Vincent, but maybe I can find someone or something to help lessen the pain.

That night, I kiss a stranger at a party; it feels awkward. It's my attempt at assuming the ritual of a typical college girl. The girls in my dorm do this all the time, and they seem to be carefree and without troubles, lighthearted and living a life where nothing is taken too seriously. A hookup gone wrong is hilarious. Sex with someone's boyfriend is due to drunkenness. Life is simple.

The clock ticks and time passes. Who am I?

It's Friday night. I walk into a party on campus with my friends when I see a man. He's tall and dark. Built. "Who's that?" I ask Molly, my neighbor in the dorms.

"That's James Dogman. He's the lacrosse captain." She bobs her head up and down. "Crazy hot, right?"

I don't respond.

Physically, he resembles Vincent more than anyone else I'd ever seen. My traitorous body hums. I feel disloyal. Still, I'm dying to feel an emotion other than emptiness.

He catches my stare and smiles, a deep dimple forming in his left cheek. He pushes through the crowd, seemingly to get to me. This man is bigger than everyone else by at least five inches. He takes my hand, knowingly, and walks us to the staircase. It's quieter here. He makes a joke and I laugh. He asks about my major. I tell him pre-law. He asks for my number and I give it. He tells me to take his too, and I say, "Okay."

"You're fuckin' gorgeous." His voice isn't deep like Vincent's.

He moves his hand to touch my hair and I quickly tie it back in a low ponytail. He looks at me funny, but I smile like it's nothing.

The lights are off. I'm burying myself into his wide muscled chest. His smell, a fancy and sharp cologne, is all wrong. I look into his dark brown eyes, searching for a connection. But all I find is a stare as empty as my heart.

I leave before he wakes, shaking with stress as I dress and telling myself that it will be better next time.

The following week, he asks me to his game. I watch him from the stands with friends, doing my best to have fun. We draw hearts on our faces in the school's colors, posing for photos and taking selfies. But it's all a ruse. Turns out, I'm good at faking it. Weeks pass, and he notices nothing.

A month goes by. Everyone tells me I'm so lucky. I internally shrink.

Another night. Movies and chill. James is above me, but my mind starts playing tricks. It's James, and then it's Carlos. Naked and sweating, pushing against me. Hurting me. Tattooed teardrops down his wild eyes. I'm too afraid to scream.

With a burst of energy, I push all two-hundred-some pounds of man off me. Jumping out of his bed, I trip over my own feet as I dress in panic. Underwear. Jeans. Bra. Tank top. My heart—it may explode. I hear static. Running down the steps of his off-campus house, I sprint to my dorm, sweat pouring down my face. I go straight into the shower, turning the dial to scalding. I drop on the tiled floor, clothed and crying.

I finally get back to my room and dial Janelle. I'm shivering.

"Eve, please speak with a therapist. You still have so much unresolved shit, and it's all catching up."

I hang up.

I need to move on again and find a new set of friends. Still, I want to try to live. I want to be happy. James keeps calling, but I avoid him.

Vincent invades my dreams. I hate that I can't let him go. All I want is to forget him! But he plagues me.

Vincent's hands...Vincent's eyes...Vincent's voice.

"You're young," Janelle reminds me the following day over the phone. "You'll find a new man again; I swear it."

"Angelo sent me care packages of expensive clothes and makeup. He even sent me a fancy coffee maker. Do you think he's doing all of this because he feels guilty about lying?" I lift up a gorgeous pair of J Brand jeans as I hold the phone between my ear and shoulder. "Maybe all this stuff is his form of apology."

"No, Eve," she insists angrily. "It's because he wants you comfortable.

Why is that so hard to imagine? Angelo loves you. That's why he sends you stuff."

I need to believe her. But deep down, I don't. "You're right. I'm being crazy."

A few weeks later, I'm hanging out with my new friends, who are interested in philosophy and being "deep." They all grew up in cushy households but love to talk about the "struggle," as if they'd been there. We get high on Mexican marijuana while sitting on five-thousand-dollar couches and discussing the merits of higher tax rates for the rich. I stay quiet, leaning on a beautiful silk pillow. Missy told me earlier that it's Armani home. I'll need to look that up.

I take a sip of my fancy imported beer, reminding myself that I'm lucky. I have a life. I'm not lying in a ditch in the Blue Houses or floating in the Hudson River.

Life goes on in a rhythm of classes and parties. A year passes by. And another. And slowly, the ache for Vincent starts to numb. The want and the need—that never leaves. But the heaviness in my heart is lessening. It's almost as though my body went through an unconscious healing process where all emotion was crushed out of my body. I'm harder now, but at least I'm not crumbling.

* * *

A CAR HONKS its horn and I'm brought back to the moment. "I'm not a kid anymore. I'm a woman now," I exclaim into the empty car, slamming the steering wheel with the palm of my hand.

The me of seven years ago would be out of my mind with this new information. The old me would be wracked with tremors with her head in the toilet, vomiting from the stress. But the me of today is able to rise above the pain. Maybe it isn't Vincent behind this deal. And if it is? I wouldn't be the first person to work with an ex-boyfriend. I'll just figure it out, like I have everything else in my life. I will not allow this problem to become me. It's simply just an event in my life and I will deal with it as such.

I have a job that pays more money than I ever dreamed, a nice boyfriend, who may not give me toe-curling sex, but it's still good enough. I even have an apartment, which I bought all on my own. I shut my eyes, focusing on the feeling of relief. When I'm centered, I pull back into traffic and resume the drive to my apartment.

Friday morning comes faster than I'd hoped. I go through my usual morning routine of a hot cup of coffee at six o'clock while skimming the news headlines on my phone. After my three-mile treadmill run, I take a hot shower followed by a quick blow-dry of my hair. My tan skirt-suit is impeccably tailored and I know I look both professional and stylish. After securing my hair in a tight and sleek bun, I apply Bobby Brown tinted moisturizer all over my face, NARS concealer under my eyes, and Two-Faced bronzer beneath the hollow of my cheekbones. Work at the firm is a battle, and my hair, makeup, and clothes are my shields.

The entire office is buzzing when I walk in, the possibility of landing the Milestone is obviously generating excitement. Lauren and I make eye contact as she jumps up from her desk.

Walking a step behind me, she starts without any preamble. "The meeting has been shifted to nine thirty."

My head is down, eyes glued to my phone as she hands me a cup of coffee. I put out my right hand to take it from her. "Did you get the file for Bearwoods Resort?"

Lauren has a friend at the firm, Scranton and Arps, who did work on another casino complex on Native American lands. I knew it would be a big help for me to review a development that is comparable to the Milestone.

"Yup. It's on your chair. Everything that's not confidential." I look up as she winks, letting me know with no uncertain terms that the entire file is there, confidentiality be damned. It's a dog-eat-dog world I work in, but as Jonathan always says: If you don't play, you can't stay.

I finally take a seat at my desk and Lauren hands me my protein bar before quickly leaving the room. I always need quiet before a big client comes in; silence helps me focus.

I take a sip of coffee before shutting my eyes. Leaning my elbows on my desk and massaging my temples with my fingertips, I repeat: It's just a client. I can handle it.

My door swings open. It's Lauren.

"Oh my God!" she exclaims. "I know I shouldn't be in here when you're doing your mind focus or whatever, but holy shit!" She leans against the door, fanning herself with two hands. I take a deep inhale through my nose. It's *him*. The blood in my veins turns cold as I swallow the bile rising in my throat.

"The man outside. Holy hell!" She practically skips to my desk in excitement. "You know those guys that are all dirty and rough? Like, he looks like he probably smokes a pack a day for breakfast, fucks you ten ways by lunch, and works hard labor under the sun?"

"Jesus, Lauren. You're out of your mind." I let out a shaky laugh.

"Oh, come on. You know what I mean. The guy out there for the Milestone. He's like, dark and brooding. Like he hasn't shaved in a week because he's too cool to care. His sleeves are rolled up and his forearms are all corded muscle and all these black tribal tattoos! And not like these hipsters. He looks like the real deal. I'm equal parts turned on and scared right now. I bet his dick is like, a foot long. So hot!"

"When's your romance novel coming out Lauren Love Joy?"

She puts a hand on her slim hip. "Oh, please. When you see him, you'll understand. Trust me on this, Eve. He's the kind of hot that any straight breathing woman can appreciate." She's absolutely giddy.

Before I can speak, my door reopens. It's Jonathan in a perfectly tailored navy suit with his lucky blue silk tie. "Hey sweetheart, it's show time," he exclaims.

Jonathan loves this part; wheeling, dealing, and finessing are his specialties. I remind myself to calm down. *It doesn't matter if Vincent is here. This is my life's work, and nothing he can do will take this away from me.*

Entering the conference room, I smile at Jonathan and the rest of the real estate team, who sit facing the door. I stand tall, channeling serious and sophisticated attorney. It's a role I can play. Before I round the table to take my seat next, Jonathan pipes up.

"Eve, before we begin, can you get all of us coffees please?" His voice is my command.

I turn on my heel and run into the kitchen, willing my heart to slow down as I pour the coffee into the carafe. Re-entering the room, I do my best not to trip. Even though I see the DBC chuckle to each other, because apparently me carrying their coffee never stops being funny, I keep my back straight and pretend I don't notice.

Jonathan already set my legal pad in front of my chair. I take my seat and immediately drop my head to review my notes.

A throat clears and my head pops up. My eyes practically bug out of my skull and a soundless gasp comes flying from my mouth. Gone is any resemblance to the man I knew. The lower half of his face is covered in dark scruff; if not for his sharp cheekbones and eyes, he'd be unrecognizable.

As his deep and soulful stare bores into mine, I know he hasn't changed much at all. All at once, I'm that innocent girl again. Small pieces of me that have been dormant for years vibrate in my chest. With just one look, Vincent moves me. He's coarser but still utterly gorgeous. There's a hardness about him now, which wasn't there before. Clearly, prison changed him. But I guess I've changed, too. *Can he see me?*

Jonathan clears his throat. "Vincent, this is Eve. She's an attorney on our team." Vincent leans forward and we each put out our hands to shake. The moment he takes my hand, a spark of an electrical charge surges through my body before simmering into a warm and slow buzz. A few seconds pass and my palm is still encased in his; he isn't letting me go.

Nervously, I wriggle my hand free. Sitting back in my seat, I feel like crying. Anger boils up on sadness's heels.

I can't believe he has the audacity to show up at my work. I harden like I've trained myself to do. A shadow crosses his face as he realizes I'm closing myself off from him. I want to stomp my feet and scream, "I'm not a naïve little girl living in the projects! I'm not the girl you knew."

Jonathan continues to introduce Vincent to the rest of the team.

"Vincent is the man behind what will be the most incredible hotel and casino complex in the country. It's really an honor to meet you." Jonathan is in full kiss-ass mode.

Vincent lifts a hand politely in thanks before casually resting one foot on his opposite knee. Raw masculinity drips from his pores while his eyes are savagely trained on me. As if he's able to control me with only a heated look, my entire body floods back to life. I cross my legs tightly, telling the pulsing ache in my lower body to stop. But of course, the little traitor doesn't listen.

For years now, I just assumed I wasn't a sexual person. I chalked up my time with Vincent as adolescent excitement, figuring adult relationships don't have that kind of heat. Wild attraction is for kids, not adults with mortgages.

And now, with one look at Vincent, my blood stirs straight into my core, abruptly waking up my sexuality without consent.

I'm snapped out of my trance as Jonathan speaks. "Eve. Offer him a drink." I stand.

Vincent squints as if confused, turning his dark gaze to Jonathan. "Didn't you just tell me she's one of the attorneys here?"

Jonathan smirks. "Yes, but she helps us out too from time to time. You know how it is." He laughs jokingly. His implication that I do more than work as an attorney is obvious, and I cringe.

Vincent's face turns to ice, his eyes darkening. *Oh shit.*

"No, I'm not sure what you mean. You want to elaborate?" His glacial eyes focus on Jonathan and it's as if the whole room stopped breathing.

Most of the time when Jonathan makes these comments, the businessmen laugh. It becomes a boy's club, and I'm the woman on the outs. I'd never do anything sexual to get my way, but apparently, just the joke is enough to bond them. I have to work harder than everyone else to prove I'm more than what they see. It's a vicious cycle, but what choice do I have? I try to show the clients I'm highly qualified via my strong work ethic, but it's difficult to get respect when Jonathan and the DBC make underhanded and subversive comments meant to disparage. I'm certain, though, I'll prove myself to all of them—eventually. I *have* to.

When Vincent decides Jonathan looks scared enough, he rises from his seat. Jonathan is straight-up terrified; I see the sweat beading on his forehead. He isn't sure if Vincent is about to kick him in the face or leave the office. Knowing Jonathan, he'd rather take a beating than lose this deal. Instead, Vincent moves swiftly to the console, pouring two coffees. One is black, but he adds milk and a spoon of sugar in the second. It's exactly the way I used to drink my coffee. He places the cup in front of me, making sure not to spill a drop.

"For you," he whispers, looking into my eyes. I feel lightheaded as he takes his seat.

Moving along like nothing is amiss, Jonathan continues with a smile, adjusting his tie self-consciously. "Let me introduce the rest of our team." He clears his throat.

Pointing to each person one by one, he states their respective title. When he gets to me, I raise my head, but can't manage to make any eye contact with Vincent; the stress is unbearable.

"So, you met Eve a few moments ago." I want to laugh out loud, but thankfully keep it in check. "She has her undergraduate degree from Stanford and JD from Stanford as well. She specializes in real estate transactions."

I see Vincent's face from the corner of my eye, lips twisted into a half smile.

"I heard about her work from a friend of mine, Colin Vorghese. He told me she's quickly becoming the best in the field. If I hire you, Eve must work on the Milestone with you."

I blink quickly. Did I hear him correctly? "Of course, she will." Jonathan's voice has an excited boom. I feel lightheaded. "Eve is fantastic. She'll be with you the entire way."

The eyes of the DBC pop in shock before a few chuckles fill the room.

I can see the indignation rise in Vincent's face as understanding dawns as to what these assholes may be thinking. "Yes," he states firmly. "What she was able to negotiate for Colin was outstanding. He and his wife are close friends of mine, and they both thought Eve's professionalism, work ethic, and intelligence is rare. I can use any other firm, but Colin insisted she and you, Jonathan, are the best team in the business." Vincent stares at Jonathan before glaring at the other attorneys, daring them to say otherwise.

"I'm glad Colin was happy. Keeping clients satisfied is what we do. So, Vincent." Jonathan claps his hands together. "Let's get to it."

Vincent sits up, explaining the Milestone, which he calls *the Mile* for short. He's in complete control. The room is hyper-focused as he maps out the intricacies of the Tribe and the detailed level of work needed.

I find myself completely engrossed in the details, taking copious notes and trying to stay calm and cool. Vincent begins to ask probing questions about how our team operates: timetables and friendships with state officials. Jonathan responds easily. He may be an asshole, but he knows his stuff.

By the end of the hour, my fingers are cramped from note taking and my lower back is damp. One thing is clear: if we get this deal, we'll be working non-stop for Vincent for a few years at a minimum; the workload is enormous.

Vincent stands to shake our hands as he readies himself to leave. Again, he takes mine for a second longer than necessary. His scent hits my nose like an aphrodisiac, woodsy and dark and something uniquely *him*. Everything about this man is like no one and nothing else. He finally lets go, turning to walk out the door with Jonathan at his heels. And just like that, he's gone.

A few minutes later, Jonathan returns to the room, loosening his tie and dropping into the chair at the head of the table. "So, you think he'll hire us?" he asks, his mouth set in a straight line, eyes filled with an emotion close to anxiety.

Jonathan is so successful precisely because he's always nervous he may not close the deal. That small piece of humility keeps him working harder than anyone else in the game.

Jeff clears his throat, crossing one skinny leg over the over. "Well, I think he'll come because we're the best. But I'm no longer sure we want his business."

Jonathan stares at him incredulously. "Explain."

"I heard to get his foot in the door out in Nevada, he used serious gang connections. You all may not be familiar with the Borignone mafia, but they're the most powerful gang on the East Coast." He moves his arms in front of his chest haughtily.

Now that Vincent requested me to work on the project, Jeff has the audacity to try to stop the entire firm from getting the work. *Selfish douchebag.* A nagging voice inside my head tells me to agree with him; working with Vincent would be the worst idea on earth. This could be my out. But the words won't leave my lips. I can't. I just can't do it.

Instead, I sit up taller. "Who mentioned anything about mafia connections?" I hate his snide remarks, and I refuse to let them stand, even if they're true.

"Well, things out there on the reservation aren't exactly kosher, Eve." His condescending tone is infuriating. "The Tribal Council was sitting on that land for years. Word on the street is the Borignone mafia had the rivers running red until the Tribe agreed to give Vincent a seat at their table.

"According to my research, Vincent is the son of the big Boss, Antonio Borignone. But because his mother was Native, he has a technical stake in the lands. He graduated from Columbia and proceeded to spend half a decade in prison for a laundry list of illegal dealings. And let the record show, his probation was done just last week." He lets his eyes roam the room, making sure we're all paying attention.

I swallow. It feels like I have a pit stuck in my throat.

"Sure, the man is obviously brilliant," he continues. "Managing to build out the entire Milestone while behind bars couldn't have been easy. But think about his reach," he exclaims, throwing his hands into the air theatrically. "A normal man, no matter how intelligent, could never pull that off. Vincent Borignone is a bona fide thug." He spits out his words confidently as if he's making a closing argument in front of the jury.

I click my tongue. "Interesting how this information never left your mouth until after he said he wanted to work with me," I question. "I've read the entire file from the beginning and know for a fact that every detail of the Milestone was done legally. Nothing shady— at all. What he chooses to do on his time outside of this work is not our concern."

"I don't even want to know how many men were paid off or died so he could sit at the Tribe's table as a Council member." He turns to face Jonathan. "Are you sure you want to get involved in a business which could result in a gun to your head? The Borignone mafia is not a simple street gang. They're internally organized and smart. And they have no qualms in killing to get their way." He looks to the other associates, garnering their support. They shuffle nervously in their seats, obviously affected.

I'm outraged. "You shouldn't slander a potential client. It's totally unprofessional."

He laughs out loud. "You're calling me unprofessional? I can only imagine what Borignone is expecting to get from you in addition to legal work, huh?"

My jaw drops as a smile spreads across his face. If I could, I would jump over this table and knock out his teeth. This is a new low, even for Jeff.

"Enough," Jonathan says dismissively as if the conversation were nothing more than banter between two kids. "I don't care what he does on his own time. This man will make all of us rich if we get his work."

I'm shaking with fury. Jeff is only mad because I'll be center on this project and not him. But with enough time and hard work, my results will do the talking for me.

I wish I could report this to a higher-up, but the result would be a mark on my head. People will think I screamed "harassment" in order to grow in the firm. They'll spread rumors about me through the legal community, which is a small one. I'll never be able to get another job again. My rational mind tells me to just pick up and find another firm. But Crier is the best and my pay is unrivaled. In a few years, I can make partner and all of these issues will disappear. *They have to.*

We all leave the conference room and head to our respective offices. I shut my door behind me before pulling down the blinds and bursting into tears.

And Vincent...how could he be here? My heart races.

My mind goes back to the night I found him sitting on the bed we shared, a bottle-blonde on her knees before him.

The fallout.

I was unable to shower or eat.

Daniela's onslaught of bullying—throwing salt over the burns Vincent created.

The entire school calling me "whore" to my face.

Imprisoning myself in my dorm when I wasn't in class.

My chest clenches with memories. All of my carefully crafted walls vibrate with Vincent's reappearance in my life. My stomach cramps.

I run to the bathroom and drop to my knees onto the green and pink tile floor, emptying the contents of my stomach.

3

VINCENT

I SHIFT UNCOMFORTABLY in the black Escalade, still reeling after seeing Eve for the first time in years, wondering how it's possible for a woman to be so beautiful.

I want to storm back into her office and throw her over my shoulder. Lock her in my hotel room and fuck her for hours on end. Make love to her deep and slow, how she loves. My dick hardens and I groan. With a curse, I tell myself I've got to keep it together, at least until I get back to my hotel room.

Every single piece of that woman calls to me, both in mind and body. Just the way she listened as I spoke, taking copious notes and biting on her plump bottom lip...I saw the way her eyes took me in; she is still attracted to me. But, there was something else in her gaze too, and it wouldn't take a genius to figure out it's the pain I caused all those years ago. Buried under a ton of tough-girl concrete is damage, and it'll take serious thought as to how I can fix it. Will she even let me?

Ideas bounce around my head, but I need to think on them—analyze the possibilities of where certain paths would take us and figure out which plan has the highest likelihood of bringing her back to me.

Slade is calling, but I hit IGNORE. I'm too shaken up after seeing Eve to speak with anyone.

He and I met at the gym shortly after I got out of prison. The gym's owner told me he had come home from Iraq a few months earlier and was working as an MMA instructor while he sorted out his life.

His demeanor was angry as hell. With dark circles under his eyes, a perpetual sneer on his face, and body completely ripped with heavy muscles, he had brutality written all over him. In other words, he looked like the perfect sparring partner.

My stress about Eve was compounding by the day, along with pressure from my father to keep myself in the family fold. Probation made me feel like a dog on a leash; I couldn't get to my girl and I was stuck under my father's shadow. Training to fight was the only stress release.

At about six feet and two hundred pounds of pure muscle and an obvious slew of anger management issues, Slade was a beast in the ring—exactly what I hoped he would be. After one crazy bout, I asked him how he got to be so good. Turns out he was on the boxing team in the Navy. Later that night, we grabbed dinner and surprisingly, he was a pretty decent guy. It didn't take long for hanging out to become a weekly occurrence. Soon after, we both opened up about the shit we faced, finding more similarities between ourselves than I would have predicted.

Eventually, I introduced him to Tom, who immediately trusted him. Slade's quiet, strong, and honorable in the way we were raised to understand honor.

Last month, I let Slade know I would need someone to run security at the Milestone and he jumped at the opportunity. For me, it was the perfect setup. He's a natural leader, smart, hardworking, and has all kinds of amazing connections because of his military background.

And for Slade, working with me out in Nevada was the opportunity of a lifetime. He had no family or close friends on the East Coast and hated working at the gym.

With the steady pace of the car, my mind turns back to the first time Slade gave me information on Eve.

* * *

VINCENT: *Yo. You around? Meet me at the gym.*

Slade: Be there in twenty

I shuffle to the white cement wall, placing my phone and a bottle of water on the short ledge.

Stepping to the heavy bag, I stretch for a moment to warm up. I'm planning on going harder tonight than usual, and don't want to get myself hurt by starting cold.

I finally begin, my fists moving faster and faster against the red bag. I want to keep focused, but it only takes a minute for the bag to turn into a set of bars. The men I killed in the name of the family. The time in lockup I did for the goddamn family. The girl I lost because of the fucking family. Anger crawls in my chest as I realize how much of my life I gave up in the name of loyalty.

I punch harder, heaving as sweat pours down my face as I add in various combinations. The physical intensity should shut my mind up, but it's not working.

Eve is now an adult. A woman with her own life. And what if she doesn't want me? I'm an ex-con. A reformed killer. I tore her heart out. She has no idea I did it to save her life. I've got to be a better man for her, but I can't when I'm still locked in New York. Fuck! I continue, punching harder and harder, welcoming the burn in my forearms.

Resting my bare hands on my knees, sweat drips from my forehead onto the mat below me. I lift my head. Slade's already here; he's watching me with lowered brows. Heavily tatted-up arms are crossed in front of his chest, a thoughtful expression on his face. Shaking his head from side to side, he gives me the cue to take a break.

Stepping closer, his dark eyes zero in on my knuckles. "Glad to see you stopped wrapping your hands with tape. Your grip will get much stronger this way." Pointing to my water bottle on the window ledge, he walks over and picks it up. "Hydrate."

I grab the bottle from his hands, my big shoulders shifting beneath by soaked shirt.

"Ready to hear about your girl? I got good info from my boys out in Cali."

"Yeah, man. Yeah." I take another deep pull from the water bottle. The private investigator who works for the family is undeniably good, but I didn't want anyone finding out how desperate I've been to learn about Eve; getting her back on my father's radar is the last thing I would do. I did all the internet searching I could on my own but wanted to wait until I met someone I could trust before doing actual digging.

He leans against the cracked white wall as I pour more water down my throat.

"She's doing well. Still close to Angelo. Her phone records show calls at least once a month to him."

"Good. I was hoping Angelo would keep taking care of her," I murmur to myself.

"Your girl also managed to finish her undergraduate degree in two and a half years and went directly to law school. She's now working at one of the best law firms in the country doing real estate transactional work out in L.A."

I already knew this from my own searches but hearing it out of Slade's mouth has my chest filling with deep pride.

"She volunteers twice a week at the Kids Learning Club in Los Angeles as a tutor for underprivileged kids. Place is pretty run down, but she goes on Mondays and Wednesdays. As far as relationships are concerned, she's got herself a boyfriend. Been with him for a few months now. Last few years it's been a string of nice guys who come in and out of her life. This new one's a doctor at Sinai."

I face him, crunching the now empty bottle of water in my hands. "I'll head over to California this week."

His eyes flash, startled. "Fuck no," he exclaims. "You aren't risking your probation."

My heart beats erratically. "You don't understand what we went *through. She and I. We were only kids. I-I fucked up. She was everything. And I—" I start sweating again.*

He pats my shoulder with his hand. "I know, brother." His voice is calm as he presses his lips together. "You've explained the situation. But this is how I see it. Your girl's life was shit and she's finally gotten to a good place. Okay, so she's been with other guys. So fuckin' what?" He shrugs. "You can go get her again, but when you do, it's gotta be maturely. Not when you're out on parole, true?"

I know he's right. When I go back for her, it's gotta be at a time when shit is clear. I'm a man now, no longer an irrational kid.

"I'll keep watching her. Don't worry." He turns his face to the center of the gym. "Time to work."

We don't spar, but instead, put ourselves through treadmill sprints and weighted sled pushes. With each passing minute, the pain sets deeper in my chest until I swear to God I feel like I've got a gaping hole in my center. After forty minutes, he grabs a towel to head out.

"You gotta stop, man. It's enough."

"Nope," I reply easily, not nearly exhausted enough to give up. I step back onto the treadmill and turn up the speed, ready for more.

* * *

I GET into my hotel room and unbutton my shirt, immediately calling Slade. He answers with a "Yo," and I begin without preamble.

"She's changed, man."

"It's been seven years. Don't tell me you thought you'd see the same college girl you knew."

I drop into a chair by the window, imagining her beautiful face.

"So now you've seen her. You still want to hire her? There are lots of other—"

"Yup."

"Honestly, I'm surprised she didn't throw her legal pad at your head when you walked inside," he chuckles.

"Need her schedule," I grunt. Lucky for me, Slade hacked into her work computer and Outlook account.

"Already got it. I'll shoot you an email now."

I hang up. Opening my laptop and clicking on the browser, I immediately find his email in my inbox. Turns out Eve has a black-tie event tonight with the Kids Learning Club at the Beverly Hilton.

I move to the edge of the white queen-sized bed with my laptop open. I know I shouldn't show up to an event Eve's at; I mean, that's stalker shit right there. Then again, it'll give me a chance to see the new woman she's become. I won't stay long. Just long enough to see what she's like in a social setting so I can plan the right way to get her back. There's only so much information photographs and schedules can give me.

I abruptly stand, feeling antsy. Pacing the room in long strides, I walk from one end to the next. I always think better when I'm moving.

The truth is that yeah, I want to see her. I want to grab her and fess up to all the dirty lies I told all those years ago. But I can't rehash all that shit. If I come to her all intense like I did in college, she'll run away. The last thing she wants—or needs—is a redo of a relationship that ended in heartache. No. If I do this, it has to be wisely. I'll come to her as a new man, through business, in a setting she's comfortable and confident in. Slowly, I'll slide myself back inside her heart. When the time is right, I'll tell her the truth about how I left things before prison. I won't just shove it down her throat or force her to believe me. The truth has to be revealed organically.

I used to be an aggressive, angry kid with no self-control. I want to show her how I've grown up. I crack my knuckles, finally feeling secure in this plan. I can't force her back to me. She needs to realize on her own that the love we shared was true.

Still, I want to see her tonight. No damn way I'm sitting alone in a hotel room when Eve and I are in the same city. I pick up the room phone, dialing the concierge.

"Hello, Mr. Borignone. How may I help you?"

"I need a tuxedo for this evening."

4

EVE

I'M STILL at my desk when a hair stylist and makeup artist strut into my office side by side, each rolling a small black suitcase behind her. It's after six, and the Kids Learning Club gala starts in a little over two hours. Luckily, I already have my gown, shoes, and bag all hanging in my office closet, courtesy of Lauren. Seriously, I need to thank that girl. If not for her, I'm not sure how I'd manage a life outside the office. The gift cards over Christmas just aren't enough.

I raise my head, acknowledging their entry.

While still at risk for breaking down in tears, I continue to use my coping skills to keep my emotions afloat. Rule number one: Don't stop working, and keep your eyes glued to the page. Currently, I'm reviewing a contract for a lease assignment. It's boring as hell, but it's what I do.

"Eve, right?" the taller girl asks, bringing my focus back to her. She bites her cheek nervously. Wearing her hair long and wavy with tips dipped pink, she stares at me with wide eyes, as though I may bite her head off.

The second girl wears a micro-mini skirt, short black combat boots, and a torn T-shirt. "I'm makeup," she says, blinking behind two pounds of black mascara and a heavy row of false lashes.

I exhale, trying to relax the hard edges of my face; it's difficult to morph from high-strung attorney to easygoing and friendly. "Yeah, I'm Eve. You guys can set up over here behind me in front of the window. I'll continue to work while you do your thing." I force my lips into a smile.

"Great!" they reply in unison, looking relieved by the change in my demeanor.

Crouching down on the floor behind me, I hear unzipping. The tall one moves beside me, placing a flat iron, curling iron, a large round brush, and a blow dryer at the edge of my desk.

The girls are likely around my age of twenty-six. But where they're seemingly young and fresh and full of dreams, I'm working like a dog for a goal I'm not even sure I want anymore.

I make a few hundred thousand dollars a year as an attorney, plus a bonus. I should feel fulfilled; after all, I worked like hell to get to this spot. But deep down, I'm unhappy. They treat me like shit here. And while I'm learning a lot, I'm not remotely interested in what I'm absorbing.

I wanted to make it to this level in my career precisely so I could have stability and freedom—and I have it now. After going to college and graduate school with the upper-crust crowd, I yearned for this exact life of ease. Fancy dinners, beautiful clothes, and an apartment of my own. I thought I'd finally be happy but instead, there's only emptiness.

I stare at my computer screen, forcing myself to read while the girls prep my face for makeup and spritz my dry, but clean, hair with water.

"Girl, you are so lucky," she separates my thick locks into sections using a comb and clips, "to have this office! You must be so smart."

A cold hand spreads cream all over my face. "You're a girl boss!"

"We all work hard." I try to keep my face unaffected as she preps it for makeup. "My sister does hair in New York; so trust me, I know how hard you guys run. Don't tell her though, but New York doesn't hold a candle to L.A. beauty."

"Yasss," they exclaim, slapping each other five. "Where are you going tonight?"

"The Kids Learning Club gala."

"We just did another girl for the same event. But don't worry, you're hotter and you've got the better career."

We all laugh, but inside, my chest sinks. I want to tell them it's all just a façade. I'm not as happy as I seem. Instead, I just smile.

"How do you want to do your hair? I think beach waves would suit you best. Your bone structure is perfect for that look."

"Oh, and a smoky eye!"

"No," I reply firmly. "I want to go for straight and sleek. I want both hair and makeup to be elegant, clean, and polished. Not too much bronzer. No sparkle." They both nod quietly in understanding.

The days of wild and sexy hair and makeup are firmly behind me. My New-York self is a time of life I'd prefer never existed. But somehow, the more I try to ignore the old me, the more she haunts me.

5

VINCENT

EVE WALKS into the ballroom and my heart constricts. In a long black gown, she is a sight to behold. She's straightened that wild hair I love. I smile with the memory of how hard she always tried to tame it down. But I always loved her exactly as she was, without all the bull-shit other girls do.

My tux fits like a glove—an overly restrictive and scratchy one. I always hated dressing like this, and it's even more hellish now. I've got no patience for this shit. I lean against the darkly polished wooden bar, ordering a vodka rocks from the bartender, who won't leave me alone. She's already asked me if I'm an actor or a model about a hundred times. Normally, I'd be annoyed by this can't-take-a-hint flirting. But she provides good cover from what I'm actually doing here: lurking around my ex-girlfriend.

I turn my head as Eve steps closer to where I stand. Her dress makes her look like a mermaid; it's off the shoulder and tight down to her thighs before flaring out. I'm in awe of her; she accomplished everything she set out to do. In prison, I wished to see this moment. Here it is.

Eve's head moves around as her eyes scan the room. Absentmindedly, I rub my chest, feeling my body sway toward her like a magnet. There's a part of me waiting to see her flinch or show an emotion, as though maybe, on some level, she notices my presence.

She smiles. God, but I missed seeing this. Watching her happiness makes me feel straight up euphoric. Following her gaze, I freeze. Her eyes are locked on a clean-cut preppy boy who is half my size. Calm settles into her demeanor. My fists automatically clench as my body registers fury—*she's mine*. I move up to my toes in anger before settling myself back down.

He takes her in his arms. Holy fuck, seeing this hurts like hell. I knew the guy existed, but nothing could prepare me for watching my woman in the arms of another man. They're chatting and I take a minute to inspect this asshole.

He's sporting a navy tux that fits him too well to be rented. A white-gold Rolex Daytona watch—the same one my father wears—sits on his wrist. His hair is clean cut, his face shaven. *Is this Eve's type now?*

An old man with stark-white hair walks over to the happy couple interrupting their conversation. That boyfriend of hers stands slightly behind her, dutifully. I want to stride over and punch his lights out. Instead, I take another deep pull of my drink before grinding my teeth together.

6

EVE

"Eve!" Cyrus Nazarian walks up to me wearing a perfectly fitted black suit complete with a pink silk tie and matching pocket square. After immigrating from Iran without a dollar to his name, he worked from the ground up to become one of the largest real estate investors in L.A. Just like me, he gives back.

We kiss each other twice, once on both cheeks. As I've learned since living here, this is the typical Persian greeting. "I still can't believe the new wing," he exclaims. "I wonder if the donor is here tonight."

"No idea," I shrug. "Whoever he is though, he just changed life for these kids."

A few months ago, during a tutor meeting at the Kids Learning Club, the president let us know about an anonymous donor who handed over a forkful of cash without any demands in return.

"I doubt he's from around here," he whispers conspiratorially.

"Yeah? Why do you say that?"

"People in L.A. want their name up on everything. If they give a penny to even a remotely decent cause, they want public credit for it."

He lifts his glass to me. I have to admit, he has a good point. "You look drop-dead gorgeous, by the way. I'll see you next week."

I turn my head around and feel my skin prickle as if I'm being watched. I shake the feeling off; seeing Vincent has clearly put me on the crazy train. Marshall steps beside me, a reminder that while Vincent is in my city, nothing has changed. I'm here at a charity event with my sweet boyfriend. He's annoying me with his presence, but still, I'm safe.

I move around the bar area with Marshall by my side, shifting my hands to my thighs to lift up my gown so I can walk easier. I can feel the eyes of the expensive crowd watch me, but it only makes me raise my head higher.

Marshall's hands gently graze my lower back and I flinch from his touch. He knows how to play the part of devoted boyfriend, but tonight, he's making my skin crawl.

I clear my throat, wanting to change my train of thought. "Have you started the book I gave you?"

Last week, I lent him *The Autobiography of Malcolm X as told to Alex Haley*, by Malcolm X. Time Magazine recommended it as one of the most important nonfiction books of the twentieth century. And on top of that, it still reigns as one of the most important books in my life.

"Nah. Not sure I'll read it," he says with a quiet chuckle.

"But—"

"You know how busy I am." He squints his eyes, confused. It's not like me to push him. Everything we do is easy and relaxed.

Memories of Vincent and me discussing this exact book over dinner pop into my head. I push Marshall's dirty-blond hair away from his eyes, reminding myself that any woman would be lucky to be with a man like him. Who cares if he shares my passion for reading?

He pulls me into a soft embrace, careful not to grab too hard when he notices my sad demeanor. "Eve. You okay?"

I force a smile, but it comes out as a grimace.

"Hey," he lowers his brows, concerned. "You look upset. If you really want me to read the book—"

"No, no. I'm fine. Just a tough day at work."

"Those guys giving you a hard time?" He pats my back. "Just hang in there. Soon you'll make partner like you've always wanted. Just a few more years of the suck."

"Yeah," I reply miserably, wishing he'd say something more along the lines of 'If they fuck with you again, I'll beat their asses.' But that's just my inner Blue-House girl talking, as opposed to the respectable new me. He knows how poorly they treat me, but agrees that with enough work and dedication, I'll be able to show myself apart from the others.

Marshall orders me a glass of Sancerre from the bartender who thankfully, pours quickly. Only yesterday, I loved how easy and simple my life was with Marshall. And now, everything I thought was working is turned upside down. Maybe I ought to just try harder. A nagging voice inside my head tells me that I may as well just start fresh with another man. Why hang onto someone I don't really like? But a more mature voice chimes in, telling me I've got something good and I ought to do the mature thing and stick it out. Relationships take work. If I just open up more, maybe what we have can be *more*.

I never let him know what the Learning Club means to me and that it's not just a side gig. Sure, I've told him that I was raised in a pretty shitty part of New York City and that helping kids with potential, but limited means, is both fulfilling and necessary. But I never talked to him about my history. The result is that a huge chunk of who I am, or who I was, has been deleted. Up until today, I loved that fact.

No—I still love that fact. And I'm going to prove it to myself right now. I place my glass of wine back on the bar and squeeze his hand. "Let's get out of here," I step closer to him, an invitation in my eyes. First, I need to get my physical body on track. And then, we can talk.

"Hell yes," he smiles wide. "My place or yours?"

"Mine."

Draping an easy arm around my shoulders, we walk across the room and leave the event.

Questions and reservations knock on my head again. I take a deep swallow, telling my thoughts to shut it. Plenty of people begin relationships without digging up and sharing their old dirt. He knows the me of today, and he likes it. The rest will follow. I seal my will, determined to make a last-ditch effort. My agonizing is nothing but stress from seeing Vincent. Marshall is great. We're great. Everything is great!

We step into the car, but before we can buckle up, I grab him by the lapels and press my lips against his. I'm dying to feel that connection, and I desperately want to remember that what Marshall offers is good for me. Waiting to hook up until we reach my apartment is no longer an option. I need reassurance—now.

The minute we touch, my body recognizes his clean scent and gently melts. He's a good kisser, with soft but firm lips. Gently caressing my back, I urge him on by kissing him deeper, pushing for more. I want to want this—so badly. I let out a groan, hoping the sound will jumpstart my body.

"Eve, oh—" he murmurs.

I grab him harder, "Tell me." I pull my dress up to my thighs to spread my legs, straddling him and grinding down. I squeeze my internal muscles on a mission to get my body on board with this moment. "Tell me what you want. I'll do anything," I beg between dry kisses. I need him to make me forget.

7

VINCENT

I WALK OUT of the event a few minutes after Eve leaves when I imme-diately spot her prissy boyfriend stepping into her car; it turns on but doesn't move. I get closer before wishing I hadn't. I can see through the window that her boyfriend is all. Fucking. Over. Her.

My body lunges forward, wanting to rip the car door open and beat his ass—jealous energy coursing through my veins. I gather myself by taking deep inhales through my mouth and exhaling through my nose. The result is a sound more animal than human. But the idea of another man kissing her perfect lips. Touching her full breasts. Listening to her moans.

"She's mine!" I roar, turning from the scene and cursing.

Sweat beads on my forehead. Does he make her feel good? The thought of her enjoying what another man can do is enough to make me sick. I kick the ground, small rocks flying ahead of me. I want to break something.

I drop down to the curb, unable to stand. Eve may be the love of my life, but the truth is that as of now, I have no hold over her. She can be with whomever she wants, whenever she wants. And it's all my fault. One thing's for damn sure: I've gotta make this right between us and get her back.

I pick up my phone, ordering a car to bring me to her apartment building. If I have to wait all fucking night and day for her to show up, I'll do it. I don't give a fuck if she comes home at three in the morning with mascara smeared on her face from a late night with this asshole—or a smile and a coffee in her hands in the morning. I'll take Eve any way I can get her.

8

EVE

I'M in the process of unbuttoning his shirt when I feel his hands at my shoulders, pushing me back. "Wow, let's relax a second."

His blue eyes are startled. "Huh?" I pant, confused.

"What's gotten into you?" His mouth is parted and eyes drawn to slits. He's mad.

Embarrassment blazes through me as I think of how to explain myself. "Well, I just thought—"

Before I can finish speaking, his hands spread beneath my ass. I'm lifted off his lap and into the driver's seat. "What if we were seen?" He straightens his skinny black tie. "I mean, a kiss is one thing. But what you tried to do is an entirely other—"

"Are you kidding me right now?" I start to fix my dress as my body turns cold. It's as though the temperature between us has dropped twenty degrees.

"This isn't even about me, Eve," he exclaims, throwing his hands up in the air. "It's about you. People know your car." He turns his head to look out the window and shakes his head in disapproval. "What would they think? You're not a college girl. You're a world-known attorney for God's sake." He slicks his hair as I unroll my gown down my thighs.

Our car ride back to his upscale apartment complex is full of awkward silence. I pull up to his front door, exhausted and reeling from Vincent. Having Marshall near me is only making things worse.

"Sweetie, let's talk a second." His voice is quiet. Unbuckling his belt and leaning toward me, I raise my hands in front of my face, as if to say, don't get any closer.

"You know what? I think we're done." The minute the words leave my lips, I feel a rush of relief.

His head rears back, shock moving across his features. "What are you talking about? Done with what?"

"It's just not working between us. I've got too much happening at my office. And this isn't feeling good to me anymore." I shrug, realizing this is all coming out of left field to him. Hell, it's coming out of the woodwork for me too, but I don't want to try harder with him. I need to find someone else. Someone different.

"Because I didn't want to screw you in public?" he spits out his words furiously.

I do my best not to roll my eyes; it's not as if we ever said we loved each other. We were dating out of convenience. "No. It's not that. It's because what we had was nothing more than easy. And I'm just not happy anymore." I bring my gaze to his face, staring at him directly so he knows I'm serious. The truth hurts and no one knows that better than me. But in my opinion, it's better to rip off the Band-Aid than send someone off with a lie.

He waits expectantly for me to fight back or to show emotion, but I have none.

"I was wife'ing you up," he yells, throwing the door open before jumping out of my car. The side door swings open next as he grabs his neatly folded jacket from the back seat. "You're a cold bitch, you know that?" And with those parting words, the door slams with a *bang*.

My fingers grip the steering wheel, knowing in my gut that what he said is true. I'm not warm and soft—not anymore. Maybe I'm just meant to be alone, forever.

Shifting the car in gear, I get to my building in record time. Pulling into the parking lot, I jump out of my car and run as fast as my high heels will take me to the elevator. I just want to take off my shoes, wash my face, eat a bowl of cereal, and pass out. Sliding my keys into my apartment door, I pause. I can feel a body behind me. My old instincts immediately kick in as I turn, lifting my keys in my hand like a weapon.

He looms in front of me like a dark shadow.

"V-Vincent?"

I take a step back.

He steps closer. "I've been trying to call you the last few months, but you never answered." His voice is deep and low. All I can do is blink as he leans his huge body against the doorframe. "Why don't you invite me in? We should talk, Eve. It's been a while, yeah?"

I finally look him up and down as a lump rises in my throat. He looks like danger in a black tux—muscled thighs covered in a pair of tapered black pants and a wide chest encased in a crisp white tuxedo shirt. I crane my neck to look up at his face. God, he's *gorgeous*.

I lean my weight onto my right leg and lift my chin, needing to get a grip on reality. "No." The word flies out of my mouth like a whip. My feelings are all across the map, and I can't get a hold of them. I move to my safe default: bitch mode.

"No?" He looks at me incredulously, crossing his huge arms in front of his chest.

"I'm not a kid anymore, Vincent." I swallow. "You can't just boss me around. I have plans for myself and they don't include you. Now, if you'll go back to your hotel or wherever you're staying, you can send me an email and we can find a good time to talk. I assume this is work related, right?" My voice comes out as high and mighty, but I've got to harden myself as much as I can around this man if I want to keep myself straight.

"Let's talk for a minute. Touch base." He squints, and I can see the slight formation of crow's feet at the corner of his eyes. Vincent is a man now.

I do my best to stay composed, but I'm grasping on every strand of my self-worth to keep from crumbling. "Who the hell do you think you are, Vincent? You left me seven years ago after ripping my heart to shreds and forcing me out of the only city I ever knew, after feeding me to the dogs, no less." I throw my hands up in the air. "I'm not a teenager anymore. You can't just—come here!" I slam my foot onto the ground, angry and hurting so badly. I bite my lip, even more upset when I see the pity cross his face.

He stares at me, remorse coating the darkness of his eyes. We're silent, but my heart pounds a mile a minute. Can he hear it?

Lifting his heavy arms, he links his hands behind his neck before dropping them back down to his side. "Eve," he starts, licking his lips. "I know you've grown up, and I'm glad for that. You've achieved your goals and you're astounding." He lowers his voice and I strain my ears, subconsciously trying to hear every word.

My body, on its own accord, leans toward him. "You are allowed to be angry, but I hoped we could talk tonight. I know you aren't a teenager anymore, okay? We've both grown. I didn't mean to piss you off by coming to your work. But in my defense, I tried to call you. You wouldn't answer." He touches the edge of my face so gently—I have to wonder if it happened or if I was hallucinating.

I clear my throat. I should pull off my heel and stab him in the stomach. Call the cops, maybe. But I don't want to show him just how angry I am. He shouldn't know how much he affects me. I refuse to let him know.

I focus on small mundane things because the large issues are too much to handle. "You don't shave anymore?"

A lazy grin spreads across his mouth. We're barely a few inches apart now, and I can smell him, woodsy and clean.

"You know I don't like to shave when I don't have to," he whispers. "And you keep your hair back tight or straight, but I know that after you wash it, it's long and curly." His nostrils flare as his eyes move down to my lips and back up again. I keep my eyes focused, not giving in. Still I notice how huge he is. Arms. Wide chest. *God.*

My face instantly flushes—I need to change the subject. "You're making it out west like you wanted."

"Yes. And you became a lawyer. You graduated early from Stanford, magna cum laude. You finished second in your law school class. Janelle has her own salon—"

"Wait, what?" It's as if the music just stopped. I ball my hands into fists as I'm snapped back to reality. "You've been keeping tabs on me?" I take a step away from him, feeling violated. Vincent has been watching me for years. He ruined my life, and what, did he stick around to watch my unraveling?

He squints his eyes again and slightly tilts his head as if he's confused.

"I'm not yours to watch, Vincent." His name flies out of my mouth like a whip. "So, I should assume you know the hell I went through after you ruined my life?"

Honestly, I can't believe how much rage I have inside me right now. It's bubbling up and I feel the sudden urge to slap him across the face. I may have told myself that my hatred and resentment disappeared and that I grew up and out of the pain he caused, but clearly, it was only lying dormant.

His face flashes hot with his own anger. "For fuck's sake, Eve. I did the best I could to protect you. And that part of my life is over now." I watch him clench his jaw.

"Protect me? By cheating on me and making me believe we had a- a future?" I stutter before letting out an ironic laugh. "No. I'm not letting you in." I look him up and down, registering his clothes. "And why are you wearing a tux?" I drop my hands to my hips, the thought momentarily stunning me that Vincent may have been at the gala tonight, watching me.

He smiles with that faraway look in his eyes; I recognize it as the one he makes when an idea is taking shape in his head. "Let's rock-paper-scissors. If I win, you let me in. If you win, I leave."

"You're kidding." This man is infuriating. He thinks he can just change the subject? "This isn't a game. This is my life," I exclaim.

One of my neighbors, an older woman in her seventies, pokes her head out her door. "Keep it down!" she shouts angrily.

I want to point at Vincent—tell her it's all his fault. Instead, I attempt to channel a civilized person. "Everything is fine," I smile tightly. "My apologies."

"Well, it's after eleven and I'm doing a commercial tomorrow!" She slams the door and I look back at Vincent. Chuckling, he reaches out his hand. "Come on. Let's play."

Tears prick my eyes. I'm proud of him, but it also hurts. His dream was also mine, once. We were supposed to be about truth and honesty, but in the end, he gutted me. If he thinks he can bring out the old me with a stupid game we used to play, he's mistaken. That girl was burned alive years ago and there's no trace left of her.

He stands tall, his stance almost playful.

"Okay. Fine. On three. But if I win, you're gone, right?"

He smiles. I'll call him on it if I think he cheated.

I put out my hand reluctantly. "Rock-paper-scissors says shoot!" My fingers morph into a fist to make rock, and of course, the asshole's hand comes out straight to make paper. He wins.

I open and close my mouth like a dead fish, wanting to find fault. Instead, I open my front door. Pulling off my heels, I leave them by the door before walking barefoot to my kitchen table.

"Prison," I say point blank, taking a seat. Vincent sits in front of me, his long legs stretching out below the table. I cross mine, making sure not to accidentally brush against his.

"Yes. I got out six months ago, but had to stay in New York for probation. The last seven years have been dedicated to the Milestone. I worked my ass off in lockup and continued the work after I got out. And now I'm finally there, out in Nevada and living on the rez."

"And how's your father?" I press my lips together firmly, trying to compose my trembling body.

"You cut to the chase now, yeah? No more running and hiding?" His lips quirk in a grin.

I smile back sarcastically. "Nope. Those days are done and gone, Vincent."

"Though nothing can bring back the hour of splendor in the grass, of glory in the flower..." He pauses, waiting for me to finish the poem.

"I'm not here to quote Wordsworth," I exclaim, "Jesus." I shake my head angrily, but my heart flutters; he knows I love poetry. And of course, he's quoting from "Splendor in the Grass," a poem that speaks of childhood as a time when we're the most able to see clearly, before adulthood comes and jades us. But that's the thing about adulthood —we can't escape the loss of innocence. Our bodies change, but so do our minds.

He laughs, shrugging his massive shoulders. "What can I tell you? I did a lot of reading in prison."

I cross my arms over my chest, giving him my best I'm-a-lawyer-and-I'll-nail-your-balls-to-the-wall glare. There's no way in hell I'm letting him sweet-talk me right now.

"Okay, okay!" He lifts his arms up in front of him like a shield. "We're business partners in the Mile. The family is silent, of course. Aside from that, we've got nothing else between us. I've separated."

"Separated?" I ask inquisitively. "How did you manage that?" I shake my head in disbelief.

"Well," he sighs. "I guess when I met you, I started doubting the family. But I figured I made my bed and had no choice but to sleep in it. My senior year of college, when we were together" —he says, gesturing between us— "I thought it would be possible to keep one foot in and one foot out. I figured once I left New York, I'd be able to have the freedom."

I lean forward in my chair, wanting to look disgusted and angry over his mention of that time. Instead, I listen with bated breath.

"But in prison," he says, clearing his throat. "Shit started unraveling within the family. They got involved with things that I wouldn't stand behind. I was growing the Milestone and knew that I wanted no part of the family anymore. Told my father he could kill me if he wants. Or, he can let me run the business and we can be partners. But the Borignone table isn't mine to sit at anymore. Don't want that shit. And truthfully, you and I both know that I never did."

My jaw practically hits the floor with his utterly honest confession. His head stays raised, exuding strength. "I'm secure now, doing what I want."

I shift in my seat, my eyes darting to the floor. This is his lifelong dream he's about to live. I want to ask him if he remembers our first conversation over dinner the night we met. About changing one's path, and now, here we are—changed. But have we, really?

I clasp my hands together, gathering my wits. "Look, Vincent—"

"You sure do like to say my name a lot, Eve." Again, that roguish grin.

I blow air from my lips, exasperated. "Look," I repeat. "You can tell me anything you want. But let me get one thing straight." I lift a finger in the air. "Firstly, I have built a life here."

He looks around the apartment as if he's calling bullshit. My blood grows hot. How dare he judge me! Skimming my open floor plan, all of my furniture is modern and useful in clean beiges and soft browns. I'm just not a warm type, and I guess my apartment shows that. But that doesn't mean I'm not happy. Anyway, since when do throw pillows and blankets mean happy home? I own this place and I'm proud of that.

My hands grip the edge of my chair. "If you want to work with my firm right now, that's fine. But our relationship will be strictly business. You don't know me anymore, and I don't know you. And all those promises we made when we were kids are just that, promises made between kids. They don't matter. Your business is important to me—to the firm. So, I can make this work if you can." I shut my mouth and wait for his agreement.

He hums his assent calmly. "I understand the way I left all those years ago was..." he pauses, not finishing his sentence. "But for the sake of our dealings, I agree we must keep ourselves as strictly business. Actually" —he leans forward in his chair— "that's why I'm here. Your office is widely known as the best, and I need you for the Milestone."

My stomach sinks with his agreement, but I don't show it. I guess what else did I expect? That he'd come here and beg forgiveness?

"Well," I clear my throat. "I am good at what I do." I sit taller, doing my best to act as if I'm completely unaffected.

He shifts toward me, and I try not to swoon from how good he smells. "I like your gown. But you should have the straps tightened. They keep falling." His fingers graze against my bare skin as he lifts both straps back up my shoulders. My entire body freezes before melting from his touch.

He gets up to go and I stand up after him. We're facing each other and I internally groan, wishing I didn't take off my shoes earlier. My eyes dart to his feet; he's wearing a pair of steel-toed black boots, completely at odds with the tux. It doesn't match the outfit, but he makes it look rugged and sexy. He's impossibly tall and imposing. I'm struck by how small I feel. Almost at his mercy, and all at once, a blast of lust shoots straight through my blood. I'm hot and wet. *For him.*

He smirks wickedly. "I'll see you at the office, then." And with those words, he walks out my door.

9

EVE

I STEP into the office building's elevator with a grande coffee from Starbucks in my left hand and my Chanel purse slung over my right shoulder. It's Monday morning, and I'm wearing my extra-large and round black Dior sunglasses to hide the bags under my eyes; even my heaviest-duty concealer couldn't cover my dark circles today. Now that Vincent has reappeared, all I can do is agonize over every possible scenario in my head.

Thankfully, Marshall only called twice; his begging did nothing but turn me off even more, making it deadly clear that we are absolutely done.

The elevator door *dings* and I walk out into the hallway. I push through the firm's front doors expecting the hum of cold air conditioning to greet me. Instead, I feel as if I've just walked into an alternate universe.

The office is buzzing with noise. Instead of sitting, everyone is congregating together at reception. Lauren is perched on top of the front desk, feet dangling off the edge while Max, the young office tech guy, is giving her fuck-me eyes. The mergers and acquisitions group laughs together off to the right, clapping their hands in glee.

"Um, what the hell is going on here?" I push my sunglasses up on top of my head as my gaze works the room. "Did I miss something?"

Lauren's smile is joyous. "Oh. My. God, Eve! Vincent emailed the contract early this morning. He's already sent a four-million-dollar retainer, and this is just the beginning. The entire firm is trying to angle their way to work on the Milestone to get a cut of billable hours. Isn't this exciting? The best part is, the bosses are out celebrating together over a breakfast meeting, and they'll probably be out today golfing! Do you think bonuses will be larger this year?"

I roll my eyes. "I guess while the cat's away, the mice will play," I say quietly under my breath. I don't have the energy to get caught up in the party, and there's a ton of work on my desk I should be getting to. I walk as quickly as I can toward my office, but stop short when I see the DBC opening up beers in the conference room. They have their bottles raised high, about to cheers. Before they can notice my presence, I run into my office, slamming the door shut behind me.

The day passes quickly as I work on finalizing the details for a huge condominium closing I've got with the bank on Friday. I'm back and forth with the seller's attorney, haggling over contractual language. After filling out the last of the forms, I realize how badly I need to pee.

I get up, straighten my skirt, and head to the ladies' room. Luckily, the office has calmed down a bit as most people have already left. When I'm about to wash my hands, Lauren steps inside.

"There you are! I've tried to reach you all day. How was the gala?"

"Oh, it was fine. Broke up with Marshall." My voice is nonchalant.

"What?" she practically screams.

I shrug my shoulder before turning the water on.

"Is that why you're locked up in your office instead of celebrating?"

"No way." I shake my head. "You know I never really liked him," I reply, resigned.

"Well, everyone has been in the best mood. You should be, too."
She sounds annoyed.

"I have a closing this week, and I had to finalize everything. My
client wanted me to push for a lower purchase price before closing,
and I wasn't happy with the contract language, so I had to negotiate
the hell out of the sellers." I dry my hands on a paper towel before
pulling the clip out of my hair and twisting it back up again.

"Tell me you're coming out with us to celebrate. Jonathan is
already at the bar. I was just about to barge into your office after I
finished freshening up." She drenches her hair with texturizing spray
and fluffs up the roots with her fingertips.

I open my mouth ready to tell her that there is no way in hell I'm
going out tonight. But before I can start, she pushes her bottle into
my hand.

"Please use some for tonight. Your hair is super limp and you
need va-voom if you're going to pick any guys with me after the
douchebags leave."

Ah, there it is; she needs a wingman. I want to laugh, but all I
have the energy for right now is a half smile. "I don't think so. What I
really need is a long hot shower and dinner. I would be terrible
tonight, anyway. I mean, look at me." I gesture to my rumpled
appearance.

She pouts in an over-exaggerated way. "First of all, you're
gorgeous even when tired. And second of all, Vincent put in a
contractual request that guarantees you work on the project." Her
high voice turns to pleading. "You need to be celebrating like crazy
right now. You're like, the woman of the freakin' hour. No—the
woman of the year." She claps.

I frown.

She huffs, exasperated. "I'm not sure why you look so pissed off.
By the way, you're going to wrinkle if you keep making that face.
Don't say I didn't warn you when you've got lines in your forehead
that even Millennial Plastic Surgery can't get rid of."

Now it's my turn to roll my eyes.

"Eve," she says emphatically, holding me by the shoulders.

"Imagine the hours you're going to bill. Not least, Vincent is insanely sexy. I was dreaming of him last night. I wonder how his beard would feel rubbing against my thighs."

"Oh, come on, Lauren. He's a client." Her comment has my heart squeezing.

"Well, I'm not his attorney. Unlike you, I don't have any obligation to keep a distance." She moves her eyebrows up and down like she can't wait to get down and dirty with him. It's as if I can't breathe.

"Anyway, I tried to Google him, but the man has like, zero social media presence. So annoying. Who in this day and age is this impossible to find?"

What I want to tell her is she's absolutely correct. Vincent is, for all intents and purposes, virtually nonexistent; I know this for a fact because I looked him up myself, hoping maybe I would see his new life since he got out of prison. For a guy who used to have thousands of followers on social media, it's crazy how he was able to just erase that entire part of his life. Unfortunately, I even found myself snooping on Daniela—something I haven't done since I left New York City. I was pleasantly surprised to learn that she was busted for cocaine possession and sent directly to a rehab facility. After a six-month stint, she went to Colombia to help in her father's business. I tried to find out more, but she too seems to have vanished from the social-media stratosphere.

Lauren looks at me happily as though she's waiting for me to joke about Vincent's hotness or illusiveness, but I can't chat with her about Vincent. I can barely think about him when I'm all alone, for God's sake.

"You look like you're having an entire conversation in your head right now. What's wrong, babe? Come on, let's go out and have fun," she begs. "A drink or five will do you good."

I grimace. "But—"

She raises a hand, cutting me off. "Women stick together, right? Don't leave me alone with those savages."

"You sure you want to call in the girl card tonight?"

"If I use it, will you come? Because I look really good tonight and I don't want it to go to waste," she pouts.

I laugh. "Fine. Let me get my bag."

"Yay!" She sprays my hair quickly before dropping the can back into her purse and links her arm into mine. Clinging to me like a barnacle, she ensures I don't duck and run as we walk back into my office.

"Maybe a drink is in order, even if it's with the DBC."

"That's my girl!" she says with glee as I take my bag from underneath my desk before fluffing my own roots. I sling my purse over my shoulder, ready for a break.

"Let's just go get this over with."

She leads me out the front doors and into the elevator.

Luckily, we don't have to walk too far to the bar since it's only a few blocks from the office.

The entire place is packed with suits. Moving toward the back, we find Jonathan and the DBC sitting together at a long wooden table in the corner. They shift over grudgingly to make space for us. Jeff pushes an open Corona Light in my direction and I grab it and bring it to my lips, not pausing before taking a long gulp.

"Thirsty?" He chuckles. I ignore him. The truth is, the ice-cold beer is seriously hitting the spot right now.

I turn to Lauren, who's staring at the menu. "Are we ordering any food? I'm starved."

Jonathan puts his hand up to call the waitress over. When she gets to our table, he orders three baskets of fries, an assortment of cheeses, two orders of beef sliders, and shots of tequila for everyone. The liquor choice is a pretty aggressive move for a Monday, even for Jonathan.

He takes a nice long look at the waitress's ass before turning back to me. "Who would have thought you, of all people, would bring in our biggest client to date? You're a brilliant girl, Eve. I don't tell you enough." Even though it's backhanded, I still smile from the compliment and take another gulp of my beer, hoping the bottle covers the blush that has taken over my face.

The drinks arrive. We all bring our shot glasses up in the air, ready to toast the Milestone when the table goes quiet. Everyone's heads crane up. I swivel my head to look where they're staring. The moment I see who's coming, I gasp, startled by the huge, hulking form walking toward me.

My eyes greedily travel over every inch of him. He's wearing dark denim and a gray button-down shirt. His hair is incredibly mussed, as if he recently put his hands through it. If Janelle were here, she'd say he looks like he just fucked the shit out of someone. I swallow hard. *Vincent.* My heart pounds his name, almost painfully. *What is he even doing here?*

Jonathan stands to welcome him. I glance around the table, noticing that no one else looks surprised. Plastering a fake smile on my face, I do my best to act like nothing is amiss.

"So glad you were able to make it out tonight." Jonathan takes Vincent's hand in a firm shake. "I wasn't sure if you'd be able to find the time," Jonathan exclaims. "Come and sit down. Oh, Eve, scoot over."

I move myself to the left as Vincent sits down to my right. He angles his body toward me and puts out his hand for a cordial hello. I shake it calmly without making any eye contact before glancing around to make sure no one sees our handshake as anything more than strictly business. I finally look up at his piercing gaze.

Before I can cross my legs, his denim-clad leg presses against my bare thigh. I'm taken aback for a moment, silently cursing myself for wearing a skirt today. Sure, it's appropriate work attire since the length hits mid-knee. But sitting down, it has ridden up and left most of my legs exposed. I'd be lying if I said the contact didn't heat me up inside, but it also makes me vulnerable. I can't have any skin-on-skin with this man if I want to keep my sanity. *Business. Everything with Vincent is now strictly business.*

Jonathan pipes up, immediately garnering Vincent's attention. "We're going to be spending a lot of time together. I'm glad you came out tonight." Jonathan lifts his drink to cheers, and Vincent responds with a nod. I shoot back my drink in one swallow, ignoring the fact that I've barely eaten all day.

The truth is, I shouldn't be surprised that Vincent is here. Jonathan always aims to be friends with clients, and a few nights a month, he expects us to come out and schmooze. It not only buys us leniency if there are delays, but it also makes for an easier work environment when we're all friendly.

"Eve just arrived, too. This girl can outwork anyone else. She's the perfect person for the work you've got, and I must say, you were absolutely right to request her." Jonathan's face is turning red from drinking, but it's clear that he's in his comfort zone.

"So, Jonathan." Vincent clears his throat and the entire table quiets, seemingly waiting for his next word. "I think it's important for her to see the Milestone."

"Yes. I was planning to email Eve tomorrow morning to let her know that she should head over to Nevada right away. She'll be able to do lots of due diligence on the project; she's already read the files you sent over prior to our meeting. It's all good. How long do you think she'll need?" His voice is all excitement. I feel shell-shocked, as though his words are bombs.

"I think a week would be sufficient for this first trip," Vincent replies casually.

"A week?" I shout, practically leaping out of my chair. My eyes immediately move around the table; everyone stares at me as if I've lost my mind. "Oh..." I smile, letting out a small self-conscious laugh and tucking a stray hair behind my ear. "I don't think a week is really necessary. I mean, I could do it in two or three days. I'm sure. Or one day, even."

Jonathan's mouth spreads in a wide grin, but behind his eyes, he's telling me he will cut me if I anger our client. "Yes, it's true Eve, you are a fast worker." He laughs, trying to ease the awkwardness. "But if Vincent thinks a week is necessary, I'm sure a week is what you'll need."

Jonathan cranes his head looking around for the waitress. Unable to find her, he turns to me with a request on his lips. "Eve, the waitress is so damn slow. Why don't you go to the bar and find out if the drinks and food are coming soon? Vincent, what do you want? Eve will order for you while she's up there."

I make a move to stand when Vincent's heavy hand grips my bare thigh locking me down in place. It's huge and hot and incredibly strong; there is no escape. Without any preamble, warmth travels straight into my belly and down through my legs, the strength of which I haven't felt in ages.

Vincent turns back to Jonathan, his voice short. "Why don't you just flag down the waitress? Eve doesn't need to get up."

Jonathan's mouth snaps shut as his nostrils flare. I don't need Vincent to be my champion. If he keeps this up, everyone is going to assume what we have between us. And they'd be thrilled to spread a rumor that the reason I got this job is because I spread my legs. I hate the fact that I have to think this way, but what else can I do? I'm in this position and it forces me to keep all my hackles up.

I need to do damage control before anyone gets the wrong idea. "It's no big deal. Let me go check on it; it's my pleasure." Vincent's hand squeezes on my thigh again, a little higher this time and I swallow, my throat running dryer than the Sahara.

I tell my body to relax, but my mind wanders to what those hands can do. I flush, the heat moving up my collarbone and into my face. I'm powerless. Once my mind gets the memo, I relax into his grip.

Vincent looks at me with confidence, as though he's proud of me. Luckily, the conversation turns moot as the waitress shows up with a huge tray filled with more drinks and food. The moment she places everything out on the table, he lifts his hand from my leg; I want to say I feel relief, but I don't. Instead, it feels like loss.

Vincent looks up at the waitress, his body language casual. "I'll have a Blue Label on the rocks, please." The waitress smiles seductively, eyes noticeably widening as she checks him out.

What's he going to do? Will he flirt back? I mean, he's a gorgeous single man. Wait. Is he single? Maybe he isn't. He probably isn't. Not that I care.

He turns his head to dismiss her, and I quickly look to Lauren as if I'm about to tell her something enormously important, hoping he didn't catch me staring.

It only takes a few minutes for the waitress to return with his drink. I watch him from my side-eye as he picks it up with his right hand, bringing the clear glass full of ice and amber liquid to his full lips which are more sensuous than any man's has a right to be. Tilting his head back slightly, the drink goes straight down his throat.

"So, Vincent, where are you originally from?" Jeff sits up eagerly, hoping to make conversation. Now that the asshole knows the work is ours, he'll probably try to angle himself to get involved and get a cut of billable hours. What an asshole.

"New York," Vincent replies, clipped.

"Born and raised in California," he smiles. "Eve is from New York, too. Aren't you?" He looks between us questioningly, as if it's oddly coincidental we're both from the same state.

"Yes, I am." I try to keep my voice even as if there's nothing I'm hiding.

Jeff continues, his sharp eyes focusing on Vincent. "What part? I have family in Great Neck."

"Oh?" Vincent stares at him dead on and Jeff immediately cowers, his pupils widening in anxiety. I have to admit, between the tatts, the scruff, and the muscles, Vincent is intimidating. Add in his death stare and he's got all the ingredients for how-to-be-scary-as-hell. But it's not just his physical traits that make him so intimidating. It's more than that.

Vincent moves his body as if to say: this is me—I dress, walk, and act, as I truly am; if you don't like it, you can go fuck yourself.

Vincent turns to Lauren as she asks him how long he's staying out here in L.A. His reply is muffled, but she giggles. Making eye contact with the waitress, I lift my beer and put up a finger, miming "one more please." Luckily, she nods in understanding.

"You should hang out with me and Eve tonight. We're celebrating." Lauren's eyes sparkle.

"Oh yeah?" He takes another gulp of his drink before looking between us.

"Eve broke up with her boyfriend and I'm totally single. We're celebrating our freedom." She winks at me and my stomach drops.

After a polite smile, I face forward. Still I try, as shadily as possible, to hear every word of their conversation. Unfortunately, all my worries gather together, clamoring for headspace. *He ruined you once; he could do it again. The only thing you can count on anymore is your work.* Fucking emotions!

Thankfully, the waitress returns, handing me another drink. I wrap my hands around the cold bottle, ready to lift it to my lips when I realize I'm a few sips away from drunk. Water—I need water. I pick up my cup of tap and drink.

The conversation flows and Vincent looks totally relaxed. Everyone wants to impress him, but he maintains his laid-back and even-keeled demeanor. His calmness is *infuriating*. He obviously put our past behind him. Watching him act so calmly is making me realize there is only one truth: Vincent never cared about me. If he did, how could he possibly be so nonchalant right now? I need a break. On shaky legs, I manage to stand, albeit swaying a little bit first.

"I'm going to use the restroom; if you'll excuse me," I politely tell the table. I beeline to the bathroom, relieved to find it empty. After peeing quickly, I stand in front of the sink to wash my hands. But when I look up into the mirror, I realize I may cry. The last few years I've been unshakable. And now Vincent is back and I can already feel the tears welling. I bring my hands to my lips, puffy and red. I hardly recognize the woman staring back at me; I'm everything I wanted to become...yet more unfulfilled than ever. I feel ungrateful, confused, and stressed out. I have to leave.

I open the door, pausing as my eyes register what's in front of me. She's tall, with gorgeous red hair and a tight black dress. If this isn't a sign, I don't know what is. I'm about to lose it.

I do my best to politely say goodbye to the table, feigning a headache as an excuse and avoiding Vincent's prying eyes. I walk away with a casual wave, as if I'm in no real rush, but once I'm far enough out of sight, I run out the front door and cross the street. I

need to create physical distance between me and my shitty coworkers, who treat me terribly but I'm too scared to report—and Vincent,
the only man on earth with the ability to break me into pieces.

I use my arm to wipe my tears away before pulling out my phone
and clicking on the Uber app. Glancing back to the bar, I see Vincent
jump out the front door, his head swiveling from left to right as if he's
searching. I hear him loudly curse before turning back inside.
Leaning against the building, tears blur my vision. I just want to
go home.

* * *

I GET BACK into my apartment and pick up my phone to call Janelle. I
haven't spoken to her in a week. I hit FaceTime on my phone,
needing to see her. She answers after the third ring, her hair tied in a
white towel-turban. She looks exhausted but happy from a long day
and night at her salon. I know that no matter how tired her feet get
from standing all day, she's fulfilled. Things aren't always easy, but
neither she nor I have any doubt this is her life's calling.

"Hey, sissy!" She smiles, blue eyes shining. They dim as she
assesses my state.

"You look drunk. Bad drunk."

"Yeah, you can say that," I swallow. "But there's more."

"How much more." There's a question in her voice.

"More more," I reply, dread webbing my insides.

"Talk," she says in that no-nonsense way of hers.

"Well," I start, pulling off my heels and planting myself comfortably on my bed. "Vincent's back."

She gasps.

I fill her in on all the details of the Milestone and how he's now
technically a client of mine. When I get to the part of him showing up
at my door after the Kids Learning Club gala, she looks downright
furious.

"Jesus," she replies, her forehead crinkling. "What does he look
like? I wanna get a good visual."

"He's physically rougher. Bigger, even. Tatts and dark scruff like he couldn't be bothered to shave. But I guess when he talks, he's still sort of the same. Brilliant. What he built out in Nevada is pretty unbelievable."

She purses her lips. "You've got a job to do, Eve. Don't let that piece-of-shit-dickhead-motherfucking-asshole come between you and your work." I can see the sneer on her face, but I'd bet money that she's got a finger pointing at me.

"He wrecked me. My entire life was thrown into chaos because of Vincent Borignone." I can feel a headache coming on along with a serious dose of anger.

"No shit."

"And now," I exclaim, standing up with the phone in front of me as I unzip and then shimmy out of my skirt. "He comes back and wants us to be normal. But how can I be normal? Is he insane?" I question angrily, unbuttoning my blouse before flinging it onto the floor.

"Listen, Eve. Do not let him steamroll over your life again. If you can't handle working with him, just pass him over. Either give him to one of those assholes you work with or tell your boss that it's dangerous to do business with him. You don't need this—"

"No," I reply quickly, cutting her off as I walk over to my dresser and pull out a pair of pajamas. "If I let his business go, he'll win. He's the biggest deal to come through my door and I'm not going to just back down."

"You know what? You're right," she shouts, pumping a fist in the air. "Anyway, he's the one who should be scared. Not you. Let me remind you: you did nothing the fuck wrong."

"Exactly. But, Janelle, what if he didn't actually—"

"Good, so it's settled," Janelle decrees. "Wash your face. Sleep. Tomorrow morning go for a run and drink your coffee. And when you get dressed, put your big-girl panties on because we are not letting him take even one more thing from you."

I nod my head in solidarity. "You're right."

"Of course, I am."

"I'm gonna sleep. My hangover tomorrow is going to suck."

"Take an Advil now."

I change into cozy sleep clothes, wash my face, and climb into bed. It only takes a moment for me to burst into tears; it's an assault. Salty water runs through my sinuses and floods my face like a torrential downpour. Whatever strength I had from my phone conversation is now nothing but dust.

I spend the rest of the night awake in my bed, feeling my emotions like waves as they come and go from the forefront of my mind. I want to block them, but it's not possible. As though I were a bystander in my own life, I replay the ending of Vincent and me, and my heart manages to break all over again.

10

EVE

IT'S BEEN a week since the disastrous night at the bar, and now I'm sitting on Vincent's private plane on my way to Nevada to visit the Milestone. Per Jonathan's orders, I'm to complete due diligence that cannot be done remotely. I already spoke with Vincent's assistant, Kimber, to ready all the files.

This is my first flight since I came out to California. Once I got out here, I never left. Janelle asked me to come back to New York for Christmas and other holidays, but I always refused—too much pain and memories in my home city that I don't want to deal with. *Can't* deal with.

I let my fingers glide against the beautiful tan leather seat, the type of luxury poor-girl dreams are made of. The plane is so roomy and beautiful. Although I wanted to fly commercial, Kimber advised it would be easier to fly private as it would decrease my travel time. I was hesitant at first but ultimately agreed.

Staring out the window and watching us ascend, I grip the wooden armrests. With shaking hands, I put a piece of gum in my mouth, taking Janelle's advice so my ears don't pop. I shut my eyes and lean my head against the cushy seat, not letting myself think about the plane crashing. But the second my mind starts to run, I wish I had death on my mind, because all I can think about is Vincent and what will become of this trip.

The plane finally stabilizes and I open my eyes, slowly at first. Staring out the window, I'm in awe of the blue sky with nothing but the clouds below me.

Pulling out my laptop, I read about Nevada's history with the Tribe. Regardless of what is or isn't happening between Vincent and me, I've been paid to do a job and I'm nothing if not competent. I always stay on task, no matter what craziness is going on around me. This way, if things go belly up, I have my work to fall back on.

"Hello. I'm Alina, your stewardess for the flight. Are you comfortable?"

I hum out a "Yes," not looking up from my screen.

"Would you like a drink?" Her soft voice asks.

"Sure," I continue to stare at my monitor.

"Water? Orange juice? A cocktail perhaps?"

"Huh?" I look up at her, exasperated at the constant interruptions. My eyes lock on her face and I pause. She's gorgeous and tall, with long blonde hair and clear blue eyes. Her tight navy dress shows off her slight curves. Deep in my gut, I know this is Vincent's type. Or at least, I always figured this was the type of girl who suits him best. Model perfect. I immediately feel stung, wondering if he's been with her. I can just imagine the two of them on this plane, her listening to his every command. *I can get on my knees, Vincent. You want me to bend over like this, Vincent?* Bitch! Between these wide seats and the private bedroom in the back, he would have opportunities abounding.

She gives me a small smile, and I do my best not to glare. I want to strangle her.

"Non-carbonated water is fine, thank you," I reply, my voice curt. I watch as she glides to the back of the cabin, narrow hips swaying with each step.

I'm momentarily embarrassed by my rude behavior as well as angry at myself for even caring. This woman has done nothing wrong. Okay, so maybe Vincent fucked her a million times on this plane—it shouldn't mean anything to me. She comes back to my seat and hands me my drink with a courteous smile. I take it and swallow back my tears before facing the window.

My email *dings* letting me know I have a new message in my inbox; the Wi-Fi on the plane makes it incredibly easy to refocus on my tasks. I refresh my browser, seeing five new messages from Jonathan. He's forever working like crazy to keep his spot as partner.

After Jonathan's divorce, he told me of his utter relief not to have a wife annoying him any longer to come home for dinner or spend time with the kids. His words were, "I can finally work in peace."

Is this how I'm going to spend my life? Alone with my work, nothing but the work, so help me God?

The plane lands smoothly. I walk to the door, rolling my suitcase behind me and politely thanking Alina and the captain for the trip. I step outside into the sunlight, finding a huge guy with a buzz cut, black T-shirt, jeans, and heavy work boots watching me from the bottom of the steps. I drop my sunglasses over my eyes and pop a fresh piece of gum into my mouth as I take the stairs from the plane's door onto the tarmac. He immediately grabs my bags as he leads the way to an extra-long black Escalade. As he places my things in the trunk, I make myself comfortable in the plush black leather seat.

He finally gets into the car, sitting in the chair next to mine. "Hey Mark, we're ready to go." His voice is deep.

The car begins to drive. "Welcome to Nevada. You must be thirsty." Pulling out a bottle of water from a cooler on the floor, he hands me one. Before I can take it out of his grip, we make eye contact—it's almost like a standoff. "So, you're Eve, huh?" His green eyes squint like he knows exactly who I am. I'm momentarily surprised, wondering what he's heard.

I raise my eyebrows, pursing my lips as I pull the water away from him. "Yes. And you are?" I look him up and down, noticing his body is corded with heavy muscle and his arms are sleeved with colorful ink. I can only imagine Lauren right now; she'd be going insane over him.

"Slade," he says, introducing himself. "I head security for the

Milestone." A small smirk forms his lips, but it's clear he isn't hitting on me. An alarm rings in my head: who is this man to Vincent? I gather my wits and get into questioning mode.

"So, where did you work before this?" I cross my legs and type out a quick message to Lauren about landing, trying to act as if I'm making casual conversation and don't care too much about his response. Meanwhile, I'm on complete alert, waiting to hear what he says so I can accurately gauge who he is in Vincent's life.

"I was in the Navy. Came home and met Vincent at the gym. The rest is history," he replies, not unkindly.

I tilt my head to the side, wondering if he's Borignone muscle. "Well, you must know him and his family." I'm watching his face intently to see if he understands my implication.

His body stiffens before letting out a quick laugh. "I know you've got lots of grit. But let's get one thing straight. I'm not here to hurt you. In fact, it's the opposite. While you're here, if there's anything you need, don't hesitate to ask me." He pulls out a card from the pocket in the seat in front of him and hands it to me; I scan it with my eyes. It has all his contact info on it.

I stop my bitch routine for a second and take a good look at the man next to me. He's scary looking and big. His light eyes are kind, but there is damage lurking beneath their depths—as though he's been to war and back. For a strange reason, I trust him. This isn't another friend of Vincent's whom I should be afraid of.

I nod my head silently as my internal fume meter simmers down. The rest of the ride, I do nothing other than stare out the window, watching the magnificent red mountains ahead. I've never seen natural beauty like this in my entire life.

When we finally reach our destination, Slade pulls out my suitcases from the trunk and hands them to me. I thank him graciously.

Strutting into the lobby with my heels clicking against the floor, I take stock of what's around me. The hotel is beautiful and impossibly serene. The lobby is all tans, whites, and creams. Limestone floors and walls give the entire place an upscale but earthy feel. Glass windows encase the north side of the lobby, showing spectacular mountain views. It's simply perfect.

I check in with the concierge, a brunette, thank God, who accepts my firm's credit card along with my driver's license. Within seconds, my bags are taken and a cold towel is offered to me by a member of the hotel staff. I press it against my neck and forehead in relief as I'm told my room is ready.

Following the bellboy through an outdoor hallway, we stop to enter room 403. It's a stunning suite facing the desert land; tall sand-colored mountains loom in the distance. As he sets down my luggage, I step onto the terrace and see a small, round private fire pit and two chairs. The room is the epitome of seclusion and comfort. I wonder if this is the style Vincent is going toward for the Mile. From the work I've done so far, I know it isn't obvious and in-your-face bells and whistles like the Vegas Strip. Instead, it has all the gambling and excitement minus the phony factor. The files mentioned building the Milestone to blend with its surroundings, and I can't wait to see what he came up with.

I hand the bellboy a tip and he nods his thanks before exiting. Pulling off my shoes and shift dress and letting them drop onto the floor, I unceremoniously plop on the fluffy white bed to find a printed schedule on the pillow. Apparently, reservations for dinner have been made for me at six in the hotel lobby. Lauren must have taken care of this, thank goodness.

After showering, and put on a clean pair of jeans and a fresh shirt. After applying a minimal amount of makeup, I secure my dark hair with a clip. Grabbing a black cashmere sweater, I make my way to the hotel bar.

I try to relax in the black barstool, ordering a glass of white wine from the bartender. After my first sip, I decide that I can't let Vincent rule me. I have to separate my emotions from reality and just set out the facts. I pull out my phone and open my Notes app.

Since Vincent has returned...

- I have a large new client and will likely make a lot
  more money
- He and I have agreed to leave the past where it belongs
- I still have my fantastic career and apartment

I want to write more, but I can't, because there IS nothing more. I shake out my shoulders, feeling satisfied. Just as Janelle and I discussed, there is literally zero to do other than get the work done; our history can't have any bearing on my career. Regardless of why we ended, we're finished. Today, I am Vincent's attorney, sent here to conduct due diligence on the Milestone. And Vincent is simply an important client.

Another sip of the wine and I smile confidently, feeling proud of my clear thought process and dissection of the issue when someone takes the seat next to mine.

"Hi. You're here."

I turn to the deep voice. The smile on his lips practically throws me off the seat. Fluttering takes over my stomach. I swallow hard, trying to regain a semblance of control.

"Y-yes, I-I guess I am. Here, I mean. I'm here."

Vincent's eyes crinkle at the corners, as if he's trying not to laugh at my stuttering.

"Come with me," he whispers with a smile. But I stay cemented in my seat, unmoving. A few moments pass and I watch as his initial happiness becomes tinged with apprehension.

More time is needed to sort this out—clearly, my list wasn't nearly expansive enough. This is Vincent Borignone, not a grocery list. The beat of my heart picks up its pace. "Actually," I start, clearing my throat. "I have a reservation soon. I shouldn't cancel."

We both turn our heads to peer inside the restaurant. My hope of delaying this meeting is smashed; the restaurant is completely empty. *Shit.*

"Dinner is with me tonight. Come." I can tell from his tone that he's annoyed with me. Standing up, he gives his large hand for me to take. I stare at it nervously, as though it may bite me.

He presses his lips in a firm line before exhaling. "We've got work to discuss, okay?"

"But, where are we—"

"For once in your life, don't think. Just come."

"Anytime a man tells me not to think—"

He cuts me off with deep laughter and I roll my eyes, trying to stop my smile. Does he remember the time at Goldbar when we had a similar conversation?

"We'll discuss work, yeah? I'm not trying to get you naked, Eve. There's no reason to be nervous." His dark eyebrows move up his forehead as if he's daring me.

I let out an awkward laugh. "Naked?" I swallow hard, the visual of a nude Vincent steamrolling through my head, down my body and settling in my core. "I don't think you're trying to get me... naked." I shake my head vehemently. "I mean, obviously not." A shiver runs up my arms as I force my eyes away from him.

"Exactly," he says, his voice deep and seductive. "We're doing business." He's so rational. I want to strangle him!

I internally huff, gathering myself. "Well, maybe I don't believe it's appropriate to do business in the evening hours." I want to sound haughty, but instead, my words come out like a nervous question.

His eyes narrow. *Oh, shit.*

Instead of cowering like the rest of the universe would likely do, I lift my head in defiance. The last thing I want is for Vincent to believe I'm anxious around him. I mean, if anyone should be awkward, it's him. I've done nothing wrong. If he's okay with seeing me, I'm more than okay to see him.

"Fine. If you think there is certain work better to do this evening, then I guess so be it." I hop off the stool, pretending that his hand isn't in my line of sight and that he isn't offering it to me. We get to the front of the hotel when I see a huge motorcycle sparkling under the orange lamplight; it's silver and chrome with a heavy black leather seat. I turn to Vincent with uncertainty, but he only smirks. We walk to the beast of a motorcycle and he lifts a small helmet from a bag hanging off to the side, securing it on my head before putting on his own. Jumping on, he gives me his hand. I remind myself: *Work purposes.* Holding onto his warm palm, I gingerly climb onto the back of the bike; our bodies are flush.

"Make sure you lean with me on the turns, okay? Don't be scared. There's no traffic. Driving on open roads is a dream."

I say a little thank you for this fully covered helmet because if he saw the look on my face, he'd know I'm dying inside. Between pressing against Vincent's hard back and the way my legs are splayed across this vibrating seat, the throb that started up in the restaurant is now pulsing.

I tentatively wrap my hands around his midsection, because hey —I don't want to die. Fortunately for my body, my hands immediately find the ripped muscles of his abdomen. God, he feels so good. It's almost like holding onto an unmovable wall. Moments later, we're off; the wind rushes around us like a curtain as the bike roars, my hair flying out from beneath the helmet.

"Oh, fuck it," I think, pressing my face against his muscled back and taking in his scent. *So good.*

11

VINCENT

I PULL up to my trailer; it's on a quiet sandy patch on the rez. Getting off the bike first, I move to lift Eve in my arms, not wanting her legs to touch the hot pipes. I've burned myself before, and it sucks. Once she's steady on the ground, she pulls off her own helmet, shaking out her hair like some sexy shampoo commercial; except when she stops, it isn't perfect bouncy strands. Nope. It's a wild tangled mess. I smirk; her hair is exactly how I like it—natural and crazed.

"Shut it, Vincent." She giggles while trying to tame it down with her fingers.

"Let's go inside. I've got some meat marinating and ready to grill. You still like steak?"

She nods, her face tightening with anxiety. What Eve doesn't realize is I'm just as nervous as she; I'm just better at hiding it.

It doesn't take a genius to recognize that anytime Eve feels as though we're moving away from business, she freezes. I've got to slow the moment down for her. Keep us at a steady pace—for now. Every ounce of me wants to just *talk*. Get it all out there. But she's not ready to hear it.

"I've got a few files we should work through." I say the last part slowly, knowing that work will keep her comfortable around me.

"Yeah. Okay." She pushes back her thick hair, securing it with a clip. I give myself a mental pat on the back, glad to know that my plan for easing Eve is working.

I open the door, stepping directly into my living room. I turn, watching her eyes widen in surprise before turning back to me. Luckily, she isn't horrified. Actually, her face looks somewhat settled in relief.

Seven years ago, I shattered this woman and ruined her life. Everything she threw at me that night after the gala was deserved. No. I deserved worse. And now I'm back, and somehow, she's still here. I want to pull her in my arms and thank her. If she'd just give me a chance, I'd show her that I've given it all up. But I've got to make her believe that I'm true.

"Nice place," she tells me, a soft blush on her cheeks as her eyes zero in on my couch. Nothing is fancy, but it's all clean and comfortable.

I point to the left. "Kitchen." I turn, pointing to the opposite side of the trailer. "Bedroom and bathroom." I walk a few steps to the sink, seeing my two large marinated rib steaks have defrosted nicely. "How about I'll grill these out front and you make a salad?"

"Okay." Again, the hesitant nod.

My smile grows as I watch her straighten her back and walk toward the fridge with her head raised. Opening up my refrigerator as though it's her own, she pulls out some chopped red cabbage and washed spinach leaves, dropping them on the counter. She plunges her head back inside, probably noticing containers filled with grilled chicken and beef before coming back out again.

"Do you have mustard, olive oil, red wine vinegar?"

"Yeah." I pull out what she needs, my heart pounding—she remembers this is my favorite dressing. I open my small liquor cabinet, taking a bottle of red wine, two glasses, and an opener. Grabbing a handful of files we can review together, I finally step outside to fire up the grill.

While the meat cooks, I watch the mountains in the distance, taking a moment to thank God for my life. I never considered myself a God-fearing man, but between these vast mountains and the clear sky, it feels like denying the existence of a higher power is impossible. Compared to New York, where everything is man-made from the people to the buildings, it was easy to believe that I was in control of my own life and destiny. God's work is obscure in the big city. Out here though, is nothing but the truth. I look around and witness creation on a daily basis. I imagine Eve living with me here. Loving me. I picture her in my bed every morning and night.

I turn the steaks over, finding a perfect sear. A few minutes later, I pull them off the grill and onto the plate. Eve is sitting at the small picnic table to my right, watching me with a glazed look in her eyes as if she sees something more than just...me. The sun has set behind her, and she looks like an angel.

I take a seat, immediately moving to open the bottle. The last thing I want is to show my desperation for her, which would probably send her running into the mountains. I clear my throat. "I wanna take you hiking tomorrow around the area. See the land. Some cold beers and I'll pack lunch. Yeah?" I pour her a full glass, but only half for myself. I'm driving her back tonight and want to make sure my head is clear.

"I'm not so sure that's necessary."

"Well, it is," I reply firmly before clenching my fists to calm down. "It's important for you to know the surrounding area." She presses her lips together in contemplation.

Standing, she fills my plate with salad—taking care of me. I stare until she finally brings those big brown eyes to mine. *I miss you. I fuckin' love you, babe. Come back to me. Forgive me.* The words sit on the tip of my tongue, but I refuse to mess this up. I can't push her.

I clear my throat as she takes her seat. "I don't want you thinking I'm doing illegal shit here, anymore."

"I don't think that, Vincent." She shakes her head from side to side, her words sounding genuine.

"Well, you should know the score. If you're going to work for me, I don't want you ever wondering if you'll be implicated in something." I continue, giving her the details of how I set everything up in order to safeguard the Mile from any possibility of seizure. She listens quietly as I fill her in on details. I make sure to include the fact that I'm no longer in the family and have cut myself out of all their dealings, legal and not. She listens intently, seemingly hanging onto every word.

"Well, that's pretty crazy. I mean, I never thought you could—"

"Well, I have. Thank you for taking this chance on me. For working with me on this. Seriously."

We stare at each other, an emotional and heavy silence between us. Her brows furrow before she lifts the glass to her lips. Slicing up her meat, she brings a piece of it to her lush mouth. I blink, knowing that I'd do anything to have this woman's lips on mine. She catches me staring, but I don't look away. *I can't.*

When we're finishing up, I pull out a set of architectural plans for one of the spas. The designers submitted their ideas a few days ago, and I've been reviewing them to decide the best option.

I move our plates to the end of the table before unrolling the large sheets of paper, securing them with our glasses on opposite corners. "I wanted to hear your opinion on this. There are two spa companies that want to take over the space, but each of their lawyers put in clauses that I'm not so sure about. They also have different visions for the space."

"Retail leasing. One of my specialties." She smiles confidently, moving to my side of the table so we're both looking at the plans from the same view.

An hour passes and we're pouring over the minutia, keeping focused as a team. Fuckin' heaven. I keep letting my arm brush against hers and yet, she stays by my side.

When we finally leave to take her back to the hotel, I don't even remember to clean up the table or bring the dishes in. All I see is her.

12

EVE

VINCENT BRINGS me back to my hotel, the perfect gentleman. I check my phone, seeing three missed calls from Janelle and one from Lauren. Nosy girls they are; obviously both want to know about the day. I take off all my clothes before walking into the beautiful bathroom to wash my face and brush my teeth. The cold marble feels amazing against my feet, hot from riding.

The next morning, I wake up with my phone next to my head; clearly, I forgot to call anyone back. I pick up the room phone and dial room service, ordering a hot coffee and an egg-white vegetable omelet.

I take my time in the shower before finding a plush bathrobe hanging behind the door. I try it on, reveling in its softness. Dropping in the terrace chair, I let myself daydream about Vincent's life out here on the rez—simple, yet straightforward. No frills, yet incredibly satisfying.

No one has ever taken care of me in the way Vincent has. Behind the size, the strength, and the tough façade, he gives me this...

warmth. I've been stressing so much about him lately, and I just want to relax. He isn't pressuring me, and I have no reason to feel nervous.

My doorbell rings, and I pad over to the door barefoot. I open it, expecting breakfast.

"Rise 'n shine." His black hair is windblown, and his skin a perfectly dark tan. My throat dries. "Gotta get going early before sun gets too hot," he tells me with a smile.

"You could have called." I'm annoyed. Tightening my robe around my waist, shyness comes over me. Vincent, on the other hand, doesn't seem fazed in the slightest.

"Nice room," he states casually, welcoming himself inside. Taking a seat on the white couch in front of the bed, he leans back cool and calm as though he's the one staying here.

"I'll wait. Get dressed," he states succinctly. I roll my eyes before taking a good look at the man before me. Scanning him, my feet suddenly grow heavy, keeping me rooted to the spot. Every single thing in this room from the slept-in white sheets to the beautiful terrace to the gorgeous floors fade away—everything except him.

The old Vincent would give me a smirk, telling me with a cocky expression that he's reading me like an open book. Instead, what I see in his face shows something closer to yearning.

I clear my throat and turn around, entering the small changing area that's connected to the bathroom. I change into a pair of Lululemon black leggings, a fitted sports bra that gives me great cleavage, and matching spandex tank top. Finishing off the outfit with a pair of sneakers and my hair in a high ponytail, I check myself out in the bathroom mirror.

Feeling confident, I step back into the bedroom, noticing my room service already arrived.

Vincent looks me up and down. "Sorry babe. As good as you look in those pants, you're gonna need jeans to ride." He shrugs a huge shoulder as a sexy half smile forms on his lips.

I groan, turning back into the bathroom to change, albeit grudgingly. Truthfully, I loved riding on his bike. I'm itching to get back on, but he doesn't need to know that. I come back into the room, updated. "Better?" I ask, my voice syrupy sweet.

He stares at me mutely as his eyes rove up and down my body. "I want to take you to the Mile," he starts, his voice rough. "After, we'll hike the valley of Fire State Park."

Sitting up and turning his eyes away from me, he pours two cups of steaming coffee from the large silver carafe, finishing mine with cream and sugar.

"Where's the park?" I ask as he hands me a mug. Putting my nose to the coffee, I smell the sweet and nutty aroma. With just a whiff, I feel refreshed.

"It's a nature preserve about sixteen miles south of Overton. I'd show you a photo, but it's better if you're surprised."

"Are there snakes?" I ask nervously. "I'm not down with snakes."

"Nah," he shakes his head. "I mean, they exist. But chances are slim we'll see any."

"Slim, like, slim to none? Or slim, like, there's a possibility greater than two percent?"

He lets out a deep chuckle that I feel straight down in my belly. "Chill, city girl. I'll be with you the whole time. Nothing to be afraid of when I'm with you, yeah?" His words come out slow and thick, feeling and sounding like truth.

"Okay." Lifting the coffee to my mouth, I watch as his gaze moves to where my lips press against the cup's rim. It dawns on me that this man—New York City mobster, has morphed into an outdoorsy biker. I try not to smile at the irony.

"What are you thinking about?" He leans closer to me.

"Wouldn't you like to know," I sass.

"No, actually." He shakes his head in mock seriousness and I slap his arm, laughing.

Sitting down beside him on the couch with nothing but a sliver of space between us, I lift my fork and knife to enjoy my omelet. He's scanning headlines on his phone while I eat and I read my own work emails, but our quiet is filled with comfort. Everything about this moment feels natural.

* * *

WE GET off his bike and I immediately take out my phone to see if I have any missed calls.

"I forgot how obsessed you are with being on time. Do me a favor and give me your phone." He puts out his hand.

"No way," I exclaim, looking up into his face, warmed and slightly sweaty from the helmet.

"Come on. What are you afraid of? Missing a call from work? If anyone complains, just say the phone service was shit." His eyes are mischief.

I bite my lip, considering his dare. I haven't taken a vacation for myself in years, choosing instead to spend any days off just lounging in my apartment and reading. What would happen if I actually listened to Vincent right now? Normally, I am diligent in following all timelines and schedules. Every billable minute counts. Truthfully, I'm tired of it.

I do the unthinkable, handing him the phone.

"Ah!" he shouts. "The girl listens." His voice is triumphant. I roll my eyes as he opens a bottle of water and hands it to me.

I look around. "My God, Vincent. This is..." I'm at a loss for words. I simply cannot believe the beauty of what's in front of me. Other than the size, the style is similar to the Freedom Towers in New York City. Four low buildings nestle into the mountains. With glass and steel façades, they act as mirrors, picking up the oranges, reds, silvers, and golds of the mountains. They're incredibly modern, but because of the play of light, look seamlessly woven into the Nevada desert. Simply unbelievable.

He clears his throat and I stare back up at his strong and serious demeanor. "You like it?"

I nod my head.

"It occupies roughly one mile of land, hence the name Mile-stone..." He continues, and I listen, completely enraptured. The boy I knew has evolved into a captivating and mature man.

He brings me to each of the buildings, showing me what's

completed. Everything is both modern and five-star, but the complex stays true to the mountains and the desert; it's unlike anything I've ever seen. Vincent has really done it. He's astounding. After the tour, we jump back on his bike and head toward the State Park.

We arrive, and Vincent steps off his bike first before helping me down. It occurs to me that he doesn't need to carry me, but I can't seem to tell him no. Once he sets me onto the ground, he pulls out some food from his saddlebag. I walk by his side until we reach the park.

He points forward and I look up. "Red sandstone. Amazing, right?"

In front of me are red-and-silver-swirl mountains. He takes my hand gently, bringing me over to a shaded picnic table and sets out our food, making sure I'm sitting with the best view.

We eat and joke around, my mood lightening. All of our past is on the backburner as we get to know the updated versions of ourselves.

He tells me more about Slade, who he says is like a brother to him. It turns out that Slade had a rough stint after spending over six years with the Navy.

"He seems really decent," I tell him in all seriousness.

"Yeah. The more you get to know him, the better he gets."

I raise my eyebrows and purse my lips, a facial combination that's got New York City Blue Houses written all over it. "Don't tell me you've got a bromance."

Vincent laughs. "Well, he's a good-looking guy. Can you blame me?" We both laugh as he squints his eyes in that cocky New York way and here we are again, just two city kids playing around.

He gives me a wicked grin. "It's getting hot, right?"

Before I can answer, he pours a bottle of water all over my head. I take a sharp inhale before screaming, and he just laughs.

"You're gonna pay for that," I exclaim. My hair is going to frizz like crazy now that it's been doused with water. I didn't even bring my hot tools with me, figuring that dry shampoo would secure me for the week. *Shit!*

I get up, pouring my own water over his head and feeling highly vindicated. The water drips off the tips of his black hair, hitting his sharp cheekbones. He stares up me hotly. *Holy shit.* Vincent is so sexy it's insane.

"You still like looking, huh?"

His comment makes me angry and I give him the stink eye, which makes him laugh louder.

We spend the rest of the day hiking. Each time he helps me up a tall rock, my heart patters. His hand is just so massive and swallows my tiny one so easily. My body loves it.

Over a few hours, we get to really talking. Vincent tells me about his life in prison and how the Mile came to be; he talks about his unlikely friendship with the warden and how much that support meant to him. I know there's more he isn't telling me, but still, he's opening up more than I would have imagined.

We find a nice large, high, and flat rock to take a break. Sitting down together, our legs dangle off the side as we stare out at the setting sun.

I want to talk to him, too. Something inside me aches to connect; it's been so long since I've had that with anyone. "You know," I say nervously. "I worked so hard to be in this position at work—" I pause, giving my attention to a group of three making their way up the mountain, packs on their backs. I let myself take another second or two, needing to sort through my thoughts before continuing. Vincent sits quietly, giving me time.

"I should feel fulfilled, right?" I question. "Instead, though, I just feel exhausted and totally...burned out." I put my finger on the rock, moving some dirt around.

"After my first large paycheck, I bought myself this beautiful silver desk clock from Tiffany's. Actually, I bought myself a lot of stuff. And now, when I see them, I want to burn it all. I thought those things would make me happy, but they don't. It's like..." I lift my head and hands in aggravation. "Whenever I hit a milestone, I find myself looking to the next thing, because the satisfaction I was supposed to have never comes. When can I just stop and be happy where I am? I thought once I had the material things, I'd feel like I arrived or some-thing. I worked for this. I bled for this. But it's not...enough."

He turns his head, sadness coating his eyes. I wait for him to speak, but instead he stays silent, urging me with his eyes to continue.

"Still," I say. "I love the independence the job brings. I love the fact that the money I make is all my own. I'm sorry to say this, but I just love making money. Sometimes I check my bank account and I'm like, so relieved. And thrilled. And I worked my ass off to get it, too. After being poor all my life..." I pause a second before continuing. "I also helped Janelle with the down payment on her salon, and...I think I'll make partner one day..." my voice trails off.

Vincent moves his arm, brushing it against mine. He leans so close, I can smell his scent: dark and woodsy. He's almost close enough to kiss. I wonder if the dark scruff on his jaw is rough or soft. I drop my hands on the rock, keeping myself from reaching up and touching him.

"I understand your need to feel financially secure," he says softly. "But there are other things you could do that would give you all of those benefits as well. Something you love that would also give you satisfaction. You've worked hard and I get it's difficult to step back after clawing your way to the top. You thought this is what you wanted, but it isn't what you thought it would be. Why should you have to make yourself suffer? Fuck it. You've got one life, and you are allowed to change your mind, Eve. Money can be made in many ways —trust me."

"But, what would I even do?" I ask questioningly, eyes fixated on his face. Yes, he's gorgeous. But in this moment, all I see is the man inside.

"Well, you're part of the Kids Learning Club, right?" A small smile plays on his lips.

I blink, the new wing coming into the forefront of my mind. Like the sun in front of me, the truth sets. "Vincent? Have you donated anything recently?" I stare into his eyes, wondering if it's possible he would do such a thing. What I see shining back at me is a definite yes.

"Sure," he shrugs casually. "I may have donated something for someone I've been missing."

I stare up into his handsome face, speechless. I open my mouth to speak when he lifts his hand up.

"No. Don't give me that. It means something to you and the truth is, it means something to me, too. Those kids deserve a chance. I believe in the Club's mission, okay?"

I nod my head, wanting to believe him. He admitted before that he kept tabs on me—which still infuriates me to no end. Still, I'm glad that at least the Kids Learning Club benefited from it.

He stands, wiping the back of his jeans with his palms before taking my hand to help me up. It's getting dark as we shuffle down the trail. Vincent supports me as we walk; it's trickier on the way down than it was on the way up. Finally, we make it back to his bike. After handing me my phone and watch, his phone rings. Lowering his head, he checks the caller ID. Instead of answering, he clicks IGNORE. The ringing stops, and I immediately go on alert.

"Who was that?" I ask probingly.

He turns as though ready to speak. But, he doesn't.

"Well?" I ask again, a little annoyed.

"It was Tom."

"Oh?" My hands move to my hips as my imagination starts gearing up for level-ten-magnitude anger.

"I'm out of the family, Eve. He's still my boy, though," he says with a decided finality.

I let my eyes move up and down his body. "Are you packing right now?"

He stares at me, amused, before bringing his hands down and lifting his dark shirt. There's only gorgeous tan skin and mouth-watering muscles; no guns in sight. My gaze moves down his jeans next, stopping at his ankles. I look back up at him pointedly. "Lift your jeans, Borignone."

He laughs out loud, the sound lighting something up in my chest that I thought was dead.

"You used to help me, remember?" he winks. *Oh God, do I.* Bending down, he brings up the bottom of his pants to show me his ankles, proving to me he no longer carries weapons.

I try not to show it, but my heart wildly pounds inside my chest. I want to stop it, but I can't.

13

VINCENT

WE STOP AT HER HOTEL. I get off the bike first to lift her off, taking an extra few moments to hold her before setting her down. Staring into her eyes, I want to kiss the hell out of her. But the look I see in return is still tinged with some anxiety. I swallow, knowing the key to Eve is still patience.

She saunters away without a backward glance and I'm left staring mutely at her perfect ass. She enters the hotel lobby and my phone rings again. I check the caller ID. It's Tom again.

"Yo."

"Vincent. How many fucking times do I have to call you? Look man," he sighs. "Things are getting hot here, and you're not answering your goddamn phone."

"I've told you too many goddamn times. I'm not part of that shit anymore."

"It's your father. He's getting angrier. Darker. Doing shit you wouldn't imagine. And he's still fuming over your leaving—"

"Look, I've got some work to do. I'll talk to you—"

"Don't you fuckin' hang up the phone!" he barks. "Your father is a dangerous man, or have you forgotten? I can feel bad shit coming your way. You know I've got a sense for these things. He blames you, Vincent."

"Me? What the fuck did I do? I'm not the one who aligned with lunatics. I'm not the one who got into business with untrustworthy men."

"You left—that's what you did. And I can feel it in my bones. He's comin' for you."

"No," I growl back. "I'm all the way out here. I've got Slade by my side nearly every damn moment. When the Mile opens, money will pour in and he'll calm down."

"Open up your eyes, brother." I can hear the stress in his voice over the line. "Because you aren't in the fold, you don't know the shit that's heating up. You've gotta trust me on this," he says desperately. "Your father has changed. You said it in lockup, but I didn't really see it until now. He's got a serious screw loose."

"I know who my father is. But I can't care anymore. I just can't."

"And Eve? You still tryin' to get her back?"

"Yup." My voice leaves no room for negotiation.

"All right, man. What can I say?" he says dejectedly. "Just do me a favor and watch yourself. Don't let your guard down."

I hang up and head directly back to the Mile. There's a large art installation coming tomorrow and I want to make sure the space is ready.

14

VINCENT

One Year Ago

"Vɪɴᴄᴇɴᴛ," *the warden calls my name, shaking me out of my work-induced trance. When I'm focusing like this on the Mile, I'm on another mental plane. I don't need to eat, drink, or take a piss for hours on end when I'm in this zone. I look out the barred window, noticing what looks like a torrential downpour.*

I turn my head to face him, straightening my back. "What's up?"

"Dinner's on. I didn't want to interrupt you, but you know how the inmates talk when they don't see you at meals."

"Yeah, I know." *I stand, cracking my neck. Tension is always higher when people are stuck inside all day.*

No one knows the warden and I are friends, not even my boys. Hell would land on me if word ever got out. But I'm thankful for the guy. Our weekly chess sessions where we talk about current events helps to keep my mind sane. Otherwise, I'd probably rot in here, like so many men do.

Our friendship started simply. He'd been reading my emails about the Mile, as prescribed by the judge, and started to ask some questions. Before I knew it, he became a great source of information. His brother is a builder and father an architect, so he knows a thing or two. And while the family negotiated the computers and email access for me with the DA before my entry, it's my friendship with the warden that actually gives me the time and space I need to build the Milestone.

We shake hands before he cuffs me, passing me off to a guard who brings me down the steps to the chow hall. My crew bangs on the table as I enter, a show of respect. The men around us quiet for a moment, looking down in a combination of terror and worship. Between fucking up Crow and creating the Mile, I've developed a reputation of power. I may be in handcuffs, but I'm the one leading the guard to the table and everyone here knows it.

"Fuckin' stop that shit," I tell my boys, annoyed. The banging immediately stops. I turn my head around the room, feeling a change in the air. Everyone seems twitchy.

I turn to Tom, who's laughing at something Chris is telling him. "What are we eating tonight? Ribs?" I stare at the gruel in their plates. The guard removes the cuffs from my wrists and thanks me before stepping away.

"Sorry Vincent," Tom replies. "Tonight, we've got Veal Milanese with a side of fried garlic and artichokes. Elios delivered your favorite a few minutes ago. Even brought a nice chunk of Parmigiana with fresh crusty bread and butter."

I chuckle. Elios is our favorite Italian on the Upper East Side of New York City, and Tom and I have been dreaming of it for years now.

I walk over to the line still filled with people waiting for grub. The first guy notices me and immediately steps back so I can cut. There is a pecking order here, and things move smoothly because of it. My eyes scan the shitty food options when—seemingly out of nowhere—a fist comes barreling into my cheek before a weapon is plunged into my thigh. I'm caught off guard, momentarily stunned.

"Fuck you!" the guy screams. I throw an arm around his neck and turn his back to my front, incapacitating him while gaining my bearings. The entire place is silent, watching in shocked confusion as a little pissant tries to fight me.

Seeing as he's black and this entire place is divided by color and race, the white inmates start to mumble, likely taking his act as a personal *attack. He's struggling, but I keep him in my hold, waiting for a guard to break this up and take him away. The last thing I want to do is spend a few weeks in the hole for fighting back.*

The talk in the room turns louder. The yelling begins.

One.

Two.

Three.

That's all it takes for the entire chow hall to turn on each other. I can hear the walkie-talkies going off around me as an alarm bell turns on. It's deafening.

Meanwhile, this guy—who I've never even seen before—keeps trying to get out of my grip. He moves his head around, trying to bite me.

"My f-f-fam," he attempts to speak, but I shut his mouth with my hand, holding him against my chest. Moving my head to the side, I take a good look at his tear-stained face. He's nothing but a kid, barely looks eighteen. And fuck, but he's crying. I'm restraining him, but not causing pain.

The chaos continues around us when I realize he's trying to actually tell me something.

"What is it?" I ask tightly, lifting my hand as blood soaks through my pants. I'm still keeping him in my clutches, but letting him tell his message to me.

"Fuck the Borignone mafia!" he says, saliva dripping from his mouth onto my palm. His forehead is in my grip and I'm holding his head tightly. One twist and I could break his neck. I pull his head tighter, letting him know if he tries anything, his life is done.

He takes heavy pants through his nose. "Killed my whole family. Burned my whole house down with them in it. Just because I was short. I hope you all die and rot in hell!"

Before I can process what he just said, tear gas is thrown into the hall, and we all go down.

* * *

I'm WAITING in the cafeteria for my father's bi-monthly visit. I got a corner table by a window. Prime real estate.

The family's business has been deteriorating in the last few years and it's obvious to me that as of late, it's only gotten worse. The men in here with me are organized and follow the proper command. But from what I've been gathering, disorganization is starting to reign back in New York. Worse, the family has been inducting sloppy kids with no sense of decency or respect. Rumors have circulated about the Boss Brotherhood MC getting in touch with my father on the outside and have struck some sort of deal. It's hard to believe, considering the fact that here on the inside, we're enemies. I'd never imagined the family would work with a bunch of skinheads, but my sources don't lie.

My father comes across from me, sitting down in the blue plastic chair and pulling it closer to the table. "Vincent," he says calmly, "I want to know if—"

"Not today," I say, effectively cutting him off. He squints his eyes in confusion. Clenching and unclenching my fists, I know I'm going to need to keep calm in order to have this talk.

He leans back into his chair, casually draping one leg over the other as though he were sitting at the opera as opposed to a prison.

"I wanna know why I keep hearing about our nephews getting more...excited around town." I say the word 'excited' slowly, so he understands I mean more aggressive. "Nephews" has always been our code word for younger men in the family. "Word is, they're losing control. Control is paramount, yeah?"

"I guess you can say the new nephews are more excitable. Especially these days," he replies casually. "With the changing times, this is the path the family is taking."

I sit back in my chair, crossing my arms over my chest. "You have to get rid of them. They're nothing but tr—"

"Well Vincent, if you want to keep growing your family, new children are a must."

My heart pounds as I turn my head away from my father and toward the sea of convicts. This fuckin' life.

"I don't like this route," I practically spit the words out. "You know I'd never okay this. I hear some of them have priors." I move myself closer to

him and lower my voice. "Sexual assault? Stalking? Petty theft? What the fuck is that about? It's unacceptable," I say quietly with gritted teeth.

"Too bad you're not home and don't get a vote." He puts a hand in his jacket pocket, casually pulling out a piece of spearmint gum.

I shake my head disbelievingly.

He looks me over. "It takes numbers to maintain a stronghold. Otherwise, new kids come from other places and try to take what's ours."

"But that was never our way," I say tightly. "We're better than that. Than them." I point my finger to the men around us.

"It's where we are," he states succinctly, chewing his gum and watching me pointedly, daring me to disagree.

"You know the guys I grew up with and always fucking despised?" I draw a large B with my finger on the table. He sits up, nodding in understanding that I'm talking about the Boss Brotherhood. He knows our beef with them here in prison is dark. "Inviting them for a birthday party is the biggest mistake yet. I won't attend if they're included."

He leans forward, clearly aggravated. "You better fuckin' be there, Vincent. Birthday parties are. Not. Negotiable." His voice is a threatening growl.

"I'm not sanctioning this." I seethe, trying to keep my voice low despite my pounding pulse. "Neo-Nazis? These guys are dirty. You want to contaminate our lives with parasites?" I question. My body grows hot.

"What you fail to realize is while you've been gone, the landscape has changed. We've got to make sure these new kids on the block don't take our candy."

I move closer to him, our heads practically glued together over the table.

"These new nephews of ours are nothing but trouble," I say, keeping my voice measured. "They'll never be effective members, and they'll only bring us down in the end." My mind rails. "Who the fuck is even in control of bringing in these morons? Good men are hard to find and even harder to train. The muscle we hired to help us out for the Mile were ex-Israeli Defense Force men. I spent months scouting them out and interviewing to make sure they were legitimate. These choices you're making are fucked. Ya hear me?"

Shock and anger mar his face; my father was always a narcissist, but his ego has grown tremendously in the last few years. I can tell I'm pushing him right now, but he's gotta hear it.

The bell rings, letting us know our time is up.

"Listen to me," I tell him as I stand, pushing my chair back aggressively and pointing my finger in his face, "show a little integrity—"

"No, son. You listen to me." He stands up quickly, grabbing me by the collar despite the no-contact rule. I can see a vein popping in the center of his forehead. "This is my goddamn show. My fucking party. Who's invited? I say who's invited! You're nothing without me. I'm the leader. You don't take a fuckin' piss without my okay," he exclaims.

A guard pulls us apart, cold cuffs linking my hands behind my back as I'm roughly escorted away. I look around quickly. Luckily, with everyone hugging their loved ones, our altercation has seemingly gone unnoticed by the other inmates.

I get back to my cell, sitting down on my cot as I'm locked back inside the cage. The bars close with a clang. Lifting my head to the small window, I stare up at the blue sky—free and clear of clouds. Somehow, in what feels like the first time in my life, I see things for what they are. I've had flashes of this truth, but now, it's here.

What the hell am I doing in here? Paying a debt and taking the fall.

Why did I leave the love of my life, stage an ending, effectively ruining Eve's world? To keep her safe from the life I live.

I grip the side of my bed. I've got to get out of the family, or sooner or later, I'll be back behind bars or dead.

Ever since I came to prison, things on the outside with the family have disintegrated. The new guys they're bringing into the fold? Sloppy. Hiring the BB to run guns for us? Disgusting. Over my dead body would I ever align with those fucks.

I used to believe leaving the East Coast and beginning gaming would allow me to stay as part of the family without dealing with its day-to-day business. I figured my physical departure would be enough. I was wrong. The only way to be free is to leave the fold completely.

I've told myself, all my life, that love and loyalty are who we are. Borignone mafia is power and strength. Borignone mafia is allegiance. I never considered us on the same level as these dirty street gangs. But now, *it's obvious the only family glue is greed. My father doesn't care what he does, so long as the family stays on top. If that means selling us out, he's willing. I'm not sure if Antonio Borignone was always this way, or if he's changed. But regardless, this is where we stand—on opposite sides of the bay. I'd never imagined myself totally breaking free from the family; the stakes alone could mean my life. But for true freedom? It's worth the risk.*

I drop my head in my hands. I've got to think strategically. If the family is doing business with that scum, it's ten times more likely our work on the outside has turned into disorder. Luckily, the Milestone is set up and so tightly organized, it can't be affected by any of their illegal business endeavors. My chest loosens. I'm glad to know the Mile's secure.

Ideas come and go into my head until I finally see a light go off. I've got to continue making myself invaluable. So much so, they can't kill me without risking their own business. My father prizes money above all things, and he'll do whatever he has to—so long as I line his pockets.

I'll leave the family and turn myself into their business partner instead. I won't have to take any fall of theirs as my own. I will give them that option as the only one. Otherwise, I'll take death. But if they choose to kill me, they'll be losing out on all the money. I'd bet my father will take what I offer.

Another thought jumps front and center: I need to call my lawyer and have him remove me from every single deed and business owned by the family. My ties must be totally severed. I raise my arms, grabbing the bottom of my shirt and pulling it up and off my head to stare at the tattoo on my arm. I'm sure I can find a way to blend it into something else. Get a nice sleeve when I'm out—cover this shit up and at least make the insignia less noticeable. I see Eve's name blended into the swirls and feel an immediate sense of calm.

Eve. Jesus, I miss her. I shut my eyes, ignoring the fact that I'm in a cold dark cell and picture her face. If I focus hard enough, I can even smell the coconut scent of her shampoo. What would she say if she knew I left the family? I imagine her smile when she hears the news. She wraps her arms around my neck, squealing with delight. I keep my eyes screwed shut, smiling at the images moving through my mind's eye.

15

VINCENT

"Vincent," she says, opening the door to her room. Her voice is smooth and sweet in the way I love. My name was meant to be on those lips.

I bend down, kissing her soft cheek and taking in her clean scent. Her body shudders. "Hey." She smells absolutely perfect. Like fresh soap and coconut cream.

"C-come in," she turns and I follow her inside. "So, what are we doing for today? I know Kimber mentioned plans to look through files at your office?" She moves around quickly, not making eye contact as she grabs her tablet off the desk along with her phone and e-reader, dropping them into a black bag.

Instead of replying right away, I just stand there, staring. How many years did I spend imagining her just like this, doing something mundane? My fantasies were never overly done. It's Eve in her normal habits: freshly showered. Sweaty after our workout at the gym. Cooking in my kitchen. Reading in bed next to each other while she compulsively highlights passages in a textbook, wearing my shirt. We don't have much time before she heads back to California. The clock on our week is ticking, and I've got to solidify us before she goes.

She smiles innocently as I clear my throat. "We'll go to my office first."

"Okay cool. Are we gonna ride there?" Her voice is hopeful.

"Hell yeah," I grin, noticing she's already wearing her jeans.

Instead of walking out, we both hesitate by the door. The air between us changes. I stare at her full lips and round brown eyes. I need her mouth on mine. I grip the keys in the palm of my hand, attempting to maintain control.

Throat moving in a hard swallow, I can tell she wants this, too. Instinct says to throw her on the bed. Rip her clothes off. Make her come so hard until she's yelling my name. But what if she refuses and everything comes crashing down? There's still so much to talk about.

"Take her," my blood roars, dick hardening in my jeans.

Licking her lips, her eyes scan me from head to toe. Her face is flushing, eyes dilating and body begging. She needs me. I can feel it.

I need to gather myself. I clench my fists, the keys digging into my palm. *Not now*, my mind pounds.

She brings her bag to her hip and I turn to the door, holding it open for her to walk through. After a long pause, she does.

16

EVE

VINCENT'S OFFICE isn't fancy. In fact, it's just another trailer on the rez. When we walk in, Slade's stepping out, talking on the phone. I hear him mention something about camera equipment. He raises his palm to us in "hello" before getting on his bike and driving away.

Vincent steps behind me. He's so near, I can feel his body heat; I'm warming from the inside. Today, things are different between us. The tension is becoming impossible to bear. I know there are still so many issues. But overarching everything is my need for him. I want to feel that closeness again. I can't believe how long I've gone without it —without *him*.

He points to the left. "Kimber works out of here with us, but she's on-site today. Slade takes this front area, and I use the back. Files and everything you need are where I am."

I scan the room, realizing the screens and computers they're all using are seriously high-tech. As relaxed as Vincent is, I'm reminded that he's running a multi-million-dollar industry.

We walk together into his office, closed off by a door from where Slade and Kimber work. The entire room is filled with bookshelves, and they're packed to the brim. I have zero doubt Vincent has read everything in here. Against the window are silver file cabinets, which I assume are what I'll be going through. There's also a large desk outfitted with two large monitors, and a brown leather couch off to the side.

"When did you get all these books?" My fingers lightly graze their spines as I read their titles, one by one.

"I kept notes of what I read in prison. And whatever I loved, I ordered for myself when I got out here."

I want to ask where he wants me to begin when my bag falls off my shoulder, clattering onto the floor. I drop down to my knees, meaning to pick it up. But when I raise my head, what I see freezes me to the ground. Vincent stands tall above me, tatted up and rough. The look on his face has me so turned on, I'm afraid to blink. The slightly reserved man from the last few weeks has been uncovered and in his place is the real Vincent—raw and intense. My gaze moves to his thick-corded neck, tan from riding, and down to his jeans where I come face to face with his enormous erection, punching through his jeans.

"Vincent?" My voice shakes with nerves. *God*, but he is just colossal, making this small room look more like a dollhouse than a small office. I want him so badly my brain literally clouds over with lust.

"Yeah, baby." His voice is deep as he extends a hand to me. On shaky legs, I rise. There are conversations to be had. But right now, I can see and feel nothing but us.

The last seven years, I gravitated toward men I could control. Clearly, that isn't going to happen here. But—I want to try. What would Vincent do, if for once, I was the one in charge?

"Wait," the word leaves my lips and he pauses—for just a second. His eyes assess the situation as my body trembles from his proximity. He takes another step, closer still. Could it be as good as it was back in college? So much time has passed; I'm not even sure what was real and what was simply my imagination.

He lifts me into his arms effortlessly, placing me on the leather couch, so I'm sitting, facing him. Dropping to his knees before me, he takes my head in his hands. Pushing back my hair so all he can see is my face, his dark eyes bore into mine.

"Say yes," he asks. His voice is gravel, almost desperate. "I'd never touch you unless you wanted it."

I blink once, twice, and slowly move my head up and down. My body has taken over.

He inches closer until his mouth is pressed against mine. I can feel a small sliver of tongue slide between my lips. "Oh, God," I moan, shifting my body horizontal and pulling him onto me. He rubs his mouth over mine gently and whisper-soft. Not entering. Not going fast like I wish he would.

I'm shaking. He's barely moved and my panties are drenched. He continues to do nothing other than tease. My legs open wider in anticipation, but he's taking his damn time.

He licks at my ear, sucking down the column of my neck. I think I'm begging him to undress me, but I can't be sure. *Is he really here?* I shut my eyes and inhale, everything feels right. I know—it's Vincent. Mine.

I shift my body, trying to align us. Moving my hands down to unbutton my pants, I'm yearning to get naked. I need skin on skin. He moves his fingers to where mine are, unfastening my jeans for me before pulling them off. Lifting me up with a muscled arm, my shirt and bra fly off next. We're fused, breathing each other in until our inhales are completely synchronized. I grip his back beneath his shirt and lightly score my nails against his skin. He hisses and I smile at the power I feel.

I'm desperately waiting for him to get naked. I pull at the waist of his jeans and luckily, he takes the hint. His leather jacket comes off first, followed by his black Henley. The air in the room leaves as I take the biggest inhale of my life. I thought I knew the body beneath the shirt, but apparently, my imagination didn't do him justice. Vincent is absolutely ripped. The leanness of his youth has been replaced with heavy muscle and swirls of black, riotous tattoos. I notice a long scar on his lower abs, but there's no time to examine. I need his hands on me. My mouth dries as I watch his pants fall to the ground. His underwear is next. Vincent's dick is a sight to behold—perfect. Mouthwateringly thick and long. His body is a work of art.

He moves to the edge of the couch, nostrils flaring in desire. My heart pounds. I'm naked and for the first time in seven years, completely vulnerable and at a man's mercy. Control? Gone. Nothing could ever prepare me for this. His dark gaze roams every inch of my body and I subconsciously arch my back, thrusting my full breasts toward him. I yearn for him to see me in the way only Vincent ever has.

"Your body. You're so beautiful, baby. Your nose. Your lips. That mouth. Everything about you..." He moves his large palm down from my stomach all the way to my toes and back up again. "I'm insane for you. Stupid for you. God, Eve, everything about you calls to me. We need to talk, but I can't stop right now."

Talk? I can barely breath.

He lowers his mouth to my nipple and my entire body convulses with his first suck. I'm turning mindless as he shifts, lining himself up with me and sliding his dick up and down, agonizingly slow, my wetness coating us both and driving me insane. I clutch at his neck, wrapping my legs around his waist and raising my body higher, angling myself to catch him. But I can't. Why won't he just get inside me already?

"Vincent!" I yell.

I can feel his smirk against my shoulder. "I fuckin' missed you." Back and forth, he drags his heavy cock over that bundle of nerves, wreaking havoc on my insides. My body pounds with desire and need.

"Missed the way you smell. Your soft body in my hands." His voice rumbles at my ear as he gently pulls my hair, moving my head back before dropping his head to take another deep suck of my nipple. My pussy clenches. "You're my life," he growls. "My everything. Do you know that?" His damp breaths move to my ear. "I've been dreaming of you nonstop. In every move I make. It's always you. Only you. Since you, there was no one else. Do you hear me?"

This man owns me.

I want to speak, to tell him everything, but I can only whimper. Every ounce of blood has left my brain.

His eyes, now coal black, lock on mine. "I need to know you hear me. That you want this. Tell me again," he insists.

I shiver, realizing he isn't going to continue until I give him full consent. I grab the back of his head in an attempt to force his lips back to mine, but he won't move.

"For fuck's sake, Vincent. Now!" I beg.

He chuckles. "Just what I need to hear." He fills me entirely, all at once, and my insides pulse against him. It's so good, it's shocking. His fingers move down to my clit and I throw my head back, moaning loudly. My body wants to bind itself to his. Seal us together.

"Good girl," he whispers as I tighten my legs around him. "Need to hear you. Need to hear those moans, understand? Been waiting seven years for this. For you."

He drives into me hard and deep only to pull back in a slow drag as if he were savoring me. Pleasure like hot lava pools in my core, a feeling I haven't felt since Vincent himself all those years ago. No, it couldn't have been this good.

"...Don't stop," I groan as he mumbles a soft curse, pushing deeper.

Beads of sweat drip from his body and onto my breasts. I stare up at him, wanting to memorize his face—just like this. I can scarcely believe I'm on my back with Vincent above me.

"I have to taste you," he mumbles, voice heavy.

Sliding out of me, he moves off the couch and drops to his knees. I can feel his hands, hot against my skin spread my thighs apart. The warmth of his lips and wet tongue fall directly on my center and with a firm and hot lick, my lower body clamps like a vise, ankles locking around his head. My entire world shimmers while he continues to drink me in.

In a sex-drunken daze, I'm brought onto his lap on the floor. I wrap my arms around him tightly as he begins to fuck me in earnest with too many years' worth of tension. Bending his body, he captures my mouth in a deep kiss. It's desperate, our tongues swirling together.

I can taste a trace of myself on him. Our hands clasp, fingers lacing together. Clinging to his huge body, I take everything he gives.

He pants as his movements deepen. Rolling his hips, a heavy hand cups the underside of my breasts as his angle shifts. He's hitting *that* spot. Like a cyclone, another wave of pleasure moves through me. My world explodes as he roars, collapsing on top of me with his own release. We're a bundle of sweat and pounding hearts.

"Thank God," I say out loud, tears rolling down my face as I press my cheek against his shoulder. *This*. We have so much to talk about, but I feel the truth now. My heart always knew it.

Vincent wraps me up tightly in his arms, pressing a hot kiss against my lips. "Fuckin' love you. Always will."

After we somewhat stabilize, we stand. Vincent presses his lips on every inch of my body before covering me with my clothing. *This man.*

"Let's stop. Get you some stuff you'll need at my place."

"Why not the hotel?" My voice comes out as a rasp.

"Takes too long. Need you in my bed," he grumbles, voice low and deep.

"My clothes?"

"Not necessary."

We get back onto his bike and ride to the nearest pharmacy. Vincent struts up and down the aisles, picking up a toothbrush, shampoo and conditioner, and face and body wash with quick efficiency. I'm laughing as I practically chase him down, trying to keep up with his pace. Finally reaching the register, Vincent takes out his black wallet to pay. I pause, noticing a pulse in his neck as he hands over his credit card for the cashier to swipe.

I stop smiling.

He looks worried and anxious, brows lowered in that dark and brooding way of his.

"Vincent," I touch his arm, "I'm here, okay?"

A line has formed behind us, but I couldn't care less. He swallows hard, the scruff on his face thicker than a few hours ago. Under the bright lights and white walls, his eyes are practically savage. "Don't want to waste time," he whispers with his teeth clenched, grabbing the back of my neck possessively as if he can't help it. I'm struck again by my tiny size compared to his. His grip isn't painful, but still, it's strong. The cashier looks at us nervously as the line grumbles in annoyance.

I focus only on Vincent, nodding gently in understanding. Stepping against him, I remove his hand from my neck and loop our fingers together.

"I'm still here," I swear. "We'll talk about everything later, okay?"

He nods and visibly relaxes before finally taking the plastic bag from the cashier.

We ride another ten minutes to his home. Pulling up to the side of his trailer, he lifts me off the bike and doesn't put me down until I'm on my back. I grab his soft sheets, fisting them as my body reignites. He moves to his knees, pulling me into his chest with so much emotion it steals my breath.

He's everywhere. Eyes closed. Licking and sucking at my neck so deep, marking me how I know he loves. A few beats.

"I'm gonna fuck you now, yeah? Can't wait anymore." His voice is desperate, our mouths melded.

"Please, Vincent. Yes," I whisper into his lips, wrapping my legs around his waist.

He enters me, groaning. "You're fucking gorgeous. Goddamn." He pushes in and out again, harder still, settling himself inside me and staking claim. Picking up one of my legs, he throws it over his wide muscled shoulder. My eyes practically roll back as he hits that spot so precisely; every inch of my body clenches tight, coiling. Bending down, he brings his mouth to my ear.

"Only me and you. Forever. Got that?" he growls, swiveling his hips in circles and grinding down on my clit. I'm moaning—out of my mind. Like a fire, the flames rove straight through me and down into my toes until they curl up in sweet agony.

Before I can catch my breath, he pulls me on top of him. I bring myself up and down on his cock, so slow. He's buried so deep, it's almost painful. So fucking good. He's cursing, begging me now.

Holding my hips with his hands and watching me fall down on him over and over again. We're drunk on each other. His grip tightens as he finally moves me the way he needs, grinding me down hard before raising me up again. My heart is about to beat straight out of my chest; pleasure mixing with emotional openness giving me a sublime high.

"Vincent," I moan, my voice hoarse.

The thought crosses my mind—if he ever left me again, I'd die. Vincent turns me desperate. He makes me *insane*. I drop my head down into the crook of his neck.

"Fuck," he groans, squeezing my hips hard enough to bruise as he presses me down harder and not letting go until he fills me to the brim.

My entire body is like lead in his arms, heavily sated. He slowly runs his calloused fingers over my skin, as if he can't bear not to touch. With his large hands, he cups my breasts and slides his fingers along my curves, humming deep in appreciation. I lay soundlessly, letting him take his time. Overcome by emotion, I find myself swallowing back tears. I never thought—

"Eve," he says, interrupting my internal voice.

"Yeah?"

His hand spans around my throat. He's gentle and yet, I'm completely at his mercy. "Never letting you go. Never," he commands. I know Vincent is dominant, always in charge. It isn't because of who his father is. And it isn't because he was raised in the Borignone mafia. It's just something within him. Anywhere Vincent goes, he's the king.

I lift my eyes to his, submitting. We wrap ourselves back up in each other until our lips are numb, all thoughts of the world around —my office, my shitty coworkers, our past—silenced.

The clock ticks and the sun begins to set. I turn, pressing his hand between my thighs. The room glows.

"We should talk about that night."

"Not yet. First, I want you to tell me about lockup. Let's start there." My voice comes out in a whisper. I want to know.

17

VINCENT

ALL SHE DOES IS ASK, and within seconds, I'm opening up about the worst time in my life. At first, it's as if I'm telling someone else's story. But somewhere between explaining the Boss Brotherhood and the look in her eyes, acute anxiety settles in my chest. I open my mouth to continue, but my throat is uncomfortably dry.

Sensing the change in me, she kisses my shoulder before hopping off the bed. I hear kitchen cabinets opening and the sink turning on. She comes back to me with a tall glass in hand, full to the brim with water. I drink the entire thing in one swallow.

After taking the glass from me and setting it on the side table, she curls up into my chest like a kitten. I press my forehead against hers, keeping our lips separated by mere centimeters. Her breaths enter my mouth, and it gives me strength.

"Prison. It was worse than you think. I did horrific shit without blinking an eye. Luckily, after I stood my ground with the BB, everyone knew who I was. They all stayed back. Still. I-I don't know what to tell you. It was like there was a constant war on—" I stop, unable to manage. I know I have to talk to her about everything, and I want to, but it's too fuckin' much and I wasn't expecting this kind of emotional onslaught. She puts her hands on my shoulders. So gentle. So perfect.

"We have sex and now I'm unraveling." I laugh, but we both know it's not funny.

She pulls back, touching two scars in my left eyebrow. Moving her hands down my body, she lets her fingers graze over all my new wounds, pausing at the deepest one in my lower abdomen. We are both silent, but her eyes fill with pain at the sight.

"Oh my God, Vincent," she says, her face distressed. Fingers moving downward, she finds the stab wound in my thigh.

"Look at me," I say with as much strength as I can muster. "Things were bad. But they're over now."

"But how can you be so sure your father really let you go?" She's shaking her head from side to side, wild hair framing her face. "You said it once—no one leaves without a body bag."

"Believe it, Eve. I left and I'm still alive."

She moves closer, melting into me. But I'm not done with her—not yet. I move off the bed and drop down to my knees.

"Vincent, wait—"

"Don't deny me. I need to drink you in." I immediately slide my tongue inside of her, and she lets out a low moan. Time ceases to exist. Stopping myself isn't an option. I need to lose myself in her.

"Vincent. It's too much," she begs. God, she tastes so fucking good. I keep up my pace until her entire body is pink, flushed and shaking. She liquefies into my mouth and I savor every drop. When she's finished, I kiss back up her body and bring her to my chest. She fits.

"Eve, I need you."

"I know. I'm here." Strength and emotion shine from her voice. But behind it, is love.

18

EVE

I CLUTCH onto Vincent's back as we ride up the bright highway, nothing but open road and mountains ahead of us. The last forty-eight hours have been spent watching TV and alternating between fucking like crazy and making slow, savory love. We didn't talk much —we just *lived*. I'm not ready to open up about how he left me before prison. Discussing the details would only ruin this moment. Still, I'm worried that if we get into the past, everything between us will break down. Maybe I'm falling back into an old habit, but I trust we'll figure it out when the time is right.

He grilled steaks and corn for us every night, and I always made a big salad. I wanted to cook more for him, but he didn't want me busy in the kitchen. Doing work for the Milestone was nearly impossible, but we managed to get a bit done while tangled up in each other.

With Vincent, it's that mind-body connection. He takes me over on every single plane.

His home is tiny and perfect and we agreed that more than this just isn't necessary. What a relief not to deal with anything material. We have each other, delicious food, and a safe, warm home. What else is there? Over coffee this morning, he mentioned building us a house with a backyard one day—when we have kids.

I had burst into tears. He got down to his knees, holding me tightly around the waist. Not talking. Pulling off our clothes. Making love to me on the floor of his kitchen. Cold tile becoming slick with our sweat.

Gripping him as the wind whips around us, I let myself imagine our future. Vincent. Three children. A son and two daughters, because every girl deserves a sister. I hope they have his eyes. I want them to have his heart and strength too.

Our bike pulls into a dirt and cement parking lot, kicking up dust as we take a corner spot. Staring up, I see a huge red, white, and teal neon sign: THE BLUE. With nothing other than a gas pump and a handful of motorcycles, I'm equal parts excited and nervous. This life isn't what I'm used to, but still, it feels like it's where I'm meant to be.

Walking into the dimly lit restaurant and bar, country music plays on the speakers as I tightly clutch Vincent's hand. Being next to him fills my heart with pride—this brilliant, handsome, strong man is mine. I finally look around, eyes widening in surprise; the bar resembles an old New York City deli counter.

"This place is one of the few around here that's typical America." He walks us to a small booth in the center of the restaurant.

"Are most of the people here locals?" I sit down across from him, placing my hands on the table for him to hold; he immediately takes them.

"Yup. Believe it or not, most of the people here are Native Americans, but there's a range of blood degrees from full-blooded to practically blond, yeah?"

I gaze around the room and stare at the other patrons before settling back at the man in front of me, whose dark eyes haven't left my face. I flush, thinking about an hour ago when he was on top of me, going deep and slow.

Sexually, we're explosive. But it's so much more than that, and it always has been with him. I've known Vincent from when I was a little eighteen-year-old in the Blue Houses. The man took me for pizza and ice-skating, for God's sake. No one knows me like he does —so fully.

But I'm no longer a kid, and the realization is worrying. I'm a level-headed woman with a job and an apartment with a mortgage; my life is set on a track. But where does that leave us? The last few days have been spent in a dream world. Now we're out of his trailer and at a restaurant with the real world upon us. Our past—we'll deal with. But what about tomorrow? What about my work and the life I built? Anxiety brews.

19

VINCENT

SHE'S STRESSING; I can see it in her eyes and in the tiny crease in her forehead. I'm done with tiptoeing around. There's no way I'm going to stop myself anymore around her.

"Come here," I say. I need to feel her, and she needs to feel me, too. Smiling with a little hesitance behind her eyes, she stands up to come to me. Before she can make another move, I grab and pull her into my lap.

"Vincent!" She giggles. I throw my arm around her shoulders as she nestles herself into my side. Her life gives me mine.

As much as I love disappearing from the world and staying in bed all day with Eve beneath me, I don't want to hide her like I had to back in college. Never again.

"We've gotta really talk now, babe." My voice comes out like gravel.

Her body shivers as I press my lips to her collarbone, snaking out my tongue to get a taste. So sweet.

The waitress comes over. "Hi! Do y'all know what ya want?" Her smile turns down as she stares at us with a look of confusion and nerves and I try not to laugh out loud. My girl is fresh with clear skin and shining eyes. So tiny and right now—cute as fuck with her hair in a high ponytail. Meanwhile, I've got my resting murder face, tatts, and four-days-worth of dark stubble.

Eve stares up at me, all trusting and innocent without any care that people are judging us. She's too good to me. Too good for me. Jesus Christ, *this woman*. I move an errant hair from her forehead before turning back to the waitress, asking for a few good things on the menu I've eaten before. Eve cuddles closer, letting me take care of her.

The waitress leaves, giving us privacy once again.

"So, when should I come back?" Her voice is whisper soft. She moves her nose to my shoulder, inhaling. "If you want me to negotiate some agreements for you, I can probably stay long—"

"Eve," I laugh, cutting her off. "I don't just want to hire you. Hiring you and your brilliant mind would be a perk. I want you in my bed every night." I rub the back of her neck as I stare into her eyes. She's hesitant, but still, she's going to have to hear this.

"I've been to hell and back, just as you have. I've got scars. And the truth is, my days of living in big-city luxury are behind me. I like the simpler life without all the goddamn noise. I'm happy with cash in the bank and you on the back of my bike. I'm not a clean-cut doctor. I've been in lockup. I've got a laundry list of sins." I pause, noticing she isn't panicking. I drop my hand on her thigh.

"I ran you from New York and ruined your life. No one knows it better than me. You need to hear now how sorry I am." I swallow. "But I couldn't drag you into that shit, and I think you know there was no other way to make sure you were safe. I also didn't want you coming out here and wasting your life waiting for me. But now I'm back, and I want you. Need you. Fucking love you babe and always have. It's time you move here with me."

20

EVE

THE WAITRESS RETURNS CARRYING PLATES, interrupting Vincent from his speech. I take a minute to contemplate his words as the food is set in front of us. But with each passing second, I feel my temperature rise. We've been stuck in our own cocoon for days. But reality just punched through my door.

"Am I just your puppet?" He tilts his head to the side as if he's confused. "Is my life something you can control at your discretion?" The updated version of myself rears its head.

His eyes soften as he shakes his head. "No, it was never like that. It's still not like that. In fact, I need to tell you the truth about that night—"

I put up my hand, silencing him. "Tell me you're joking," I say angrily, pushing one of the plates away from me. A minute ago, we were drenched in love. He seems surprised by my hurt, but what can he expect? I'm still aching and it's not ignorable. "Forget college for a moment. Did you consult me before showing up at my office? Nope. You just came and stomped on my emotional well-being and sanity. Meanwhile, it's been seven years, Vincent. Seven fucking years."

I can feel my heart racing with an avalanche of emotion. "You waltzed into my office and threw millions at my firm—the one I worked my ass off to have a desk at—and I'm supposed to leave everything I've studied and worked for and come running back into your arms?"

We've been loving each other so hard the last few days, but with his admission, all of my resentment bubbles to the surface.

He pulls on the ends of his hair. "You have no idea the hell I was enduring in lockup, huh? I called you the second I got out and you didn't answer your fucking phone." His eyes flash.

"You knew where I lived, Vincent. You could have shown up to my apartment. But no, you had to come through work?"

"Hold up." He shakes his head, as if I'm not understanding him. He looks frustrated. "I only did that because I thought it would be a more comfortable way for you to—"

"—And you think I don't know what you must have gone through in prison? You threw me away." My voice breaks. I can't stop the words even if I wanted to. "I died for you, Vincent. Without you, I wasn't functional. I was basically s-suicidal." I squeeze the napkin in my fist, remembering my younger self wading into the ocean. Everything around me turns into a blur as pain slams into my bloodstream. The look in his eyes was cold. A girl on her knees before him. The imagines flash, turning my stomach.

He grabs the back of my head with his hand, keeping me tethered to him. "Well, I lived for you, Eve." His hold tightens, but I feel stricken. "I went through hell and back, and your face kept me alive. I told you all those years ago I would never be done with you. That I'd kill for you. Die for you. And baby? I'm no liar. You can be scared right now. You can be nervous. You and me, Eve, we'll never be over. And now that shit is finally clear out here, you're deluding yourself if you think I'll ever walk away from you again." He takes a sharp inhale through his nose. "I hurt you. I know it." His head moves up and down, once. "It was for your own good. And if as an adult, you can't see that? Well, you n—"

I let out a loud sarcastic laugh. "You don't get a choice anymore. I'm leaving here tonight."

"Leaving?" The word falls out of his mouth with surprise.

"Yes. I'm going." I throw my hands up. "You can't just expect me to uproot my life. I've built a whole world out in California. Working my ass off at work to make partner. And anyway, I think it's only a few more years away—"

"Fuck them," he presses his lips together, voice vibrating. "Come here and open your own law firm. Or don't. You love the Kids Learning Club. The teenagers on the rez could use your help, too. Half of them drop out of school and unplanned pregnancy is rampant. You could start a tutoring center."

"You can't just decide this for me." I turn my face around to see if we've garnered any attention. Luckily, the place is filled with patrons and the music is loud, drowning out our words.

He grips my hand in his. "I'm not blind. You hate working for that dickhead. And they treat you like shit, too. Let me guess, you think it'll get better? You can prove them all wrong?" His voice is accusing. "They harass you in that office, babe. I hate how you stay there. You need to quit that place. Now's a good time."

I sit back, pulling my hands away as if I've been slapped. He's so honest and accurate in his assessment that it momentarily jars me. "You have no right throwing that back in my face. I can deal with the way they treat me. I'm not weak." I grit my teeth.

"Of course, you're not. You're as strong as they come. But you don't have to eat shit in order to prove strength." He looks up at the ceiling as if to gather himself. "Okay. You need more time. Fine. Go back to L.A., a city I despise, and we'll do the long distance. That's what you want? Once or twice a month? Fuck like crazy before returning to some cold apartment? Newsflash. That's not the life I want and it isn't what you want, either. We've been separated long enough. That shit's gotta be done now. It's time." His voice is urgent.

"No," I shake my head from side to side. "No, it's not time. If I can just work for a few more years, I'll finally—"

"—make partner? And then what? So, you can continue as a cog in their bullshit machine? We both know it's not your calling. Yes—be a boss. But not there. Not for them."

"Don't say that," I gasp. "Don't come here and step all over my life and my work." I cross my arms over my chest, trying to stabilize myself. He's speaking truth, but it's butting heads with what I've been telling myself for years. It's too much.

"I'm not stepping on you, babe," he replies, his voice calmer. Gentle, almost. "You should have more than what they're giving you. You want to keep doing contractual work, I'll pull my money from Jonathan and give it all to you. The Milestone is yours. Do you hear me? Everything that's mine was yours and still is yours." His words are promises. I believe him. "I'm the one who messed up and lied to you. But come be with me now and let me make it right."

I drop my head down low, staring at the white-tile floor. Vincent puts his thumb under my chin to lift it back up before staring into my eyes. "If you don't want to do law anymore, just stop. I'll support anything you choose. You don't have to keep running to reach some goal you don't even care about. I know you, Eve. I know the real you. Real Estate law isn't your end game."

I touch my forehead, feeling totally out of sorts. I have no idea what it is I even want. I've been dreaming of this career for so long. Even if law in this capacity makes me miserable, it's all I've focused on. And now, am I supposed to just let it go? How can I?

I lick my lips, facing the window in the back of the restaurant. "This is too much, too soon. We just started seeing each other again. We haven't even talked enough about the past. And you've obviously thought all the details through. But I haven't."

"The past? It's simple. I staged the party to make sure you moved on. I wanted you safe and free. If anyone knew we had ties? If anyone knew you were mine? The backlash would have been a hundred times worse than what Daniela gave you. You'd be dead by now, Eve. My father alone was enough of a threat. Everyone had to know we were done. I didn't have a month to convince you to leave me. It had to be hard."

He puts his hand back under my chin, forcing me to look at him.

"Do you love me, Eve? Because you're the breath in my prayers. In my mind, it's only ever been *us*." His hands dig into my hair, gentle yet dominant, as his dark eyes fill with so much adoration, it stops my heart. "Do you love me?" he repeats.

I blink, the answer sitting on my tongue. I'm afraid to say it now. I'm scared of what it'll mean and what I'll have to give up. He waits, staring at me searchingly. Pleadingly. When he realizes I'm not replying, he sits back, looking knifed.

"I just need some time, okay?" My words fall out in a rush. "Let me go back to L.A. and just, s-sort it all out."

He lifts his hand, asking for the check as our entire meal sits untouched before us. Before the waitress can bring it over, he drops a few twenties on the table and stares at me expectantly, waiting for me to move from the booth. I feel like crying. Screaming. Telling him to just... hang on and wait, dammit! But Vincent waits for no one. It's who he is and why he's so successful. But right now? I'm the one getting stomped by his drive.

I move out of his way. He wastes no time in striding out of the restaurant, people stepping left and right to avoid getting run over by this beast of a man. He pushes through the front doors and I run behind him. I'm so mad, but still...

"Vincent, please—" I beg, practically chasing him to his bike.

He drops the helmet on my head, closing it tightly while refusing any eye contact. Climbing on, he waits with a look of impatience for me to join him.

Our entire drive is cold. I grip his waist as tightly as I can, wishing that somehow, I could open his brain and pour my feelings into him so he could understand.

Stopping in front of my hotel, he lifts his helmet. "Don't burn your legs when you get off." His words aren't said cruelly, but they are final. He's mad. He's so fucking mad.

Shakily, I climb off, trying not to crumble onto the ground as he rides away, leaving nothing but dust in his wake.

Fifteen minutes later, I'm still standing in the spot he left me—my body in a trance. Is Vincent gone?

* * *

I FINALLY RETURN to my hotel room. Packing my clothes and checking out is taking longer than expected.

Sitting on the white couch in the hotel lobby, I barely notice a single thing other than the desert, dimmed to gray by my sunglasses. This is exile.

"Miss?" One of the hotel staff touches my shoulder politely. "Your car is here for you."

I turn around, noticing a long black Escalade waiting in the hotel's driveway. I stand, walking out the sliding glass doors while the bellboy carries my bags.

The driver runs around the car, opening my door. I step in. Slade is here. He looks happy at first, but his mouth quickly turns down at my demeanor. I pull my sunglasses back over my eyes; the last thing I need is to talk to someone on Team Vincent. Taking a seat in the third row, I stare out the window, doing my best to avoid any conversation. Luckily, he stays silent.

Halfway to the airport, I sit up, pushing my glasses on the top of my head as an idea takes shape in my head.

"Sir," I call to the driver, clearing my throat. "Can you take me to the main airport, please?"

Slade turns around. "The private jet is ready for you." He sounds confused.

"I want to go to the regular airport," I repeat with as much strength as I can muster. "I no longer want to go back to L.A. I need to get to New York." My voice comes out strong and determined, and as words leave my lips, I feel an immediate sense of relief—as though I'm doing right.

I have a weekend before work Monday morning, and I want to go home—my real home—and sort this out. I actually believe every word Vincent said, but I need confirmation and answers from someone other than him. Angelo is in New York. It's time I hear the truth straight from his lips.

Not least, I'm sick and tired of running away from my past. It wasn't until I saw Vincent again that I realized how much pain I was carrying. Until I clear it up, I can't move forward with my life the way I need. I grip my purse, bringing it to my chest as I try not to bawl.

21

EVE

LaGuardia is gray and cold. Within twenty minutes of landing, I'm sitting in the back of a yellow cab telling it to take me to Seventy-Fifth Street and Second Avenue.

I enter Janelle's boutique hair salon, smiling wide, all of her white chairs are filled with clients getting cuts, color, and blow-dry. The place evokes a cool downtown style with 90s supermodels like Christie Brinkley, Claudia Schiffer, and Naomi Campbell gracing her walls in oversized black-and-white prints.

The salon is located uptown and designed to cater to rich girls who don't want their hair done by their moms' snooty colorists. I smile, trying not to roll my eyes at these teenagers and early twenty-somethings scrolling their phones, probably checking out the latest social media posts while having their hair brightened blonde. As Janelle likes to joke, these little shits are the ones paying top dollar for her services. So, as far as she's concerned, God bless 'em!

Before the girl at the front desk—who looks more model than human—can ask me who I'm seeing today, Janelle comes barreling toward me from the back of the salon.

"You bitch! You came without telling me!" she squeals, jumping up and down and throwing her arms around me. "How was Nevada? Ohmygod you look gorgeous!" She takes my hand, dragging me to the couch by the door.

We sit with our knees touching. She's still the light to my dark. The free spirit to my seriously focused.

"It was cool," I start. "I got a lot done—" I open my lips to continue, but the words catch in my throat as tears gather in the corners of my eyes. She encases me in a warm hug. Janelle smells like a floral vanilla. It's different from her usual scent, but it's still my sister.

Letting me go, I take a hard swallow as she pulls the clip from my hair. "You need a haircut." She grins. "I love it long like this, but let me trim your ends. I know we've got a shit ton to talk about, but everything will be better with good hair and some wine."

I can only nod, afraid that if I even try to speak, I'll cry. Luckily, Janelle knows this by just looking at me. "Quick wash first. I'll squeeze you between clients." She turns around, raising a hand in the air.

A young girl with a white crop top and pink streaks in her platinum hair comes running to us nervously. "Yes, Janelle?" She bites a glossy pink lip.

"Hi, Angeline. Wash. Two shampoos." Janelle's voice is commanding as she stares at the girl in that no-nonsense New York way. I missed this and can't believe how long it's been since I've been here. I'm quickly escorted to a chair in front of a small white sink. Once seated, Angeline places a warm towel behind my back—a nice touch.

The water turns on and I try and relax. The moment she scrubs my scalp with her fingertips, I have to try not to moan out in pleasure. Holy shit but this girl can wash!

Finally sitting in Janelle's stylist chair, Angeline taps my shoulder. "Can I bring you a coffee or tea? We have cappuccino, latte, regular, and decaf. Teas include green, black, and chamomile."

I turn to Janelle, smiling at her as if to say—damn girl, you did well!

"I'll take a cappuccino. Skim, please," I ask politely.

She walks away as my sister begins trimming my ends. Janelle tells me it's called *dusting*. "Hopefully you won't notice any change in length, but the hair, in general, will have bounce and freshness."

There's so much I want to tell her. I open my mouth to start.

"Just sit tight for now, okay? Let me do your hair. Tonight, when I'm home, we'll talk. I'm assuming this is about Vincent, right?" She shakes her head in anger.

I pull out my e-reader and open up an old favorite, reveling in the comfort of a good book while my sister takes care of me. I can be the big boss all I want in L.A. But within a second of being near Janelle, I'm back to being the baby. I would expect that feeling to annoy me, but it doesn't.

Forty minutes later, she tells me to lift my head and take a look. My hair is shining; dark waves fall down to the center of my boobs. I feel like...me.

She hands me a set of keys. "Go to my apartment. I'll be there around eight."

"I may go see Angelo early tonight." I step in for a hug.

"He's going to be thrilled. Always complaining that you never come home." She raises her eyebrows accusingly.

"Yeah, I know." Guilt rises up. It's been seven years since I've been back to the city. If Janelle hadn't come to visit, I probably never would have seen her. But, I'm here now.

I tip Angeline as she hands me my luggage. Walking the few blocks to Janelle's apartment, I let my mind wander to Vincent.

Deep in my gut, I know that he's right about my work. I'd be happier doing something that actually helps people. It's not as if real estate transactions were ever my dream. In fact, it came to me by happenstance. A friend in law school mentioned that Crier, the best firm in Los Angeles, was hiring. I went ahead and applied. When they offered me a job in their real estate department, I felt like—how could I turn it down? The money was phenomenal and it was so well known. So, I said yes. And now, here I am.

Using my legal degree to actually benefit the world is obviously more my speed. But I couldn't do it just because Vincent said so. Can't he see that? This is something I've got to think about for myself. I've spent the last however-many years of my life planning to be a lawyer; making partner was always the big goal. And it's so close, I can smell it. Sure, it's nothing like I thought it would be. And Vincent's not wrong that I'm unhappy. Still, it was always "the plan." Truthfully, I'm not even sure why making partner is so important. I can continue practicing law in a different capacity, and like he said, be my own boss.

Finally getting to Janelle's, I take the elevator up to the third floor and walk down the narrow hallway to apartment 6B. The space is a small one-bedroom, overlooking a courtyard with a wooden bench and patchy grass. It's not fancy, but it's just right—so much warmer than my apartment back in L.A.

A small photo of us hangs in her hallway; it's the two of us on the Blue Houses' stoop making kissy faces to the camera. I smile in surprise, having no idea she had this picture. We look so young. My baggy sweatshirt reaches my knees. God, I've come a long way. We both have.

I drop my things in the corner of her blue and white bedroom and pull out my phone from my purse. Disappointment ravages through my chest; he still hasn't called. Of course, he hasn't. I tried not to compulsively check my phone, but now that I've broken the seal, I'll probably be staring at it every other second.

Dialing Angelo, I let him know that I'm home. He's surprised, but also excited. I ask him to meet me for dinner tonight at a small Italian place I noticed on my walk over to Janelle's. We agree on six o'clock.

* * *

THE RESTAURANT IS warm and cozy, complete with interior red-brick walls and candles lining the white-clothed tables. I scan the nearly empty room, finding Angelo at a table in the back corner. Walking toward him, he stands to greet me. We talk regularly, but I haven't seen him face to face since he brought me out to California. To my relief and happiness, he still smells and looks the same. Red and blue striped shirt and dark slacks. Aqua de Gio cologne. I couldn't stop my smile if I tried.

After a long and drawn-out hug, I take my seat across from him.

"Look at you! Fancy and gorgeous," he says with pride, lifting up a cup of tap water and taking a sip.

"Oh, please." I shake a hand in front of my face dismissively. "You know I just clean up well."

I took my time getting dressed this evening by putting on my makeup as meticulously as I could and choosing the classiest outfit in my suitcase. I guess I just wanted to show Angelo that I really and truly changed my life. Maybe I also wanted to prove it to myself.

My white button-up shirt is sheer, but not see-through. With my jeans in Janelle's washer, I opted for a pair of tan straight-leg trousers and nude Louboutin round-toe pumps.

"I missed you, doll," he tells me earnestly, his eyes crinkling in the corners. Finally, I notice the guilt swimming in his eyes. I swallow hard, knowing in my gut what's about to happen.

"Angelo," I start, clearing my throat. "I'm here for a reason." The waiter steps over, dropping a basket of bread and a small plate of olive oil in front of us. We both look up to thank him before he walks away.

"I figured." He shrugs sadly as if he has an inkling of what I need to discuss. "Talk to me." With elbows resting on the table, he shortens the distance between us.

"Well, I've seen Vincent." I stop to gauge his reaction—he's surprisingly calm. "I've been helping him on the Milestone, as his attorney. And he hinted at some things about our past. So, I'm ready to hear it all from you. Because you know how much I love and trusted y—" my voice breaks. "And you swore over and over. You swore it, Angelo. And—"

He shakes his head, putting out a warm hand to cover mine. "I never wanted to hurt you." He speaks quickly, defending himself. "I just wanted to help. Vincent knew how close me and you were..."

Tears drip down my face as he finally tells the whole agonizing story, hands moving quickly through the air as he delivers the painful details. After so adamantly swearing to those lies all those years ago —that Vincent was cheating and a liar, he's shockingly forthcoming with the truth: it was all a sham. Then again, a lot of time has passed.

Finally, he stops. I stare at him in silence, noticing sweat beading on his forehead. It's clear no one wanted to propel the lie, but neither Angelo nor Vincent thought there was a better option. My life was on the line because of our relationship. I was too young, too in love, and too invested in Vincent to just walk away from him.

"I trusted you, though, Angelo. And Vincent, he could have spoken to me." I sniffle, dabbing the napkin under my eyes.

"Well, he told me he tried. But you weren't going to give up on him. I mean, shit. If you stuck around and people found out about you, it would have been bad. And if you left to Cali and promised not to contact him, but you waited for him, that would have been fucked-up too." He drops a heavy fist on the table. "How could he ask you to wait and give up your life? Plus, Eve, I was angry with him for takin' you. I felt that he took advantage. It wasn't fair—you finally got that school and deserved time to grow. Instead, he took you as his own. Hid you. I wanted you freed from him." He licks his dry lips and I can feel my face turn down. "Come on, doll, you were just a kid." He fidgets with his collar.

"Angelo, what me and Vincent had wasn't just some small little fling." I am angry and shocked that he would ever be so dismissive. "We were in love. Real love. The soul-shattering, once-in-a-lifetime kind."

"But Eve, you were a baby. And so was Vincent. What's love between two kids? Losing your virginity under the stars?"

Shock moves through my insides, but he continues, backtracking to explain. "You know, that love that feels intense, but then you take time apart from each other and the dust settles and really, it was all just surface?"

I turn away and he shifts his chair, leaning closer. "I'm not saying it didn't feel serious, but I figured you were a lovesick child. Vincent is magnetic; we all know that. He's all brains and looks and power. I figured you'd leave and find someone else to take his spot. Someone who doesn't have gang connections for God's sake."

"You've got gang connections, Angelo, and I still love you. Or have you forgotten?"

"Doll, you know I fuckin' regret it every damn day. I was a kid when I got into it with the Borignones and now I'm stuck paying 'em and helping 'em 'til the day I die. They ruined my goddamn life. Did I want them to ruin yours, too?"

"No, Angelo," I exclaim. "But..." I pause. "Vincent and I may have been young. But we were real. We were honest and open and it wasn't about where we came from or who we knew; it was more than that. I love him for who he is beneath the exterior and he felt the same—" I stop, swallowing hard. Vincent loved the old me. And he loves the new me, too.

"We read books together," I add, my voice cracking. "We studied; he helped me in my classes. We laughed. We spent months just talking and eating and making love. We used to dance together in his kitchen because he knew how much I loved to dance. He brought me to his gym to learn MMA. He always empowered me—"

Like an avalanche, my feelings for Vincent hit me so hard, I'm practically floored by the force of it. I love Vincent. Why am I running from him? How could I even consider letting him go? He isn't trying to take my life away from me. He wants the best for me, still. I don't want to run anymore.

They lied, but both of them thought it was the only way. And outside of that, they've always been honest. I want to forgive.

I move my hair over to one shoulder, gathering myself. "Regardless, you had no right to lie, Angelo. No. Right. You played with my life."

He drops his head for a moment. "I'm sorry for the lies." His eyes move to mine, watering. "So many times, I wanted to apologize to you, doll. But I figured it was just water under the bridge. You became an adult and made it so far in life." He lifts his hands, gesturing to the new me. "Fancy job and decent boyfriends and that nice apartment. You stopped asking about him," he shrugs. "I thought you just moved on."

"But I didn't. I never did." Desperation tinges my voice.

"So, you think you still love him?" he questions.

I nod my head *yes*.

He stands, taking his brown wallet out of the back pocket of his jeans before sitting back down again. Opening the worn-in leather, he pulls something out. "This is yours. Vincent stopped by the pawn-shop and gave it to me before he went into lockup. Wanted me to hold it for you." I put out my hand as the thin gold chain collapses into my palm. A gold crucifix shines on top of the golden pile.

"I hung onto it 'cause it made me think of you. It's yours again, doll, if you want it."

My hand stays open, eyes trained on the necklace sitting in the center of my hand.

"H-he tells me he's out of the fold," I tell Angelo.

"Yup." He bunches a napkin in his hand. "I don't know all the details, of course. But I know Tom stepped up. Antonio ain't happy about it, either. It's all anyone talks about these days—how the prince left his throne." He lifts a hand, pushing his hair back. "Antonio's gotten a hell of a lot crazier, too, since Vincent left. Anyways, maybe you gotta give it another chance. No one's a kid anymore. If you still feel it with Vincent, who am I to say otherwise?"

The waiter comes to take our order, but my stomach is rolling; there's no way I can eat right now. "I have to go, Angelo. I need to call him." My chest squeezes as I finally clutch the necklace in my warm palm, swinging my head toward the door. Even if I don't know all the details of how we'll make it work, I can't walk away.

Angelo lifts his hand, telling me to wait. "And I'm sorry. With all my heart, doll, I'm sorry I lied. All I can say is I thought it was the right thing. For *you*." He opens both his hands to me, pleadingly.

"Okay. I'm going to go now though, all right?"

We stand up and hug before I hesitantly pull away. Dropping the necklace into the small zipper pocket of my purse, it now sits beside the silver boot charm that I never leave home without.

"Bye, Angelo."

"Always love you, doll."

I pull out my cell phone as I move to the door. I have to call Vincent—now. I need to hear his voice. He has to know I love him. I still don't have all the answers, but I can figure those out. He'll give me the time I need. He just needs to know I'm in this with him.

The city streets pass in a blur, tears clouding my vision as I run through the hectic blocks filled with people. Upper East Side moms push wide strollers with huge wheels. People returning from work are hustling to cross the street before the light changes. Rumpled suits wave down cabs. I forgot about the New York City hustle, and the feeling is both heart-pounding and claustrophobic. I practically trip over a kid scootering on the sidewalk in my haste to get to Janelle's faster.

The phone rings and rings, but Vincent doesn't pick up. Taxis honk like mad at a traffic jam ahead. One Starbucks turns into the fourth I've seen. Still, he hasn't answered. *Where is he?*

22

VINCENT
Thirty Minutes Earlier

I DROP myself at the bar while Sam Hunt blares on the speakers, taking my phone out of my pocket and leaving it on the old bar top. I'm looking forward to getting completely hammered. I don't make a habit of it, but now that Eve basically told me she isn't ready to commit, I feel like this is the only viable option. My phone rings, blinking red. Checking the caller ID, I see it's Slade.

"Yo," I answer.

"Hey man. Where you at?"

I lift my chin to the bartender, trying to get his attention. "Come join me for some drinks. I'm at The Blue."

Turning my head around, I spot the table Eve and I were at just a few hours earlier. My stomach clenches. I should have found a different bar, but coming here is second nature at this point.

His voice comes out scratchy; I can barely make out his voice through the static. "Be the-r- la—" The line cuts out.

Christ, but I need to find a way to get better cell phone service out here. It's annoying as hell. Hanging up, the bartender moves in front of me. I order myself a Jack and Coke.

I finish my first drink when Slade drops into the seat next to mine.

"Dude, what the fuck happened? Eve ran off like she was heading to a goddamn funeral." He raises a hand and the bartender nods in acknowledgement. "Oh, and she didn't go to L.A."

"What the fuck you talking about?" I turn to face him.

"Dropped her off at the regular airport. She went to New York City."

"She must have gone home to talk with her sister. And Angelo." I grab my glass, squeezing it so hard my knuckles hurt.

"You gonna tell me what happened?" Slade asks before ordering his drink. I go through the general outline of events, ending with the shitty way I dropped her off in front of the hotel. Repeating it like this, out loud, makes me realize that I may have seriously fucked up.

"Listen, brother." He clears his throat. "She's worked pretty fuckin' hard to get where she is right now. You gotta understand that. You can't just throw it all at her and expect her to say *yes*."

My heart beats erratically. "You don't get it. I've waited for an eternity. And she hates her job, anyway. There's nothing out in L.A. for her. If she wants, she can do law out here, too." I sound like I'm making excuses, but still, it's the truth.

"Come on, man. That may be right, but it's gotta be a conversation. Not an edict."

"It's been long enough," I grumble. "If she wanted—" I close my mouth, dropping my head into my hands and pulling on the ends of my hair. "I should call her. Apologize again. Ask one more time if—"

"No. Just chill and let her work it out. She'll come to you when she's ready." He pats me on the back. "No doubt."

I exhale, long and slow. He's right. How could I have given her the cold shoulder after telling her to end her career? I went about it all wrong. I curse under my breath, rubbing my face. I'm goddamn impulsive. She didn't say she loves me, but I know she does. Of course, I know. I was supposed to go slow. But instead of keeping up that pace, I ran over her. I shake my head, angry at myself.

We drink together in silence until Slade stands up, dropping money on the bar. "Wanna head out?" he asks.

"Nah, not yet."

He leaves, and I continue to agonize.

I try to relax, bringing forward memories of Eve.

SHE'S TRYING to sit up in bed, but I keep grabbing her waist, pulling her down to me.

"Vincent, I've gotta get to class!" She giggles. Again, she tries to get up, but I don't let her. Throwing her on top of me as if she were my own personal blanket, I wrap my arms around her back.

"Need you, babe," I grumble.

"And I need an A in Ethics." I can feel her smile against my chest.

I sink my teeth into her shoulder and she cries, "Ouch!" My tongue laves the mark. Love how she tastes. Even though I can't see her, I feel her epic eye-roll.

"I'll tutor you," I move my lips to her neck. "You'll get the A; I promise. Skip class."

She struggles to get free, but I only laugh.

"There's got to be a way to get out of your hold."

She's turning angry, and I love her angry face. I turn us around so that I'm straddling her. She lets out a huff of annoyance. I place my large hand around her wrists, locking them above her head. She immediately quiets.

"I'm not so sure that's possible. Seeing as I'm over a foot taller than you." I trail my palm down to the valley between her breasts, moving down the curves of her hips. "Much heavier than you, too." I let go of her hands as I lift her bottom half into the air, bringing myself to the edge of the bed.

"You never play fair, Vincent." She tries to maintain composure. As usual, she knows what I want. Her eyes are trained on me as I stare at her body hungrily, dragging her soft white cotton underwear down her thighs...

A BLONDE TAKES the seat next to me, interrupting my dreaming. "Hey," she says in a sweet voice.

I ignore her, wanting to go back to my daydream, but she introduces herself to me anyway. "I'm Emma."

Turning toward her, she places a small pale hand on my arm. I stare down at her fingers, ready to pry them off. Before I can, I look up at her and see her smiling. Eve runs into my thoughts and the way I treated her today. The last thing I should do is be a dickhead to some innocent girl. She's wearing a cardigan for fuck's sake.

"What are you drinking?" She turns red, seemingly embarrassed by her forward behavior. She lifts her fruity-looking cocktail to her mouth before continuing. "I moved here last year from Idaho. My grandfather lives on the rez." Fuck, she's trying to make small talk. I gulp down my drink and ask the bartender for another.

"I live in town now," she continues, taking another sip. "I'm a teacher at the elementary school. Third grade." She pauses, staring at me hard as though she's trying to place me. "Wait a sec—are you Vincent Borignone? The Milestone?" Her voice and eyes are starstruck.

"Yup," I nod.

Girl's got a strange glint in her eye, but she keeps talking as if I'm some goddamn celebrity. I continue to act like I'm listening, as though I were a decent guy.

I press my lips together. Fuck, but I miss Eve so badly. She's probably with Angelo and her sister right now. I should just call him. But I can't interfere any more than I already have. Slade's right, anyway. She has to decide this for herself. Still, it's hard to sit back and wait when I know that she'd be happier doing something else. Doesn't she know I would never take things away from her? I always have and always will put her first, and I know she'd do the same for me.

I want to shift in my seat, but somehow, I can't move. It's as if my arms and legs are paralyzed. I try to kick out my feet again, but they do not budge. *What the fuck?*

I stare at my phone on the bar. It's blinking red. I see Eve's name on the screen; she's trying to call. I want to answer, but my body is no longer taking direction from my mind. *What is going on here?* I only had a few drinks, not enough to get me hammered like this. Sweat breaks out on my forehead as nausea turns my stomach.

"He's Vincent Borignone. Just confirmed it." I hear Emma smugly talk to someone behind me.

"Crow's gonna be thrilled we got him so quickly. Nice job, sweetheart." From my side-eye, I see money exchanging hands before a pair of strong arms pull me off my stool. Two men I don't recognize, both wearing leather vests, hold me by the shoulders. I want to get free, but it's a losing battle. My head lolls to the side as they grip me, lugging me out of The Blue. I can vaguely hear them tell the bartender they're my friends, here to get me home safely.

Moments later, I feel the warm Nevada air, and my entire world goes black.

23

EVE

IT'S BEEN over twenty-four hours of calling Vincent, but I can't get through to him. In my gut, I know something's wrong. He was angry and lashing out before I left. But after what he told me about the way he feels, I don't think he'd just stop answering. No. I know he wouldn't. I pace Janelle's small bedroom while she watches me with sadness in her eyes. She ordered sushi that's sitting in the kitchen, untouched. I can't eat.

I already spoke with Kimber, who can't get a hold of Vincent either. I called the number on the business card Slade gave me the day I came out to Nevada, but he also isn't answering.

I told Janelle all the details of what happened between me and Vincent. She hates him for everything he's put me through and swears she always will. Regardless, she's sitting with me as I stress out, and that has to be enough.

My phone rings and I answer without checking the caller ID. "Hello?" I pray to hear Vincent's voice.

"Eve. Something's up. It's Slade." His voice is clipped but calm.

"Is it Vincent?" I swallow, moving my free hand to my bottom lip.

"I've been trying to call him and he won't answer." My voice comes out in a rush. I can practically feel the mounting pressure in my head.

"You've gotta get out of New York tonight."

"W-why?" I stutter.

"There's a lot going on. Vincent's been taken, Eve. I'm sending a car right now to bring you to Teterboro airport. The jet will be waiting to—"

"Wait a second. Vincent's been taken?" I drop into Janelle's desk chair. "Where?"

I can hear his loud exhale over the phone. "I got a call from Tom. Turns out Antonio's anger over Vincent reached a crescendo. He hired the Boss Brotherhood to kill Vincent. They've got him now, most likely at their clubhouse in Nevada."

"But, why would he do that? Why would he—"

"—Tom tried to warn Vincent that Antonio was losing it, but he didn't want to listen. Antonio doesn't care about his son, Eve. Shit went south during the years Vincent was in lockup. And when Vincent came home and told his father he was backing out of the family, Antonio lost it."

Bile, like liquid acid, rises up my throat.

"You know the line, cut off your nose to spite your face?"

"Mmhmm," I manage to hum.

"Well, that's Antonio. He knows how important Vincent is for business. But he's mad, Eve. He's mad that Vincent walked away from him. Not because he gives a shit, but because no one walks away from Antonio Borignone. It's a loss of control. And to an egomaniac, nothing could be worse. Do you understand me? I'm sorry for rushing through this, but we don't have time right now. Vincent is in the hands of lunatics. You've gotta get him out of there."

"M-me?" My head spins.

"Yes. Antonio knows who I am and that I've got Vincent's back. The likelihood that the BB knows my face and that I'd be coming for Vincent is high. But you—you're unknown."

Janelle bends her knees to come face to face with me. "What's going on?" she mouths.

I widen my eyes and shake my head at her, but don't reply.

"I'm going to email you details so you can study on the ride over," Slade adds.

"What?"

"I was able to put together a map of the clubhouse. If you go in there as a girl looking for a wild night, there's a chance you can get into one of the bedrooms and then into the basement." His voice is confident, leaving no room for negotiation; this is Slade in his natural element, military training on point.

I turn my head to the floor, staring at the silver diamond pattern on the carpet.

"Eve?" His voice is urgent. "You in?"

My breath exits my mouth slowly as I gather my wits. If I go in there, I'll be risking my life. But without Vincent, there is no life. And regardless of the drama and pain of our past, I would never turn my back. Could never. No amount of self-knowledge and reflection can change the outcome of my choice because—Vincent.

"Okay," I respond, my mind made. "Send the car. I'm at Janelle's on—"

"I know where you are."

I hang up the phone. "Well?" Janelle asks curiously.

"Vincent's been taken." My voice comes out shaky as our eyes lock. "I'm going back to Nevada tonight. He's at some motorcycle clubhouse right now. Slade wants me to go in there and get him out, but I have to look like a girl there for the party. He has a plan—"

She raises her hand in the air, cutting me off. "Oh, fuck you Vincent Borignone!" she screams to the ceiling before training her angry gaze back on me. "You can't risk your life for his, Eve. I'm not letting you go."

"Janelle," I reply quietly. "I love him—"

"Love shouldn't mean that. Love shouldn't bring you down or kill you, for God's sake. And Eve, take a look at yourself. Nothing about you spells *club slut* looking for a good time with bikers."

"I'll figure it out—"

"No. I'm coming with you. You'll need help turning yourself into one of these girls and that's something I can do." Janelle jumps off her bed and immediately takes out a small duffle from her closet shelf and drops it onto the floor. Gathering her makeup cases from the bathroom, she places them into the bag before running back into her closet and removing clothes.

She pauses, turning back to me. "Pack your shit, Eve. And call that fucker, Slade. Tell him that I'm going to need his plane to bring me back here when I'm done with you. I've got appointments I can't miss."

"Janelle, I can't ask this of you. It's too much. It's too risky. I don't even know all the details—"

"The only one at risk right now is you. You're my sister. I'll be there to help you get ready and I want to see you walk out of there in one piece. Maybe I'll even come inside with you. Afterward, I'll come back to New York. As much as I despise Vincent, I love you more. If you're gonna do this, I'm there."

We leave the apartment together, taking the emergency steps to the lobby. The street corner is quiet. Minutes later, a black Escalade pulls up to the curb.

Janelle takes my hand and squeezes three times—our version of a promise. The tinted window opens. "Eve?" The driver's eyes dart from Janelle to me.

Without replying, Janelle opens the back door and climbs inside; I step in right behind her and shut it with a forceful *slam*.

24

VINCENT

W<small>HEN</small> I <small>COME TO</small>, I find myself on my knees in a dark and rank holding cell. My black T-shirt sticks to my skin, heavy and cold with salty sweat.

Moving my arms proves impossible; I seem to be connected to the wall behind me—the cuffs and chains feel like hard iron as I try to maneuver myself. I attempt to tug and pull with all my might—but the handcuffs bite into my wrists, making me cringe. I stop, knowing it's useless. A lesser man may yell or scream, but not me. Licking my cracked and dry lips, I wait patiently for whomever it is to show himself.

Sometime later, the light flips on, temporarily blinding me. I want to cower from the brightness, but instead, straighten my spine. My knees cramp from the position, but I show nothing but strength. A group of men in identical leather vests saunter into the cell, the door shutting behind them when none other than Crow steps up to where I'm kneeling. I come face to face with his legs, covered in tattered blue jeans.

"Welcome to hell, Borignone. No crew to back you now. No fists, either." He grabs the roots of my hair and pulls upward until our eyes lock. His pupils dilate from excitement.

His jaw is still fucked up, courtesy of me from the prison yard. I try not to smirk.

"What do you want?" My voice is firm. I may be tied up and at his mercy, but I'll never show weakness. There are some things I can't unlearn; being unshakeable in the face of a threat is one of them.

"What do I want?" he repeats mockingly, shaking his head to his crew like I just asked the most ridiculous question on earth. As though it's happening in slow motion, he turns toward me and strikes his black boot straight into my stomach. I double over, but my chains keep me from collapsing.

Leather vests surround me—a move meant to intimidate. There is no longer a doubt that these men want my blood and suffering. But to what end? Information? Death?

"The question is, Vincent, why did your father call me a few days ago, requesting I kill you?"

Before I can process his words, his fist rears back and slams into my face once. Twice. Three times. My pain threshold heightens— brass knuckles. I can feel the warm blood pouring thickly down my face. I blink, trying to replay what I heard amidst the physical agony.

"Men like you have no goddamn morals. No code of ethics," he shouts close to my ear, spraying spit into my beaten face. "When we're done with you, MOTHERFUCKER, you'll wish you had your father to answer to instead of us. Your time is up!" He's bouncing on the balls of his feet.

"The fact that I hate your guts and get to torture you before I kill you?" His laugh is slow and maniacal as he lifts his head to stare at the ceiling. "Bonus," he cries, his voice echoing around the small room. It doesn't take long for my eyes to swell shut. Darkness.

I hear the flick of a lighter before the smell of cigarettes hits my nose.

The hard butt of a gun slams across my face and more blood flows into my mouth.

I can hear the pounding of music somewhere above me as two

men push me forward until my arms are splayed straight. What feels like a hundred heavy boots begin kicking my back until I can barely inhale; my ribs are cracked.

The men pause, seemingly to take a break. Someone unceremoniously unchains me, and I crumble onto the cold ground. Her name pounds its way into my head. *Eve. She's my life.* Maybe my father will arrange to have her taken, too. I'm not afraid of my own death. But, I am afraid of hers. The idea of her dying is enough to take away my strength. Since I met her, she is the one who gives order to my life. Eve is stability amidst chaos.

I keep myself still, focusing my thoughts. "Please, Eve, forgive me. For everything I've done. Jesus, keep her safe." Nowhere other than with Eve have I ever felt peace.

I hear a *zipping* sound. My breath hitches as I feel a body step in front of me. I try to cling to the picture of her face, but my brain muddles from what is to come. She's sobbing in my arms after we made love on the floor of my office. Something slams down onto my knee—the *crack* shocks me until I see stars behind my eyes. I want to tell Eve not to cry, but she can't hear me. She's detaching. Am I screaming?

My stomach tightens and a smoke-like numbness spreads in my lower half until I can barely feel the blows.

I'm silent—checked out and taking the beating like the man I was raised to be. But when I feel the point of a sharp knife digging beneath my eye and carving its way down my neck, I roar.

25

EVE

JANELLE and I sit in the back of Slade's blue pickup truck as he drives to the Boss Brotherhood clubhouse. According to two of Slade's friends, who recently surveyed the scene, the party is raging tonight.

"Okay, so you got it all now, Eve?" Slade asks for the hundredth time.

"Yes," I reply with confidence. I know he's worried about me right now. I'm hopped up on a ton of adrenaline and feeling like I can take on the world.

"The club whores should help you, got it? Those girls know all the ins and outs. Find them first and make nice. They'll point out the important guys. But don't look threatening or they'll never let you in." He sounds like a drill sergeant.

"Right," I respond at the quick.

Clutching my full purse like a lifeline, I remind myself that everything I need is safely tucked away in this bag—goodies courtesy of Slade—loaded pistol, sharp knife, a handful of condoms, and two vials of pentobarbital, according to Slade it's a common barbiturate that will incapacitate a man. Of course, I also have my phone, and per Janelle's orders, a tube of red lipstick to reapply if necessary.

On the flight over, Slade sent me an email complete with attachments of the clubhouse map along with a detailed plan that I've since sworn to follow to the best of my ability. Operating under the assumption that Vincent is in one of their holding cells in the basement, it's my job to go in and get him out of there.

"Slade," Janelle calls out. "Are you sure me or one of your friends can't go in, too? I don't like the idea of her being alone in there."

"No," he replies forcefully. "The party is closed to any men who aren't either part of the club or typical hang-arounds. And your presence may lessen her chances of finding Vincent. It's more likely the men will see Eve as easy meat if she's alone and without a friend."

I turn to Janelle, squeezing her hand. "I'll be okay. Don't worry."

Janelle sits back and purses her lips. I know she's angry and worried, but there is no room for negotiation.

Slade turns up the rock music, Papa Roach blaring on his speakers. We're speeding; no one is out on the road right now other than us. Still, I wish I could snap my fingers and just get there already.

The phrase "time is of the essence" pops up in my head, a line I've used millions of times at work in relation to parties signing contract agreements within a stated time. I start to laugh, thinking about how ridiculous it is that I ever thought anything in this life could be time sensitive. Compared to this, that part of my life feels like a joke.

Slade turns his head back and forth between the road and the back seat. "You hanging in?"

I laugh harder, tears dripping down my face like thick drops of rain. "I'm f-fine." I don't even try to hold in it—I can't. Unfortunately, this crazy nervous laughter is something I never completely grew out of.

"She does this sometimes. Annoying as hell," Janelle voices loudly. Slade lets out an awkward chuckle, but unfortunately, it does nothing to stop my hysterical laughter.

About twenty minutes later, we pull into the dark driveway of a wooden ranch house in The Middle of Nowhere, Nevada. I grab the small mirror from Janelle's handbag and take a good look at the woman staring back at me. I'm not recognizable, not even to myself: blood-red lips, dark-brown eyes rimmed heavily with coal-black liner, and heavy foundation, two shades lighter than my natural skin tone. Contouring has my nose looking miniscule and cheekbones razor sharp. There is no other way to describe my look except to say that I'm *changed*. I'm about to clean the black mascara that smeared below my eyes when Janelle grabs my hand.

"Don't touch it. You look like a girl down for *anything*—it's perfect." The anger in her gaze is gone and in its place is confidence. "You got this, girl. Navigating this shit is in your blood. It's time to channel it now."

The *click* of the door unlocking is my cue. I pause to compose myself.

"I'm ready," I tell them both, voice sure.

"I'll be waiting by the emergency door out back. Once you have Vincent, text me—"

"I know, Slade. Trust me."

I turn to go when Janelle pipes up. "Eve? You better come back. I'm waiting for you."

I nod solemnly before swinging the door open and jumping out. The weather is warm and balmy and the night sky sprinkled in stars. Rows of black motorcycles line the front of the clubhouse like a foreboding fence.

I strut toward the front door full of attitude, bringing forth Blue House-girl-on-the-stoop. My boobs pour out of my slinky red tank top and my skirt is so short, I'm sure any of these guys could see the underside of my ass.

Janelle's clothes were obviously what I needed for a night like tonight. If she didn't come with me and bring all this stuff, I'm not sure how I would have made this work. After I changed, she did my makeup in the back seat of the car. She even packed a pair of sandals, if you can call a pair of patent-leather six-inch spike heels with a platform, a sandal. Janelle explained the entire outfit and shoes was from a Halloween costume party a few years ago called "pimps and hoes." *Whatever.* My sister turned me into sex on legs tonight and nothing else would have done it. I'm sure our mom would be proud.

The front door is flanked with two youngish-looking guys wearing white T-shirts beneath black-leather vests. They scan my body and I seductively purse my lips while pushing my tits out, making a visual promise. Luckily, after their eyes get their fill, they step aside.

"Come on in," the taller one says, his voice heavily laced with a southern twang.

I strut by them and walk straight to the bar, the smell of stale beer assaulting me. Guns N' Roses' "Sweet Child O' Mine" plays in the background as goosebumps erupt on my arms; I know it in my bones that Slade is right—Vincent is here, somewhere.

I act as though I'm holding back a smile as men turn their heads, rubbernecking to get a good look at me. A huge wooden swastika painted gold and red, hangs on the wall. It catches my eye and sickens me, but also serves to make my mission more real.

Seven years have gone by without Vincent. College. Law school. One man. Other men. But my hope never completely died; there was always a sliver of faith that he'd come back. That he didn't lie. That our love was real. And now he's so close. I can't let him go again —I *won't*.

I lean forward against the badly damaged wood—the words WHITE POWER etched deeply within and sticky from spilled drinks. My stomach clenches and I send a silent prayer to Janelle, thanking her for the heavy makeup that's lighter than my olive skin.

Looking to my left, there is a blonde girl with hair in high pigtails next to me. She's wearing a triangle American flag bikini top and ultra-tiny jean shorts. An opened beer rests happily in her hand.

"You're new here." She takes a swig. "I'm Heather. How did you hear about the party?" She smiles kindly.

"Met one of the guys at the supermarket. Told me to come on down." I shrug, my New York accent nice and sharp.

"Ohmygod are you from New York City? I love it there! Not that

I've ever been, but it's always been my dream." She bounces up and down excitedly. New York City is always a big hit with girls like these.

I stare at Heather, who may be called beautiful—if not for a wide and deep scar running from her nose to her ear. She caked her makeup for cover, but it didn't work. Her eyes are genuinely kind, though.

"Where are you from?" I need to keep the conversation rolling.

"Oklahoma. But I haven't been back there in years." She lets out a small and awkward smile before taking another long sip. "I'm with Guns. He takes care of me."

I click my tongue. "I could use that too, if you know what I mean. Haven't exactly had an easy go of it lately." I drop my head for a moment, my voice down and out.

"Oh, girl, I've been there." She touches my shoulder in solidarity. "You see that guy over there in the green baseball hat?" She moves closer to me, bringing her voice to a whisper.

I scan the room and immediately spot him. "Yeah," I reply. "You mean the one standing under the swastika?"

"Yeah. Him. He's the treasurer. But all the girls say he's into some crazy kinky shit. You're not into that, right?"

"No. No way." I shake my head vehemently.

"Unless you're real desperate, I would skip him. The guy next to him? That's Crow." Both our eyes widen, but for different reasons. I recognize his name from what Vincent told me about his time in prison. "He's the president and the one to latch onto. Got out of lockup six months ago and I know for a fact he isn't interested in the club whores who come and go often. He's always into new girls who haven't been touched by any of the other members." She's enthusiastic as if she likes the idea.

"Thanks, Heather." I smile wide. "I really hope he likes me."

"Oh, he will. You're exactly his type."

I stare at her a moment, wanting to take her by the hand and run her out of here. She's such a nice girl—and so young, too. She shouldn't be here.

"Oh!" she starts, interrupting my thoughts. "He's comin' over here. This may be your shot," she squeaks.

As luck would have it, the men move to my right. Heather takes that as her cue to leave.

"... bleeding out in the basement."

I inch closer, pulling out my phone and keeping my eyes trained on it while listening as keenly as my ears will allow.

"Let's head down in another hour or so. Let him sit in his own piss a while."

I hear a grunt that sounds like agreement. "Should we send one of the boys in there to watch him in the meantime?"

"Nah. No way in hell he can move." Dark laughter ensues.

My blood burns hot, but I don't freak out. Instead, I let out a breath of relief. My mind flickers to Vincent's face and I vow to be the greatest actress there ever was. That's my man they're talking about, *and he's alive.* I'm getting Vincent out of this hell hole.

Crow turns forward, presumably to order a drink. He rubs his forehead with his palm thoughtfully as I angle myself in a way so he can see me.

I catch his eye. Raising an eyebrow in appreciation and surprise, he takes a long slow look from my feet up to my face.

I smile, all coy, playing with Vincent's cross around my neck as I quickly read the patch on his vest for confirmation. Jackpot. Anger streams through me, but also something else—excitement. I want to take this asshole down. I loathe to think about the scar he gave Vincent in the yard, the story still making me ill.

He creeps up to my side and I give him another sexy smirk. He's tall. Not as tall as Vincent, but still big enough that I have to crane my neck up to see his face. Small brown eyes peer down at me through narrow slits, gazing as if I were a fresh piece of ass he can't wait to taste. His head is shaved smooth, showing bluish veins along pasty skin and a slightly crooked jaw. A dark swastika is tattooed on the front of his neck along with a set of numbers below. I feel a surge of hatred so strong, it outshines any possible fear.

I slide my tongue slowly across my front teeth, lips slightly parted, eyes trailing his body as though I like what I see. That's when I notice the collar on his white shirt is stained with what looks like blood splatter.

"Hey," he says in a raspy voice, leaning a tattooed forearm on the bar. His knuckles are bruised. "Having fun?"

"I am now." My voice is quiet enough to bring him closer. I need this to happen—quickly. There's no time to waste.

After a few seconds of eye contact, he turns his head. "Yo, Chub!" he yells to the big guy with a beard pouring people drinks. Chub immediately stops and turns to Crow, waiting for his command. "Natty Light," Crow simply states.

Chub's blue eyes widen before turning to a huge trash can and pulling out two beers, wet from condensation, and handing them to Crow.

"Glad you came tonight. Got a name?" He cracks a can, the *hiss* sharp and quick. I let my fingers cover his for just a moment before taking it for myself.

"Yeah. I've got one." My voice is seductive as I bring the drink up to my mouth nice and slow. There's noise all around us, but I'm completely focusing my attention on him. I want him to feel like a king right now.

"You gonna give it to me?" His thin lips quirk up.

"Depends on how badly you want it." I raise my eyebrows flirtatiously and he laughs out loud.

He moves closer to me. "Waiting, sweetheart. And a man like me doesn't like to wait. Even if it's from a sexy-as-fuck woman like you."

"Irina." My voice is soft as I look up into his eyes. The irony that I'm using my mother's name isn't lost on me.

"Crow."

I hum, the vibration fluttering around my lips.

His smile reaches his eyes. I can feel it—he actually likes me. "So, you ever ride?"

"Nope. I've always wanted to, though. Looks like fun." I cock my head to the side.

It's a few more minutes of small talk before he takes my hand and walks me out of the party, straight into the quiet white hallway where the bedrooms are located. I grip his damp hand tightly, as though I don't want to let go. He squeezes mine back, and I know I've got him just where I want him.

"Don't normally bring anyone back here." His voice is gruff.

Crow pushes open a door. Before stepping inside, I make a mental note that we're in the third room on the left. The light flicks on and I take stock of the situation. Queen-size mattress on a box spring pushed against the wall. Black sheets and two white pillows. A wooden cabinet in the corner with an old boxy TV perched on top. A small table in the corner.

We're alone.

The light is dim and yellow.

This is dangerous. Every internal alarm I have in my head is screaming for me to run. Not only is this man a complete stranger, but he has Vincent's blood on his shirt. Still, my heart tells me to stay clear and straight. Step one, get him relaxed. I go on hyper-focus, bringing forth everything I've got.

I purse my lips as my fingers lightly caress my breasts. I let my hands roam over my nipples; they harden under the thin fabric of my shirt. He grumbles like a pitiful dog.

"You want?" I'm all innocence.

"Fuck yeah," he grunts, voice hoarse from desire. Unbuckling his belt, he pulls down his blue jeans, kicking off his ratty black boxers next. Sitting his pale and scrawny ass down on the edge of the bedspread, his white legs part. I walk to the corner of the room, placing my purse on the small table. Opening the zipper pocket, I pull out one vial of pentobarbital along with a condom.

I turn to him seductively, slowly walking forward with the foil packet in my fingers.

He's grinning excitedly and hardening; I try not to gag. Dropping down to my knees before him, I come face to face with under six inches of scrawny dick. The scratchy carpet rubs against my knees, keeping me on my game.

"Close your eyes," I say in a sing-song voice, a request full of promise. I inch my face forward and hold my breath, exhaling as he shuts his eyes. Without any hesitation, I shoot him in the thigh with the needle.

First comes shock — wide eyes and a mouth open in an "Oh." Anger flashes in his face but before he can act, he drops back onto the bed, disabled.

"Bye motherfucker," I hiss.

I'd punch him, but there's no time. Quickly standing, I grab my bag and focus on getting down to the basement. Opening the bedroom door and looking both ways to make sure no one is around, I count the fourth door to the left from the bathroom, which according to Slade's map, should be the basement entrance.

I open it. There's a long narrow staircase—dark and full of shadows. I move onto the first step, shutting the door behind me and praying there are no cameras trained on me. Then again, nothing about this place is high-tech or organized. I'd say these guys are sloppy, especially on a night like tonight when there's a party going. I shiver as I walk. Nothing but dead silence surrounds me.

What if someone other than Vincent is down here? There could be another man. What if one of the bikers is hanging around? Fear tries to grip me, but I tell it to shut up. Reopening my purse, I take out my loaded gun.

I scurry my way down the steps until I reach the bottom. Light is pouring out from beneath another door. I wrench it open with one hand, my gun lifted high in the other.

The heavy stench of grime and rot coats the air and my stomach twists. Shuffling inside and looking left to right, I keep my pistol up in front of me.

Small room. Old walls. White paint, chipped. Scattered garbage. A random red and silver Nike sneaker alongside an empty Domino's box. Moving forward, my eyes dart around as I kick trash out of my way. Another door. I open it.

It's a small dark room. My eyes adjust. The first thing I see is something large, crumbled on the floor. The smell in here is burned copper. Is it blood? Silence is everywhere.

"Vincent?" I run forward, dropping to my knees. My heart stutters. He's lying in a fetal position. I touch his skin; it's clammy and cold. There are chains behind him, but thankfully, he isn't locked up.

His body is unmoving. I bring my hands to his back. "Baby?" My fingers move to my mouth as I stifle a cry. "Vincent...Vincent." I whisper his name.

Is he dead? I gently push his blood-matted hair away from his face. I must be in shock. My mind isn't fully comprehending this scene. On instinct, I touch his chest. I can feel a slow and ragged breath—it's barely there.

Hours ago, I was sitting at an Italian restaurant with Angelo. And now I am in the basement of a motorcycle clubhouse rescuing Vincent, who could die. It's as though I'm an outsider looking in— there is no more logic to the storyline of my life.

Pulling out my phone, I turn on the flashlight and shine it directly on his face. There's a gash from his eye down to his lip, still oozing.

"What did they do to you?" His eyes are closed. I wish they'd open.

Looking down to his hands, there's just so much blood. His pinky is gone and bone protrudes. I gasp, unable to find a single word to explain this feeling. I want to throw my arms around him and scream —rally against fate, destiny, whatever!

Still, he's alive.

I gather myself, knowing it's time for action.

"Don't worry, baby. I'm getting you out of here." I kiss his bloodied head before lifting my phone.

Me: Basement. It's bad. With Vincent.

Slade: Find door now. I'm west.

I shut my eyes for a brief second, refocusing. It must be on the other end of where I am.

I stand up and run forward, leaving Vincent behind. Pulling open a door, I find a closet—full of guns and ammunition. Their arsenal. And left wide open? *God.* I turn my head around, sweat beading on my forehead. Sloppy or not, these men are dangerous and armed.

"Where the hell is the door? How much time do I have before

they come back down? What if Crow wakes up? I should have shot him twice...fuck!"

Another door. I open it. Fresh night air pours in along with Slade.

"Follow me." I'm on autopilot. The door slams shut behind us with a *clang*.

We're back to Vincent. Slade drops to his haunches, deadlifting my life in his strong arms. We walk outside and straight into his black truck, where Vincent's head is placed on my lap in the back seat. I barely notice that Janelle is in the front. She speaks, but I can't hear her.

"I'm here, now," I tell Vincent, my tears dripping from my eyes onto his face. If I were in a fairytale, my tears, full of love and heartbreak, would shatter the spell. The water would drip from my eyes and onto his face and just like that, he'd be brought back to life. But this isn't a fairytale. This is life in all its grittiness.

"Vincent," I start, my voice croaking. "I'm so sorry for leaving. I love you so much," I hiccup, leaning forward and kissing his bloody head. "I can't believe you were unarmed," I quietly wale, remembering being happy at the fact he wasn't carrying. How stupid was I? "I'm never leaving you again. Ever. Please stay with me. Please, baby."

He hasn't budged—not once.

I keep his hand on my bare thigh. For a moment I think he's moving, but I realize his body is only shaking with the car's movements. I pull him closer to me.

We get to the hospital and it all moves in a rush. Vincent is taken away and I collapse into Janelle's arms, the stress finally engulfing me.

"He's safe now, Eve. He'll be all right. You did it." Her soft arms keep me from falling. "Slade's with you now. I'm gonna call a cab to take me back to the plane, okay? I'll be back when I can." She kisses my head before squeezing my hand three times and hands me off to Slade, crying her own tears.

I burst into sobs as we make our way into the stark-white waiting room; the bright lights make me dizzy. Slade brings my small body close to him. I'm so cold. He nestles me tighter. At one point, I look up into his eyes. He's so hard and complicated, but there's something incredibly good about him, too. He's so solid from the outside in. If I ever had a brother, it would have been nice to have one like this.

Hours pass. My heart feels like it's leaking. I finally notice Slade's clothes are bloodied. Mine are, too. Vincent's blood. *Oh God.* Slade tells me to wait a minute. He leaves me alone in the waiting room and returns with two sweatshirts, presumably from the gift shop, and hands one to me. Sliding it over my body, I shiver.

A nurse shuffles out in a white uniform, asking for the family of Vincent Smith. Slade immediately gets up. I'm too dazed to ask any questions about Vincent's alternate name. My anxiety of what will come of Vincent has me close to incapacitated, but I lean on Slade's strength to pull me forward.

The nurse takes us into a small and quiet waiting room when a doctor enters; he looks sixteen, give or take a few years. Is this a joke? Vincent's life is in the hands of a... teenager? I blink hard, trying to cool myself down. Slade's warm hand grabs mine in solidarity.

"Who are you two?" the doctor asks, staring us down condescendingly as if he were the adult and we're bad kids in need of punishment.

My annoyance at this child-doctor has me vibrating. "Vincent is my brother," I reply full of attitude, crossing my arms in front of my chest defensively. I will kick this kid's ass! He stares at me skeptically, eyes zeroing in on my outfit. I look down at myself, noticing that I'm not in one of my tailored suits. I look like a hooker in a man's sweatshirt. But so what? He should be giving me information, not judging me. I fume. What a fucking asshole! The heat of indignation continues to rise as Slade pulls me backward, slightly behind him.

"We appreciate you helping Vincent, doctor. Can you tell us his status?" Slade's voice is all business—exactly what we need. I exhale, letting him take the reins.

"Either of you care to tell me why your *brother* is sliced up like a Thanksgiving turkey?"

"We just found him like that," Slade shrugs a shoulder, his huge muscles bunching beneath his shirt. He's got black circles under his eyes and dark scruff lining his jaw. He looks highly threatening. I cringe, realizing that our current state coupled with Vincent's situation doesn't bode well. I'm sure the cops will come to investigate this eventually. I look up at the doctor as laughter starts to bubble up again in my throat. It's all just too much. Slade gives my hand a squeeze which says: 'you better not fucking laugh right now.' I swallow it down obediently and drop my head to the white-tiled floor.

"Well," the doctor starts, lifting up his blue pen and clicking it twice. "Your brother's pinky is severed. He has a deep knife wound down his face. His cheekbone is broken..."

I stare at the doctor blankly. The entire scenario feels surreal. I can hear the words leaving his mouth, but nothing sinks in.

"...we've put him on serious antibiotics to cure infections—knives can be extremely dirty. He's also got broken ribs, a shattered kneecap, and of course, there's the severe head trauma..."

I step closer, trying to hear better—for some reason, his words sound muffled.

"...we've put him in a coma in order to decrease the intracranial pressure."

I blink. Slade clears his throat. "And how long do you think it will be until you can remove him from the coma?" His dark brows furrowed together. "You will remove him, right?"

"Well, that all depends. I'll monitor the numbers and when it's safe, I'll turn off the sedation."

I find a large white circular clock on the wall. It's five minutes after four in the morning.

"A-are we talking hours? Days? Months?" Desperation has my voice cracking. The doctor may be a kid, but right now, he's all I've got.

"You never really know." He shrugs his shoulders sadly. "Hopefully it won't be more than a few days."

Slade and I turn to each other again before looking back at the doctor. "C-can we go see him?" I cower, embarrassment finally hitting me over my indecent state of dress. The sweatshirt hits my legs in such a way that it looks like I'm not wearing pants.

"Sure," the doctor replies. "He's in 304."

"Is he in any pain?" My voice comes out crackled with intense emotion as I wrap my arms around my middle.

"No. He's not." His voice is decisive.

Slade and I take the elevator to the third floor. The hallway is cold, white, and completely sterile.

We walk into the room. The man in the bed can't be Vincent. It just can't be. His head is bandaged. I can hear the heart monitor beeping. He's technically alive, but he's... gone.

26

EVE

Three Days Later

"HOLY SHIT, EVE." Lauren walks into the hospital room wearing tight denim jeans and a sexy, off-the-shoulder black T-shirt. A jumbo black Chanel purse is slung over a small shoulder as she pulls a black carry-on suitcase with a small duffle on top behind her. Parking everything in the room's corner by the window, I realize she's here— for me, and I burst into a set of fresh tears.

She quickly moves to me and bends down, hugging me to her chest. "Babe, we gotta get you out of here. Showered. Changed. And food." She's whispering, as though she's afraid to bother Vincent. I'd tell her that he won't wake up no matter what, but the words won't leave my lips. It's too painful.

"N-no." I shake my head. "I c-can't leave him."

"Yes, you can." Pulling out a tissue from the small white cardboard box by Vincent's bed, she hands one to me.

"How did you know to come here?" I sniffle.

"Janelle called—all shady, telling me not to let anyone know I was coming here. But she was so worried about you." She places a hand on my back. Janelle and Lauren have never met, but after the hundredth time of calling my office and speaking to Lauren, they developed an easy friendship.

She takes stock of my outfit and grimaces. I'm wearing a pair of black leggings, a loose yellow T-shirt, and a pair of black rubber flip-flops courtesy of Slade. After refusing to leave Vincent's side, he stopped at Target and grabbed these clothes and even a toothbrush and face wash for me. Two days ago, the clothes were clean and I was physically back to a semi-normal state. Now, not so much. Adding insult to injury, I have leftover mascara under my eyes that won't come off.

"I went to your apartment and picked up what you need." She points to the rolling suitcase.

"Thank you," my voice shakes. "I don't even—" I pause, feeling an incredible amount of guilt. Lauren is better to me than I deserve. We've worked together for so long and I never gave her enough credit. Never let her into my life the way she deserved.

"Shh," she rubs my back. "Let me pull out clean clothes so you don't have to leave here looking disheveled." Unzipping the bag, she removes a pair of soft navy sweatpants, a fresh nude bra and under-wear, and a white cotton T-shirt.

"What did Janelle tell you?" I clutch the clothes to my chest.

"Just that you and Vincent have a long past and he is seriously hurt in the hospital. Also, that you're desperate for clothes and a shower." She stares at my outfit and rumpled, disheveled appearance.

"A-are you mad I didn't tell you about him?" I swallow hard, my mouth feeling dry. I really don't want her to be angry with me. I sniffle.

"Don't tell me you're about to cry again? Ohmygod!" She shakes her head and rubs the beautiful solitaire diamond necklace she always wears around her neck. "Eve doesn't cry. Eve is strong and makes shit happen. And to answer you, no, I'm not mad. I know how weird it must have been having him as a client. And all you were dealing with, making sure none of the DBC wouldn't catch on. I mean, if they knew about the two of you, they would have pounced. They're disgusting."

Her understanding has me breaking down in another round of tears. We joked about the way they treated me, but both of us knew that none of it was actually funny.

"I was horrible in that office," I mutter, hiccupping. "I'm so sorry—"

"Oh, please," she waves a manicured hand in front of her face. "There was no other way to be. It was like a sanctioned cage fight. Now, go to the bathroom and clean up so we can get out of here for a little while and you can get some fresh air."

I have such a good friend in her. Still, I don't think I'm ready to leave Vincent's side. "I'm afraid to leave him alone. What if he needs me?"

She looks at him sadly. "He's under for now. The best thing you can do is take care of yourself. If you don't, you won't be well enough to care for him when he comes out of this."

I haven't showered or eaten in days and the truth is, I feel on the verge of collapse.

"Okay. Not for long, though." My voice is full of hesitation.

She tucks a long blonde hair behind her ear. "By the way, Jonathan is freaking out. His biggest client is quiet for days, and then you email him about a leave of absence yesterday?" She blows out a puff of air. "I didn't tell him anything, though. Janelle swore me to silence."

"Jonathan can go screw himself." I feel a combination of anger and anxiety. This morning I let him know via email that I had a family emergency and wouldn't know how long I'd need. He replied, but I didn't read it. "This leave will likely turn into my quitting."

Lauren's eyes pop open in surprise before settling in understanding. "Honestly, I don't blame you. You've been dealing with way more than you should. All that harassment. It's seriously out of control the way they treat you in that godforsaken place. You'd think it was still 1987." She shakes her head. "By the way, I emailed the Kids Learning Club for you before I got on the flight over."

"Oh shit, I totally forgot." Guilt crashes through me that I didn't contact them right away.

"Don't worry." She rubs my arm. "They've got people filling in for you. Right now, it's just about the hottie in the hospital bed." She winks and I have to consciously stop myself from laughing out loud.

Lauren takes a chocolate brownie protein bar from her purse and opens the foil wrapper before handing it to me. I slowly bring it to my mouth. Taking a bite, my stomach clenches. Nausea follows.

I must make a face because she pulls the bar from my hand. "You'll have to eat slowly. Actually, why don't you clean up first?"

I swallow, wondering how I manage to eat this garbage every morning. If I never ate another protein bar again, it wouldn't be soon enough. Moving to Vincent, I bend my head to his left hand, kissing each of his fingers slowly, one at a time.

"I'll be back soon, okay baby?" I press his warm palm against my forehead before gently placing it back to his side.

Making my way to the bathroom, I take off my dirty clothes and rinse my face and hands with soap and water. Sliding on my own fresh things, a horrible thought crosses my mind: Does changing mean I'm moving on? "No," I tell myself out loud. "I'm not moving on. I'm only cleaning up. I'll be back—soon."

"Let's go, honey," Lauren calls, hurrying me. On shaky legs, I step out of the bathroom and into the hallway. Two huge guys sitting in chairs by the door notice me and stand at attention. I suck in a breath of air, scared shitless that these guys are from the BB. *Did they find me?*

"Hey Eve," the bigger one starts gently, raising his arms as if surrendering. His navy spandex T-shirt highlights his muscles. "I'm Cole, and this is Ax. We're friends of Slade." With their military haircuts and serious demeanors, they've got armed forces written all over them. "Ax will accompany you wherever you need to go."

We all look up to see Slade marching down the wide hallway toward us. His back is straight, gait quick, and he walks with purpose.

"Hello," he turns to Lauren, faltering for a moment as he takes her hand in a friendly shake. "Slade," he introduces himself, a redness creeping up his neck. "Janelle told me she asked you to come out." He gives her a genuine smile.

Her jaw slackens. "Y-yeah. No problem," she stutters. "I love you. I mean—Eve! I love Eve!" She lets out a nervous giggle and I bite my cheek.

"Good friends are important," he replies calmly, ignoring her slip.

"Eve, let's talk a second before you go." Slade moves back into Vincent's room, waiting for me to follow.

The moment I re-enter, I can't help but look again at Vincent's still body. My chest constricts.

"Eve," he states, bringing my attention back to him. "A lot has happened in the last few days. I didn't want to bombard you so soon, but now that you're leaving the hospital, you need to know."

"Um, okay," I reply nervously.

"Antonio found out that Vincent escaped the Boss Brotherhood alive. According to Tom, the moment Antonio heard, he ran out of New York City like a bat outta hell. Went rogue. The entire Borignone mafia is on hold right now—no one's sure what's going on."

My hands fly up to cover my mouth.

"Crow was shot in the head yesterday."

"What?" I exclaim in shock.

"Yes," Slade moves his hands to his narrow waist. "It was Antonio, angry that Crow didn't complete the job. He's out for blood. And at this point, it's no secret he blames you for Vincent leaving the family, and apparently, for everything else that's gone wrong."

My heart pounds so hard, I can feel it in my throat.

"Be thrilled that Crow is dead. Otherwise we would have had to worry about him finding out who you are or potentially coming after you."

"Well, what about the rest of the BB?"

"Vincent was only a job to them. Their main focus right now is most likely avenging Crow's death."

I want to feel relieved, but Antonio is the bigger threat. "D-does Antonio know Vincent is here? In this hospital?" My voice shakes.

"Well, I don't know just yet, which is why I want you protected."

He presses his mouth together tightly. "You've been so attached to Vincent, you never left to notice I've had his roomed guarded all this time."

I need to take a moment to think. Everything happened too quickly. I never took a second to consider anything other than Vincent. There will be massive repercussions. What kind of backlash could fall on me, or even Janelle back in New York? These gangs are known to intimidate family.

He points to the door. "I've got one of my boys staying here to watch over Vincent and another to be with you, wherever you go. There's a third, his name's Gavin. He'll be doing hospital nightshifts."

"Okay," I reply, my voice small. "Can you arrange a guard for Janelle, too?" I bite my bottom lip. If he says no, I'm sure there's a bodyguard service I can call.

"I've already taken care of that. She'll have Jose by this evening."

"Does she know about it?" I raise my eyebrows nervously. I know the next time I speak with her, I'm going to get hell.

"Yes, I called her yesterday." He tries not to laugh. "That sister of yours is something else." He smirks. "She chewed me out."

"Oh, God." I raise my face to the ceiling. "Are you okay?"

He chuckles. "Don't worry about me, Eve. I can handle her."

"So, she agreed to the bodyguard?"

"Yes. Eventually, she did."

He reaches into his pocket, pulling out a set of keys. "This is for his trailer so you can stay there. I'll text you the address." Nervously, I take them from his hands; the keychain is cold in my palm. I lift it, noticing a small silver boot dangling off the ring.

"Slade, what's this?" My voice catches in my throat as I stare at the charm.

"Oh," his voice is casual, "Vincent picked that up back in New York. He told me he gave the original one away before leaving for prison. When he got out, he bought an identical one for himself."

He gave it to me. It wasn't an accident. Vincent must have wanted me to know that he'd follow me anywhere. And...he did. He came back. But now, he's gone. I can feel the room start to spin.

"Whoa, whoa." Slade pulls me toward him before gently lowering me into a chair. He sits on his haunches in front of me so we're eye level, keeping his hands on my arms to steady me. A terrible thought runs through my head.

"He'll come out of this, Eve," he says, reading my mind. "It's time to be brave. I know you're beat up, but you can't give in to that feeling."

I look directly at him, wanting to agree. But I don't. If Vincent doesn't make it through, I don't think I can go on.

Once I'm steady, Slade helps me to stand and passes me off to Lauren, who links a skinny arm in mine.

"Ax is going to accompany you ladies." Slade keeps his face passive.

"Okay," she smiles wide, "nice to meet you." Waving, Lauren gives him her best cool and calm goodbye.

"Slade got me a hotel room for the night," she whispers conspiratorially as we walk toward the hospital exit. "You think maybe he'll join me if I'm feeling lonely?" She raises her eyebrows and giggles, but I don't reply.

"I think it's where you stayed when you originally came over. Was it nice?" She's trying hard to be friendly and lighthearted. I want to scream at her—tell her that right now isn't the time to be fucking chipper. But I collect myself, knowing my exhaustion and sadness are talking.

"It's beautiful." My voice is machine-like, without intonation. With every step, I feel farther away from Vincent; the distance making my anxiety rise. I should go back to him. I don't want to leave.

"You know what?" I start, my mind officially changed.

She stops walking and faces me. "No," she shakes her head. "You aren't backing out. A shower and a hot meal will do you good. No one is telling you to leave his side. Just take a little break, okay? Plus, think of my life. Janelle will kill me if I don't take you out of here."

Before I know it, Ax is helping us inside the large black Escalade. I'm silent as the driver brings us to the hotel. Lauren, God bless her, is her usual talkative self, keeping him occupied.

I stare out the window, picturing Vincent and me on his bike. Gripping his back while the wind blows over us. The warmth in his eyes when we're in bed. They lighten when he's happy but turn near black when he's emotional.

The car stops in front of the hotel, shaking me out of my daydream.

After a steaming shower, a few bites of a vegetable omelet via room service, and Lauren insisting on blow-drying my hair—two hours have passed. I'm clean, but my emotions feel like roadkill.

We set ourselves up by the wood fire pit on the small terrace. I promised Lauren I'd spend three full hours away from the hospital to revive. The entire setting is the epitome of calm and relaxing, but my heart won't settle. I'm staring at the orange flames as Lauren sips a glass of cold wine from the minibar, likely scanning her social media pages.

She sits forward, putting her empty glass down by the fire. "Okay. Talk to me."

I tell her the whole story. She cries along with me, insisting that love will conquer all. It's exactly the type of thing I'd expect Lauren to say, and I love her for it.

We turn quiet as I stare at the darkness. The mountains, so monstrous in size, can no longer be seen. The night is jet-black with nothing but stars pebbling the sky. I wish I had never left Vincent's side after The Blue. If I only said yes to him right away. I touch my chest, my heart actually squeezing as tears refill my eyes. *I can't lose him.*

And oh, *God*, this shit with Antonio. It took a few hours, but Slade's warnings finally sink in. I stand up and move inside the room, opening my purse. My gun is still here. I clutch it in my hands the same way I did all those years ago in the Blue Houses. But this time, I'm not afraid to use it.

My phone rings and I jump from the sound. I slide the gun back into the bag before taking out my cell. It's Janelle on FaceTime.

I click ACCEPT, and Janelle's face pops up in the center of my screen, blonde hair in perfectly messy waves, face crazy angry.

"Holy fuck, Eve!" Her free hand flies up in the air. "I want you to know how pissed off I am that you haven't called me in three days." Her teeth clench.

"You spoke to Slade though, right?" I know he already told her I'm just fine. And right now, I don't have it in me to argue.

"Yeah, I did." Her reply is both grudging and sad. "Is Lauren with you, now?"

"Yeah, she got to the hospital a few hours ago and brought clothes and forced me to come shower. Thanks for having her come, by the way. And for everything, Janelle. I owe you." I turn my head, seeing Lauren with her head bowed reading on her phone.

"Lauren is seriously the shit," Janelle states. "I'm glad she was able to come. Anyway, move your phone up and down. I want to make sure you're still in one piece."

"Oh, come on—" I nag.

"Just do it. Make your momma happy."

I roll my eyes before moving the phone so she can see my toes up to my face. "Happy now, Granny?"

"I said *momma*, not granny, you bitch." She chuckles and a small snort escapes my mouth.

"As you know, I'm back and alive and fine and Vincent's—" My voice cuts off. I can't say it. I gasp, tears taking the place of words.

Her mouth turns down. "I know. You love him. Just relax. He's...he's going to be okay."

While her words are hopeful, I know she has doubt. In the world we grew up in, life isn't just given and expected to continue until you're old. People die—all the time. Vincent dying young, especially considering the life he used to lead, shouldn't be a surprise.

"I don't know, Janelle."

I wish I could, but I can't escape her pitiful gaze.

"And what about Antonio?" Her voice is gentle. "If you ask me, he's the bigger issue and the looming threat. I've got Mr. Beef watching TV right now in my living room and eating Chinese take-out. Tell me you got a plan?"

"Plan?" I ask her, confused.

"You've seen a million *Law and Order* episodes. Can't you like, go after the bad guy and put him in jail for life? You're the hot blonde lawyer, but obviously, with dark hair." She looks at me as if putting Antonio behind bars is the simplest thing in the world. "He probably has a laundry list of bad shit he's done that the feds can't catch, right?"

"I can help you!" Lauren screams into my ear. I shudder from surprise; the girl obviously has ninja powers because I didn't even realize she was next to me.

I lick my lips, brain turning. "I don't know, Janelle," I say to the screen. "Let's see."

Lauren brings her face to the camera. "Whenever Eve says 'let's see,' what she really means is, 'I'm doing it!'"

* * *

I PUT my hand in Vincent's hair, brushing back the dark strands as my nails graze against his scalp; I know he loves when I do this.

"Vincent," I whisper into his ear. "I want to quit the firm. Because I hate it. You were right. They treat me horribly. And I took it all because I thought there wasn't a choice. But there is a choice, and I'm making it now." My hands move to my neck. I rub his cross between my fingers.

Standing up, I pull out a small, portable MacBook. Opening the screen on Vincent's bedside table, I begin typing my resignation.

Once I start, the words flow. I detail the harassment and intolerable work conditions I endured as an associate at the prestigious firm. I'm not looking for any kind of monetary compensation. Instead, I want to specifically pinpoint the failed options for reporting, explaining that I was scared to be punished and therefore stayed silent. My hope is for other women never to have to undergo this abuse.

Draft after draft gets written until I click SEND. It's after two o'clock. I pass out in the wooden chair beside Vincent, holding his hand in mine.

The following morning, I'm leaning my head on Vincent's chest when Lauren walks inside the hospital room carrying two hot coffees in a tray along with a white paper bag.

"You know I'd never touch these sugary carbs. But I figured, if not now, when?" She puts the coffees down on the small side table before handing me the bag full of breakfast desserts.

I sit up to peek inside: croissants and blueberry muffins. "Let me wash up quickly."

"Hurry so your coffee doesn't get cold."

I make my way into the small en-suite bathroom and try to avoid the mirror.

"Lauren?" I ask, walking back toward her. "Would you be able to put up my apartment for sale and maybe hire movers to bring all my clothes out here?" Maybe it's presumptuous of me. Still, where Vincent is, is where I want to be. I have faith he's going to come out of this. And when he does, I need to be here.

"Of course, I can. Did you already resign?" Her eyes are wide.

"Last night." Surprisingly, admitting that I resigned doesn't cause the earth to shatter.

"Harassment is real and shouldn't be tolerated. I hope your letter goes all the way to the top."

"Me too." I press my lips together firmly, nodding in absolute agreement.

Twenty minutes later, she stands to leave. After lots of hugging, one of Slade's guys steps in, letting her know that he'll be escorting her to the airport. With a wink, she leaves my side for California.

I know Slade's army is probably sitting outside, but I pretend they aren't. Reopening my computer, I brainstorm ways to take down Antonio Borignone. I'm not ready to commit to this plan, but a little thinking couldn't hurt. Before I know it, I'm completely in the zone, mapping out ideas.

My phone *pings*, shaking me out of my trance.

Lauren: Eve, it's 9pm. Have you left the room to eat?
Me: okay, okay.

Janelle's name pops up on the screen and I groan. I hate group texts.

Janelle: Go now!

Me: I'm leaving! Je-sus!

Janelle: LOLLLL. Now go.

Lauren: By the way, Janelle, should I use coconut oil on my scalp or will it make it too greasy?

I shut my phone. For a moment, I consider falling back asleep again on the chair. But my back feels like hell. I know that Vincent would rather me stay in a bed. And plus, it'll be HIS bed, so maybe it won't feel so bad.

* * *

I ENTER Vincent's trailer with Ax behind me, who's holding my stuff. I open Vincent's fridge and offer him a cold bottle of water or a beer. Luckily, he declines both and tells me he's going to hang out in his truck to make a few calls and sleep. I already noticed that the back of his pickup was set up as a bed. He walks out and I shut the door behind him, relieved. Not that he isn't a super nice guy, because he is, but I want privacy.

I hesitate at the doorway in front of Vincent's room, slowly taking off my socks and sneakers before finally entering. Pulling a white undershirt from the drawer by his bedside, I slide it on, drowning in worn-in softness. His scent is everywhere, and I'm immediately brought back to last week.

* * *

VINCENT JUMPS OUT OF BED, picking me up in his huge arms and carrying me into the bathroom, my entire body feeling completely satisfied after last night. "Vincent put me down, I want to brush my teeth!" I giggle, heart soaring.

Last night. I can't even think the words without flushing. Vincent made love to me as if the world was ending. He's so commanding and dominant.

Completely thorough. I'm sure that not one inch of my body was left untouched by his worshipful mouth. He sucked, licked, kissed every piece of me. And when I thought he was done? He simply gave me more.

Holding me up with one arm, he puts toothpaste on two brushes. I start to brush my teeth, still securely nestled in his chest. I can tell he loves watching me do these random mundane things. His lips move to my neck, as though this simple task is too much for him.

"How am I going to spit like this?" My mouth is full of suds. He grunts, finally lowering me down. I rinse my mouth with water a few times. After drying my face with a small white towel, he lifts me up piggyback style. I press my minty lips against his shoulder as he starts brushing his own teeth.

Glancing in the mirror, my hair is an absolute mess and for the first time in maybe ever, I love it. Our eyes lock. I love this man to no end.

"Your body, Vincent. I still can't believe how much bigger you've gotten." I swallow hard, staring in the mirror at his gorgeous wide chest, down to his six-pack of muscles. "And tan. You're just..." I stop talking, suddenly overwhelmed.

"You didn't notice last night?" He bends his head down to spit in the sink.

"I mean, I did. But..." I can feel a blush creeping into my face. He laughs at me, bringing more water to his mouth while I cling onto him like a little monkey.

Back in the bed, Vincent holds me tightly in his arms; I can barely move a muscle, not that I'd want to. We're not simply embracing—we're fusing.

"I'm keeping this shirt," I speak into his neck.

He pulls away and I watch the smile move through his face and settling in his eyes. "Everything that's mine is yours." He rubs his nose against mine.

"You told me that once before," I remind him. Swallowing, I stare into his deep and dark eyes. It's love.

"And it's still true. Always will be." He pushes a stray hair off my forehead. I'm home.

* * *

I BLINK and the memory disappears, leaving me all alone in his trailer. My mouth opens wide as tears stream down my face; it's an ugly and painful cry. I manage to fall asleep a few hours later with his pillow over my face, inhaling his smell and praying he'll come back to me.

27

EVE

THE NEXT MORNING, I awake to a knock on the trailer door. I shuffle out of bed, his shirt like a long dress reaching the center of my calves. I move my hands to rub the sleep from my eyes but wince; they're raw.

I peek through the window shade before opening the door.

"Hey, Ax."

The sun shines over the mountains, casting a reddish-orange glow all around. It's so beautiful, but still, I feel a deep sense of sadness. I need to get back to the hospital. I raise a hand like a visor on my forehead, trying to shield my face from the brightness of the sun.

"Sorry to wake you, but I can't leave without your knowledge. I'm gonna run to the store for a very quick errand. Need anything?" He leans against the doorway, a black leather jacket in his hands.

"Nah," I reply. "I want to head back to the hospital in about thirty minutes, though. Think you can drive me over?"

"Yup. Should be back in fifteen." He turns to go, but stops, looking back at me. "Just so you know, Slade installed cameras around the outside of the trailer. I just let him know that I'm heading out for a few, so he'll be watching." Walking to his pickup, he drives away, sand kicking up at the huge wheels as he takes off.

My skin prickles. I look left and right nervously, not noticing anything out of the ordinary. All this shit with Antonio is obviously affecting me. Shutting and turning the lock, I put on a pot of coffee before getting into the shower. Instead of using the shampoo and conditioner Vincent and I picked up together, I use his Dove Men's shampoo and body wash, wanting to smell like him. In some strange way, it makes me feel closer. I step out of the shower and put on a comfortable pair of relaxed-fit jeans and a white T-shirt, texting Ax I'm ready to go.

I hear a noise. Someone else is here. My breath stops as I listen intently.

Bending down, I grab the gun from my purse. Water drips from the ends of my dark hair, soaking the back of my white T-shirt. The silence is eerie, but my instincts are on high.

I step to the bedroom door and stare through the sliver of an opening. My eyes focus on a familiar man with salt and pepper hair, sitting at Vincent's small and round kitchen table. I keep watching as he slowly turns his head, licking his full lips like a wolf.

A sneer is settled on his chiseled and cruel face; I'm taken aback. He looks so much like Vincent, it's staggering. But those eyes, a cold electric blue, are vacant.

Antonio Borignone.

"I know you're watching me, Eve," he says loudly, body turned toward the bedroom door. "Come out," he says in a sing-song voice.

My heart slows as I realize there is nowhere to go. I consider jumping out the bedroom window, but there is no way I can fit through. I briefly consider hiding, but if he already knows I'm here, he'll surely come and find me. I've got to strengthen myself and move forward. Ax will walk in any minute now—I just need to stall. Tucking the gun in the back of my pants, I take a tentative step out of the room.

"The girl who shook my empire." He starts a slow clap as I walk closer to where he sits. "Sit," he commands. My heart beats straight into my throat.

I take a seat, doing my best not to show any emotion or weakness. I know from Vincent there's no quicker way to get myself killed.

"Look at you." His voice is unnervingly calm as he stares me up and down, considering what's before him. Pulling a cigarette from a Marlboro Red pack at the center of the table, he lights up and takes a deep inhale.

I remember the first time I met him at Angelo's pawnshop; he's still just as frighteningly magnetic. But I'm no longer the scared girl I once was. I straighten my back, waiting to hear what he has to say. If I'm going to die, I won't go down as a scared child. He notices the shift in my demeanor and smiles.

Still, I try to keep my face unreadable.

"The little girl from the hood has risen," he says, seemingly to himself. His fingers tremble as he brings the cigarette back into his mouth for another long drag, the smoke billowing from his mouth as he speaks. "I remember you as a terrified kid. And now here you are —trapping my son with that pussy of yours."

His fist, resting on the table, clenches.

"He went to prison seven years ago." He leans back into the chair and crosses one leg over his knee. "I figured that would be the trick to get you guys separated for good. You see, a woman like you is terrible for business. Love? I hate the word. In the same way I hate all pathetic and needy people." He grinds his teeth, pitching forward. "But could he just forget you? Nope. Vincent comes out of lockup and heads straight here." He lifts his hand like an airplane and flies it toward me. "You fucked up his head, girl."

His eyes are unfocused. He's on a rant, so much in his own mind that I wonder if he even realizes I'm sitting in front of him. Antonio Borignone is no longer the self-contained man I knew. No wonder Vincent thought the family was a losing bet.

"What a joke," he hisses. "To think my son now lives in a fucking trailer on an Indian Reservation. Left the family for this fuckin' shit. And with a woman from the goddamn gutter."

He stands up and walks to the wooden kitchen cabinets, pulling one open. With a sweep of his hand, spices and cans clatter onto the ground and roll around the floor.

"He should be living like a king, running the Milestone while readying himself to run my empire." He laughs, shaking his head as he turns back to me. "He should be the prince I raised him to be. But for you, he gives up his life and all the possibilities and the money and the power and the women. It's sickening."

I glance up at the clock. *Where is Ax?*

"If you're waiting for that moron to come for you, you're wasting your time. I shot him in the head just as he left." He shrugs casually, sitting back down in the chair.

Before I can feel terror, a thought hits me like a freight train: It's not my time. Vincent is going to come out of his coma and when he does, I'm going to be by his side. I'm not letting this lunatic take it all away.

And for maybe the first time in my life, I know I deserve better. All my life, it was about working hard and getting out of the ghetto. But no matter how high I climbed, I never believed I was actually *worth* more. I've been pushed around and bullied for years. My mother's emotional abuse. My near rape with Carlos. Daniela, the bitch from hell. Even Jonathan and the DBC. And now this psycho—who sent his own son to jail and tried to murder him—blames me for Vincent and me falling in love? I'm finished with this shit. I know who I am and I know my value. The days of letting people run over me are done. I shift in my seat, steadying myself. If I go down today, it will not be quietly.

"You have anything to say before you die?" He pulls out his gun and grips it in the palm of his hand. The look in his eyes completely unhinged. A voice inside my head tells me to keep him talking and delay our standoff. If the camera was on like Ax had said, Slade should have seen Antonio entering. Still, if one of us has to die, it won't be me. To make it out alive, I'm ready to do whatever it is I have to do.

"Vincent told me that your uncles started the Borignone mafia."

My voice comes out stronger than it has the right to be. "It's so impressive what you've accomplished. Clearly, you took what they started and created an empire. How did you manage it?"

If my memory from Psychology 101 serves me right, egomaniacs are possessed by delusions of prominence, but frequently feel a lack of appreciation. Hopefully, this should get him talking.

He places his gun down on the table and turns his head toward the window, staring at the mountains.

"I began as a kid. Let me tell ya, my uncles were the real deal. I met your mother shortly after I started with 'em. She was gorgeous and wild, recently came from Russia with a baby. Danced at one of our clubs. Enzo had a thing for her." He taps the end of the cigarette, ash snowing on the floor. "Threw a vase at one of the doors in your shitty apartment, once." He laughs as if reminiscing about the golden days. My heart slows to a steady pound. *It's working.*

"She used to party with us. Hot as fuck. Into the drugs, of course." He takes another smoke from the pack and lights it up. "Complained a lot about you. That's why she got you the job with Angelo. Figured if you stayed in our hold, you'd keep it in mind who you were and stop dreaming." He blows upward, smoke circling around his head like a devilish halo.

"There are people in this world who eat shit. And because they do, they think that every other person on the planet should, too. They hate anyone who tries to do better because they themselves can't do better. That's your mom. And let me tell ya, she wasn't wrong.

Lifting a finger, he points at my face. "Your mom and I were always on the same page. Sure, I lived like a king and she was addicted to meth. But both of us set our lives in motion. Your mother was a crack whore. Why should you be allowed to just escape or do better? She had no choice but to stay in the life—why should you be able to just leave when she couldn't? And why should Vincent be allowed to just do whatever-the-fuck he wants?" He slams his hand down on the table and his cigarette flies out of his mouth and onto the floor. I don't allow my body to jump.

"I created a kingdom," he shouts, looking at me with crazed eyes.

"Vincent doesn't get to just walk away. I'm the creator. I'm the ruler."
He pants, his mouth foaming white at the corners.

My hand steadily presses against the gun in the back of my jeans.
The man is so involved in his words, he wouldn't notice the entrance
of a wild animal. I internally smile.

Life isn't just about escaping my past circumstances but thriving
despite them. With confidence I never knew I possessed, I remove the
piece, aiming it straight in front of me. I can't stall any longer.
Antonio pauses, mouth settling on a smirk. The asshole thinks I don't
have the guts.

"You see, Antonio." I lick my dry lips before pointing the gun at
the center of his head. "Me and Vincent aren't in your hold anymore.
And now there is another thing you and my mother have in common.
She's dead. And so are you."

I pull the trigger on the exhale. Blood, black like tar, and pieces of
bone and brain matter spray across the room. I'm not sure how long
I'm sitting there with the gun clasped in my hands, but the next thing
I know, Slade is running into the trailer saying something I can't
understand.

He's got me in his arms and I feel warmth and safety. I turn to him
as he speaks. "The doctor called—he's waking Vincent up today.
Antonio is dead, now. You're free. Do you hear me, Eve? You're free."

"V-Vincent?" I manage to stutter out, shaking.

"Just calm down now. You'll be all right."

I hear an ambulance in the distance as I hang onto Slade, clinging
to him as my body trembles in shock.

* * *

Twenty-Four Hours Later

Slade accompanies me to Vincent's room, leaving me at the
doorway to give us privacy. The nurse shuffles out. "Be gentle, darling.
He doesn't remember much of what happened." I make my way
inside, slowly.

Vincent turns his head to me and I can't stop my gasp. Dark, red-rimmed eyes. Heavy black scruff along his jaw. Slash down his face, stitched. Hair overgrown.

But, he's here.

"Come." His voice is a dry and broken rasp.

I run toward him and drop my head on his chest, thinner from drugs and ventilation.

"Tell me. What happened?" He asks.

I take a piece of ice with my fingers from a cup on his side table and bring it to his cracked lips. He shuts his eyes in relief as it melts into his mouth. He stares at me again, waiting for me to speak. I drop the cube back into the cup before breaking down and spilling everything. How the BB was hired by his father to take him. Entering the clubhouse. Crow. When I get to killing Antonio, his shock and relief are palpable as tears fill his eyes.

I grip his hand. "We're free."

"We're free," Vincent repeats my words slowly, as if he needs to come to terms with them, too.

"I've been here since yesterday morning. The tribal police—they had so many questions. I was stuck here, answering everything. I k-killed him. Antonio is dead now. Self-defense, of course. The cameras show him entering and—"

He hums, shutting his eyes. Seeing Vincent so weak is devastating.

When it's time for discharge, I tell the nurse to leave. I'm going to help him dress. His entire body seems broken and yet, here he is—with me. I know he'll heal.

We get into the car and take the back seat as Slade drives us back to the trailer.

I begin crying into Vincent's shoulder.

"I wake up from a coma to see you constantly crying?" His lips quirk in a small smile, different from his old one—almost, weary. His entire face is so bruised, I can barely recognize him.

I cry harder. "I'm crying because I love you. I'm crying because I'm so happy you're w-with me." I keep my arms wrapped around his chest because I can't let go. If he isn't comfortable, he doesn't say.

"Are you staying tonight?" His words come out insecure.

"I'm going to stay here until I figure out my next steps. Lauren's selling my apartment and I resigned from work. I'm here now."

"We'll work it all out together, yeah? We've got time. If you want—"

"No. I'm doing this for me. I'm going to figure out another path for my life. That one wasn't making me happy and I have ideas, you know." He squeezes my hand in his.

I'm emotionally crumbled, but Vincent is with me. It's the best day of my life.

28

VINCENT
Six Months Later

ANGELO STANDS ON A FLAT ROCK, smiling happily in a black pinstriped suit as beads of sweat drip down his sideburns. In order to officiate this moment, he became ordained. As the only father Eve has ever known, I know it means the world to her that he's doing this. He stares at me in deference and I nod my head back in reply. It's a little piece of my old life.

The mountains surround us, giving us privacy, yet looming large and serving as a reminder that there is something greater out in the universe above us all.

Eve and I hiked here when I was well enough to walk. She made us sandwiches of fresh-baked bread, roasted turkey, and vegetables. Packing it all together with two miniature wine bottles and chocolate chip cookies, she managed a perfect feast. It only took half an hour for her to get tipsy and giggling. My heart got so fuckin' full, there was nothing left to do but get down on a knee and swear my never-ending love and devotion. I would have begged if I had to, but luckily, she only wrapped her arms around my neck and cried.

Lauren and Janelle stand on the left side of Angelo, both in short colorful dresses. Slade and I are situated on his right, wearing khaki slacks and white shirts. Janelle gives me a half smile as if she's saying, "Let's make peace." I chuckle, knowing that beneath that nice-girl façade she's cursing me. She is going to have to learn to deal with me, though. Eve's about to be my wife, and I plan on never letting her out of my sight until the day I die.

Slade taps my shoulder. "Any minute now, brother." He faces ahead and I watch him flush. He's staring at Lauren, who's adjusting the straps on her dress. I've never seen Slade as anything but serious, and truthfully, I like it. Lauren's a good girl.

I was angry at him for risking Eve's life to save mine, but she convinced me to forgive him. Eve made it clear that she is her own woman, and she was the one who chose to come to my rescue. "...I'm not a doll Slade can control. He put out the option, and I took it." I can't stop the smile spreading across my face because Eve is everything, and then some. *Damn*, I love my woman.

It took her time to come to terms with the fact that she killed Antonio, and emotionally, she wasn't doing so well. While the feds—down to the local police—knew that she acted out of self-defense, killing a man, no matter how deserved, is a sickening feeling and something I understand all too well.

Returning from the hospital, she began having dreams that she killed me instead of my father. Sweating and crying out, I tried to wake her gently, not wanting to shock her. When she'd come to realize I was still next to her, she would only cry harder.

The last few months, she's been getting much better. With the help of a fantastic psychologist, who she speaks with a few nights a week on video chat, Eve's beginning to cope with everything from her mother's abuse up to killing Antonio. Finally living together without any constraints or secrets helps, too. We cook and work and love each other daily.

My fingers move to my face, the scar from my eye down to my chin is raised and still slightly tender. The pinky on my right hand is gone, although I do have phantom pain. My limp is here to stay, thanks to my shattered kneecap. While my physical body has taken a serious beating, I'm lucky to say I've still got all my mental faculties. The Milestone is no longer encumbered by any Borignone interference. Life is better than ever.

Tom stepped up as the new boss. He and I spoke. He swore no one will ever touch me again; the entire underground knows that I am no longer affiliated. Turns out one of the newer members had an idea of how the family can clean and house their dirty cash out in Argentina and the Milestone is no longer necessary for their operation. Regardless, I know Tom would never keep me tethered. The family may be my past, but Tom and I will always be brothers.

At any rate, today is not about yesterday. It's about starting my life with the only woman I've ever loved. The photographer I hired comes over to where the five of us stand, taking snapshots to memorialize the moment. The lone violinist, sitting a few feet away from us, plays the instrumental version of "Next to Me" by Imagine Dragons. My heart pounds. This is our song.

I blink and she appears—Eve. A long white gown with delicate straps falling off her slender shoulders, she glides down the small aisle filled with white flower petals. She slightly bends her head to stare at her feet, all innocence and truth. I couldn't stop my own tears if I tried. I already know she's wearing no jewelry. Our mutual commitment is based on who we are as people, not on any material possessions.

I remember her as a kid sitting with me in a pizza shop, eating together and talking about Italy. Teaching her to skate in Central Park while she gripped onto me for dear life. Studying in our bed down in SoHo, buds in her ears as she memorized mathematical formulas beside me. The woman I found her to be when I returned from prison. Brilliant and so beautiful.

And now? My wife.

Solo, she makes her way to the center of the aisle. I feel a pang in my chest—Eve shouldn't walk alone. Not anymore. My feet move on their own accord as I limp into the aisle. She smiles as I reach her, eyes full of joy. Taking her hand, we walk together to where Angelo and our friends stand. Janelle steps forward, handing her a soft white shawl.

"Wrap this around our shoulders," Eve tells me, smiling. "Let it symbolize that we're bound."

I do as she asks, covering us in soft cloth as Angelo begins the ceremony. When it's time, I kiss every finger of her left hand before placing a plain gold ring on her finger. It has no blemishes or stones, serving as a symbol that our marriage will be one of simple beauty. My voice is stronger than ever as I swear to always love and protect her.

After placing an identical ring on my finger, she too swears to always love and protect me. We say the words but both know, deep down, we've already proven our vows to each other. I'm struck by the fact that she's next to *me*. Loving *me*.

Our friends clap as we kiss, cheering. I bend down to press my forehead against Eve's, raising the shawl above our heads and repeating over and over again against her lips how much I love her. It's no one but us.

We all walk to the picnic area of the park where I surprise Eve with a party filled with music, all of her favorite foods, and twinkling lights. I told Kimber how I envisioned the night, and she managed it perfectly. Eve's always had a thing for delicious meals and dancing. Even though she said she didn't need or want a party, she should have it all tonight while surrounded by the people she loves.

"Vincent, how could you?" She slaps my shoulder and I laugh. Her face is warm and utterly euphoric.

"There was no way I was going to let this moment go without celebration." I wrap my arms around her tiny frame, bringing her against me. "Plus, we've gotta dance together, yeah?"

The violinist is joined by a drummer, guitarist, and keyboard player. I hired a DJ as well, because the band couldn't play all the music Eve loves. Janelle wrote out a list of songs for him and I laughed when I saw the lineup. The girls have a serious thing for Drake that's been going on for years. Slade told a few of his friends to come as well, and they meander over to where we are with beers in hand, clapping me on the back in congratulations.

We're all dancing to OutKast's "Hey Ya!" when Claire and Ms. Levine, Eve's high school English teacher, walk over. Eve's jaw drops in shock as she runs to hug them wholeheartedly.

Eve hasn't seen Ms. Levine in years, but they've kept in touch via email. As the woman who picked up my girl by the bootstraps and got her out of Blue Houses hell, I'm forever indebted. When I called her with the news of our wedding, she was over the moon with happiness.

Claire and Eve haven't seen each other since Columbia, but they've kept in touch for all these years, too. Claire was in Algeria with Doctors Without Borders and it was purely coincidental that she was back in the states for a two-month vacation while our wedding was happening. Seeing her is bittersweet; she was part of the best and the most terrible of times.

As the guests eat and hang out by the bar, Eve and I continue to dance under the evening moon, our own pace nice and slow despite the beat of the music. My hands stay on her at all times. I know I'm greedy, but I just can't let her go.

"Eve?" I bring her closer.

"Mmm?" she hums, smiling.

"You gave yourself to me." She squints in annoyance. I know it drives her insane when I talk macho, but her mad face is just so damn sexy.

"Vincent," she says my name all angry, and I have to stop myself from dragging her out of here and taking her to bed.

"Now that I'm your husband, I'll be more protective. Extra crazy, too. Gonna need you next to me all the damn time." She gives me another face. "Can't help it, babe."

"Is it too late to back out?" My mouth turns down and she giggles, slapping my arm. "Oh, come on. As if I don't know you."

"Well, that's why I think we should build out your center next to my office trailer. This way I can always be near."

"You were able to get the land?" She lets out an adorable squeak.

I nod slowly and her eyes flash in excitement. The last few months, Eve has been planning logistics of her domestic violence shelter. With five short-term residences and a specialization in building life skills, employment assistance, and legal counseling for battered women and their families, she hopes to give families a safe place to restart their lives and rise above their current situations.

Eve went through hell by the hands of her own mother, but with an iron will and the support of her sister and Ms. Levine, she was able to claw up and out. Still, most people aren't so lucky or as strong. This shelter will be a support and savior in the way these families need.

I touch her gorgeous dark hair, down and wild the way I love, and feel immeasurably lucky. "I'll spend my life making myself worth it. I swear." I kiss the top of her head softly before she tilts her head up, giving me those warm, full lips. My entire soul stirs.

"Vincent. Vincent. Vincent," she says my name over and over like a blessing.

"Yeah, baby?"

"We're married." She looks at me then, in a way only Eve ever has. And with every ounce of love within me, I kiss her.

AFTERWORD

I am crazy about tortured heroes. I mean, what woman doesn't love a Navy SEAL hero, home from war, who's damaged, broken and sexy as hell?

Remember Slade and Lauren from REDEMPTION (VINCENT AND EVE BOOK 3)? Well, they've got their own book in WARRIOR UNDONE!

If you haven't had a chance to read WARRIOR UNDONE yet, you can check out the first few chapters in the back of this book. Just keep swiping, and you'll find it at the end!

Oh, and by the way...Vincent and Eve are in there too!

Warrior Undone

I have no intention of finding happily-ever-after. At least, not anymore.

Fighting for my country was an honor, Returning home is a curse.

My demons need to be fed. How else can a shattered man stay afloat?

When a wild night in Las Vegas with the sexiest woman I've ver met turns into hell, she attaches to me as though I'm her savior.

But what happens when a woman hangs her hands on broken glass? She bleeds.

*Warrior Undone is a stand-alone spin-off from the Vincent and Eve series. This is a full length novel.

WARRIOR UNDONE is available NOW on Amazon and FREE with Kindle Unlimited!

Purchase **Warrior Undone** here: https://amzn.to/2JI5gHW

Thanks for reading!

-Jessica

STAY IN TOUCH WITH JESSICA

You can check out all of my books on my Amazon author page:
https://amzn.to/2MwV7eF

Want to know about all the sales, updates, or news I have? Sign up for my newsletter:
http://jessicarubenauthor.com/newsletter/

Interested in hanging out with me and chatting all-things bookish? Join my Facebook group, Jessica's Jet Setters:
https://bit.ly/2lHuCaZ

I love to hear from readers! Please reach out to me via my website:
http://www.jessicarubenauthor.com

ALSO BY JESSICA RUBEN

Vincent and Eve Series:

Rising (Vincent and Eve Book 1)

Reckoning (Vincent and Eve Book 3)

Redemption (Vincent and Eve Book 3)

Stand-Alone Novel:

Warrior Undone

Coming Fall 2019:

Light My Fire (A Sex Rock Mafia novel)

LETTER TO THE READERS

Readers,

Did you know the Vincent and Eve series was my debut series? As a brand-new author who independently publishes, reviews have the power to make or break a book. If you have the time, please drop a line! It would truly mean the world to me.

Amazon:
https://amzn.to/2MwV7eF

Goodreads:
https://bit.ly/2Ksoof8

BookBub:
https://bit.ly/2CGAvPi

With Love,
Jessica

WARRIOR UNDONE

Prologue

Slade

The helicopter descends into the brown-and-gray peaked mountains that jut between the Afghanistan-Pakistan borders. Shifting forward, a tightness fills the circulated air. Systematically wringing my hands, I move them left before right. I'm a man of rituals.

The door opens into extraordinary heat. It rushes forward and seeps beneath layered clothing. As I step off, my head focuses forward while my eyes do a snapshot perusal of the vast earth where people have lived and fought for centuries on end. When I slide on my sunglasses, the bright world dims.

Images of the compound flash on the projector. It doesn't look different from the hundreds we've raided beforehand.

"We're set to clear." The commander's hands move behind his back. He clasps them as he paces. "Marines are coming, too. They'll be inserting with us and setting up a perimeter of defense. Covering while we do our work." A cough rings through the room as coordinates are mentioned. "Intel says they're abandoned."

But first, sleep.

A sudden sensation of falling. Hard grains of sand nestled within the sheets move against my calves and between my toes. It's gritty. It's home.

A hard knock on wood before the door swings open.

Someone shouts, "It's go time, boys!"

I throw my legs to the right side of the bed and rise. Water to the face and brush my teeth. Time to suit up. My heart settles to a steady rhythm as I gather my weapons. The methodical movements are where I find my peace. M24 is strapped to my back. Heavy enough to make a dent but not too heavy to slow me down. An American flag sits on my bed, pre-folded. I place it between my armor and uniform. It settles inside my chest cavity. My body is its cocoon, reminding me of who I am, what I love, and where I came from.

As a team, we enter the thick darkness, a perfect cover.

A few kilometers into our hike, we sit to break. Rex is to my left, his photographic and video equipment resting on his side. He grumbles, spitting on the rocky ground before taking a swig from his green canteen.

"How you doin', brother?" I take a drink from my own.

"Fuckin' A," he replies but not for nothing. Rex hauls some heavy shit. Between the weight of his communications equipment and the high altitude, he is miserable.

He looks up at me. It's so dark, but I can still make out his shining eyes and sharply gritted teeth. Rex is probably the angriest corpsman on the Teams. Yet his complete stability in the face of a firefight has always transcended any anger—probably why we work so well together. Always have and always will.

I rise before holding out my hand. He takes it.

The team gets back on its feet.

As I'm walking, sweat pours down my face.

Our commander turns to me. "The caves are near, and we haven't encountered a single person yet. Luck of the Texans, eh?"

The sun rises as we reach the complex. It's huge, circular, and wet with riotous colors. Looking up, I imagine who else around the world is staring at it, too.

We start in, four of us entering in formation. Before I step inside, my rational mind reminds me there could be an ambush ahead. This cave could be booby-trapped.

I turn to Rex.

His eyes say, *I've got your back.*

I clench my fists and walk inside.

It's dimly lit, but my adrenaline ... it burns. I pivot.

Wooden chairs and desks are organized neatly in rows facing a chalkboard. I'm in a classroom. Posters line the walls, full of anti-American slogans. Bin Laden's smile graces the largest poster in the center as two planes crash into the Twin Towers behind him. DEATH TO AMERICA!

Lives are dictated with propaganda. The systematic washing of brains.

We clear the room and step out to report.

Onto the next.

It's a fanatical dedication. They're pursuing a brand-new type of combat the free world is only beginning to understand. My father fought in the trenches. He rolled across deserts with huge ground forces. But us? We're up against decentralized cells. Guerrilla warfare on a scale of infinity.

The work is nerve-racking and tedious. Sweat saturates everything from my wool-blend socks up into my North Face jacket. It cools me.

Hours later, our job is complete. We gather what we need before stepping out. Phil rigged each room. When he clicks, it'll all blow to hell.

We easily hike down in a comfortable quiet.

Phil pushes the button.

The explosion causes a wild fireball against the sky, rocking the ground beneath my feet. The world is an echo.

Have I been here before?

The gunfire begins, and the ground shifts again. Liquid black oozes from Rex's mouth, and then his face is ablaze. Through a flaming mask, blue eyes stare as his mouth widens in terror. I move to him but fail to go quickly enough. An enemy comes up behind me. I jump and turn, muscles pulsing. I grab his throat with my left hand and my gun with my right. My mind tells me to forget the gunman and go to Rex, but my body is now on auto. Years of training take control away from my conscience.

He's carrying an AK-47 and a brown wool blanket. Motherfucker is going to die. I squeeze my grip, the world zeroing in on the two of us. He's thrashing. The smell of burning flesh infiltrates my senses as I squeeze ...

Rex. Something in the recesses of my mind knocks frantically. *He's dead. Your friend is dead. You turned away, and now, he's gone. It's all your fucking fault.* I want to scream, but nothing comes out of my mouth. I'm a dying fish.

The cemetery is cold, and everyone is gone. I've killed him. It's my fault. The sun sets, and I'm on the ground. Take me instead.

Open your eyes. Open them. OPEN YOUR FUCKING EYES, my mind screams.

On an exhale, I do.

A room ...

My room.

I drop my gaze. I'm inside a bed where a thick hand is wrapped around a slender, pale neck. My hand? Teardrops pool beneath her pale eyes. The room is still dark, but nature's light illuminates her in sepia. Bare, pointed breasts quiver, and goose bumps cover her soft flesh. I gently let go, my coiled muscles unraveling as my mind recognizes the pace change. Consciousness is restored.

Another night terror. My God.

I trip off the bed before righting myself and flip on the light. "I'm so sorry. Holy fuck," I exclaim. I turn back to her and pause at her unmoving form. Shaking her. "Lilly. Wake up. Wake up."

She's unconscious. I take a sharp inhale through my nose as I check her pulse. Alive. Next, I raise her bare legs over my shoulders to promote blood flow to her brain. Years of boxing and ten years in the SEAL Teams have taught me a thing or two.

Sixty-four seconds, and her glossy blue eyes open. She's looking at me, confusion in her irises, as though she isn't sure what's happening. I turn my gaze to the bedside clock. It's 1:04 a.m. It takes a few seconds for her puzzlement to leak into fear.

My handprints—I can see them against the column of her white throat. Her breathing is somewhat normalizing.

Sweat drips from my forehead. "I hurt you. I didn't ..." I pause, my hands rubbing against the back of my buzzed hair. "You'll be okay. It's happened to me before. Getting choked out, I mean. You might have a headache later, but you'll be okay."

She stares at me, dumbstruck, not unlike the deer I used to shoot every October.

"S-Slade?" Her voice is hoarse as her delicate hands move up to her neck. She winces, white-blonde hair twisted above her head like a wild halo.

We just met tonight. I stayed until closing, just watching her wipe down the bar top.

With a little T-shirt that shows off her midriff and red-painted nails, she bends down to grab something below the bar. The last few tired patrons leave some cash for her before walking out.

"They're pulling out their keys." She nods toward the door. "I've got a crazy good sense of hearing."

"My younger brother, Aaron, had a keen sense of smell as a kid. Like a dog, he could sniff what the neighbor was cooking in the house next door. No joke."

I drink more of my beer, and her heart-shaped face laughs.

"Where's he now?"

"Who?" I polish off my drink, not wanting to speak anymore.

I want to get this woman into my bed and lose myself in her body. We've only met tonight, but she's sweet and pretty. Reminds me of the girls I used to know.

"Your brother?" Light eyes squint in curiosity.

"Oh." I clear my throat, rubbing the back of my neck. "He wanted to be like me. Join up. But ..." I lick my lips, not finishing my sentence.

"Oh shit. Sorry." Her gaze nervously darts to the side.

"Yeah." I get off the stool. "Ready to go? My bike's outside, and my place isn't too far."

Presumptuous of me, sure. But women are strange. They claim to want freedom, but most of them just want to be told what to do. Not that I mind. I'm a decent man, but I know what I like—to be in charge.

"Sure. Let me just grab my bag?" Her voice is hesitant with question, as though I might change my mind. She's sweet but insecure.

I nod before stepping outside and lighting up a smoke.

When she's on the back of my bike, her fingers grip my waist in excitement and fear. She tells me, "I've never been on a bike before," as I put a helmet on her head. Yet she trusts me.

And, now, look what I've done.

"I don't know what happened. I was ... dreaming. Let me bring you home. You shouldn't stay here with me."

I could have killed you, I think. Another round of sweat coats my forehead.

I jump out of bed and move around the room, steadying my trembling hands as I grab her strewed clothes off the gray-carpeted floor. My place isn't much, but I always keep it spotless and organized.

"Rituals," I mumble under my breath, the word leaving my mouth without any thought.

My dream hits me again, ricocheting around my brain. The force is so strong; it stops my breath.

I exhale, focusing on the task at hand—dressing Lilly. Slowly, I guide long and lean legs back into lacy black panties, trying to remain gentle. Her black miniskirt goes on next as guilt hits me like a freight train.

She's moving slowly but thankfully letting me help. Next, I clasp her bra behind her back and slide her white T-shirt over her head. It says, *Stumble Inn. Have a drink.*

Millions of emotions threaten to take me down, but I tell them to shut the fuck up. Right now, I have to make sure she gets dressed and goes home safely. I'll deal with myself later. When she's clothed, I throw a pair of jersey sleep pants onto my legs and a blue T-shirt with the word *NAVY* in bold white letters.

I help her into my red pickup. Some country song plays on the radio as I try not to drive over any potholes. Like it's hard for her to speak, she tells me her address. I force myself to stick to the speed limit.

Getting to her home, a simple bolted-down trailer, I park the car in front. She opens the car door herself, but I run around to the side before she can exit, taking her hand in mine to help her down. I hold the small of her back as we walk. She fumbles with her keys, a massive chain, but quickly finds them. The door opens to a clean home with white walls and flowery furniture.

Her feet turn toward her bedroom, and I swiftly follow her lead. Hitting the bedroom lights, I lift her in my arms and gently place her on top of the bed, pulling off her short boots. The bedspread is pink. A large framed photo sits on her wooden nightstand. She is smiling in a blue cap and gown next to an older man with a wide, proud grin. Lilly is someone's daughter.

I head to the kitchen and find a glass in the cupboard, filling it with ice from the old white freezer and water from the sink. I take it to her room before asking, "Any Advil?"

"Motrin. Bathroom." Her voice rasps. It hasn't returned.

I immediately find it and remove two pills. Placing them in her hand, I finally ask, "Are you okay?"

She swallows the medicine with a large sip of water, wincing, and then rolls away from me. My cue to leave.

I hightail it back to my place. Shit's been going south in my head for too long, but this is a new low. Dirt kicks up around the car when I pull up to my small home, but I don't wait for it to settle before jumping out.

Within seconds, I'm rummaging through my own kitchen and pulling out a bottle of tequila, twisting the cap open. I need it to function.

"God is watching," my father loved to remind us at our wooden dinner table. He'd built it himself. Chewing his collard greens closed-mouthed with buzzed hair and his back ramrod straight, he'd lecture.

I grew up well. Football captain. Great friends. Church every Sunday. Both my parents were hardworking and God-fearing. When kneeling for Holy Communion, I'd shut my eyes, just as I'd been taught, regardless of the fact that I was constantly restless from sitting too long. When I confessed to the priest, there was nothing I'd withhold.

I believed in God back then. I still want to, but how can I now amid the shit I've seen?

I take a few more gulps, aiming to drown myself in liquor and old-time memories ...

Aaron beating me in a shoot-out—it was one time, damn it, but he never forgot. That time when Dad drove his truck into a ditch, and the whole football team came to help push it out. Or the time Mom baked that zucchini bread for our new neighbor, but Aaron and I found it sitting hot in the oven, just waiting to be eaten.

"She can make another one," I said, slapping each other five.

We used our hands like spoons, shoveling the warm bread into our mouths until there wasn't even a crumb remaining. It was so damn good; we didn't pause to get forks. Mom found us there with our hands in the oven, and boy, did she yell.

I take another swig, laughing.

Aaron standing at the door next to my father, watching me as I readied myself to leave for boot camp. His blue eyes were full of hero worship for his older brother, who was willing to risk his life for God and country.

As he was three years younger than myself, life with Aaron was a continual test of strength and strategy. And, by that, I mean, we basically beat the living shit out of each other on a daily basis. Still, we were tight when it mattered.

The Twin Towers had fallen weeks prior, and we'd watched a documentary on television about the strength and pride of our Navy.

After all, good ole boys like us had been raised to represent our country and do it proud.

After I made my choice to go, he swore to join me after he turned eighteen. We shook on it.

On the brick steps leading to our front door, my father hugged me to his chest. "It's what we do," he said into my ear. As a Vietnam veteran, he'd seen and done his share.

My mother's tears weren't silent as I left home. She was proud but terrified.

"I'm proud of you. But what about school? Your football scholarship?" She reminded me of my old plans, worry etched within her words.

"When I come home, I'll finish it all up. I swear." I hugged her, but she shook in my arms as I kissed her good-bye.

Four years later, Dad died of prostate cancer. One year after that, my mama died from breast cancer. And, two years after that, Aaron was gone when a roadside bomb went off in Iraq.

And my world turned.

Some hearts are full of gratitude and joy, eager to make the earth a better place. My heart? It's disfigured, and it can no longer be trusted.

I retired to an empty house with nothing inside but furniture, photographs, and ghosts. In my bed that first night, between stale sheets that smelled vaguely of my high school gym locker mixed with my mom's detergent, I stayed up late to watch TV, hoping to adjust to the time change. A commercial came on for gourmet cat food served in a shimmering crystal bowl. In my mind's eye, I saw children rummaging, barefoot, through trash, looking for scraps to eat. Meanwhile, here in the USA, cats ate salmon out of gemstones.

What is this world coming to?

I became angry.

It took a few weeks, but I called friends to try to reacclimate.

Reading the pamphlets, I was urged to reconnect. But it was all in vain.

I called my high school girlfriend, Sally.

She had been the cheerleader, and I had been the football captain. Cheesy, sure. But we had some real good times. We were innocents back then. Not that we weren't partying, having sex, and drinking beers from kegs because we were. I'd always been the type to enjoy life. Still, we were innocent in our thinking. All I thought about were grades, college, sports, and getting laid once or twice a day by my sweet and super-hot girlfriend. It had been a fun life. A simple life.

I picked up the phone and dialed with hope in my chest. Turned out, she was married with three kids. I could barely hear her over the sound of children screaming in the background.

Next, I called Tex.

He told me he was running the town auto shop and married to Jane, his own high school sweetheart. "Let's get a beer sometime."

Sure.

Hanging up, I called Billy. A CPA now living in Connecticut with his wife, whom he'd met at Yale. Always was a smart guy.

Hell, I am, too. But, with no college degree or work experience in the field, I'm behind.

Shannon was next. His mom answered and told me he'd died in a car accident during his senior year in college. I was floored. No one had told me.

Some friends from the SEAL Teams wanted to connect, but I didn't. Could barely look them in the eye after Rex's death. Loneliness and guilt threatened to pull me under at every turn.

Like my father, physical labor was a go-to. I refinished the wooden staircase in my family home, repainted the shutters blue, fixed some shaky white tiles in the bathrooms, and finally sold the house in an auction.

It was time to hit the road. Bouncing from spot to spot, I found myself in New York City and did a little fighting for cash.

"It sucks to have to train these Wall Street fucks," a guy tells me after an underground bout beneath a shitty bar on the outskirts of Times Square. A gash over his blackened eye trickles blood as men yell and jeer around us. "But it's a good way to ease back into the real world after leaving the military. Money and hours are pretty good, too. And the guy who owns the place, Joe? He's a decent guy." Lifting a small, clear plastic cup filled with water, he swallows it down like a shot of tequila. "He was in the Navy himself. I think Special Forces. He gets it," he adds.

Blood continues to ooze.

"You need stitches." I point to his brow with my forefinger.

He shrugs. "Whatever," he says like it's the least of his worries. "It's just one of many."

I hand him my sweaty white towel. It's better than getting blood in the eye. Lifting it to his brow, he presses firmly to stop the flow.

I pull the gun from my pants, spinning the black piece on the wooden table. What's the point of life really? My bladder reminds me it's full. I lean against the wall, letting it support me as I make my way to my small, blue-tiled bathroom.

"Want a smoke," I say to no one.

Unzipping my jeans, I lean my hand against the sink to keep steady.

Heading back into the kitchen, I check the junk drawer by the fridge. I push random keys and takeout menus around until I find the pack.

Shit. It's empty. I crunch it in my hand as my phone buzzes.

On shaky legs, I make my way to the table where my phone and gun sit. It flashes red. I've got a message.

Vincent: Yo. Dinner at my place tomorrow night? Eve's cooking.

It only took a few months of training and sparring with Vincent at

Joe's Gym, and I was lucky enough to call the man my friend. As it turned out, Vincent was living in New York while out on parole, but he was in the midst of completing construction on the Milestone, a large-scale hotel and casino complex out on Nevada's tribal lands. When he offered me the job to head security, I jumped at the chance. Even though I had no prior experience, Vincent trusted me to figure it all out. Luckily, my extensive military background easily translated into the security business. I connected with some of my brothers from the SEAL Teams, and together, we began VST, the Vulcan Security Team.

Would I let Vincent down? The Milestone is his life as well as mine. Vincent gave me this opportunity on a silver platter. He and I have a good thing going, and more is yet to come.

Bringing fresh water onto the reservation is next on our agenda, and hiring veterans to do the work will be a great thing.

I continue to spin my gun, dark thoughts pushing through. I wonder ... Why wait? Others can take my spot with Vincent. I'm not afraid of death. In fact, it would be better there. Valhalla. No more nightmares. No more waiting for the last shoe to drop. I almost killed a woman tonight. She could have died. I'm a loaded gun.

My hands shake as I lift my phone. I type and delete. Put it down. Spin the gun. Pick the phone back up again.

Finally, I type, **Yeah. I'll be there.**

Send.

CHAPTER 1
Lauren

Las Vegas is completely phony but fun if you buy into its game.

When Sanam said she was getting married to the super-wealthy Reza Nader, everyone begged for a bachelorette party in Vegas. It seemed like it would be a fun idea at the time, but now, I'm seriously regretting saying yes. They're all in amazing places in their lives while I'm stuck in the same spot I've been for the last ten years—a legal secretary at Crier, one of the most prestigious law firms in LA and completely single. I've had boyfriends, of course. But none to love. I'm thirty-two years old, and I want to settle down with a smart, intelligent, kind, and handsome man who loves me. Where the hell is he? I've dated men who checked every box in my credential list. And yet all of them have turned out to be utter assholes.

The heavy rap music bounces against high concrete walls, painted to look like marble, and bursting against my eardrums. Bodies, costumed and practically nude, gyrate on the dance floor. A life-sized metal birdcage dangles from the ceiling by our table. A woman dances inside, if you can call spreading your legs and grinding against the bars dancing. It's Cirque du Strip. I don't want to stare, but it's hard not to. I mean, how the hell does she contort herself in these positions? The theme of the party tonight is Turn a Trick, Get a Treat, and my entire group, along with the rest of the club, is dressed accordingly.

I turn toward my friends, simultaneously cringing at their antics and wanting to make sure they've had enough water. They're all rolling on Molly, and their happiness has reached cloud-nine status. Apparently, Roxy and Allie got it from Sandy, who swears up and down it's as pure MDMA as you can get. The alleged result? The euphoria of ecstasy without any down. I know because I did all the research beforehand. Everyone's been texting for weeks about the party favors tonight, and of course, I immediately looked up all the details. I'm not planning to partake, but I'm also not one who appreciates a surprise. If everyone around me is going to be on drugs, I need to know what to expect.

Sanam moves to where I stand, hugging me with more empathy and love than I ever thought she was capable of feeling. I'm furious with her for rolling on drugs, but her kindness right now makes it hard to be angry. Her expensive perfume moves through my nose, making my eyes tingle. It's the same scent she's been wearing since we were in college, reminding me of when we lived together during our senior year at UCLA. Memories of how we'd find lunch specials from the fanciest restaurants and eat there, waiting for rich businessmen to see us and ask us out for dinner. It was all fun and games for me but not for Sanam. Over time, finding the man with lined pockets became *everything* to her.

We used to be inseparable. But our priorities changed drastically over time, and at this point, we couldn't be more different. I want to still love her because of what was, but it feels as though I can no longer trust her. In fact, everything in my life these days looks and feels like filler, overstuffed with fleeting conversations and pretentious hellos.

She pulls back, smiling. "I know I'm getting married, and you're not. I mean, not for a really long time at least. But we have to stay best friends forever, okay?" Her voice is high-pitched and haughty.

For the millionth time tonight, I ask myself if she has always been this bitchy and I never really noticed or if it's a new development in her personality now that she's about to be Mrs. Reza Nader.

Pushing her thick black hair over one shoulder, she smiles like she just won the lottery. Technically speaking, she has. Reza is rich.

I let out a, "Mmhmm," as I try not to slap her off the metaphoric high horse she's sitting on. Turning my body to the side isn't a choice but done for her preservation.

From my side-eye, I see her duck lips purse. She clears her throat, as though she's trying to get my attention.

"I'm telling you this because I love you. You're getting older, and it's time to wake up. There's no such thing as love. What's real is money. You are beautiful right now, but in a few years, you'll be older. Newer stock is going to rise. Just get in the game and close the deal with one of these wealthy men we know."

I swing around, facing her head-on. "I can't just—"

"Yes, you can," she interrupts. "You can, and you should. I know you believe that love will conquer all and blah, blah, blah. I thought, over time, you'd grow out of it, but you're still stuck in that stupid mindset. Why should you live in a small and crappy apartment with a man who'll eventually cheat on you with some dumb slut in his office? News flash: whether he's loaded with money or poor and hood, they all do the same shit. At least with the rich one, you'll be able to live an amazing life of travel. Parties. Dinners. Private planes. Reza has a lot of friends I want you to meet at the wedding." She smiles excitedly.

Sanam doesn't realize that it's not about money. It's that I'm sick and tired of eating shit from men who think that, because they buy me nice things, I have to say yes to their demands. I'd explain this to her, but how can I? Sanam's entire life is a transaction. She'll be a good wife in the ways Reza expects, and in return, he'll take care of her materially. She's followed this pattern since college. Sure, the trips we took in our twenties to St. Barts and the South of France with handsome and rich men were fun. But, for me, that's all it ever was— fun. As I got older, it became less and less so.

"We've always done everything together. I know we've separated some since I met Reza, but let's get you on my train. All you have to do is pick one of his friends. You're brilliant and beautiful and the nicest girl ever. It's all so simple! The only person to convince is yourself." The look in her eyes is full of honesty.

Before I can reply, Daniela comes over. Long red hair and completely coked up, she's totally out of her mind. She just got out of rehab, but clearly, it didn't help her. Anyway, I heard she's leaving for South America to help her father do some business. Good riddance! She opens the flap of her designer purse and dips a black manicured nail inside. Slowly pulling it out so as not to spill a grain, she sprinkles white powder in Sanam's palm. I try not to cringe over their blatant drug use. I love Sanam, but I hate some of the girls she surrounds herself with.

After she rubs the white crystals on her gums, it's only moments before a bright, demonic smile fills Sanam's face. Still, her crown continues to sparkle. On anyone else, it would look tacky—*Bride-to-Be* spelled out in shining, faux diamond letters. But, on Sanam, it's perfection. She's so attractive that, even drugged up and starving, she looks perfect.

"Most of Reza's friends are assholes," I add.

They're all big in California and New York City real estate, and they come to my law firm for closings. Any chance they get, they hit on me. As the head legal secretary on the real estate transactional team, it's my job to know every single client who works with the real estate team. Unfortunately, it's also my job to make sure they're comfortable and happy. This means that, oftentimes, I have to plaster a smile on my face—even if it hurts.

"And they'd do anything to get into your pants. This has never bothered you before. What's changed?" Her eyes plead before sparkling at someone or something over my shoulder.

I turn my head and groan. There's a man behind me, tall and muscular, with an interested smirk on his face. He stares between the two of us, implication clear that he wouldn't mind some fun with us both. I quickly turn away, not wanting to give him any ideas.

"Anyway"—she brings her focus back to me—"I know your office has strict rules about dating clients, but, girl, get a clue. Every secretary on earth is working to meet a rich businessman. No one is actually working to work."

"I'm not just a secretary. I'm a legal secretary," I huff, feeling defensive. "And, while I'm not crazy about my job, it isn't just to meet some—"

"Whatever. Same difference," she interrupts, circling her hips to the music.

I narrow my eyes, wanting to shake her back to reality and then stab her with my red Louboutin stiletto. Sanam isn't cruel; she's just clueless.

Or maybe it's me who's dense. No. It's her.

The girls around me flit in excitement as some rap song I've never heard comes on. I can feel my despair seeping through my thighs, heavier than I wish they were.

Should I just take some Molly? Maybe, if I did, I could actually be happy again.

I bite my lip, running through my usage checklist for the millionth time. I have no preexisting health conditions. I am not taking any medication that interacts with MDMA. I'm aware of the dosage guidelines, and I know that the positive effects of this drug are maximized between eighty-one to one hundred ten milligrams. I will be sure to drink two cups of water. My costume is thin, which should keep me cool to avoid heatstroke. Molly could be the pause my body yearns for, but my mind won't allow.

Sanam brings her skinny, hairless arms high above her as the music thumps.

"I never really liked this rap music." She shakes her tiny ass as sweat beads at her unlined forehead. "But I love the vibrations. Can you feel it? We're all one. Humanity is meant to become a single body, full of unity!"

I cock my head in confusion at her spiritual words, so unlike her.

"And I'm getting married. And that house he just bought me? God! Can you believe it?" she squeals.

In front of us, Allie climbs up onto the rectangular table overflowing with liquor and ice. Lowering her own diamond-encrusted hand, she brings Sanam to stand up with her. A few bottles of vodka topple to the ground, the glass shattering near my feet and soaking the floor. The girls only laugh at the mess they made. Reza, of course, is footing the entire bill for the weekend. Meanwhile, they're dancing like they're starring in a porn, making *come fuck me* eyes at any man with a pulse. Okay, maybe not that bad. But still.

Sanam screams to me, "Come up, Lauren!" She's enjoying the attention she's receiving from partygoers, her moves exaggerated and overly sexy.

I click my tongue, turning away. No way in hell am I dancing on a table. Jesus, but I need an escape right now. Still, I wish I weren't the way I was. I want to just take the drugs and be happy like everyone else. I want something to shut me up for once, so I can actually enjoy life instead of questioning and thinking of all the possible outcomes. I want to dance without a care, too. But ... I can't.

Sanam's laughing. She's got that squinting-eye look as her hands clap together, mouth parted. I can't hear it over the loud music, but I know the sound is high-pitched. I tap her slender hip, getting her attention.

I shout, "I'm going to use the restroom!"

She lifts a finger in the air, the universal sign for *wait one second*.

Jayme takes Sanam's hand as she daintily steps off the table.

Picking up a bottle of tequila, she fills a full shot glass and lifts it up between her perfectly manicured fingers. "At least take another drink before you go. I hate seeing you so miserable when we're all happy." She pouts.

Rolling my eyes, I take the drink from her hand and swallow it down in one gulp.

Chapter 2
Slade

I gave my friends shit when they told me we were going to a costume party, but apparently, this is tonight's hot spot. A well-known rap artist, whose name I can't even remember, is performing.

Hip-hop blasts around the dimly lit club as we step into the throng teeming with sweaty, half-naked bodies. The dance floor is full of women in lingerie and men who look like they just left lockup. People see us walking forward and immediately make way, parting to steer clear. Lots of guys on the SEAL Teams aren't big. But we are.

At the Mile, we work our security team with a single-minded purpose that borderlines on insane. Working for Vincent Borignone means staying in complete control all the time. But, tonight, we're in Vegas to let out some of that pent-up steam, and we aim to tear it up.

I lean on the black lacquered bar. "Three tequila limes."

The bartender wears a black push-up bra and micromini. She's got a throwback 1950s *Playboy* centerfold thing going for her. Retro or whatever the word is. Jet-black hair with straight-cut bangs. A black line on her eyelids that flicks up at the end, sort of like a cat eye would look. She's even got bright red lipstick. I let my eyes take their fill, her practically nude body on display. I'll be able to enjoy it more when I'm drunk enough to relax.

"Anything else you want?" She leans forward against the shiny bar top, putting her massive fake tits closer to my face. Her question is filled with possibilities that have nothing to do with my drink order.

"I can think of a few things. Let's start with those drinks though, yeah?" My voice is gravelly.

She smiles wide. "I'm Candice."

"Slade." I want to grin, but my mouth refuses to turn up. I'm so damn tired. I drank my body weight in liquor last night and slept like shit. My liver is angry as fuck, but here I am, planning on doing it all again. But harder.

Turning around to pour the drinks, she makes a nice show of bending over, showing me her tight, pert ass.

Nice.

Rob rubs his hands together, scheming. "Bachelorette party, twelve o'clock." He points north, his white button-down shirt rolled up to his tatted forearms. "Could be just what we need tonight."

After I choked out Lilly, Rob and I spoke. He hooked me up with some benzos a doctor prescribed to his brother-in-law for anxiety. Men like us don't need to be psychoanalyzed. I can take care of myself. I didn't spend the last twelve years engaging and prepping for war, only to come home, crying to some doctor who doesn't know shit about shit when it comes to what I went through overseas. If I saw a shrink, he'd smash my head open. Memories that I never want to discuss—ever—would be called out and brought into the real world. And once those demons are freed? There's no putting them back. That would fuck me up more than anything, no doubt. Luckily, Rob understood me perfectly.

The drugs have been a huge help, pausing the never-ending leak of memories that plague me at night. Still, I'm careful not to have any women or friends stay over. While the meds work wonders, they're not foolproof.

I just need a little more time to get myself back under control. I can handle it. I'm going to find a hot girl or two tonight, get laid, and release some of this stress simmering under my skin. It'll work.

I hear laughter next to me and turn toward it. Ultra-slutty attire has my eyes widening. Sparkling white angel wings, lacy white bras, and thong panties. I'm enormously enjoying the view until I see their faces. They're girls, and they all look about sixteen, smiling and taking selfies. My jaw drops.

"Tell me all the women here aren't teenagers," I grumble, rubbing the back of my neck and feeling like a creeper.

"I hope they are," Mike replies with an evil grin, doing his vampire costume justice.

"Sick fuck."

I laugh, lifting my hand to slap him behind the head. He ducks quickly and chuckles as my hand makes a clean sweep, slicing through air.

"Yeah, as if you haven't done some crazy-ass shit yourself, motherfucker. Who could forget Candy, eh?"

We continue to talk smack when my eyes pause on the bachelorette party. I tune out my idiot friends and focus on the bride-to-be, wearing a sparkling crown. A one-night stand with one of these women would be good. Exactly what I need. I admire the half-naked nurse. The slutty devil. Oh, *Risky Business*—always a good costume. And then I pause at the flight attendant, who might not be dressed as scantily as the rest of her group, but whose body is straight-up sexy. Legs for miles into a small waist. Perfect tits. I move my eyes to her face, marked with a scowl, and pause.

Holy shit. *Is it her?*

The strobe lights move across the group, making it difficult to be sure. I wait patiently for colors to shift. Finally, yellow hits her face in just the right angle, and I can confirm. It *is* her. Still hot as fuck, but angrier than before. A hand flies to her hip as she talks to her crown-wearing friend. Yeah, she definitely isn't happy right now. Luckily for her, I can change that.

Her hair is long and wavy, like she just came from the beach. It looks damn good. Last time I saw her, it was pulled back tightly for Vincent and Eve's wedding in some fancy style. Actually, after I was done with her, it looked a lot like this. I can't help but chuckle at the memory. Was it really only a few months ago? She's just so ... beautiful. Something about the shape of her brown eyes, large and almond, makes my dick twitch. I adjust but keep my eyes trained on the prize.

I asked her what her ethnicity was, but she was shady as hell about it, playing around and never giving me a straight answer. I continue to stare, vividly remembering the night of the wedding.

"Let's go for a walk." Grabbing two wineglasses from the wooden bar, I stuff them in the back pockets of my khakis before taking a cold bottle of white from the bartender. "Thanks, man."

We pound fists. He's the son of one of the board members on the tribal council, and Vincent and I both spar with him from time to time. He's never fought competitively, but he is pretty quick on his feet.

"A walk?" she repeats.

I face her and notice her pink lips, nice and full. My eyes trail down to her nipples, which have pebbled beneath her gown. She catches me staring and immediately drops a hand over a slender hip, daring me to keep looking. Good thing I'm not the type of man who hides. I'm not into cryptic shit. If I want something, I go for it. No excuses and no bullshit. The last hour has been spent taking shots and making jokes. It's been great, but I'm ready to move on.

"Yeah," I start. "You know, put one foot in front of the other. Walk." I raise the bottle of wine in my hand and lift my brows, promising more fun. "My truck isn't too far."

"Well, I don't walk in heels like these," she sasses back, shrugging.

I look down and laugh. She wasn't lying. Those shoes are pretty damn high. Strappy and pointy and who the fuck knows what.

"Take them off." I stare at the death traps on her feet. "I'll hold them for you. Why did you even put that shit on tonight? You're in the mountains, if you didn't notice."

She squints. "Shit? They're my shoes."

I grunt, feigning understanding.

Her eyes roll. "You don't get it."

"Guess not." I tip my head, trying to charm my way around the fact that I have zero clue what she's saying.

The women I grew up with had three pairs of shoes—flips, sneakers, and work boots. Lauren wears the kind of fancy shit that I can barely get my head around. I guess they're sexy, but she'd be hot in anything.

She huffs, "Fine. I'll take them off." A flirty kind of annoyance is written on her face. "But only because you served my country. Don't want to seem ... ungrateful."

I laugh, and she bites her cheek, not wanting to let on. This girl. She crouches down, and after a few moments, she stands back up again. She's a lot shorter than what I'm used to. I'm well over six feet, and she looks about five foot three. Surprisingly, I like it.

We walk away from the twinkling Christmas lights outlining the wedding area.

Her bare feet, softly arched, slowly pad forward. "If I get something stuck in my foot, you'd better be ready to remove it."

"No worries. I've got a whole kit in my truck."

"Boy Scout."

"You know it."

I take the shoes from her hands before sparing a glance at the newly married couple, who are so up in each other's love that they can barely see straight. The music is fast, but Vincent and Eve are at their own leisurely pace.

Walking toward my truck, I smell vanilla and citrus. It's her. I want this woman. And it's not just because she's gorgeous. She actually makes me laugh, which is rare. Smarter than she seems, too. She plays it off to be all simple and sweet, but if there's something I've learned tonight, it's that there's more than meets the eye. The fact that she's here for a limited time doesn't hurt either. We can have a great time, and then she'll head on home to LA. No stress.

I turn to her as she breathes in the fresh air around us. It's so dark.

"This is it," I tell her as my red truck comes into view.

She leans against the side, looking sexy as hell. I just spent the last hour trying to make the girl smile, and now, with the way she's staring at me, I feel like yelling, Hooyah! I love completing a good challenge, and the finish line is so close; I can taste it.

"So, is this where you wanted me?" Her tongue teases through parted glossy lips.

Before she can open up that pretty mouth of hers again, I lift her round ass into my hands and place her on the car's bed. Her legs spread apart, making room for me. My lips press against hers, and she immediately grabs my back, moaning. Fuck, she tastes so good. Like wine and berries.

I start pulling on the straps of her dress, wanting it off, as I move my mouth to the side of her neck.

"Wait, wait. My dress. The buttons—"

I'm panting. "Huh?" My dick strains against my jeans.

"Don't rip it. It's Mendel."

I remove my mouth from her collarbone. "Mend-who?"

"Like, a serious designer."

I curse. "Turn around. Let me take the thing off."

"You can't do it in the dark, Slade." Again, that annoyed voice.

Why it turns me on, I don't have a clue. The girls I grew up with are down-home and relaxed. Not snooty upper class. I have no idea how a woman like her operates, but right now, I'll do basically anything to make us happen. My dick and I, we're in agreement. We want this girl.

I slide my hand up under her dress, pushing her panties to the side to feel her soaked, hot center. She sucks in a breath as my fingers circle her clit.

"I'm going to fuck you so good. You'd better tell me how to get this dress off before I grab my knife and cut it off," I growl.

She brazenly puts her hand down my pants, stroking my cock while my hand stays up her skirt. I thought I was hard, but her soft hand on my dick has my brain short-circuiting. I can hear her gasp as I reach up higher and curl my finger up, hitting her spot.

"Don't you have a flashlight or something? Isn't survival, like, your thing?" Her voice comes out strangled as she lets go.

I laugh. The combination of wanting to fuck like crazy and this stupid dress has my wires crossed. I lazily pull my hand out of her wet heat before moving away.

I run to the side of my car, pants and belt undone with my dick hanging out, and pull the flashlight from under the passenger seat. I've got my knife here, too, *but something tells me she wouldn't appreciate this dress getting sliced in half. I make it back to her and freeze. She's sitting on her knees, facing the dark mountains. Finally moving her head to me, her brown eyes blink in amusement.*

"Are your parents Middle Eastern?"

God, she's beautiful. That thick hair is a beautiful shade of golden blonde, but I can see the darkness at her roots.

She smirks. "Just take it off, Slade."

Holy fuck, if this girl isn't the sexiest woman I've ever seen, I don't know who is.

I move behind her, letting my hands rove over her creamy, nude thighs. My callous fingers skate against her delicate skin. She's perfect. A large part of me wants to take her just like this with her dress around her waist. But the other part of me—the smarter one—wants to get her totally naked.

Button by button, so slowly, I begin opening her dress. I'm surprised to realize that I've never undressed a woman like this before. I touch her bare back and kiss the spot between her shoulder blades. She's getting antsy, so I slide my hand into her pussy again, taking my time. Still soaked.

"You're enjoying this?" *she asks, trying to mask her arousal with a steady voice. She can't hide from me. Her body betrays her—wet.*

"You bet I am." *I continue to touch her with one hand and continue to open her dress with the other.*

Finally, the last button is undone. She gasps as I blow across her nude back. She shivers.

"Turn that off?" *Her voice is all breathy as she stares at the flashlight, the mouth on her suddenly stilled to a whisper.*

As the straps of her dress fall from her slender shoulders, I'm silenced. For the first time in my life, I want to make sex amazing for the woman in front of me. It's not just about getting off and having fun. I don't know what it is I'm trying to prove, but I want to show her that I can do it better than any of these prissy fucks she's had before me. Because I'm better than them. And I'm the best she'll ever have.

"No." *I shake my head from side to side.* "Stand up. And pull your dress off nice and slow. For me."

I step back to watch, shifting the flashlight to face her. She's on display, standing like a vision from my dreams. Listening to my commands, the way

I like. And, just like that, her dress falls. Perfectly shaped breasts. Flat, defined stomach.
"Now, come suck my dick before I fuck you."

"Yo, dude. Earth to Slade. Those drinks are sitting on the bar, man." Mike gestures to the shot glasses sitting before me.

I take them off, holding two in each hand, and pass them out, completely ignoring the bartender, who is expectantly staring at me.

Lauren. It's her.

* * *

Purchase **Warrior Undone** here: Warrior Undone

ACKNOWLEDGMENTS

This book has been an incredible journey. Without certain individuals, the finish line would never have been reached. Firstly, I need to thank my husband for giving me the space and support I need to follow my dreams. Jon, you're the breath in my prayers. I love you more. I must also thank my children, who make me believe in the purity of human beings. Because of my family, I know that love is truth.

I want to thank my team. First on the list is Leigh Ford, my master Beta reader. When things got stressful, you were the one talking me through my words. Helping to outline and brainstorm. You're the scaffolding for not only these books, but also for life. I also need to thank Andrea at Hot Tree editing, Candice, Caitlin, Jana, Roxy, and Jayme for Beta-reading. Your support in these books gave me the strength I needed to plow forward.

Now here comes the part when I talk about the big gun. Autumn at Wordsmith Publicity. You are fierce. You are brilliant. And you literally picked my debut books by their binding and threw them, with all your might, onto the map—all with class and determination. You're amazing. I am so thankful to call you my Publicist, but even more thankful to call you my friend.

I have to thank Ellie from Love N' Books for reading the earliest draft of my work and encouraging me to split the novel into three. Your guidance and knowledge of the book world is second to none. From small wording changes to large plot issues—I'm lucky to say my books were all in your excellent care.

BilliJoy Carson at Editing Addict. You are so skilled at what you do. You dissect my work like a book surgeon! And your attention to detail are what took my books from "good" to "as good as they could be." I thank you.

The bloggers. You ladies are amazing. You shouted my books from the social media rooftops and brought me to Kindles around the world. You're the gatekeepers of the book community and I admire all of your hard work, dedication, and most of all passion for the craft. I may tell a story, but you guys shed the light. I am so grateful you all took a chance on me.

The READERS!! Thank you, thank you, THANK YOU for reading. For clicking on an unknown and taking that risk. I hope you enjoyed the journey of Vincent and Eve. While this is the last of their story, you can catch them again in my standalone spin-off, Warrior Undone.

ABOUT THE AUTHOR

Jessica Ruben lives and works in New York City, where she spends her days dominating in the court room as an attorney. Come nightfall, she writes romances centering on gorgeous alpha males and the intelligent women who love them.

Jessica is an insatiable reader, and will devour a few books a week without batting an eyelash. Books have always been her drug of choice, and she has no plans on detox anytime soon.

She has three wildly delicious children and a husband who, for reasons unimaginable to her, loves her brand of crazy.

Printed in Great Britain
by Amazon

53582231R10357